Demon's Dream

A STANDALONE NOVEL

ELLE KAYSON

Want to be a part of the
Grand Penz Family?

To submit your manuscript to Grand Penz Publications, please send the first three chapters and synopsis to grandpenzpublications@gmail.com

Acknowledgments

First of all, this is my little sister's (Kizzy's) birthday book. Happy Birthday to the Leo I love most. She asked for this and some chicken and dumplings. Chyle…

I love my Mama and her support. That's all!

To my favorite Sugar Daddy, Aubry Jackson. Bet you I buy me something pretty! Thank you, fellow BWB. And to Author Jas B.—thank you for being the best pen (little) sister. It's you and me against the Legion of Doom. I love our joint toxicity. Thank you both for your help with this book.

And speaking of the Legion of Doom, Tava, I love you. You been there in sickness and health. You probably deserve an engagement ring, hell.

To Videssa, Ericka, Monica, and Joi, thank you for reading this 973 times over two whole years! I love y'all and your influence and input has been so crucial.

To the women who are my cousins and closest friends— y'all stay ready to uplift, support, promote, and rejoice. I love y'all and am glad to be among your ranks.

As always, thank you to Monique Pearson and Crystal Nicole Collier!

And for my readers… y'all have held on for almost three years. Where would I be without y'all? I hope it was worth the wait!

CHAPTER 1

Marshall McLemore

(*TUESDAY*, *May 11*)

I jumped as the loud rumble of thunder cracked outside. I was antsy tonight, didn't like being in this house by my-damn-self. Eve's bitch ass was missing, had ducked out with my seed this evening and wouldn't answer my calls. The bitch was lucky it was raining. I knew she had probably run to her grandmother. If it weren't storming so hard, I'd go get her. But tonight was the kind of night I might break her fucking face. The rain was probably a blessing in disguise, keeping me out of jail for murder. Another peal of thunder boomed, knocking me out of my thoughts.

"*Fuck!*" I cursed, shaken up by the violence of the storm.

I grabbed my phone again and tapped Eve's name. The call went straight to voicemail.

"Bitch, you better get your ass home, got my son out in this weather! I'ma fuck you up for real, Eve," I growled before disconnecting.

Reluctantly, I climbed into bed, hating to go by myself. I knew I probably wouldn't get any sleep as the storm shook the old house, making the windows rattle. I had just calmed my nerves a little bit when I thought I heard knocking.

Frowning, I laid there, wondering if I had imagined the shit. I had almost decided I had when the bell rang.

Eve. Stupid bitch had probably forgotten her house keys and had the nerve to disturb my rest. Getting out of bed, I didn't even bother to pull on my sweatpants. No one else would come here this time of night. Dressed only in a pair of boxer briefs, I ran down the stairs and toward the front door, ready to teach this bitch another lesson. I wouldn't have to handle her the way I did if she wasn't so fucking slow about some shit.

Unlocking the door, I yanked it open, a scowl already on my face.

"Where the fuck you been with…"

My voice trailed off as I looked at the person standing on the other side of the screen. He was tall, taller even than my six-foot-one. He was dressed in all black—a hoodie, pair of jeans, and sneakers—but it didn't hide that this nigga was ripped. His head was slightly bowed, covered by the hoodie. He lifted it slowly and my eyes tangled with the coldest gaze I'd ever seen. Green eyes stared back at me, dripping ice. This nigga was the shit nightmares were made of. I knew who he was from the one old picture Eve had and from the word on the streets. I cursed myself for coming downstairs without my gun.

"D-D-Demon?" I stuttered.

"Open the screen," he ordered, his expression blank.

"Eve's not here. I'll let her know you came by."

It was a desperate try, almost a plea. He didn't move. Of course, he didn't.

He wasn't here for Eve.

For one minute, I debated opening the screen. I knew his presence meant that I was fucked. But it would probably be even worse if I didn't do what he said. Hesitantly, I reached out, unlocked the screen, and pushed it open. He slipped into the house silently. His eyes scanned the room. Checking for what, I didn't know. Finally, they landed on me again. I had the sudden urge to piss, my nerves sitting somewhere in my stomach.

He walked further into my house. I took anxious steps backward, my eyes never leaving him. I bumped into the sofa table, almost falling over it. Scrambling, I steadied myself.

"I saw Eve," he said.

I knew that. And I knew what he saw. I wasn't trying to hit her in the face, but when I realized I was out of my favorite cologne and she acted like she didn't give a fuck, I had to get her attention. I needed a better story than that for this maniac, though.

"Demon" was a childhood friend of Eve's. Apparently, he grew up hard. Real hard. Eve had given him food and tried to treat his wounds anytime she was at her grandmother's house, who was Demon's mother's next-door neighbor. But Eve's kindness hadn't been enough to change how he turned out. Demon was a killer. Ruthless. Violent. Fearless.

And he was here for me.

According to Eve, he had promised to never forget what she did for him. Even after she told me that, I had pushed my luck. Tonight, I knew I would pay. I just hoped it wouldn't be with my life.

"Demon, you gotta understand—"

"I saw MJ, too," he cut in. "Li'l nigga is what, five? Six?"

MJ... my son. He'd tried to stop me from punishing his mother. I wasn't proud of what happened after that. I lifted my hands as I tried to explain. "Th—that with MJ, that was an accident."

"Accident, huh?"

He stroked his chin with his hand like he was thinking. His voice was calm, conversational. Maybe he wasn't *that* mad at me. Maybe he *could* understand. Hell, he had an anger management problem himself. I felt a little hope as I looked at him.

"Yeah, an accident. He got in the middle of our... argument."

"We gotta make sure that doesn't happen again," he said.

I nodded, my head moving up and down so fast, I almost got dizzy. "You right. I will."

"Seems like you like to fight, but Eve and MJ don't."

I knew better than to respond to that, so I just waited. My hand on the sofa table inched closer to the lamp that sat there with its metal base. It wasn't much, and I'd have to move fast, but it was better than facing this sick muhfucka empty-handed.

"So... since you like to fight, fight me."

My eyes widened and I froze as he walked closer to me. Even before I got my voice back, my head shook "no." *Hell no.* The last thing I was was suicidal. I watched as he stretched his fingers, like he was loosening them up for what was to come. For the first time, I noticed he wore gloves, despite the summer heat. My heartbeat sped up, fear shooting through me. His lips twisted into a sinister little smile, and his eyes suddenly held some kind of emotion.

"Demon—"

"Stop talking. Act like I'm Eve. Hit me, nigga."

"I don't want—"

"*Hit me!*" he growled.

Agitated, I blinked back tears. I could hit him, try to give myself a chance, or I could stand here and be beaten by a man known for killing people with his bare hands. Shit, I had to at least try. I squared up, then swung, throwing the weight of my whole body behind the punch. It landed on his jaw.

He didn't even flinch.

"My turn."

My heart dropped as he spoke. I would not stand here and let him fuck me up without defending myself, but I knew I was outmatched. I—

Thunder roared outside as his fist flattened my nose,

sending blood streaming toward my mouth. I coughed and spat blood, every thought gone from my head. His next blow connected with my lips, and I fell backwards, landing hard on the tile floor. That same twisted smile graced his face as he looked down at me.

"Please..." I whispered drunkenly.

He kneeled over me, his smile now a grin.

"Is that what she said? Please?"

"Demon, I swear I'll never touch her... them again. Please, just—"

My words were cut off as his knuckles crashed into my teeth.

"I know you won't."

I lost count of the number of times he punched me. He didn't stop as my bones broke beneath his fist, didn't stop as my eyes swelled shut, didn't stop as I gurgled on my own blood. At some point, as blackness closed around me, I realized...

...he wasn't going to stop.

CHAPTER 2
Dream Dior Castle

(*WEDNESDAY*, *May 12*)

"You did what?"

My father's voice roared across his office as he glared at my younger brother, DeAngelo. I blinked twice behind my reading glasses before rubbing my temple. I was shocked, but maybe not as shocked as Daddy was. It was clear from the moment DeAngelo met Crystal where they were headed. The fact that they eloped was not the surprise; the timing was. Well, that and the fact that she had gone against her father, Dante Ware. It was no secret that Dante had had Crystal on the market for the highest, most powerful bidder. DeAngelo wasn't even a contender. Beautiful, educated, and reportedly a virgin, Crystal was worth a lot in a world like ours, especially because her father was one of the biggest players in the "underground economy."

My father's wild gaze swung to Crystal.

"Have y'all told Dante?"

She shook her head. Daddy sighed loudly.

"Of course, you haven't, because this fool would probably be dead," he said, pointing at DeAngelo.

"My daddy wouldn't do th—" Crystal began, but a look from Daddy silenced her.

She shouldn't have even wasted her voice. Dante would kill DeAngelo as soon as he looked at him, especially now that my brother had taken his prized possession.

"So, what's your plan? Huh? You think you gon' just stroll up in Dante's crib and make this same little announcement? You think he gon' give a damn about your marriage? You lucky if he don't get it annulled and make D's ass disappear," Daddy raged.

"He can't get it annulled," DeAngelo shot back.

I gave him a warning glare. He needed to shut his mouth and let Daddy just go off. Then, we'd figure this out logically. Daddy looked at him incredulously, then started laughing.

"You dumb muhfucka! He can't get it annulled? Why? Cuz y'all done had sex? You think he can't get around that?"

He laughed harder. DeAngelo's eyes narrowed, and I knew he was about to say something. Why couldn't he just be quiet?

"D—" I started, about to try to calm this shit down.

"Nah. Cuz he doesn't want his daughter walking around pregnant and unmarried."

The room went totally silent. Even I had no immediate comment for that one. Instead, I focused on the sound of raindrops pelting the big office window and the beautiful lines of the K. Reid painting across from me, trying to get my thoughts together. Daddy leaned forward and grabbed his desk like he needed the support. All eyes were glued to him, ready for him to blow his fucking top. But he surprised us. Slowly, he lowered himself into his chair. I watched as he dropped his face into his palms for a minute, before lifting his head again and staring at DeAngelo and Crystal.

"Please, *please* tell me y'all ain't that stupid. *Please*," Daddy said, voice low.

They looked away from him, then directly at me. I wanted

to squirm in my chair, wanted to leave the room, but I knew I couldn't. In my family, I was the fixer, the one who smoothed things over, the one who found even the hardest solutions. That's the only reason I was in the office right now—DeAngelo had begged me to sit in while he and Crystal told Daddy their "big news." Not my mama, not my sister, who was his twin, but me. I wracked my brain for something, but I really had no ideas. Dante was dangerous and deadly. DeAngelo might have bitten off more than he could chew.

I abandoned that idea as soon as I thought it. There was no way I was going to sit back while Dante Ware got rid of my brother. I would come up with something. My brother was counting on me. Hell, at this point, even Daddy's eyes were on me. In the last couple of years, I'd become like his right hand. It didn't matter that I didn't want to necessarily know all the shady shit he was involved in. I rubbed a hand across the back of my neck.

"Well…" I stalled. "I don't think the two of you should be there when Dante finds out."

DeAngelo's head snapped back. "I'm not afraid of Dante, and I want to approach him like a man—"

"He'll shoot you before you can finish telling him," I cut him off.

I started to tell him that if he wanted to approach him like a man, he should have done that *before* he eloped with his daughter, but I figured he got the point.

"So, who gon' tell him?" Crystal asked.

"I will," I said.

Daddy and DeAngelo started shaking their heads simultaneously.

"No!"

"Hell no!"

I held up a hand. "I'm not going by myself. Daddy's going, too."

He nodded at that. "Maybe I should take Jimmy. I don't

even want you around Dante."

"No. I definitely should be there. Let's be for real—it never hurts to have a pretty woman around to deliver bad news. Might keep him from flipping all the way out. And you"—I pointed at my father—"you have to be there because, hopefully, he wants to make a deal."

"A deal?" Crystal scoffed. "What, like I'm an object?"

I almost snapped off on her ass, but I let a tight smile cross my face. "With all due respect, Crys, the rumor is that your dad was trying to give you to that Smoke nigga to secure their alliance. I have no doubt that he loves you, but he has no problem with using you, either."

Her eyes narrowed at me, but she said nothing else. She knew I was telling the truth or else she wouldn't have felt the need to run off with my brother.

"We need to handle this as soon as possible." Daddy broke the tense silence.

I nodded. "I agree. Can you set something up?"

He let out another deep sigh. "Yeah. I might have to call in a favor to see him on short notice without letting him know all the details."

"And can you two continue to stay off his radar?"

I looked at Crystal and DeAngelo. They nodded. I honestly was surprised that she had gotten from under Dante's thumb long enough to pull this off. I didn't want to know how they did it. I gave them a half-smile.

"Let me make some plans with Daddy."

DeAngelo frowned. "Why can't we know your plans? I don't like this shit at all. You shouldn't be going in—"

"If you don't like it, you shoulda thought about that before you did what you did. Dream always cleans up your messes. Don't act like this gon' be any different," Daddy snapped.

DeAngelo opened his mouth to argue, but I shook my head slightly. He needed to get his ass out of here and let me figure this out. I could tell he wanted to say something else, but he didn't. Instead, he grabbed Crystal's hand. With one last look at me, he stalked out of the room. Daddy's attention swung to me.

"Mind telling me what the fuck you think we can offer Dante to save that crazy muhfucka's life?"

"He's not—" I paused as the sound of thunder cracked through the air. "He's not crazy, Daddy. He's twenty-one and in love. Dante didn't give a damn that Crystal loved him back. You know he's all about what brings the greater advantage."

Daddy sucked his teeth. "So, you saying you understand what he did? Come on, Dream. I expect more from you—"

As usual, his words cut me. He expected more. That's why I could never act on my feelings, to just wild out and do what I wanted. Instead, I'd been pushed into this role, training for his position when, in the end, it would go to DeAngelo. I ignored my feelings as I looked up at him.

"I don't understand, exactly, because I've never been in love. But I get it. They were desperate. Imagine if Grandpapa was going to marry Mama off to somebody else just because he had more money and power. What would you have done?"

He didn't answer, so I knew I had made my point.

"I'm gon' see if he'll see us tomorrow," he said instead.

"Dante's old school. You gon' have to insist that I be there."

"He does business with women, if he thinks he can get something out of it."

I blew out a breath. "I just gotta figure out what he can get out of this."

———

Grasping tightly to the railing, I stood on the balcony outside my bedroom, enjoying the warm breeze. My mind was so occupied with thoughts of Dante and the meeting my father had arranged that I almost didn't hear the soft whir of the mechanized chair as it glided into my room. A smile spread across my face as I waited for him to join me. It didn't take long. In my peripheral vision, I saw the lower part of the chair and a pair of motionless legs. I waited for him to speak.

"What in the world have you let that boy get you into?"

The question was part concern, part scolding, his voice slightly shaky with anger. I knew he didn't need an answer—Daddy had no doubt filled him in on everything.

"Don't fuss, Grandpapa," I said with my most persuasive smile.

"Don't try that smile on me, girl. You ain't gon' be happy till that boy get you in a situation that smooth talking can't get you out of!"

"Well, I don't think we're there yet."

"What you mean? A man like Dante will kill you without another thought. You putting your life on the line for—"

"Wouldn't you?"

He sighed. "This ain't about me, girl."

"Grandpapa, what did you expect me to do? Dante might still put a price on D's head, even after we meet with him. I at least have to try—"

"You always gotta try, let you tell it. Let them handle their own shit!"

"Next time—"

"Dream Dior! Don't lie to me!"

He raised his normally calm voice, only to have it dissolve into a bout of coughs.

"Grandpapa!" I turned to him, immediately moving to rub his back.

The last thing I wanted was to upset him. My grandfather was my favorite person in the world. He waved me off, rubbing his broad chest as his coughs lessened. Finally, he looked up at me again, his hazel eyes angry.

"Stop tryna save everybody."

Before I could say anything else, he turned his chair around and left my room. Sighing, I watched him go. I had pissed off the one person who was always on my side. And I *still* didn't know what we were going to bargain with Dante Ware with. I needed to go to bed before the night could get any worse.

CHAPTER 3

Dante Ware

I TOOK a long pull on the blunt clutched in my right hand. I needed my nerves as calm as possible before I met with this crazy muhfucka. Truth be told, I was surprised he agreed to see me on such short notice. Shit, I was surprised he agreed to see me at all. His ignore game was strong and, no matter how much I tried to get him to see the family's "business" as our legacy, built from the gifts left to us by the father we shared, he wasn't interested.

He wasn't interested in much. He didn't let people close, so there weren't many personal attachments. I didn't fool myself that my brother loved me. I didn't know if he could even love anything after the childhood he'd survived. My father hadn't found out about him until he was a half-wild teenager who had already claimed his first body. He never learned to fully trust us, and our relationship showed that.

I leaned back in my seat. I knew he knew I was here, probably knew the moment I drove onto his property. Knocking on his door would do no good. He'd come when he was ready. I put on some music and waited. Five or six minutes later, his front door opened. I got out of my car and ashed the blunt on the concrete before walking up the driveway. He stood in the doorway, looking. I wasn't a scary nigga, but as usual, his empty green eyes fucked me up. I was used to niggas looking down and away when I approached them. I was used to them trembling and begging in my presence. Nobody fucked with Dante Ware...

...except my cold-eyed, cold-hearted "little" brother.

"You gon' let me in, Demon?" I finally asked, using the nickname he'd been given long ago.

He didn't say a word, just stared at me for a few more seconds before he finally backed up. I already knew to walk in front of him. He didn't like giving anyone his back. I crossed the dimly lit, freezing cold room to sit on the couch. He walked more slowly—Demon didn't get in a hurry for anybody. I watched as he settled on the loveseat. Silent and still, he waited. He hadn't asked for this meeting, so he wouldn't be making small talk to get it started.

"I got a job I think you'd be interested in." Might as well get to the point.

His cold, green gaze never wavered. "What made you think that?"

"This muhfucka Marvin owes me, right?"

Demon smirked. "Of course, he does."

"Anyway, I had Li Jun searching all his computers and shit, looking for where he might keep his money. We didn't find no new accounts, but we did find... look, that nigga into nasty shit with kids, man. Little ones."

Li Jun had shown me pictures that would make you hurl everything in your stomach. I would've beat the nigga to death myself, but I knew my brother had a thing for taking out niggas who hurt kids. I wasn't a dumb muhfucka—I figured it was because of the way he came up. Before he'd tatted most of his body, you could see the scars from beatings and burns all over him. I looked at him now, waiting for a response. Demon said nothing, but I could tell that his body tensed, just a little bit. I knew not to rush him.

"Where is he?" he finally asked.

"In the guest house."

The "guest house" used to be the servants' quarters on my estate. We used it now to handle shit related to family business.

"What time?"

I shrugged. "It's up to you. I only got one meeting at home tomorrow and the guest house is far enough away... anyway, anybody meeting with me knows not to talk about anything they hear."

He was quiet for another minute.

"I'll call you when I'm on my way."

I nodded, then stood. He wouldn't want me here any longer than necessary. I'd gotten what I came for, so it was time to make my exit. Demon followed me to the door. We didn't say anything else to each other and he closed the door as soon as I crossed the threshold. I exhaled deeply as I walked toward my car. I realized it felt like I'd been holding my breath the whole time I was in my brother's house.

He had that effect. Nigga was so distant and so cold. He needed to connect with somebody. I wished he had some kind of weakness, a soft spot. Crazy muhfucka needed to fall in love or some shit.

But not Demon. He'd never be that human. Ever.

CHAPTER 4

Dream

(*THURSDAY, May 13*)

Luxurious. There wasn't a better word to describe Dante Ware's home. I had grown up well-off, the daughter of one of the biggest gun runners in the South and the granddaughter of a former kingpin. Even after my mama asked my daddy to step back, money was still plentiful. But this... My eyes moved around Dante's huge office with its solid wood furniture, silk wall coverings, one-of-a-kind rugs, and priceless Black art. He'd probably spent more decorating this room than Mama had on most of our house. And the glimpse I'd had of the living room with its high ceilings and sky lights—this man was richer than God.

The door opened suddenly and the man that most of the city feared was there. He walked in slowly, two men trailing behind him. I watched as he took a seat behind the big desk, across from my father and me. His chair was throne-like, and it suited him. He really looked like he ruled over all he could see.

His eyes settled on my daddy, and he nodded once. Daddy nodded back silently. I waited as Dante's gaze roamed over me appreciatively. He had a wife who was rumored to be as homicidal as he was, but that didn't stop him from eyeing me up and down. My father sat stiffly, hating the whole situation, but I had endured worse.

"Ms. Dream Castle. I've heard a lot about you, young lady."

I smiled. He'd heard the same things about me that people said about Crystal. I knew I was a hot commodity, wanted by many of the men who lived this life. I came from a family that had been in the business for a long time. I was pretty, had a degree with honors from one of the best schools in the nation, and had a solid reputation. The only difference between me and Crystal was that my daddy would *not* be trying to pick my husband. Oh, he wanted to. He'd hand-picked my sister Dayana's fiancé—luckily, she cared about him. But I had made it clear that I wasn't going for it. When I got married, it would be about trust and love, not some business arrangement. Life owed me at least that much romance.

"All good, I hope," I said, keeping my smile.

"Of course," he agreed, giving me one more look before returning his attention to my father. "To what do I owe the pleasure of this meeting?"

Daddy sighed and Dante frowned, realizing something was off. The awkward silence stretched for a bit, the quiet fucking with my anxiety. I drummed my fingers against the arms of my chair, then stopped, realizing I was betraying my nervousness. Dante was a predator. If he knew how I was feeling, he'd move in for the kill. I had to play this shit off. I sat up even straighter and met his eyes.

"Mr. Ware—" I began.

"Your daughter Crystal and my son DeAngelo… eloped."

I looked at Daddy, shocked that he had just blurted that out. He didn't even try to couch it in pretty language, which was why I wished he'd let me break the news. For a moment, Dante sat, stunned. But he recovered quickly, and Daddy and I shot each other glances as he laughed. His deep voice sounded throughout the room, and he even had tears in his eyes from laughing so hard. Then, the laughter stopped just as quickly as it had begun, his face smoothing into a blank mask as he stared at us.

"You expect me to believe that my daughter... my *baby* defied me and sent you here in her place?"

He nodded once, and suddenly, my father's head was being yanked back and a gun pressed under his chin.

"Wait!" I tried to inject authority into my voice as Dante's guard pushed the gun deeper into my father's skin.

My heart was somewhere near my stomach even as I tried to hide my terrified reaction. I'd told myself to expect the worst, but damn! They moved so fucking fast, and I knew they'd blow Daddy's head off without a second thought.

"No, you wait," Dante said calmly.

He pulled out a phone and dialed a number. The call seemed to take forever to go through, but it was just seconds later when he asked, "Crystal... where are you?"

"Hey, Daddy! How are you? What you doing?"

Her voice came over the speakerphone, nervous and faster than it usually was. She knew her secret was out, and her fear of her father's reaction was clear in her unsteady tone.

"Answer my question!" he demanded.

She paused for a minute. "I'm... I'm at my place."

"And who's with you, sweetheart?"

Another pause. Then, "Daddy, I can explain—"

He hung up without another word. He did it so calmly, I would've never realized the extent of his rage if I hadn't seen his eyes. It should've been impossible for the color brown to look so cold. Those icy eyes flickered over me and my father.

"Tell me why I shouldn't go to my daughter's house and kill that thieving son of a bitch right now?"

"He's not a thief—" Daddy argued.

"He took what wasn't his!" Dante snarled, standing and pacing.

I wanted to point out that Crystal and DeAngelo loved each other, but Dante didn't strike me as the type to care about love.

"Look, Mr. Ware, there has to be something we can offer you. Something to help make up—" I began, but then that cold gaze swung to me.

"Something as valuable as my daughter? You ain't got shit," he hissed. "Do you realize how bad they fucked up? Do you know the two families Crystal was supposed to bring together? And she betrayed me and her legacy! For what? A nigga that's beneath her!"

He spat the words out, and I felt my own anger stir. We might not have as much money or clout as his or Smoke's operation, but that didn't make my brother beneath them.

"If you take the gun off my father, we can talk about this—"

"I oughta blow his head off for raising such a disrespect-ful, sneaky ass *boy*," he growled.

"No!" I objected. "He was as upset as you are. This is not his fault."

Dante glared at me. "You sure seem to have all the answers, Ms. Dream. But you still ain't told me why I should spare your brother's life."

"For the sake of your grandbaby."

The words tumbled out before I knew it. I hadn't planned to reveal that yet, but this nigga wasn't playing. Just like my daddy had, he went totally silent and fell back in his seat. For a minute, we sat in a tense silence, my father under a gun, Dante's eyes narrowed on me. He studied me for a couple of minutes, his gaze so intense, I had to fight the urge to fidget in the chair. I wanted to say so much, but I didn't want to set him off. Finally, he looked at the guard holding Daddy and shook his head once. Immediately, the man backed off, and I sighed my relief.

"You owe me," Dante said calmly, his eyes back and forth between me and Daddy.

"We know. And we'll make good on this," I vowed.

"Just give us your terms," Daddy offered. "I know DeAngelo insulted your family. My family will fix it."

Dante sat up. "You fucking right you will. You owe me twice, Castle."

Daddy looked at him for a moment before nodding. It wasn't like we had much choice.

"I'll collect for the second time at a later date. I'ma need several RPGs and M2s, and that's just the beginning. But the first…"

He gestured for one of his guards to come closer. They had a quickly whispered conversation, one that had the guard looking at him crazily before he straightened his face and walked out of the room. We sat quietly for a few minutes until I couldn't take it.

"The first?" I prompted Dante, anxious to know what he had planned for us.

"Patience, Ms. Dream," he said.

I felt a shiver creep down my spine as he started smiling again. I didn't know what he was plotting, but I could tell I wasn't going to like it. His attention turned back to my father.

"Castle, your son took my daughter. Ruined a lot of my plans. Destroyed what would've been a beautiful alliance. So, you know what I think would be fair?"

Daddy met his eyes. "What?"

Dante's eyes landed on me again. "A daughter for a daughter."

His smile widened as he made his announcement, like it was the most brilliant shit ever. *A daughter for a daughter?* My heart dropped again. I had no interest in sleeping with a married man, not even a handsome, filthy rich one, to even the score. Daddy was already shaking his head.

"My daughters are not part of this deal. Hell no."

Dante relaxed into the chair, his smile growing bigger. "Yeah, I think I like that idea. Ms. Dream came here to bargain for her brother. Let's see how far she's willing to go."

"What about your wife?" Daddy asked, his voice tight.

"Oh, Dream's pretty, but she's not for me," he said.

I frowned. "Who…"

I stopped as the office door opened and the guard came back in. But this time, he was followed by someone. My jaw dropped as the second man stepped in. He was literally blood-spattered, which only added to his terrifying look. He stood well over six feet and every inch of him that I could see, aside from the smooth, light brown skin of his face, was tattooed. Shoulder-length locs framed a face that might actually be handsome if his expression weren't so cold. Green eyes took in everybody in the room before settling on Dante. I was glad they were off me. This man gave me chills. Still, I couldn't look away from him. It was like I was mesmerized, a victim of his commanding presence.

"No," my father said, shaking his head hard as hell. "Hell no. Not him."

Dante chuckled. "You know how this works, Castle. You think your daughter is better than mine?"

"No, but she's in no danger from my son. Can you guarantee my daughter will be safe with him?"

With him? My eyes flew back to the man who had just walked in. Surely, they didn't think I was about to lie down with this cold-eyed, crazy-looking stranger?! His bloody t-shirt and jeans said all I needed to know. And his eyes… I shuddered again. They held nothing. I'd never seen someone look so blank.

"I'm sorry, but I can't—" I spoke up.

My voice trailed off as Dante's smile disappeared. His eyes narrowed on me, and I shivered under his glare.

"C'mon now, Ms. Dream. You want to save your brother.

His life is in your hands. All you have to do is make the same sacrifice my daughter did."

"Your daughter didn't sacrifice. She loves DeAngelo—" I began.

"She sacrificed the plans I had for her. The same kind of plans I'm sure your father has for you. She's damaged goods, now. Her reputation will never be the same. So, neither will yours," he said coldly.

I winced inwardly at hearing how he talked about his own daughter. But that was the way men like him and my father thought. Women were possessions to them, things to be fucked, traded, or used as they saw fit. I'd fought against that my whole life, and now, here I was, about to be part of some negotiations. Bitterness rose in my throat, but I swallowed it down.

"I'm not ready to get married—" I tried again.

Dante waved his hand, cutting me off. "No marriage. Something short term. Just long enough to…"

His voice trailed off and I waited for him to finish. Instead, he gave another one of those mysterious smiles.

"Dante, I understand how you're thinking. But pick somebody else in the organization. Not Demon. For fuck's sake, he's not even sane half the time," my father bargained.

Demon? They called him *Demon*? My heart dropped even further. Those green eyes were on my father, and I was surprised to see "Demon's" mouth twist up in a smirk.

"Anybody wanna tell me what the fuck is going on?" he asked suddenly.

His voice was deep and rough. It fit him perfectly.

"His fuckboy son eloped with my baby. Now, they owe me. And Ms. Dream here is gon' pay part of the debt if she knows what's good for her brother," Dante explained abruptly.

Those green eyes were suddenly gazing at me again. This time, they weren't so empty. I couldn't identify everything I saw in them, but I knew one thing: these were the eyes of a man who had seen and done some terrifying things.

"A daughter for a daughter," he said softly, like it made sense.

What was wrong with these people?

Dante nodded.

"Exactly. I thought you could do the honors. That is, if Ms. Dream consents."

Their eyes were on me again and I couldn't find my voice. I could hear my father objecting, could feel my own reservations. But a pair of green eyes had me stuck.

"What do you say, Ms. Dream? Are you gon' save your brother?" Dante goaded.

I knew then that he would not let the idea go. He was determined that I give myself to this man whose sanity my father questioned.

"What happens if I don't?"

I still had to ask. Some crazy part of me needed to hear the words before I made this deal with a devil.

His smile turned even deadlier. "You know what will happen, Ms. Dream. You know your family can't stop me."

My father made a strangled sound, evidence of his rage, but he didn't have the power or the reach that Dante had. I had no doubt Daddy would try to avenge DeAngelo, but his efforts would be in vain, and he'd probably end up dead, too. I would not let it get that far.

"And… and the baby?" I asked softly. "You would just take your grandchild's father—"

"Oh, he'll have a father. I'll marry my daughter off—not as good of a marriage as she could have had—but one where the nigga will adopt her baby and be the only father the kid ever knows. So, your brother will not only have no life; he'll have no legacy."

He would do it. I knew he would. Dante was known for his ruthlessness, for his willingness to kill anybody to protect his empire and his pride. My eyes flitted to Demon who was looking at me intently. I swallowed as I looked away, unable to handle the enigma of his eyes.

"Two favors will save him, right?"

Dante nodded. "So, what you gon' do, Ms. Dream?"

"Dante. You know it'll be like she's been marked. No one else will ever—" my daddy started.

"I asked Dream," Dante interrupted.

I needed to answer. It was, what, a few nights at the most, I told myself. A few nights out of the rest of my life. I could do this, help my brother, and move on. I could do this with a blood-soaked, cold-eyed stranger and come out okay. I looked up into the green eyes again and found myself drowning.

"I...okay," I whispered.

Dante smiled. "Glad you see it my way." He turned to Demon. "Well?"

He looked at me again, green eyes holding mine for what felt like forever before he nodded. Then he left as quietly as he'd come.

I pressed a palm against my chest where my heart was racing with a strange combination of fear... and anticipation. Dante grinned again as he steepled his fingers under his chin and rested his elbows on his desk.

"Now. Let's make some arrangements."

CHAPTER 5

Dante

(*AN HOUR later*)

I flicked the engraved, solid gold lighter on and off, my eyes focused on the flame as the night's events replayed in my head. Every once in a while, a nigga could admit he got too cocky. I never would've thought my baby girl would've played me like this. Sherrilyn and I kept a tight rein on Crystal and our teenaged son DJ. I had plans for my kids, plans that would keep them on top of shit, ensure that their kids and their kids' kids would be all right. Crystal had thrown that away for what? Some love shit? I laughed quietly. Silly ass girl. I should cut her ass off, let her see how far love would get her. The Castles were rich, but they didn't have money like mine. Take away a few of her luxuries and see how deep her love was. But even as I thought it, I knew I couldn't do that to my baby... my *pregnant* baby, if they were telling the truth.

Sighing, I shook my head. I wasn't expecting the message Darius Castle delivered. He'd supplied guns for me in the past and, truthfully, when he requested the meeting and mentioned bringing his daughter, I thought he wanted to introduce her to one of his customers, maybe show her how deals were made, bring her into the business as he expanded. No way in fuck I'd let the women in my family be involved in the business like that but, as Crystal liked to tell me, it was a new day and age. Women were running a lot of shit that they hadn't when my pops first brought me into this world, and I thought that Dream may have been part of that. Castle had scaled back his operation years ago, although he was still one of the best-known gun runners in this part of the country. Now, he was looking to grow again, to make the alliances that would bring him more business and the kind of protection he'd need. Hell, I would've been willing to make some kind of deal with him. But not for my daughter. She deserved bigger, better, more. And DeAngelo Castle had fucked that up. Usually, nothing would satisfy me but bloodshed. Tonight, they got lucky.

I knew Darius, but I'd had to get information on his daughter quickly. Dream was impressive on paper and even better in person. Beautiful and composed, she'd mostly kept her cool during everything that unfolded. In a couple of years, shorty would be a true asset to the empire her father was trying to re-build. The only thing that seemed to shake her was Demon and that nigga had everybody shook. Recognizing that she was something special as I sat there looking at her, I'd come up with this crazy idea.

Just last night, I'd been thinking about how Demon needed a soft spot, a touch of humanity. Knowing the life he'd had, I was protective of my brother, even though he'd probably kill me for thinking like that. If I couldn't do anything else, I wanted to help the nigga find some peace, some little bit of happiness in his fucked-up life. I didn't get to be one of the richest niggas in the state just because I followed my head —I also knew when to follow my gut instincts. And my instincts told me that Dream Castle—smart, pretty, outspoken, loyal—might be just the connection my brother needed.

Now, if he would've been as uninterested as he usually was, I would've left the shit alone. Demon had never had a girlfriend that I'd known of, never been out with a woman, or brought one around the few family events he attended. I'd seen bitches shoot their shot and he'd look right through them. The one time Sherrilyn's nosy ass tried to ask about his love life, he'd grilled her so hard that I would've killed the nigga if he weren't my brother. So, I knew it was a long shot. But then he'd walked into my office and saw her. He'd stopped for just a second, a pause anyone else would've missed, but I'd been studying this nigga since he was fourteen. His frozen eyes had changed when he looked at her. I watched him watch her and I felt like I was on the right track. And when he agreed to the shit instead of cussing me out for interfering in his life like he usually would, I *knew* I was.

I flicked the lighter on and brought the flame to the tip of the blunt I had been holding. I laughed to myself again. He was gon' fight it, but Ms. Dream might be the one to prove this nigga had a heart.

I couldn't wait to see it.

CHAPTER 6
Damien "Demon" Montana

I TENSED as the water hit my body, then let out a slow breath as I adjusted to the steaming hot temperature. I had just finished handling the sick nigga that Dante had come to me about. I should've made Dante send a driver for me earlier since I didn't want blood in my car. But I didn't like people knowing where I lived, so I was stuck showering at his house before I could leave. I let the water hit me from all sides for a few minutes before I picked up the washcloth and body wash. The red stains on my hands had already disappeared, but I lathered up and rinsed off three times to wash the night's work away. I usually felt satisfied with a job like tonight's, ready to get home and sleep as the adrenaline faded. But not tonight. Tonight, I felt restless, ready for something else. I already knew what it was, but I refused to accept that she had that much power.

Dream, Dante had called her. She was the first thing I saw when I walked into that room, and instantly, I wanted to take her, figure out what it was besides fear in her chocolate eyes. It wasn't like I needed Dante to recruit pussy for me. Any other time I would've told him fuck no. My interactions with women were clear cut, no feelings allowed. The high-end escorts I used knew they weren't getting conversation or spending the night. I got my dick (well, my condom) wet; they got paid.

But Dream... she sat there, beautiful and a mix of bold and scared. My dick responded instantly to that combination. It stirred now as I closed my eyes and thought of her, hardening as I remembered her full, glossed lips and those doe eyes. Reaching down, I grabbed my dick and pulled it slowly, envisioning her on her knees in front of me, her pretty mouth wrapped around me. Willing... submissive... *mine*...

My eyes flew open at that last thought. I didn't want to own her. I *couldn't* want that. I had no interest in holding on to any bitch for the long term. I just needed to get her, fuck her, and see that she was nothing special.

Speaking of fucking her... I stroked myself rhythmically as I imagined her bent over and spread, her pussy stretched around my dick. I wanted to fuck her hard and fast, make her scream with pleasure and pain. My hand moved faster as I thought about destroying her prim and proper look, fucking up her hair, smearing her lip gloss, marking her smooth skin as I pounded into her mercilessly.

"Fuck!" I grunted as I felt the telltale tingling in my balls, letting me know I was about to cum.

I aimed at the drain, letting my thick release wash away with the water as her image danced in front of my eyes. Finally, I fell back against the shower wall, waiting for my heartbeat to return to normal. I finished minutes later. Stepping out, I dried off quickly before getting dressed and going in search of Dante. He was still in his office, smoking a blunt, looking like his mind was a million miles away. I took a seat across from him and he gave me a half-ass smile.

"You change your mind?"

I ignored the question and the blunt he tried to hand me. "Who is she?"

He smirked at me.

"Pretty, ain't she? You lucky I thought about you. I woulda kept her for myself—"

"No."

I wouldn't even entertain that possibility. The one word got his attention, and a smug smile crossed his face as he looked at me.

"Her time is yours whenever you want it," he said finally.

"Soon," I said.

"Of course."

He sat back and studied me for a moment. I waited, the only sound in the room the slow ticking of the grandfather clock in one corner. I knew he didn't like the silence, wished I would talk more, but he was the one who should have more to say.

"Not much to tell about her. She's twenty-four years old and works with her father's money. Graduated from Yale three years ago. No serious boyfriends. Good reputation, so I'm sure Castle was planning to marry her off in some kind of deal. That shit's not happening, though. You get thirty days with her, on your terms, whatever you want—well, no permanent markings, modifications, or damage."

My head snapped up and I frowned at him. "I don't hurt women."

That was true... except for one time. One time that couldn't be helped. One time I'd never forget. I knew Dante was thinking the same thing as he stared at me. Finally, he spoke again.

"Starts when you say so."

Nodding, I stood.

"Address and phone number," I said abruptly.

"I'll send it. She's a good girl. Still lives at home."

I turned to walk out, but he called my name. I faced him again.

"I want Castle to lose what I've lost—the ability to arrange his daughter's marriage to benefit the family. I don't mean to offend yo' crazy ass, but you know yo' reputation. People respect you, but they fear you. If you show interest... more than you usually do, they'll assume she's yours. They won't touch her," he said.

He was asking me to make this shit public, knowing I didn't fuck around about my privacy. Part of me liked the idea of keeping other niggas away from her, though. That realization fucked with me, and I wanted to leave, figure out what the hell I was thinking. Without saying another word, I left his office and his house. By the time I got in my car, he had sent the information I requested. I was tired, but that didn't keep me from taking off in the direction of her house.

Thirty minutes later, I sat across the street from the mini-mansion, in the not-so-secure-gated community, wondering which room was hers. Suddenly, a door on the second floor opened and someone stepped out onto the balcony. It only took a moment for me to realize it was her. Dressed in a dark-colored, silky-looking robe, she was thick in all the right places, her body matching the beauty of her face. My dick jumped in response to her. She walked up to the railing and wrapped her arms around herself, staring off into the darkness.

What was she thinking about? The deal she had made tonight? The crazy nigga she was supposed to spread her legs for? Was she scared? That thought bothered me for some reason, but I shook my head sharply. A nigga was tripping. I thrived on people's fear. Why should she be any different?

For ten minutes, she stood on the balcony. I sat, unwilling to move, looking at her. I watched as a dark-colored Mercedes pulled through the open gates and onto her driveway. Some lame looking nigga in a designer suit emerged and looked up at her. He said something and she stepped closer to the railing, a smile on her face. Was that why the front gate was open? Had she been waiting for him? *No serious boyfriends,* Dante had said. Then who the fuck was this? My jaw clenched as she disappeared into the house, and he walked to the front door. A minute later, she was opening the door and he pulled her into a hug.

Something dark and cold spilled inside me as my hands balled into fists. One word churned inside my raging brain: *mine*. She stepped back to let him in before closing the door. Was she about to fuck him when she had just agreed to fuck me? That shit wasn't happening. Until I was done with her, she was done with other niggas.

I got out of my car and jogged across the street to her house. I knocked once and waited, turning to look at his license plate and commit it to memory. Seconds later, the door swung open, and she stood there. My eyes were stuck on her face with its pretty brown eyes and plump lips. Her smile slowly disappeared, replaced with a small frown. I didn't like that shit.

"You," she said softly.

"Yeah. Me."

CHAPTER 7

Dream

HEART RACING, I looked up into the blank face of the man in front of me. He was the last person I was expecting, despite that disaster of a meeting with Dante. He had cleaned up, but he looked just as menacing in his dark clothes. He was so tall and built as solidly as a football player. Without the blood and gore covering him, he was almost beautiful... in a scary kind of way. I wasn't a big fan of tattoos, but this close-up, I could see how intricate and beautiful his were, his light skin the perfect canvas. My body reacted instinctively, heat spreading through my veins. I feared him but, if the sudden, slow throbbing between my legs was any indication, I wanted him, too. Green eyes peered down at me, waiting. I shook off the haze of lust I was feeling.

"I thought I would have some time—"

His gaze cut me off. My hand went to my throat as I stared at him. Nervous, I could feel myself shaking, but I moved back to let him in. He walked through the doorway, his eyes immediately darting to where Isaac sat on the couch.

"He needs to go."

The words were a low rumble. I wanted to open my

mouth and tell him he didn't get to dictate who was at my house. The look in his eyes robbed me of words, though. I nodded slowly.

"Dream? What's going on? You okay?" Isaac asked, walking closer to me.

I felt Demon tense, knew Isaac better tread carefully before he set him off.

"It's fine, Isaac. Can we catch up tomorrow, though?"

I touched his shoulder. Demon cleared his throat, and I raised my gaze to his. His eyes were fixed on my hand on Isaac's shoulder, a small frown on his face. Slowly, my hand fell away.

"If you're sure…" Isaac said hesitantly.

"I'm sure. I just have some business with…" my voice trailed off as I gestured toward the man in front of me.

Isaac's eyes narrowed. "You got business with Demon?"

My eyes flew to his face, surprised Isaac's strait-laced self knew who Demon was.

"Ain't that what she said?" Demon inquired calmly.

Isaac eyeballed him with a mix of fear and disgust on his face. Demon smirked at him and waited. Isaac didn't know what to do. He didn't want to leave me alone with Demon, but it was obvious he didn't want to fuck with him either.

"Does Mr. Castle know about this?" he asked finally.

Demon moved suddenly, walking until he was inches away from him.

"Noooo," I whispered.

Isaac took a step back and swallowed, but he caught himself and met Demon's gaze. I had to give him credit. He looked like he wanted to disappear, but he was trying to stand his ground. Unfortunately, I didn't know if that was brave or stupid as hell.

"Leave," Demon snarled.

Isaac shook his head. "I—"

Demon's hand shot out and grabbed him by the throat

before squeezing. My mouth fell open in surprise as Isaac gasped for air, his hands flailing around helplessly. Finally, I grasped Demon's arm.

"Stop! Please!" I begged.

I didn't think he was going to listen to me. He was going to kill Isaac in my living room, in front of me, and I couldn't stop him. I panicked, dots dancing in front of my eyes and my breath heaving in and out as I opened my mouth to scream for help. He looked down at me and all the air left my body. Suddenly, his hand opened. Isaac fell to the floor, coughing and clutching his throat. I squatted beside him, trying to see if he was okay. Before I could utter a word, a strong arm was around me, yanking me up. I stood with my back pressed to Demon's impossibly hard front.

"Leave," he repeated.

This time, Isaac nodded. He scrambled off the floor and quickly straightened his clothes. I twisted out of Demon's arms and walked him to the door, apologizing softly the whole time. He was silent until he stepped outside. Still holding his throat, he turned to look at me, his face twisted into a nasty scowl.

"That's the kind of nigga you wanna be involved with?"

My eyes widened at the accusation in his tone. "Isaac, I—"

"Be careful, Dream," he muttered, before walking off.

I closed the door behind him slowly, then locked it, stalling. Anger surged through me at Demon's actions. I understood he had a reputation, but this shit was uncalled for. I whirled around and walked back toward him. Yes, the nigga was scary. But I was one who always spoke my mind.

"Was that really necessary?" I snapped.

His expression never changed as he shrugged. "It is when niggas make me repeat myself."

I sighed and rubbed a hand across my face. Maybe the best thing to do was to go ahead and settle this debt, start this thirty-day sacrifice. I didn't want this man in my life any longer than he had to be.

"Look, let's just get this started. My whole family lives here so we can't... do anything. Do you have somewhere to... to take me?"

I could feel myself blushing as I spoke, my eyes dropping to the marble floor. He didn't answer me for a minute. I lifted my gaze, confused.

"I'm not here to fuck you, Dream."

My head snapped back as I frowned. "Then what are you here for, Demon?"

He shook his head immediately. "No. You don't call me that," he told me, his voice tight. "Damien," he said. "My name is Damien."

"Damien..." I repeated. "Why are you here?"

He shrugged. "To talk to you."

I felt skeptical, but I said nothing. Instead, I chewed on my bottom lip and waited. He stepped closer to me and reached out his hand. Using his index finger, he pulled my mangled lip free of my teeth.

"You made a deal tonight."

"I-I know that," I stuttered, caught off guard by his warm touch.

"You need to understand a couple of things," he continued, his finger sliding upward to caress my cheek.

Something sparked between us, something I tried to ignore. Still quiet, I raised an eyebrow. He leaned forward, bringing his lips closer to my ear.

"I want to make sure I have your consent."

I swallowed, surprised that mattered to him. "It was implied when I took the deal. I'm a willing participant, Damien," I promised.

"When I'm ready, I'm gon' fuck you however, whenever, wherever I want to," he said in that low, unexpectedly sexy voice.

I sucked in air, the warmth of his breath against my ear and his erotic words making me shiver. I wanted to argue with him, deny him that much control over my life, but the words wouldn't come. Instead, he spoke again.

"Until then, you won't be entertaining any other niggas. You mine until this deal is done. Understand?"

He stepped back so our eyes could meet. Slowly, I nodded, against my better judgment.

"Good," he said softly.

I watched as his gaze trailed over me again, his eyes warming as he took in the fullness of my breasts and hips in the clingy robe.

"You always answer the door like this?" He reached out and touched my silky lapel.

"When... when are you going to want to... start this?" I asked, ignoring his question.

The thirty-day clock wouldn't start ticking until he said so. Dante had been insistent about that. He seemed to take a strange pleasure in working out the details of this deal.

"Why? You anxious?" Damien teased, surprising me.

I sucked my teeth. "I just want it to be over with. I don't like owing your brother."

Rather than answer me, he leaned in, bringing his nose closer to my throat, inhaling the scent I wore. His skin grazed mine and I felt the electric energy running between us. I gasped and moved back so quickly that I stumbled. He grabbed me to keep me upright, pulling me against his body.

Solid. He was so fucking solid and warm that I wanted to feel more of him. Despite my fear, my body was responding to his, my curves melting against his muscular frame. I looked up at him, chewing on my bottom lip again as I felt color flood my face.

"You good?"

I nodded, but didn't move. I wanted him to hold me

tighter, let his fingers explore my thick figure. Instead, he dropped his hands.

"I'll be in touch," he said abruptly before striding toward the door.

He didn't wait for me to follow before letting himself out.

CHAPTER 8

Demon

HOLDING her in my arms knocked a nigga off game. I had to leave because I didn't like the way she made me feel. It had already fucked with me when she grabbed my arm while I choked that nigga out. Something about her touch calmed the demon inside me. I felt my anger rolling back, the desire to kill that nigga fading. No one had ever had that much power over me.

I hopped in my car and sped away, intent on clearing my mind. Heading toward my house, I opened the glove compartment and grabbed one of the pre-rolled blunts that I kept in there. I sparked up and brought it to my lips. As I faced the blunt, I replayed all the shit that had happened tonight. Dante may have set this in motion, but it was going to go how I wanted. Just like I told her, I was going to fuck her when I got ready, then walk away.

Twenty minutes later, I pulled into my garage. I made my way into the house and checked out everything. Finally satisfied that no one had broken in and that I had no surprises waiting, I grabbed a bottle of water from the kitchen and jogged upstairs to my bedroom. I changed into a tank top and ball shorts, brushed my teeth, and slid under the covers. Sleep came quickly. And because I'd killed a child predator tonight, so did the dreams...

———

My mama didn't have any clothes on. I wasn't surprised, not even by the naked man behind her, who was slapping his body against hers. I knew I wasn't supposed to bother her, but my baby sister, Kiana, and I were hungry. I stood in the door of the living room, hoping she would hurry up and get done. The man was pulling her hair and she was screaming like he was hurting her. I wanted to help, but the last time I tried, her boyfriend Silas had beaten me with his belt until I started bleeding. Said something about I was "messin' with" his money. I wanted to kill him, but I couldn't at seven years old. One day, though.

I knew I shouldn't be looking at her. It made me sick to my stomach, made my chest hurt. My eyes darted around the filthy room as I tried to block out their grunting. Clothes were everywhere. I knew they were dirty—we never had clean clothes. Stains covered the gray carpet, and the black furniture was patched with duct tape. Empty fast-food bags covered the coffee table and my stomach growled as I thought about the scraps they might have. Mama never finished all her food...

"The fuck you doing, you little freak? You get off seeing your mama get banged?" Silas's voice hissed from behind me, breaking me out of my thoughts.

Damn! I couldn't believe I was stupid enough to get caught. I started shaking because I knew I was in trouble. Scared, I made a little sound as he grabbed the back of my shirt and pulled. My mama looked up, right at me.

She didn't stop what she was doing. The way her eyes looked, I bet she didn't even recognize me.

Silas dragged me into the bedroom he shared with my mama, a cigarette hanging from his lips, his face twisted into an ugly frown.

"What I done told you about messin' with my money, nigga?" he asked me.

"I just wanted to ask her about some food—" I tried to explain, even though it wouldn't do any good.

"Then you ask her when she not busy, you stupid fuck!"

He backhanded me and I flew against the wall, pain shooting through my body. I slid down slowly, feeling tears well in my eyes as anger grew in me. I shouldn't even have to go through all this. I could've fixed me and KiKi some food, but Silas had padlocked the refrigerator and cabinets, claiming we ate too much. I needed the keys from Mama.

"Get yo' ass up!" Silas roared.

I pulled myself up off the floor as he came to tower over me.

"When you gon' learn not to fuck with me?"

His voice was calm, but I knew the worst was coming. I didn't say anything.

"Take that shirt off," he ordered.

My hands went to the bottom of the shirt, about to obey him. But something stopped me. I looked up at him, tired of all of it. I suddenly felt braver than I ever had with him.

"No," I said.

I could tell I had surprised him. He just stood there for a minute. But then, he started smiling. I knew that was bad. Very, very bad.

"You said, 'no,' boy?" he asked, laughing softly.

Swallowing, I nodded. He walked out of the room. I didn't know if I was supposed to stay there or go back to my room. Just when I had made up my mind to leave, he came back, KiKi in his arms. My heart sped up and I felt hot and cold all at once.

"I'll take it off," I said, reaching for her. "Please, I'll—"

He took a deep pull of the cigarette. I watched as the tip glowed bright, red hot, before he took it out of his mouth. At two, KiKi just had on a onesie, leaving her chubby thighs exposed. He brought the cigarette down, stopping a half-inch away from her skin.

"You wanna think about what you said?"

I nodded, yanking my shirt over my head as fast as I could. He gave me half a smile.

"That's what I thought. Don't you ever tell me no, nigga."

He stuck the cigarette back in his mouth. I sighed in relief, glad to save my sister from him, even if it meant more pain for me. Then, his smile widened and, moving quickly, he yanked the cigarette from his mouth and buried the tip against my sister's skin. She frowned in shock, then screamed. My tears spill over as I yelled, "No!"

I grabbed KiKi from his arms, holding her close to me as we both cried. Silas grinned at us.

"Don't fuck with me, boy! I ain't one to play with!"

He walked behind me. A second later, I felt the burning sting as he jabbed the cigarette in my back. My knees buckled, but I stayed upright, holding on to my little sister as her body shook against mine. I wasn't going to fall. The more I reacted, the more Silas enjoyed it. I blinked back tears and stood still as he added more wounds to the ones that he'd already burned and beaten into me. I lost count at some point, focusing on the stains on the sheet that covered the mattress where it lay on the floor. He was going to pay for this. For everything.

I promised myself that.

———

I sat up suddenly, sweat pouring off me, as my heart thudded in my chest. I glanced around the room, searching for the source of my nightmare, even though I knew that shit was past. My locs hung in my face, blocking my view. I pushed them back with one hand, grabbing the water bottle off my nightstand with the other. Popping the top, I swallowed half the bottle as my pulse slowed and I woke all the way up.

I hadn't thought about Silas Andrews in a long time. I hadn't let myself think about KiKi in forever, either. Refusing to let my thoughts stay on either of them, I stood up. I grabbed clean sheets from the linen cabinet and changed my bed. But when I finished, I didn't want to get back in it. Not alone, anyway. I thought about calling the escort service I occasionally used, having them send someone who would already know what my likes and dislikes were. I liked the type of woman who got up and left without all the clinging and whining and trying to get a nigga to make promises. But I didn't want an escort. I wanted...

Dream. I remembered how she had made me feel earlier, how her touch brought me peace. I needed that on nights like tonight. I could have her. She was mine whenever I chose to take her. A month of her beautiful face and her calming presence. I reached for my phone. My finger was hovering over her contact when I shook my head suddenly, rejecting that idea. I didn't need anything or anyone as a crutch. I had dealt with memories before, and I could again.

But I didn't sleep anymore the rest of that night.

CHAPTER 9
Dream

(*FRIDAY*, *May 14*)

My brother narrowed his eyes as his gaze drifted over me. It was the day after our meeting with Dante, and DeAngelo was pressing me for information. Trying to act nonchalant, I picked up my glass of iced tea and took a sip before turning my attention to the sandwich and chips I had fixed for my lunch.

"I wanna know what he wanted," DeAngelo finally spoke.

"D, I told you he didn't tell us yet!"

I hadn't told him about the deal Dante had made involving me. He'd go crazy and I wasn't about to let him ruin this.

"So, he let y'all walk out of his office with no details?"

I shrugged. "He said he'd collect later."

"And Dad accepted that?"

"What choice did he have? That man was about to kill him in your place!" I fussed.

He exhaled sharply, frustration clear on his face.

"I'm sorry I got y'all—"

I held up a hand, not wanting to hear the bullshit.

"Don't even worry about it."

"You say that now, but what if he asks for something crazy? What if…"

I lost track of DeAngelo's voice as I thought of what Dante was asking—no, *demanding*—of me. A daughter for a daughter, he'd said. I couldn't lie—I was conflicted. Daddy had told me more about Damien and his reputation for killing people. Then, seeing him choke Isaac like he was willing to kill him without a second thought hadn't helped. What if he snapped on me? What if I didn't please him? Would I end up like the person whose blood was splashed over him last night?

But then… there was the way he held me against him, after I'd almost fallen. And the look in his eyes when he told me to call him Damien. Part of me was convinced that he wasn't all crazy. That part was actually kind of fascinated by the so-called demon.

"Dream! Hello! Where the hell your mind at?" DeAngelo asked, annoyed.

I shook my head to clear it before frowning at him.

"Stop yelling at me! I'ma…"

My sentence faded as my grandfather entered the room. One look at his face and I knew he knew what was up. He clearly wasn't happy about it. He eyeballed me and said, "Hmph!" before wheeling himself to the refrigerator.

"You want me to fix you something?" I asked him.

He ignored me. That shit never happened. DeAngelo shot me a puzzled look before getting up and walking to Grandpapa.

"What's up, old man?" DeAngelo greeted, rubbing his back.

Grandpapa glared up at him and mumbled something.

"Did you just call me a fool?"

"Does that shit fit?" our grandfather snapped.

"That's how you doing me, Papa?"

"Get out my face, boy. Go back over there with yo' silly ass sister."

I didn't say a word, just lifted my sandwich as DeAngelo walked back toward me. *What's wrong with him?* my brother mouthed. I shrugged and bit into my ham and cheese. Which was exactly why I had a mouth full of food when my grandfather turned to stare at us.

"Of course, she might not want you next to her. I wouldn't blame her for being mad at yo' ass," he spat.

I chewed quickly, wanting to stop where this was going.

"Grandpapa..." I tried to cut in.

"Hush, girl. You gon' act like it's no big deal, trading yourself for his debt?"

The kitchen went completely silent then. I shifted my eyes from DeAngelo, who was looking at me with his mouth hanging open. He grabbed my chin, forcing me to meet his gaze.

"What... what is he talking about, Dream?"

Grandpapa snorted. "She ain't told you?"

DeAngelo shook his head.

"Dante says you 'took' Crystal, so he's taking yo' sister. Or, at least, his crazy ass brother is."

DeAngelo stood there for a minute, and then his eyes widened.

"Demon? He's matching you... with Demon?"

"D, it's not that serious—" I began, reaching toward him, but he was already shaking his head.

"No. Hell no! Whatever you agreed to, un-agree. Crystal and I will go see him—"

I sucked my teeth.

"So he can kill you in front of her? Nigga almost blew Daddy's head off already. You know there's no backing out of a deal with Dante!"

"Why would you accept that shit? And where the fuck was Dad?" DeAngelo raged, pacing back and forth.

"We ain't in a position to say no, D! I don't know why you

and Crystal act like you don't understand that!" I snapped, tired of his shit.

He looked at me for a long moment before striding out of the kitchen. I rubbed the back of my neck as I shook my head.

"Why did you do that?" I asked my grandfather quietly.

"He needed to know. He don't get off like this ain't costing you," he said unapologetically.

"You know he gon' do something stupid!"

"He already did something stupid, running off and marrying that girl."

I sighed, unwilling to argue.

"You feel like fixing me some of whatever you eating?" he asked, like he hadn't just blown shit up.

Silently, I got up to make his lunch. My plans for the day circled through my mind as I worked. I needed to check on Isaac and explain to him what was going on. I had been about to let him cuff me, so I wanted to tell him, before the rumor mill did, about my arrangement with Demon.

Damien, my mind corrected instantly. The minute his name popped into my head, I thought of his tall, imposing figure. He made my heart beat faster and I didn't want to acknowledge some of the reasons why. As scary as he was, he was also sexy, in a crazy kind of way. I found myself attracted to him even as I was put off by what he did. It didn't make sense, but here I was.

I finished quickly, setting my grandfather's food on the heavy wood table before pouring him a glass of tea.

"Eat with me?" he asked.

I nodded and went back to my seat.

"You mad at me?"

"No, sir. Of course not," I answered him truthfully.

"Good."

"I just don't want D to do anything—"

"Dream, DeAngelo is grown. You can't protect him from

everything. He knows Dante is pissed off right now. If he takes his stupid ass over there, that's his fault."

"But, Grandpapa—"

He held up a hand, silencing me. "Eat. I don't want to argue about that boy."

Sighing, I followed his directions.

CHAPTER 10

Demon

RED ROSE IN THE GRAY PAVEMENT

Young black nigga trapped, and he can't change it
Know he a genius, he just can't claim it
Cuz they left him no platforms to explain it

NIP'S VOICE spilled from my speakers as I parked a block away from my destination. It was the middle of the day, but this place always seemed dark to me. I took in the boarded-up houses, broken chain-link fences, and overgrown grass. Shit never changed around here, no matter how hard some people who lived here tried.

Grabbing a manila envelope, I hopped out of my customized truck and crossed the street to the cracked side-walk. I hated being here, hated the memories this neighbor-hood dug up, but I had shit to handle. Strolling the sidewalk, I ignored the people who stepped down into the street rather than walk close to me. I'd heard the rumors myself that I would kill someone for bumping into me or looking at me crazy. Shit made me smile.

My feet slowed in front of an empty lot, although I refused to turn and look at it. A house was there once. An ugly, green shack where trash littered the yard and the inside, the property and the people who lived there abandoned and neglected. It had finally been deserted, condemned and boarded-up like so many places around here. But that hadn't been enough. It needed to be gone, every trace of it wiped the fuck out. I had made sure that happened. But removing it from this space hadn't removed it from the place it took up in my mind.

Shaking my head, I walked the few yards to the next house. I watched as two fiends rushed through the gate, smiling hard as hell. They were on their way to get fucked up, floating in their own idea of heaven until they came crashing down and the search for more started again. I stopped as they got closer to me, their heads bowed as they talked to one another. They didn't even notice me until the woman ran right into me and fell down. Both of them looked up, and I smirked as their eyes widened.

"Demon," the man whispered as the woman scrambled up and tried to hide behind him.

I knew them. They were only a couple of years older than I was. This nigga, Trent, was supposed to be somewhere playing ball, living a hood kid's hoop dreams. He'd been that good. Instead, the coke he'd sniffed in college had led to heavier shit. And now, here he was, front teeth missing, smelling like death, and about to scratch a hole in his skinny, tracked up arms.

"Ay, we sorry, man. I done told Sheka about watching where she going, but—"

"You buying from Ms. Hazel's house."

It wasn't a question. I already knew the answer as my eyes settled on Ms. Hazel's porch and saw her sorry ass, wanna-be-kingpin son, Jyrell, standing there.

Trent nodded hesitantly. I looked down at him for a minute, long enough for him to start squirming and sweating even harder.

"You come to this house again, it's gon' be your last high," I told him calmly.

"O-o-okay. I'm sorry, Demon. I didn't know. He said to—"

I walked off, not interested in his stuttered apologies and excuses. I had said all I intended to say to him. I opened Ms. Hazel's gate and made my way up the walkway. Flowers decorated the sides of the path, leading up to the rose bushes that set her house apart from her neighbors'. Ms. Hazel was always looking for the beauty in shit. It was naïve to me, but she was seventy-something and still optimistic. It kept her going.

I jogged up her porch steps and noticed one was sagging. My attention was on Jyrell right now, though. He was out here doing this shit with his sixteen-year-old nephew Bryson on the porch with him. Bryson and his little sister Breshay lived with Ms. Hazel, two of the many kids she'd taken in over the years.

"You bringing that shit to your mama's front door?"

My voice was low. I didn't want to alarm Ms. Hazel if she were near the front door.

He held up both his hands. "Look, Demon. I'on want no problems. It was a onetime thing. I gotta get this money when—"

I stepped closer to him, shutting his stupid ass up. He cleared his throat, looking up at me with big eyes. I smiled at the fear I saw there. I wanted to hurt him. Bad. But that would mean hurting his mama and I didn't want to do that.

"Respect yo' mama and her house. Understand?"

His head bobbed up and down quickly.

"Yeah. I was finna get outta here, anyway," he mumbled.

"Good," I said.

"You ain't gon' tell Mama bye?" Bryson piped up.

I could see the smile he was trying to hide as he watched Jyrell creep past me and bolt down the steps. He knew his uncle wasn't about shit.

"Sup, Demon?" he greeted as Jyrell peeled off.

I nodded once and handed him the envelope with five stacks inside.

"Give this to your grandmother. Y'all get that step fixed."

"A'ight."

He stood and walked toward the front door. It was time for me to leave. Ms. Hazel was going to want to see me, and I didn't like that shit. She always wanted to thank me and talk and ask questions. That wasn't me. I walked out of her yard and was halfway down the block when I heard Bryson call my name. *Fuck!* I ignored him, but the little nigga had the nerve to call me again and add, "Mama want you!"

I paused for a moment before turning around and making my way back. Bryson waited at the door for me, then led me through the spotless house and into the kitchen. Whatever the hell she was cooking smelled good as fuck. I posted up by the kitchen doorway, waiting. Turning, she smiled at me.

"Hey, Damien."

Ever since I was younger, she had refused to call me "Demon." "*You ain't no damn devil,*" she fussed at me one day. "*We not speaking that into being.*" I didn't tell her it was too late.

"Come sit down," she invited as she settled down at the kitchen table.

"I'm good."

She showed no reaction to my abrupt tone, just kept smiling at me. "I was just about to ask how you doing."

"Fine."

"I know it ain't gon' do no good, but I keep telling you, you don't have to bring me money. You don't owe me, Damien. Not for anything," she said softly, her brown eyes gazing into mine.

I shrugged. We disagreed on that; I owed her *everything*. I wasn't going to argue, though.

"Anyway, I just wanted to tell you thank you. For the money… and for Eve."

Ms. Hazel was Eve's grandmother. They were tight as hell, so I wasn't surprised she told her about Marshall.

"You ain't gotta thank me for the money. And I ain't done nothing for Eve," I lied.

She smiled again. "Okay, baby. You want something to eat?"

I was tempted—the aroma of the food had my mouth watering. It would taste just as good as it smelled. She'd fed me enough for me to know that. A long time ago, her kitchen had been the best, safest place in the world to me. But I needed to get out of there, away from Ms. Hazel's eyes. She saw too much, made me feel uncomfortable in a way.

I shook my head.

"You still don't say much. I guess you never will," she said. "You take care, Damien. I would ask to hug you, but—"

"Bye, Ms. Hazel."

This time, I made it to my truck with no issues. But just because I got away physically didn't mean I had mentally. My mind was twisting and turning, trying to take me somewhere I didn't want to go. Closing my eyes, I leaned back against the headrest as the memory assaulted me…

———

"Mama!"

Eve's voice was a high-pitched shriek as she helped me into her grandmother's house. She didn't care that I was dripping blood all over Ms. Hazel's gleaming floor, didn't care that my heavier weight was making her stumble as she half-dragged me into the kitchen.

"Eve, I'on need this shit. I'm all right," I hissed through my blood-coated lips.

"Shut up! You not all right! And you better stop all that cussin'! MAMA!" she yelled louder.

I shook my head at her but didn't say anything else. Eve propped me up against the wall just inside the kitchen. Weak as fuck, I fell to my knees, then bent forward, resting my aching head on the cool floor.

"Evangeline Miller, what I done told you about coming in my house with all that... Oh, my God!"

I saw Ms. Hazel's feet as she rushed toward me. Embarrassed, I closed my eyes. I was ten years old, and everyone said I was big for my age. But I still wasn't big enough... I felt Ms. Hazel turn me over gently and lay me out on my back.

"Eve, come hold his head up," she ordered.

Eve obeyed, resting my head in her lap as she kneeled behind me.

"Damien, who did this to you?" Ms. Hazel asked softly.

I shook my head, even though she already knew, then moaned as a sharp pain stabbed through my skull. Eve's little palm rubbed my forehead as her grandmother's hands quickly checked me for injuries. I winced as she probed my ribs, but that was the worst spot. I would be okay. This wasn't shit compared to what I had lived through.

"Open your eyes, baby."

I ignored Ms. Hazel. It was hard to lie to her with my eyes open, and I couldn't admit who had fucked me up like this. I had more than myself to worry about.

"Damien, you could be hurt inside, baby. I need to call 9-1-1—"

Hell no. That couldn't happen. I couldn't be separated from Kiana. I tried to sit up, but she held on to me.

"Be still, love. You gon' make something worse," Ms. Hazel tried to calm me.

"I'm good. Ain't nothing broke—I can tell. I tried to tell Eve, but she don't listen—"

"You couldn't even walk by yourself!" Eve popped off.

I opened one eye and mugged her. "I can now."

She glared back at me but went silent. Her grandmother snapped her fingers at her, and Eve gently laid my head on the floor before standing up.

"Bring me a bowl of warm water and a towel. And Damien, I am calling 9-1-1 —"

This time, I sat up. Everything felt like it hurt, but I tried to keep my face together.

"No! I just had a fight, Ms. Hazel. Three nig—boys, I mean, tried to jump me," I lied.

Her eyes narrowed in disbelief. "What boys?"

"I'on know. They were older than me. They don't go to our school or nothing."

I was spinning shit off the top of my head, but she didn't look like she was having it. I stared into her eyes. If I dropped mine, she'd know I was lying.

"Damien, this looks bad, baby. You need—"

She stopped as we heard a knock on the door. Eve set down the stuff that her grandmother had requested before going to answer the door. Ms. Hazel was wiping my face when the visitor walked in behind Eve. I looked up into my mother's face. She looked worried, paler than even usual. Mama was white and Mexican, but she had none of my Mexican grandfather's brown skin. She wore a long sleeve shirt even though it was the middle of a Texas summer, and her green eyes were everywhere.

"Demon—" She cleared her throat as Ms. Hazel frowned. "I-I-I mean, Damien! There you are. I was so worried! What happened to you?" she asked.

I watched silently as she crossed the room and squatted beside me, cupping my cheek in her hand. I moved my face.

"Nothing," I mumbled.

She laughed nervously, scratching at her covered arms. "Don't lie, boy! We can all see. You been fighting again? De- Damien, what have I told you about your attitude?"

She looked at Ms. Hazel and turned on her best smile. "Thank you for everything you've done, but I got him now. I'm going to get him home and take care of him—"

"He needs to go to the hospital," Ms. Hazel said dryly.

"No, he's fine. He's always fighting. This isn't even the worst, is it Damien?" she asked, touching my hair that needed a cut badly.

Looking down, I shook my head.

"So, I'll just take him—"

"No," Ms. Hazel said.

My mother dropped the fake grin. "Listen. You don't tell me what to do with my—"

But her attempt to act all hard wasn't shit compared to Ms. Hazel's attitude. The older woman held up a hand and Mama's mouth snapped shut.

"This is what I will tell you. I don't believe that shit about a fight. But I'll make you a deal. You gon' get out of here and let me take care of him or I'll call the police and you know where they gon' look first."

I looked up, surprised to see my mother's eyes widen. She looked scared. She kept opening and closing her mouth, but Ms. Hazel just stared at her coldly.

"But he fights all the—"

"Eve, can you walk Damien's mother to the door?"

"Yes, ma'am," Eve said.

My mother squatted there, frozen, for another few seconds. Finally, another little smile covered her mouth.

"I-I know my way out. Thank you for helping my son. Just make sure he's home by—"

"He'll be home when I send him," Ms. Hazel cut her off again.

Mama stared before finally nodding. Turning, she almost ran out of the house.

I looked at Ms. Hazel, relief flooding me. "No 9-1-1? Please, Ms. Hazel."

She watched me for a long minute. "No 9-1-1... right now," she finally agreed. "But if you get worse—"

I shook my head fast. "I won't. I won't."

———

The sound of my phone ringing through the Bluetooth brought me back to the present. Dante was calling. I answered before I even thought about it.

"What?" I snapped.

"Hey, to you, too, brother. How you doing?"

His voice was smooth and unconcerned, but I knew he wanted something. I wasn't in the mood to play the games he loved.

"Dante, the fuck are you calling me for?" I demanded.

"How's our deal going?"

The question pissed me off. "I agreed to handle it. I do what I say."

He sighed. "I know you do, Demon. I was just—"

"Is that all?"

"Not that you give a fuck, but I've heard that her brother wants to see you. He's been looking for you."

DeAngelo Castle was the least of my worries.

"Yeah, you right. I don't give a fuck. I'll talk to you later."

"Demon—"

I hung up on him, ready to get the fuck out of this neighborhood.

CHAPTER 11
Dream

(**MONDAY**, *May 17*)

I looked up at the light knock on my door. Smiling, I waved for my co-worker, Parker, to come in. I had known Parker since middle school, and we'd always vibed. She was funny and cool as hell, a down-to-earth baddie with a heart of gold.

"I'm here to propose that today be our extended lunch day," she said, walking up to my desk.

Once a month, Parker, our co-worker Paul, and I took a long lunch together. I looked up at her, curious.

"Why today?"

"Because I'm craving The Jerk Shack on the Westside soooo bad."

She rubbed her stomach for emphasis, looking at me hopefully. Really, I should say no. I had a lot of work to do, and we usually coordinated this better. After these lunches, we didn't get a damn thing done. But the thought of those jerk ribs and sautéed cabbage had my mouth watering. Nibbling on my bottom lip, I debated it while she waited. Finally, I sighed.

"Damn you, Parker," I mumbled.

She grinned, clapping her hands. "Be ready in fifteen," she ordered, switching out of my office.

Exactly fifteen minutes later, we climbed into Paul's BMW X5. Parker put me in the front because she got a kick out of the way Paul constantly tried to shoot his shot with me. He started as soon as we were buckled in for the thirty-minute drive.

"That dress must've been designed specifically for you. You look like an angel," he complimented.

I rolled my eyes at his corny ass. Paul was so good for me on paper. Harvard MBA. Tall and so handsome that he was almost pretty. Stable, well-off family background. He even took care of his little cousin and her mother. My father had tried to push us together more than once. Despite all his good qualities, Paul aroused nothing in me. I tried to let him down gently several times, but, at this point, I believed the flirting was like a game to him, so I let him carry on.

"Thanks, Paul. Can you drive now?" I asked.

"Whatever my future wife wishes," he said.

Shaking my head, I sighed.

"Play some music, Dream," Parker suggested.

"Your phone hooks up to the Bluetooth, too," I shot back.

"I mean, if I DJ, I'ma focus on setting the mood for you two."

I turned around to glare at her as Paul simpered and told her thank you. She shrugged unapologetically and settled against her seat. *Messy ass*, I thought as I connected to Paul's system and chose a song by Chloe x Halle. The drive passed by quickly as I kept the music mellow. The Jerk Shack had a little lunch crowd, so we sat for a minute at one of the outdoor tables, talking and sipping our drinks. I sat across from my co-workers and Paul started in about that.

"You sure you don't feel alone over there, beautiful? Because I'd be happy to come keep you company," he offered.

"I'm good," I assured him.

Parker mushed his head.

"What?"

"You're pathetic," she said. "But it's fun to watch."

"Keep thinking it's a joke. I'm not gon' stop until Dream is mine."

The sincerity in his voice surprised Parker and me. She and I glanced at each other as an awkward silence surrounded us. Finally, she cleared her throat.

"I need you to look over something for me tomorrow. I know we ain't gon' be good for nothing else work-related today. But these numbers—"

Parker's voice trailed off as she looked behind me. "Ahh, *fuck*. I forgot to stop sharing my location."

I frowned, confused by her statement.

"What is—"

I stopped as Parker's on-again, off-again fuckboy of a boyfriend, Jory, approached our table.

"I told you I wanted to take you to lunch today," he spat, not bothering to speak to Paul or me.

That was fine because I wouldn't have said shit to him. Parker deserved so much better than this slimy, lying, cheating piece of shit, but he'd hooked her in high school, and she'd never been able to shake him fully.

"And I told you I probably had plans, Jory," she said calmly.

"Plans? With them? I'm your man, Parker. I come first."

He looked at me and Paul in disgust. My hand balled into a fist on the table as I bit my tongue. Paul reached across and grabbed it, trying to keep me calm.

"My man?" Parker scoffed. "Jory, you once again proved that your ho ass is for everybody. Go be Cherice's man. That's what you been doing."

She'd caught him cheating *again*, this time with a girl she considered a friend. Parker said she was done for real, but I didn't believe it.

"I'on want no fucking Cherice. And why you put them in our business?"

"You the one putting everyone in y'all business, out here fucking up left and right."

I didn't even realize the words were coming until they spilled out of me. Paul squeezed my hand as Jory turned his angry eyes on me.

"Nobody was talking to you, Dream," he gritted out.

"That's okay cuz I'm talking to your sorry ass. If you don't want people in your business, keep your dick in your pants," I said with a shrug. "It's simple."

He took a step closer to me. I smirked. Jory was a bully, but he didn't scare me.

"Jory, back up," Parker demanded.

He ignored her. "Maybe you should let a nigga in your pants, so you'll have some business of your own."

His comment stung a little, but I refused to show it.

"If that comes with putting up with a weak ass *boy* like you, I'll pass," I shot back.

He moved closer and Paul spoke up.

"That's enough, Jory."

"Nah, somebody needs to show this bitch her place. She always got some shit to say, and I'm tired of it."

I laughed in his face. "First, you can back up because you don't intimidate me, Jory. Second, I'ma always say what I gotta say and I don't care if you fucking *exhausted*. You ain't about nothing, never have been, even before the injury that ended yo' weak ass career. You shouldn't even be breathing the same air as Parker, and I definitely don't want you in my atmosphere. So, why don't you leave our table and don't bring yo' stalking ass back over here. Understand?"

I was ready for him to push back, but, to my surprise, he just nodded. I smirked at him, feeling smug about his back-down. I was about to add a few more points, but I realized his eyes weren't on me. Neither were Parker's nor Paul's. All of them were staring behind me. Now that I wasn't caught up in my little speech, I could feel the electric tingles zapping through me, smell the scent of Dove soap and man. Turning my head, I looked up. My heart forgot to beat for a moment.

"Damien..."

His locs were down, framing his perfect face. The V-neck t-shirt he wore put his neck tattoos, Cuban link chains, and a little of his chest ink on display as it hugged his muscular body. His lower arms were left bare, except for the colorful images that decorated them. The denim of his jeans outlined long, solid legs. He looked so damn good that I couldn't even say anything after his name. His attention was on Jory, anyway, his eyes freezing.

"Apologize to her," he ordered.

Jory held up his hands like he was surrendering. "Look, Demon, it ain't—"

"Back the fuck up off her and apologize."

Damien's voice, his whole appearance was calm. But there was something deadly about the way he spoke, and Jory quickly stepped back.

"I... I'm sorry, Dream," he muttered.

I nodded, unsure of what to say.

"Now, do like she said and leave," Damien instructed.

With one last look at Parker, Jory did what he was told. Three sets of eyes, including mine, swung to Damien, amazed. Jory never gave in that easily. Usually, he and Paul would be on the verge of fighting before Parker could get him to back down. Damien looked at me for a minute, then down to where Paul still held my hand.

"Stop touching her."

His rough voice issued the command calmly. I wasn't ready for that, and neither was Paul.

"Excuse me?" he said.

"You heard me."

They eyed each other for a moment. Paul looked away

first. He let go reluctantly and I pulled my hand back. Damien was taking this a little too far.

"Can I talk to you?" I asked him.

He didn't say anything, just raised an eyebrow. Standing, I walked a few steps away. Thankfully, he followed.

"I could've handled Jory," I began.

"Okay."

I waited for him to say something else, but he didn't. He was so damn frustrating. And gorgeous. It was hard to look at him without embarrassing myself.

"Damien, people are going to touch me—"

He shook his head, cutting me off.

"Nah. These niggas not about to be out here touching what's mine."

I scowled at him. "I'm not—"

"You are until your thirty days are up."

"But—"

He gave me a look that silenced me. Reaching out, he tilted my head back so that his eyes could drill into mine. My skin warmed at his touch, and I bit down on my bottom lip. He used his thumb to pull it free.

"I don't say shit I don't mean, and I don't repeat myself. Understand?"

I stared at him before hesitantly nodding. He nodded in satisfaction.

"Good."

"Are you following me?" I blurted.

He looked down at me, a small smile around his mouth.

"Why would I do that? I can have you whenever I want," he said cockily.

I frowned, hating... and loving the sound of that.

"Hey, Demon! Your order is ready, and I know it's right cuz I packed it myself," one of the waitresses interrupted us, holding out a bag.

She was smiling so hard at him, fluttering her eyelashes

and sticking out her ridiculous rack. Shit pissed me off. I mean, was I invisible?

"Thank you," he said.

"You're welcome," she cooed before slowly walking off, swinging her wide hips extra hard. I rolled my eyes.

"Anyway, we should talk—"

"Enjoy your lunch, Dream. Tell that nigga at your table to keep his hands to himself."

He walked off without saying anything else, just left me in the middle of the floor. Speechless, I made my way back to the table.

"Girl, who the hell is that fine ass nigga?" Parker asked, bouncing on the seat.

"Nobody," I mumbled, waving a hand.

She and Paul looked at each other, then back at me. Parker opened her mouth to speak again. I stood up abruptly.

"I'ma go check on our food," I announced.

I didn't care about our lunch, didn't even have an appetite anymore. At least, not for food. Nah. What I was hungry for had just walked his fine ass out the door, leaving me standing there, hot, bothered, and wishing I were going with him.

CHAPTER 12

Demon

(*MONDAY*, *May 24*)

I knocked on the door and waited. It was one of the few courtesies DeAngelo Castle would get from me today. Dante had told me first, but then the little nigga had put word out that he needed to see me in the last week. I'd debated meeting him. I wasn't a you-call-I-come type of nigga, but I already knew what this shit was about. I didn't expect the nigga to be happy about me eventually fucking his sister, but I didn't give a damn about his opinion. I just hoped he didn't step out of line during this "conversation." I stepped back as I heard the door of the condo unlock. A second later, my niece's eyes met mine.

"Demon?" Crystal said, like she was surprised to see me.

I offered her a half-smile and she opened the door wider. I didn't bother walking in, at first. If DeAngelo wasn't here, I wasn't going to stay.

"Come in! It's good to see you."

I knew she meant it—I had an okay relationship with my niece, better than I had with most people. She hugged me and stood back.

"I know you not just in the neighborhood."

"Your husband wanted to see me."

Her smile slipped and I saw the worry cloud her eyes.

"Yeah. About... about that. He's really protective of his sisters and—"

"Is that nigga here?" I interrupted her as nicely as I could. I didn't usually worry about doing nice.

She nodded. "Come in. I'ma go get him."

I nodded as I stepped over her threshold and waited. My eyes moved around, taking in my surroundings as always. She was the daughter of one of the richest men in the city and it showed. My niece was definitely living well. Crystal was back in seconds with a tall, skinny ass nigga who was frowning. He didn't stop walking until he was too close to my personal space. I tensed, ready for anything, then tried to convince myself to relax. I didn't want issues with this nigga, but I wouldn't run from it.

"Ay, you know this bullshit agreement y'all got with my sister is outta line," he said, not holding back.

I shrugged, trying to stay calm. "It's not yo' business."

"She not keeping that agreement."

I smirked at him. "That's up to her."

I didn't have to say anything else. If she broke the deal, they all knew the possible consequences.

"DeAngelo," Crystal said softly, touching his arm. "You know she can't walk out on a deal with Daddy—"

He spun around and glared down at her. My fists clenched. The last thing he wanted to do was come at her wrong. Her husband or not, I'd lay his ass down.

"I'm tired of hearing that. Who is Dante supposed to be?" he spat.

"The nigga you ran off from," I reminded him.

Nigga wanted to act bad now but hadn't been willing to face Dante before, and then sent his sister to clean up his mess. I had no respect for his bitch ass.

"That wasn't my idea. I wanted to go—"

I waved a hand. "I really don't care about all that shit. Is that all you wanted with me?"

"Don't touch my sister, Demon. She's too good for you. Too clean. You ain't nothing but—"

I didn't let him finish. I promised myself a long time ago that I had been insulted and discouraged enough when I was a broken down, beat down kid. I didn't let the shit happen now that I was grown. Still, the punch I landed on his jaw was not as hard as anyone else would've earned. He was my niece's husband and Dream's brother. I didn't know why the last part mattered to me, but it did.

Crystal screamed as he stumbled back.

"I ain't the nigga you wanna come at crazy," I warned him.

He touched his jaw and then his eyes met mine, blazing. I knew that look. I was going to have to fight his stupid ass. *Oh, well.* Maybe I'd stop myself before he quit breathing. Sometimes, I did. Crystal moved in front of him, facing me.

"Demon, just go," she pleaded as he lifted her, and she struggled.

It took a minute for her words to sink in and make sense. I had never just walked away from a fight, so the idea was strange to me. I almost ignored her.

"Uncle... *please.*"

Crystal had tears in her eyes as she begged. Shaking my head, I relaxed my stance. I didn't want to kill this little nigga, anyway. With one last look, I backed out of the condo and walked toward my Jag. Climbing in, I peeled off. Crystal may have kept me off DeAngelo's ass, but his words still pissed me the fuck off.

Because they were the same thoughts I'd been having. Because they were the reasons I hadn't called her to make plans. Dream looked like something pure and good and a nigga like me could only ruin that. I didn't want to see her ruined. I needed to stay away.

But I couldn't. My thoughts were full of her, and I hated that shit. I'd watched her a couple more times, standing on her balcony, thinking. I wanted to bend her over that railing and take shit off her mind, but I didn't think she was ready for that. Hell, she was so much of a good girl that I didn't know if she'd ever be ready for the things I wanted to do to her. I said I didn't want to ruin her, but I wouldn't mind seeing her a little dirty.

Almost like I couldn't help myself, I headed toward her house. She should be done with work—her daddy rented a little office space for her and a few other employees, including the ones I'd seen at The Jerk Shack, I'd found out. I parked in my usual spot, waiting for her to walk out onto the balcony. She didn't disappoint, stepping outside with her phone in one hand, pressed to her ear, and a wineglass in the other. The little tank top and shorts she wore showed off her thick figure and I watched her appreciatively, feeling the tension from my run-in with her brother leaving my body. She paced back and forth for a couple of minutes before she stopped suddenly. She walked closer to the railing, and I could swear she looked straight at me. Suddenly, she ran back into the house, closing the glass doors behind her. Frowning, I wondered what that was all about. I waited a couple more minutes to see if she came back. Settling back in my seat, I closed my eyes. They flew open a minute later at the sound of banging against my window.

What the fuck?

I sat up immediately, my hand already closing around the gun I kept on me, my mind in kill mode. I relaxed when I looked up to see Dream's scowl outside my window. Even with a mug, she was pretty. I sat back, just observing her, until she hit my window again.

"Get yo' ass out this car!" she yelled.

Any soft thoughts flew out of my head. I'll be damned if I let her handle me. I wasn't going to hurt her, but she needed to learn that I wouldn't play with her ass, either. I moved to open the door. At first, she looked like she wasn't going to step back. I looked up at her, hoping she could read the warning in my eyes. She moved just enough to let me open the door and slide out. I loomed over her, keeping my face expressionless. She didn't need to know how being close to her again made me feel. She looked scared for a minute, but she didn't back down. That little show of fire had my dick instantly hard. Focused on the wrong head, I missed her hand swinging toward my face until the slap cracked against my cheek. I wasn't used to being caught off-guard, so I just stared down at her, shocked. While my brain processed it, she lifted her hand again. I caught it, then used my other hand to grab her around the throat. Switching our positions, I pushed her against the car.

"Don't ever put your hands on me like that!" I warned her.

"Why? You put your hands on people!" she spat.

Leaning in, I brought my face close to hers. "You don't worry about who the fuck I touch."

"You touching me right now. Get off me."

She struggled against me, trying to buck me off. That shit made me harder. I pressed closer to her, putting the slightest pressure against her neck. Anger sparkled in her eyes, but so did something else, and her body softened against mine. Immediately, my mind went elsewhere, images of me choking her while she came all over my dick flashing in my head. I squeezed again and got the same reaction. I smirked at her.

"You like that shit? You like a nigga being rough with you?"

She shook her head quickly and pushed against me again. "I don't like anything about you."

I laughed softly. "Wait till I fuck you."

Dream opened her mouth to protest, but I spun her around so that her front pressed against my car. I crowded against her so that she couldn't move much, then slid a hand around her body to rest on the softness of her stomach. I lowered my mouth to her ear. She shivered, her body responding to my touch.

"You won't put your hands on me in anger. I don't allow that. Understand?" I whispered.

"You hit my brother!"

She was showing out over that weak ass nigga? Shit pissed me off. She needed to learn that it wasn't her place to fight his battles.

"His bitch ass called to snitch on me?" I asked, chuckling. "Mind your fuckin' business. Lucky I didn't do worse."

I felt her tense and she turned her head, trying to look at me.

"Don't threaten him!"

"Or what?" I goaded her.

"You're not untouchable, *Demon*," she snarled.

That shit ran me hot. Snaking my hands through her braids, I pulled her head back.

"What's my name, Dream?"

Stubbornly, she kept her mouth closed. My hand tightened the littlest bit, tugging on her scalp. I let my other hand creep downward to the waist of her shorts. She sucked in a deep breath as I slid two fingers beneath the fabric.

"Wh-what are you doing?" she stuttered.

"Making sure you know what to call me, especially when I'm touching this pussy. What's my name?"

I pressed my face against the side of her neck, savoring her soft, sweet scent. My hand descended into her panties. She grabbed my wrist.

"People can see us!"

"Say my name," I demanded as my fingers brushed the top of her mound.

She shook her head, then whimpered as I parted her folds. I drew slow circles around her clit. She bit down on her bottom lip as her head fell back further. I felt my dick responding, hardening against her back.

"Demon…"

Stubborn ass. I brushed my lips against her neck.

"What's my name?"

She held out longer than I expected. Long enough for my fingers to slide lower and feel how wet my touch had her. Long enough for me to pick up the pace at which I stroked her clit. Long enough for her body to shiver and her breathing to speed up. She was about to cum against my hand when she finally whimpered, then spoke.

"You have to stop… *Damien.*"

My name whispered past her plush lips. Reluctantly, I stopped, easing my hand out of her shorts, letting it rest on her stomach for a moment. She was trembling, her body pressed into mine. I gave her a minute to recover before picking her up by her waist and setting her on the curb. Opening the door, I hopped into my car and pulled off while her eyes were still glued to me. My dick was still rock hard.

Soon, I thought. I was going to have her soon.

CHAPTER 13
Dream

I STOOD FROZEN, like I couldn't move away from the curb, his touch still tingling against my skin. I'd just had the most intimate part of me stroked on the street in front of my house and, instead of being horrified, I wanted more. Damien was dark and dangerous, but I had some kind of craving for his domineering ass. He touched me like he really believed he owned me, like he had some kind of right and I—

"You gon' stand out here all evening?"

My sister Dayana's voice interrupted my thoughts. She stood across the street, at the foot of our driveway with a bat in her hands. Shaking my head, I walked to her.

"What you doing with that, Yana?"

"I saw that nigga had you hemmed up against his car. I was coming to help you."

I tilted my head to the side, curious. "So, why didn't you?"

"Shit... you didn't look like you wanted my help," she teased.

The warmth of a blush heated my skin as I mushed her head. "Shut up," I mumbled.

"So, that's the famous Demon?"

I nodded as we walked back into the house.

"Damn, Sister, he fine. You think they'll let Daddy's other daughter fulfill the deal?"

"Umm, Yana, how would your fiancé feel about that?" I asked dryly.

She shrugged. "Some things a nigga gotta understand. Swear I'd lick every one of them tattoos!"

"Remember, he kills people, too."

"I like a little thug in my niggas."

She definitely did, even though you couldn't tell by the preppy fiancé my daddy had chosen for her. That was one difference between us. I just wanted a nice, respectable, business-minded man. I didn't want to spend my life in the world of my father, Dante, and Damien. It was too uncertain, too hazardous. I wanted a man whom I could be pretty sure was coming home to me every night. Isaac's family had dabbled in some illegal activities, but he was mostly a stand-up guy. He had his MBA and dreams of establishing his own business. I could work with that. But none of that explained why I responded to Damien like I did. He could just look at me and something sparked. And, Lord, the few times he'd touched me...

"Why was he holding you like that?" Dayana asked suddenly.

I waved my hand dismissively as I walked over to the couch and plopped down. She followed.

"It was nothing."

"It looked like something. Stop holding out."

Sighing heavily, I rolled my eyes at her, while reaching in my bra for my phone. On silent, it showed eight missed calls and four texts, all from DeAngelo and Crystal. Crys had been on the phone with me, telling me about Damien's "visit" to their condo, when I hung up suddenly after seeing Damien's car. The last message was from DeAngelo. **Call me or I'm**

coming over there, he had demanded. Shaking my head, I FaceTimed him.

"See? No damage done," I said as soon as he picked up.

"What was he doing there, Dream?" he asked, his face one big scowl.

I ran a hand over my braids as I settled back against the couch. "I don't know, D. He's come by a couple of times. I don't think he knew I knew."

"How could you not know?"

"Because… he just sits in his car for a little while, then drives off."

"Like he's watching you?"

"I guess."

I shrugged the question off. I had no idea why Damien did what he did, and I wasn't about to try to figure it out.

"What did he say to you?"

"Not much. Told me not to hit him again."

"You hit him?" Dayana hissed in the background, sitting up higher on the couch.

I heard a gasp, then suddenly, Crystal's face was filling my screen.

"You hit him?" she repeated Dayana's words.

"Yes. Is that so hard to believe? He hit my brother!"

Good for him, Dayana mouthed. I looked at her, surprised.

"Hold on, y'all," I told D and Crys, muting the call before turning to my sister. "What you mean, 'good for him?'"

"DeAngelo deserves to be hit. Got you all up in this mess."

"Yana, that's our brother—"

She stared at me defiantly.

"I don't care. I said what I said. You need to let him be a man sometimes, like Grandpapa says, Dream."

Shaking my head, I returned to the phone call. I'd deal with her later. Everybody was mad at my brother, but, hell, I'd decided to fuck with Damien.

"I just can't believe you hit him, and he let you make it. I never heard of that happening," Crystal said. "I mean, I guess I never heard of him hitting a woman, but still, I bet he don't play that shit."

"Oh, well. I don't know what to tell you. I hit him and I'm here to talk about it," I said smugly, neglecting to mention how he yoked me up.

"Dream, you can't be doing that. You could trigger his ass. People used to beat on him, burn him, do all sorts of shit to him. He ain't stable and he don't let people touch him like that," Crystal warned.

"I don't plan to do it again, Crys. Chill."

She sighed. "I just don't think you know what you done got into."

"Well, I'm in it now. We just have to see how it plays out."

CHAPTER 14

Demon

WET. Warm. Silky. That's how her pussy felt beneath my fingers. I was ready to explore her more, to feel that wet heat wrapped around me. I wanted to fuck shorty until she was hoarse from screaming my name. Her sweet smell had me wanting to taste her, too, something I hadn't done in a long time. I didn't know how or why, but Dream had my fucking number, and I didn't like it.

Not ready to go home yet, I headed toward a local bar owned by one of the few niggas I could tolerate for more than five minutes. I pulled up in the parking lot and just sat there for a minute. I wasn't a nigga for socializing, but the crowd here would know not to approach me. Hopping out of the car, I walked toward the door. I stepped in and observed the room for a minute. Gazes turned toward me, and the buzz of conversation faded a little. Dozens of eyes watched as I strolled slowly to the bar. I knew they were wondering what havoc I'd come to wreak. I stood behind a couple of niggas who looked nervously over their shoulders at me. If I said "boo," I had no doubt they'd pass the fuck out. One of them swallowed hard before speaking to me.

"Demon... you can go—"

I shook my head, cutting him off. I was cool with waiting. My eyes were sweeping the room again when I heard a familiar voice.

"Who you looking for?" Smoke Salinas asked me, extending his fist.

Smoke owned this bar, one of the legal businesses that washed the millions of dollars he made in his other pursuits. He was a straight shooter, one of the closest things I had to a friend. I dapped him up, a small smile dancing around my mouth.

"I come in peace."

He raised an eyebrow, skeptical. I met his eyes wordlessly.

"Aw, shit. You serious. What you drinking?"

"Louis XIII."

He requested a bottle from one of the girls passing by, before leading me to a little ducked-off booth.

"I know you don't fuck with niggas like that, so I wanted to give you the most secluded spot I got."

"You right, but you got a minute?"

The question shocked us both. To his credit, he didn't say anything, though, just slid his tall frame across from me. The bottle girl came with the cognac and one glass but hurried and got another. Once both of us had been served, he looked at me expectantly. I didn't even know where to start; I just knew the shit with Dream was taking up too much of my mental.

"Dante all right over there? I know he was ready to set shit on fire when he called to tell me about it," Smoke said.

I shrugged. "That nigga all right. He getting revenge and some deals out of this situation."

"Revenge?"

"A daughter for a daughter," I explained abruptly.

He let out a low whistle. "So, he took one of Castle's girls? What the fuck is Sherrilyn saying about that? I know she ain't going. I don't blame the nigga, though. Both them bitches fine."

My eyes narrowed on him when he called Dream out of her name.

"He didn't take her for himself. And she's not a bitch. Her name is Dream," I said before sipping from my glass.

He frowned. "Then who he give her..." His head snapped back as he realized. "To you?"

I nodded. "Thirty days, whenever I decide. Whatever I want."

The look he gave me implied I was crazy.

"She agreed to that? Shit sounds like a dream come true, but you don't look too happy. She a bad fuck?"

I was silent for a moment, staring at the bottle.

"I ain't fucked her," I finally admitted.

"You don't want her? Shit, I'll take her as a consolation pr—"

"No."

My expression didn't change as I cut him off. I'd kill this nigga before I let him touch Dream, though.

"Got it," he said, sitting back and eyeballing me. "So, you feeling shorty."

I refilled my glass before answering. "I'on know her, really."

"But you sitting in this bar, talking to me about her."

"Nigga, it ain't like I need therapy or some shit—" I said, starting to stand.

Shit was stupid and I didn't know what the fuck I was doing here. Smoke touched my arm and I stared at his hand.

"Nigga, you definitely need therapy, but I know that's not why you here. Chill. Enjoy your drink."

Slowly, I sat back down. We sipped in silence for a minute.

"Let me ask, why you ain't fucked?" he inquired suddenly.

I sighed. "I'on know. She keeps saying she wanna get it over with, but…"

"But what?"

Shrugging, I didn't answer at first. This was too much talking, too much emotional shit for me. Smoke drained his glass as he waited.

"She not the type you fuck and walk away from," I finally admitted.

"So, you worried about getting caught up?"

I frowned. "Fuck no. That ain't me. I ain't tryna be with no chick like that."

Nodding, he was silent for a minute. Finally, he met my eyes again.

"I ain't gon' flatter myself and think you want my advice. But just in case, if I were you, I'd give her what she was asking for. Enjoy your thirty days and collect what they owe your family," he said. "They lucky Dante feeling merciful. Surprised he didn't kill that little nigga."

"Me, too," I agreed. "You okay with—"

He nodded abruptly. "It could've been a good business deal, but she probably wouldn't have been happy with me. Shorty is too young to spend her life miserable. It was nothing but business for me—a nigga ain't tryna be in love. I already had my soulmate. Let her do the same."

I knew he was talking about his wife, who had died from cancer. It was fucked up, but I hoped Crystal appreciated the fact that he wasn't demanding some sort of payback for the shit she and DeAngelo pulled.

Smoke slid out of the booth. "I got some shit to check on. Grab some of the bar food and whatever else you want. It's on me."

I shook my head. "Nah, I need to get home."

Ten minutes later, I sat in my car, still in the parking lot, thinking about what Smoke had said. What was I waiting for? Dream was willing, and I wanted to fuck her. At this point, I *needed* to fuck her so I could drop her and get past having her stuck on my brain. That's all that mattered. Pulling out my phone, I called her.

"Hello?"

Her voice sounded breathy and half-asleep. I didn't say anything for a moment.

"Who is this?" she demanded.

"Damien."

She paused. "Oh. Yes?"

"I don't play about my fucking health. I want you to get tested for everything and I wanna see the results," I said.

She paused again. "I want the same."

I knew I was good, so that wasn't a problem.

"Is that all?" she asked. "I mean, I'm busy."

My next words were meant to shock her since she was acting so bold, brushing a nigga off and shit.

"If you not on birth control, get on it. I'ma fuck you raw. Every day."

She sucked in a deep breath before disconnecting the call.

I smiled.

CHAPTER 15
Dayana Dionne Castle

(**MONDAY**, *May 31*)

"Raw? Every day? That nigga gon' fuck around and shoot up the club," I said, laughing at my sister as she mugged me.

"No, the hell he ain't. I got my pills and I ain't gon' miss one," Dream vowed before walking into the dressing room. "Yana, I can't find anything!" she complained a minute later.

Sighing, I rolled my eyes. This was the fourth store we'd been in, and Dream was being more difficult than usual. I loved shopping, but not with my ultra-picky big sister.

"If you quit being scared to show your figure in public, this would be a lot easier," I told her.

"But my thighs—"

"Are thick. Get over it. So are mine. Niggas love that shit."

"I ain't worried about what niggas love," she snapped.

I sighed again.

The Wares had hit us with an unexpected invitation. They were hosting a party to recognize—I wouldn't say celebrate—Crystal and DeAngelo's marriage. It was only three days away and Sherrilyn Ware had requested we wear black. I already had the cutest off-the-shoulder jumpsuit I'd picked out a couple of stores ago. I was still shopping for other pieces as Dream looked around, though.

"Come out," I told her as I moved closer to her dressing room.

It took her a few seconds, but she finally appeared. My sister looked like a brick house in the simple, above-knee-length body con dress she wore.

"Bitch, if you don't buy that!"

"It's too tight!" she complained.

"No, it's not. It fits perfectly."

We argued for a few minutes until I enlisted two of the sales ladies on my side. Reluctantly, Dream bought the dress. I wondered if Demon was going to be at the party. Nigga was going to be amazed when he saw her, if so. I hadn't said anything to Dream because she would kill me, but silently, I was cheering for them. She needed someone who could shake her up and handle her bossy ass. And from every little bit I learned about his life, he needed a strong woman, someone he couldn't break, to love him. I could tell my sister liked him. I was counting on him feeling the same.

Dream and I grabbed a quick dinner at Jason's Deli.

"You coming home now?" she asked as we got ready to split up in the parking lot and head to our cars.

"I'ma pop up on Jordan first," I said, speaking of my fiancé.

He had called to let me know he was breaking our movie date because he didn't feel good. That wasn't like him, so I wanted to check in and see if I could take care of him for a little bit.

Time had flown by, but Jordan and I were getting married next Saturday. My mother was going crazy with last-minute details, but for some reason, I was calm. I was actually glad the shit with my twin took some of the focus off Jordan and me. It was like I was marrying a good friend. We didn't have a traditional romance—our marriage was arranged by our fathers. But we grew to have some type of love for each other. He was thoughtful and quiet, a real sweetheart. I looked forward to being his wife and having his children. Plus, our union would solidify a strong partnership between our families.

Twenty minutes after leaving the restaurant, I stood outside his condo. I had a key—he'd been wanting me to move in. My father wasn't going, though. He wanted Dream and me at home until we were officially married. He was so old school in some ways, insisting we live with our parents, preaching the importance of "saving" ourselves, always warning us about protecting our reputations. The shit was boring and one reason I was ready to be married at twenty-one was to have more freedom.

I let myself in quietly, in case he was resting. Tiptoeing across the living room, I made my way to the hallway where the bedrooms were. I shook my head as I heard moaning and a rhythmic slapping. This nigga wasn't too sick to watch porn, I guess. That was one of my few issues with him—he had a little porn fetish that I didn't like. I mean, even I watched some, but Jordan watched A LOT. I opened the bedroom door, ready to fuss at him about the need to get some rest.

At first, my eyes couldn't make sense of what was in front of them. Like, why was he up, wearing leather boots and pants, and it was almost June? And, oh, why was he standing between the thighs of a woman who was tied up and suspended from some kind of swing? My jaw dropped as my slow brain realized the sound of skin slapping against skin hadn't been coming from the TV.

"Dayana... what are you doing here?" he asked lamely.

That stupid ass question triggered something in me. Suddenly, rage filled every inch of my body. This cheating bastard! I had been worried about him and this was what he was doing? Had the nerve to call off our date to fuck a bitch a week and a half before our wedding? Where the fuck was my bat when I needed it? *Oh, well, these hands gon' have to do*, I thought as I charged toward him. Catching him off-guard, my first punch snapped his head back. The second sent him to the floor. I was about to climb on top of him and beat his ass when I realized his dick was out, wet and semi-erect. The bitch hadn't had time to pull those tight ass pants up all the way and he wasn't even wearing a condom! I didn't want to get close to that. Instead, I kicked him as hard as I could while his bitch tried to scream around her ball-gag.

He was yelling for me to stop, curling himself into the fetal position.

"You lying muhfucka!" I shrieked, aiming for any part of him I could reach.

"I'm sorry, Sweetness. Let me explain. Please... let me explain," he begged.

"Explain? *Explain?*"

I kicked him harder. I had just lifted my foot, ready to crack his damn ribs, when another voice called out, "Stop!"

I looked toward the door of his en suite bathroom. Incredibly, there was another naked woman standing there, shaking, with a phone in her hand.

"So, what, you over here having a whole orgy?" I screamed at Jordan.

"I'm calling 911. Y-you need to l-leave," she stuttered, fear all over her face.

I realized I must look crazy as hell, but I didn't give a fuck. The bitch was right to be scared—her ass might be next!

"No, Angie, don't!" Jordan barked at her.

She whimpered, "I'm sorry, sir. They're on the line."

His eyes darted back to me.

"Dayana... you need to go. You can't get arrested right before our wedding."

I looked at him before the most ridiculous giggles escaped from me, turning into deep, slightly crazy laughter. I knew I sounded hysterical but finding your supposedly shy fiancé dressed in leather with women who were clearly his submissives would do that to you.

"Wedding? You crazy or something? Nigga, the wedding is off!" I spat.

He sat up calmly, like I hadn't just been kicking his ass.

"No, it's not. You're upset, understandably. But we still getting married. I'ma explain all this to you later. For now, you have to go," he said.

Standing, he grabbed my arm. I was so shocked that I let him lead me to the front door.

"Don't worry, Sweetness. Everything will be okay. My father will make this shit with the police disappear."

He picked up my purse and phone from where I'd left them on the table, beside the door. Handing them to me, he opened the door and gently pushed me out. I stood there, feeling like I had just escaped from some alternative world. My adrenaline was starting to die down, taking my anger with it. Confusion clouded my brain as I slipped into the elevator. What the fuck had just happened? And how the hell was I going to tell my father?

CHAPTER 16

Cartier "Smoke" Salinas

"JENESIS, don't go to sleep, mama. You gotta go to your GiGi's in a minute."

Silence greeted my announcement, and I knew my four-year-old daughter was already asleep. I lay on the couch, and she had spread out on my back to watch some cartoon. I'd picked her up from her pre-school summer program early and took her to lunch and a trampoline park because I hadn't been able to spend enough time with her lately. Before my wife Jenna died, I'd promised her our baby girl would always be my number one priority. I was going to live up to that or die trying.

"Jeni-face, wake up," I said, moving a little bit, hoping to stir her.

She finally woke with a soft whine. "I'm sleepy, Daddy."

"I know, but you can take a nap at GiGi's."

Little arms shot around my neck, holding me tight.

"I don't wanna go to GiGi's! I wanna stay with you!"

Guilt filled me as I sat up gently.

"Daddy gotta go to work today, baby. I'm sorry."

Her arms tightened around my neck as she sniffled.

"Come here," I said, reaching behind me, trying to slide her around.

My stubborn baby wouldn't move.

"Jenesis, come on, now."

A few more tears, then she climbed down and crawled into my lap.

"If you be a big girl and stop crying and be real good for GiGi, I'll pick you up from school real early tomorrow and we'll spend the whole day together," I promised.

She sniffed and looked up at me, her eyes sparkling with tears. She looked so much like Jenna that I almost couldn't take the shit some days.

"Really?" she finally said.

"Really. Daddy needs for you to pack your iPad and grab your overnight bag so we can go, okay?"

I hugged her tightly for a minute before setting her down to run off to her room. Sighing, I slid back into my shoes and shirt before grabbing my keys, phone, and wallet to wait on her. I didn't have time to take tomorrow off, but my baby had been good about the extra time she was spending at my mother's house. I owed her more than a day of my time.

The ten-minute drive to my mother's place passed quickly, and I helped Jenesis settle in before I got ready to go. Mama followed me out the door and grabbed my arm.

"What's wrong, OG?" I asked, instantly on alert.

She pursed her lips as she looked me up and down.

"You working too much. Getting pale and skinny. You sure you eating enough?"

Laughing, I dropped a kiss on her forehead.

"I'm good, Mama. How 'bout you plan a getaway for me, you, and Daya? A week to wherever you wanna go."

She nodded her approval. "When?"

"We could leave next weekend, maybe. Shit shoulda slowed down by then. The new bar will be a month old and some… other things will be in place."

"Mm-hmm. It's them 'other things' that keep me worried," she fussed.

I didn't want to hear this lecture. I kissed her again and made my escape. I needed to check on my bars this evening, but I had some "other things" to handle first.

———

I stared at the nigga in front of me as I toked on the blunt, letting the relaxing smoke flow through me. We were surrounded by a few niggas who worked for me, all of them quiet, waiting to see what I was going to say.

"Garett... you're a courier, right?" I finally said to the man who stood, shaking and unable to hold my gaze.

He knew he was in trouble, the kind there was no coming back from. No one had put a hand on him, except to snatch his ass, but he knew shit wasn't good. Why else would we be standing in front of a four-foot-deep hole a mile into the woods?

"Y-y-yes, sir," he finally stuttered.

"So, your job is to carry shit back and forth. I explained to you that it's not your concern what you're carrying or who you carry it to, as long as you get paid," I continued before pulling on the blunt again.

"I didn't want to get in trouble—" he started.

I held up a hand, cutting him off. "You knew what you signed up for when you took the job. You making ten times as much as a regular delivery person. I don't want to hear the bullshit. Why did you open my package, Garrett?"

He looked lost as he searched his brain for an answer I might accept. He wouldn't find one. I didn't like this part of my life, but I never backed down from doing what needed to be done.

"I wanted to see what was worth so much," he finally admitted.

"But you didn't just see. You stole from me," I reminded him.

"I wanted to try—"

"You got greedy, Garrett. That's never a good thing."

"But Mr. Salinas—" he started again.

"Do you pray?" I asked him, stepping forward.

He stumbled back, twigs snapping under his feet as he moved away from me.

"W-what?"

"Pray, nigga! Do you pray?"

My patience for his ass was wearing thin. I wanted to get this over with and go check on some other shit.

"Not really."

I smiled. "You may wanna start. Get things right with God."

His eyes darted around our group, then widened as I pulled out my favorite weapon: a bad ass little switchblade I called "Scarlet." I strolled toward him casually until only inches separated us.

"Please... no. You don't have to do this, Mr. Salinas. You don't have to—"

I severed the arteries in his throat before he could finish the sentence. He fell backwards on the edge of the grave. One of my niggas, Anthony, kicked him and I watched as he rolled into what would be his final resting place.

"We got it from here, boss," Anthony said.

I nodded. Turning, I walked back toward the road, already putting what had just happened out of my head. Guilt and remorse had no place in this business. Thieves had to be dealt with. The counterfeiting plates Garrett had stolen were extremely valuable. He took the risk and paid the price. Once I made it to my car, I changed shoes before taking off.

An hour later, I stood in my new bar, glad to see that business was good. My eyes moved over the happy hour crowd, lingering on one table in particular. One of the Castle sisters sat alone, looking like her mind was a thousand miles away. Shorty was beautiful, with her smooth, pecan brown skin, pouty lips, and dreamy looking eyes. I hoped this wasn't Demon's Dream. If it was, I would step back. But if she were the other one...

Long strides took me to her table, where I studied her up close, still marveling at her beauty. This close, I could also see the rock on her left ring finger. I usually respected that, but I didn't see a matching wedding band and something about this girl had my attention. Demon hadn't mentioned Dream being engaged, but it's not like Dante would have cared. I opened my mouth to say something, but she spoke first.

"Sorry, but I'm not interested."

Her voice was cold, as distant as her eyes. I shrugged, about to walk away. I wasn't one to chase a bitch. They'd been falling at my feet for as long as I could remember. Shorty could keep looking crazy with that foul ass attitude. But then, I saw the tear tracks on her pretty face.

"You don't have to be interested to tell me what's wrong, ma."

She picked up her glass, swirling around her drink. I waited.

"I don't even know you," she finally said.

"I'm Smoke."

Her eyebrow lifted. "The owner?"

I nodded, then took it upon myself to sit across from her. Almost immediately, a server appeared.

"Hello, Mr. Salinas. What can I get you?" she asked, the interest in her eyes clear.

"Our guest needs a refill. And get me a Patrón on ice," I instructed.

"Yes, sir."

Once she walked away, I turned my attention back to the woman sitting with me.

"Now, what nigga was stupid enough to make you cry?"

She frowned. "How do you know it was a nigga?"

"Ain't it always? What's your name?"

She hesitated before answering me. "Dayana."

Good. I wouldn't have to kill Demon.

"Dayana," I repeated. "Tell me what happened."

Five minutes later, I sat there, rubbing my chin. The shit she had just told me was crazy. What the fuck did that nigga have going on?

"Damn, baby girl," was all I could say.

She shrugged and took another sip of her drink.

"It's whatever. At least I got to kick his ass."

"So, what you gon' do?"

"What I'ma do?" she scoffed. "That nigga is over with."

I kept my thoughts to myself. She was angry and hurt now, but when that shit died down, it might be a whole other story.

"Listen, beautiful, I can't undo what happened to you today, but I can make you forget it for a little while. Drinks on me, okay?"

A small smile lifted her pretty lips. "On one condition," she said.

I raised an eyebrow. "What's that?"

"You drink with me."

I had a million other things to do. I had somewhere I needed to be in an hour and a half. The last thing I had time for was sitting down and getting buzzed. Knowing all of that, I smiled back at her.

"You got that," I agreed.

For the next couple of hours, we drank and talked. Shorty opened up in ways I hadn't expected, from telling me about how her father arranged her marriage to mentioning that she loved to sing to admitting that she thought she wanted to be a teacher and her father didn't approve. I mostly babysat my glass while she made her way through three coconut mojitos. Her eyes were low, her cheeks flushed when she finally decided she was done. We stood up and she stumbled a little in her heels.

"Whoa," she mumbled, then giggled. "Maybe I should call an Uber. I can get my car later."

"You definitely not driving," I agreed.

"Let me just call—"

"Nah, shorty. I'll take you."

"You don't have to do that, Smoke."

Frowning, she shook her head, but I wasn't trying to hear that. I was feeling little Ms. Dayana and making sure she got home okay was my pleasure.

"I want to do it. We friends, now, right?"

She bit down on her bottom lip. "Shit. That's cool. I don't have many friends as fine as you."

I hid my smile. I knew she was going to regret saying that shit, *if* she remembered later.

"Well, thank you. I need you to just sit tight for like two minutes while I get my stuff and talk to my staff, okay?"

She nodded and eased back into the chair. It took me closer to ten minutes, but finally, I was back at the table. I held out my hand and she took it, letting me guide her out of the restaurant and out to the parking lot. I got her into my BMW M8 Coupe and helped her strap in. As soon as I was settled in my seat, I asked for her address. It was a good thing I did because she was sleep almost as soon as we took off. I hated to wake her up when the twenty-minute drive was up. I got out and opened her door, and she still didn't move.

"Dayana?"

I had to call her name a few times before she replied with a soft, "Hmm?"

"Wake up. You home, ma."

Her eyes popped open, and she looked around, confused. She blushed, embarrassed, but I wasn't having it.

"You good. No snoring or slobbing," I teased.

She shook her head but smiled up at me. I handed her my

phone. She already knew what to do, and I watched as she locked her number in.

"Thank you for bringing me home," she said as she climbed out.

"Anytime."

She walked up her driveway a little bit before turning around. "Smoke?"

"Yeah?"

"Thank you for everything else, too."

I nodded and leaned against my car as she made her way to the door. She looked back one more time and gave me a little wave. I waved back and she disappeared inside the house. Shooting her a quick text, I told her goodnight. I was surprised when my phone vibrated with her response.

Dayana: *Goodnight, finest friend.*

Chuckling, I pulled off, already wondering when I could see her again.

CHAPTER 17
Dream

(*SATURDAY, June 5*)

I could already tell that tonight was going to be fucked up. I had no interest in going to a party at the Wares. Then, I still wasn't comfortable in this close-fitting ass dress Dayana had me wearing. And speaking of my sister, something was wrong with her. She'd been unusually quiet the last few days, even when we went for our final dress fittings, but she wouldn't tell me what was up. When I tried to bring up her bachelorette party next week, she waved me off. I counted on her to be the life of the party, but that obviously wasn't happening tonight. I looked over to where she sat in the passenger seat. She was staring out the window, probably focused on nothing.

"So... when you gon' tell me what's on your mind?" I asked.

"I told you, I'm good."

The lie rolled off her tongue, sounding totally unbelievable. I would let her make it tonight, but tomorrow, we were having a come to Jesus meeting.

"You think Demon gon' be here?"

I shrugged at her question. "I don't know. I mean, the nigga don't look like the party type."

I hoped I sounded nonchalant, but I felt exactly the opposite way about the prospect of seeing him again. Butterflies danced in my stomach and heat sparked along my skin as I remembered his touch. I'd been waiting for him to reach out ever since he called the other night.

I shivered as I thought about his last words to me. *I'ma fuck you raw. Every day.* He was so blunt and vulgar, and I should be disgusted. Instead, his words had turned me on as I imagined him inside me, with nothing between us. I bit down on my lower lip, holding in a moan at the thought of his hard, inked body between my thighs. I didn't exactly choose Damien, but I'd be lying if I said I wasn't fascinated by him.

"Look at you, over there daydreaming about him! You need to gon' and let him fuck," my sister teased.

"Yana!" I gasped.

"For real, what you waiting for? That nigga looks like he can—"

"Yana, shut up!"

She giggled as I blushed. I was so glad to hear her laugh that I didn't even cuss her out.

We pulled up in front of the Wares' mansion, where an employee checked our IDs and a list, then took the key fob to park my car further back down the long driveway. I noticed the Wares had security out in full force as we approached the front door. I raised my fist to knock, but it opened as if someone knew we were waiting.

"Come in, come in," a gray-haired man with a friendly smile urged us in. "Let me show you to the ballroom."

Dayana and I looked at each other and mouthed, *"Ballroom?"* as soon as he turned his back to us. These people really lived lavishly. Money and excellent taste were displayed in every inch of their home, from the obviously handmade, one-of-a-kind furniture to the contemporary art on the walls. I recognized works by a couple of famous Black artists, including my favorite, K. Reid. Security guards strolled back and forth as we walked, protecting the Wares' treasures.

"If we're rich, what do you call these folk?" Dayana whispered.

"Wealthy," I whispered back as we were ushered into the ballroom.

A quick glance around the room revealed that it was filled with the who's who of the "underground economy." Black-suited security patrolled the perimeter of the room while guests mingled in the center, accepting drinks and *hors d'oeuvres* from circulating catering staff. I spotted our parents and pulled Dayana toward them.

"Only fifteen minutes late! It's a miracle," our mother, Lucia, quipped, giving us both air kisses.

Daddy hugged each of us, but I noticed Dayana didn't hug him back. Maybe they had had one of their famous arguments. That would explain her mood. I grabbed a glass of champagne and chatted with my mother for a minute, my eyes still scanning the room. Disappointment settled in my stomach as I realized Damien wasn't here. I tried to dismiss the feeling, even moved around the room and talked to several acquaintances. But I missed his presence, and I was ready for this night to be over.

"Awww, fuck," Dayana cursed under her breath, standing next to me.

"What is it?" I asked, following her gaze.

I frowned. All I saw was her fiancé, Jordan, approaching. That usually made her smile, but tonight, she was stiff, and her resting bitch face was in place. Yeah, something was definitely off.

"Dream," Jordan greeted me, before pressing a kiss to my cheek.

"Hey, Jordan," I said dryly.

I was in whatever mood my sister was in when it came to this nigga. I liked him just fine, but if she wasn't feeling him, I wasn't either.

"And my beautiful bride-to-be," he said, stepping closer to Dayana. "Hello, Sweetness."

She stepped back. "I have to go to the bathroom," she announced before damn near running out.

Jordan and I looked at each other. He gave me a guilty half-smile.

"We had a little argument—"

"Don't fuck with my sister, Jordan. I don't play about her," I warned.

He nodded and drifted off from our awkward run-in. I stood there for a couple of minutes, people-watching and plotting how I could leave.

"Dream," Daddy called from behind me.

I turned to see him a few steps away with Eric Vaughn.

Great, I thought. He was definitely matchmaking. Eric was the son of Mario Vaughn. That man moved more pills than a major pharmaceutical company. I pasted on a smile.

Daddy stayed just long enough to start a conversation before he lied like Mama was trying to get his attention. Alone with Eric, I searched for something to talk about, but I really wasn't interested.

"They—" I began.

"Ay, Dream, it's cool. I know what your pops tryna do. Mine be on the same shit. To be honest, you fine as fuck and I wouldn't mind getting to know you a little better, but I can see you ain't feeling it. So, I got a proposition," Eric said.

I smiled. "What's that?"

"Let's hang out for tonight, so they don't hook us up with nobody else. Then you ain't gotta ever fuck with a nigga again."

"You got that," I said, extending my hand for him to shake.

We talked about a little of everything. He was funny and smart, but definitely destined to be a drug lord, a turnoff for me. I looked up one time, searching for my sister. She and Jordan were in the middle of a discussion that looked like it was getting heated.

"Hold on a minute, Eric," I said, about to march over there.

Before I could, a tall, slim man who I vaguely recognized moved behind Dayana and leaned down to whisper in her ear. She visibly relaxed as she looked over her shoulder and nodded at him as she said something. Oh, yeah, this bitch had some explaining to do.

Eric caught my hand, grabbing my attention.

"Everything okay?" he asked.

I was about to respond until I felt the tingling that let me know eyes were on me. My body tensed as my eyes darted around and nervous anticipation flooded me. Only one person could cause that response, that strange sense of aware-ness. Still, I almost jumped out of my skin when a possessive hand cupped the back of my neck, and the tantalizing smell of Dior Sauvage greeted my nostrils. Eric frowned.

"You touching her. Why the fuck you got your hands on her?" a rough voice questioned him.

I looked up, way up, and met Damien's cold, green eyes.

CHAPTER 18
Demon

FIVE MINUTES AGO, I had no problems with Eric Vaughn. But then, I'd walked into this fake ass party my brother had invited me to and saw him talking with Dream and holding her hand. Now, we had an issue. I didn't want to be here anyway, only came because I knew her ass would be here, and I walked in to find him all over her. Hell nah.

"You touching her. Why the fuck you got your hands on her?" I asked him.

She looked up at me. "Damien! Why you so—"

"Shut up," I told her softly, squeezing the back of her neck gently.

I could tell by the way her mouth fell open that she was shocked. She didn't say anything, though, and she pulled her hand out of his. She was going to learn that I meant what I said. First, I had to deal with this nigga.

"I asked you a question."

"And who the fuck you supposed to be that I owe you an answer, Demon?" he shot back.

This nigga wanted to talk crazy? That shit made me smile. Slowly, I released Dream's neck. I didn't feel the need to answer him in words—he knew my name, so he knew who I was. Before that nigga could blink, my fist connected with his fly-ass mouth. Blood spurted and Dream gasped. He staggered but remained upright, and I took a step closer, ready to finish him. She moved in front of me quickly, her hands going to my chest.

"Damien, no!" she whispered.

I looked down to where her fingers were splayed against me. Already, I could feel the calming effect of her touch, but I refused to admit that shit. Security surrounded us. Two of them grabbed Eric and the rest looked at me like they didn't know what to do. Every one of them niggas knew if they laid a hand on me, it'd be the last time they tried to restrain anybody. The room was suddenly quiet, all eyes on us, and I saw Dante stalking toward me, frowning. He could get fucked up, too, if he wanted. Eric struggled to get free, his eyes shooting daggers. My smile widened.

"Let him go," I ordered.

"Damien," Dream spoke again.

"Move."

She shook her head. "You can't here. Please."

My hands went to her waist, ready to move her out of the way. Then, I made the mistake of looking into her eyes. *Fuck!* Shorty was pleading with me and, simp ass nigga that I was turning into, I was about to give in to her.

"Damien—"

"I'll see you again," I promised Vaughn, before looking down at her. "Let's go," I snapped, grabbing her hand and heading for the ballroom's double doorway.

"Wh-where are we going?" she asked.

I ignored her, mostly because I didn't have an answer. All I knew was that I needed to get out of this pretentious ass house, away from all these damn people who were staring at us. Two steps from the exit, her brother stepped into my path, a mug on his face.

"You good?"

He was looking at me, but his words were directed at her. I wanted to put this nigga down permanently, show him the consequences of staying in my damn business. But once again, I found myself considering her feelings. I hated that shit. Dream was making me soft. I didn't tolerate the bullshit Eric and DeAngelo were on, and here I was, letting both of them make it tonight. DeAngelo crossed his arms over his chest, like he could really stop me. I laughed softly.

"I let yo' ass live one time," I told him. "It won't happen again."

"D, I'm okay," she reassured him. "Tell Yana to get my car."

Still frowning, he slowly stepped out of the way. I half-walked, half-dragged her outside until she stood beside my car. As I made my way around to the driver's side, I heard her voice.

"You not gon' open the door for me?"

"I look like that lame ass nigga Eric or some shit? Get in the car, Dream."

She hesitated and I walked back around to where she was.

"Get in the muhfucking car before I put you through the window. Glass up and all."

I didn't mean the shit, but she didn't know that. Her eyes widened, and she hurriedly opened the door. By the time I slid in, she was in the seatbelt, staring out the windshield with her pretty mouth in a pout. Fuck it. She could sulk all she wanted. I wasn't in the mood to talk, anyway. Loosening the tie around my neck, I pulled it off and threw it. Sherrilyn had me paying four thousand dollars for a suit and tie, and I couldn't stand to keep the shit on for an hour.

I drove for forty minutes in silence. Finally, I felt her gaze fall on me.

"Damien, you know—"

"Shut up," I cut her off.

She exhaled loudly. "You—"

"Ay, yo, Dream, I said shut up. I'on wanna hear shit you gotta say."

I raised my voice, something I never did. Pissed off, she crossed her arms over her chest and turned her body toward the side window.

A few minutes later, I pulled off onto a narrow, private road that could barely be seen from the highway. A mile down the road, the lake finally came into view. Out of my peripheral vision, I saw Dream shift in her seat, her arms falling, her body turning toward me. I ignored her as I pulled up, parking between the lake house my father had left me and the edge of the lake.

"Get out," I told her as I opened my door and slid out.

As soon as I closed the door, I heard the lock engage. Scowling at her, I walked around to the passenger's side. I knocked on the window and she shook her head, her cocoa eyes wide with fear.

"Get out the fuckin' car, Dream!"

"No!"

I rubbed my temple and sighed. This girl was giving me a headache. Reaching in the pocket of the suit pants, I grabbed the key fob and unlocked the door. I opened it and stared down at her.

"Dream—"

"I'm not getting out."

I guess the shit was a game to her. Reaching in, I pulled her out of the seat. She started struggling and swinging immediately. One of her wild throws popped me in the eye. I'd had enough of her shit. Wrapping both arms around her, I squeezed until she stopped fighting.

"What I tell you about putting yo' hands on me? The fuck you hit me for?" I raged at her.

"I'm not stupid! You brought me out here to kill me and dump me in that lake. I'm not dying without fighting!"

I let her go, then stood back to look at her.

"The fuck you talking about?" I demanded.

She shook her head again and looked down.

"Why the hell would I kill you?"

"Because I was talking to Eric and I kept you from killing him and you think you gon' take it out on me," she snapped.

It was the stupidest shit I'd ever heard. I couldn't help the low chuckle that escaped me at her dramatic ass. Her head popped up as I laughed at her, a mug on her pretty face.

"Ay, shorty, you gotta stop listening to them rumors about me. I ain't tryna kill you, crazy ass girl. Come on."

Reluctantly, she followed me to the house. We climbed the steps and crossed the porch. I unlocked the door quickly and we stepped into the living room. Darkness greeted us, the only light spilling in through the front picture window. It illuminated her beautiful face and outlined the thick curves covered by that tight ass dress. I could feel my dick responding already.

"Are you going to turn the lights on or..."

Her voice trailed off as I backed her against the wall.

"What I tell you about entertaining other niggas before our deal is done?" I asked, pressing my body against hers.

"It wasn't like that. If you would stop being so rude—"

"Fuck that!" I nuzzled her cheekbone and she sucked in a deep breath. "I own you until our time is up."

"I'm not property, Damien!"

I smiled down at her.

"I'm serious. We have a short-term deal. I could never belong to a crazy, rude-ass nigga. I swear, I be wondering what kind of woman raised you—"

I didn't hear anything she said after that. Grabbing her chin, I tilted her head back roughly, making her meet my eyes.

"What the fuck you say to me?"

Her eyes widened as if she suddenly realized what she'd said.

"Damien—"

"Nah. You wanna know what kinda woman raised me? She was a little like you. Every time I see you, you barely dressed, and a different nigga got your attention. All y'all bitches the same, fucking for a come up. She fucked for drugs. What you fucking for? Huh, Dream? To pay off deals and to make sure your bank account stays fat? Swear you probably more of a ho than the escorts I fuck with. At least they real about theirs."

I smirked at her as tears welled in her eyes. Her stubborn ass didn't let them fall, though.

"Fuck you, Damien. Fuck yo' ignorant, assuming ass. I—"

I cut her off by slamming my mouth against hers. She fought me at first, twisting and turning, refusing to part her lips. But it only took a minute for her body to betray her as she softened against me, opening her mouth to let my tongue slide in. She moaned in the back of her throat as her hands gripped my locks.

Deepening the kiss, I reached down and eased the dress up her thighs. My hands slid to her fat ass, squeezing her tight. She whimpered as I lifted her, balancing her against the wall as I pressed myself between her legs, letting her feel my body's reaction to her. I was ready to sink inside her, fuck her until she didn't remember anything but my name. She rolled against me, the seat of her panties rocking against my print.

She moved to lock her legs around my waist, but I stopped her. Pulling back, I smiled down at her. Her words from before, about my mother, were stuck in my head. I wanted her, but I wanted to hurt her more.

"See?" I taunted. "Just like the escorts. But I'm not sticking my dick in you until I know you clean."

The desire in her eyes faded instantly, replaced by anger

and more than a little pain. For some reason, it didn't feel as good as I had expected.

"Take me home," she whispered.

"Shit. Say less."

CHAPTER 19
Dream

HUMILIATED, I fixed my dress, doing my best to ignore the dampness between my thighs. My emotions were all over the place. I didn't know whether to cry, scream, or pick up the huge vase to my left and bash Damien in his damn head. Instead, I held my head high and walked out the door and got in the car. I didn't bother looking at him when he got in. As he started the car, I could feel his eyes on me. Unwilling to give him the reaction he wanted, I stared out the window, telling myself to calm down inside.

But my brain replayed tonight's events. As soon as I saw him at the party, looking darkly beautiful in his perfectly tailored Brioni suit, I'd been stuck, heart racing, eyes glued to him. His touch on my neck, his possessive words to Eric, the heat of his eyes on me had sent chills through me. And even if he tried to deny it, I knew he held back on Eric and D because of me.

I had almost convinced myself that I was more than a deal to him, that he might be feeling something for me. I don't know why it mattered, but it did. His calling me a ho had dashed all those hopes. Yeah, I was wrong for what I said, but his reaction was savage. He was so fucking wrong about me, it was laughable. My pride wanted me to correct him, but I convinced myself that it wasn't worth it.

Fuck what he thought about me.

As we reached the city limits, he messed with the radio and Li'l Baby's voice flowed through the car, rapping "Emotionally Scarred." It took all my strength not to roll my eyes at the irony. By the time Damien pulled up to my house, I was more than ready to get out and get away from him. But for some reason, I didn't reach for the door handle. I heard him laugh softly.

"Waiting for me to open it again?"

"No, you've proved that you don't have the common decency and manners to do that," I insulted quietly.

I saw his hand tighten on the steering wheel.

"Get the fuck outta my car, Dream."

"I am. I wanted to say that I'm sorry for what I said about your mother. I was out of line. I know how to apologize when I say shit I shouldn't."

He turned to look at me, his top lip curled into a sneer. "I ain't apologizing to you for shit."

"I don't expect you to. But I do have a question for you."

I had to say what I was thinking, had to know if I'd been reading him right at all. I lifted my eyes to his.

"Since you claim I'm like the bitches you pay to fuck, do you care this much about who else they might be fucking?"

Silence met my question, and I smirked at him. He refused to give the answer I already knew.

"Yeah. So, I guess I'm not *just* like them after all."

I opened the door then and climbed out. He surprised me by waiting until I made it to the front door. Slipping inside the house, I kicked off my shoes and made my way toward the stairs. All I wanted was a hot shower and my bed. Halfway up the staircase, I stopped when I heard my grandfather behind me. He maneuvered his chair to the foot of the stairs. Turning, I smiled at him. He looked me up and down before saying anything.

"How was the party?"

I shrugged. "It was fine."

"Where is everyone else?"

"Still there, I guess. I left a little early."

His eyes pierced mine. "Alone?"

I hesitated before answering, but I didn't make a habit of lying to him. "With Damien... Demon."

"Hmm," he said, before he started to roll off again.

Suddenly, he stopped. Without turning, he called my name.

"Sir?"

"Be careful."

It was much too late for that. Of course, I didn't say that to him. Instead, I made my way back downstairs and kissed the top of his head. This man was so precious to me, and I didn't want to worry him. I watched as he disappeared down the hallway to his room.

Starting back up the stairs, I paused again as my phone vibrated. I pulled it out of my clutch, expecting to see my sister's number. Instead, it was Isaac. I still hadn't told him about my situation with Damien. I debated answering, thinking about how our last meeting had ended with Damien's threats. Then I thought about how Damien had just treated me. Why should I ignore a man who respected and was kind to me because an asshole said so? I answered.

"Hey," I greeted.

"Hey, you," he responded. "What you up to?"

"Nothing. How are you?"

"I'm fine. You feel like company? We could grab some food and watch movies."

I closed my eyes as I reached the landing. Part of me was exhausted. But I *was* hungry, and I had no doubt Isaac could get me out of the funk I was in. Anyway, I needed to tell him about Damien.

"Sure. But let's find something open late on DoorDash. I've already been out tonight," I suggested.

"Whatever you want, Beautiful. A nigga just wanna chill in yo' lovely presence. See you in half an hour?"

I smiled. "I'll be waiting."

I took a quick shower, moisturized, and changed into a tank top, pajama shorts, and fuzzy socks. I made my way to the theater room, ready to choose one of the cheesy, indie movies that Isaac hated on Amazon Prime. A couple of minutes later, my phone vibrated as he announced he was outside. I jumped up from the plush, reclining chair and walked up front to let him in. I didn't know how he was going to greet me since Damien had damn near killed him the last time he was here, but seeing the smile on his face relaxed my nerves.

"So, what do you wanna eat?" I asked him when we were back in the theater room.

"I'm not falling for that. You pick," he said.

I giggled as I opened the app on my phone. After ordering a crazy amount of Mexican food, I started the movie. Isaac groaned as soon as the opening credits rolled.

"Dream, you gotta be fucking with me!"

"This one gon' be good, boo," I coaxed.

He shook his head and sighed. Fifteen minutes later, I had to admit... it was pretty damn bad. From the stiff acting to the poor lighting and ridiculous plot, the movie was a mess. By the time the food arrived twenty minutes after that, I was ready to take a break from the bullshit. Isaac followed me into the kitchen after we got our food. I grabbed plates, utensils, and paper towels, and we settled into the breakfast nook. We ate in almost silence. I was going to let him get a full stomach before I told him the shit about Damien. He wasn't going to like it, but hopefully, he would understand why I had to do what I had to do.

As if our brains were connected, Isaac and I moved at the same time to clean up the small mess we'd made.

"This damn salsa was made in hell. I'ma pay for that later," he said as he picked up the empty containers that once held the extra-fiery salsa verde.

"I got some acid reflux stuff you can take before it kicks your ass."

He nodded and I moved to run some dish water. Caught up in what I was doing, I didn't realize he'd moved behind me until he called my name. I jumped, then laughed at myself.

"What's up?"

"The last time I was here—"

Sighing, I wiped my hands on the drying towel before turning to face him.

"Yeah... I need to talk to you about that."

He frowned. "Do you know who he is? What he does?"

I nodded slowly.

"Then what kind of business could you possibly have with him?"

I had made up my mind to tell him, but now that it was time, I was stalling, not sure how to put the words together.

"I-I owe him."

"Owe him what?"

I looked up into his brown eyes that were dark with confusion. Biting down on my bottom lip, I searched for the right words, a way to make this ridiculous situation make sense.

"Dream? What do you owe him?"

I closed my eyes. "Me."

"What the fuck does that even mean?"

Reluctantly, I explained the whole fucked up deal to him. When I finished, I looked up at him, hopeful. That hope died instantly. Isaac was damn near shaking with anger. Without a word to me, he stalked toward the living room. I ran behind him, grabbing his arm before he could open the door.

"Isaac, you have to understand—"

"Understand what? You out here hoing yourself out for DeAngelo's ass?" he snapped, yanking away.

I felt my anger simmering. That was the second time tonight I'd been called a ho. I wasn't going to be too many more of those.

"I was saving my brother's life!"

"What about your own life, Dream? I thought we were working toward something."

"We are! It's just a month, Isaac. A month and then—"

He glared down at me, freezing my words in my throat.

"A month of that nigga fucking you however he wants and then I'm supposed to be happy to get his sloppy seconds?"

My jaw dropped open at his words. *Sloppy seconds???* That's what he thought of me? He walked closer and I backed up, stopping before I was pressed against the wall.

"You been making me wait for months now, fucking tease. I can't even touch the pussy, but I'm supposed to want it after that nigga uses you up? Girl, please."

I was stunned. I'd never heard him talk like this. I mean, I knew he was pissed off, and yeah, I saw occasional flashes of his bad temper, but still! He didn't even look like himself, with his face twisted into a mug and his brown eyes blazing.

"Isaac—"

Suddenly, his face cleared a little as he looked down at me. "You wanna make this right?" he asked.

Really, after the shit he'd just said, I was re-thinking everything about him. I didn't give a fuck about making shit right. But maybe I was overreacting. I couldn't really expect him not to be mad, could I?

"How?" I asked grudgingly.

He smiled as he curled a hand around the back of my neck.

"Let me fuck first."

My jaw dropped at the audacity. *This nigga!*

"That's what you worried about? Being first?"

He shrugged, like it was no big deal. "I think I earned it."

Dropping a kiss on my lips, he tried to pull me closer. *Okay, that was it.* He had me all kinds of fucked up.

"You need to go," I hissed through my teeth, pushing him off me.

His frown returned immediately.

"I was trying to, remember?"

My head snapped up as I heard the soft hum of my grandfather's wheelchair approach. He rolled slowly into the living room and my eyes widened when I saw him. His face was calm, but the Desert Eagle in his lap let me know he knew shit was off.

"You all right, granddaughter?" he asked, his eyes on Isaac.

I nodded. "It's fine, Grandpapa," I lied, trying to control my agitated breathing.

"Fuck this shit," Isaac said, wrenching open the door.

He looked back at me once and mumbled, "Bitch," under his breath.

Ah, hell naw! My grandfather called me as I followed Isaac out the door.

"Bitch? *Bitch?!*" I repeated, walking behind him to his car.

He stopped by the door. "Yeah. Bitch. Get the fuck away from me."

"Fuck you, Isaac. Who was the bitch when Demon was choking yo' ass out, you bitch ass nig—"

The backhand landed across my right cheek, surprising the hell out of me as I stumbled backward. The pain of the blow seared across my face, and tears welled in my eyes. My hand went to my mouth, and I looked in shock at the blood on my fingers. Isaac had jumped in his car and that broke my daze. Enraged, I balled up my fist and hit his window as hard as I fucking could. That nigga still pulled off, barely missing my feet. I screamed in frustration, but the sound stopped abruptly as I saw the sleek body of a Jaguar F-Type speed past my driveway. I recognized it instantly.

Damien. Oh, shit!

CHAPTER 20

Dayana

(*A little earlier*)

The last place I wanted to be was this stupid party, especially in the presence of my father and Jordan right now. I wasn't feeling either of them, and if I hadn't wanted to show my twin support, I'd be home in my room.

The day I found out Jordan cheated on me, I told Daddy I needed to talk to him. He suggested we have lunch the next day. Imagine my surprise when I showed up and Jordan was sitting at the table with my father. He'd already admitted what he'd done and was in apology mode.

But what was even more shocking was my father's response to my idea of calling the wedding off. I would never forget his words. *"The man made a mistake, baby. It's time you grow up and realize that it probably won't be the only time. But he will still be a good husband and father. There's too much at stake with this marriage to give it up. Find it in your heart to forgive him, Yana."*

When I had resisted the idea, my father, the king of my world, had looked at me coldly and said, *"You need to make a good match. I'm not taking care of you forever. You gon' marry*

Jordan and you gon' get over this bullshit. If you don't, I'll cut your ass off."

Everything I'd ever thought I knew crumbled as my heart broke. The idea of being disowned terrified me. I wasn't Dream with an Ivy League education and some lucrative career ahead of me. I had no real idea of what I wanted to do and hadn't thought much about it since I accepted the idea that my marriage would be arranged. So, I gave in and agreed to marry Jordan after both of them kept talking. It felt like something inside me died.

"Dayana, you at least have to talk to me," Jordan said, snapping me out of my thoughts as he grabbed my arm.

"Don't touch me," I hissed, trying to yank my arm away discreetly.

"I'm not going to make a scene at this party. But remember, you'll be my wife in one week and you crazy if you think I'ma put up with your attitude and the way you been acting."

I glared up at him.

"Then maybe you should find another wife."

He chuckled, knowing he had the advantage.

"And how would your father feel about that?"

Before I could answer, I felt a warm presence behind me, then a low, smooth voice in my ear.

"You okay, shorty?"

I looked over my shoulder and into the handsome face of Smoke Salinas. For one moment, my heart stopped as I took him in. It restarted with a rapid beat, and I had to fight myself to keep from turning around and stepping into his arms.

"I'm fine," I said softly.

He didn't move immediately, and I heard Jordan clear his throat.

"Smoke, good to see you. How do you know my fiancée?" he asked, his voice fake and bright.

Smoke looked down at him with disgust.

"Just know that I know her," he said coolly before turning his attention back to me. "You sure you good?"

Hell no, I wanted to say, but I nodded.

"I'll be around if that changes," he said before strolling off.

I couldn't help it. I watched him. People stepped out of his way as he walked, tall and slim in a perfectly cut dark suit. His aura commanded attention, and I wasn't the only woman watching his lean, muscular frame.

Jordan cleared his throat again. I looked at him in annoyance.

"You need some water or something?" I asked sarcastically.

I could see anger glittering in his eyes as his mouth pulled into a thin line.

"Nah. I need to know what that shit with Smoke was about."

I waved him off. "He's a friend."

"Since when?"

"Bye, Jordan."

I moved to make my way back to Dream, only to see Demon beside her, his eyes on Eric Vaughn. The next minute passed in a blur as Demon punched Eric and security swarmed them. Before I could move, I saw my sister being pulled along by Demon. DeAngelo tried to stop them, but finally stepped back. He was frowning, so I hurried to see what was up. On the way, my phone buzzed in my clutch. I pulled it out and smiled when I saw Smoke's name.

Just say the word, he had texted, and my smile grew bigger. Feeling bold, I typed back, *The word is, I wanna see you.*

"Yana, Dream left with that lunatic. She said for you to get her car."

I didn't even realize DeAngelo had walked upon me.

"She good?" I asked.

He shrugged, looking agitated. "She left willingly."

"Then why you pissed off? You got her into this shit, D. Let her make the best of it."

My phone vibrated again.

Smoke: *Tell me when and where.*

I bit my lip as I thought about it. I had an idea growing in my mind, a way to say "fuck you" to my daddy and Jordan, to prove to myself they didn't have all the control in my life.

"I know that look. The hell you up to?" DeAngelo inquired suspiciously.

"Hmm? Oh! Nothing. D, I'm not feeling so hot. I'ma go, too."

"Yana—"

I damn near ran out of the ballroom before he could protest. Halfway down the hall, I stopped to text Smoke back.

Now. Meet me at the Westin.

————

My breath left me in a whoosh as I was slammed against the wall. Before I could recover, he had our mouths fused together again, kissing me like his life depended on it. I grabbed his shoulders and kissed him back, heat flooding my body. I moaned as I ran my hands over his chest, feeling the muscles ripple beneath my palms. He lifted me up and I wrapped my legs around his waist, grinding my pussy against his dick, cursing the material that separated us.

Our outer clothes were already gone, ripped off and thrown all over the posh suite. Suddenly, I wanted my lacy black bra and the matching panties gone. He must've read my mind, because he pulled me away from the wall, and I held on as he reached behind me and unhooked my bra. He flung it somewhere—I didn't give a damn; I'd find it later.

He pressed me against the wall again, sliding me up so that my breasts were near his mouth. I sucked in a breath, waiting in anticipation. He didn't make me wait long. One hand cupped my left breast and he lowered his mouth to it. I arched away from the wall as his lips closed around my nipple. I felt the wet lash of his tongue and then he sucked me hard.

I always imagined gentle when I thought of this. I thought I wanted to be handled delicately, made love to slowly. But that's not what was happening in this room. He was rough and I was loving it. Whatever this was that was burning between us was too hot for slow and gentle. I had known that from the minute my eyes fell on him in his bar days ago.

I grabbed his head, feeling the silky waves of his hair as I held him close to me. I moaned as he shifted his attention to my other breast, giving it the same delicious treatment. His mouth was so magical that I almost didn't realize that he was walking with me wrapped around him. He unhooked my legs from behind him and threw me onto the bed. He joined me a second later, his hands already on the sides of my panties. I lifted my hips impatiently as he pulled them down.

"Your pussy is pretty as fuck, shorty," he said, his gaze focused between my legs.

I don't know what came over me, but I spread my legs wider for him. He slid his fingers up my thigh before moving to cup my pussy in his big hand. My heart beat faster, a beat I could feel in the throbbing between my legs. He moved his palm in a circular motion, right above my clit, and I moaned again.

He teased me like that for a couple of minutes, close but not close enough.

"Smoke," I finally pleaded.

He smiled at me like he knew exactly what I wanted. And he did, because a second later, his thumb was on my clit. He rubbed it as his gaze met mine. I felt myself get wetter when I saw the look in his caramel eyes. Smoke looked like he wanted to devour me, and I wanted him to. My hips moved against his hand, wanting more, wanting the orgasm that was already building inside me.

He pulled back suddenly, and I whined my protest. I watched greedily as he slid out of his boxer briefs. But then, my jaw dropped. I mean, I could tell through his underwear that he had a nice package, but he was bigger than I imagined. I felt a moment of fear, a little uncertainty, but then he was climbing over me, making room for himself between my thighs.

He lowered himself to give me a hard kiss. His dick pressed against my pussy, and I sighed, moving my hips to rub against him. His fingers slipped between us, and he found my clit again. I shuddered as he rubbed his fingers over the little nub, getting me extra wet for him. His lips trailed down my neck to my shoulder, then the tip of my breast. He sucked my nipple into his mouth, dragging his tongue against it. I sighed his name.

Slipping two fingers inside me, he pumped them fast and hard, dragging soft little sounds out of me.

"You so fucking tight."

My legs spread wider at his words, and I bit down on my bottom lip, my body shivering.

"Smoke, *please*..."

"Please what?" he teased me, brushing his lips against mine.

"Please. I need—"

My voice trailed off as my body shook even harder.

"You need me to fuck you?"

I nodded, then pulled his head down for another kiss. He broke it long enough to reach for the condom he'd put on the nightstand, open it, and roll it on. And then he was bending my legs, pushing my knees to my shoulders as he rose above me. My pussy was wide open to him, and I felt nervous for a minute. He grabbed his dick and I felt him drag it along the seam of my soaking wet center.

"I don't do soft," he told me.

I shook my head. "I don't want soft."

"Safe word," he mumbled.

"Wh-what?"

"In case it gets too rough, too intense. You need a safe word, so I know to stop."

I was in no mood to think; I just wanted to feel. I pulled myself together enough to say, "Mango."

The head of his dick parted my pussy lips then, and I could feel his tip pressing against my opening. Before I could take that in, he drove into me, burying himself balls deep with that one hard thrust. I jerked beneath him, and a whimper escaped my lips as pain burned through me. He looked down at me and I blinked tears away.

"Okay?" he asked.

It took a second, but I nodded. He moved then, stroking in and out of me. My pussy clenched around him as the pain started to disappear, replaced by something else, some kind of pleasure I'd never experienced. He let go of my legs as he fucked me. I locked them around him. Catching his rhythm, I moved my hips against him.

"Fuck, Dayana," he growled as he picked up his pace.

He pounded into me, and I still wanted more, my earlier pain forgotten. My nails in his back encouraged him to go deeper, harder. Leaning forward, he smashed his mouth into mine, catching the little sounds I was making. I kissed him, loving the softness of his lips.

He lifted and grabbed the top of the headboard, using it as leverage as he fucked me hard. Our bodies slapped against each other, the sound loud in the room. Part of me couldn't believe this was happening. The other part was so happy it was.

"Smoke," I whispered.

I felt my pussy contracting around him, my body shaken by uncontrollable shivers as tingles spread all over me. I knew he could feel I was close because he smiled down at me.

"You about to cum, Dayana?"

"Y-yes," I stuttered, my legs tightening around him.

He let go of the headboard and found my clit. He swirled his thumb around it until my body seized up and I cried out.

"Good girl," he said. "Cum on this dick."

I came hard, holding on to him tight as he continued to slam into me. I think I screamed his name. He grabbed my hips, holding me up as he fucked the hell out of me, my pussy still contracting around him. Heat twisted through me as he stroked me. I could feel another orgasm building already. My hands on his back pulled him closer and deeper into me. My hips were grinding in sync with him. I closed my eyes, focusing on the feeling of his dick inside me, stretching me. The shivers started again, and I didn't know how long I could hold out.

Suddenly, his smooth strokes were rougher, like he was losing control. Knowing he was about to cum triggered something inside me. I fell apart beneath him, his name on my lips as I came again. I felt him let go, felt him jerk inside me. He didn't stop moving, though, until the last of his seed erupted. Falling forward, he let himself rest against my body for a minute. I was breathing as hard as he was, my chest rising to meet his. Finally, our breathing evened out and Smoke dropped a kiss against my lips. He stood and headed toward the bathroom.

I smiled as I snuggled beneath the covers. *Mission accomplished*. I had done it. I had decided about who I was going to give my virginity to, and I followed through. It was one less thing my father could sell, one less thing Jordan could claim. I'd known from the moment I saw Smoke in the bar I wanted him. He'd looked at me and my body felt like it was on fire for him, even as I was fuming over Jordan. I was glad I'd decided to come to this hotel, to this room.

And it had all been worth it. Yeah, it hurt like hell at first, but Smoke knew what he was doing. I lost myself in the feel of his dick stroking in and out, faster and faster until I exploded. My first orgasm with a man inside me had been worth the wait.

But now I needed to wash up and go. Back to my perfect, but suffocating life, where most of the decisions were made for me. Back to my perfect, but lonely bedroom. Back to my worthless fiancé. I really didn't want to think about it.

I sat up as he walked out of the bathroom naked, muscles rippling all over his slim body, his huge dick swinging between his legs. Immediately, that slow throbbing began between my thighs, and I had to squeeze them together as I watched him. Maybe I didn't have to leave so soon. Maybe we could go for a round two. Smoke was so fucking sexy, with his smooth, light skin, low-cut, wavy hair, and caramel brown eyes.

Right now, those eyes were on me, and he was frowning. For some reason, that made me nervous.

"Is something…" I cleared my throat and tried again, my hands twisting in the covers. "Is something wrong?"

CHAPTER 21
Smoke

I WASN'T ready for what I saw when I got in the bathroom and got ready to roll the condom down. Streaks of bright red blood were on the latex, and I thought back to her reaction when I'd first pushed inside her. I knew she was tight as fuck, but I never expected...

A virgin.

Goddamn. But how? There was no such thing as a twenty-one-year-old virgin, especially not one who would fuck a nigga after only knowing him for a couple of days. I stood in front of her now, wanting answers.

"Ay, why you ain't tell me?" I demanded.

She looked like she wanted to pretend that she didn't know what I was talking about, but one look from me killed that. She shrugged.

"Does it matter?"

"Fuck, yeah. I'on fuck virgins, ma. I like women with a little more experience."

She frowned and I knew I had pissed her off, but shit, it was the truth.

"I might not be experienced, but you seemed to enjoy yourself," she snapped.

I shook my head. "I'on like how virgins get in they feelings. I learned my lesson a long time ago."

I'd punched a couple of V-cards only to watch those chicks turn into stalkers. I was *not* trying to deal with that shit again. I didn't have time for needy women and boring ass relationships. Dayana was gorgeous and I was feeling her, but I'd promised my heart to Jenna forever.

"Trust me, being in my feelings is the last thing you have to worry about from me."

Her voice was cool with her little attitude, but I wasn't moved. She climbed out of the bed and started searching for her clothes. Now, that was a shame—I hated to see her cover up that bad ass body. She found her bra and panties and slip into them quickly. She was looking for her jumpsuit when I decided to ask the question on my mind.

"Why?"

She stopped and turned to look at me. I walked to where she was and waited.

"Why what?"

"Why lock your shit down for twenty-one years, then give it to a nigga you don't really know?"

I already knew the answer. She'd used me to get back at Jordan's bitch ass. While I had enjoyed the sex, I didn't appreciate that shit. I didn't want another nigga on her mind while I was fucking her.

"Because…"

She looked away from me, her eyes on the floor. I tilted her chin up so that she had to meet my eyes.

"Because what?"

"Because I wanted to. I saw you and I wanted to," she said, staring at me defiantly.

"That's your reason?"

"Yes. I saw something I wanted, and I got it. It's really not a big deal like you tryna make it."

I knew there was more to this situation than that, but I

decided to let her make it... for now. Seeing her stand there in her lacy ass underwear had me re-thinking. She still smelled sweet, like candied apples and cinnamon. And even though I had worked her ass out, she still looked good. Big brown eyes, full, pretty lips, smooth, brown skin, long, dark hair—shorty was beautiful as a muhfucka. I grabbed her hips and pulled her closer to me, making my dick rise. She looked up at me, confused.

"I thought you didn't fuck with virgins."

That's how I usually moved, but fuck it. I could make an exception. I wanted to get inside her again.

"Shit, the way I just banged that little pussy, you definitely not a virgin no more."

Rolling her eyes, she pushed at my shoulders. "Nasty."

"Let me show you nasty," I said, walking her backwards to the bed.

She talked shit, but she didn't fight me. I turned her around.

"Bend over and put your hands on the bed."

She looked over her shoulder, like she wanted to say something. I waited. After a minute, she slowly did as I told her. I pulled her little panties down to just above her knees, keeping her legs close together. The position put her pussy on display, and I could see that it was already glistening with her juices. My dick jumped. I wanted to slide in her raw right then, especially knowing she had been a virgin. But a nigga had no plans on any more kids, so I held back. Lazily, I smacked her ass. She jumped, then moaned as I did it again. I wondered briefly how she'd respond to a real spanking. I'd love to see her fat ass marked by me. But that wasn't for now.

"Don't move."

I walked to the nightstand and grabbed another condom. I slid it on as I walked back to her. This time, I eased into her. I wasn't a gentle nigga, but I knew she was probably sore. She moaned as I filled her up, then slowly pulled back. My fingers dug into her hips as I slid back in. Her pussy was so wet, so tight, I had to control the urge to fuck her hard and fast.

Yeah, she was definitely worth breaking my "no virgin" rule.

———

Fresh out of the shower, Dayana yawned and pulled the covers over her thick body. I expected her to try to cuddle up to me—women always did before I let them know no mushy shit would be going on—but she stayed on her side of the bed. The shit kind of bothered me for some reason, but I shook it off.

"Make sure I'm up in two hours. I wanna do my walk of shame in the dark," she said, eyes already closed.

That was a surprise, too. Usually, chicks wanted to broadcast it if they slept with me, make it seem like they had some kind of claim. That's why I was careful not to spend the night and be seen leaving the next morning. Since Jenna died, women were just a basic need. I fucked 'em and left 'em, but here I was, lying up in bed with a girl who didn't even want to be seen with me. I needed to shake back.

"Set your alarm. I'm about to head out," I told her.

She opened one eye and looked at me before nodding. No whining, no arguing, nothing. She was definitely something different. I dressed quickly and made my way to the door. I called her name and she rose slightly.

"Come make sure it locks," I said.

She sighed, but threw the covers back. I watched as she walked toward me in nothing but my undershirt. I started to change my mind about leaving. Nah, fuck that. She already had me out of my element. She stood there for a minute before putting her hands on my shoulders and standing on her tiptoes. She brushed her lips along my jawline.

"I enjoyed tonight. Thank you."

I had never been thanked for fucking someone, like it was a business transaction. I frowned at her, but I didn't say anything. Instead, I opened the door and walked out. I made sure it was locked before I took off down the hall. My mind was still in the room I had just left, though. Dayana was the kind of chick I'd bang more than once—pretty as fuck with some good ass pussy. But something told me Ms. Dayana was different from my usual. I wasn't ready to deal with what that meant.

CHAPTER 22

Demon

THIS MUST BE what having a conscience felt like. I hadn't been bothered by shit like that in years. But here I was, on my way back to her house. I had gone home, expecting to shower and go to bed. Instead, I was restless, unable to sleep as the night replayed in my mind. All I could see was her standing in the lake house with the crushed look I'd put in her eyes.

I didn't know why I was going back. I didn't know what the fuck I was going to say to her, if anything. I wasn't the type of nigga to apologize or explain or try to make shit up. This little trip was probably pointless, but for some reason, I wanted to see her.

I turned into the subdivision where Dream lived, thoughts still scattered as I drove past the guards. Slowing my car to a crawl, I inched forward. The three homes on her street seemed quiet as usual, but as I got closer to Dream's house, I could see a car I knew instantly. *Isaac Stone.* I'd done my research on the nigga after I got his license plate number. He was a mid-level employee at an IT firm. His father and grandfather had fucked around in some shady shit, but, after a few run-ins with the police when he was younger, Isaac was trying to stay on the straight and narrow... on the surface.

The nigga wasn't above getting his hands dirty, as long as his involvement was well hidden.

He had another involvement, too, one he was hiding from Dream and their circle. Isaac Stone was fucking a chick named Natasha. Nothing really stood out about her—she was from a middle-class family and worked as a personal assistant. Too bad for her that her sorry ass nigga was trying to come up. I had no doubt Stone saw money when he looked at Dream, the kind of money Natasha didn't have access to.

My attention turned back to his car. The last time he was here, I had told him to leave. Tonight, I'd make sure he knew not to come back. And Dream… she really thought this shit was a game. I'd been too easy on her—her last little comment earlier made it clear that she knew I had a weak spot for her. That shit was about to stop. I was getting close to my usual spot when the front door opened. Stone walked out, Dream right behind him. I couldn't see their faces clearly, but the tension between them was obvious. She followed him to the car door, and they exchanged words. She never saw the slap coming, didn't even take time to step away from him. For a moment, it was like time stopped as her pretty face canted to the side. Then, the fury that had been building in me since the moment I saw his car spilled over, sending ice through my veins. He had fucked up. Badly. No one else touched her, especially not like that. He would learn that tonight.

He hopped in his car like the bitch-made nigga he was. I sped up, block him in, and reach out and touch him right there. But some small corner of my mind reminded me I didn't want to bring attention to her and her home. He pulled out and I followed. I looked over at Dream as I passed her driveway. She covered her mouth as she recognized me. A minute later, my phone was ringing through the Bluetooth. Seeing her number, I silenced it. She called three more times. I rejected it each time. I needed to focus.

I had work to do.

Stone surprised me. Instead of going home, he pulled into the closest Smoke's bar. I had followed him from a safe distance, but to make sure he didn't catch on to me, I drove further down the street before doubling back. Studying the parking lot, I parked as far away from the door and any streetlights as possible. I sat in my car at first, plotting on this nigga. I could handle this shit simply, wait for him to walk back out and take his head off with the Heckler & Koch I kept on me. Smoke would take care of any video issues. But that seemed too easy for Stone. I wanted to hurt him for hurting her. I wanted him to see my face as I killed him. I wanted to watch the blood leak from his worthless body and see the light disappear from his eyes.

With murder on my mind, I decided I would go to Stone's house and wait for him. Nothing like a good ol' ambush. I needed to get some shit in place, so I called Li Jun, Dante's tech guy, first.

"I need a rush job," I said as soon as he answered.

"How much of a rush?"

He didn't sound surprised to hear from me at all. Working for Dante meant that Li Jun was always ready for whatever.

"Like, right now. I need your team to sweep a house, possibly disable cameras and an alarm system."

"Address?"

Pulling my phone away from my ear, I opened the file that Dante's information team had compiled for me about Stone. I rattled off his address.

"Can you keep the target away for at least an hour?" Li Jun asked.

I looked over at Stone's car. Shit, I didn't want to wait an hour, wanted to end the nigga right now, but I knew how to bide my time.

"Yeah."

I hung up without saying anything else. Reaching in my back seat, I grabbed one of the black hoodies that I always kept with me and slipped it on. I opened my glove compartment and retrieved the Ka-Bar hunting knife there and a pair of gloves before climbing out of the car and making a quick survey of the parking lot. I didn't see anyone outside, so I moved quickly toward Stone's car. I planned to flatten two of his tires to buy Li Jun the time he had asked for. Just as I made it, a car swung into the lot. I stood silently, head down, as the driver parked. I heard a door open and slam and waited to hear the bar's door open. Instead, it sounded like footsteps were coming toward me. Tensing, I tightened my hand around the knife in my hoodie's pocket.

"Ay, can I help you?"

My head snapped up as I recognized Smoke's voice. I relaxed as he came closer. He finally realized who I was and stopped.

"You gon' fuck up and become a regular," he greeted.

"You just leaving that bullshit?" I asked, noticing that he still had on the suit he'd worn to Dante's party.

"Left a little earlier. Got sidetracked," he said nonchalantly. "You and Dream disappeared fast as hell."

I didn't say anything. He could think what he wanted.

"You coming in for a drink?"

"Nah. I'm here on business."

His eyes lit up with interest. "Something I can help with?"

I started to tell him no, stick to my original plan. I didn't trust easily, and I was used to working alone. I fucked with Smoke, though, even if it was on a limited basis. I knew he was solid. With his help, I might be able to handle shit here, get it over with.

"Your cameras—"

"Only see what I want them to see," he assured me. "Just like the traffic cameras around here. I know people."

I nodded. "You got a customer in there. Isaac Stone. He... touched something that belongs to me."

"Dream?"

This nigga made me feel so obvious and the shit was aggravating me. I mugged him.

"Why you so worried about her?"

He held up both hands, but the smirk on his face let me know he wasn't fooled. "You right. It's none of my business. But I know he gotta pay for touching what's yours."

"Yeah."

Smoke pushed his hands into his pockets and stood there, head bent, like he was thinking. I wanted to hear what the nigga came up with. Finally, he looked at me again.

"There's a side door, mostly used for deliveries. Opens into an alley. It's dark there this time of night. Nobody can see what they don't need to see."

I nodded. That would work. I might not be able to take as much time as I wanted, but I could make sure Stone knew who was ending his useless life and why.

"How you gon' get him out there?"

He smiled. "Got a little chick that works for me named Tamia. We go way back and she real. She don't see what she ain't supposed to see and she don't remember what she ain't supposed to remember. Li'l mama so fine, a nigga will follow her anywhere," he explained.

I nodded again. All I had to do was lay in wait for this nigga while Tamia lured him outside. I'd take over from there.

"Can you describe the nigga?"

"I can do better," I said.

Returning to my car, I grabbed my phone. Ignoring the fact that I had more missed calls and texts from Dream, I opened Stone's file again. I showed Smoke a picture and he studied it a minute before nodding once. He walked toward the front of the bar as I made my way to the alley. He hadn't lied. It was dark as fuck back here, except for the light by the door. There was a dumpster near the back, and I went to stand next to it, waiting. I texted Li Jun a brief message, letting him know plans had changed, then called for cleanup to come to my location. This might be where Isaac Stone died, but it wouldn't be where he was found. Smoke didn't need his bar getting a bad reputation.

Twenty minutes later, the door finally opened, and I watched as a short, curvy chick walked out, laughing. Stone was right behind her. He wasted no time trapping her against the wall and kissing her. She played her role perfectly, looping her arms around him as I silently approached them. Nigga was clueless as hell. He didn't even realize I was there until my arm was around his neck, choking him.

"Oh, look at that! My break is up," Tamia said, winking at me before she disappeared into the bar.

"Look, just reach into my pocket and get my wallet. You can have everything I got on me. Just don't—"

I let him go and pushed him into the side of the building hard as fuck.

"I ain't here for your money."

He turned around slowly. For one moment, his eyes were so clouded with fear, I thought he was going to piss himself. But then he tried to hide it.

"What, Dream call you and tell on me?" he spat.

I said nothing, just looked at him, crouching against the building. The silence made him uncomfortable, and he squirmed, the brave face he put on disappearing.

"L-look, Demon. She told me about your... arrangement. I love Dream. How was I supposed to react?"

"Natasha know you love Dream?" I asked him.

His light skin paled. "Th-th-that's not what you think—"

"I don't give a fuck what it is. Dream told you about our agreement. So, you knew what was up between us. That means you knew she was mine, and you still put your hands on her."

He shook his head rapidly, his chest rising and falling so fast, he had to be about to hyperventilate.

"She said it was just a deal. I didn't know... how was I supposed to know... I'm sorry. She's yours. You ain't gotta worry about me—"

I crashed my fist into his side, aiming for his ribs. He whimpered as he balled up tighter and I chuckled.

"Nigga, what makes you think I'm worried about you?"

I hit him again, in the same spot, and heard the air leave his body as he doubled over. It took a minute, but he finally stood upright again, his eyes wide and pleading.

"I get it. I swear I do. She's yours. I'm—"

I guess he thought his words were going to distract me. In the middle of his little speech, he suddenly threw a punch, aiming at my jaw. I sidestepped it easily before hammering my fist into his ribs again. He heaved forward, putting his strength behind an uppercut that glanced off my chin. I smiled at him as he aimed a quick flurry of punches at me, most of them missing. And then, I was tired of playing. Grabbing his fist, I hit him in the side repeatedly, not stopping until I felt his ribs crack. He fell to his knees, and I kicked him in the forehead, splaying his body on the ground. Once he was all the way down, I stomped on his ribs, determined to drive them into his lungs. They would collapse, robbing him of breath, making him feel like I did when I saw him hit her.

Finally, when his breath was labored and slow, I squatted beside him. I wanted to leave him like this, let him die slowly and painfully, but I knew I couldn't take the chance. His eyes were still open, glazed with pain. I pulled the Ka-Bar out of the hoodie's pocket and laid it against his neck.

"You fucked up, Isaac," I said softly.

He tried to say something, but the words wouldn't come. I shrugged.

"Must not be important."

I swiped the knife across his throat, smiling at the spray of blood. He was still bleeding as I wiped my blade on his shirt and stood to exit the alley. Crossing the parking lot, I got back into my car as if nothing had happened. I texted the head of the cleanup crew, then watched as a dark, tinted van cranked up and pulled toward the alley. They'd been waiting for me to confirm that the job was done. My phone buzzed and I saw Dream's number. This time, I answered.

"Damien," she said, sounding breathless. "Did you—"

I cut her off. "You gon' learn not to play with me, Dream."

"Oh, my G—"

I hung up.

CHAPTER 23

Dream

(*MONDAY*, *June 7*)

I stretched my arms above my head and yawned before standing up from my desk. Silently, I walked over to the windows that made up the wall of my second-floor office. I had so much work to do, but I couldn't focus. I needed to get my shit together because I was taking off Wednesday for Dayana's wedding weekend. I already hated Mondays, and this one was even worse because I couldn't get past the huge distraction occupying my mind… Damien.

When the weekend news shows started reporting on finding the body of Isaac Stone in his car in one of the roughest neighborhoods in the city, my heart plummeted. My grandfather was the only person I had told what I suspected, and he outright approved of Damien's actions.

"Nigga shoulda never laid hands on you," he'd said coldly before going to destroy all the night's surveillance footage.

The truth was, I didn't know how to feel about what had happened. On one hand, the murder made my fear of Damien resurface. I mean, part of me had been scared of him from day one, but I had got more comfortable. Too comfortable with someone as crazy as he apparently was. But on the other hand, I knew Isaac lost his life for violating me and part of me romanticized that shit, like Damien was some knight, protecting my honor. On some level, I accepted that that's the way things went in our world—if it hadn't been Damien, one of the men in my family would have handled it. The whole thing was confusing, and I was tired of feeling torn.

Then there was the fact that I was still thinking about our last encounter. I was glad I got the last word after we left the lake house, but I was still pissed at the way he talked to me. No disrespect to escorts, but I didn't sell my time or anything else. And as far as his comment about my being around rich men, in our world, that was who I came into contact with.

I sighed aloud. He was confusing, fascinating, crazy, dark, and sexy, and he was taking up too much of my mental energy. We needed to get these thirty days started ASAP, so I could get him out of my mind and out of my life. Walking back over to my desk, I grabbed my phone. I found his contact and tapped, trying to gather my thoughts as the phone rang. I got no answer, even after my sixth call. Aggravated, I sent him a text that said, "We need to talk" before trying to get back to work.

Two hours later, he still hadn't replied, and I was getting ready to run a few errands before going home. He was lucky that I had no idea where he lived or if or where he worked. Otherwise, I'd pop up on his rude ass. He'd had my life in limbo for too long. Our deal was three-and-a-half-weeks old. It was time I took charge. Damien was going to have to be on my time.

I opened the bottom drawer to dig for my purse. Retrieving it, I stood up, grabbed my briefcase off my desk... and almost screamed when I looked up. I hadn't heard him open the door, much less step into my office.

"How... how did you get back here? Rayleigh didn't even call—"

Damien glared at me, and my words dried up. He was too fucking big to move so quietly. *Bet that's why he so good at killing people*, I thought. He probably crept up on them and—

"Don't ask questions about how I'm here when you called me. What do you want, Dream?" he asked, breaking into my thoughts.

My heart raced like it did every time he said my name. I stood there, looking stupid, unable to respond as I took him in. He was dressed in all white, his locs pulled back, highlighting his perfect face. High cheekbones and a square jaw were a beautiful backdrop for his thickly lashed eyes and juicy lips. His shirt was short-sleeved and clung to his rock-hard abs, displaying the colorful, inked sleeves that decorated his arms. I saw a muscle in his jaw move as he waited for me to say something. When my voice failed me, he walked toward me. He didn't stop until he was way too close. A thrill raced down my spine as he lifted a hand and grabbed my face, tilting my head back. He frowned as he brushed a thumb over my lip where it was still slightly puffy from Isaac's blow. His touch made me shiver and feel hot all at once.

"I don't like it when people waste my time."

I cleared my throat, forcing myself to remember how to speak. "I-I'm not wasting your time. I told you in my text that we need to talk."

"So, talk," he ordered.

"I have something to do now. We can talk like civilized people. Later, over dinner."

I didn't know where the words came from, and I almost regretted them as his frown deepened. Almost. I was taking control, I reminded myself, refusing to look away from his cold eyes.

"Over dinner? Like a date? I'm not dating you, just fucking you, remember?"

His words pissed me off, but I refused to show it. Instead, I shrugged nonchalantly.

"That's okay. I can find someone else to do both."

He stiffened and his eyes turned stormy. I swallowed. It was the response I wanted, but that didn't mean it didn't shake me. I wasn't expecting his next move, though. I shrieked, my briefcase and purse falling from my hands as he lifted me and damn near slammed me on my desk.

"Didn't I tell you to stop fuckin' playing with me, Dream?" he growled, wedging his solid body between my thighs.

A little bit of fear arced through me, but more than that, I was excited about what he might do next. Already, my hips were shifting, trying to bring our bodies closer. The hand that had just been clutching my face was suddenly around my throat and I sucked in a breath as his head lowered toward mine. I shouldn't want this, should still be mad about how he treated me this past weekend and scared for how he did Isaac. But here I was, waiting for his kiss.

"You wanna make me kill a nigga?"

His warm, minty breath brushed across my mouth. I licked my lips in anticipation. Boldly, I wrapped a hand around one of the Cuban link chains encircling his neck and pulled him closer.

"Another one?" I goaded, unable to help myself. "You didn't have to do that."

He shrugged, brushing my swollen lip again. "Somebody shoulda taught the nigga to keep his hands to himself."

"But—"

He stopped me with a finger across my lips. "We don't talk about this shit. Ever. Understand?"

I backed down as I saw the warning in his eyes. Nodding, I traced the single black rose that adorned the front of his throat with my fingertip. I inhaled as his body brushed me. He always smelled so good. Sometimes like cologne, but mostly his own natural scent and Dove soap, of all things. A half-smile stretched his lips before he pressed them against mine. His tongue glided across my mouth, and I opened for him, wrapping my arms around him. Like him, his kiss was forceful, claiming so much of me. I couldn't pretend that I didn't want it, that I didn't want him, because he wasn't having it. Damien took my breath away, made me breathe through him. My heart raced as he continued his assault on my mouth. I moaned aloud as I pulled him closer, my body melting, desperate to merge with his.

He broke away and I whimpered in protest. His hand tightened around my throat, and reluctantly, my eyes fluttered open. He nuzzled the side of my neck before nipping my earlobe. Then, his warm mouth rested against my ear.

"You don't control shit, Dream, unless I let you. Understand?"

"Damien." My voice sounded soft and drugged. "It's just dinner."

He paused for a long moment before resting his forehead against mine. I closed my eyes again, enjoying the feel of him against me.

"I'll meet you at Signature at eight. You better be on time," he said, then pulled out of my arms.

I sat motionless as he walked out of my office. I didn't move until I heard a knock and Parker stuck her head in.

"You okay in here?"

Sighing, I nodded, sliding off my desk before reaching for the stuff I had dropped.

"You so lucky. He entirely too fine for a light-skinned nigga. I bet—"

I glared at her, stopping her mid-sentence.

"I told you it's not like that."

She waved me off. "Dream, you a terrible liar."

I rolled my eyes. "Bye, Parker!"

"Fine, I'm going. But if you ever need to talk about this

non-relationship relationship, I'm here for you," she said before ducking back out.

Shaking my head, I wondered was I that obvious. I didn't realize I had said that out loud until she called out, "Yes! *That* obvious!"

"Bye, Parker!"

I grabbed my stuff again, then groaned as the intercom sounded. I debated picking up—I could just speak to Rayleigh when I walked out. But even as I was thinking, I sat back down in my chair and answered.

"It's good to know this thing works," I snapped sarcastically.

"C'mon, Ms. Castle, don't be like that. You know I'm from the hood. I know better than to mess with Demon," Rayleigh explained unapologetically.

Squeezing my eyes shut, I shook my head.

"What if he were here to hurt me?"

This heifer didn't wait a minute before throwing me under the bus!

"You was gon' have to take that 'L', Ms. Castle. Ain't no use in both of us getting messed up."

"Rayleigh!"

She laughed like shit was funny. "I'm just playing, Boss Lady. He don't mess with women like that."

"Mm-hmm," I said skeptically. "Why you buzz me?"

"Oh!" Her voice dropped to a whisper. "The opps here to see you."

I frowned. "What?"

She cleared her throat before putting on what I called her professional voice. "Detective Poole and Detective Jiménez are here to see you, Ms. Castle. Shall I send them back?"

Cops? What the fuck? I scowled as I wracked my brain, trying to figure out why they were here. I was beyond good at my job, could wash and hide money with ease. What—

"Ms. Castle?" Rayleigh's voice broke me out of my thoughts.

"Yeah, send them back," I answered reluctantly.

My father and grandfather would have a fit if they knew I was sitting down with the police with no lawyer. I probably should've made them schedule something so I could have my attorney there, but I was too curious. Plus, I knew how to watch myself.

I stood as two tall men—one Black, one Latino—walked through my open door.

"Ms. Dream Castle?" the Black man asked.

I don't know if he was trying to intimidate me or what, but he was frowning, his brown eyes glaring at me. Too bad for him, I didn't scare that easily.

"Yes, how may I help you?" I inquired coolly.

"I'm Detective Nick Poole. This is Detective Jorge Jiménez. We're from Homicide. We'd like to talk to you about Isaac Stone."

Ahh, shit, I thought, but I made sure my face and my body gave nothing away. I nodded and invited them to have a seat.

"I'm sure by now you've heard about his untimely demise," Poole said.

I sighed. "Yes. It really was unfortunate for him and his family. I know he'll be missed," I said carefully.

"You were one of the last known people he contacted. He spent some time with you shortly before his death."

I noticed he wasn't really asking questions, just making statements as if he were fishing for something.

"Yes. We had a late dinner and watched a little TV. He didn't stay long."

"Why not?" Jiménez asked.

I frowned. "What do you mean?"

Poole smiled. He looked like an oily, evil shark.

"Man comes over to spend time with a woman late at night, he's not usually trying to leave quickly."

Another statement. Another pause as he waited for my response. I gave him a fake ass smile.

"As I'm sure you know, Detective Poole, I live with my family, including my parents and grandfather. I don't have overnight male company. And my relationship with Isaac was not sexual. We were more friends than anything."

"Hmmph," he grunted, like he was debating whether or not to believe me.

"So, the two of you didn't have a little argument or anything that may have caused him to leave?" Jiménez pressed.

Yeah, this had gone on long enough.

"No. We parted on good terms," I lied smoothly. "I was tired because I'd been to a party celebrating my brother's wedding and then, I'm sure you know how the -itis works. I was ready for bed. Like I said, Isaac's death is really sad. I'm glad I got to spend some time with him before he was so tragically taken away. I have no idea where he went when he left my house. Now, if you gentlemen will excuse me," I said, standing, "I have somewhere to be. If I can be of further assistance, please let my attorney know. You can get his card from my receptionist."

Another fake smile and I was ushering their scowling asses out the door. I exhaled deeply once they were gone. I handled myself okay, but if they came back, I'd definitely be lawyered up.

And I'd definitely have to warn Damien.

CHAPTER 24
Demon

BUTTON-DOWN SHIRT. Slim-fitting slacks. Simp ass nigga. I saw all that when I looked in the mirror, checking my appearance before I left to meet Dream's annoying ass. She was getting too comfortable, demanding dates and shit. *But you gave in,* my brain reminded me. I pushed that thought away fast as hell. This wasn't a date. I wasn't picking her ass up, she wasn't getting any flowers, and I wasn't trying to talk her out of any pussy. That was already mine. She'd be lucky if I paid for this shit since it was her bright ass idea.

I was still thinking about what the fuck I'd gotten myself into ten minutes later as I drove toward the restaurant. I'd gone to her office to see what she wanted and to tell her not to blow me up like that. I ended up kissing her and agreeing to what was technically my first date. Shaking my head, I thought about that kiss that definitely wasn't supposed to happen. But every time I got near her and saw her pretty, glazed mouth, I wanted it somewhere on my body. I didn't even kiss bitches on the mouth like that, but I couldn't keep my lips off hers. Thinking about the fresh, sweet taste of her— all apple and mint—made me brick up instantly.

In fact, it felt like I'd been walking around with a hard

dick since the first night I saw her. That problem could be easily solved, though, and, the other night, when I'd instructed her to get tested, I had every intention of getting her under me as soon as she got her results. But, for the first time, I wasn't so sure of my decision. Not because I didn't want to fuck her senseless, but because of what might happen afterwards. She had me off my fucking square already and I had barely touched the pussy. If I fucked her...

I shook my head. I felt lame just thinking the shit. But I always kept it real with myself and Dream had an effect on me I wasn't used to. Maybe I could do her like I did other women—fuck her and lose interest. But something was telling me that wasn't going to happen, and I'd be damned if I was out here in my bag about some chick. Even as I thought the shit, I knew it was a lie. If I weren't already in my feelings, Isaac Stone wouldn't be dead.

My phone rang through the Bluetooth suddenly and I looked over at the number. *Dante.* What the fuck he want? That nigga had been calling a little too much lately. We were cool, but I didn't fuck with him like that. I know he wanted to play the role of big brother, but it was too late, and I was good on that. I started to ignore the call, but something made me answer it.

"What's up?" I greeted him.

"Not much. How you—"

"Why you calling me, Dante?"

I could hear Dream calling me rude in that bourgeois voice of hers. She had a point, but I didn't have time for bullshit and making small talk.

"Well, damn," Dante said, chuckling. "I'm reaching out because some... interesting shit has come up. Keep your eyes open. And I have a business proposition for you—"

"Nah. I'm good."

I turned him down easily. He was always trying to get me more involved with the "family business," especially because our father had been clear that he wanted us to share the profits. But Dante liked playing the kingpin role, liked the flashiness and the power. That shit wasn't for me. I handled a few situations for him every year and that was enough involvement for me. I wasn't stupid—I didn't turn down the money our "interests" earned. Other than that, I was good on all of it. As far as his telling me to keep my eyes open, I knew he'd tell me more when he felt it was time.

He was quiet for a minute, probably thinking about pressing me a little, but he knew that shit would do no good. Finally, he sighed.

"I just wanted to extend the offer—"

"I know. But look, I gotta go. I'm meeting Dream—"

I stopped immediately. Now, why the fuck had I said that? It wasn't his business, and it wasn't like me to share my movements. I could almost see him sitting up.

"Ah. Young Ms. Castle. Is she as good as she looks?" he asked.

Anger boiled through me as he laughed lowly. I knew he thought Dream was beautiful, but she was mine now, and I didn't play that shit.

"That's something you ain't gotta worry about," I responded tightly.

His laughter cut off abruptly. "Chill, nigga. I'm just fucking with you. I knew what it was when you took her out of the party and away from Eric Vaughn. Her father looked like his dreams went up in smoke cuz every nigga there noticed."

He sounded way too pleased with himself. That shit wasn't helping my mood. I wasn't one of Dante's pawns and I didn't like feeling like he was using me. That made me want to walk away from all this shit. But that would mean walking away from Dream and, as much as I didn't want to admit it, I wasn't ready to do that shit.

"Is that all you wanted?" I asked him.

"Shiii, I can take a hint, brother. Enjoy your night."

I disconnected the call as I took the exit for the restaurant. Signature was an upscale little place that I only knew about because I snatched a nigga out of the restaurant's parking lot one night. I didn't know why I picked it for tonight, going through the trouble to call in a favor to get a reservation. Should've taken her bossy ass to IHOP or somewhere. It was 7:55 when I valeted my car. I started to walk in, leave her to fend for herself. But something had me pulling out my phone to call her.

"Where you at?" I asked as soon as she answered.

"I'm almost there," she said, her husky voice soft.

I hung up but waited outside under the portico for her. A minute later, she pulled up in a Mercedes Coupe. She climbed out slowly, her beautiful face smiling at the valet. She exchanged a few words with him, but I had no idea what she said. I was too focused on her thick body in the cream-colored dress that skimmed every curve. Physically, Dream was perfect, and I could see myself peeling that dress off her and enjoying all she'd been blessed with.

She turned toward me, and her smile faltered a little bit, but she lifted her head higher. I watched as she walked toward me, wide hips swaying, pretty legs taking sure, confident steps, eyes never leaving mine. So, that's what she was on? It was clear she'd come to do battle about something. I might actually entertain it for a minute. She stopped inches away, and the familiar, sweet scent of her floated around me.

"Hello, Damien. You look nice."

Instead of thanking her or returning the compliment, I raised one eyebrow and looked down at her. Sighing, she shook her head and moved toward the door. She didn't wait for me to open it, not that I planned to. Despite what Dream thought, I'd lived with my father long enough to know how to treat women, had watched him and Dante open doors, buy gifts, and say all the right things. But this wasn't a relationship and I refused to handle her like it was. I had to do something to keep my head straight.

We were seated quickly, our drink orders taken, and menus placed in our hands. I really didn't give a fuck what I ate. Growing up eating out the trash and stealing other people's scraps, I wasn't a picky eater. I ate because it was a basic function, not for pleasure. It was obvious that Dream's background was totally different from the way she studied the menu and made little exclamations.

"What do you think? The duck breast or the lamb loin?" she asked.

I shrugged, offering no suggestions. She narrowed her eyes at me and opened her mouth like she was about to say something, before shaking her head and returning her attention to the menu. Finally, she put it down, like she'd made up her mind.

"So, how was your day?" she tried again.

"You gon' pretend like I look like the type of nigga to make small talk?" I shot back. "You don't give a damn about my day, and I don't give a fuck about yours. Now, what you wanna talk about?"

She blew out a frustrated breath, shaking her head at me. Turning, she reached for her big ass purse and started digging in it. I took the time to watch her, the angles of her pretty face revealed because her braids were pulled up into a bun. I liked looking at her way too much. I wondered what she was looking for, but my attention was quickly diverted when I felt eyes on me. Suddenly tense, I scanned the room again, looking for a familiar face. A pair of hazel eyes tangled with mine and I relaxed. Her name was Juliette Nicholson, and she owned the escort agency I used. Before I'd sampled any of her employees, I'd fucked her. Juliette was cool, though. She knew how this shit went, so I was a little surprised to see the small frown on her beautiful face. Probably shock because I never took women out. It didn't matter what she thought, though. She was discreet, and she knew better than to cause a scene. She smirked at me, and I nodded once. Dream cleared her throat. Looking over at her, I noticed she was paying attention to the silent exchange between me and Juliette.

"Who is that?" she demanded.

"None of your business," I said calmly.

"But you think the other men I'm around are your business? I—"

"Why are we here, Dream?"

Scowling, she pressed a couple of papers into my hands. I frowned.

"Fuck is this?"

"My test results. As you can see, I'm disease free."

"And?"

"And I need to know, when do you plan to fuck me?"

CHAPTER 25
Dream

SIGNATURE WAS CHARMING. Set on a local resort, its exquisite views and lovely architecture were matched by the stunning interior décor, with its huge chandeliers, heavy wood and leather furniture, and massive windows. I hated to be so vulgar in the middle of such a breathtaking place, but I was fed up with Damien's attitude. Plus, apparently, he needed something to snap his attention away from the woman who held it. The bitch was beautiful, I had to admit grudgingly. Her toffee-colored skin glowed and the hazel eyes that were glued to Damien were bright and tilted up at the corners. Her bow-shaped lips were painted a perfect, deep red and I watched as she tucked a piece of her bone straight, jet black hair behind a small ear. She quirked an eyebrow at me, and I hurriedly turned back to Damien.

"Well?" I pressed.

"Do you know how fucking thirsty you sound right now?" he jeered.

I sucked my teeth. "Please. I'm just ready to get on with my life. Don't nobody want your ass."

He smirked at me, like he knew I was lying. He could believe what he wanted—I wasn't admitting shit. I made sure my expression didn't change as he stared at me. Defiantly, I stared back. I was so caught up in our battle of wills that I didn't realize our server had returned until she set our drinks in front of us. I waited as Damien ordered, then made my own request. The tension between us was thick and the waitress damn near ran away from the table. Settling against the leather back of my chair, I waited.

I felt the heat of the mystery woman's gaze on us as I lifted my drink. Slowly, I took a much-needed sip. The bittersweet taste of Campari mixed with the tartness of the pomegranate juice was refreshing. I sighed appreciatively, then gazed at Damien again. God should be ashamed of Himself for making this man so beautiful. I squeezed my thighs together, trying to ignore the sudden throbbing between them. I knew the seat of my panties was probably drenched. It always was when I was around him.

"Can you tell your girlfriend that staring is rude?" I popped, wanting to focus on something else.

"You always comment on shit that you don't know nothing about?" he returned calmly.

I waved a hand, like it was no big deal, but I was curious as hell about how they knew each other. I wasn't naïve; this nigga had fucked her. I could tell that by the intensity of her gaze and the way her eyes seemed to measure me. The idea bothered me for some reason that I refused to try to identify.

"Whatever. Back to our deal—"

"Enjoy your drink, Dream."

His attempt to dismiss me ran me hot. I didn't know what he was used to, but I wasn't some little docile woman that he was going to ignore. Narrowing my eyes, I glared at him.

"No! You're going to—"

He laughed softly, interrupting me. But that laughter didn't reach the suddenly cold eyes that robbed me of my voice.

"Watch who the fuck you talking to before I hurt your

feelings in front of all these people. You used to the soft ass niggas around you who wait on you to fix shit and defend them or whatever. I'm not that nigga. You don't run shit here, Dream. I do. You understand?"

I wanted to argue, wanted to object to the way he described my father and brother, but something in his eyes had me nodding slowly. I knew Damien had a soft spot for me and it made me bold. But moments like this, when his green eyes were freezing and his voice was menacing, I remembered the Demon he was at heart.

Silence, dark and edgy, descended over our table. Maybe I was the only one who felt it. Damien seemed totally unbothered as he sipped his Hennessy Paradis, while I had to fight myself to keep from tossing my drink back to calm my nerves. Abruptly, I pushed back my chair and stood up.

"Going to the restroom," I mumbled.

I didn't even wait for him to respond as I hurried off. Once I was behind the door, I closed my eyes and sighed.

"What are you doing, Dream?" I whispered, frustrated.

He wasn't responding like I had imagined. I envisioned coming to dinner and demanding we agree on a date to begin our... entanglement. Instead, he shut me down at every turn. I massaged my aching temple. I couldn't keep doing this. The anticipation and uncertainty were killing me. I—

"He has that effect, doesn't he?"

My eyes flew open as the sultry voice spoke. I was so caught up in my thoughts that I hadn't even heard the door opening. My eyes met the hazel ones of the woman who'd been staring at us.

"Excuse me?" I said, barely able to keep the attitude out of my voice.

She smiled, revealing perfect white teeth, as she walked closer to me, her hand extended.

"I'm Juliette. I'm not sure which agency you work for, but

I believe we could do wonderful business together. You're beautiful with that... *Rubenesque* figure."

Caught off guard, I took the business card she was offering me. Across the top, I read *Juliette's Gems*. But it was the tag line that caught my attention: "Fulfilling Our Clients' Every Desire." My eyes flew to hers.

"What is this?" I asked suspiciously.

She laughed. "Girl, you with Demon Montana. You know what this is."

No, this bitch didn't. Her condescending attitude pissed me off, and I wanted to slap the smug little smile off her face. She was trying to get under my skin, though, so I would never show her she was.

"No, I don't know what *this* is. Why don't you tell me?"

"Everyone knows Demon likes... *professional* women and you must be exceptionally good," she said, looking me up and down again.

Blood boiling, I returned her little smile.

"Why do you say that?"

"Because you got him to bring you on a date. That's a Demon no-no—he's always clear about that. Excuse my language, but that pretty mouth—or maybe it's that pretty pussy—must be phenomenal," she mocked. "Based on that alone, I'd love to add you to my roster."

Forcing myself to take deep, calming breaths, I fought to keep my hands from balling into fists and punching this trick in her eye. She was mocking me, but there was bitterness in her tone, too. The bitch was jealous. Two could play her little game.

"Actually, he hasn't had either... *yet.* And I'm not a 'professional.' Damien just knows I have standards, and dating me is a minimum."

Yeah, I was exaggerating, but she didn't know that, hell. Something flashed in her eyes, but she hid it quickly. I didn't hide my petty smile. To her credit, she smiled right back.

"Oh, honey," she said with fake sympathy. "He made you feel special. Don't fall for it. He doesn't give a fuck about you. It's not in him."

Her words made my stomach sick, but I kept my smile.

"Don't compare our experiences," I said sweetly.

"Oh, I'm not. I knew exactly what I was getting. I feel bad that you don't."

She was walking toward the door before I could say anything. Pausing, she looked over her shoulder.

"Keep the card. Call me if you want to know what he likes. I know how to make that dick cum. And if you're a good girl, I could make you cum, too."

She winked at me, then left. I counted to ten... and still had to bite back a scream.

CHAPTER 26
Demon

WHAT THE FUCK *was Juliette up to*? I knew it wasn't a coincidence when she bounced her ass up a minute after Dream stalked off. I wasn't worried about that shit. She was always the ultimate professional, and if she ever wanted my business again, she wouldn't discuss me. I figured she was caught up in the fact that I was out publicly with a woman. Probably wanted to see her up close.

Dream came back, attitude all over her, and I realized I overestimated Juliette's professionalism. She sat down and looked at the plate that had been delivered to her, ignoring me. I started to ask her what was wrong, but I didn't want her to assume I cared that much. My eyes flickered over to Juliette's table. Before, she couldn't keep her gaze off me. Now, she was avoiding my eyes, acting like she was caught up in the conversation with the woman who was there with her. Yeah, she'd definitely done something she had no business doing. I'd deal with her ass later. I looked at Dream as she pushed her food around her plate, clearly agitated.

"So, you gon' suggest dinner, then play with your food? Remember what I told you about wasting my time?" I taunted.

She dropped her knife and fork and glared at me. "We can leave. You won't address what we need to discuss, so fuck it," she said in a low voice.

"You wanna discuss our deal? Let's discuss it."

Shaking her head, she reached for her purse. "Nah. It's fine. I don't think there is any more deal. I don't want to do this with you."

I sat back, eyeballing her. What the fuck had Juliette said?

"What about your brother?"

"Dante is obviously over being angry. He had that party for them and everything. He can name his other favor and my family will settle that. I—"

She stopped as I laughed softly. "You think Dante has forgiven that shit just because he let Sherrilyn throw a party? It's a set-up, Dream. Nigga makes it look like he approves of their marriage, so if DeAngelo comes up missing, he won't be the prime suspect. Your brother fucked his daughter, knocked her up, and stole her away. Dante's ego ain't going for losing that much control. Part of him will never get over that shit.

"At this point, it's not just about DeAngelo anymore. It's about your family keeping your word. Your daddy is in an interesting business. If Dante spreads the word that he can't be trusted, a lot of that business stops. You wanna be responsible for that?"

She froze for a second, thinking about what I was saying. Slowly, her hand dropped from her purse. Frustrated tears filled her eyes and she closed them for a minute as she rubbed her temple. Then she picked up the knife and fork, cut into her food, and slowly chewed another bite before saying anything else to me.

"I just want this to be over with. You should want it, too, so you can get back to the Juliettes of your world. Apparently, she's a pro at making you cum," she spat.

I smiled. "You will be, too, when I finish with you."

Her mouth fell open as her hand tightened around her

knife. She was probably imagining sliding it between my ribs and into my heart. As long as it was just a thought, I'd let her make it. I watched as she lifted a piece of lamb and brought it up to her mouth, her pouty lips closing around it. They'd be closing around me like that soon. That thought had me needing to adjust my dick in my pants.

We ate in silence, interrupted only by our server checking on us. I looked over at her a few times, but she never lifted her head. Her body was tense, and every movement was stiff. She was definitely not happy. I shouldn't give a fuck, but, for some reason, I did.

"Dream."

She froze and for one moment, I thought she was going to ignore me. Finally, she lifted her gaze to mine.

"What?"

"Tomorrow."

She frowned. "What?"

"Your thirty days starts tomorrow."

I watched her face. She looked relieved at first, but then I saw doubt and fear in her eyes. I shook my head.

"Ain't this what you wanted?"

She dabbed at her mouth before speaking. "Yeah. Where—"

"I'll let you know tomorrow. Finish your food."

"Stop giving me orders," she snapped.

My mouth twisted into a smile. "I haven't even started. Wait till tomorrow."

She dropped her napkin. "I'm done."

She really was done. No dessert, no coffee, nothing. Dream was ready to go and, fifteen minutes later, we stood outside, waiting for the valet. I turned to look down at her.

"So, you don't like the thought of me giving you orders?" I teased.

She narrowed her eyes, her full lips in a tight line. "I know what our deal is, but I'm not doing no crazy shit, Damien."

I chuckled at her mad ass. "You gon' do what I tell you, Dream."

She opened her mouth to snap back.

"I'ma make you feel so good that you gon' want to," I promised her.

Her mouth closed as quickly as it opened. She dropped her eyes, and I could see the blush staining her cheeks. All this talk about being ready and she couldn't deal with me even talking about sex.

"You—"

I stopped as Juliette's voice sounded from behind us, talking to the woman who was with her. Dream mumbled something under her breath, and I smiled.

"Damn, what she say to you?"

She crossed her arms over her chest and stared at me angrily. "Apparently, you're such a good customer that she offered to hire me on the spot. She just knew I had to be a 'professional' because you don't date other women."

"I don't date, period," I corrected.

"She also told me don't get my hopes up about you. Something about you being incapable of giving a fuck about me."

She shrugged like it was no big deal, but I could tell Juliette struck a nerve. It pissed me off. This bitch had really overstepped. I looked over my shoulder at her and she gave me a half-smile. I looked forward to wiping that shit off her face. She read my look and her eyes widened as she hurriedly turned her face away from me.

As if that would stop me.

"Juliette," I called her name calmly.

"What are you doing?" Dream whispered.

Juliette brought her hand to her throat, fear obvious in her eyes. "It was a misunderstanding, Demon. I—"

"Yeah, you definitely misunderstood." I took a step closer to her. "You don't discuss me. Ever. Understand?"

She nodded so fast she looked like a damn bobblehead.

"And this one right here..." Reaching out, I grabbed Dream's hand. "Don't ever say shit to her. When you see her, you don't see her. Or else you gon' have to see me."

She looked at Dream and I saw a spark of jealousy in her eyes before she blinked it away and nodded at me again. Is that what this was about? Bitch considered herself a professional and she out here feeling some type of way? I smiled at her coldly as she and her friend stared at me, speechless.

"Damien."

Dream pulled on my hand. I looked at her and she pointed to where her car had pulled up with mine right behind it. She took a step toward it, but I tightened my hold on her. She looked down at my hand, then up at me, surprised. Aware of Juliette's eyes still on us, I pulled Dream closer and leaned forward to brush my lips against hers.

"I'll call you tomorrow," I said. "Be ready."

Swallowing, she nodded once before running to her car.

CHAPTER 27

Dayana

(*TUESDAY*, *June 8*)

I slung my backpack over my shoulder and grabbed my purse out of the little closet. I almost jumped out of my skin as I walked back into the classroom and nearly bumped into the teacher, Ms. Adriana, and her aide, Ms. Maria. They were grinning at me like they were crazy, and I couldn't help smiling back, even as I wondered what the fuck they had going on. Suddenly, Ms. Adriana pulled a bag from behind her back and pressed it into my hands.

"We got you something for your honeymoon! Ignore the Target bag. I couldn't walk up in this pre-school advertising Victoria's Secret," she whispered before giggling.

"Thank you! You didn't have to do that!" I said, hugging them both quickly.

Today was my last day volunteering with my four-year-olds before the wedding. I was going to miss them over the next three weeks. I'd spent the last three years working on a business degree, just doing what DeAngelo and Dream did, but more and more, it seemed like I might be changing my major to early childhood education. I loved working with these babies. Daddy would have a fit but, for marrying Jordan's bitch ass, I better get whatever the hell I asked for.

"Of course, we did!" Ms. Maria exclaimed. "We had to get you a little something else to help you enjoy the next few weeks."

She wiggled her eyebrows suggestively and they laughed again. This time, I didn't join them. I was dreading my upcoming nuptials and honeymoon and I tried to think of them as little as possible. Of course, that wasn't happening, given that the big day was this Saturday.

One of the things that made Ms. Adriana such a great teacher was her empathy and ability to read people. She immediately picked up on my mood.

"You good?" she asked, touching my arm.

I forced a smile. "Yeah. Just a small case of cold feet."

Ms. Maria waved her hand dismissively. "Ah! Happened to me, too, girl. But now me and Eduardo have been married thirty-two years and I don't regret a moment! You'll be fine."

"I know," I murmured. "I'ma get out of here. I have to meet my sister and my mama—"

"Of course! I can't imagine all the stuff y'all have to do. Go ahead," Ms. Adriana said, hugging me again.

Five minutes later, after some naughty suggestions from Ms. Maria and loud goodbyes and "Love you, Ms. Yana!" from the kids, I was sitting in my little carmine red Boxster, trying to get my nerves together. I rested my forehead on the steering wheel for a minute, fighting back tears. Dayana Dionne Castle was not a crier. I was making this bed and I was going to lie in it. With one last sigh, I started my car. Before I could pull off, my phone buzzed. I pulled it out of my purse. Dream was calling. I shook my head—I already knew what this was about.

"Bitch, I'm coming!" I answered.

"Trick, if you don't hurry up, I'ma lay yo' mama out!" she hissed.

"What she doing, Sister?"

"Acting like this her wedding. Panicking over everything."

"Somebody might as well be excited," I mumbled.

"What?"

"Nothing!"

"Bitch, I heard that! You gon' stop holding out on—"

"Dream, I'll see you in twenty or thirty minutes. Just hold her together till I get there," I quickly changed the subject.

"Yana—"

"Please!" I said, then disconnected before she could cuss some more.

It was hard not telling my sister the whole story. Dream was my best friend, my confidante. If she knew what Jordan had done, she'd have a fit. No way would she support the marriage, and I didn't want her worried about me. So, I was trying to hold it in, hard as it was. I was about to toss the phone on the seat when I noticed a text notification. My heart rate sped up as soon as I read his name.

Smoke. I had been avoiding him, knowing that I had to go on and get ready for my role as faithful wife. He'd texted me Sunday morning and I'd sent back a message letting him know I was less than a week away from being married and what had happened between us could never happen again. He'd called after that, but I refused to answer. He sent me one text yesterday that simply said, "You deserve more." I'd almost broken down.

Today's text was one sentence, too. *You don't have to marry that nigga.*

"Yes, I do," I whispered to myself as I threw the phone on the passenger seat and took off.

I had wanted individualized gifts for my five bridesmaids and, while I should've been done selecting them, I wasn't. Mama, Dream, and I were going to pick up their jewelry today and shop for the last two gifts. It was something I could have done on my own. But left up to me, with the way I was feeling about this wedding, it might never have gotten done. Anyway, Mama insisted on going and I was not dealing with her by myself.

She started as soon as I walked in Tiffany. Turning, she gave me a look that was half irritated and half anxious.

"Dayana!" she whined as she air kissed me. "You're late!"

I tried to ignore my stupid ass sister who was behind her back making faces and flipping me off.

"Five minutes, Mama. It's okay," I said.

"No! No, it's not! I need you to feel more of a sense of an urgency. For God's sake, Dayana! It's Tuesday! You're getting married Saturday!" she fussed.

That's pretty much how the rest of the afternoon went, with her fluttering and whining and freaking and Dream and me trying not to kill her or ourselves. By the time we were done, I needed a drink. Several of them. Dream agreed. Mama was meeting Daddy for dinner, so that left the two of us.

"Let's go to the Smoke's close to here," she suggested.

The man had three bars and other businesses. There was no telling what he dabbled in on the side. So, I had no reason to believe he'd be at this particular location. Still, I didn't want to take the chance.

"Can't we just go to Kona Grill? It's right here and it's still happy hour," I pleaded.

"I don't want sushi, Yana. I want some of those damn smoked wings and the sweet and spicy shrimp. Please!"

I was already shaking my head. "Dream—"

"If we go there, I'll give you the Damien updates," she said slyly.

My ears damn near perked up. "Damien updates?"

She smiled. "I'll meet you there."

Forty-five minutes later, we were seated, drinks in front of us, and I was looking at my sister expectantly. She traced the rim of her glass with her finger, then shot me a coy look.

"What?"

"Dream, don't play with me."

Sighing, she sipped her drink. I drummed my fingers against the table. Finally, she began to talk.

"So, we went to dinner last night—"

"Wait… like a date?" I jumped in.

"It's Damien. It was *not* a date," she said dryly. "Anyway, we decided when our deal would start."

She lifted her glass again, leaving me hanging. I watched as she drank a little, then looked at me.

"So, now, what's up with—"

"WHEN?!" I interrupted her.

Dream frowned. "When what?"

"When does your thirty days start?"

"Oh!" She paused for a second. "Tonight."

My mouth fell open, but I recovered quickly. "Tonight? In a few hours tonight?"

She nodded.

"Dream! Oh, my God! What are you going to wear? Why aren't you getting ready? What—"

"Yana!" She cut me off. "There's nothing romantic or anything about this shit. It's a business deal. I'm just going to meet him wherever and… you know."

I leaned back against the soft brown leather of our booth and glared at her.

"Bitch, you are *not* meeting that man in white cotton underwear!"

She smirked at me.

"Mind your business, Sis!"

We argued until our food arrived, then continued to argue between bites. Finally, she agreed with me, a little. She promised to pull out some lingerie and I already had a baby doll in mind that I could give her. It had been an early wedding gift, but fuck it. By the time we were done, I was more excited than she was about her night. I was also breathing a sigh of relief that I had dodged Smoke.

I should've known it wasn't going to be that easy.

Our server reappeared to ask if we needed anything else. Dream requested the check and the woman smiled.

"Oh, no, ma'am. It's already been taken care of."

My sister frowned as I froze.

"By whom?" she asked.

"The owner—Mr. Salinas."

Dream's frown deepened. "But why—"

"Girl, why you looking a gift horse in the mouth? Let's go!" I urged, sliding to the edge of the booth.

He was here. I needed to get out before he caught us. Of course, her nosy ass didn't budge.

"I don't—"

"Dream!"

"Everything okay, ladies?"

I closed my eyes as the deep voice sounded behind us. When I opened them again, he was standing there, beside our booth. God, this nigga was so fucking fine with his tall, slim build, slightly bowed legs, and perfect face. I pasted on a smile.

"Everything is fine, thank you."

His caramel eyes lingered on me, and a slow burn started somewhere in my center and spread throughout me. Images of Saturday night flashed in my head and suddenly, I wanted to feel him again, over me... inside me.

"You sure, Dayana?" he asked, his tone soft.

"Y-y-yes," I stuttered, fidgeting in my seat as his voice washed over me.

Dream cleared her throat as she stared at me, the question in her eyes clear. I didn't stammer. I was a shit-talker, non-stop, but this man had me almost speechless.

"Oh, um, Smoke, this is my sister, Dream. Dream, this is Smoke, the owner," I introduced awkwardly.

They shook hands, and Smoke's attention turned right back to me.

"Can I talk to you for a minute?"

I picked up my glass and drained the lemon drop martini it still contained. I had been about to leave it, but I suddenly needed the liquid courage.

"I-I don't think that's a good idea. And my sister is—"

"Oh, I'm fine. Go ahead," Dream said, smirking.

I narrowed my eyes at her before looking up at Smoke. "I guess I got a minute."

He moved back and I stood up, following him as he walked. He led me down a long, polished wood hallway to what I assumed was his office. I closed the door behind us, then sucked in a breath when I turned around and he was right there, crowding me against the door.

"What you doing, Dayana?"

I scowled at him. "What you mean, what am I doing? I was having a drink with my sister before you—"

He pressed a finger against my lips.

"You know that's not what the fuck I'm talking about. What you doing, still marrying that tired ass nigga? I thought it was over?"

I shrugged, trying to look nonchalant. "I changed my mind."

He stared down at me, his caramel eyes seeing shit I didn't want him to see. I looked away, embarrassed.

"You changed your mind, or your daddy and that sorry ass nigga changed it for you?" he challenged.

"Does it matter, Smoke?"

He placed a hand on each side of my head. "Hell yeah, it matters. This shit gotta be your choice."

"It *is* my choice," I lied.

"That's why you can't meet my eyes?"

He tilted my head up, making me look at him.

"Look, this really isn't your business—"

"Yes, it is."

"And how you figure—"

My words disappeared in his kiss. His lips were soft but insistent against mine, and I whimpered as he sucked my bottom lip into his mouth before sliding his tongue against mine. Helplessly, I kissed him back, drowning in his taste. I moaned a complaint when he pulled back.

"You been my business since you walked in here last week."

"Smoke..." I whispered, burying my face in his chest. "Please don't make this harder."

"If it's already hard, you know it ain't right," he pressed.

"I have to—"

"You ain't gotta do nothing, Dayana. This is *your* life. Any nigga that would cheat on you, don't deserve you. You can—"

"I can what?" I cut him off, then laughed bitterly. "What can I do, Smoke? I have nothing. No education, no job, no home, nothing. I knew what I was agreeing to when I accepted Jordan's proposal. I can't embarrass our families like that. It's too late."

He cupped my face and I wanted to press my cheek against his palm, absorb his warmth.

"Dayana—"

"*It's too late!*" I repeated. "Now, please. Move back and let me go. My sister is waiting."

He refused at first, just looked down at me, his caramel eyes angry. Angry... and hurt. I pretended not to see all that.

"Smoke, please. I need to go."

Another minute ticked by before he finally stepped back.

"I have to go. I'm... I'm sorry," I whispered before flying out of his office.

Dream was waiting, so fucking curious that as soon as she saw me, she started.

"Yana, what the hell—"

"Not now, Dream," I pleaded, grabbing my purse and heading for the door. "Not now."

CHAPTER 28

Smoke

STANDING IN MY OFFICE DOORWAY, I watched as Dayana hurried her ass away from me. *What the fuck am I doing?* I had almost refused to let her go and I hadn't given a fuck about a chick walking away since my wife. My sex-life since Jenna died had consisted mostly of one-night stands—I had a couple of repeaters, but they knew wasn't shit coming out of our situations. What happened with Dayana should've been perfect for me. Pretty woman, good pussy, no strings— all the shit I was looking for. So, why wasn't it enough, all of a sudden?

Maybe it was the circumstances. I couldn't believe Dayana was about to let that nigga wife her after what he did. I knew how this game went, though, had almost walked into a marriage of convenience myself. In her kind of family, Dayana would have had little choice about who she was marrying. Hell, I wondered how her sister didn't find herself married off first. Men like Darius Castle and Dante Ware treated women like pawns. I guess I was guilty, too. But now that it was Dayana's turn to be manipulated, the shit made me feel a way.

I closed the door and walked behind my desk to take a seat. She refused to think about what I was saying, and I had work to do. Sighing, I rubbed a hand down my face. Fuck it, she was a good lay, but there would be more, starting tonight. Grabbing my personal phone, I opened the text app and searched for a contact named Sienna. She wasn't as beautiful as Dayana, but she was cute enough. Plus, she had tight, gushy walls, a super wet mouth, and she didn't seem to have a problem playing her role. She would do. I texted her and I swear she responded before she had time to read the whole thing. I made arrangements with her before turning my attention to my computer.

An hour later, I gave up on the shit. My focus was shot, all because of one little stubborn woman. I started to text her, try again to make her see shit my way, but something stopped me. I could admit that I was feeling Dayana way more than I had felt a woman in a long time. That shit made me feel guilty, though. When I had to stand there beside my bed, all those years ago, and look into the face of my dead wife, finally at peace, I had promised her that no one else would ever take her place in my life or Jenesis's. I always planned to keep that promise. No one had come close... until now. The fact that Dayana had me so open seemed like a betrayal of my beautiful Jenna.

I stood up abruptly and gathered my shit. My plan was to go to my OG's house and chill with her and my daughter for a minute, maybe get some perspective and settle my mind. But on my way there, I found myself taking a detour. The drive to Beautiful Flower Cemetery passed in a blur. Before I knew it, I was walking into a Greek Revival-style mausoleum, my steps leading me to Jenna's final resting place. Touching the front of her tomb, I bowed my head for a minute, and let the memories of the girl I'd loved since the moment I saw her across a kindergarten classroom wash over me.

In terms of my heart, Jenna had been it. Yeah, as a dumb ass young man, I got caught slipping a couple of times, but all them bitches got was dick and their feelings hurt. That shit caught up with me, though. I swear I never knew real fear or pain until Jenna walked out on me for cheating. Losing her had a nigga sick. It took a year of begging and promising for her to even look at me again. I didn't waste the opportunity. I never gave another woman a second look and I married her as soon as she said yes. Jenna had been my world and Jenesis was the living evidence of our love. We were supposed to be together forever, but fucking ovarian cancer had other plans. Watching my love die little by little had almost killed me. I learned right then that life wasn't fair, that human plans were nothing. For all the money and power that I had, I couldn't save her. I felt like I failed her when it came down to it. But I had promised her forever and I wanted to keep that promise.

"Hey, baby. I wasn't planning to stop, so forgive me for not bringing your flowers. Hope everything is okay in heaven… but I guess it wouldn't be heaven if shit wasn't all good," I said, tracing my fingers over her name. "I'ma have to bring our baby soon. I know you watch over her. You see how big she getting? And she your twin, Jenna. Beautiful and smart, just like you, baby girl."

The mausoleum was silent, the stillness broken only by a sudden breeze, the wind brushing gently over my face. I smiled, knowing it was her.

"I can't stay long. I gotta go pick her up. Mama done had her all day. But I was just thinking about you, and I wanted to stop by and let you know…" I swallowed, fighting the dampness I could feel in my eyes. "I love you. Nothing will *ever* change that, baby girl. I promise."

I pressed a kiss to my fingers, then rubbed it against her tomb. "Keep resting easy, baby."

I needed to get out of there before the memories overwhelmed me. Looking up at the roof of the small building, I whispered a quick prayer for her soul and mine, then left. The heaviness I felt every time I left her didn't lift until I was pulling into my mom's yard and saw her and Jenesis outside. I was barely out of the car before my baby was racing toward me, hugging my legs.

"Daddy! Look at the 'biscus me and GiGi just planted," she yelled proudly as I swung her up in my arms.

I covered her face in kisses before oohing and ahhing over the plants she pointed out.

"I can tell they gon' be beautiful, Jeni-face," I lied. I didn't know a damn thing about flowers. "What you do at school today?"

She chattered for a few minutes about all the stuff she'd learned earlier and the homework her GiGi had helped her with. The whole time, I pretended not to feel my mama's eyes on my face. She knew something was up. She always did, and I hated that shit. Finally, she wouldn't let me avoid it anymore.

"Jenesis, go on in the house, wash up, and get your stuff together," she instructed.

I set my daughter down and she looked up at my OG in confusion.

"But GiGi, we eating dinner with you."

"So? You can have everything ready to go for when we finish," Mama said, shooing her off.

My baby had barely closed the door before Mama was narrowing her eyes at me.

"I cannot wait until we leave for this vacation this weekend. You walking around here, looking crazy as hell. What's the matter?" she demanded.

I shook my head. "Nothing, OG. What you cook? A nigga hungry as—"

"Boy! Don't play with me. You think I don't know my own child?"

Rubbing my head, I sighed. Might as well get this over with. I knew my mama and if there was one thing about Stephanie Salinas, she wasn't going to stop until she got to the bottom of shit.

"I went to see Jenna," I finally said.

Her eyes softened. "Oh, baby. What happened?"

"I just wanted to talk to her."

I hoped that was the end of the conversation, but she just stood there, eyes glued to me. This lady, man! She saw through *everything*.

"I met a girl last week, OG," I admitted reluctantly.

Something flashed in her eyes, but all she said was, "Mm-hmm. And?"

I shrugged. "And nothing. It's nothing, for real."

"But you felt the need to see Jenna? Cartier Alaric Salinas, don't play with me! You must like this girl!" she snapped.

"Yeah, Ma. I like her, but it don't matter. She getting married Saturday."

She put her hands on her hips, dirt trickling off her gardening gloves. "First girl you done told me about since Jenna and you just gon' sit back and watch her marry somebody?"

Shaking her head, she huffed out a breath and mumbled something. I had no doubt she was calling me some kind of fool.

"Yep. I ain't got nothing to offer her. I ain't tryna love nobody else. It's me and Jenna forever. This girl… Dayana… she deserves somebody who can give her 100 percent. That ain't me," I explained, turning toward the front steps.

Yeah, I had entertained the thought of marrying Crystal Ware, but that was no love match. That was all business. She was pretty and, if she'd been my wife, I would've fucked her, but there were no feelings between us. But this shit with Dayana…

"Because you won't let it be," Mama said from behind me. "And stop running from this conversation."

"Ma, I'm not running."

"Yeah, you running. You so focused on what you *think* Jenna would want that you forgetting how she truly was. Ain't no way Jenna would expect you to live your life alone, without loving someone and having someone love you. Ain't no way she'd want her baby girl to never know what it's like to have a mother—"

I turned around, cutting her off.

"She *had* a mother and she got you. That's enough."

She shook her head. "Cartier, Jenna gon' always be with you, in your heart, in your memories, in Jenesis. But it's okay to move on. If you like this girl—"

"Did you miss the part about her getting married?" I asked sarcastically.

"Don't get smart with me, boy. You better take out your frustrations somewhere else."

I blew out a deep breath. "Mama, can we just eat? I hear what you saying, but I don't know about all that."

She mugged me but started toward the porch. "Fine," she muttered. "But don't you miss out on your future holding too tight to your past."

"Who said Dayana's my future? I just told you I liked her. Obviously, she ain't feeling the same."

She snorted. "Boy, please. You my son. Handsome, smart, rich, a boss nigga. What girl don't like that?"

I smiled down at her. "What you know about boss niggas, OG?"

"Tuh! You the son of a boss bitch. You can't help it," she popped.

My mouth fell open and I stared down at her. "Mama!"

She bumped me with one of her hips as she walked past me. "Move out the way, Cartier. My baby probably in there hungry. She been working hard today. But you think about what I said. Don't mess around and let your second chance slip away. Not everybody is lucky enough to get one."

She gave me a hard look before strolling into her house. I knew that meant she had said all she was going to say about the subject. I heard her. I really did. But I was still confused as hell.

CHAPTER 29
Dream

MY HEART WAS CURRENTLY LIVING in my stomach, beating so hard that I thought I was going to pass out. He'd sent me an address. That was it. Oh, and the letters "ASAP." Bossy muhfucka! I watched as Dayana packed a bottle of coconut and cocoa butter body oil for me, along with the matching body wash.

"Yana, I'ma shower before I go," I pointed out.

She looked at me like I was the stupidest person she'd ever seen. Plopping down on my black and butter yellow comforter, she sucked her teeth.

"Dream, are you serious right now?"

"What? I really don't see why I need this bag. We can handle our business and I can come back to my own shower and my own bed," I argued.

"Girl. I've only *seen* the nigga. Haven't talked to him. Haven't even really been close to him. And I still know he got BDE!"

I frowned. "BDE? What is that?"

She shook her head. "Big Dick Energy. If you think that nigga gon' fuck you once and let you go, you crazy. Yo' legs or yo' ass about to be in the air all night."

"Yana!"

Shrugging, she went into my closet and came back with a pair of new slippers that she packed.

"Dream, stop being naïve. Shit, you better be over there doing some stretches or something while I'm packing."

She stopped and clapped her hands suddenly, a big smile on her beautiful face.

"What, bitch?" I asked suspiciously.

"This yo' first spinnanight bag!"

Sighing, I rolled my eyes. "I been to sleepovers before."

"But not with a man!" she exclaimed as she packed more toiletries.

"You act like I'm leaving for a week. Chill, girl! And how you become an expert on all this?" I asked.

My sister thought she was slick, but I hadn't forgotten about her run in with Smoke Salinas earlier. I was going to let her make it until after her wedding, though. She waved a hand at me.

"You know I'm more streetwise than you."

That was true. I couldn't even argue.

"Yana?"

"Hmm?" she said as she dug through my underwear drawer. "I want you to put on some cute underwear when you leave in the morning, too."

"You really think he's gonna want to... all night? And I need to be comfortable in the morning; I'm going to work," I whined.

"Girl, yes. That nigga looks like 'stamina' is his middle name. I hope yo' ass don't be limping for my wedding, since he said he gon' beat that back in every day."

I decided right then that I hated her.

"Go shower, Dream Dior. I got this. And make sure you shave everything that needs shaving."

My jaw dropped at her directions. Yana was doing too much, now.

"Bitch, I regularly groom myself. I don't—"

"That nigga gon' wanna taste straight pussy, not a hairball."

"Ugh!" I groaned aloud as I marched to the bathroom.

A few minutes later, I stood under the steaming water, nervous as hell. I hadn't thought about all the shit Yana was teasing me about. What if he did want to fuck me repeatedly? Would I enjoy it? Would I be too sore? How bad was it going to hurt? Was he really going to put his mouth on my... I stopped that idea in its tracks as I felt my body heat just from the thought. Really, *all* these kinds of thoughts about Damien, about his mouth or his hands on me, about him inside me, made my body react like it belonged to a damn thot.

I finished my shower and moisturized my body before making my way back into my room. Dayana lay across my bed on her phone. She looked up as I walked in and smiled.

"He said 'ASAP.' You need to hurry up so I can give you a light beat."

"Dayana, I'm not doing all that!" I objected as I started to put on the lacy black panties that had been a spur-of-the-moment purchase one day when I was feeling risqué.

Ten minutes later, I sat still as she finished my face. She walked over to the dresser and grabbed a scrap of black silk and lace off it.

"Here."

I raised an eyebrow at her. "What is that?"

"Put it on, Dream."

"Dayana—"

"Dream!"

I couldn't believe myself, thirty minutes later, when I pulled up to what I assumed was his house. Dayana had convinced me to wear only a robe over the baby doll and black panties she'd approved of. My feet were encased in some high-heeled Giuseppe Zanotti sandals. I had argued with her that all of this was unnecessary, but she had insisted that I make the best of tonight.

"Just because it's a business deal don't mean y'all can't enjoy it," she popped.

I let her win. But now, even with Megan the Stallion rapping in my ears for encouragement, I was five seconds away from hyperventilating, feeling stupid and like I tried too hard. Grabbing my phone, I texted him that I was here. His response came a few seconds later.

Damien: *I know.*

I watched as one of the doors of the four-car garage lifted. Once it was all the way open, I drove inside. I turned off my car, grabbed my duffel bag, purse, and phone, and got out. Dayana had also packed a garment bag for me with a dress for work in the morning, but I was not being bold enough to bring that in! The duffel was too much—he probably planned to fuck me and turn my ass right back around, despite what my sister said. And anyway, I was not about to make a habit of spending the night with him for the next thirty days.

If I expected him to let me in, I was disappointed. Nigga was just unnecessarily rude. I opened the door that led into the house and stepped into his kitchen. *Oh, my God!* His house was freezing and dark. The light above the stove was the only illumination, but I could see that the kitchen was big, with shiny black counters and stainless-steel appliances. I took a few steps in.

"Damien?" I called, feeling shyer that I had in a long time.

He appeared in the kitchen doorway suddenly. I swallowed hard as I looked at him. His lounging clothes were all black: black tank top, black ball shorts, black socks, black slides. Damn, this nigga was so fine. I wasn't sure if the goosebumps suddenly decorating my skin were from the house's arctic temperature or from looking at him.

"Come here," he said.

I hesitated for one second and he tilted his head to the

side, waiting. Slowly, I crossed the stone floor until I was a few inches away from him. He looked me up and down, saying nothing. Then he reached out and untied the belt of my robe. I blushed, embarrassed until I saw the lust flare in his eyes. I had been about to pull it closed, but my hands dropped. He slid the bag off my shoulder and slung it over his own. Wordlessly, he walked off. Unsure of what to do, I clutched my bag and trailed behind him. We made our way upstairs and I followed him into the second room on the right. The moon, through the huge windows, and one of his nightstand lamps provided the only light in the room, and I was glad. The less attention on these thighs of mine, the better. The room was done in a dark color—black or navy blue—and what looked like cream. His furniture was wooden and sturdy and the bed... Oh, God, I couldn't look at that huge bed when I thought about what was about to happen to me in it. There wasn't much in terms of decorations, no pictures, no rugs, no knick-knacks. Of course, he didn't look like a knick-knack sort of man. He placed my bag on the dresser, so I set my purse and phone beside it.

The covers had already been pulled back. I watched as he settled on the side and looked at me.

"My paperwork is behind you on the dresser."

I nodded, then turned to grab it. Slowly, I walked closer to him so that I could see in the lamplight. A quick scan showed me he was clear of everything. I set the papers on the night-stand and waited. I felt an invisible clock ticking in my head as he just looked at me for a long moment. Finally, he spoke.

"Take your clothes off," he ordered.

Well! I guess we getting right to it, then, I thought. My mouth went dry, and I squeezed my hands together.

"Can we... can we turn the light off?"

He chuckled. "Nah, shorty. We can't turn the light off."

Oh, God. My hands trembled as I pushed the robe off my shoulders and freed my arms. Folding it, I laid it on the nightstand. Shivering, I gathered the bottom of the baby doll in my hands and pulled it over my head in one jerky movement and lay it on the robe. My breath was coming in spurts as I stood there in just my shoes and panties. His eyes never left me. Bending over, I unbuckled my shoes and slid my feet out of them, then moved them to the side. I had hooked my fingers in the sides of the scrap of lace I called panties when he surprised me by pulling me closer to stand between his legs. His hands moved from my waist to my breasts, and he pulled on my nipples. They were already hard, thanks to how cold he had it. Looking up at me, Damien twisted them slightly. It hurt, but it also felt good. Moisture flooded my center, wetting the panties, and I bit down on my lip to hold back a moan. I couldn't hold it back, though, when he replaced one of his hands with his mouth, pulling my stiff nipple against the warm, wet heat of his tongue. My hands tangled in his locs as he sucked me, the feeling unlike anything I had ever experienced. My eyes drifted closed as he released me with a soft pop, turning his attention to my other breast.

He teased me like that for long moments, until I almost couldn't take the heavy throbbing between my thighs and my knees felt like they were about to buckle. Finally, he moved me back a little, then stood up. I stood still as he eased my panties over my hips and down my legs, then I stepped out of them as he squatted in front of me. For a moment, he just looked at my freshly shaved pussy before leaning forward and pressing a kiss against my mound. I gasped, feeling another blush heat my skin. He rose, his green eyes glued to mine.

"Take your hair down."

I removed the pins quickly, shaking my head so that the honey blonde braids cascaded around my shoulders. He ran his fingers through them, then tugged gently, pulling my head back. For a minute, we just looked at each other. I trembled under his gaze, anticipation uncurling inside me.

"Get in," he instructed.

I climbed into the bed, the black silk sheets feeling decadent against my skin. I lay back, watching him, unsure of what to do. Then, he pulled his shirt off, and I was stuck. Damien's body was a living piece of art, from the beautiful ink that covered his light complexion to the well-defined muscles that rippled beneath his skin. His shorts were next, and his legs were just as cut up and powerful as his upper body. I squeezed my eyes shut as his hands went to the waistband of his Ethika boxer briefs and he chuckled. The underwear was gone when I opened my eyes again and I sucked in a sharp breath. His dick was impossibly thick and long, swinging from his body with a slight curve in it.

He gon' kill me, I thought, pressing my thighs together.

"Touch it."

My eyes widened at his words, and I bit down on my lip. Slowly, I extended my hand and tried to wrap it around him. My fingers almost didn't meet, and I had to bite back a panicked moan. I moved my hand up and down in a smooth glide, looking at him to judge how he felt. He covered my hand with his, making me squeeze tighter and move faster. Incredibly, he got even harder and longer in my hand. I watched as a drop of clear liquid beaded on the head. Licking my lips, I wondered what it tasted like, then blushed at the thought. My skin got even warmer when I looked up and he was smiling at me. He knew what I was thinking. His hand stopped suddenly, and my eyes met his.

"Did I… did I do something wrong?" I asked shyly.

Being shy was definitely not me, but, hell, I was out of my element. He shook his head.

"Move over."

I obeyed instantly and he got in beside me, propping himself up on one elbow. I had to resist the urge to move closer to his warm body. Damien looked down at me as his other hand settled above my knee and slowly stroked its way up my thighs.

"Spread your thighs, Dream," he ordered softly.

Last night, when he implied that he'd be giving me orders, I couldn't have imagined how erotic they'd be or how much they'd turn me on. I let my legs fall open for him and his hand moved between them. The kiss of the cold air against my pussy had me trembling. The first brush of his finger against my clit had me sucking in a deep breath, the cold chased away by the warmth of his touch. The second had me moaning as my fingers clenched the sheets. Then, my back was arching off the bed and I was whispering his name as he slowly circled the little bud with his thumb. He eased down so that his face was even with mine, then buried his lips against my neck, biting and sucking me on the sensitive skin there. That shit felt so good that I whimpered, releasing the sheet and pressing his head closer to me. I had closed my eyes, but they flew open as he slipped two fingers inside of me, teasing the throbbing walls of my pussy.

"Damien…" I moaned.

"*Fuck!* Yo' shit so tight and wet," he whispered against my ear.

As if they had a mind of their own, my hips moved against his hand, grinding my clit against his palm and sliding my pussy up and down his fingers. The rhythm he set was slow at first, but as his speed increased, so did the movement of my hips. My body tightened as I felt a tingle in my stomach and between my thighs.

"Damien, I—"

"Ay, let that shit go," he whispered as he worked me like he'd known my body forever.

And my body responded like it knew him and craved his demands. My pussy pulsed as I came all over his hand, soft, hungry sounds escaping my mouth. He didn't stop stroking me until my body stilled, limp and satisfied beside him. He brought his hand up to my lips and painted them with my juices before he leaned down to kiss me, sharing my flavor between us.

Damien rose over me without breaking the kiss, his hard, intricately inked body settling between my thighs. Nervous, I closed my eyes. I had barely realized that his hand was between us, lining his dick up with my entrance, before he pushed forward, making me take all of him in a single, powerful stroke. My eyes flew open, and a scream ripped from my throat as pain tore through me.

CHAPTER 30

Demon

HER SCREAM... I pulled out of her immediately, my dick already missing her impossibly tight walls. She was shaking, her breath coming fast, tears clouding her chocolate eyes. All that shit pissed me off. I moved away from the warmth of her thick, brown thighs and sat on the side of the bed.

"What..." she paused as she sniffed. "What are you doing? Why did you stop?"

I grilled her ass. "You just screamed like a nigga was killing you. The fuck yo' old ass doing still a virgin, Dream?"

She sat up slowly, pressing her back against my head-board and pulling her knees up, wrapping her arms around them.

"What kind of question is that?" she asked.

"A real one."

"M-m-my parents always said we should save ourselves for marriage. I didn't think I'd last that long, but I wasn't going to just give it away to the first nigga that came along, either," she said, still sniffing.

"But you traded it away for yo' bitch ass brother? I oughta kill that nigga for even putting you in that situation," I spat.

Her head flew up. "You can't do that! I'm here and I'm holding up my end of the deal—"

"Shut up, Dream!"

"Stop yelling at me!" she hissed before dropping her forehead to her knees and letting her braids fall forward, forming a curtain around her.

I looked at her, shaking my head. This wasn't how this shit was supposed to go. Hell, I was fucking with her when I compared her to an escort—I didn't think she got down like that. But I wasn't expecting her ass to have *no* experience. And then, she didn't even say anything.

"Ay, why you go through all that getting tested and shit?"

She shrugged, head still down. "Because you asked for it."

"You couldn't have just said it wasn't no way in hell you had anything? How you just forget to mention that ain't nobody ran up in that shit?"

Finally, she looked up. "Do you have to be so nasty? And does it matter? I'm sorry I'm not as skilled as your fucking Juliettes!"

Hell yeah, it mattered. But not for the reasons she was probably thinking. Yeah, I was mad that she wasn't experienced, but not because I needed her to be a pro. Nah, I was already possessive and now, knowing I was the first nigga to have her, I could feel that shit growing. I was supposed to let her ass go in thirty days, but the thought of leaving her for another nigga to grab her up? That shit wasn't sitting right with me.

The sound of her sniffing brought me out of my thoughts. I looked at her bowed head in disbelief.

"I know yo' ass ain't crying."

She didn't say anything, just hugged her knees tighter. I pulled on her braids, trying to make her lift her head. She resisted.

"Dream. I'm talking to you."

Her only response was silence. Standing, I walked to the

end of the bed. I leaned forward and grabbed her ankles and pulled her flat, dragging her until her ass was near the edge. She shrieked as I parted her legs and kneeled between them.

"Leave me alone, Damien."

"Shut up," I said, right before I lowered my head and buried my face in her pussy.

Her body tensed in surprise, and I heard her soft gasp. Slowly, I trailed my tongue between her lips, licking her from her entrance to her clit. Pulling back, I blew on her softly, then stroked her again with my tongue. She moaned, her body writhing against the bed. I grabbed her, my fingers sinking into the silky skin of her thighs, holding her in place as I continued the assault with my mouth. The tempting scent and taste of her was going straight to my dick, had it rocking up harder than ever. Her hips tipped forward, pressing her pussy tighter against me, silently asking me for more. I gave her what she wanted, letting my lips encircle her pearl and pulling it into my mouth.

"Damien..." she cried, her hands tangling in my locs as my tongue teased her.

I loved the sound of my name on her lips. For long minutes, the only noises in the room were her heavy breathing and the sound of me sucking on her pussy as it got wetter and wetter. I wanted to make her feel good, take her mind off the pain she felt when I slid up into her. When her legs shook under my hands, I knew I was succeeding. A second later, her body tightened up. I dropped one last kiss on her clit before pulling back. Yeah, I knew she was about to cum, but she was going to do it on this dick.

I stood up and looked down at her lush, brown body. Dream was perfect with her smooth skin and fucking crazy curves. She moaned her protest at my stopping, squeezing her thighs together to try to finish the job. I pushed them apart.

"Nah, shorty. Slide back," I said.

She obeyed, and that shit turned a nigga on even more. Dream thought she ran shit everywhere else, but in this bedroom, she did everything I said. I climbed over her, using my knees to spread her legs. Reaching between us, I slipped the head of my dick between her lower lips. Her eyes were wide open, and I could see that the lust in them was mixed with fear. That stopped me. I wasn't a nigga who was into fucking women who didn't want to be fucked.

"You want me to stop?"

She shook her head and grabbed my biceps.

"Can you just go slow?" she asked.

I didn't answer, just eased inside her. She tensed as she sucked in a sharp breath, her nails digging into my arms. I pushed deeper. I needed an award for taking my time because this girl had heaven between her legs. Warm and wet, she sheathed my shit tightly.

Still, I needed her to ease up and let me all the way in. I brushed my lips against hers before trailing kisses to her neck. She moaned, but her hold on me tightened and her pussy still had me in a vise grip. I couldn't go further without hurting her.

"Put your hand between us," I whispered in her ear before sucking on the lobe.

She hesitated, but she did it.

"Touch your clit for me."

"Damien—"

I pulled back a little to look at her. Her eyes met mine and she looked away quickly. Little bossy ass had the nerve to be embarrassed.

"You gon' pretend you never did that?"

Burying her face against me, she shook her head. "I didn't say that. But... not in front of anyone."

"Dream."

She stirred slowly, but a gasp escaped her mouth as her fingers touched her pearl. Her hand moved in a small, unhurried circle. I looked down, the sight of me spreading her open while she rubbed herself making me harder. She stopped suddenly, and my gaze clashed with hers.

"Don't look at me," she pleaded, a tinge of red on her cheeks.

Careful to stay inside her, I rose to my knees. Grabbing her hand, I guided it back, keeping mine on top. We moved together, her wetness drenching our fingers. She bit her bottom lip and moaned. I felt her tighten around me and I struggled to concentrate on what we were doing. Her breathing became heavy as she enjoyed her own touch. Moving my hand, I watched her bring herself closer to cumming. I slid further into her as she got wetter. Halfway in, I moved back and forth, going deeper with each thrust. Her back arched suddenly as the orgasm sneaked up on her, her pussy contracting and releasing around me. Grabbing her hips, I pulled her toward me as I thrust forward, finally burying myself inside her. *Fuck!* Her pussy was everything. Nothing had ever felt this good.

I fucked her slowly, giving her light strokes until she got used to having me inside her. Her hips rolled against mine and she reached for me, her hand stroking my cheek before easing down to my neck to grasp one of my chains. I leaned forward, pressing my mouth to hers. I kissed her way too fucking much, but it was like I couldn't help myself. Her arms went around my neck as she kissed me back. I slid my hands under her, squeezing her ass and angling her body so I could go deeper, hit every inch of the hot, wet walls stretched around me. Her nails slid along my back and shoulders, encouraging me to go harder, faster as I claimed this pussy I never wanted to leave.

I pulled my mouth away from the softness of hers. I wanted to hear her cries, hear my name on her lips. Her soft moans echoed around the room, accompanying the sounds of my body driving into hers. I circled my hips, hitting a spot that made her eyes roll in the back of her head.

"Damien," she whimpered.

"You like that?" I teased her, doing it again and again until she trembled beneath me.

"Y-yes. Damien, please…"

A nigga was trying to stay in control, not lose myself before she got hers, but the sound of her pleading had me about to fuck up and moan.

"Fuck, Dream," I hissed as she squeezed around me.

I pressed my face against her neck again, sucking hard against her soft skin, marking her before my lips traveled lower. I kissed the top of her breast before pulling her nipple into my mouth, twirling my tongue around it, then gently nibbling on it. Her nails bit into my skin and she screamed as she came. I fucked her through her orgasm, my hands clenching in her hips, holding her still as I pounded into her. This time, I couldn't hold back the groan as I started to cum. Holding her against me tightly, I released my seed deep inside her.

CHAPTER 31

Dream

I'D HEARD my girlfriends talk about sex, seen porn, read romance novels. But nothing could have prepared me for the sensations Damien introduced me to. The slick, wet feel of his tongue against my clit, the pleasure and pain of him stretching me out, the glide and friction of his dick against my walls, the warmth of him cumming inside me… *Oh, my God,* I wanted to feel it all again. Suddenly, I understood what the big deal about sex was.

"You gon' let me go?"

His voice brought reality crashing down. The insides of my thighs were hugging tightly to his hips and my arms were still around his neck. Embarrassed, I let go quickly and he rolled over to lie beside me. *Soooo, what happens now?* I wondered. It wasn't like I was an expert at this. The silence and my feelings of awkwardness were a cold reminder that this was nothing but business. If it were anything else, he'd be cuddling me or talking to me, right? Or running bathwater for me to soak after my first time. Yeah, my assumptions were based on what I'd heard, but I knew he should do something else other than lie beside me quietly. It was time to put on my professional face. I sat up, pretending not to be self-conscious about the facts that I was naked and that I had enjoyed our… *session* so much that the silk sheets were damp beneath me, and it wasn't sweat. Snatching my baby doll and robe off the nightstand, I climbed out of the bed and damn near ran into the bathroom, flinching at the unfamiliar ache between my legs.

Lucky for me, his linen closet was in the bathroom. Grabbing his Dove soap and a towel, I looked longingly at the freestanding garden tub, but I was ready to go. I washed up quickly at the sink and slid back into my clothes. God, I didn't want to make this walk of shame. I inhaled and exhaled deeply a few times before pulling the door open. Walking into the room, I refused to look toward the bed. Instead, I made my way to his dresser and opened the duffel bag, pulling out the slippers Yana had packed. I wasn't getting back in those heels; I didn't even want to go by the bed to get them. I quickly put on the house shoes and was about to shove my purse inside the duffel when I heard him move. Unable to stop myself, I looked in the mirror. I froze when I saw him walking, naked, toward me.

Damien stopped behind me, his eyes tangling with mine in the mirror. I was already shivering from the cold and his nearness only intensified my shaking.

"Where you going?"

I swallowed, fighting not to drop his gaze.

"Home."

He smirked. "Oh, yeah?"

"Yeah. We already… I mean, I figured you were done…"

My voice trailed off as his smile spread, fucking with me. This was a joke to him? That pissed me off. Squaring my shoulders, I stared back at him.

"You got your nut. What else you want with me?" I snapped.

His smile disappeared and, a second later, his hand was in

my hair, pushing me forward. I grabbed the edge of the dresser, trying to steady myself.

"Damien, what—"

The feel of the cold air against my suddenly naked ass stopped me. He had bent me over and shoved my skimpy little outfit up. I opened my mouth to protest, but he smacked my ass hard. Gasping, I tried to pull away from him. He spanked me again.

"Be still," he ordered.

I wanted to argue, but his hand tightened in my hair. I stared at his reflection, a pout on my full lips. He looked down for a moment and suddenly, I felt him easing inside me. I winced as he bottomed out, the stretch still somewhat painful, although it was nothing like that first time. I wondered if I'd ever get used to it. Then, he dragged himself backward and thrust forward again and I forgot all about the hurt. My fingers tightened on the wood of the dresser, and I bit down on my bottom lip.

"Look at me, Dream. Watch me fuck you."

Slowly, my eyes lifted, and I watched him in the mirror, his hips moving at a slow, steady pace, filling me over and over. The feel and the sight of him had me gushing around him, more turned on than I had ever been. I moaned softly as he tightened his hold on my hips, dragging me back against him. My body caught on and suddenly I was the one moving, meeting his deep strokes.

"We not done until I tell you we are, understand?" he said, his eyes piercing mine.

I nodded, my eyes closing as I shuddered around him, loving the feel of him inside me. He pulled on my hair.

"Open them."

I obeyed immediately, looking at him again, at the rippling muscles and swirls of ink, before lifting my eyes and getting lost in the mystery of his green gaze. Damien fucked me for long, slow minutes against the dresser, pulling out only when my body began to rhythmically tighten around him. I held back a whimper as he lifted me and carried me to the bed, tossing me against the sheets. He had me spread open beneath him, my legs in the bend of his arms, before I could blink. I moaned as he slid inside me again.

"You sore?" he whispered.

Hesitantly, I nodded. He smiled down at me.

"You gon' stay like that for the next thirty days," he taunted.

His words made me blush... and made me wetter. His mouth descended on mine, and I parted my lips for him, my arms encircling him as I got lost in the allure of his touch.

———

I realized two things as I squeezed my eyes shut against the sun. One, I was having the completely new experience of waking up naked in a man's bed and two, the sunlight streaming through the window was way too bright for it to be early morning—I was late as fuck for work. And, oh, as I stretched, there was a third realization—I hurt... *everywhere*. I opened one eye, peeping around me cautiously. Damien was nowhere in sight, and I sighed in relief. That man was insatiable, I swear. After the second time we had sex, I had given in to temptation and soaked in the tub. He joined me... and fucked me there, making me ride him until both of us came. He'd changed the sheets on his bed before laying me down and taking me again on the fresh linens. I'd finally fallen into a dead sleep, only to wake up when the sun was just lighting the sky. He'd buried his face against my neck and slid into me while we lay on our sides, fucking me silently as the sun rose.

I pulled a pillow over my face as I admitted something to myself. He may have been the instigator, but I wanted him each time, opening for him whenever he touched me. At this rate, I was going to be addicted to him. But I didn't have time to lie in this bed and think about that. I had so much to do at work before I could take off for the wedding. Hurriedly, I jumped out of the bed, making my way to my phone. *Ten forty-three AM.* Shit! I had to get moving. I decided to get my dress from my car before I hopped into the shower.

By the time I made it to the top of the stairs, the scents of bacon and coffee were teasing my nose. *Damn!* I was going to have to pass him in the kitchen to get to the garage. I wasn't ready to see him—I was too embarrassed after a night of letting him have his way with me repeatedly. *Fuck that, Dream Dior. You're a grown woman. You have just as much right to enjoy sex as any man,* I hyped myself up. Blowing out a deep breath, I made my way downstairs and to the kitchen. The goosebumps on my skin were a mix of nervousness and cold—this crazy ass man kept this house arctic!

He was standing over the stove with no shirt on, his legs covered by a pair of gray joggers. I took a minute to admire the tattoo inked deep into his skin. I had noticed a few of the ones on his front—a bird escaping a gilded cage, the face of a lion, and a grinning skull were just a few that adorned his sculpted chest and abs. But his back only sported one that covered the whole surface. It was the snarling, terrifying face of a demon. I studied it, fascinated by the elaborate, beautiful work that had gone into making such a hideous vision. I dropped my eyes quickly when he turned around and slid some scrambled eggs on to a waiting plate. Suddenly, I knew why some women were so fascinated with gray sweatpants. Damn, was he even wearing underwear?! I hurriedly lifted my eyes to his face. He smirked at me like he knew what I was thinking, before turning to open the oven and pull out the bacon. I watched as he moved it from the sheet pan to another pan covered in paper towels. I jumped as four slices of toast popped up from the toaster. Two mugs sat beside the burbling coffee maker, waiting to be filled. His timing was perfect, everything done at once.

I shook my head, realizing I had come to a stop just to stare at him and his handiwork.

"Umm... good morning," I said softly.

He raised an eyebrow but didn't return the greeting. I swear I was getting used to his rudeness. Sighing, I headed toward the garage door.

"Where you going?" he asked.

"To my car. I need to get my dress for work—"

"Sit down."

He gestured toward the breakfast nook where two plates sat before plating the toast and grabbing the eggs. I watched as he carried them to the table and went back and got the bacon. I caught his eye as he approached the table and gave him a small smile.

"Thank you, Damien. This is really nice, but I'm already late. Maybe I can fix a breakfast sandwich or—"

"Sit down, Dream."

My smile disappeared. He was so damned bossy, but he was going to have to learn that I wasn't good at following orders... outside the bedroom, at least. I fought back a blush at the thought.

"No, really, I have to go to work."

"What do you like in your coffee?" he asked, ignoring what I said as he poured the dark, rich liquid into the mugs.

Damn, it smelled good and the steam curling above the cups called out to me—I was tired as hell. But I really didn't have time.

"No, seriously, I'm going to work—"

He walked toward me, not stopping until he was a few inches away and I could smell his clean, manly scent mixed with Dove.

"No, you not," he said calmly.

"Damien—"

"You got about, what? Three, four hours of sleep? And that's cuz I fucked your ass until you were too tired to do anything else. So, you about to eat this damn brunch and then, you going back to bed."

I shook my head. "I'm not—"

I sucked in my breath as he stepped closer. His hand closed around the back of my neck and his lips hovered right above my ear. "You are. Then, if you lucky, I'ma fuck you again when you wake up," he said, his voice low and rough. "You understand?"

If I had on panties, they would've been flooded at the erotic promise. I shivered as his mouth grazed my ear. I was supposed to be arguing, putting my foot down, letting this arrogant, demanding man know he didn't run me, and NOTHING interfered with my job. I opened my mouth.

"Dream."

Just the one word sounded so commanding. I swallowed, dropping my eyes. I knew right then that I wasn't going to do any of the shit I should be doing. *Weak ass girl.* But fussing at myself wasn't doing any good. I looked up at him again.

"I... I just need to call Parker," I whispered.

CHAPTER 32
Demon

Curled up against my sheets, her braids all over my pillows, Dream was beautiful. She was asleep, not even the cup of coffee enough to keep her awake. That was probably because she made it with more milk and sugar than coffee; my stomach hurt as I watched her stir that shit together. I looked at her one more time before I walked out of the room, closing the door softly so I wouldn't wake her. That was the shit that had me pausing in my steps. When had I ever given a fuck about disturbing some-body else? There was something about this girl with her butter-soft, brown skin, sweet smell, and irresistible taste.

And fucking her... she had the kind of pussy I'd heard about but never experienced. The kind that would have a nigga feeling shit and making promises, have him up doing stupid stuff like cooking breakfast and making sure she got her rest. If I had the ability to feel guilty, I might feel bad for keeping her on my dick all night long. After finding out she was a virgin, that wasn't my plan. But then, she'd tried to leave, and I realized I didn't want her to. I wasn't about to give her any ideas by just admitting that shit, so I kept her busy until she was too tired to do anything else but fall asleep next to me.

Until last night, that was shit I hated. I needed my space. I fucked women in hotel rooms and left them there. I didn't touch them after I was satisfied, didn't shower or bathe with them, didn't feel them shivering with cold in the middle of the night and pull them close to me. Dream fucked all that up. If I was thinking with the right head, I'd wake her ass up, put her out, and never see her again. Instead, I walked downstairs, into the sunlight-filled room I considered my sanctuary. For several minutes, I looked at the blank space in front of me, already knowing what I wanted to fill it. I closed my eyes, let it take shape behind my lids. Sliding in my AirPods, I went to work.

I was so caught up in what I was doing that I almost ignored my phone when it rang three and a half hours later. I grabbed it off my desk and looked down at the number. *Eve.* I answered because she rarely called, and I wanted to make sure no one was fucking with her about her recently departed baby daddy.

"Hey," I answered.

"You busy?" she asked, getting right to the point.

"What's up?"

"Can I come over?"

For some reason, I thought of Dream. Yeah, she was sleeping, but— I shook my head, dropping the thought. Eve had always made time for me, so I made time for her.

"Yeah."

"See you in thirty."

She hung up without saying anything else. Eve was hood enough not to trust phones, even if it was nothing major. I needed to get ready before she popped up. Opening the door, I stepped out into the hallway. I stopped in my tracks when I saw Dream standing there, looking around. She tried to peek into the room I'd just come out of, but I shut the door quickly and made sure it was locked.

"What you doing?" I asked her.

Looking up at me, she bit down on her bottom lip. I noticed she did that shit when she was thinking... or when that little pussy was getting hot. I waited for whatever she was about to say, my eyes sliding over her curvy frame. She had that thin little robe pulled on over one of my wife beaters that she'd slept in after she ate and showered. That whole little get up left nothing to the imagination. Her pretty double D-cups were sitting up, straining against the shirt, lifting it so that her smooth thighs were on display. It took everything in me not to back her against the wall, make her wrap her legs around me, and fuck her senseless.

"I was looking for you. My sister is getting married this weekend and we have a lot to do. I need to go," she said, twisting her hands in front of her.

I nodded at her. "I'll see you tonight, then."

Her eyes flew to mine in surprise. "Tonight? Damien, I can't spend every night here, at least not this week..."

Her voice trailed off as I moved closer to her. Lifting both her hands, she pressed them against my chest, like that would hold me back. I tilted her chin up with my finger, making sure she didn't drop her eyes.

"You asked for this to start. So, you gon' stay when I want you to stay."

"Fine, but it can't be like today. I have an appointment to get my braids taken down in the morning so I can get my hair done Friday," she protested.

"You'll make it."

She sucked her teeth, disbelief all over her. I smirked at her.

"You will. As long as you stop spreading those thick ass thighs every time I touch you."

Her mouth fell open in shock, before she wrinkled her

nose and frowned at me. "I do not... Ugh! You so nasty. And don't be looking at my thighs."

Her lips were saying one thing, but her body was on something else. Reaching out, I stroked a finger across one of her suddenly hard nipples before pulling on it. I raised an eyebrow at her. Embarrassed, she pushed my hand away.

"Whatever! My body is just reacting to how cold you keep it in here!" she snapped.

I didn't even respond to that lie. Instead, I walked past her toward the stairs. I needed to get cleaned up and dressed before Eve got here. After I showered, I dried off quickly and left the bathroom, a towel wrapped around my waist. Dream was in front of my dresser mirror, getting ready. She glanced up when I walked out. Seeing me in just a towel, she looked away so fast that I smiled. I walked up behind her, pressing my body against the back of the yellow, sleeveless dress she wore. The material hugged her ass and set off the glow of her pretty brown skin.

"W-what are you doing?" she stuttered.

"You in the way. I need underwear."

"Sorry. Excuse me."

She waited for me to move so that she could step away. I took my time, getting so close to her, I heard her breathing pick up and saw the quick movement of her chest in and out. Finally, I let her move. She stood back, waiting without looking at me. I wasn't that polite. I stared at her for a moment in that dress that hugged her body. The top crossed over itself, leaving a vee that put her cleavage on display. Dream was blessed up top and watching her breasts jiggle as I moved inside her had to be one of the sexiest things I'd ever seen.

I grabbed what I needed and went into my closet to get dressed. By the time I had put on some jeans, a black t-shirt, and a pair of Dior sneakers, she was still putting on makeup.

"You slow," I told her.

She glared at me. "If I didn't have to spend ten minutes covering up all the marks on my neck..." she mumbled.

I walked out of the room. I had barely made it into the living room when the doorbell rang. I could count on one hand how many people had my address, but I checked my phone anyway and made sure it was Eve. She smiled as I opened the door and stood back to let her in. Plopping down on my couch, she crossed her legs before looking up at me.

"So. How you doing?" she asked.

I sat on the love seat, waiting for her to get to the point. She sighed.

"One day, you gon' learn how to carry on a normal conversation."

I shook my head. "People use all them words and don't be saying shit. I'm good."

She rolled her eyes before fluffing her burgundy hair. "Anyway, I just wanted to come tell you—"

She stopped suddenly at the sound of footsteps on the stairs. Her eyes flew to me, curiosity on her face.

"Why you didn't tell me somebody was here?" she hissed.

I shrugged. "You didn't ask."

Dream came into view a few seconds later. "Okay, I'm—"

Her eyes landed on Eve, and she frowned before quickly smoothing out her face. Eve looked back and forth between me and her, a smile slowly spreading across her lips. She popped up off the couch and walked toward Dream, who stood there looking stiff and proper, her duffel bag over her shoulder and a garment bag across her arms.

"Demon, you got a girl up in here? Nigga—"

"Chill," I warned her.

Eve ignored me, of course, holding out her hand to Dream. Dream took it hesitantly, shaking it like she didn't want to.

"Hey! I'm Eve, Demon's—"

"Eve." I cut her off, standing and walking closer to them.

Our relationship was none of Dream's business. I watched as they eyed each other, Eve, nosy as hell and probably happy —she was always telling me I needed a woman—and Dream, making her own wrong assumptions. I didn't feel the need to correct her.

"I'm Dream," she finally said coldly, pulling her hand away.

Eve's smile faded a little as Dream turned her attention back to me. Her face looked cool, but her brown eyes were blazing.

"Have a good day, Damien."

She turned on the high heel that matched the shade of her dress perfectly, thinking she was about to walk out and dismiss me. Shorty had me all fucked up.

"I'll see you tonight, Dream."

She froze for a second before slowly facing me again, a fake smile on her face.

"I really don't think that's a good idea. Like I said, I have a lot to do—"

"Like I said, I'll see you tonight."

I could feel Eve staring, wondering what the fuck was going on.

"We'll see," Dream said.

I let her leave, unworried about whatever she was talking about. Her heels clicked across the stone floor of my kitchen, and I heard the door to the garage open. Eve waited a few seconds before pushing my shoulder and starting to run her mouth.

"Nigga! Who is Ms. Bourgeois? You really let a bitch know where you lay your head—"

"She not a bitch."

She covered her mouth with both hands, her eyes getting big. "And you defending her? Oh, shit—"

"Eve, why are you here?" I asked, trying to redirect her.

"She really was *not* happy to see me. I don't blame her,

though. Let me come out of my nigga's bedroom and another bi—woman standing there. She reacted better than I would have."

"I'm not her nigga," was all I said.

Sucking her teeth, she pranced back over to the couch and sat down.

"I'm ready. Tell me all about her."

She knew that shit was not about to happen. I just looked at her. Finally, she sighed.

"Fine. You always such an asshole, Demon."

"Thank you," I said. "Wassup?"

Her face softened, her eyes filling with tears before she rubbed them away. "I just came to say thank you. I wasn't expecting that but—"

"Eve. I don't know what you talking about," I said, ready for this conversation to be over.

"Whatever, Demon. You saved me. Again. One day, I'ma pay you back."

My head snapped up. That shit pissed me off. Eve could never owe me because she'd saved me a hundred times in my fucked-up childhood. But I didn't know how to tell her that, so I just ignored her comment.

"Anything else going on?" I asked.

She looked down for a minute and all my alarms went off.

"What, Eve?"

She cleared her throat. "It's just... his... umm... his brother been asking me stuff, saying little shit—"

"I'm sure that nigga will stop being curious," I told her.

I knew he would. Dead niggas didn't ask questions.

"Demon! No! It's okay. For real. He's, like, twenty and he goes to college up north. He's just annoying."

I looked at her skeptically. "You gon' let me know if he gets more than annoying."

It wasn't a question. I didn't get in her business, but I felt some type of way about not knowing that sorry ass nigga was hitting on her. She should've told me long ago. If his brother turned out to be a problem, I wanted to handle that shit quickly.

"Yes. I promise."

She stood up then, grabbing her purse. "I know you ain't one for company and MJ probably driving Mama Hazel crazy."

"Shit. Ms. Hazel can handle any damn kid that comes through. How's he doing?"

Seeing his little face bruised like that fucked with me, made me remember shit better left buried.

Eve laughed. "True about Mama. And he's okay, Demon. But I'ma go because you got some explaining and begging to do."

I didn't even bother to respond to that ridiculous shit. She walked up to me and, before I could step back, threw her arms around me in a quick hug.

"See? That didn't kill you," she said. "Now, go get yo' girl. And you gon' tell me one day."

"Tell you what?" I asked, walking her to the door and opening it.

She slid on the sunglasses that had been resting in her hair before stepping outside and looking at me. "Why you the fucking roughest nigga out here and you gon' go get you a bourgeois li'l princess."

I closed the door in her face, ignoring the sound of her laughter.

CHAPTER 33

Dream

DAYANA WAS GOING to be a beautiful bride. I watched as she stood in the mirror, looking at herself as the dress-fitter flitted around her. The strapless, hand-embroidered, feather-trimmed, silk organza gown by Oscar de la Renta showed off her hourglass figure while looking impossibly classy and chic. Her flawless brown skin was radiant against the white. She looked perfect, except for the lack of a smile on her face. I knew she was keeping something from me, and I'd been trying to wait until she was ready to talk about it. I didn't know how much longer I could hold my questions and my thoughts in, though.

But, hell, who was I to offer her advice about anything man-related? I had just spent the night with a man who fucked me countless times, then had the next bitch at his house hours later. My heart had dropped when I made it to the bottom of those stairs and saw her sitting there. It didn't help that she was beautiful and bubbly with her wavy burgundy bob, smooth tan skin, and big, sparkling eyes. And then, the way she'd been about to introduce herself, *"I'm Eve, Demon's..."* He'd cut her off, but I wondered what she was about to say. Surely not his girlfriend. She was way too calm for that, given the fact that I'd come down from his bedroom carrying bags. Maybe Juliette had sent her. The thought pissed me off and then I got pissed off at being pissed off. Damien was not my man. This was a deal, a thirty-day fuck before I moved on with my life.

"What you doing over here, frowning?" Dayana inquired, breaking into my thoughts.

"What were you doing over there, frowning?" I shot back.

Rolling her eyes, she disappeared into the back of the store to get out of the dress. Thirty minutes later, we were sitting in the Tahoe we'd borrowed from Daddy to make sure we had room for our dresses.

"Where we going for dinner?" my sister asked, reapplying her lipstick in the visor mirror.

I side-eyed her from my spot in the passenger seat before settling back and closing my eyes.

"Who said we were going to dinner?" I mumbled.

I felt a sudden, sharp smack. My eyes flew open as I grabbed my injured shoulder.

"Ouch! Yana!"

"Bitch, you playing! You come waltzing yo' ass in the house after four o'clock after being out all night, popping that little pussy. We didn't have time to talk because we had to rush to get our dresses, thanks to you. So, you crazy if you think we ain't about to go somewhere and you give me alllllllll the details," my sister ranted.

It was my turn to roll my eyes as one of the employees opened the back door and another arranged the bags that contained our dresses.

"Do you have to be so dramatic?" I hissed.

She just smiled and waited until our dresses were loaded. As soon as the door closed, she glared at me.

"Whatever. Now, where we going?"

I sighed. "I'm kind of tired."

"I'll bet," she muttered.

"Let's just go home, order something, and talk in my room."

She sucked her teeth like I was getting on her nerves.

"I mean... unless you want to go back to Smoke's place," I taunted.

She pulled away from the building. "You think you so funny. Just open DoorDash and find something good."

———

Dayana had barely chewed the mouthful of baked rigatoni before she looked at me expectantly.

"Okay. Start talking."

"You know, if Mama could see you eating all that pasta and cheese three days before your wedding, she'd die," I said.

She waved her hand, frowning. "Girl, fuck that dress. Don't try to get off the subject."

I grabbed my favorite yellow throw off my bed and pulled it down to the floor where we were sitting. Wrapping it around my shoulders, I eyed her.

"Fine. Ask what you want to know."

She clapped her hands. "Tell me everything."

I shook my head. "I'm not doing that. Ask me something."

"Whatever! Okay. Was it good?"

"It was fine, Yana," I said reluctantly.

She looked at me in disbelief. "You stayed gone that long and it was just *fine*? Why you holding out?"

"Yana—"

She stood up suddenly and I saw the look of hurt on her face. Picking up her plate and cup, she looked down at me.

"It's cool, Dream. It's your business and I know it's not like it was this grand romantic thing. I just thought—"

"It was good, Yana. It was better than good. Like, that rose toy you gave me has *nothing* on him," I blurted.

"Biiiiitch," she whispered, slowly sitting back down.

"I-I mean, it hurt at first—"

"I know," she mumbled.

I paused, the forkful of chicken piccata halfway to my mouth as I eyed her suspiciously.

"Bitch, what you mean you know?"

"Girl, nothing! I just meant that I've heard," she said, brushing off my question. "Go ahead."

I frowned at her but decided to let her make it... for now.

"Once I got past the pain, oh my God, Yana! And you were right. He's definitely got Big Dick Energy. Girl, I finally understand what people mean when they say a third leg."

We squealed at the same time, then giggled before she clapped her hands again.

"Okay. Yo' ass was gone all day, so he got stamina like I said, right?" she asked excitedly.

I blinked my eyes at her, my smile widening. "I really shouldn't kiss and tell..."

"Dream!"

"Five times. I spent the day recovering, hell."

Her mouth fell open. "Oh, my God! You must be so sore!"

"Sore is not the word. I just want to sit my poor little kitty in a tub full of Epsom salts or something. And it doesn't help that he likes to bite."

"Really?"

"Yes!" I smiled at her again. "But I like it, too."

We laughed again, stopping only when there was a soft knock on the door.

"Come in!" I called.

The door opened and my father stepped in. For a minute, the room was silent. I hoped my face didn't look as guilty as Dayana's or he'd know just what we'd been talking about.

"Sounds like y'all having a good time. What's up?"

"Just girl talk," Dayana said mysteriously.

"Mm-hmm," Daddy said before turning his attention to me. "You didn't come home last night."

I glanced up at him, suddenly uncomfortable. "I… umm… I was with Damien," I admitted softly.

He looked confused. "Who?"

"Demon," my sister volunteered.

I could tell the minute he realized what that meant. He frowned before quickly trying to hide it.

"You okay?" he asked.

"I'm fine, Daddy."

"You—" He stopped and shook his head. "I'm sorry, Dream." He sighed before closing the door.

He looked so dejected and sounded so worried about me. Here I was, about to dish about my multiple orgasms, and my father was concerned for me. I—

Dayana waved her hand in front of my face, interrupting my thoughts.

"Girl, stop looking like that. They rely on you way too much to fix stuff, from money problems to other shit. You deserve to get some enjoyment out of it."

I nodded slowly, although I still felt kind of bad. "Yeah. You right."

"I wanna know one thing, though," she said, tilting her head.

"You wanna know a lot of shit. What is it, Dayana?"

"If it was so good… why didn't you want to tell me at first?"

"Oh," I said dryly.

"Oh?"

"Yana, he made me breakfast, then told me to take a nap because I didn't get much sleep."

"Awww!" she cooed. "That's so sweet."

"Bitch! I woke up and he had a hood super model there!"

Her smile turned into a scowl so fast that it was funny. "No, this nigga didn't! Did you have to fight or—"

I could see my sister hyping herself up. I held up a hand, trying to settle her down.

"No, no, Yana! It wasn't like that. She was friendly and shit. Introduced herself and everything."

"Oh," she said with a shrug. "So, she wasn't his girlfriend. The nigga can have friends."

"He can have whatever he wants. It's not my business," I said, hoping I sounded nonchalant.

Dayana sucked her teeth. "Whatever, girl," she said, shoveling another bite of rigatoni into her mouth.

We talked for another hour before I fell asleep on her. Once she left, I took a quick shower and slid into a tank top and pajama pants before collapsing across the bed. It felt like I was only asleep for five minutes before Dayana was back in my room, shaking my leg and jumping up and down. I rubbed a hand over my face, trying to wipe the sleep out of my eyes before glaring at her.

"Bitch, what is wrong with you?"

"Bitch, get up! The doorbell just rang and guess who the security system shows it is?" she asked, sounding too excited about my level of sleepiness.

"Dayana, I don't know," I whined. "Can you just—"

"It's Damien, Dream!"

"What?" I sat up so fast that I got dizzy. "Yana!"

"I know!"

"Can you go get the door before Daddy does? Did you see him earlier? If he sees Damien, he gon' have a heart attack," I whispered, scrambling out of bed and shoving my feet into my slippers.

"I got you." She turned to walk out.

"Tell him I'm asleep. But wait till I get down there!"

I hurriedly ran into the bathroom. I splashed my face with

cold water, gargled some Listerine, and ran a hand through my braids… just in case. I crept down the stairs.

"Now?" Dayana hissed.

"Wait," I said, ducking into one of the hallways off the living room. I could hear them from here, but I wouldn't be able to see them. "Okay!"

Seconds later, I heard the door open.

"Heyyyy! Damien, right?" she said brightly.

"Nah. Most people call me Demon," he corrected.

"Right… okay, *Demon*. I'm Dayana. Please, come in."

"I'm good. Where's Dream?"

"She's… ummm… she's asleep."

That girl was a terrible liar, because she usually said whatever the hell was on her mind.

"Go wake her up."

Silence. My sister didn't know how to deal with a man that just gave orders like that. I knew because I was still getting used to it.

"I… don't think that's a good idea. She's tired, as I'm sure you know," Dayana finally spoke up.

I was going to kill her, I swear! And again, with the silence! I knew his ass was probably just standing there, waiting to be obeyed. *Ugh!* I had just decided to reveal myself when I heard Grandpapa behind me.

"Dream? What the hell you doing? You didn't hear someone at the door?"

Oh, my God! I couldn't believe how loud he was! I felt myself blushing, knowing I was busted. Taking a deep breath, I stepped forward and stumbled over my own feet.

"You clumsy now?" Grandpapa snapped.

I glared at the old man before I looked toward the door. Dayana stood there smirking, the raggedy heifer, and Damien's eyes were focused on me. I cleared my throat.

"Hello, Damien. I told you I—"

"Go get your shit, Dream," he said.

His voice was quiet, but commanding.

"I—"

"So, one night of defiling my granddaughter wasn't enough, huh?" Grandpapa asked from behind me.

I dropped my head.

CHAPTER 34

Demon

THE NIGGAS around her had obviously been letting her run shit for too long. I didn't care what she did in her office; I understood women had to be tough and independent to get ahead in that world. I didn't care what she did with the other niggas in her life. If their weak asses let her dominate, that was on them. But the fact that she ignored what I said? That shit was unacceptable.

Which was why I stood outside her door at ten o'clock, ready to make sure she understood I meant whatever I told her. She was coming home with me tonight—and any night that I wanted her—no arguments, no explanations. I wasn't expecting to deal with her grandfather, though.

Lucien Dumont was legendary. He'd started out in his hometown of New Orleans and took over the city before branching out and making deals all over the South and Southwest. Dumont was rich, respected, and ruthless. And, just like any nigga in his position, he had people out to get him. Years ago, some nigga who had started making a name for himself decided Dumont was his main competition. He caught Dumont out with his wife at a jazz concert at a spot that had been declared neutral. The nigga ignored it and had his team light Dumont and his wife up. She died instantly. Dumont survived. If the rumors were true, he did some shit that even I admired. He had his crew kidnap the nigga who ordered the shooting and made him watch as he tortured and killed every member of his family before taking him out. And then, Dumont walked away from it all, leaving his empire to his right hand.

He stared at me coldly, and I could see the savage he used to be. I respected that.

"Come in," he said.

I nodded once, then stepped over the threshold. Dayana closed the door behind me.

"Grandpapa—" Dream said, her eyes darting back and forth between me and him.

He held up two fingers, silencing her.

"You made a deal, granddaughter. Our word is our bond. Go get your things."

She gasped, her eyes big as hell, unable to believe what he said to her.

"But—"

"Dayana, go help her."

They both looked at him like he had grown an extra head or some shit, but finally, Dream stalked off toward the stairs, Dayana on her heels. Lucien turned back to me.

"I won't ask you what your intentions for my grand-daughter are. The fact that you're here this time of night tells me what they are."

I didn't say anything, just waited for him to get whatever he needed to off his chest.

"But, then again, you came for her, and you handled Isaac Stone, so I'm thinking this... *situation* might be more than you expected."

I opened my mouth to deny what he said, but he shook his head.

"Don't waste your time telling me it's all about a fuck or

some good pussy. A man with your money and reputation has access to plenty of good pussy. I know. I lived that life once. But anyway, let's get some shit straight. I love my son-in-law. I stand behind him on most things. But he has a soft spot for DeAngelo. That boy has always gotten away with murder and Dream is always trying to fix what he fucks up. This was not her deal… her sacrifice to make."

"I know," I admitted.

"But you still took her," he pointed out.

There was nothing I could say to that, and he knew it. A small smile crossed his lips.

"I love all my grandchildren, but it's no secret that Dream is my heart. I hate to see anything bad come her way. I hope she makes it through this month with you without losing herself. You're a powerful man, Demon Montana, and a dangerous one. But don't underestimate an old man in a wheelchair. I won't insult you by threatening you. But I *will* make you a promise. If you hurt her, you will regret it. Deeply."

No one talked to me like that. Ever. I didn't know anyone brave enough to try it. It was enough to get a nigga killed. But looking at Lucien Dumont, I knew he meant every word. And for some fucked up reason, I felt my respect for him grow.

"I'm not trying to hurt her," I finally said.

He nodded. The sounds of footsteps on the stairs ended our conversation. Dream appeared first with her bag, her body tense, her cocoa brown eyes glittering. She was mad as fuck, but I didn't care.

"You ready?" I asked.

Refusing to speak, she crossed her arms over her chest and walked to the door. Yanking it open, she left without saying anything to her family. She walked to her car and was about to get in when I called her name. She looked over at me, frowning. Silently, I walked to the passenger side of my truck and opened the door. She huffed out a breath.

"I told you, I have places to be tomorrow—"

"You gon' get there. Come get in."

She stared at me. I raised my eyebrow and waited. Mumbling, she marched over to the truck and climbed in, throwing her bag in the back. I waited until she was buckled and settled in before closing her door.

"Nigga, don't be acting like you got manners now," she snapped through the window.

Shaking my head, I walked around to the driver's side. She was quiet for the first ten minutes of the drive. Then she turned in her seat so she could glare at me better, I guess.

"My deal is with you," she announced.

"I know that. I was there, remember?"

"Nobody else. So, if you came and got me because you got some little threesome planned, that's a no."

I shot her a quick look, frowning. "Fuck is you talking about now?"

She sucked her teeth like I was being slow. I really had no idea what she was talking about. Hell, if she knew how I felt about that little pussy, she'd know sharing it was the last thing I wanted to do.

"Your little girlfriend from earlier. If she still here, I am not—"

That's what she was on? I wanted to laugh at her little mean ass.

"Eve? You talking about Eve? You stay making assumptions, huh? You sound crazy as hell."

"I don't give a fuck how I sound. Just know that I mean it," she popped.

"You was just a virgin yesterday. How you know you don't want some pretty girl sucking on that clit while I fill up that pussy?" I asked, fucking with her.

"You so vulgar. Don't say shit to me with that nasty mouth."

But when I looked over at her, she was biting on her bottom lip. *Little freak.*

"And, FYI, my grandfather is right. I keep my word, but just so you know, fucking you is the last thing I wanna do right now."

I guess I was supposed to be fucked up by that, but I was too close to laughing at her dramatic, lying ass.

"Oh, yeah?"

"Yeah."

After that, she gave me the silent treatment all the way to my house and into my bedroom. She stood beside my bed, shivering and glaring at me. I watched as she rubbed her arms, trying to get warm.

"If you wanted somebody to come stay in this big ass house with you, the least you could do is turn the AC up from arctic blast to deep freeze," she snapped.

That shit hit a little too close to home. For some reason, I wanted her ass here, but that was none of her business.

"Who said I wanted somebody to come stay with me? You feeling yourself too much, shorty," I said, my voice low.

"Whatever. Why am I here, then? You could've left me at home, asleep."

Smiling, I stroked a finger across her cheek. She looked like she wanted to bite my hand off. I was about to relieve her of that attitude real quick.

"Don't worry, Dream. I'ma put yo' ass back to sleep."

She made a soft sound as I reached for the hem of her tank top and pulled it over her head, revealing a silky green bra. I found the matching panties as I pulled her pajama pants down her legs. I stripped the panties off, too, leaving her standing there in her bra. I eased my hand between her legs, my fingers finding the softness of her pussy. She was soaking wet, despite her attitude. I smirked down at her as I worked two fingers inside her. Her eyes fluttered closed as she bit back a moan and rocked against my hand, her hungry walls clamping down on my fingers. I withdrew them slowly and she whimpered a protest. Pretty brown eyes tangled with mine as I slid my fingers into my mouth, greedy for the taste of her.

"Damien," she whispered, her voice and her eyes glazed with lust.

I didn't answer, slipping my index finger between her lips instead. She inhaled sharply, surprised at the move. But then, her mouth closed as she sucked the last of her essence off. I withdrew my finger before my lips met hers in a quick, hungry kiss. Satisfied, I lay back on the bed.

"Come here," I ordered.

She hesitated for a moment, but she finally climbed on top of me, straddling my thighs as she looked down at me.

"Nah. I mean here."

I slid my hands under her and picked her up. Surprised, she shrieked as I carried her forward until her smooth lower lips were right above my mouth, her soft thighs on each side of my face.

"Damien, no! I'm too heavy for—"

My tongue snaked out. She stopped talking as my mouth explored the sweetness between her legs. She came twice, bucking and grinding against my mouth before I pulled her under me. I trailed my dick through the slickness between her thighs, tapping against her clit as she twisted against the bed.

"Damien—"

I pressed inside her a little bit. She moaned, lifting her hips, inviting me all the way in. Holding her down, I leaned forward, resting my lips against her ear.

"You don't wanna fuck me right now, though, remember?"

She whimpered, her nails gripping my back as she tried to pull me closer.

"Tell me to stop, Dream," I teased, moving back and forth just a little bit.

"Damien—"

I loved her voice when she sighed my name like that. It took everything in me not to pound into her.

"Tell me again you don't want it right now."

Her eyes were half open, her teeth locked on her bottom lip. I brushed my mouth against hers.

"Dream… you want me to stop, right?"

She gave in finally, her legs locking around me as she said, "No, don't stop… please… *Damien…*"

She barely had the words out before I was deep inside her, stroking her as I felt her cum around me. I buried my face against her neck, inhaling her as I tried to imprint myself on her walls.

This girl, man. This girl.

CHAPTER 35

Dayana

(*THURSDAY*, *June 10*)

It was the opening everyone had been waiting for all year. The establishment was simply called Bliss and it was predicted that, next to Dante's Inferno, it would be the hottest spot in the city. My bachelorette party would end there tonight, hopefully with us so fucked up that I forgot about this wedding… and Smoke Salinas, at least for a little while. But first, we were partying and pre-gaming at Parker's house. Dream, my bridesmaids, and a few other friends were all there, sipping on mixed drinks that I swear had only a splash of juice or whatever mixer Parker lied like she was using. I was mostly holding mine—no use in getting drunk before we even headed out. Poor Crystal was nursing a glass of orange juice.

"Smile, trick. You supposed to be having fun," Dream said, standing in front of me with her hands on her hips.

"Damn, Dream, didn't anybody tell you yo' ass ain't supposed to outshine the bride?" I asked, grinning up at her.

On some real shit, my sister looked fabulous. Her hair, light brown with gorgeous blonde highlights, fell past her shoulders in its natural spiral curls. She'd let me buy her outfit for tonight and her curves were everything. She wore a fitted, slightly cropped, black and gray camo top with the word "Glamorous" lettered in red above her breasts. Her bottom half was poured into a pair of tight black jeans—she'd fought me on that, but I won, as usual. And I was going to steal the red, patent leather Impera pumps by Louboutin she wore. She might be modest with her clothes, but my sister's shoe game was everything. Her face was lightly made up, but it wasn't the cosmetics that had this bitch glowing. Business deal or not, Demon was obviously fucking her right. You could just tell. She rolled her eyes at me before taking a sip of her drink and dropping onto the couch beside me.

"Girl, no one ever outshines you. You look so damn perfect that I'd hate you if you weren't my baby sister," she said.

Okay, I had to admit that I looked good in the coral-colored, satin mini dress I wore. It was cut higher and ruched on one side—revealing most of one of my thighs—and had a plunging neckline that put the girls on display. Because it was my night, I wore a tiara in my wavy hair and Parker had draped a "Bride-to-Be" sash over me. The neutral, crystal-embellished Gianvito Rossi pumps I wore were the perfect complement to the bold color of the dress.

"I think it's safe to say we'll be the baddest bitches there," I said smugly.

"Oh, definitely. Now, drink that. We getting to' up tonight. Crystal just triple-checked with DeAngelo that we'll have a driver to and from Bliss."

I sighed. "Dream—"

She shook her head, refusing to listen. "No, ma'am. No excuses. We never really cut loose, always worried about our reputations and shit. Daddy just gon' be mad tonight, cuz I'm trying to make sure we known as 'them wild Castle sisters.'"

She tapped her cup against mine and I decided not to argue. By the time we arrived at Bliss two hours later, I was slightly buzzed and loving it. I felt sorry for the people lining the block to get in, but money brought privileges, and I was about to enjoy them. We were escorted to our VIP section on the third floor where it was clear, from the multiple screens to the plush leather couches and chairs, that no expense had been spared on this place. Bliss provided security, but two of our own guys guarded the entrance to our area.

"This shit is nice," Laina, one of my bridesmaids, commented.

"Hell yeah," Parker agreed as we settled on the comfortable furniture.

Bottle girls appeared not long after we were seated, their hands full of sparklers and bottles. Dream had mostly ordered liquor and mixers, but one of the girls set a bottle of Opus One in front of me. Looking up, I grinned at my big sister, who was already mixing something. She winked at me.

"You know I always got you," she said.

Her words unexpectedly brought tears to my eyes. She did always have me—me and DeAngelo—no matter the cost to her. That's why it was so hard keeping the shit about Jordan away from her... and the truth about Smoke.

Walking out of his office the other day was the hardest thing I'd ever done. I wanted to stay with him... hell, I wanted to *be* with him again. He hadn't texted me since that day and I missed him. Some crazy part of me wanted him to fight for me. But fight for what? One stolen night of passion? That's all we had. At least, that's what I was telling myself. But damn, it felt like so much more and it seemed like he felt it, too. It was all so confusing. And so impossible, I reminded myself as my eyes fell on my engagement ring.

Dream cleared her throat. I looked up and her eyes were glued to my face.

"What's wrong?"

Blinking away the tears, I smiled at her.

"Girl, nothing. I'm 'bout to pour up."

I did just that, taking a sip before I stood up and began to vibe with City Girls. With my crew acting as hype women, I had a mini twerk session with my sister right beside me. Feeling conceited, I was loving the lyrics. I don't know how I managed to dance and empty my cup, but I did. One of my girls refilled it and pressed it back into my hand just as Li'l Durk's voice surrounded us. I slowed down and closed my eyes, rapping along in my head.

"You look like you're having a good time."

My eyes sprang open at the voice. Remembering that we were in public with an audience, I kept the scowl off my face. I wish I had told our guards not to let him in, but I knew they assumed it was okay since he was my fiancé.

"What are you doing here, Jordan?" I asked dryly.

He stood there, fine as ever, in a black blazer, gray button down, and fitted black slacks. But his looks did nothing for me anymore. Jordan disgusted me—not because he was into BDSM; I had no issue with that and had always been slightly curious. It was the lying and cheating for me. I had no respect for him. I noticed two of his brothers and a few friends with him, circling my girls like vultures. All of them made me sick.

"Bachelor party tonight, remember?" he said, pulling me into a hug.

Swallowing my disgust, I returned the embrace quickly before moving away from him.

"Couldn't you just be cliche and go to a strip joint?"

He looked offended.

"You know my brothers don't do cliche. And I saw where Parker tagged you in a post about where y'all were headed so—"

"So, you followed me? Are you serious, Jordan?" I hissed, unable to hide the frown this time.

I cleared my face quickly when I noticed Dream's eyes on me. I could tell by how she shifted her body and tightened her lips that she was ready to go to war. I wasn't going to let her, not tonight. Jordan looked down at me, his expression frustrated.

"Damn, Dayana, it's the only way I've been able to see you—"

"I been busy."

"We're getting married in less than forty-eight hours. You—"

I blocked out the rest of his words, the mention of the wedding enough to make me sick. Closing my eyes, I took a deep breath and took a minute to get my shit together. When I reopened them, I had pasted a smile on my face.

"Jordan. Please go to your section with your friends. Let me enjoy my party and I'll see you at the wedding shower tomorrow," I said.

He stared at me for a moment before sighing.

"Yeah, okay. But this attitude better be gone by tomorrow. I—"

"See you later," I interrupted him.

Leaning forward, he kissed me before I could escape it. I swallowed the urge to throw up. I'd never noticed how cold and lifeless his lips felt. Maybe because now, I was comparing them to Smoke's warm, smooth ones. *Stop it, Dayana,* I scolded myself. Clutching my cup tightly, I watched as he and his crew left our section. Dream was in my face a second later.

"You good?"

"Hell yeah. Let's go dance," I said, not giving her time to go into one of her interrogations.

By the time we made it to the main floor, the DJ was playing a dance mix. I was glad because I wanted to bounce my ass and forget about this coming weekend. Most of my wedding party had followed us downstairs and we danced and laughed together. Dream was serious about letting her hair down and I loved to see it. I was cheering her on when Parker elbowed me.

"Ouch, bitch! What?" I snapped.

"Girl, do you see how that nigga looking at your sister? I knew that day at the restaurant something was up, with her lying ass. Then, he showed up at the office and she was looking star-struck when he left! Is she fucking him? She better be fucking him!" she whispered.

My eyes swept the area around us, and I froze when they landed on Demon. His gaze was stuck on Dream and her ass was fucking clueless. So clueless that when this fine ass, chocolate, Greek god of a nigga asked her to dance, she happily started grinding her ass against his pelvis. I yanked her so hard that she stumbled. The only thing holding her up was the guy's fingers in her back pockets. I frowned at him trying to touch my sister's ass.

"Yana, what the fuck—"

"I'm ready to go back upstairs. I need a refill," I lied.

"And, umm… I got something for y'all, too!" Parker added.

"Y'all full of shit," she muttered, but she started toward the spiral staircase.

"Hol' on, li'l mama. Let me get yo' number," the guy said.

My eyes widened as she turned around, smiling, and accepted his phone. But Demon just watched. This nigga would probably be dead later. My sister didn't see it, but the stories she told me about her "Damien" let me know the nigga was crazy possessive. Dream put her number in and then switched her ass over to the stairs.

Parker really had something for us. Once we were back in our seats, she pushed a small piece of candy in both our hands.

"Remember, it just takes a little. It gets you up there quicker than smoking," she instructed before walking off.

Dream looked at me.

"Did she mean just a little, like this whole candy because it's small, or did she mean break a piece off the candy?"

I shrugged. "I don't know. It can't be that bad, little as it is. Plus, we getting fucked up, anyway."

"You right," she agreed.

We popped the chewy candies in our mouths, eating them quickly before we stood to dance some more. For twenty minutes, I was unimpressed. It was my first time eating an edible and I didn't feel shit. Then, suddenly, I felt... different, like I was outside my body, looking at myself. I danced a little more, but everything was moving crazy, and my legs felt funny. I glanced at my sister.

"Dream? I think I'ma sit down," I announced.

She nodded. "Yeah, me, too."

Slowly, on unsteady legs, I made it back to one of the couches. Dream sat down beside me. We looked at each other, then burst out giggling.

"Oh, my God. What did she give us?" I asked.

"I'on know, but I'on want no more," Dream mumbled back.

"Me, either."

I lost all sense of time as I sat there, watching people around us move in slow motion. I wanted to get up and walk or dance or something, but I didn't trust my legs. Hell, I wasn't even sure I could feel them. Looking down, I sighed in relief when I saw they were still there.

"It is so colorful in here, Yana. Just colors, colors every-where," my sister said suddenly.

"Like a kaleidoscope," I agreed.

"It's kinda moving like that, too."

"Mm-hmm."

I knew we sounded fucked up as hell, but I couldn't do anything about it. I giggled, then slapped a hand over my mouth. Dream pulled it away.

"Noooo! Please laugh. You ain't been laughing. You supposed to be happy right now, but you seem like you got so much on my mind. I mean, *your* mind. I been worried about—"

"Dream, I fucked Smoke and I liked it a lot," I blurted out.

She blinked several times, processing what I'd said. Then she just stared at me, speechless.

"I know. It sounds bad. But I caught Jordan cheating first and I met Smoke after that and he kinda took care of me that night and then I saw him again and he was in that suit, and he looked so good, and I fucked him and—"

I knew I was rambling, so I stopped when she held up a hand.

"Bitch, I'm high. Lemme catch up."

I dropped my head in my hands as she mumbled to herself, trying to make sense of what I said.

"Okay, I'm ready," she finally said.

"There's nothing else to say. I'm getting married Saturday."

"Do you wanna get married?"

I shook my head. She shrugged.

"Then, don't get married. If you liked fucking Smoke, just do that some more, hell."

I knew we were high as fuck because she sounded perfectly logical. I shook my head, trying to clear it. Dream popped up suddenly as that Pop Smoke joint, "The Woo," came on.

"This still my shit," she said, gyrating her body.

She looked cute... until she stumbled and fell against Crystal.

"Dream!" I hissed as she and Crys laughed.

"Chill, Yana. Girl, I'm good," she said, waving the shit off.

"Come sit down. It's safer," I coaxed.

Shaking her head, she started dancing again, rapping along with the lyrics. I put my head down on the table—her twisting and turning were making me dizzy.

"I think you're ready to go."

It was Jordan's voice again, and I sighed.

"Can you just go back to your own shit?" I asked without looking up.

"Dream."

My head snapped up then at the sound of my sister's name in that deep voice. Demon stood there behind her. She turned around slowly.

"Damien," she said, mocking him.

"Let's go," he said, his face and voice expressionless.

He sounded so calm—that shit was scary. I'd rather he snapped at her. When I'd first seen him up close, I didn't understand how his cold, vacant eyes didn't freak her the fuck out. But now I understood, because those green eyes were anything but icy when they were on her. Still scary to me. I guess fucking him made her brave, though, because my five-foot-four, never-fought-a-day-in-her-life sister looked up at this muhfuckin' killer, who towered over her by at least a foot, and said, "No. I'm not ready."

I laid my head back on the table and prayed.

CHAPTER 36

Demon

(*A LITTLE WHILE earlier*)

I looked around the room I called my sanctuary, unable, for once, to find any peace there. It was the same story for everywhere I went today. At first, I couldn't figure out why. Nothing was really different. I followed my usual routine, except for the fact that I had to drop Dream off. I went through the motions, working out, showering, cooking, checking on a few investments, but none of it felt right. Finally, I realized what had thrown me off. My ability to be at ease had been fucked ever since *she* made her little announcement. *"Damien, I know we have a deal, but tonight is my sister's bachelorette party, tomorrow, we're busy all day, and Saturday is the wedding. I can see you Sunday."* I was okay at first. I didn't even fuck with people like that, so a few days' break should be fine.

And then the reality set in.

No seeing her. No arguing with her. No tasting her. No feeling her soft body melting into mine. No hearing her sigh my name against my skin or into my pillows. *Fuck, no.* I didn't like the idea of that shit, but I knew from the way her eyes lit up when she mentioned Dayana that they were close.

Even I wasn't enough of an asshole to intrude on her sister's celebrations.

Even if it meant I was sitting here looking stupid as fuck.

I tried to focus on the shit I'd done before she ever stepped foot in my house, but it was useless. I couldn't lie like she wasn't taking up a big piece of my head space. I hated that, wasn't used to wasting my thoughts and my time on women I fucked. They were there for one purpose, and when that was over, I was done. Not with this bossy girl, though, and I couldn't figure that shit out.

I tried to get rid of any sign of her. I changed my sheets twice, hoping not to smell the soft sweetness of her Prada perfume, slid the heels she'd left into the back of my closet, put her lip gloss in a bathroom drawer. None of it did any good. It couldn't erase the memory of her on top of me this morning, moaning as I coached her while she rode my dick slowly, my hands full of her thick hips and ass as I drove up into her.

Before Dream, I hadn't slept with many women more than once. I fucked and lost interest, ready for the next one who caught my attention. But she was different. Yeah, I'd only been fucking her a couple of days, but I'd been drawn to her since I saw her in Dante's office almost a month ago. For now, the more I touched her, the more I wanted her. The thought of not being inside her again until Sunday was fucking with me. But that shit had to wear off in the next few weeks. All pussy got old. Dream would be the same.

She had to be.

My phone vibrated in my hand, and I looked down to see a message from Dante. For once, I was glad. Fucking someone up might take my mind off all this shit. But his text wasn't what I was expecting.

Dante: *Our new place opened tonight. I know you don't give a fuck, but you should come see what you putting your money into.*

I shook my head. It wasn't that I didn't give a fuck. Dante

was good at what he did, and I always had a feeling about what I should invest in. Between his skill and my intuition, I'd made a lot of money. I felt no need to check up on him. I started to turn him down—clubs had never really been my thing. I stopped before I hit send, though. I didn't have shit else to do, so why not?

A little over forty minutes later, I valeted the truck and approached the front of the building. I ignored the line behind me and heard a few voices popping off. Shit went silent when I turned around, though. The guy at the door took one look at me and shook his head.

"Gentlemen are not allowed in in denim," he announced.

I knew the place was upscale, but I hadn't wanted to change out of jeans and my t-shirt, so I didn't.

"That's cool. I'm not a gentleman," I told him.

He sighed and rolled his eyes. "Sir, please don't make me have you escorted off the property."

I shrugged. "You can try."

Pressing his lips together, he mugged me before snapping, "Carl! Lex!"

I watched as two of Dante's black-suited goons appeared in the doorway, scowls in place, ready to threaten someone. I smiled as their faces changed.

"Let me holla at you right quick," Carl told the guy letting people in, yanking him back into the building.

Of course, when he reappeared, a nigga's whole attitude had changed. I watched his weak ass fall over himself to let me in and congratulate me on my new business venture. Bitch made nigga.

Dante had the place laid out. That was no surprise. If nothing else, he and Sherrilyn had good taste. Shit, Sherrilyn was my stylist for the few fancy events I agreed to attend. Opening night looked like a success, from the line outside to the packed dance floor in front of me. He had texted that he was on the third floor. The nigga and I didn't hang out, but I would acknowledge his presence. I spotted the staircases bracketing each side of the floor and made my way to the closest one until someone in my peripheral vision caught my eye.

She stood under one of the spotlights, winding her curvy body. Her back was to me, and I didn't recognize the thick, highlighted hair, but I knew that shape anywhere, especially the round ass filling out the skintight black pants. Apparently, so did my dick as that shit bricked up instantly. I moved around the floor until Dream's face was visible. She was dancing with a group of other women, a cup clutched tightly in her hand as she bounced along to DJ Chose and Megan. The shit she had on hugged every inch of her body, revealing a little bit of the softness of her stomach. I wanted to grab her, drop one of my hoodies over her head, and hide her from every thirsty nigga staring at her.

I watched as one of them asked her to dance. I knew the little nigga. His name was Smith, and he was Dante's cousin by marriage or some shit. She nodded and turned her back to him, rocking her hips against the nigga before her sister shot me a look, then yanked her away. The shit was vaguely funny because I had no intention of confronting Dream tonight, but I might knock his ass the fuck out. His hands were in her back pockets, and I felt a familiar icy calm wash over me. I hated to see other niggas touch this girl. He said something, handing her his phone, and she gave him her number. I was going to make sure he lost that.

Dream disappeared upstairs with her little crew. Making my way toward the opposite stairwell, I stopped at the feel of a small hand on my arm. I looked down at it for a moment, hating the feeling of someone touching me without permission. Finally, I let my eyes follow the arm up to the face of its owner. A pretty, chocolate shorty stood there, smiling at me. She was everything I usually liked—beautiful, brown-skinned, and built like a model, but I wasn't interested.

"I bet you can't be as mean as you look," she leaned forward and spoke.

I shook her hand off. "You bet wrong."

I found Dante a few minutes later. As usual, the nigga was being a little too extra for me. Security stood all around his section while barely dressed dancers performed for him and his guests. Thousands of dollars' worth of liquor bottles covered the tables and lavish trays of food were spread out. His wife sat in his lap and, while their jewelry was understated, it probably cost as much as this club. Every member of his team had eyes trained on me, but they didn't stop me from walking up to him. He was sitting in a darkened corner, talking to some younger members of his crew, including that Smith nigga. Good. I needed to see him, anyway.

Voices faded as I approached my half-brother. Niggas knew I didn't make idle conversation, so other than a few nods, they didn't greet me. I hid a smile as most of them walked off. I was used to making niggas uncomfortable. Dante patted Sherrilyn on her thigh, and she popped up, walking toward me as he stood.

"Demon," she said, touching one of my shoulders and giving me a half-smile.

"Hey."

I had no issues with Sherrilyn. She'd been with Dante as long as I'd known him, and she'd always been cool to me. I liked that she matched his crazy.

Dante dapped me up, stopping just short of hugging me. Yep. Extra.

"Demon, you made it just in time," he said, turning back to his employees.

"For what?" I asked, voice flat.

"Smith was just telling us about some chick he met downstairs, named Dream."

My eyes clashed with Dante's as a smirk lifted his lips. Nigga was always trying to get a reaction out of me, and I knew exactly how eager he was to see this Dream shit play out publicly. I returned his smile and shrugged. I planned to deal with Smith privately. But then he opened his mouth.

"Dante said it might be this chick you get off with. I told him, 'shit, that's cool.' I ain't never seen you give a fuck about a bitch and who got next."

He laughed as he extended his hand to me, like I was about to shake that shit. I just looked at him until his smile and his hand fell.

"Bitch is fine, though. I know she spent some money on that body—" he kept on, trying to fill the awkward silence.

"Nah, she didn't. And she ain't a bitch," I said calmly.

I slid my hands into my pockets to keep them off of him. I had never given a fuck about shutting shit down, but I kept thinking about how excited Dream had sounded about tonight. For some reason, I was trying not to ruin it. Smith needed to shut the fuck up, right now, though.

"Ohhh. So, that's how shit is?" he asked, chuckling. "I'on blame you, my nigga, especially if that shit all natural. That jiggle must be nice."

My mouth twisted. "I suggest you find something safe to do."

It was the closest thing he was going to get to a warning from me. He held up both hands, like he was done. But a young nigga's pride will fuck him up and he was too stupid to let shit rest.

"I felt that soft ass and them hips. Let me know when you ready to share. We could spread that bitch out and—"

Ice flooded me at his suggestion that I would share Dream with anyone. I stepped forward before he could finish, reaching out before he realized he was speaking his last words. His neck snapped in my hands, freezing everyone around us, except for Dante and Sherrilyn.

"Catch his ass," Dante ordered some of his men before Smith could hit the floor.

They scrambled to obey, getting his body out a side door before most of the people in the section even realized what had happened.

"I guess I should be glad you did that back here in the dark," Dante said wryly.

"Demon! How am I supposed to explain this to my uncle?" Sherrilyn whined.

I lifted my shoulders, unbothered. "Tell him it's what your husband wanted," I said, my eyes on Dante's smirking face. "You enjoying this shit, but that's the last time you fuck with me," I warned him.

His silly ass smile disappeared. "I wouldn't say enjoying it, but seeing yo' cold-hearted ass actually give a fuck about somebody? Yeah, I like that."

Opening my mouth, I started to deny what he was saying, but fuck it. What or who I was feeling was none of his business. I turned to walk away, but a scene in one of the other third-floor sections had me stuck. Dayana's bridal party was diagonally across from us, chilling in their own section. She and Dream were sitting behind one of the tables, talking to each other. Even from across the room, they stood out and I let my eyes roam over Dream's new hairdo and her made-up face. Shorty looked flawless. I thought about asking Dante for the key to his office and pulling her ass in there for a few minutes. She stood up, revealing her body in that tight black shit that had me wanting to strip her and fuck her on the table in front of this whole damn club so all these niggas would know who she belonged to. She was dancing, but not as smoothly as she had downstairs. Then, she bumped into Crystal and all my urges to fuck her disappeared as anger, cold and instant, rose in me.

She was high or drunk. I hated seeing women fucked up like that, even though I refused to acknowledge why. I moved toward her section without thinking, frowning as I saw their guards let a few niggas stroll in, most of them with eyes on her. I walked in behind them, daring the weak ass detail to stop me.

"I think you're ready to go," the one in the front announced.

I followed his gaze to Dayana, whose head was resting on the table.

"Can you just go back to your own shit?" she snapped, sounding like her bossy sister.

I wasn't worried about them, though, as my attention focused on *her*.

"Dream."

I didn't raise my voice, but she turned around, her glazed brown eyes meeting mine. She looked at me for a minute before smirking.

"Damien," she said.

I could hear the little attitude in her voice, but I tried not to react.

"Let's go."

Rolling her eyes, she kept dancing.

"No. I'm not ready."

Cold trickled through me as I debated just snatching her ass and walking out. She stumbled again and I started moving toward her.

"Oh, shit," her co-worker said, her eyes widening on me.

Crystal stepped forward like she was about to say something, then paused when she looked up at me. Good choice. She just didn't know, if it was up to me, she'd be leaving, too. She didn't seem intoxicated, but shit was too crowded—anything could pop off. Dante must not have seen her because her pregnant ass had no business being here. My opinion of DeAngelo dropped even more.

"Dream, maybe you should—" Dayana began.

"Mind your business, Dayana," the nigga who had spoken to her a minute ago interrupted.

Dream's eyes flew to him at the same time Dayana stood

up, her face a mass of frowns.

"Jordan, who you think—"

"Nigga, I *am* her business—"

The sisters spoke at the same time and Jordan's eyes flashed on Dream.

"Stay out of this, Dream," he snapped.

This nigga had life fucked up. I looked at him coolly. "Don't address that one."

He looked like he wanted to say something, but thought better of it. I walked behind Dream, pressing my body against hers as my hand tangled in her soft hair. Pulling her head to the side, I lowered my lips to her ear, tired of her friends in my conversation.

"Did it sound like I was giving you a choice?" I asked, drinking in her sweet scent.

"I told you I was spending this weekend with my sister," she whispered.

"You will. But you done for the night. You can barely stand up."

"Damien—"

"You want me to drag your ass out of here in front of all these people?"

"You wouldn't!"

I smiled as she lied to herself. "You know damn well I'll do that shit. You can walk out or be carried. That's the only two options you get."

The pout on her full lips was the only answer I got. It was the only one I needed.

"Get your shit," I said.

Sighing, she grabbed a little red clutch off the table before turning to her sister.

"Yana, I—"

"It's cool," Dayana said, hugging her.

"You're going, too," Jordan told her in his preppy ass voice.

"I know," she said. "Demon's taking me."

I side-eyed shorty. That shit was news to me, but I didn't say anything.

"You're riding with me," he insisted. "Stop arguing and get your stuff."

Nigga was trying to play tough with a woman when it was obvious that he was pussy. That shit aggravated me.

"Ay. You heard what she said," I cut him off.

I had no idea why I was backing this girl up. She seemed as annoying and out of line as her sister. Jordan's eyes flashed to me.

"This is between my fiancée and me."

The nigga was suddenly bold as his crew came closer.

"J, what's up?" one skinny ass nigga asked him, staring at me like he wanted problems.

I smiled, waiting.

"Nothing's up," Dayana spoke up hastily. "I'm leaving and Jordan was saying goodbye, right?"

Jordan looked at me again before swallowing. Finally, he nodded.

"Text me when you make it," his weak ass instructed her.

She ignored him. Twenty minutes later, I had the Castle sisters buckled in my truck when Dayana spoke up again.

"I'm not going home," she said. "Take me to Smoke's place."

Shit, her eyes were as low as Dream's.

"I'm not taking yo' drunk ass to a bar—"

"Not one of his bars!" she broke in. "His... his house," she added in a softer voice.

I looked over at Dream. She shrugged, like it was normal for her sister to be going to one nigga's house when she was marrying another one the next day. What the fuck did they have going on?

"I'on know what Smoke got up. I can't just take you to that man's house and he got shit goin' on—"

"I already asked. Look."

Seconds later, her phone was on speaker as she dialed someone. He picked up.

"Hey."

I recognized Smoke's voice.

"Hey. My ride just wanted to make sure it was okay that I got dropped off," she said.

He paused for a minute. "Dayana, I don't like a bunch of people knowing where I lay my head. I'll come get you from—"

"It's Demon."

Another pause.

"Montana?"

"Yeah."

I could tell her answer surprised him. All this shit was surprising to me, too, especially the fact that I was sitting here calmly waiting to play chauffeur while they talked.

"I sent you the address," he said.

She smiled.

"I'll see you in a minute."

The ride to Smoke's house was silent as Dayana slept. I swear Dream struggled to stay awake out of spite, just to make sure I knew she wasn't speaking to me. She kept dozing off, her head falling, then snapping back up. Close to Smoke's spot, I called Dayana's name. She woke up slowly to text him she was almost there. He gave her a gate code and was waiting for her at the foot of the driveway. He pulled the back door open, his eyes meeting mine as he helped her out. I shrugged. It was none of my business.

"Thank you," he said.

I nodded. We pulled off again and Dream turned on the radio before hooking her phone to it. Of course, Beyoncé was the first voice out of the speakers. She still didn't say a word to me. *Fuck that*, I thought. She was about to talk to me, and I knew how to make her do it.

CHAPTER 37

Dream

I WATCHED as Damien turned down the radio a little, ready to ignore whatever he had to say. I wasn't ready for his next words, though.

"In case you on that same shit your little sister is on, remember that pussy is exclusively mine for a few more weeks."

My reflexes had been kind of off, but my head snapped around like I was auditioning for *The Exorcist*. *This nigga!*

"What the fuck are you talking about?" I demanded.

I didn't play about Dayana, not even with his ass.

"That fucking two niggas shit she got going on? You can save it," he replied.

I wrinkled my nose at him before sucking my teeth. This nigga had the nerve to be making assumptions, like he knew Yana like that. I was ready to set his judgmental ass straight.

"You don't even know what you talking about."

He looked at me from the corner of his eye.

"She didn't just leave her fiancé to go be with another nigga?"

"She ain't even fuckin' Jordan, so don't be judging her."

Okay, I was high, for real. No other way would I be

spilling Dayana's business like that. I crossed my arms over my chest and got quiet.

"Her fiancé the one she not fucking? That shit is crazy," he commented.

"Don't—"

He shook his head. "I'on need to hear anymore. That shit is not my concern."

I turned the music up just as Toosii and Summer Walker's "Love Cycle" came on. At first, he surprised me by rapping along. But I could feel a blush warming my skin as I listened to the lyrics and realized he was fucking with me. He smirked and gave me a peripheral glance as the words flowed from him.

That pussy so wet, I don't think that this good timin'
I'ma nut in that pussy, buy you Gucci and some red bottoms
We gon' have the bed rocking, take off them leg stockings

I bit down on my bottom lip as I turned toward the window, trying to ignore him. He chuckled behind me. I noticed we were headed for his house. I was getting my hair done today and had the wedding shower on top of other last-minute shit before the rehearsal, but I didn't even argue. Damien was going to do exactly what he wanted to do. He just better make sure I didn't miss a damned thing. Anyway, between the alcohol I drank and his sexy voice rapping about nutting in this pussy, I wouldn't mind ending up in his bed right now. That edible had me sleepy. If I let Damien fuck me first, I would sleep so well. He made me sick with his high-handed ways, but I couldn't lie—the sex part of our deal was everything.

I guess I drifted off at some point. I woke up in the truck as he got out and made his way to the door that opened into the kitchen. Shaking my head, I opened my door.

"Back to your usual rudeness, huh?"

He shrugged. "Shit, I was about to leave your ass in there. Hurry up."

I couldn't hurry, though. My arms and legs felt a little heavy, and I debated sleeping in the truck for real. Finally, I stumbled out. He shook his head as he waited. As soon as I stepped into the kitchen, I took off my shoes and damn near ran to the stairs, ready for the warmth of the shower and his bed. I didn't know why this crazy nigga insisted on keeping the temperature subzero. Damien followed me upstairs and into his room.

"You getting too comfortable," he commented as I opened his drawer and pulled out a wife beater.

I glared at him over my shoulder.

"In your bedroom? I'm supposed to, right? It's not like you want me for anything else."

For just a minute, he gave me a strange look, but it was gone by the time I blinked. Hell, it probably was the THC, anyway.

Stepping carefully, I made my way into the bathroom and started the water. I laid his shirt and some towels between the double sinks before a sense of boldness came over me. I walked back into the room and over to him, looking up at him expectantly.

"You wanna shower with me?" I offered.

He surprised me by shaking his head.

"Nah. I'm good. You go ahead."

Frowning, I stared up at him. Had I missed something? He hadn't been able to keep his hands off me the last couple of days, but now he was telling me no?

"Soooo… you can initiate shit, but I can't? Why you make me leave the club, then?"

He looked at me like I was stupid. For a minute, I didn't think he was going to answer. But I stood there, just waiting.

"The last time we fucked, you climbed your ass on top of me and sat on my dick, so obviously, I got no problem with you initiating shit. I made you leave the club cuz yo' ass was drunk, and all kinds of shit be happening to drunk chicks at parties."

I felt myself blushing at his words, but I wasn't embarrassed. I was feeling him not wanting anything to happen to me. I took a shaky step closer to him, then balanced myself by reaching out and touching his chest. My legs still felt kinda crazy, but I didn't have to be standing for what I had in mind.

"So, you'll be waiting once I get out the shower?" I asked in what I hoped was my sexy voice.

I must've failed because he shook his head.

"I don't fuck drunk pussy, Dream."

"My pussy's not drunk," I countered, letting one of my hands slide down to the front of his pants.

"Go take a shower so you can go to sleep."

"Damien! So, you don't wanna fuck me?" I squeezed his stiff dick. "Why is this hard, then?"

"I told you I'm good, shorty," he dismissed me, pushing my hand away. "This ain't even you."

Emboldened by the alcohol and weed, I grabbed him again.

"Dream."

I ignored the warning in his tone.

"What if I suck your—"

I didn't even get to finish my offer before his green eyes turned icy. That should've scared me, but I thought my intoxicated ass was reading him wrong, especially when he scooped me up and carried me toward the bathroom. Usually, I would fuss because I'm not a small girl, but I was basking in my victory. I thought I was about to get what I wanted. Instead, he carried me into the shower, clothes and all. I shrieked in protest, and suddenly, the water was cold.

"Damien!" I yelled, hitting him and trying to push him off.

Of course, I couldn't move his solid ass. He had one hand tangled in my hair, holding my head back, and the other gripped my shirt. I was mad at first, fighting his ass with everything in me. Crazy nigga probably thought this shit was funny.

But when he wouldn't let me go, my heart pounded as my anger became fear. Was he going to drown me? I choked as water streamed into my mouth and nose. *Oh, God.* I really had gotten too comfortable, let myself forget who he was. My screams turned into sobs and pleas for my life. Scared, I tried to call his name as I struggled against him.

He was so strong, and I could barely move. I was already slightly dizzy from the edible. My head was spinning crazily now, wondering what he was going to do, how I could get away, why he had snapped. My knees buckled, but he kept me upright, holding me relentlessly beneath the cold stream. Terror spread through me as I tried to blink water out of my eyes and look at him.

"Please," I begged. "Don't kill me."

Suddenly, he let me go. I stumbled backwards, collapsing into a crying heap against the shower's back wall. I don't know how long I sat there, soaked and frozen while the water still ran. I was vaguely aware that he left, but he came back and turned the water off.

"Dream..."

His voice was soft as he reached for me, a bath sheet in his outstretched hands. I flinched away from him.

"D-d-don't touch me... *don't.*"

He ignored my whisper, lifting me and carrying me out. Cold and fear combined, leaving me shaking harder than I ever had. Damien set me down and tilted my head back to look into my eyes. Something like regret darkened his, but I looked away, tears still pouring down my face.

"I wanna go home," I said, my voice hoarse from screaming and crying.

"No," he responded simply, putting the bath sheet on the counter.

I dropped my head and cried harder. My phone had been in my jeans, so I knew calling for a ride was a lost cause. I was trapped here with a crazy ass man who had just tried to kill me. Who knew what he planned to do next? And then his hands went to the hem of my shirt. My heart dropped.

"Damien, please... *no*. I don't want this. *Please*."

He couldn't really think... Hell, I didn't even know how I was going to finish this deal. I never wanted him to touch me again.

"So, now, I'm a rapist, Dream? I told you before this shit started that I wanted your consent. You think that shit changed?"

His voice was low, and he had the nerve to sound almost hurt. I didn't answer, didn't even look at him.

"You shaking. I'm just trying to get you out these wet clothes."

This time, when he reached for my top, I was silent. The shirt and the bra came off quickly. But the pants—they were already tight and now that they were wet, it took him what seemed like forever to work them past my hips and thighs. Finally, he ordered me to step out of them and I obeyed. My panties were next, and then I was naked and shivering uncontrollably in front of him. Taking the bath sheet, he ran it gently all over my body before tucking it around me. He grabbed the towel I'd had and rubbed it over my hair, squeezing out as much water as he could until he was satisfied. The bath sheet came off and he slid his shirt over my head before tilting my chin up again. This time, he held the small towel I had taken out. He had dampened it and proceeded to wipe my face gently.

"Stop crying," he ordered.

But I couldn't. My emotions were too raw. Rage and fear battled inside me, and I didn't know if I wanted to kick his ass or run as far away as I could. I stood there, weeping silently, until he picked me up again and carried me to his bed.

"I don't wanna sleep with you," I told him, trying to sit up.

He looked down at me, that same regretful glint in his eye. Ignoring my movements, he pulled the covers up around me.

"I know. I'm not gon' touch you."

Walking around the huge bed, he climbed in on the other side. I turned my back on him, curling myself into a sniffling, freezing ball as far away from him as I could. My sleepiness was gone as my mind swirled in confusion and anger. A long time later, he spoke.

"Dream."

I didn't say anything, just laid there, miserable.

"She... Melanie... m-my mother..."

His voice trailed off, but he had my full attention because I'd never heard him hesitate or stutter before.

"She had this nigga... he used to pimp her out. She had to get fucked up first. So high that she didn't recognize shit. And then she would offer to do anything to anybody... even in front of me and my sister."

Oh, my God. I couldn't even imagine. I wanted to say something, but what could you say to shit like that?

"Fucked up part is—I mean, it's all fucked up—but the *really* fucked up part is that nigga would get mad at her for doing what he made her do. And she'd try to make it up to him. So fucking high that she could barely stand up and she'd be offering to fuck him or suck his dick, almost begging his bitch ass. She..."

He stopped, but he didn't have to say anything else. I realized what he must have thought of me standing there, high and a little drunk, and insisting on fucking him. I couldn't help it—my heart felt for him, for the little boy he had been, and for the part of him I triggered. But that didn't erase what he had done, or the fear that consumed me, or the anger that simmered even now. I wanted to reach out to him, but I couldn't. We laid there for a while, a few inches apart physically but miles apart mentally.

"I'm not her, Damien," I finally whispered.

"I know."

More silence. And then he reached for me, pulling me into his warm, solid frame. I didn't even struggle against him. I was too tired to fight the truth—I was mad as hell at him... and I *still* wanted to be close to him.

"You said you wouldn't touch me," I reminded him, needing to put up some kind of resistance even as I settled against him.

"I know. You cold and shaking the whole bed, though."

I sniffed. "You worried about me being cold, but you were gon' leave me to sleep in your truck."

He sighed.

"Nah. I was gon' prop the door open so I could carry you in," he admitted.

I ignored how melted me a little bit.

"I'm still mad at you," I said softly.

He didn't say anything for a minute. Then, I heard, "Go to sleep, Dream."

Exhausted and confused, I went to sleep.

CHAPTER 38
Smoke

I HAD no idea what the fuck was going on. When Dayana first texted, I was half-asleep after a day of handling some of the unpleasant aspects of my "business." Hearing my phone buzz, I almost ignored it, but my OG had Jenesis and I answered everything when my baby wasn't with me. The message caught me off-guard.

Dayana: I need to see you.

I stared at it for a minute, confused. Shorty had made it clear what her plans were, so I honestly hadn't expected to hear from her again. I guess I took too long to reply because she followed up that first message with *"Please."*

And now, here we were, standing in my living room, staring at each other. I don't know how long we would've stayed like that, but she swayed on her feet, and I moved to catch her. I knew from the walk outside that she was a little tipsy. She fell against me, burying her face in my chest with a soft moan. Part of me wanted to lock my arms around her and hold her, but I hadn't forgotten that she was the same chick who brushed me off and walked out of my office the other day. I straightened her up and stepped back.

"What you doing here?" I asked.

She frowned up at me. "You said... you said I could come."

"But why you wanna come? Didn't you just tell me you were getting married? Ain't that shit this weekend?"

She held up a hand, like she could stop me.

"Wait! You asking too many questions. I'm a little slow tonight."

"You mean a little drunk?"

She tilted her head, like she was thinking. "More high, I think."

"Is that why you here?" I demanded.

"No!" She shook her head to emphasize her point.

"Then why, Dayana?"

Looking down, she took her time to answer. Finally, she mumbled something I couldn't hear. I slid a finger under her chin and pushed her head back.

"What?"

"I wanted to see you, Smoke," she repeated.

Hell yeah. Satisfaction spread through me. I knew she felt something. But I refused to let her see my reaction to her words.

"Why? Shouldn't you be focused on your wedding? I bet you got a lot to do today."

Sighing, she rubbed her head.

"Can we just... I really don't wanna think about that. Let's just..."

Her voice trailed off as she looked down. She looked shy, but I wasn't about to make this easy for her.

"Just what?" I pressed.

She didn't say anything for a minute, and then she turned her back to me and pulled her hair over her shoulder.

"Unzip me," she whispered.

The shit was tempting. My dick was hard just thinking about seeing her body again. But, hell nah. Shorty wasn't about to keep using me. Plus, she was drunk. I moved closer, pressing my lips to the shell of her ear.

"You want me to unzip this dress, and then what?" I asked, filling my hands with the curves of her hips.

Her breathing picked up as I pressed a kiss to the side of her neck, then made my way up to her ear and nipped the lobe.

"Y-you know," she stuttered.

"Nah, tell me."

She gasped as my hands moved up to squeeze and cup her titties.

"Go to your... to your bed."

"And do what?"

"Smoke!" she whined, her curvy body shivering against me.

"You want me to fuck you?"

She nodded so hard, I was surprised she didn't get dizzy.

"You want me to lay your thick ass down, eat the fuck out of that sweet, tight little pussy, then slide this dick in you?" I teased.

She shuddered, a moan escaping her pretty lips.

"Y-yes."

I dropped my hands. "Then you run out of here and go marry that nigga? Hell nah, shorty," I said coolly.

Her eyes flew open as her jaw dropped. She whirled around to face me. She looked pissed off... and hurt. I ignored that shit.

"Smoke—"

I shook my head.

"I'm not yo' side nigga, Dayana. I'm possessive—I don't share. The only reason you not in an Uber right now is cuz I don't trust them niggas like that, especially with you half-drunk. Now, I can unzip you, you can take a shower, and go to sleep. That's all the action yo' ass getting tonight. You wanna do that?"

My mind was feeling the shit I was saying, but my body...
my dick was hard as fuck from how soft she felt and how
good she smelled. I had to get her ass away from me fast
before I said fuck all my principles.

Tears brimmed in her eyes, but finally, she nodded. I led
her up the stairs to my bedroom. Jenesis and I had just moved
in here, so while the guest rooms had furniture, my OG
hadn't fixed them up yet or anything.

I showed her where everything was in my en suite bathroom before grabbing a t-shirt and boxers for her. She gave
me her back again, and this time, I pulled the zipper down
slowly. I pushed the material apart before running my fingers,
then my lips down her spine. A nigga was principled, not
perfect. She sucked in a breath and whispered my name, but I
walked my ass out of there.

She stayed in the shower forever, but I couldn't fall asleep.
Knowing she was about to climb in my bed was enough to
keep me woke as hell. By the time she came out, I thought I
had my dick under control. One look at her in my underwear
had that shit hard as fuck again. It was going to be a long
night. Silently, she got in beside me.

"Can we... can we listen to some music?" she asked shyly.

I didn't answer her, just got up to grant her request. I
fumbled around with my phone until some 90s R&B poured
out of the house's speakers. Instead of getting in on my side, I
climbed over her, stopping above her to drag my erection
against her plump ass and whisper goodnight in her ear. She
sighed, then grabbed my wrists when I moved.

"No! Just lay right there for a minute. You feel warm."

"Dayana—"

"Please?"

Her voice was soft and sweet, and I gave in to that shit.
Keeping most of my weight on my forearms, I lay on her
back, trying to ignore the scent of my soap on her skin and

the way her body relaxed as she drifted off. Only when her breathing was smooth and deep did I move.

Rolling over, I stared at the ceiling. I wanted her, I admitted to myself. Not just to fuck her—I wanted her to be completely mine. Yeah, it made me feel guilty as fuck, but it was what it was. My mama's words ran through my head: *Ain't no way Jenna would expect you to live your life alone, without loving someone and having someone love you.* But Dayana's little stubborn ass refused to back down about this marriage, and I wasn't a nigga to beg.

Eventually, I fell asleep, only to wake up to her ass wrapped around me like cling wrap. Pushing her hair away from her face, I just stared at her. Shorty was so pretty, it almost hurt to look at her. It had been a long time since I woke up with a woman in my bed and I low-key wanted to just lay there and hold her. I shook that weak shit off immediately. Dayana was someone else's woman, and I didn't need that headache. I gently shook her awake. It was after seven and I knew she had a busy day.

"Hey, wake that ass up. You getting married tomorrow!" I taunted.

I watched her eyes slowly open as she stretched.

"Ugh, Smoke! It's too early for rudeness," she complained, turning over and burying her face in the pillow.

I looked at her in disbelief. "What's rude is you bringing your ass to my house to fuck the day before your wedding to a lame ass muhfucka. That's what's rude, Dayana."

She mumbled something, but I didn't hear as I made my way to the bathroom to piss and handle my hygiene. I hoped she was up and getting ready. The sooner I got her little ass out of here, the less likely I was to give in to temptation. Opening one of the drawers, I pulled out a new toothbrush for her. Then I snagged a small towel so she could wash her face or whatever. I strolled back into the room, but stopped when I heard her soft snores. Shaking my head, I walked over and touched her again.

"Ay, Princess! It's yo' big weekend. You need to get up. I know you don't wanna miss—"

"Fuck you, Cartier Salinas. Nobody feels like your sarcastic ass bullshit!" she snapped, sitting up, frowning.

Even with the frown, the messed-up hair, and the bare face, she was still the prettiest woman I knew. But that thought took a backseat to my need to check her.

"Who the fuck you talking to, Dayana?" I asked calmly.

She stared at me defiantly for a minute before dropping her eyes. Good. She knew better.

"Look, I'm sorry. I'm not a morning person at all and that wedding is a sensitive subject right now."

She sighed, running a hand over her tangled weave before meeting my eyes again. I shrugged.

"I figured it was since you waking up in my bed."

She cleared her throat. "About that... you know, I had been drinking and ate an edible—"

"Nah. Don't even try it," I cut her off.

"I'm just saying, I wasn't making the best decisions," she insisted, looking everywhere but at me.

"So, you didn't come over here because you wanted the dick?"

Her eyes widened at my blunt question. I smirked at her, liking to shock her still too innocent ass. She recovered quickly, though. Pursing her lips, she looked at me boldly.

"I mean, the dick is good, but I wasn't in my right mind."

I moved closer to my bed, where she sat, gripping my covers.

"So, you in your right mind now?"

She lifted her shoulders. "Mostly... Just a little foggy from sleep."

"And now that you in your right mind, you ain't on the same shit you were last night?" I asked.

Shaking her head, she peered up at me. "Nah, I'm good."

Liar, I thought, before reaching out and grabbing the covers off her.

"Smoke! What are you..."

Her voice trailed off as I climbed on top of her and buried my face against her neck. She tilted her head to the side, making room for my kisses even as her hands pushed against me weakly.

"Cartier—" she whispered.

It was the second time she used my real name and I wondered how she knew it. I was too busy proving a point to ask, though. My lips glided up her neck to her chin and then her lips.

"So, you don't want this, right?" I asked against her mouth.

"Nope," she said, before pressing her lips to mine.

I let her take over, contradicting her own lie. She sucked my bottom lip into her mouth, brushing her tongue against it as her arms wrapped around my neck. Deepening the kiss, she moaned softly. The sound went straight to my dick, and I tried to pull back before I forgot all those principles I bragged about. Shorty wasn't having it, though. Her arms tightened and she kissed me harder, her tongue sliding against mine as she pressed her soft body into my much harder one.

Fuck that. Using my knee, I spread her thighs before settling between them. She circled her hips, the warmth of her pussy dragging against my dick. My hands went to the waist of the boxers I'd loaned her, ready to slide underneath. I froze as my bedroom door flew open.

"Daddy, GiGi and me are here!" Jenesis announced.

Dayana squealed as she tried to push me off her. For a second, I didn't move. Finally, I rolled over, and she pulled the covers up to her neck.

"Jenesis, what have I told you about knocking? You—"

My OG's words stopped as she appeared in the doorway.

Her eyes darted from me to Dayana before a smile lifted her mouth.

"Good morning, Cartier," she said before shifting her gaze to the mortified chick beside me. "You must be Dayana?" she asked.

Dayana shot me a confused glance before stuttering, "Y-yes, ma'am."

My mother winked at me before extending her hand toward my daughter.

"Mm-hmm. Jenesis, come on out of here!"

But my nosy baby girl wasn't having it. She eyed Dayana up and down before her gaze landed on my nightstand on the tiara Dayana had been wearing. Her eyes got big, and she looked at me excitedly.

"Daddy! Your girlfriend is a princess?"

Dayana pulled the sheet over her face as I laughed. My mother finally got Jenesis out of the room and Dayana used the bathroom, then slid into her dress and heels so fast, my head spun.

"I'm calling an Uber," she announced, grabbing her purse and making her way toward the door.

I waved at her. "Have a nice life, Princess."

"I will," she snapped, slamming my bedroom door.

Shaking my head, I walked into my closet. By the time I came back out, my mother was there, staring at me.

"What, Ma?" I asked.

"She didn't look too happy. You hadn't told her about Jenesis?"

I shrugged as I laid my clothes on the dresser and started making my bed.

"That shit ain't got nothing to do with my baby. She unhappy because she hooking up with a nigga who already cheating on her."

My OG walked to the opposite side of the bed to help me. "Wait... so the wedding isn't off?"

"Nope."

"She *still* marrying someone else?"

"Yep."

"And you gon' let her?" she asked incredulously.

"Not my business, OG."

She sucked her teeth before pulling the sheet a little harder than necessary. I looked up to catch her rolling her eyes at me.

"So, now you got an attitude, too?"

Her eyes narrowed. "I just don't want you to make a mistake—"

I stood up and stared down at her. "I ain't the one making a mistake. If that girl wants to—"

"Daddy, the princess gone! She coming back? Can I have some cereal?" Jenesis interrupted, popping into my room.

My mother gave her a look. "Daya, you just ate!"

I listened to them argue for a minute, glad for the distraction. Dayana Castle had made her choice, and I was going to respect that. But why did that make me feel like I was missing out on something I shouldn't?

CHAPTER 39

Demon

(*FRIDAY, June 11*)

"I need you to go to Ms. Angela's house for me."

My head snapped up at Melanie's words. Ms. Angela lived down the block and I sometimes did shit for her to pay her back for money Melanie borrowed. She would always give me something extra, so I usually didn't mind. But today was my thirteenth birthday. We wouldn't celebrate, no cake or gifts or shit, but that didn't mean I wanted to spend it running errands and doing yard work.

"Why?" I asked.

Melanie glared at me. "Because I said so. I owe her, and she wants you to do some things for her."

I frowned at her, wanting to say no. But Ms. Angela's brother was one of Melanie's dealers. If he found out Melanie owed his sister and didn't pay, he'd have somebody beat her ass to teach her a lesson. I shouldn't give a fuck, but, sorry as she was, Melanie was still my mother. Shaking my head, I moved toward the door.

"Demon?" she called.

I stopped without turning around.

"You thirteen today. No more little boy. Remember that."

She hadn't even told me happy birthday, but she wanted to say some shit like that? I hadn't felt like a little boy in a long time. And, *already six feet, I didn't look like one, either. I shook that shit off and made the ten-minute walk to Ms. Angela's. Her big ass house sat off by itself on a little plot. It was like she was in the hood but living above it.*

She answered the door, looking like she had just come from running or something in some shorts and a tank top. Smiling, she invited me in and pushed me into the dining room. There was a plate of food and a cup on the table. The smell of fried chicken had my stomach growling. As usual, I hadn't eaten today.

"My mama said you wanted me to do some stuff for you—" I started.

"I do, but that can wait. You should eat first. You tall, but you so skinny," she fussed.

Pride made me want to tell her no, but I was so fucking hungry. I sat down and she sat next to me. I wanted to show that I had some manners, but I was too far gone. I shoveled the chicken, mashed potatoes, and green beans into my mouth as Ms. Angela watched, patting my back and talking.

"Your mama told me you turned thirteen today."

I nodded as I inhaled another forkful of food. Ms. Angela was pretty, and she could cook. No wonder niggas were always hanging over here.

"You've grown up on me, handsome," she continued.

I nodded again, tuning her out as I finished my plate. She let me have seconds and finally, I was full enough to run her errands or whatever. She led me upstairs and into a pink and white bedroom. I figured she wanted me to move some stuff again. I stood in the middle of the floor, waiting.

"Demon, do you have any idea how much your mama owes me and my brother?" she asked, circling me.

I shook my head. "Nah, but I can work until it's paid."

She smiled up at me. "That's what I'm hoping. That's why she gave you to me."

That shit didn't sit right with me. I shook my head again.

"She can't give me away," I mumbled.

She walked up and patted my cheek. "She did, baby. And it's time to work off her debt."

I shrugged. I didn't like what she was saying, but this part, I could handle.

"What you want me to do?"

I wasn't ready for what happened next. Ms. Angela smiled again… and reached down and squeezed my dick. Stumbling back, I pushed her off me.

"Wh-what you doing?" I asked, the food she'd just fed me suddenly churning in my stomach.

"You don't look or feel like a little boy, Demon. I'm gon' make you a man," she whispered, walking up on me again.

"Nah, Ms. Angela. I ain't doing that. You—"

Her smile dropped. "You gon' do whatever the fuck I say when I say it if you don't want that hype ass mama of yours to die. Now, strip."

Heart pounding, I shook my head. "I don't think this is what my mama—"

Her laughter stopped me.

"It was her idea."

I wanted to accuse her of lying, to deny what she was saying. But I knew. Deep down, I knew. Melanie sold her own body. Why not mine? If she couldn't snort, shoot, or smoke it, she didn't give a fuck about it. She never pretended she gave a fuck about me. Still, I didn't want to do this shit.

"Ms. Angela—"

"Strip or I'll call Keith," she said.

Keith was her brother. I'd seen him beat Melanie's ass before, beat her so badly, she was unrecognizable. I wished I didn't care, wished I was as selfish as she was. But… she was my mama. I wanted to throw up all that food I just ate. Instead, I swallowed and started to slowly remove my clothes.

"A few more meals and you gon' be fine as fuck. This body is mine for now. I'ma feed you and fuck you. And if you tell anybody,

you can say goodbye to that junkie and your little sister," she said, her eyes so hard and cold. "You understand?"

I wanted to say no. Wanted to ask her how she'd feel if someone did this to her son. But for KiKi, I could take anything. I nodded. Her smile returned.

"Good. Trust me, you gon' like this part," she promised before dropping to her knees in front of me.

———

I woke up with a jerk, heart still racing, stomach sick at the memory. Moving to sit up, I realized Dream was still pressed against me. I pushed my face against her hair, inhaling the scent of the fruity shit she used as I tightened my grip on her. The feel of her calmed me down, wiped away the last of that dream-memory. I should've known it was coming after I talked about Melanie earlier. That's why I worked hard not to think about my past.

The tension in my body was just starting to relax when she woke up. She was soft at first, yawning and stretching, but I could tell when she remembered what happened. She stiffened and whispered, "Let me go."

I wanted to ignore her, but she had every right to be mad. I had sat through enough of the therapy sessions my father insisted on to know that she had triggered me. My response had been fucked up, though. Reluctantly, I moved my arm. She scrambled away from me, not even looking back.

"I need to borrow your phone to get a ride. And some shorts or something because I'm sure my clothes still wet."

Her voice was low, but I heard her.

"I'll take you home."

"No, thank you."

"It's not an option," I said, standing from the bed.

She mumbled something, but I was already digging in the

dresser for a t-shirt, some socks, and a pair of ball shorts with a drawstring. I tossed them to her before going into my closet to get something else. By the time I came back out, she was in the bathroom. The water ran for a little while before she reappeared with a damp face, dressed in my clothes. I walked over to where her clutch rested on my nightstand and dropped the ten stacks that I had pulled out of my closet safe. Her eyes flew to me.

"What—"

"I fucked up your phone, your clothes, and your hair," I said, even though I liked the riot of spiral curls around her face.

She shook her head.

"I don't want your money, Damien."

I shrugged. "I don't care what you want, Dream," I said before going to handle my business in the bathroom.

I brushed my teeth and showered quickly. She sat on the side of the bed quietly as I got dressed.

"You ready?"

The ride to her house was silent. She hopped out of my car without even looking at me. I let the window down as she started up the driveway.

"Dream."

She stopped but refused to face me.

"Get a new phone first. Answer when I call you."

"Fuck you, Damien."

I smirked. Guess that was better than silence.

"You heard what I said," I warned.

But I wasn't going to call her today. Nah, she could have her time to cool off. She couldn't stay mad. Hell, I'd done some shit I never do—tried to explain myself. That was as apologetic as I could get.

Remembering that it was Friday, I swung by Comfort Cafe. It was only open on the weekends and the breakfast was banging. On my way there, I called Eve. She answered on the first ring.

"Hello?"

Her voice had me ready to change directions and go to her house. She sounded scared and anxious.

"The fuck is wrong with you?" I demanded.

"I'm wondering the same thing about yo' ass," she clapped back.

I frowned. "Why you think something wrong with me?"

"Because you calling me. Since when you call people? You don't even like to talk!"

She had a point. It wasn't even like Eve and I talked to each other too regularly. Sometimes, we ran into each other, like the day I realized that nigga was hitting on her. Every once in a while, she sent a "Just checking on you" text. I couldn't remember ever reaching out to her first.

"Demon!" she snapped, bringing me out of my thoughts.

"Huh?"

"What's wrong?"

I ignored the question to ask my own. "You want breakfast?"

For once, Eve was silent. I probably shocked the shit out of her. I was definitely surprising myself.

"You... calling at eight o'clock in the morning and you wanna bring me breakfast?" she said slowly.

"Yeah."

More silence. Then, "Cough twice if you need help."

"Fuck you, Eve."

"Nah, fuck you. I'm about to drop MJ off at school. You wanna meet me at my place with this unexpected breakfast?"

I was glad she wasn't asking too many questions right now. I didn't have any answers for her. The shit I was about to do was way out of my element.

"Yeah. What you want?"

A little over an hour later, I was at her door with the bag of food. Eve let me in and led me to her dining room, where she already had plates and forks sitting out. The room was as bright as the rest of her house, the sunny yellow and spring green almost blinding me.

"Coffee or juice?" she offered as I washed my hands.

"You got apple juice?"

She sucked her teeth. "You and that damn apple juice. Yeah, I got some. MJ likes that nasty shit, too."

We passed the first few minutes eating in silence. Finally, she looked up at me and cleared her throat.

"As much as I am enjoying this omelet, I'm still wondering why you decided to bring it to me this morning. What's up with you, Damien Montana?" she asked, laying her fork down.

I took another bite of my breakfast potatoes, chewing slowly. I couldn't believe the shit I was about to do. I'd never given a fuck before, but the shit that went down with Dream wasn't sitting right with me.

"I need to ask you something," I admitted.

She nodded. "Anything."

I leaned back in my chair and rubbed a hand down my face, stalling. I felt weak even thinking about this shit. But fuck it.

"Ay, when a nigga makes you mad, what he gotta do to get back on your good side?"

She stared at me for a full minute. Just looking, like one of us had lost our minds. Then her mouth dropped open. I felt myself getting defensive, ready to tell her to forget this shit.

"Eve—"

"Oh, my God! That bourgeois girl got yo' ass like this?"

"Man, fuck this—" I began, pushing back from her table.

She grabbed my wrist and held up her hand.

"Wait, wait, wait! I'm sorry, but don't act like I ain't supposed to be shocked. You don't care about being on nobody's good side except my grandmother's!"

I didn't say anything, waiting for her to offer something helpful.

"You gotta realize I was messing with a fuck nigga off and on for the last few years," she finally said, speaking about her recently departed baby daddy. "But I've had a couple of decent ones. And what I remember most is appreciating when a nigga said, 'I'm sorry,' and meant that shit."

An apology? I shook my head. I didn't do that shit. Eve sighed.

"Do you at least regret what you did?" she asked.

I thought about that. Dream had pissed me off acting so fucking drunk, reminding me of Melanie. I just wanted to teach her ass a lesson and sober her up. I didn't feel bad for sticking her ass in there, but I wasn't trying to make her think I was going to kill her. That shit bothered me. Rather than tell Eve that, I shrugged.

"What else can I do?"

She rolled her eyes. "I mean… I guess you can buy her some shit. Flowers or—"

She stopped as I grilled her.

"What?"

"Do I look like a flower-buying nigga?"

"Nah, smartass, but you don't look like a bourgeois-girlfriend having nigga, either," she snapped. "You gon' have to do something different with that one. Give her some money for a shopping spree or something. Them rich girls expect that."

"She don't want my money."

Eve looked at me like I was stupid. "Oh, she pissed off for real. Ain't no bitch turning down money. Offer me some and see."

Sighing, I rubbed a hand across my face. "Stop calling her a bitch. And do you need money?"

She waved me off, dismissing what I asked. "I'm good. Look, maybe you need to let her cool off, then talk to her. When you gon' see her again?"

Shit, that was a good question. Dream probably was planning never to see me again. Too bad for her. I shifted in my chair as some shit clicked in my head.

"Ay. What you doing tomorrow?" I asked.

Eve narrowed her eyes and just stared at me for a minute. "Nothing," she admitted finally.

I smiled. "You got plans now."

CHAPTER 40

Dayana

(*SATURDAY*, *June 12*)

God... please don't let me throw up on this dress. The noise, the swirl of activity around me, the brightness of the mint green and silver dresses—everything was making me sick. Of course, what was really turning my stomach was the fact that I was about to become Mrs. Jordan Middleton. I was five seconds away from hyperventilating when my sister noticed. Without saying a word, she walked over to me, grabbed my hand, and led me to another room, away from the bridal party and stylists and our frantic mother.

"Breathe," Dream instructed as she leaned against the door.

Nodding, I took a few deep breaths, in and out, calming my nerves. Eyes closed, I tried to relax all the tense parts of my body. After a couple of minutes, I felt calm enough to look at my sister. She was staring right back at me.

"I'm finna shut all this shit down," she said.

I could tell by the look in her eyes that she meant that shit, too. Dream did not play about family, and especially not about me and our grandpapa.

"Dream, no," I said softly as she reached for the doorknob.

She blew out an exasperated breath, pressing her fist against her forehead before glaring at me.

"Tell me why you doing this again."

Fidgeting with my bouquet, I dropped my eyes. "I'm just keeping my word."

"You don't have to keep your word to a cheater!"

"I'm a cheater, too," I reminded her.

She sucked her teeth. "He started this shit."

I rubbed my ring with my thumb, still unable to look at her. "It doesn't matter. And I love him, anyway."

I wasn't sure about that anymore. All I felt when I looked at Jordan was anger, annoyance, and dread. But it sounded like a good thing to say to my overprotective sister. She laughed softly.

"You love him, but you left him to go to Smoke Salinas?" she challenged.

My head snapped up. "I was dru—"

She shook her head furiously. "Uh-uh. This is me, Yana. Don't come to me with that bullshit excuse."

For a minute, I let my mind turn to Smoke. I was still trying to figure out why I ran to him. If I were honest, I'd admit that being in his arms made me feel safe and wanted, that his touches and kisses lit something in me that no one else had even come close to sparking. But I didn't want to think about that. Everything pointed to us being wrong for each other. He'd been clear about liking more experienced women. Despite his trying to tell me I didn't have to go through with this wedding, he wasn't offering anything else. Cartier Salinas was a dead-end, and the sooner I forgot about him, the better.

"I'm just having a bad case of nerves—" I started again.

"Dayana Dionne Castle, don't you go out here and do something you're going to regret for the rest of your life."

Dream's voice was low and serious, her gaze glued to mine. Her warning shook me, but so did my father's threats and the realization that I had nothing to fall back on. I found the energy to pin a fake, bright smile on my face.

"I'm not. That's why I'm getting married."

"Yana—"

Frowning, she stopped as someone knocked on the door. She opened it to reveal Daddy and the wedding planner. He looked back and forth between us, and his expression wasn't happy.

"It's time," he said in a cool voice.

"Give us one more—" Dream began.

He shook his head, scowling at her.

"I said it's time. You're supposed to be somewhere lined up," he cut her off.

Dream turned around to give me one last look. I kept my smile in place. She wanted to say something, even opened her mouth to speak. But then she stormed out, the wedding planner on her heels.

Daddy walked over to me. For a minute, he just looked down at me. I swallowed, feeling small under his gaze.

"You remember what we talked about?" he finally asked.

"Yes, sir," I said softly.

He smiled. "Good. Good matches are important, baby. You're building wealth and dynasties. You and your children will be taken care of forever. You understand?"

I nodded wordlessly.

"This marriage will be what you make of it. Don't go in holding grudges and expecting the worst."

"Okay."

Leaning down, he kissed my forehead before pulling my veil over my face. Then, he offered me his arm and we began the walk toward a future I didn't want to think about. I was glad I had his arm. It was the only thing that kept me upright as we glided down the aisle a few minutes later. Everything seemed to happen in slow motion, and it was like I could hear things only from a distance. While most of the bridal party was smiling, Dream looked pissed off. As I took my spot at the front of the church and surveyed the crowd, I realized her anger wasn't all on my behalf. Demon had crashed my wedding and some girl was whispering in his ear. That was... interesting. Then my attention turned to Jordan. He stood there, smiling at me triumphantly. I had to look down to keep from punching his ass.

The minister said something. Someone sang. The door of the venue opened again, surprising me because we'd been clear about no late arrivals allowed. I didn't care enough to be mad as I looked toward the door. But then... my heart flew up and out of my chest and a million butterflies beat their wings furiously in my stomach. Smoke Salinas winked at me and leisurely took a seat. I heard Dream gasp behind me, and Jordan's smile slipped. He covered it quickly because it was time for him to say his vows. As he repeated after the minister, my mind whirled. What was *he* doing here? I mean, I remembered his name being on my parents' endless invitation list, but why did he want to see this? Oh, God, I felt weak. I took some deep breaths, trying to calm my nerves. I dared another glance toward the back.

He was really there, tall and gorgeous as ever, his eyes pinned to me. I couldn't look away. Dressed in a slim-fitting, cream-colored suit, he was perfect. I wanted—

"Dayana!" Dream hissed.

I blinked, snapping out of my daze.

"You need to repeat after me, sweetheart," the minister said kindly.

I hadn't even realized it was my turn. I blushed, unable to meet Jordan's eyes.

"I, Dayana Dionne Castle, take thee, Jordan Daniel Middleton to be my wedded h-h-husband," I stumbled.

The minister said something else that I obediently tried to repeat.

"To have and to... to... hold, from..."

It was getting harder to say the words. Dozens of pairs of eyes were on me, including Jordan's angry ones, but I could only feel the heat from one caramel brown pair. I struggled to draw in air, to breathe like I wasn't marrying one man while thinking about another.

"Are you okay?" the minister whispered.

Nodding, I cleared my throat, tried again. "From this day forward, for better, for worse, for richer, for poorer, in sickness and in health, to love and to cherish, till death... till... till..."

Say it, Dayana, I told myself. *Commit to this man forever and get it over with.* I swallowed, started trying again. Jordan grabbed my hand and squeezed it for encouragement.

From my peripheral vision, I saw a tall, lean figure rise. I couldn't help turning my eyes to Cartier Salinas as he stood up.

"Dayana," he said.

He didn't raise his voice, but everyone heard him. The whispers started as heads snapped around to look at him. I just watched as Jordan's grip on my hand tightened.

"Come here," Smoke commanded.

The two words shocked me, took the little bit of breath I had left. I couldn't possibly...

My eyes flitted from my enraged fiancé as he muttered, "What the hell?" to my father, who looked ready to tear shit up.

And then, I looked back at Smoke, where he stood waiting patiently. I shouldn't. It would ruin so much, destroy my father's plans, leave my future unsettled. The right thing to do was turn around and finish this ceremony and forget Cartier Salinas existed. That's what I should do. That's what I was *going* to do. But...

Somehow, my hand slid from Jordan's.

"Dayana!" he hissed, warning me.

Suddenly, I had taken the three steps down from the stage,

and I was still walking, my heart lightening with every step. Jordan's father stood up.

"What the fuck? Castle, you better stop her!" he ordered.

I saw a couple of men who'd been near the back start to approach. Smoke's hand immediately went to the back of his waistband. Before I could even process that, Demon stood, which meant that Dante Ware rose, too. One small hand signal from him and more men came to their feet.

"Nah," Demon said, looking toward Jordan's father. "She good."

I decided right then that he was going to be my brother-in-law and best friend. And then, I was standing in front of Smoke. Smiling, he held out a hand to me. I took it.

"Dayana!" my father called, loud enough to be heard over the buzz of the wedding guests.

"Let's go, Princess," Smoke said.

"Okay," I said, finally smiling for real for the first time today. "Okay."

CHAPTER 41

Dream

WOW. *Did that really just happen?* I wondered. But watching the back of my sister's white dress disappear out the door, then looking over to see my father ready to explode as my mother and DeAngelo tried to soothe him let me know it was real. The guests were still milling around, whispering about Dayana's unexpected departure, not sure what to do. Jordan was surrounded by his family, including his clearly pissed off father. Jordan looked shocked and miserable. *Good,* I thought, pressing my lips together to keep from smiling, happy for my sister.

The urge to smile disappeared when my eyes tangled with Damien Montana's. *This muhfucka.* My hands tightened on my bouquet, wishing it was his throat. Not only had he had the nerve to crash my sister's wedding, but he also brought that escort Eve with him. And why? Why was he trying to fuck with me when he was the one who pissed me off? It didn't help that he looked so fucking good. Damien didn't come across as someone who liked to shop or even cared about clothes, but the gray suit was designer and obviously tailored to fit his tall, solid frame. His locs were divided into two neat braids, a style that put his square jaw and high cheekbones on display. With his full lips and cool green eyes, he truly verged on beautiful. But that adjective was too soft for him. He was too savage, too powerful, too primal to be beautiful. As always, my body responded to just the sight of him, my posture softening as my center melted, ready to submit to his dominance. He knew it, too. The bastard smirked at me.

I looked away from him as I moved to climb down from the elevated platform. I smiled as one of the groomsmen, Ray, grabbed my hand to help me down.

"Whoa. That shit was crazy, huh?" he commented.

Laughing softly, I nodded. He grinned, shaking his head.

"That damn Smoke."

"He's definitely bold."

"Nigga is bad on his own, but working with Demon and Dante? That's like a gangsta dream team."

I rolled my eyes, unwilling to give Damien that much credit.

"I know you gotta go, but I been having a question for you," he continued as we stopped a few steps away from the platform.

"A question? For me?"

I really didn't have time for small talk. My mind was already in "fixer" mode, thinking about how I could calm my father down and wondering about the terms of his deal with Jordan's father. I was glad Dayana had backed out, but we didn't need Talton Middleton as an enemy, either.

"Yeah."

Confused, I looked up into Ray's handsome, chocolate face. The look in his espresso eyes relaxed my frown. His interest was clear as he let his gaze sweep over my thick frame in the short green dress. He reached into his pocket and withdrew his phone. Unlocking it, he handed it to me.

"You gon' let me have your number?"

Why not? I figured. He was cute and I knew he owned a

couple of successful detail shops. I opened his contacts list and started typing my name.

Suddenly, a chill tripped over my skin and the familiar scent of Sauvage teased my nose.

"Give that nigga his phone back," Damien ordered quietly.

Ignoring him, I kept typing. Fuck Damien. He was out here trying to kill me and flaunting bitches at my sister's wedding and still trying to tell me what to do? Hell nah.

"Dream."

Damn. I hated when he said my name like that, like a one-word command. I rolled my eyes before looking up at him. His green gaze pierced mine, the warning in his eyes clear.

"What?" I snapped.

Ray looked back and forth between us before speaking up.

"Demon, this you? I don't want no problems—"

I glared at him, his weak ass words changing my opinion of him. "First of all, I'm right here. Ask me. Nah, 'this,'" I pointed at myself, "ain't him. Don't you see him here with someone else?"

I started typing again.

"I suggest you ask what happened to the last nigga you gave yo' number to at Bliss."

Wait, what? I looked up at him and the ice in his green gaze froze me. I didn't even resist as Ray took his phone back and disappeared.

"What did you do?" I demanded. "I know you didn't—"

I stopped as my mother's voice suddenly sounded on the microphone, apologizing for the "disruption," and inviting people to stay for the cocktail hour and reception. Lord, this was a mess.

"Let's go outside," Damien said suddenly.

"Take your little escort. I'm not—"

"Dream!" My father's voice cut into my rant.

He was there suddenly, standing between Damien and

me, DeAngelo at his side. My attention flew to Daddy, but he was all about Damien.

"You already ruined one of my daughters and now you ruining the chances of the other one," he growled.

I flinched. Ruined... that's how he thought of me? Damien's eyes were on me, so I hurriedly hid my hurt. I felt a soft pat on my back and looked around to see my grandfather. I hadn't heard him pull up, but I should've known he was behind me. He was always behind me.

"Maybe if you treated your daughters like people instead of property, this shit wouldn't have happened," Damien suggested calmly.

A muscle ticked in Daddy's jaw, evidence of how hard he was clenching his teeth. He wanted to kill Damien, but Dante would no doubt wipe all of us out if he did. So, instead, he grabbed my arm.

"Come on. We gotta do some damage control."

I pulled away. "I'll meet you in a minute," I lied.

Fuck him. My feelings were really hurt and all I wanted to do was go to the guarded room with all the bridesmaids' stuff, get my shit, and get out. I started walking away.

"Dream."

Damien's commanding voice was almost enough to stop me, but I was over niggas right now. Fuck him, too. I kept walking.

CHAPTER 42
Demon

I **WANTED** to kill Darius Castle. Yeah, I knew I had hurt Dream, too, but he crushed her so effortlessly, like he didn't even see shit wrong with what he was saying. Dream was beautiful, smart, kept his businesses looking legit, fixed everything he needed fixing... and he thought she was ruined? The nigga was on some crazy shit.

"So, what makes you think she gon' talk to you out here? She wasn't beat for yo' ass in there," Eve said, breaking me out of my thoughts.

"She gon' talk," I responded, crossing my arms over my chest and leaning against Dream's little Mercedes.

Five minutes passed before she walked out of the building, a bag in one hand and her bouquet in the other. She looked beautiful in the sleeveless, soft green dress she wore as maid of honor. Her pretty face was made up lightly and she had a long weave with half pulled on top of her head and half flowing down her back. I fought the urge to adjust my suddenly hard dick in the suit pants as I watched her hips swish and sway. She clicked across the parking lot at a fast pace until she saw me. Her steps slowed and she bit down on her bottom lip. She kept coming, though. She glanced at Eve, a frown decorating her face.

"I understand that he's paying you or whoever runs the escort service, so you do what he wants, but couldn't you put up a fuss or something? Let this nigga know it's not okay to spend your date stalking another woman," she snapped.

I smirked and sat back as Eve tensed, then stepped closer to Dream. If anybody could handle Dream's smart mouth, it was Eve.

"Look, Ms. Bourgeois. I'm not an escort. You been turning yo' nose up at me since we met and you don't know shit about me," Eve said, one hand going to her hip.

Dream eyed her coolly. "I don't care to know shit about you, seeing the company you keep."

That last bit of shade was for me, but I didn't give a fuck. She walked around the front of her car, headed for the driver's side.

"He's the company I keep, but you the one spreading your legs for him? Okay, girl."

Dream froze, her back to us. I shook my head at Eve, but she shrugged. I rounded the car, catching Dream's arm just as she walked again. She tried to snatch away from me. I spun her ass around to face me. She dropped her bag.

"Let go of me!" she demanded, her brown eyes radiating anger.

My hand tightened on her arm, and I grilled her.

"Ay. Check yo' fucking attitude. You starting to fucking blow me," I warned her lowly.

Her eyes widened in disbelief. "*I'm* blowing *you*?"

Her hand with the bouquet crept up and she smacked the side of my face with the flowers. Eve giggled behind us. I ground my teeth together but let her make it.

"You tried to kill me. Then, you pop up at my sister's wedding with one of your randoms who wants to talk to me any kind of way—"

"I'm just returning the energy, love," Eve piped up.

"Eve," I bit out.

She mumbled something but shut up. I turned back to the headache in front of me.

"Dream—"

"No! Shut the fuck up, Damien, and take your hands off me before I scream!"

I blinked at her, wondering if she had lost her mind, talking to me like that. Caught off guard, I wasn't prepared for her to hit me with that fucking bouquet again. And then again and again, sending petals and shit flying everywhere. I grabbed her other arm, pushing her until she was bent backwards over her hood.

"What the fuck I tell you about putting your hands on me?" I demanded.

She stared up at me, her eyes holding a mix of anger, fear... and lust. Still, her stubborn ass wasn't backing down. That shit always turned me on with her. As pissed off as I was, I could still feel my dick getting harder.

"Technically, it wasn't my hands," she spat.

Lightly tightening my grip, I pulled her up and against my body. The sweet smell of her surrounded me, and I had to remind myself to focus.

"Keep talking reckless, Dream, and I'ma fuck you up out here," I warned.

"There's a pond over there. Maybe you can finish dr—"

I shook her, trying to get that mouth to stop.

"Shut the fuck up. I wasn't tryna drown yo' annoying ass."

She rolled her eyes but changed the subject. "Why are you even here, Damien?"

"We need to talk."

"At my sister's wedding? It couldn't wait?"

I shrugged. "I didn't want to."

"And everything is about you, right?"

I looked at her wordlessly. We stood like that for a couple of minutes, staring at each other under the brightness of the June sun, the scent of magnolias carried on the light breeze. Finally, she sighed.

"Talk about what?"

"Our deal. Just to make sure you know it still stands."

She shook her head. "No. I'm going to Dante. He has to be willing to accept something else."

My hand settled against her throat, stroking gently.

"But I'm not."

She blew out a frustrated breath. "I'm not fucking you—"

"The deal wasn't just about your body. It was about your time, too," I reminded her.

She scoffed. "And you want my time?"

I nodded.

"But why? Why are—"

I squeezed lightly, silencing her. I didn't want her asking the question I had no answer to.

"I hate you," she whispered.

"I know."

"I will never let you inside me again," she lied.

"That's cool," I lied with her.

"Get off me."

Smiling, I stepped back. She bit her lower lip and I wanted to pull it free with my own teeth. Dream had the juiciest lips and I loved biting and sucking on them. Another weakness. I had so many for this girl.

"I'll see you later, Dream."

She didn't say a word. Just flipped me off as she marched to the driver's door of her car.

"Dream."

I called her name as she opened it. Sighing, she glared at me.

"What, Damien?"

"You're not ruined."

She blinked several times, trying to hide the sudden dampness of her eyes. Then she climbed in her car and left.

"Look at you, being sweet," Eve teased as I started toward my truck.

I ignored her aggravating ass.

"Demon?"

I walked for several steps before responding. "What, Eve?"

"You know, it'd probably be easier to keep her if you didn't try to kill her," she offered helpfully.

"Fuck you, Evangeline," I muttered.

CHAPTER 43

Dayana

OH, *my God! Did I really just walk out on my own wedding?* The question was rhetorical, of course. I knew I had done it. There was no other way I could be in the back of this Phantom with Cartier Salinas if I hadn't. But now, the adrenaline that had allowed me to escape was wearing off and reality was setting in. Aside from my belongings that Smoke had ordered one of his men to grab from the car that had been waiting to whisk Jordan and me away later, I had nothing. My hands twisted in my lap as I stared out the window. What the hell was I going to do?

I jumped, abruptly jolted from my thoughts as Smoke grabbed one of my hands and laced our fingers together.

"Stop worrying," he said softly.

I glanced at his handsome face, looking for anything to reassure me. His caramel eyes warmed me, and I found myself sliding closer to him.

"I... I can't. I mean, I'm disowned. What happens now?"

His thumb stroked the back of my hand. "You gon' be fine, Princess. I'ma make sure of it."

His voice was confident, and I believed his promise, letting his words chase away some of my fears.

"Where are we going?" I asked.

He smiled down at me. "Your honeymoon."

I sat up from the luxe white leather of the seat, a frown creasing my face. "What?"

He laughed. "You trust me?"

I nodded without thinking. I did trust him. Probably way too much.

"Then, just chill, mama," he said.

Then, he started texting, leaving me alone with my thoughts again. Sighing, I closed my eyes. I guess I drifted off because the next thing I heard were the familiar sounds of an airport. My gaze flew to him.

"Cartier, I can't—"

"Weren't you going out of town for your honeymoon, anyway? Take this trip with me, Princess. Let shit die down and get your mind right. It's only for a week," he coaxed.

I didn't know where we were going. I didn't even know much about him. But I was in no hurry to face my parents and the Middletons. I needed this break to build my defenses. I guess I was going on vacation with the infamous Smoke Salinas.

We didn't head for a regular terminal or a commercial airline. My eyes widened as the smaller hangar with a private jet came into view. The car finally stopped, and Smoke ushered me out and onto the plane. For a moment, I just stood in the doorway, awestruck. Cream-colored furniture and wood trim decorated the spacious interior. There was a small dining area with a polished, dark wood table surrounded by cream leather seats. Further back, I could see beautiful cream leather couches and recliners and a little archway that led to what I assumed was the bathroom. The long, low bar and the tables were accented with mounted crystal vases that held fresh flowers. Two of the recliners were occupied and I felt a blush heat my cheeks as I recognized Smoke's mother and daughter. The little girl let out a gasp as we stepped onto the plane. She bounced out of her seat and ran straight to me, her eyes lighting up as she touched one of the ostrich feathers that trimmed my silk gown.

"You really *are* a princess," she whispered.

I shook my head. "No, baby, I'm just—"

"She is," Smoke spoke up, cutting me off. "Princess Dayana."

I looked over my shoulder at him, wondering why he'd let his daughter think that. He shrugged and I decided I'd ask him later.

"My name is Jenesis," the little girl volunteered, sticking out her tiny hand.

I shook it. "I am so pleased to meet you," I said sincerely.

"Walk," Smoke instructed suddenly.

Hesitantly, I made my way down the aisle toward his mother. She had a knowing smile on her face, and I wished the floor of the plane would open up and swallow me. Instead, I straightened my spine and pasted on my own smile as I tried to forget how she'd first seen me. She stood up and walked toward me.

"Hello," I greeted.

I wasn't ready for the tight hug she gave me, but the feel of her arms around me and the soft scent of her perfume were some of the most comforting things I'd experienced today. I hugged her back, reluctant to let go. Finally, she stepped back and touched my face with her soft hand.

"I'm Stephanie. It's good to see you again, Dayana. Everything is going to be okay, now," she said softly. Her eyes flitted to her son. "Always so dramatic, Cartier," she teased.

"I get it from my mama," he shot back, gifting her with one of his beautiful smiles. "We should be leaving shortly. Just waiting on Ammo to get here with her bags."

She nodded and settled Jenesis back into one of the recliners with her tablet before taking her own seat.

"Do I sit here?" I asked Smoke, pointing at a chair across from his mama.

"Nah. You wanna change, right?" he responded.

"When my bags get here, I'd love to."

"Come this way."

He walked through the archway, and I saw the bathroom, as expected. But there were two more doors. He opened one of them and led me into a bedroom. It was just as sumptuous as the front of the jet, done in the same color scheme with a bed that looked way too big and comfortable for a plane.

"You can get undressed in here. I'll bring your stuff as soon as Ammo gets here."

He turned to walk out. I called his name.

"Yeah?"

"I... um... I need help."

He walked over to me, and I presented my back to him. I felt him start to slowly lower the zipper. Suddenly, the room was tense, the air thick with the electricity that always seemed to hover between us. He was undressing me... again. In this room with its huge bed and lowered window cover. I swallowed, reminded myself that his family was a few feet away. But that didn't stop me from imagining what could happen in this room. *Get a grip, Dayana!*

"I bet you wish I'd invest in clothes with side zippers, huh?" I tried to joke.

"Nah, shorty. I don't mind doing this at all."

His voice was low and deep, sparking something inside me that sent heat flooding my body. I turned around when he finished. He was ready to walk out again.

"Cartier..."

He looked at me silently. I shimmied out of the dress, wanting him to see me in the lacy white strapless bra and matching thong. I wanted his reaction, wasn't disappointed when I saw his caramel eyes warm as they swept over my body.

"Fuck, Dayana—" he hissed.

I stepped over the dress, closer to him. Grabbing his hands, I settled them on my hips before cupping the back of his neck and pulling him down to me. He didn't resist as I pressed my lips against his. He kissed me back, nipping and sucking at my lips before his tongue found mine. I moaned softly. Kissing him was—

"Cartier! Ammo's here!" Ms. Stephanie called.

We sprang apart instantly, our heavy breathing the only sound in the room. I closed my eyes, counting to twenty, willing my heartbeat to slow down. When I opened them again, he was gone. I stood there for a minute, getting myself together before picking the dress up from the floor and lying it across the bed. I heard a groan from the doorway and whirled around. Cartier stood there with my bags, his eyes glued to me.

"They're not that heavy," I said.

"Girl, I was looking at that fat ass in that thong."

I blushed again, then bit back a smile when I noticed the impressive tent in the front of his pants. He pulled my rolling luggage in and closed the door before handing me the bandoulière. I set it on the bed and unzipped it quickly, pulling out my purse, a t-shirt, and some leggings. Opening my purse, I reached for my phone… and lost my train of thought as his hands settled on the bare globes of my ass. He caressed me gently and I instinctively leaned forward, resting my palms on the bed.

"Dayana… you bending over in front of me with this shit on… I'm about to fill yo' ass up, ma," he warned.

His voice was a growl and I felt moisture pool against the silk between my thighs. Lifting my knee onto the bed, I opened myself to him. He cursed behind me.

"*Fuck*… we about to take off. We don't have time…"

His voice trailed off as I waited silently. Seconds later, his fingers slid beneath the material of my thong to stroke against my slit. My breath escaped me in a whoosh as I rocked against his hand.

"White dress, white lingerie for the virgin bride. That's what they thought, huh, Princess? They didn't know how deep I've been in this tight little pussy, how it creamed all over my dick."

He teased my clit as his words teased my ears. So dirty, but it made my freaky ass hotter. I moaned softly, the part of my mind that was still sane remembering his family was close by.

"You been thinking about that, Princess? How I fucked you and made you cum? How you screamed for me?" he whispered, rubbing me in slow, lazy circles.

"Smoke..."

I whimpered as I rode his fingers, chasing the sensations he was building in me. Heat crept over my skin as pleasure suffused me. My body was splayed over my wedding dress on the day I was supposed to marry another man, and all I could think about was Cartier Salinas and what he was doing to me.

"More," I pleaded.

"More? Tell me what you want, Princess."

His breath was warm against my ear as he leaned over me, the material of his shirt decadently soft as it brushed my back. I was bold, but my lack of sexual experience meant I'd never really talked dirty to anyone. I blushed thinking about it.

"I... I want... I—"

Suddenly, he pushed two fingers inside me. I buried my moan in the dress, biting down on the white silk. Smoke pumped in and out slowly, curling his fingers so that they stroked my walls in a way that left me breathless.

"This? You want this, Dayana?" he asked softly.

I nodded as I pressed back against him, craving his touch. His hands were driving me wild, rubbing and plunging, stroking and tormenting. My fingers clenched the fabric of the dress as I fought against the scream growing inside me. My hips moved helplessly, chasing the orgasm building in me.

"Cartier," I moaned.

"Yeah, baby?"

"I'm—I—I'm about to—"

The knock on the door had both of us freezing. I was too wound up to speak.

"What?" Smoke barked.

"I'm Abbra, your flight attendant. I'm sorry, Mr. Salinas, but the pilot is requesting that you secure your guest's luggage, and we take our seats for takeoff," a feminine voice called.

"Fuck," he sighed against my ear. "Yeah, all right," he said, reluctantly withdrawing from me.

I collapsed against the bed, boneless. Smoke smacked my ass lightly.

"Get dressed, shorty. Our adventure awaits."

CHAPTER 44

Smoke

SIX HOURS INTO A DAY-LONG FLIGHT—WE'D stop somewhere to re-fuel—and the plane was finally quiet. My baby girl was settled across the way with my mother in the other bedroom. That had been a hard sell. She was fascinated with "Princess Dayana" and wanted to continue her endless questions during a sleepover. I loved my baby, but I was selfish enough to want Dayana to myself all night.

She was lying there now, half asleep, in some little sheer yellow nightie with another lacy thong. I couldn't help it—my hand was on her plump ass, rubbing it as she settled down. I could tell something was on her mind, which was one reason I wasn't trying to continue what we started earlier. I needed to come clean about some shit, too. She was silent for a few more minutes. Finally, she looked up at me.

"Cartier?"

"Yeah?"

"Why did you come to my... to the wedding?"

I lay there, not sure how to explain this shit to her. Truthfully, I had entertained the thought of busting her shit up, but I hadn't made up my mind when I got there.

"I wanted to see if you were gon' go through with that

bullshit. I felt like, if I saw you tie yourself to that nigga, I could get you out of my head for good," I finally said.

"So why did you—"

"Cuz I took one look at your face and heard your voice shaking and I couldn't watch you do that shit, not when you deserve so much better than that bitch made nigga."

She was quiet again. Then, so softly that I had to move closer to her to hear, she asked, "Are you the much better?"

Part of me wanted to tell her yes, wanted to try to be who and what she deserved. But then, an image of Jenna's pretty, dimpled face popped into my head, and I felt like shit.

"Nah, Princess. You need a nigga that's all yours. My heart is taken," I said, regret shading my voice.

She froze for a second, tears welling in her eyes. The tears disappeared quickly as a mug settled on her pretty face, and she pushed my arm away from her.

"But... but I asked you that night at the bar and you said you were single. You said... Get off me, you sneaky ass nigga! Talkin' about Jordan, but you out here cheating, too? Ugh. I swear, none of y'all about shit!"

She climbed out of the bed quickly, yanking open the door.

"Ay!" I called quietly, not wanting to wake up my moms and baby. I tried to untangle myself from the covers she had thrown over me. "Where you goin', girl?"

Finally, I was free and followed her to the front of the plane. She was curled up on one of the couches, her scowl still in place. I sighed. This shit wasn't going how it was supposed to.

"Dayana—"

"Fuck you, Smoke. No-good muhfucka," she snapped, turning her back to me.

"Come back to the room and let me explain—"

She let out a bitter laugh. "Explain? Explain what, nigga?

That you just like every other tired ass pussy out here? I'm not sleeping nowhere with you. Goodnight!"

She could have her little attitude, but I tolerated disrespect from no one. Grabbing her shoulder, I pushed her onto her back on the couch. She swung at me. I grabbed both of her wrists and pressed them above her head as I straddled her.

"You betta watch who the fuck you talking to, Princess," I warned as she squirmed beneath me before trying to buck my body off hers. "I offered to explain—"

"Don't call me that. And fuck you and your explanations. Get off me before I wake up everybody on this muhfucka," she hissed.

I grabbed her jaw and squeezed just hard enough for her to know I was serious, then leaned forward.

"If you wake up anybody on this fucking plane, I'ma spank yo' ass until you regret it."

Something hot flared in her eyes, but she stayed quiet. I stood up slowly, my eyes pinned on her. The little nightie had made its way up to her waist while we were tussling. The outline of her fat pussy was clear beneath the sheer thong. My shit was immediately hard, and she noticed. Scoffing, she sucked her teeth.

"Take that home to whoever has your heart cuz I don't want it," she lied.

I smirked at her as my fingers fell on the seat of her thong, feeling the dampness there.

"Why you so wet, then?" I taunted.

Her eyes narrowed and she turned her head. I scooped her up off the couch. She struggled silently, but I wasn't letting her go. I walked back into the bedroom, kicked the door closed behind me, and threw her little mad ass on the bed.

"I'm not—"

"Dayana," I warned.

She sighed loudly, crossing her arms over her chest. "Fine. You stronger than I am. You can make me sit here and listen.

But just so you know, I don't want to hear any of the shit,"
she snapped before lying on her side, facing away from me.

I rubbed my forehead, trying not to get frustrated enough
to let her see that other side of me. But she was pushing it. I
waited until I had shit under control to speak.

"Look, I didn't say that shit right earlier—"

"Where your bitch at, anyway? Why she not on this
flight?" she asked snidely.

One minute, I was standing beside the bed, looking at her.
The next, my hands were on her and I was pulling her across
the covers and to her feet. She shrieked as she used both of
her hands to pull on mine, but I was too strong for her. I
backed her ass into the wall and let my hand close around her
throat. Her eyes got big as fuck when I squeezed lightly. I
lowered my mouth to her ear.

"Don't you *ever* disrespect her, you understand?" I
whispered.

She trembled uncontrollably, her heart beating so hard, I
could feel it. Wide-eyed, she nodded as best she could. Stepping back, I let her go, but she stood there, frozen, her eyes
holding a mix of fear and rage. *Fuck!* That shit made me feel
bad. I didn't want her scared of me or mad at me, but her
mouth was so—

"I just really think I should lie down in the front, since
you're so mad. Like some space would probably be good.
And when we stop to gas the plane, I can leave."

Her voice was clipped and cold as she wrapped her arms
around herself. Her words and the look in her eyes let me
know I was losing her. Despite my attachment to Jenna, that
was the last thing I wanted to happen. Shit was so confusing,
but I knew I needed to do something to fix this and fix it fast.

"Dayana. It's not what you think. I was talking about my
wife—"

She frowned. "But... she's..."

I nodded. "Yeah. But I promised... Look, it's complicated."

I walked away from her to sit on the foot of the bed, dropping my head into my hands. She stood with her back pressed to the wall for a long time. I could feel her eyes on me.

"If you don't want to get in the bed because of me, I'll go to the fr—" I began.

"You could've just said it was your wife in the beginning. I know it was hard for you to lose her," she finally said.

I looked up at her in disbelief. "You wouldn't listen—"

She shrugged, like it was no big deal. "Yeah. I'm kinda like that when I'm pissed off."

The room went silent again. She finally climbed on the bed, staying behind me, near the top. Minutes ticked by, catching each of us in our own thoughts.

"I won't let anyone disrespect her... but I shouldn't have handled you like that," I eventually admitted.

"Oh, yo' ass is lucky. I believe in being armed and dangerous. Pepper spray, my straight razor, my bat, my taser. Don't let this pretty face fool you," she popped.

I couldn't help smiling as her sass came back. I liked that shit much better than seeing her fearful. I noticed she hadn't mentioned a gun, though. I know Castle didn't have his girls out here with no heat. Not with the kind of work he was into.

"Tell me about this promise you made her."

I stared down at the floor, searching for the right words. Talking about Jenna was still hard, still painful. What happened to her was fucked up and unfair, and I would never shake that feeling.

"After she..." I swallowed. "After they pronounced her and took all the medical equipment and cleaned her up a little, everyone left me alone with her for a few minutes. I felt like..."

I paused again, hating to admit how powerless I had been. I heard Dayana move, felt a soft touch on my back.

"Cartier, if you don't want to—" she whispered.

"I felt like I let her down. I had promised her so much shit, given her so much shit, but the one thing I couldn't do was give her more time. So, I promised her that our time wouldn't end just because her life did. I knew I'd have physical needs, but I promised her my heart forever. It seemed like the least I could do."

My head dropped again, the wash of memories tormenting me. Another soft touch.

"She can always be in your heart, Cartier. But you don't stop living because she did!"

I shook my head at her words.

"Dayana… I was keeping that promise just fine until you stepped into my bar."

I heard her suck in a sharp breath, but she didn't say anything, just waited. I drummed my fingers against the cream bedspread, wondering how much more I should say, knowing I'd already said too much.

"You been in my head since the moment I met you. I've walked away from so many women since Jenna died, but I don't want to walk away from you. I don't want to break my promise to my wife, but I find myself wanting to make promises to you."

A tense silence stretched between us as I waited for her response. She should throw me out of the room, tell me to take my confused ass and all my issues away from her. I was almost a decade older than she was. Dayana was too young, too innocent to be caught up in my bullshit. But she didn't send me away and she didn't run. Instead, she whispered my words from earlier.

"Come here."

I eased back until my body was planted between her

thighs, her soft breasts against my back. Her lips brushed the back of my neck.

"I only want one promise from you right now," she said softly.

"What's that?"

"Let me have this week. No Jenna, no Jordan. Just one week and you keep an open mind about us."

I turned around to face her. She looked so fucking beautiful and hopeful. In that moment, I knew I would give her anything she ever asked for.

"You got that," I vowed.

Smiling, she leaned forward and pressed her mouth against mine. It was just a soft peck. It immediately turned into something else, something hungrier and more demanding as my tongue stroked inside her mouth.

Mouth fused to mine, she pulled me down and I went willingly. I broke the kiss only to look at her. I was a selfish ass nigga—just the thought of another nigga laying with her like this made me want to kill somebody. She placed her hands on each side of my face, pulling me back into the kiss while spreading her legs wider. Shit had my dick hard as fuck.

Then, we were moving urgent as fuck, tearing off clothes and throwing them shits everywhere. With my eyes glued to hers, I pushed inside. Her body resisted at first, still so tight that her slippery wet walls didn't part easily. I pressed forward, not stopping until my pelvis met hers. She moaned softly as she opened and pulled me in. The only other woman I'd ever fucked raw was my wife, so I wasn't ready for the feel of Dayana's pussy with no barriers. She was so soft, hot, and wet; I was about to lose it already.

I couldn't stop staring into her eyes. I could see the desire, the bright sheen of tears, and suddenly, I felt a shift in my chest, like something cracking open. Shit I had refused to feel for the last three years seeped out as I thrust into her, tying me to this girl in ways I didn't want to consider. Her hips met me stroke for stroke. I kissed her hard before letting my lips trail to her ear.

"Oh, you trying to throw that pussy back to me, ma? Good girl. Gimme all my pussy, Yana."

My voice was rough, demanding as I slowly slid in and out. I bit her earlobe then sucked it as she gasped my name. I kissed her softly.

"Say it again," I ordered.

"*Cartier*," she sighed against my lips.

Smiling, she circled her hips from below as she continued meeting me. Lifting her leg to allow me deeper access, I started deep stroking her, finding her spot as my thumb circled her clit. I caught her small cries with my lips. It wasn't long before she was contracting around me, so tight I could barely move. She cried my name as she came, acknowledging the claim I had on this pussy.

I wasn't far behind her, the warm, wet suction of her insides too much for me to fight against. Hell, it took all my strength to pull out in time, spilling myself all over the fat, perfectly waxed lips of her sex.

And in that moment, I knew one thing for sure. I had to figure this shit out, get it right. There was no way in hell I could walk away from this.

CHAPTER 45

Dream

(*SUNDAY, June 13*)

Talton Middleton was not happy. Jordan's father ranted and raved as I shot DeAngelo a glance, already tired of this bullshit. Apparently, Dayana had embarrassed not only his son, but his whole family—including his damn ancestors, the way he was carrying on—and he wasn't sure about making deals with people who couldn't keep their word. I resisted the urge to roll my eyes. My father, on the other hand, listened patiently, trying to see what they could salvage of their business relationship and what ventures Talton might still be willing to pursue with him. Talton did a lot of blustering and fussing, but Daddy, D, and I realized he was the type of man who, if you let him, would eventually talk himself down. So, I trained my attention on the windows of my father's office, staring out at the trees that swayed in the unexpectedly heavy winds. I hadn't realized it was supposed to rain today, but I wasn't mad about it. Better nap weather for me. I was so tired after the last few days that all I wanted to do was crawl into my bed and hibernate. I knew Damien was expecting me later, but he could keep expecting, arrogant ass. We would finish this deal on my terms. That meant no sex and minimal contact. He better keep entertaining his precious Eve.

Several minutes into his tirade, Talton started winding down, admitting that he still wanted to work with Castle Enterprises in some capacity. Finally, I was ready to pay attention. This was the part where I was needed. But before we could hash it all out, Jordan spoke up.

"Nah. I ain't worried about all this business bullshit. I want her back."

All eyes turned to him. I barely kept my mouth from falling open as I pushed the bridge of my glasses closer to my face. Was this nigga delusional?

"I'm sorry, but did you see her walk out of the venue with another man?" I asked snidely.

He looked at me and the hatred in his eyes was clear. That was fine with me. I was glad to know how his pussy ass really felt. I had hated the idea of Daddy arranging Dayana's marriage, but as long as I thought she was happy, I dealt with it and Jordan. Now that my sister was over it and done with Jordan, so was I.

"I'm sure everyone in here knows the... situation Dayana and I recently had. I'll bet her friends were in her ear, telling her to get me back."

He shot me another scathing look. I glared right back.

"Anyway, we're even. Now, it's time for us to move on and put this behind us," he finished.

His father stared at him like he had suddenly grown two heads. Good. Maybe he could talk some sense into his silly ass spawn.

"That girl humiliated you in front of hundreds of people. Nigga, where is your pride?" Talton gritted out.

I didn't even try to hide my smirk as I settled against the wingback chair to watch father and son go at it. They argued for a couple of minutes before DeAngelo held up his hand to stop them. I glanced at my father, but he just watched, no doubt trying to see how D handled this.

"Look, Jordan, I know it might be hard to accept, but Dayana chose something else. All we can do now is—"

Jordan shook his head, cutting my brother off. "She made promises to me. She don't get to just break them and walk away."

His words sent a chill tripping down my spine. I didn't like the whole tone of this conversation. Jordan talking about what Dayana didn't get to do wasn't acceptable.

"Nobody's gon' force my sister to do shit!" I snapped at him.

"Dream—" my father finally spoke up.

"I really thought you had these girls on a tighter leash," Talton broke in, shaking his head.

Daddy tensed in his chair. Middleton had gone too far with that one, thank God. The look my father gave him let me know these negotiations were probably over. His eyes shot daggers at Talton as he clenched his teeth.

"My daughters are not dogs," he said coldly.

"I didn't say anything about forcing Dayana. I just wanna sit down and talk with her. I'm sure she'll realize honoring her commitments is the right thing to do," Jordan said, his voice irritating me more with each word.

DeAngelo was staring at him, a mug on his face. But my father... I could tell by the look on his face that he was considering what Jordan said. He'd actually encourage Dayana to sit down and talk to this asshole. I shook my head in disbelief.

"What makes you think Smoke's gonna just let her go?" DeAngelo asked, before I could object.

The elephant in the room. Nobody wanted to cross Smoke Salinas if they didn't have to. *Nobody.* Jordan was definitely no match, not even with his father's back up. The uncertain look Talton Middleton gave his son was evidence of that.

"Dayana belongs to me, not him," Jordan growled.

"Dayana is not your property," I countered.

He surprised me by smirking at me. "Why you so invested, Dream? You mad because a good nigga wants to claim your sister and settle down with her while you out here slutting it up for a crazy nigga who will never wife you?"

Yeah, that was it. I popped out of my chair, but DeAngelo grabbed me before I could slap the silly grin off that bitch's face. I struggled against my brother's hold, but he wasn't letting go.

"You betta hope I don't tell that 'crazy nigga' you insulted me. Losing Dayana will be the least of your worries," I spat.

I was exaggerating—Damien probably didn't give two fucks about me—but Jordan didn't know that. My words shook him. Fear flashed in his eyes, and it was my turn to smirk. He covered it quickly, though, and he and his father both glared at me.

"Are you threatening my son?" Talton hissed.

I laughed at him. "It's not a thr—"

"Enough!" my father's voice rang out. "Everybody in they feelings and this shit ain't getting us nowhere."

My mouth snapped shut as his angry gaze swung between me and the Middletons. For a minute, the room was silent, tension bubbling around us, threatening to destroy the potential to reach any agreements. Finally, Talton nodded.

"I agree. I suggest the two of us sit down next week. No hot-headed kids around," he said, sneering at me.

I rolled my eyes. I wanted to cuss his ass out, but my father gave me another warning look. I bit my tongue as he walked the Middletons out and D finally released me. Surprisingly, my brother didn't say a word about what just happened. He sank down into a chair and rubbed his forehead.

"Did you know?" he asked me after a moment.

I pretended I didn't know what he was talking about. D

wouldn't believe that shit, though. As twins, he and Yana
were crazy close, but the bond between my sister and me
meant she told me the stuff D never wanted to hear, especially about men.

"I knew she was unhappy because he cheated. I didn't
know about Smoke until right before the wedding," I
admitted.

D's head popped up. "What about him?"

I shrugged, trying to play it off. "They... umm... they like
each other."

My brother frowned, looking truly confused.

"Come on, Dream. They obviously more than like each
other. How she even know that ni—"

"Dream Dior, have you lost your fucking mind?" my dad
snarled as he burst back into the office.

I looked up at him as he walked until he stood over me, a
menacing glare on his face. Refusing to be intimidated, I
stood up, smoothing a wrinkle out of the Alexander
McQueen pencil dress I wore before meeting his eyes.

"What are you talking about, Daddy? He insulted me!" I
defended myself.

"After all your little comments and hostile body language!
You my clean up person, Dream, you fix shit. I mean, yeah,
you work with the money, but you work with people, too. I
need you to smooth shit out, not fuck it up even worse!" he
raved.

His words pissed me off. Daddy acted like I lived to clean
up other people's messes, like I didn't tire of plotting and
negotiating and soothing ruffled feathers. Plus, I didn't like
the shit Jordan was saying about my sister. Dayana wasn't
ever going back to him, not if I had any say so.

"I'm sorry, but unlike *some* people, I felt the need to stand
up for Yana. You said we weren't dogs, but I know you,
Daddy. You were going to go along with what Jordan was
saying, try to make her talk to him. She's over that. No one is

going to use her, not even you! Fuck that, Daddy! She's not your fucking pawn anymore, so get over—"

He lunged toward me so swiftly that I didn't even realize it until I felt his hands close around my neck. Shocked, I couldn't even move as he squeezed, robbing me of air. In twenty-four years, my father had never lain a hand on me in anger. Tears filled my eyes as my heart fell into pieces. DeAngelo jumped up, trying to move between us. He struggled for a few seconds before he was able to loosen my father's grasp. Daddy suddenly dropped his hands and D shoved him hard in his chest.

"Ay, Pop, you outta line. Y'all need to chill—"

"Boy, you betta keep yo' fucking hands off me! I'm out of line? This girl is standing flat-footed, under my roof, cussing me like she didn't come from my nut sack, and I'm out of line?" my father roared.

He stepped around D, his eyes blazing at me.

"Just because some wild ass, hood ass nigga is rutting between your legs every night don't mean you let him rub off on you and forget where you came from. I didn't pay for prep school and an Ivy League education and a six-figure salary for you to disrespect me. Dayana has a role to play for this family. So do you. Don't forget it," he snapped.

Ignoring the tears spilling down my cheeks, I met his eyes.

"My role? What's that, Daddy? Money launderer? Fixer? *Whore*? You've used me for all three, so which one do you think I'm in danger of forgetting?"

He froze for a moment, shocked at my boldness. I watched as he squeezed his hands into fists before exhaling one long, loud breath.

"Get the fuck out of my office, Dream," he said coldly.

Wordlessly, I left. I made it to the stairs before the tears came so hard, I could barely see. Pulling out my phone, I started to FaceTime Yana, then remembered I couldn't. She'd sent a message yesterday, letting us know she was okay and promising to call when she reached her destination today. Then, for reasons I couldn't figure out, I called *him*. Damien answered on the second ring. He was in his kitchen, hair pulled on top of his head, chest bare, gorgeous artwork on full display.

"I know it's too damn cold in that house for you to be shirtless," I tried to joke.

He didn't say anything at first, his eyes scanning my face. Then he frowned.

"Why you crying?" he asked, ignoring my words.

I wiped at my eyes with my free hand, shaking my head.

"It doesn't m—"

"You wanna drive or I'm coming to get you?" he interrupted.

"Damien—"

My voice trailed off as his eyes narrowed. I already knew he was going to win this argument, but I was too stubborn to give in easily. I climbed the stairs slowly, gathering my words.

"I'm fine. I just—"

He hung up. I knew that meant he was on his way. The last thing I needed was any kind of encounter between my father and him right now. Sighing, I hurried to call him back.

"Don't," I pleaded. "I'll come to you."

"You got forty-five minutes," he said before disconnecting again.

CHAPTER 46

Demon

I WAS STILL in the kitchen when she made it. She walked in slowly, eyes on me. Dream was dressed up for a Sunday afternoon. The designer dress she wore was sleeveless and hugged her curvy body, a deep V showing off the inner curves of her pretty titties and a split in the front, giving me a peek of her thick, creamy thighs. I'm sure she could see my suddenly hard dick through the black joggers I wore. I didn't say anything, just walked over and took her garment bag and duffel bag, leaving her with her small Chanel backpack. The traces of her tears were still on her beautiful face, pissing me off. But that was before I saw the bruises on her throat. *I know the fuck not.* I moved to set the bags on the counter before grabbing her chin and angling her face so I could see her neck better. Definitely fingerprints. Ice flooded my veins at the thought that someone had lain hands on her.

"Who choked you?" I asked tightly.

She shook her head. "Damien—"

"Don't play with me, Dream. Who the fuck choked you?"

"Maybe I just had a passionate encounter. You know I like a little choking," she popped off, trying to pull away from me.

I held on. "Nah. You far from stupid. Stop avoiding my question."

Sighing, she closed her eyes. "I really don't want to talk about this, Damien."

"I really don't give a fuck."

Silence. We stood there, locked in a stand-off, with her not wanting to talk and me refusing to give in. She might annoy the fuck out of me with her smart-ass mouth and bossy ways, but I would never physically hurt her. Nobody else out here was going to be doing that shit either. I let go of her chin and let my hand slide around to the back of her head, weaving my fingers through her hair. I pulled gently, making her look up at me.

"Dream."

"We met with the Middletons. It didn't go well, okay?" she said reluctantly.

Anger, cold and relentless, spilled through me. I didn't even need to know which one of those bitch ass niggas touched her. Any nigga with the last name Middleton could get it. My mind was already twisting and turning, thinking about how to lay them niggas down. I held on long enough to ask her another question.

"Where the fuck was your father?"

She was quiet for a moment, like she was trying to hide something. I knew damn well this nigga hadn't sent her to deal with a bunch of angry, aggressive men on her own. I was about to ask when she finally spoke.

"My father is the one who did this."

Her voice was so soft, I thought I must have heard her wrong at first. But the fresh tears in her eyes meant I hadn't. *The fuck?* I felt a muscle jumping in my jaw as I ground my teeth together, trying to hold on to my rage. With anyone else, I could be cold, calculating, and figure out the best angle to approach a situation from. With her, my instinct was to kill first and fuck any questions that might come later. Some part

of me—a very small part I had no interest in listening to—
knew that I couldn't kill her father. But the nigga kept asking
for it. Letting her make this deal. Telling her she was ruined.
Then choking her? Nah, he couldn't possibly value his life.

"He been putting his hands on you?" I asked.

She shook her head quickly, eager to defend his pussy ass.
"No. He's never done that before. Ever. He was just pissed,
and we argued, and he snapped—"

"Don't make excuses for that nigga," I cut her off.

She stopped immediately, her eyes dropping again. Lifting
my hand, I traced the marks on her neck with my index
finger. She shivered beneath my touch.

"He gotta see me," I told her.

Her eyes widened as she shook her head. "No. *No!*
Damien, you can't—"

"Chill, shorty. He gets a warning the first time since he's
your pops. But I told you. You mine for the next twenty-four
days. Nobody gon' lay hands on you, I'on give a fuck who it
is," I said calmly.

"You cannot hurt my father," she insisted.

"I won't... as long as yo' father don't hurt you."

"Ughhh!" she whined, before stomping toward the stairs.

"Nah. You said I wasn't getting inside you no more, so
why you going up there already? Take your ass in the living
room."

She whirled around to face me. "I meant what I said, too,"
she snapped.

I chuckled lowly. "We'll see, shorty."

She sucked her teeth before marching toward the living
room. I shook my head. Crazy ass girl had an attitude with me
because I wasn't going for anybody mistreating her irritating
ass. I wish somebody would make it make sense. I walked back
to the stove where the timer was just about to go off. Opening
the oven, I pulled out the pan of chicken, Brussels sprouts, and

sweet potatoes. Setting it on the stove stop, I picked up the little saucepan I'd made a balsamic glaze in. I drizzled it over the pan holding the food and let it sit while I pulled out plates, knives and forks, and glasses. Yeah, I might look and act like a savage, but I'd been cooking—when we had food—since I was seven or eight. It was the only way KiKi and I got to eat sometimes. I kept the shit up as I got older. For some reason, it relaxed me.

A few minutes later, I had everything ready. I walked into the living room carrying plates. Wordlessly, I set them on the coffee table before I went back to get napkins and my glass of apple juice and her glass of iced tea. Dream eyed me as I put the shit down before sitting down next to her on the couch. I handed her the brand-new Firestick remote control for the brand-new seventy-five-inch TV now suspended from my wall. I didn't watch TV, but since she was under the mistaken impression that we wouldn't be having sex for the next three and a half weeks, I figured I needed to get something to pass the time until she gave in.

"What do you want me to do with this?" she asked.

I shrugged. "Find a movie or some shit. I'm signed up for a bunch of streaming services."

Yeah, that shit had just happened today. She looked at me for a minute before turning the TV on and going to Prime video. I picked up my plate as she scrolled for a while. Finally, she picked one called *Deliver Us from Eva*. Once it started, I pointed at her plate.

"Eat," I said.

She wrinkled her nose. "Why you giving me orders?"

"I got used to it," I teased her.

Her face flamed and she picked up her plate and utensils without saying another word. I smirked at her as I picked up my fork. She grabbed my hand.

"Uh-uh! Bless the food," she said.

I looked at her sideways. I had only done that shit at Ms.

Hazel's, and I'd never been the one to say the words. But this girl was looking at me expectantly. I shook my head.

"You can say what you want over it. God ain't never listened to shit I had to say," I told her.

A sad look flitted across her face before she hurriedly whispered a prayer. She ate two bites of her food before looking at me again.

"Oh, my God. Did you really cook this?" she asked.

I raised an eyebrow. "Yeah. Why?"

"It's soooo good! I need this recipe. Grandpapa loves sweet potatoes and Brussels sprouts. He would love this!"

Her voice was enthusiastic, and she hurriedly took another bite. I couldn't lie; I liked that she enjoyed my food. I liked feeding her. This girl had me all out of my element.

"You love your grandfather."

She nodded eagerly. "That's my heart."

"And you're his."

"Yeah," she admitted shyly. "Is that bad? He's really good to Yana, too. DeAngelo gets on his nerves, but he loves him. But I know how he feels about me."

I shook my head. "Nah, not bad at all. You take care of all of them. You need somebody to take care of you. Like, I know damn well he don't know your daddy choked you."

She looked down at her plate, confirming what I said. Lucien probably would've shot Darius's ass. I really had much respect for the old man. We continued to eat in silence, watching this movie. Twenty minutes in and I was shaking my head again.

"Hell nah," I mumbled.

Dream looked at me. "What?"

"Them some simp ass, weak ass niggas, letting her get away with all that shit. Her sisters need to get her out they business. Find somebody to stroke her ass just right, get some of that attitude and anger out her ass," I said.

She rolled her eyes. "She *is* too much, but you can't fuck

the attitude out of nobody or fuck them into submission. Please!"

I peered down at her. "Oh, yeah?"

She sighed like I was a basic muhfucka or something. "Yes, Damien. Niggas be so sure about the power of they dicks! I don't know why y'all think—"

I side-eyed her, cutting her off. "Yo' ass bossy, stubborn, and stay tryna handle niggas. But all I gotta say is yo' name, and that rah-rah shit stops. And yo' personality in my room is nothing like yo' personality outside it. Why you think that is?"

Her mouth was wide open, a blush heating every inch of her face. I couldn't help smiling at her stuck look. She finally cleared her throat and glared up at me.

"So, you gon' ignore the facts that I know you a killer and you scary as hell? Maybe that's why I fall in line," she popped off.

I twisted my mouth as I looked at her in disbelief. "So, now you scared of me? Much as that mouth stay popping?"

"Ummm… you just tried to kill me!" she snapped.

"Wasn't nobody tryna kill yo' dramatic ass. And it ain't fear that has you moaning my name and wrapping them thick ass legs around me. Admit it, shorty. This dick changed yo' attitude and yo' life," I told her cockily.

She rolled her eyes and waved a hand. "Whatever, Damien. Just watch the movie."

I let her have that for now, turning my attention back to dinner and the movie. We finished the food in silence, and I took the dishes in the kitchen to rinse and stick in the dishwasher. By the time I made it back into the living room, she had scooted closer to my spot on the couch. Sitting in the sliver of space she left me, I side-eyed her.

"I need the body heat. Why you have it so cold in here?" she whined.

"Why you stay complaining?" I shot back.

Before she could say something with that smart ass mouth, I picked her up and dragged her across my lap. I sat her sideways next to me, her back pressed against the arm of the couch, her fat ass on the seat, her legs thrown across my thighs. I grabbed the throw off the back of the couch and draped it over her.

"Damien—"

"Shut up and watch these weak ass niggas," I told her.

She glared at me before turning to watch the movie. Five minutes later, she was moving around like she was restless. I could feel her eyes on my face, but I did my best to ignore her. I sighed as she called my name.

"What?"

"May I ask you a question?"

I looked down at her. "You wanna watch this movie or talk? I'm not understanding how you plan to do both."

She waved a hand, dismissing what I said.

"People do both all the time."

I expected her to ask what she wanted to know. Instead, she twirled a piece of her hair around her finger, like she was nervous. I watched her for a few seconds, my patience fading.

"Dream."

"Why do you hire escorts?" she blurted. "I mean, you're physically attractive and sex with you is... pleasant. I don't understand why you have to pay people to sleep with you."

She blushed as she looked away suddenly. I smirked at her nosy ass.

"Yo' ass be moaning and begging, but sex with me is just 'pleasant?'" I teased her.

Her skin reddened even more. "We're not talking about me. Just answer the question."

I leaned back on the couch, thinking about what, if anything, I should tell her. She waited, her eyes burning a hole in my face.

"I'on have to pay women to sleep with me," I finally said.

"Then why do you?"

I blew out a breath. *This girl!* "It's easier. Not messy. No feelings and expectations. Just... 'pleasant' sex. Women start wanting shit when you fuck on 'em. They get in their feelings. I don't have time for that."

She sucked her teeth. "That's not true in every situation!" she denied.

"I done seen too many niggas deal with the shit. It's true enough. I like having a business arrangement."

"Like ours," she said.

Hell no. Not like ours. None of my arrangements with escorts were as messy as this... entanglement. I didn't cook for them, watch chick flicks with them, or let them cuddle close to me for warmth. I didn't care if they cried or were angry or hurt, had never been tempted to kill for them. Dream had me on some other shit and I didn't like to dwell on it. She watched me expectantly, but I didn't respond.

"Damien?"

"Dream. Watch the damn movie," I growled.

"One more question," she coaxed.

I grilled her. She looked unbothered, contradicting her claim of being scared of me.

"Why did you step up at Dayana's wedding? Why did you help her?"

Damn. She didn't believe in easy questions. The truth was, I hadn't thought too much at the wedding. I just knew Dayana looked miserable until Smoke called her. I knew if the niggas who worked for her lame ass fiancé touched her, Dream was going to lose her mind. And if they tried to restrain Dream, that wasn't going to end well. Plus, I fucked with Smoke the long way.

"I don't believe in forcing people to do what they don't wanna do. She obviously didn't want that tired ass nigga. She left him to go to Smoke. And I owed Smoke a favor, anyway," I explained.

She nodded, then smiled up at me. "Thank you. She was miserable."

"Your pops got something like that planned for you?"

I was going to wreck that shit if he did. The thought of her with another nigga didn't sit right with me. She shook her head quickly, a small frown appearing between her brows.

"Hell no. He wanted to, but I made it clear I wasn't going. I'm more valuable to him as an employee. Plus, now that I'm 'ruined,' he thinks I'm a lost cause," she said with a dry ass laugh.

"Stop saying that stupid shit," I snapped. "I ain't ruin you. Shit, I gave you an important skill set."

She rolled her eyes. "Really? What is that?"

I smirked at her. "I taught you how to ride a dick and how to throw that ass back. And even though you stay running, I'ma teach you how to take dick properly."

Her mouth literally fell open and the sight of her full lips in a perfect "O" made me think of something else I wanted to teach her. Finally, she found her voice.

"You are so nasty! And you won't be teaching me anything else sexual. Remember what I said," she reminded me.

I nodded. "Okay, shorty."

"I'm serious—"

"You working tomorrow?" I changed the subject.

She nodded. "Yeah. I need to catch up, especially since I missed last Wednesday."

She shot me a nasty look that I ignored.

"Anyway, Parker and I are going to have a working dinner, too. So, a long day," she said with a sigh.

I looked at the TV, watching Gabrielle Union tell LL Cool J off about something. Yeah, that Eva character definitely needed to be fucked right. Dream yawned suddenly, then stretched, her soft legs rubbing against mine. She was crazy if she thought I was never getting between them again. But I was going to wait for her to come to me.

"I lied," she announced suddenly.

I lifted an eyebrow and waited.

"One more question, for real. What's in that locked room on—"

I went from zero to one thousand real quick at the mention of the room I used when I needed peace. She leaned away from me, against the arm of the couch as my eyes burned into hers.

"None of your fuckin' business. No one else goes in there. *Ever.* You understand?" I spat.

For a minute, she just looked at me, her eyes unreadable. Then she nodded slowly before turning to stare at the TV. I realized that I'd just fucked up whatever had been unfolding between us tonight during our shared meal and this stupid ass movie. The soft, curious, smiling Dream was gone. In her place was the cool, tense, proper woman who'd made that deal with me.

Good, I thought, *that's the way it should be.* But I couldn't even convince myself that was true.

Our conversation for the rest of the night was minimal. She chose a second movie, some action shit I guess she thought I'd like, but she fell asleep halfway through, her attitude still evident. I carried her upstairs and helped her slip out of the dress. I knew she was tired—she didn't even fight me. Just fell on the bed in her bra and panties when we were done. I went back downstairs to get all her stuff. Her backpack was on the couch where we'd been, open because she'd checked her phone a few times. I looked at it for a moment, then did some shit I'd never done before. Grabbing her phone, I put in the pass code I'd seen her enter earlier. I checked her call log and text messages. I didn't know what I was going to do if she was talking to other niggas... but she better not be talking to other niggas. Her call log was clear—

mostly calls to her family. I read through a few of her text messages. Most were from Parker, Dayana, and her grandfather. I smirked at that. Lucien Dumont was an old savage, but he sent his granddaughter funny memes, told her he loved her every day, and constantly asked what she needed. Swear that girl made niggas soft. DeAngelo checked on her regularly. Nigga apologized a couple of times for getting her "involved" with someone like me and made her promise to tell him if he needed to handle me. Shit made me laugh. But I sobered up when I read her response:

D, he's not like y'all think. I'm good. He's rude, but I don't think he'll hurt me. Stop apologizing! I almost felt bad—she'd sent that Wednesday, before I'd scared her in the shower.

Her mama had been going crazy over Dayana's wedding. Her father's messages were short and usually about business. I was about to back out of the messages when I noticed a thread under the name Paul. The co-worker who liked to touch her. My hand tightened on her phone, and I fought back the cold trickling through me as I opened the thread. He mostly talked about work, but he was always asking how she was and complimenting her. Then, a week ago, he'd sent a message after the business shit, telling her he was serious about wifing her. She sent a blushing emoji with the words *Paul, stop.* Nigga kept trying until she told him she'd talk to him later. She tried to let him down easy. I wasn't going to be so nice.

I moved to return the phone and saw the little plastic holder that contained her birth control pills. Picking it up, I flipped it open and saw the next pill was for tomorrow. I guess for a minute, I lost my fucking mind because I considered taking the little packet and keeping it. I dropped that shit back in her bag quickly as hell. Kids were nowhere in my future.

I hauled her shit upstairs and put it on the dresser. Walking over to the bed, I looked down at her, wondering if she would still be mad when she woke. Eve's advice popped into my head. I still wasn't about to become a flower-buying nigga, but maybe I could finance her dinner with Parker. A few minutes later, I had tucked a couple of stacks on the bottom of the backpack and closed it. It was a peace offering. She better accept that shit. That was something I never gave.

CHAPTER 47

Dayana

ALL THE PICTURES and videos I'd ever seen of the Maldives didn't do the islands justice. This place was beautiful, lush and green with the scent of the ocean hanging in the air. The home Smoke had rented was equally gorgeous—four huge bedrooms and bathrooms anchored by a spacious living room and dream kitchen. I wanted to explore it, enjoy the atmosphere, but I couldn't at the moment. I was too busy listening to my twin go off in my ear.

"I'm just trying to see what the fuck you were thinking, going halfway around the world with a nigga you barely know. And this shit with Jordan—why you didn't tell me, Yana? That nigga determined to have you! I know I'ma have to fuck him up," DeAngelo fussed.

Sighing, I squeezed my eyes shut, rubbing my temple. I really didn't need this shit.

"D, I didn't plan any of this. It just felt right in the moment. I just couldn't see myself with Jordan—"

"And that's fine, but Smoke Salinas, Yana? That's almost as bad as the fact that I think Dream catching feelings for that crazy ass nigga she fucking."

I frowned at that. "Dream is in that situation because of

you, but you and Daddy keep shitting on her for that. If she can find some happiness in it, good for her. And trust me, it's not one-sided. He feeling her, too! Now, let me go so I can call her."

"I think she with him right now. Pops pissed her off, and I heard her talking to Demon a couple of minutes later."

Shaking my head, I ran my fingers over the aquamarine spread that covered the huge bed in the room Smoke had shown me to.

"What he do?" I asked.

"She got a little salty and he choked her."

My jaw dropped as the beginnings of anger flowed through me.

"What the fuck?"

"Yeah. Nigga tripping," D sighed.

"He can trip all he wants, but he better be careful putting his hands on my sister!" I raged.

"Right. He gon' regret it when he calms down. But listen, you stay safe, Yana. You call me immediately if that nigga gets on some fuckboy shit."

"You know I will—"

"And we gotta have a family meeting when you get back," he continued.

I laughed dryly. "I'm disowned, remember?"

He sucked his teeth. "Ain't nobody worried about that shit. Mama and Grandpapa ain't going for it and you know Dream and I will never entertain that shit.

"You know Darius Castle runs that household—"

"With input. This ain't no dictatorship. I gotta go—Crys and I got plans. But I'm serious, Yana. You call me if—"

"Bye, Brother! I love you," I interrupted before hanging up quickly.

DeAngelo in overprotective mode was more than I could handle. I lifted one of my bags onto the bed, looking for something to sleep in. It was almost five AM here, but I was tired after a day-long flight and my session with Smoke. I would shoot Dream a text, shower, and fall into this bed. I pulled out a tank top and some sleep shorts, intent on heading for the bathroom. A knock on my door stopped me.

"Come in!" I called, expecting it to be Smoke.

I was surprised that he'd had our stuff put in different rooms, but I didn't want to crowd him. I knew he had a lot on his mind.

"Hi!" Ms. Stephanie called out, opening the door.

I smiled at her. She really was the sweetest woman. At the same time, I could tell she didn't play. Jenesis and Smoke had the utmost respect for her, and they seemed to be her world.

"Is it okay if I come in?" she asked.

"Yes, ma'am."

She stepped in and closed the door behind her. "Cartier wanted me to check on you. He had to take a call. You good?"

"Yes, ma'am. This place is so beautiful. I'm glad I came."

"I'm glad you came, too. I was so worried that Cartier was going to let you go through with that... situation." Walking across the room, she grabbed my hands and squeezed them. "Thank God he came to his senses."

Okay, now I was *really* curious about what he had told her about me. I guess she could tell by the look on my face.

"Suga, just the fact that Cartier brought you up and mentioned your name let me know you were special to him. It's about time. It's been three years—"

"And his wife still has his heart," I interrupted her, sounding sad. "She sounds amazing, so I get it."

Ms. Stephanie sighed. "She was. Beautiful inside and out. I won't lie—they loved each other hard. He was devastated when she died. But Jenna wanted Cartier to be happy. She wanted someone to love him and her baby. It was one of the last things she told me."

Her words shook me. I just didn't know if I could be that gracious. Instead of being bitter about losing her life so young, Jenna Salinas had been worried about her family being loved and taken care of when she could no longer do it.

"But he said—"

She held up a hand. "I can imagine. Cartier has survivor's guilt. He feels like part of his life should be over because Jenna's is over. That's not how life works, though. He's been refusing to care about another woman. I haven't even heard him mention one, and I'm sure he has his... needs taken care of. So, you can imagine how surprised I was when I heard your name. And how *not* surprised I was when he got you from that wedding. I knew then that you meant something to him, and I am so glad."

I could see the sincerity in her eyes. Her words reminded me of his: *"You been in my head since the moment I met you. I've walked away from so many women since Jenna died, but I don't want to walk away from you. I don't want to break my promise to my wife, but I find myself wanting to make promises to you."* I was confused, not sure what to trust. On the one hand, he wanted someone with more experience, just to fuck, and he wanted to stay committed to his wife. On the other, he seemed undeniably attracted to me in a way that was more than sexual. I should probably walk away from him after this week, get my own life together and let him find someone who could handle being his friend with benefits. But...

Ms. Stephanie grabbed my hands suddenly, pulling me out of my thoughts.

"Listen. I know it's a lot to ask. I know he probably has your head spinning with the hot and cold, but Dayana, please, just give my son a chance. He's a good man, a good father, a good son. He don't tolerate bullshit, but he loves with everything in him. And I can already tell how easy it would be for him to love you," she said, squeezing my hands before letting them go.

Before I could say anything, she was walking back to the door.

"I'm going to let you get your rest. I'll tell Cartier you're good."

"Thank you," I told her, not sure what else to say.

With one final smile, she left me with my mixed-up thoughts. I went through the motions of showering, brushing my teeth, and moisturizing my body. The whole time, my mind was whirling. I asked Cartier for this week, Jordan and Jenna free. I wondered if that was even possible, given his love for his wife. I'd definitely have no problem pretending Jordan's bitch ass didn't exist.

I slid into my sleeping clothes and pulled back the bed covers. Then, I stopped suddenly. Instead of sitting here, wondering what was on Cartier's mind, I could go find out. Shoving my feet in my slippers, that's exactly what I did.

CHAPTER 48
Smoke

TAKING a deep pull from the blunt I'd rolled while I checked in with my right hand back in the States, I lounged in one of the chairs on the patio outside my room. From the outside, I knew shit looked good. At thirty, I was a crazy rich nigga, vacationing in one of the loveliest locations in the world with my family and a beautiful ass woman. Not bad for a former corner boy with a fugitive father who'd escaped back to Mexico and a mother who'd never worked until her husband had to leave her.

But shit was never as simple as it seemed, and Dayana Castle was a complication that I hadn't counted on. She made me question every-fucking-thing I believed about my love life after Jenna. Hell, there wasn't supposed to be a love life after Jenna, which was why I had entertained Dante's suggestion of an arranged marriage. All business, no feelings. That's why I didn't really give a fuck when that shit fell apart. Then, Dayana walked into my bar and suddenly I was having to deal with something Jenna had tried to make me face before she died.

It had been one of her good days, and out of all the shit we could've been doing, she wanted to sit in the middle of the bed and shop online for me. I was a stylish nigga, but that shit was the last thing on my mind as I watched my baby dying. She noticed and raised hell. So, I sat with her between my legs as she dropped jeans in the cart on the Balmain website.

"You not about to be out here falling off," she fussed.

I shook my head. "I'm not, baby. This shit just not important right now."

She sucked her teeth. "You just better hope your next girl is as fashionable as I am."

Her tone was teasing, but the shit instantly pissed me off. She kept preaching about me coming to terms with her dying, but I wasn't ready for that shit.

"Don't play with me, Jenna. Ain't no next girl," I said tightly.

She looked over her shoulder at me, her pretty, brown eyes worried. She grabbed my hand in her too-thin one and squeezed.

"Smoke Salinas, you better promise me there's gon' be a next girl. You too fine and too good of a husband to be single forever," she whispered.

"You trippin', J. I'm not finna talk about this stupid shit."

My voice was angry, but I was gentle as I moved her to the side of me and climbed out of the bed. I didn't want to hear her right now. But she grabbed the back of my shirt and I stopped.

"Baby," she whispered. "You deserve—"

"I already got more than I deserve when I got you. Ain't shit else out there for me," I cut her off.

"Cartier..."

"Leave the shit alone, Jenna."

She sighed and let me go. I stood up, ready to walk away from this conversation.

"Baby, don't leave," she pleaded. "We don't have to talk about—"

But I was already back in bed, grabbing her up, kissing her gaunt face around the oxygen tube.

"I'm sorry," I mumbled.

"So am I," she said softly.

She was gone two months later, and a next girl had been the least of my worries.

Until now.

A soft knock on the glass doors that led to the patio pulled me out of my thoughts. I looked up into the doe eyes of the woman who had my mind so fucked up right now. In a tank top and shorts that put all her thick, curvy legs on display, Dayana had my dick instantly hard.

"Hey," I said, adjusting myself as she stepped outside.

"Hey," she responded, a shy smile creeping across her face as she walked over and pulled out the chair to the left of me at the table.

"Nah."

She frowned as I shook my head. Wordlessly, I grabbed her hand and pulled her to me and into my lap. She settled against me easily and we just sat there for a few minutes as I finished the blunt.

"Mama said you were good," I said.

"I am. I just…"

Her voice trailed off and she looked down. I tilted her chin up, making her meet my eyes.

"Ay. I want you to always speak yo' mind with me."

She nodded, then sighed. "I watched you for a minute. You were thinking hard. Am I asking too much, asking for this week? I can't tell where your mind is and—"

I pressed my fingers against her lips.

"You not asking too much and I wanna give it to you," I said truthfully, making up my mind to keep my promise to her. "I'm gon' give it to you."

She smiled again and our eyes turned back to the view of the ocean. It wasn't long before she was yawning as she cuddled closer to me.

"Let's go to bed, Princess. Whenever we wake up, we can eat and you can tell me what you wanna do and see this week," I suggested.

She nodded, then squealed when I stood, swinging her up in my arms as I started walking.

"You let this skinny nigga surprise you, huh?" I teased.

She wrinkled her nose. Shit was so cute. "You're not skinny. More like slim, but muscular."

"Your finest friend."

She giggled. "Definitely."

I set her down on the bed and she looked up at me.

"You want me to sleep with you?" she asked.

It was my turn to frown. "You don't wanna sleep with a nigga?"

"Smoke, you gave me my own room. I didn't know—"

"Shit, I was fronting. I planned to creep my ass right over there, under yo' covers and into yo'—"

"Cartier Salinas!" she gasped, blushing.

But then a sneaky little smile curved her lips.

"Tell me more."

"Shit," I said, reaching for her tank top. "Let me show you."

CHAPTER 49

Demon

(*MONDAY, June 14*)

Dante's usual dry sense of humor was missing. Instead, I was seeing the part of my brother the world outside his family saw—silent, cold, thoughtful, ruthless. I knew something was fucked up.

"What is it?" I asked.

We sat on opposite sides of his desk, Dante deep in thought, me waiting. But I was tired of that shit.

"Dante—"

"That night you told me you were meeting Dream, remember I mentioned a situation?" he finally said.

"Yeah. It's at the point you need me to handle it?"

"It's at the point I need you to be careful."

I looked at him, confused. Being careful was automatic in our world. The fact he felt the need to tell me meant shit was serious.

"The fuck is going on?"

"Just a loose end coming back to haunt us," he said.

I watched as he opened a humidor on his desk, but instead of pulling out a cigar, he grabbed one of his ever-present blunts. A flick of his gold lighter and a citrusy, herbal scent filled the air. He toked a couple of times before letting out a deep exhale. I wanted him to explain what the fuck he meant. It made no sense. Dante was known for how thorough he was.

"You don't leave loose ends," I pushed.

He looked at me, brown eyes holding something like concern.

"I didn't leave this one. You did," he said.

I frowned. That wasn't possible. My father and brother had taught me too well.

"Nothing recent. I know you're too good for that. Demon, it's Keith McKellar. Despite the reports, he blames you for killing his family. Got out of jail three months ago and immediately put a price on your head."

Keith McKellar. Angela's brother. Melanie's dealer and sometimes pimp, according to shit I heard when I was a kid. He thought I killed his family for a good reason—I did. I would've put his ass in the dirt, too, but drug charges finally caught up with him. I sat back and eyeballed Dante. I couldn't believe he waited to tell me this shit, but I knew him well enough to know he had a reason. Still, I had to ask.

"You just now thinking to mention this?"

"I wanted to handle it myself. First, that nigga either got big balls or he crazy as fuck to come for my brother. Second, you don't need any ghosts from the past…"

He let his voice trail off. But he didn't need to say anything else. I gritted my teeth as icy anger flooded through me. I hated the fact that he felt the need to look out for me. To me, the shit was pity for my childhood, and I didn't need it. I stood up abruptly, almost knocking the chair over.

"I don't need you to handle shit. I keep telling you about that big brother shit, but you keep meddling in my fucking life. I can take care of my own problems, Dante. I—"

Surprising me, Dante sprang up, his hands clenched into fists, his jaw tight as hell.

"I usually let yo' crazy ass say what the fuck you want to say. You angry, you don't trust people, you been taking care of yourself, I get all that shit. You don't need nobody, and you don't want a family. But that's too fuckin' bad, nigga. You my brother, my blood, and I'ma continue to look out for yo' psycho ass. You think I'ma hear about a nigga tryna take yo' life and sit back? You got me and this life fucked up. Get yo' crazy ass out my office, Demon!" he raged.

I couldn't lie. The shit shocked me. For fifteen years, my brother had been laid back with me. Nigga looked ready to fuck me up right now, though. Fuck it! I stretched my fingers. I didn't discriminate. Just like anyone else, he could get it. I stepped closer to him. Before I could blink, he had his gun drawn.

"Ain't nobody stupid enough to fight yo' big ass, Demon. Way I'm feeling, you can lose a knee or some shit this evening,"

I smirked at the nigga. "I know yo' daddy taught you not to pull that shit unless you ready to use it."

He aimed at my right knee and cocked his gun. "You know better than anybody. Bring yo' ass around this desk if you want to."

"So, you hunting down another nigga who probably planning to shoot me, but it's okay if you do it?" I didn't want it to be, but something about the shit was funny to me.

"I'ma just give yo' ass a little flesh wound or something. Remind you that crazy is a family trait," he said, lowering his arm.

Shaking my head, I slid my hands into my pockets.

"So, why you ain't got the nigga?"

Dante sighed. "Having trouble finding him. Which makes me think somebody is hiding him. That shit won't last though, with Li Jun leading the search. I just needed you to know, so you could watch out for yourself… and whoever."

I looked at him silently, knowing what he was implying,

then nodded. A few minutes later, I left Dante's estate. I planned to head home and start my own search for Keith before doing some work to release my tension. So, how I ended up outside Dream's office building was a mystery to me. It was almost eight, but she'd told me she and Parker would be here late. I wanted to go in and get her, but I respected her work ethic. So, instead, I sat in my car, trying to figure out how to flush Keith's bitch ass out.

A half hour later, one of the front doors of her office building opened. She stepped out first, wearing the baby blue dress I'd seen her in this morning. Parker was close behind her and they were laughing about something. A whole day at work and she still looked pretty as fuck. And the muhfucka coming out behind her was as stuck on that fact as I was. Paul Arceneau was going to make me fuck him up. Opening my door, I stepped out. Seeing that nigga's face fall almost made me smile. Dream stopped, clutching her briefcase and back-pack while she looked at me. Parker waved, grinning her ass off. I gave her a head nod and waited. Finally, Dream walked to me, a little frown on her face.

"Did you put money in my backpack?" she asked, keeping her voice low.

Some of her hair had come out of the bun-thing she had it in. The wind was strong enough to mess with it, blowing it in her face. I reached out to tuck it behind her ear. That wasn't the kind of shit I did, but something about this girl made it hard not to touch her.

"Hey, Dream. How was your day?" I responded.

She scoffed. "Oh, now you worried about manners?"

"You rubbing off on me, I guess." I shrugged.

Rolling her eyes, she moved closer to me. I didn't think she even realized she did it, like she was subconsciously trying to be near me. For some reason, I liked that.

"What are you doing here, Damien?"

"I came to pick you up. You about to take a ride with me."

She shook her head. "Nah. I gotta give Parker a ride home, and I'm tired."

I crossed my arms over my chest and leaned against my car, watching her. "Why you always assume I'm giving you a choice?"

She sighed in frustration. "Why you always such an asshole?"

I smiled at her before gesturing for Parker to come over. Paul watched everything, his eyes narrowed as he stood in the middle of the lot. Catching my gaze, he called Dream's name. She looked up as she dropped her keys in Parker's hand.

"You okay?" he asked.

"People stay asking you that around me," I commented.

She glared at me. "I wonder why."

I pushed more hair out of her face. "Tell that soft ass nigga you fine before I do."

"Damien... just... don't."

"Personally, I'd love to see what happens," Parker spoke up.

Dream gave her a nasty look that Parker just shrugged off.

"Dream?" Paul called again.

"It's fine, Paul! Go home. Thank you for staying with us," she said, smiling brightly.

"Stop grinning like that," I told her.

"First, I can't touch a nigga. Now, I can't smile at them? Fuck you, Damien," she snapped.

"Okay. You the one talking about no sex," I shot back.

Parker giggled. "On that note, I think I'll go. Dream, call me when you on your way to pick the car up."

"You can just drive it to work in the morning," I said.

Dream gaped at me. "Nigga—"

"Get in the car, Dream."

She wanted to argue so bad. The look I gave her crushed that shit, though. She made a little sound, then followed me around the car to the passenger door. I opened it for her, and she slid in. By the time I got back in, she was buckled in and looking at me.

"Where we riding to?"

"Just sit back."

———

"You trust me not to murder you and throw you in?" I teased Dream as we sat down near the end of the pier in front of my lake house.

She sucked her teeth as she scooted closer to me, pressing against my side.

"I'ma haunt your ass forever if you do."

For a long time, we just sat. The moonlight reflected on the surface of the lake, peaceful and still. Every time I came up here, it was hard to leave. This was the one place I let shit go, the one place I didn't feel the need to be Demon, that I wondered what a regular ass nigga named Damien might be like.

"Why'd you put the money in my bag?" she asked suddenly.

"To pay for your dinner," I said, giving her half of the truth.

"Damn, Damien. I'm a thick girl, but two thousand dollars for a working dinner? How much you think I eat?"

"Shut up, Dream."

"You just gave me money Friday and again today. You can't be giving me money like that. It doesn't look right!"

I frowned at her.

"Fuck you talking about? I do what the fuck I want. I'on care what people think."

She dropped her eyes for a moment, like she was thinking.

"One of the things you do is pay women for... you know. I'm not that," she finally said softly.

I shook my head. "You tripping, shorty. I know you not that."

"Then why you give me money?"

I grabbed one of the rocks I had picked up and sent it skipping across the lake's surface. She was getting too personal, and I didn't like that shit.

"I told you why. What I tell you about asking questions I done already answered?"

She pulled back a little, going cold on me. Swear her attitude stayed on go.

"I'on know why you tripping. Niggas give chicks they fuck money on the daily. Yo' little ass just gotta question shit. Anyway, you the one saying we ain't fucking no more, so how can it be that?" I asked her, skipping another rock.

"Don't act like we're regular sex partners. And what you mean, I'm the one who said it? You might as well say it, too. Acting like you don't believe me," she huffed.

I smiled at her bossy ass. "I don't."

She looked up at me, her mouth open. "You don't believe I'm done having sex with you?"

I shook my head. "Nah, shorty. I know you ain't done having sex with me."

She mumbled some shit before rolling her eyes and turning back toward the water.

"Dream, it ain't about this deal or me wanting you. You like having me in that li'l pussy. You gon' put me back in it, too."

"No, the hell—"

I dropped a quick, hard kiss on her lips to stop that lie.

"Fuck, a nigga miss it, too. You got some good pussy, Dream. Excellent."

Shit, I could hear the longing in my own voice. She opened her mouth, then closed it again. Tilting her head, she looked up at me.

"Why are we here, Damien? What's on your mind?"

"Besides your pussy?" I teased.

"Damien!"

I sighed. "I have a… situation. Somebody from my past is looking for me."

"Why?" she asked.

I debated on how much to tell her, then said fuck it. "I killed the people he loved."

She was quiet for a minute, studying the water. I could only see half her face, but I could tell a million thoughts were going through her head.

"Did they… did they deserve it?" she finally asked.

Yeah. With a question like that, she was definitely a product of this world.

"Two out of three definitely did. I'm not sure about the third," I admitted.

"Collateral damage," she whispered.

"Yeah. And now I need to watch my back… and yours."

She frowned. "Mine?"

"You're connected to me…"

I let the sentence trail. She nodded, knowing the drill.

"Story of my life. I'll tell my dad's people," she said.

"There will be other people, too. You won't know them niggas there."

Another nod. She knew better than to argue. The silence between us stretched.

"What's on your mind, El?" she asked after a little while.

"I told you not to call me that shit."

She smiled. I had surprised her ass by having some DeBarge playing in my car. She talked shit most of the way to the lake house.

"What? I'm happy that you found your yella nigga muse," she teased, a smirk decorating her pretty face. "Let me find out you some sensitive, artistic kinda nigga."

I swallowed at how close she had hit to home.

"Don't get fucked up out here, Dream," I warned her, but the shit wasn't convincing at all.

"You stay about to fuck me up," she said, completely unbothered.

I looked down at her as she curled into my side. This girl had physically touched me more in one week than anybody had in the last fifteen years. I usually hated being touched, hated the intimacy people tried to push on me by laying their hands on me. Until her. And I didn't want to think about what that meant.

"You not picking the movies tonight," I told her, needing to put my mind on something else.

"That's okay. If your taste in movies is like your taste in music, we gon' end up watching a rom-com anyway, El," she said before giggling.

"You definitely getting fucked up," I mumbled, mushing her head.

CHAPTER 50
Dream

(*WEDNESDAY*, *June 16*)

"I can't believe you're a sore loser! Big ol' pouting ass!" I taunted Damien as he drove us home from Top Golf.

He shot me a look out of the corner of his eye, a smirk decorating his face.

"Watch how you talk to me, Dream. And yo' ass cheated enough to win."

I sucked my teeth. "Nigga! How I cheat? Tell me that?"

He didn't dignify my question with a response. Instead, he turned up the music, letting the sounds of Larry June flood the car. Rolling my eyes, I let him make it. I was still in disbelief that he agreed to go and that he relaxed enough to play. We'd had fun as I talked shit to him, and he kept threatening to fuck me up.

For the last few days, I'd maintained my vow not to have sex with him anymore. Surprisingly, he accepted it. We'd been sitting at his house, watching movies and shit for a couple of days before I declared we needed to do something else. I guess he listened, because tonight, we went out.

Now, we were on the way back to his house to watch a movie, I guessed. But the way he was looking in the simple, red, V-neck t-shirt and jeans, with his throat and arm tats on display, had me second guessing my decision not to fuck him. His locs were pulled on top of his head—a style I loved—displaying his gorgeous face, and his scent was intoxicating. My pussy was a puddle and I wanted to feel his solid, warm body on mine as he stretched and filled me. I shook my head at the thought. I had it bad.

These last few days, when we'd had to find reasons to spend time together besides having sex, had been fun. Damien still didn't talk much, but he had a quiet, dry sense of humor and he was a good listener. Every little bit of himself that he shared made me want to know more. I was in danger of forgetting this was a thirty-day deal because it was almost feeling like the beginning of a relationship. Shit, maybe we better go back to fucking and arguing before I got in way over my head.

"You over there gloating?" he asked suddenly.

"Boy, please. Handling you was lightweight," I teased.

"Keep on," he said, as we turned on his street.

"What you gon' do?"

My eyes were on him as we turned into his driveway.

"I'ma..."

His voice trailed off as he suddenly leaned closer to the windshield. He tensed and the half smile he'd been sporting fell from his face. He threw the Jag in park. Alarmed, I looked forward and saw a white woman and a young boy standing in front of the house.

"Stay here," he spat as he opened the door and climbed out.

But he was the good listener in this relationship, not me. I got out right behind him, even though I didn't think he realized. He was too focused on the people in front of him. They looked harmless to me, but I knew how Damien felt about people knowing where he laid his head.

"Damien—" the woman began, holding out her hands toward him.

"What the fuck are you doing here? How you find out where I live?" he growled, walking up on her.

I could see from here that she was shaking with nerves. She was tall, probably almost six feet, and looked to be in her fifties. Her gaze shot to me, like she was asking for help, but Damien was on his way to Demon mode, and I didn't want to fuck with that.

Still, I cleared my throat and spoke up.

"Damien, who is this?"

"Didn't I tell your ass to stay in the car?" he snapped.

"I'm his mother," the woman whispered.

He moved so fast that I didn't know what was happening until he had the barrel of the gun pressed to the center of her forehead. I froze for a moment as she sobbed. Hell, I was scared for her.

"Bitch, don't you ever, *ever* say that shit again. You sold me, remember?" he asked her coldly.

"Ay, nigga, get that gun off my mama!"

Shit, I'd forgotten about the boy with her. He pushed Damien, but he didn't move. Instead, he stared down at the boy and laughed.

"Yo' mama? How old are you, li'l nigga?" he demanded.

"T-twelve," the boy stammered.

He was trying to be brave for his mother, but it was obvious Damien scared him. My heart went out to him.

"Twelve, huh? So, he got what? A year before you pimp him out, Melanie?"

He pressed the gun tighter against her forehead.

"Damien--" she started.

"Demon," he corrected her. "You don't know me like that."

"I'm clean… Demon. I have been for a while."

He sneered at her. "You think I give a fuck? You got ten

seconds to tell me why you here or I'ma empty your head on this driveway. I been dreaming about that shit forever."

I shivered at the dark iciness of his voice. Melanie swallowed. Tension swirled around us, thickening the air. I struggled to draw in a calming breath.

"Five seconds," he bit out.

I watched in horror as he flipped the safety off the gun. He was serious. I could see it all over him. I had to do something.

"Damien—"

"I don't want to hear shit, Dream. Take your ass in the house if you ain't ready to see this."

I touched his arm. "You can't... Damien, you can't do this. Not in front of your brother. Not to your..."

His eyes flew to me, the green ice cold.

"My what? This bitch ain't shit to me. And I'on know this li'l nigga. Anyway, he better off without her."

"Please. Just put the gun down, okay?" I begged.

"You playing fixer again, Dream? You gon' make everything right?" he taunted me. "I'm not them weak ass niggas you know. I don't need you to solve shit for me. I don't need you for shit but the easy fuck you supposed to be."

His words were sharp, digging into me with every syllable, but I ignored the hurt.

"I know. You don't need anybody. But you should listen to me. Don't do this."

"Please, man," his little brother spoke up.

Damien's gaze flashed to him. "Don't you ever beg a nigga for shit. Especially not this worthless bitch's life," he spat.

But slowly, his gun arm lowered.

"Get off my property, Melanie, and take your jit. If I ever see you again, it'll be your last day. On God."

Turning, he stalked toward the front door. I glanced at his mother before hurrying behind him.

"I'm sick, Demon," she called suddenly.

"Good," he shot back. "Die quickly."

"I gotta have surgery and then I'll start treatments in a couple of days. I have to be in the hospital for a few weeks."

He kept walking, ignoring her.

"Your brother—Kameron—has nowhere to go. I-I-I don't want him to go into the system."

He paused at that. I almost ran into his back.

"It can't be worse than living with you," he finally said, but I could hear the catch in his voice.

"Damien... please," she said softly.

"Ma, don't beg this nigga. I don't wanna stay with him, anyway," Kameron hissed.

Damien turned around to grill him. "At least you can tell you not wanted."

"Damien!" I whispered, mortified.

Melanie dared to look at him again.

"Look, I know I have no right to ask you anything after all I put you through. I know I'm not your family. But Kameron is. He's your brother. Please, just…"

"Shut the fuck up, Melanie," Damien snapped before turning his attention to his brother. "Bring yo' ass here," he ordered.

Kameron looked at his mother. She touched his arm, then nodded. Slowly, he walked toward us. I watched as the brothers stared at each other for a minute, green gazes clashing.

"That's all your shit?" Damien finally asked, indicating the duffel bag and backpack Kameron carried.

The kid nodded.

"You can get a room for a little while. I'on care what you eat, but don't leave my kitchen dirty. If you steal anything, leave a mess, try to get into any of my locked rooms, or talk to me too much, I'll shoot you. Understand?"

I shook my head at his rude ass as Kameron nodded again. Damien looked at Melanie.

"Now, get the fuck," he told her, before walking off.

She hesitated, beckoning Kameron back over to her. Once he was there, she hugged him tight, whispering to him. The boy nodded, reluctant to let her go.

"Unless you wanna find yourself in foster care, I suggest you bring your ass on," Damien said emotionlessly.

Kameron froze for a moment before finally releasing Melanie. She stroked his cheek one last time before turning to go. Seconds later, he was standing beside me, obviously too wary to approach his crazy ass brother. I gave him a small smile.

"I'm Dream," I said softly.

"You can call me Kam."

"You need any help?"

I gestured toward his bags. He was already shaking his head when his older brother spoke up.

"I wish that li'l nigga would let a woman help him carry some shit."

"Damien!" I snapped again.

"What? Stop calling my fucking name like I'm your child, Dream," he growled before walking into the house.

Kameron and I looked at each other before following him. Part of me was telling me to go home, to leave the brothers to figure this shit out. But Damien was way too overwhelming for a twelve-year-old. And when his rude ass disappeared, I was glad I stayed. I showed Kameron the guest rooms, letting him pick the one he liked the most. He set his stuff down before turning back to me, his green eyes worried.

"Is he always like that?" he asked.

"Like what?" I played ignorant, not wanting to scare the child anymore.

"Mean."

His voice was a whisper. My heart broke for him. He lost his mama and gained a crazy ass big brother in her wake. That had to be hard.

"He's rude and he doesn't know how to talk to people, but he's not mean. He won't mistreat you—"

"You're too nice for him," he interrupted. "Why you here? Does he hit you? I can... I can help protect you if he hits you."

Tears flooded my eyes as I wondered what this baby had seen in his years. Crossing to him, I pulled him in my arms and hugged him as tightly as I could. He hugged me back, already so much taller than my five-foot-four frame.

"I promise you, he doesn't hit me. He would never hurt me. And I know he's an asshole, but he's not going to hurt you, either," I vowed.

Yeah, I was glad I didn't leave. I was glad to be here to soothe Kameron's worries.

And... I wanted to be here when Damien dealt with the fact that he'd seen his mother for the first time in a while. It was stupid. I shouldn't care, I told myself as I showered. He'd just reminded the world that I was a "fuck." And still, I didn't want to leave him.

He came into the room silently, so I didn't bother speaking, either. I watched as he gathered his stuff for the shower before I eased into his bed. I caught up on my social media and started a new book before he reappeared. I pretended not to notice him looking at me.

"You still here?" he said finally.

Hurt swept through me at the snide words. I threw back the bedcovers.

"Give me a minute. I can definitely be gone," I said tightly.

I stood up and suddenly he was in my face, blocking me.

"Move," I snapped, pushing against him.

I might as well have pushed the wall. He cupped the back of my neck before resting his forehead against mine.

"Fuck, Dream. I don't know why I said that. I don't want you to leave," he sighed.

His words surprised me, but I wasn't letting him off that easily, though.

"Why? I'm just a fuck, remember?"

"You *are* supposed to be just a fuck."

His gaze pierced mine. I closed my eyes, unable to deal with the intensity.

"I know. So, let me leave."

I fought back my stupid tears, gnawing on my bottom lip.

"But you're not," he whispered, pulling my lip free with his thumb before sucking it into his mouth.

I melted against him.

CHAPTER 51

Demon

YOU OFFICIALLY A SIMP ASS NIGGA. This girl made me so weak. But I wasn't ready to face the night without her. Not after seeing Melanie. Not when I knew the dreams would come.

I let go of her lip, then pressed a kiss to her mouth before stepping back.

"Stop talking to me crazy," she said.

I shook my head. "I can't promise that shit."

She sighed, then climbed back into bed. I joined her a few minutes later. Lying on my back, I stared at the ceiling. What the fuck was I going to do with a kid? Especially if his ass turned out to be as bad as I had been. Melanie was always putting me in a position to be more of a father to my siblings than a brother. I hated that shit, but it wasn't the kids' fault. Kam was also another potential weakness for Keith to target.

Dream moved, sliding closer to me. Then, her head was on my shoulder and her hand was on my chest. She traced a couple of my tattoos lightly. We had never lain like this, and I was kind of surprised.

"You wanna talk?" she asked softly.

"Nah."

I didn't want to, but suddenly, I was.

"My father said she wasn't always like that... a junkie. But everything I remember..."

I swallowed hard. Dream stroked my chest and waited.

"She was mad he broke it off with her, never told him she was pregnant. She was a model, a party girl, he said. Cocaine helped her stay thin. And I guess she tried harder and harder shit. The heroin... it got her. She'd do anything for it. *Anything.* So many 'uncles' came in and out of our shitty little house. I couldn't keep up. Then, Kiana came."

I stopped again, letting my mind drift to the sister I adored, who I would've given my young life to protect.

"Kiana?" Dream prompted.

"My baby sister. She came when I was five. She was everything to me. I guess she must've been about one when Melanie moved Silas in."

Even saying his name enraged me, made ice spill through my veins, made me feel like I was suffocating in the hatred.

"He hated me from day one. Maybe because I was another male in the house—"

She lifted her head and I saw the anger in her cocoa eyes.

"You were a baby!"

When she said shit like that, I realized how differently we'd grown up. For all her sophistication, Dream was naïve, an optimist who believed she could fix anything. She had to learn some shit was too broken.

Shit like me.

"Some niggas don't care, Dream. He beat my ass regularly. Burned me with cigarettes. Cut me—just deep enough to hurt —with razors."

Tears sprang to her eyes. "Your mama—"

"Was too strung out to care. Hell, he wasn't the first one, just the worst. All I could do for Melanie was work to pay off her debts. Till I turned thirteen. Then she... she..."

"Sold you," she whispered, remembering what I had said.

"I guess it could've been worse. That lady taught me all the shit that let me turn your ass out," I tried to joke.

It fell flat. Dream was pissed off.

"It's not funny. She took advantage of you. She took something that should've been yours to give freely. She—"

"Calm down, girl," I said, uncomfortable.

The idea that Angela took advantage of me made me feel weak, less like a man. That was wrong. I knew that. But I couldn't help it.

"Damien!"

"Dream!" I teased her, squeezing her against me.

She huffed out a breath. "How did you get away?"

This part... I hated this part. I started to tell her to go to sleep, leave it alone. But I knew she'd never leave it alone.

"I was fourteen. Melanie was still with Silas. I hated that nigga. Had wanted to kill him since I was seven. But I walked in one day and he was... he was..."

I felt sick. Hot and cold and my eyes felt... wet. Dream noticed. She stroked my cheek.

"It's okay. You don't have to—"

"All I ever wanted to do was protect Kiana. And I walked in, and he was touching her, Dream. Touching her like she was grown. And she was crying, but so quiet. So, I knew he'd *been* doing it. He'd scared her into being quiet. I just wanted to get him off her. I... I hit him. And I couldn't stop. I kept hitting him and hitting him and hitting him. Even after he wasn't fighting me anymore. I killed him. And Melanie did the only thing she's ever done for me in life. She called my father. He and Dante came. They made it disappear. And they took me. I hadn't seen Melanie since I was fourteen."

I looked down at her. I never regretted killing Silas. Never would. But, for some reason, I cared what she thought. She was crying. All the tears I never had. All the tears I couldn't. Her hand was stroking me, trying to comfort me. And I felt relief. She didn't hate me. She understood.

"Damien... where is Kiana?"

I admitted the part I hated most. "I don't know. I begged my father to go back and get her and she was just... gone. I've been looking for her for fifteen years. No trace. Melanie swore to my father that she ran away. Maybe she killed her."

The same sorrow, the same emptiness I felt when I thought about Kiana's loss, tried to swallow me. But something about Dream's touch anchored me, kept me from slipping into the darkness.

"Damien!"

She rose and climbed on top of me, straddling me, pressing her arms and legs close to me, trying to hug me.

"It's cool, Dream," I said, holding her tightly against me.

We lay like that for a long time. I honestly thought she was asleep when I felt her lips press against my throat. Her kisses were light, soft little brushes that trailed from my neck to my collarbone. Her fingertips glided up and down my sides. I could feel my body stirring at the softness of her touch.

"Dream. What you doing?"

I was serious. Shorty wasn't about to be feeling me up and think she was going to stick to her "no more sex" vow. We might as well stop this shit now. But then, her little pink tongue flicked out to trace the outline of one of my tattoos and I sucked in a breath like a little bitch. Dream would touch me a little bit, but she'd never used her mouth on me, beyond kissing me back. The feel of her plush lips against my skin had me hard.

"Dream—"

"Shh. Let me take care of you," she said.

At first, her words pissed me off. I didn't need her to take care of me, had never needed that shit from anyone. I didn't want her fucking pity. I grabbed her arms, about to push her off me. But something stopped me. The soft, warm weight of her pressed against me, the wet brush of her tongue, the smooth glide of her fingers—I realized the shit was nice. I liked the way she was taking care of me. Fuck it. Why not let her?

"Damien?"

She looked up at me, the question in her voice clear. Slowly, I let go of her arms.

"Don't start shit you can't finish," I warned her.

She gave me a little smile before sliding down so that she straddled my hips, her hot center pressed against my dick. She rocked gently, rubbing her pussy against me as she nipped and sucked at my collarbones and chest. Her mouth was warm and damp against my abs as she continued her descent.

Finally, she looked up at me shyly before grabbing the sides of my boxer briefs. Shit, I hurriedly worked my way out of those, ready to see what she was going to do.

Her fingers brushed over my dick gently before wrapping around it and lightly squeezing. If possible, I got even harder in her hand. She cleared her throat.

"You have a condom?"

I went completely still. I know shorty wasn't tryna tell me she'd been busy this past week. I welcomed the familiar coldness that settled throughout my body as I stared down at her.

"Who you fuck, Dream?" I asked calmly.

That nigga had to go. Immediately. She frowned at me.

"Me? I'm tryna protect myself because you were just with that Eve chick."

"You still making assumptions," I told her, ignoring the relief I felt. "Eve and I been hanging out since elementary. We don't fuck. Never have."

She looked at me for a long moment and I guess she believed me. She started massaging my dick again and a drop of pre-cum eased out of the tip. She watched it, nibbling on her bottom lip before she leaned forward and caught it on her tongue, swirling it quickly around the head. *Fuck.* Dream better stop playing with a nigga before—

I lost my whole train of thought as she sank her warm, wet mouth around me. She just held me at first, letting her tongue explore. Then she sucked softly. She was definitely an amateur, uncertain and even kind of shy. But nothing in my fucking life had almost made me cum faster.

Maybe it was because she looked so pretty with my dick between her juicy lips. Maybe it was because this was how I imagined having her since the first night I saw her. I didn't know, but as her head bobbed up and down, her hand twisting, her jaws suctioning, a nigga had to almost fight back tears at how good the shit felt. I wanted to fuck her pretty face, test her gag reflex, but it was too soon. Then she moaned and swirled her tongue.

I sat up suddenly, unable to take it anymore. I pulled her up into my lap. She smiled as she rose on her knees and grabbed my dick, positioning it at her opening before she slowly sank down. Dream's pussy was the best kind of scientific mystery. Shit blew my mind because I couldn't understand how she could get so fucking wet and still be so tight that it felt like she was choking my dick.

"Damien," she whined, because it wasn't easy for her to take me, even as her juices leaked down her thick thighs.

"Play with your clit," I whispered as I pulled one of her chocolate drop nipples into my mouth, sucking on the little nub as she tossed her head back and rubbed between her thighs.

Slowly, her walls relented, letting me stretch her, mold her like she was made for me. A soft scream escaped her when I thrust up.

"Shhh. Yo' little friend gon' kick my ass if I hurt you, remember?" I reminded her that Kam was there.

"Ear hustling ass," she mumbled.

I smacked her ass. "Told you was gon' put me back in this pussy. Now, ride this dick."

She did, doing whatever the fuck she felt. She rolled her

hips. She bounced a little bit. She rocked back and forth. I didn't give a fuck, as long as that pussy kept gushing and squeezing like it was doing. When her movements suddenly got jerky and she was chanting my name, I lifted her off me and placed her face down on the bed. Yeah, this had started out gentle and sweet, but we had something to settle. I'd never really been rough with her, but that was about to change. She was limp from her orgasm, so she didn't object when I made her arch her back deeply. But when I slammed into her, her eyes flew open, and she squealed as she started trying to move away. My hands clamped on her hips.

"Damien, you're too deep. I can't—"

"Shut up," I growled. "I only get thirty days of this tight ass, wet ass pussy, and you made me miss a week. Tell me you sorry," I demanded, fucking her relentlessly.

"Damiennnn..." she put her arm back, trying to push me out a little.

I swatted it away.

"Tell me."

Her stubborn ass moaned but refused to say the words. I fucked her harder, my hand tangling in her hair, pulling her up a little bit.

She whimpered, her thick brown body covered in a sheen of sweat as I worked her mercilessly. All that whining and her shit was getting wetter and wetter, already contracting around me.

"Dream."

"Y-yes?"

"Be a good girl. Tell me."

For another moment, the only sounds in the room were me moving in her soaking wet pussy and the wet smack of our skin together.

Then she cried, "Oh, God! I'm sorry, Damien!"

"For what?"

"F-for keeping my pussy away from you."

My hands tightened in her hair. "Huh?" I taunted, wanting her to correct herself.

Shivering uncontrollably, she tried again. "For keeping *your* pussy away from you."

Yeah, I was feeling possessive. Had been since I met this girl. I'd figure out the shit later, but for now, she was all mine.

"You gon' do it again?"

"Noooo…"

"Promise?"

"Yes. Ahhhh! Yes, I promise. Damien, I'm cumming!" she screamed.

"Shit, me, too," I breathed, holding myself so deep inside her, I knew my seed blasted her womb.

We collapsed seconds later, nothing but ragged breaths, damp skin, and joined bodies. When our heartbeats had slowed, I stood, then picked her sleepy ass up. I damn near had to hold her up as we showered. I swear she didn't even open her eyes. Once I changed the sheets and we were back in bed, she looked over her shoulder at me and finally spoke.

"You liked the blow job?" she asked shyly.

"Fuck yeah," I mumbled.

"I was so loud. Poor Kam gon' need therapy, listening to that."

"He already need it, fucking around with Melanie."

Her expression softened. "Damien, have you ever thought about it? Getting therapy, I mean."

I sighed. She sounded like my father.

"That shit don't work."

She raised up a little. "Yes, it does! If you want, I could schedule you and Kam some sessions with this therapist, Dr. Aubry Monroe. She helped—"

"No." I deaded that shit instantly. I wasn't about to be spilling my life to some stranger who wasn't ready for how fucked up I was. "Go to sleep, Dream."

My voice sounded annoyed, but I pulled her closer.

She went to sleep.

CHAPTER 52

Dream

(*THURSDAY*, *June 17*)

"Get yo' ass up, shorty. I'on wanna hear that mouth about being late for work," Damien said from somewhere above me.

Swear he was the most unsympathetic man in the world. Gave the nigga head, let him fuck two times, and he still showed no mercy.

"I don't like y..." My words trailed off as I smelled a wonderful, delicious scent.

Rolling over, I opened one eye.

He stood there, fully dressed, looking more perfect than any human being should, and, best of all, there was a mug in his hand.

"Coffee?" I asked, hopeful.

"Man, get this shit. I put a pound of sugar and a pint of cream in there just like yo' ass like," he said, frowning.

I stretched slowly before sitting up and reaching for the mug. The dark, silk sheets pooled around my waist, exposing my breasts to him. I didn't care anymore. He rarely let me wear clothes in his bed, so my body-consciousness did me no good.

Damien handed me the coffee before circling a finger around my nipple. It hardened instantly and I sucked in a sharp breath at the electric feel of his touch.

"Fast ass," he teased.

"Please. I'm tired and sore. That's the last thing on my mind," I lied.

He smirked at me, seeing right through my bullshit, but left me alone. A little over an hour later, I was ready, dressed in a red wrap dress and nude Stuart Weitzman heels. The dress showed a little cleavage and I sighed as I stood in front of the mirror, tracing a passion mark that was visible on my breast. I really should stop him, but I loved the feel of him biting then sucking on me. Even the thought started a slow throb between my legs. My neck, breasts, stomach, and thighs all showed the evidence of Damien's oral fixation. He slid behind me, his eyes meeting mine in the mirror.

"You scared someone gon' see how I marked you?" he teased.

I frowned, somewhere between slightly offended and incredibly turned on by the idea of his staking a claim on my body.

"I'm not property, Damien," I fussed.

His hand snaked around me to clasp the front of my throat as he lowered his lips to my ear.

"You mine for a little while longer."

I rolled my eyes, even as his words made my heart race and the butterflies in my stomach flutter. Damien nipped my ear lobe before letting me go. Grabbing my purse and my briefcase, I left his room and walked to Kameron's. I knocked on the door lightly, surprised when he called for me to come in. I wondered if the poor baby had slept at all.

"Good morning, love. How are you?" I greeted.

He was sitting on the side of the bed, tapping on his phone. I knew it wasn't really my place to reach out to him; Damien and I had no real relationship and I'd only be in their lives for a few more weeks. But knowing about their mother and my natural empathy meant I had to check on him. Maybe I could help him in some kind of way in the little time I had.

"I'm fine, Ms. Dream. You good?" he asked, looking up and giving me a hesitant smile.

"I am. And don't call me Ms.! I just wanted to give you my number in case you needed anything or needed to talk to me—"

"He don't need to talk to yo' ass. Ain't nobody gon' fuck with that little nigga and you ain't about to make him pussy. Y'all come eat breakfast," Damien ordered from behind me.

I glared at him over my shoulder before giving Kam my number and having him call me so I'd have his.

"Come on," I told him. "He serious about this breakfast thing."

I shared a quick meal with the brothers, who still eyed each other warily. Kam was so sweet, I kind of hated to leave him with Damien's rude ass. I knew I had to let them figure shit out, though. With one last round of goodbyes, I headed for the office.

Work dragged by. Figuring out where to hide and how to wash the money Daddy had made from his latest shipment was getting on my nerves. He was moving more and more weapons, making my job harder. On top of that, Paul seemed to have a million questions about one of the legit accounts he was working on and kept popping into my office, barely knocking. It usually didn't bother me, but everything was irritating me today.

Because I wanted to sit up and think about Damien.

Because I wanted to daydream about how I liked the taste of him, the feel of him against my tongue.

Because I wanted to figure out what had changed between us last night when he opened up to me.

Before I could stop myself, my phone was in my hand,

and I was FaceTiming him. One ring in and I regretted it, quickly hanging up.

"What are you doing?" I whispered to myself, rubbing my forehead.

Damien was not my boyfriend. This was not a relationship. I wasn't going to be one of those women he described who got attached because of sex. I had to keep my head clear for the next few weeks, open my legs, and close my heart. I could do that, I assured myself.

I looked up at the quick knock, followed by the sound of my door opening. Paul was there with a tablet, looking as frustrated as I felt. I sighed.

"Let me see."

He walked behind my desk, and we talked over the spreadsheet in front of us. Something was definitely up with these numbers, but before I could voice that, my phone rang. I saw Damien's name and everything else flew out of my head as I quickly answered. His face appeared, stoic as usual as he stood in front of some store. But his expression shifted into a scowl.

"Why that nigga all up on you like that?"

Shit, I had forgotten Paul was right over my shoulder. I looked back with a small smile, slightly embarrassed.

"Will you excuse me for a minute?" I murmured to him.

He gave me a funny look before exiting my office. I turned my attention back to the phone.

"Damien, he and I do work together," I scolded.

He sucked his teeth. "That nigga was tryna look down your shirt. Stop playing naïve. Let me find out his hands still too friendly."

Rolling my eyes, I refused to engage that.

"What you want?"

"Shit, the fuck you want? You called me," he said.

I scrambled around in my head for a reason and came up with nothing.

"Accident," I finally lied.

He squinted at me in disbelief. "Get off my line with that bullshit."

"Seriously—"

"Bye, Dream."

"Damien, wait!" I said.

He was silent, but looked at me expectantly. I cleared my throat.

"How... how is Kam?"

"Shot that little nigga and left him for dead cuz he didn't put his shit in the dishwasher," he said with a straight face before hanging up on me.

Swear I hated him. But I bit down on my lip to hold back the smile.

———

"The next time you say we going shopping, can you let me know it's for work clothes?" Parker fussed.

I glared at her as I flipped through a rack at Nordstrom. We'd gotten off work forty-five minutes earlier and headed straight here.

"Does it matter?"

"Yes! This is boring. And you got a thousand work outfits. Why are we here?"

Parker was right. My career wardrobe was extensive. It was also at my parents' house, and I didn't want to go home before going to Damien's. My parents would try to get me to stay for dinner, my grandfather would want to have one of our talks, and, despite everything I had told myself earlier about keeping some distance, I was ready to check on Kam and Damien, tell them about a summer day camp that still had space that Kam might be interested in. I told Parker a little of the truth.

"I'm going to Damien's, and I didn't pack enough in my

spinnanight bag," I said, holding up a terracotta-colored shirt dress.

Parker's mouth fell open before she hissed, "Yes, bitch, yesss."

I rolled my eyes. "It's really not that serious."

"Girl! A few weeks ago, nobody could even see the pussy, not even Issac's tired ass—may he rest in peace—and you strung him along for months."

I clutched my imaginary pearls. "I did not!"

"Bitch, yes, you did. But look at yo' ass now. Bustin' that shit open for a real one. That nigga so fine. I bet—"

"Parker, do you like this dress?" I broke in, desperate to cut her nasty ass off.

She sighed and snatched the dress from me.

"Selfish ass. Let me live vicariously. And yeah, this will be cute on you," she said.

"Yeah, I like it."

We spent a couple more hours at the outdoor mall before going to grab some food. I spotted a couple of big ass guys eyeing us. They kept their distance, but I knew they had to be my silent detail. Luckily, Parker didn't notice. By the time I pulled up to Damien's house, it was 9:30. I called him, but got no answer. Disappointed, I put my car in reverse.

Fuck that! part of me objected. I drove all the way over here; I was going to at least knock on the door. Opening my car door, I hopped out and walked toward the front entrance of the house. I stopped at the sound of the garage opening. He was leaving? I wasn't happy about that shit, but I shook it off. Maybe I could just check on Kam. I waited for the garage door to rise all the way.

Then I froze.

CHAPTER 53

Demon

(12 HOURS *earlier*)

I needed to work today. Had something that had been building inside me that I needed to get out. But Melanie's little surprise was fucking with my plans. So, instead of doing what I needed to do, I was in the car with her son, taking him to pick up some shit. He didn't have enough luggage to have much, plus he needed something to occupy his time. One of the reasons my ass stayed in trouble as a kid, besides being pissed at the world, was because my busy mind had no outlet. I didn't want that for this li'l nigga. I didn't want to care, but I felt some of that protectiveness that I'd only felt for Kiana...

...and Dream. I hated that shit.

I glanced over at him. He hadn't said much to me, and I was cool with that. But I had to let the li'l nigga know I saw right through him.

"Ay, you can put on that front like you all shy and quiet for Dream, but I ain't buying that shit. You Melanie's spawn, so I know you bad as fuck," I told him.

Turning in his seat, he looked at me for a minute, all sad and shit. Then, his top lip curled up and he scoffed.

"Nigga, who you supposed to be that you can just talk to anybody any kind of way? Got me fucked up," he mumbled.

I had to hide a smile. "You'on know who I am? You betta ask before your li'l ass keep coming at me sideways."

"What, you done laid a few niggas down or something? That oughta be lightweight for yo' big ass," he snapped.

Yeah, this was definitely my brother. I hid a smile and decided to let his little ass make it. Last thing I wanted to hear was Dream whining about me leaving his ass on the side of the highway.

"I'm about to cop you some shit, but don't think that means I like you. Where you wanna go?"

I expected him to go to a shoe store or somewhere with video games first. Li'l nigga shocked me when he asked about some sketch pads and pencils.

"What, you an artist or some shit?" I asked.

His face shut down like he was embarrassed. I'ma heartless ass nigga, but I wasn't trying to stop anyone's dreams. I mean, unless I was killing them. I spoke up again.

"Ain't nothing wrong with that. I know a place," I told him.

"That's cool," he said, his voice low.

We rode in silence for a few minutes until I had to give voice to a question that had been bothering me.

"How long Melanie been clean?"

Not that I gave a fuck, but it ain't like he and I had a lot in common to talk about.

"Almost five years. She really—"

"I'on wanna discuss her."

I shut him down abruptly. I didn't need to know anything else. He frowned again, but let it go.

"This car bad as fuck. What is it?" he asked instead.

I smirked. "A 2018 Dodge Demon."

He shook his head, but grinned. "Nigga, you lame as hell."

"Don't get mad at me cuz ain't no vehicle got ya name."

"Whatever. I bet it would be flyer than this."

I side-eyed him. "A Kameron? That shit would be a mini-van, weak ass name."

We spent the morning buying art supplies, clothes, and shoes. I pulled out my phone to check the time and realized I had a missed FaceTime from Dream. *Ignore it,* I told myself. I was getting too attached to her bourgeois ass and I had mixed feelings about the way I shared shit with her last night. If I needed proof that I was in too deep, the jewelry store bag in my hand with the iced Cuban link chains—she was always touching mine, so I copped her a couple of feminine, diamond-laced ones—was all the evidence I needed. Shit had to stop. We were going to go back to quiet, late-night fucks. The pussy was way too good to give up, but all this spending time and spilling my soul shit was about to end. I decided, then still stood there and called her back.

Her pretty face materialized, and I almost smiled. Then, I saw that Paul nigga lurking behind her. Yeah, I definitely had to get some space between us before I was knocking off a third nigga behind her.

I hung up with her just as Kam walked up on me.

"That was Dream?"

I grilled his ass.

"You nosy, li'l nigga."

"I guess you got good taste in cars and girls," he taunted.

"She ain't my girl."

"You dumber than you look, then. She nice and she look like one of them IG models."

"Fuck you know about an IG model?" I asked as we walked toward Armani Exchange.

"And she soft and smell good," he continued, ignoring me.

I stopped and eyeballed this li'l fresh ass nigga.

"Yo, you tryna push up on my girl?"

Grinning, he shrugged.

"You said she ain't ya girl. I'm too young right now, but in six years, you gon' be over wit'."

"The fuck make you think she gon' want yo' young ass?" I scoffed.

"Nigga, she like you, for some reason. I look like you but better, and she think I'm sweet. She already texted me, telling me to have a great day while yo' ass outchea hanging up in her face."

This li'l cocky muhfucka. I mushed his head.

"Get yo' ass in this store before I push yo' shit back," I snapped.

He gave me a smug smile. Bad ass really looked like me, then. I was low key pissed at his ass because he had put Dream right back on my mind. I needed to clear my head, remind myself she wasn't the only chick out here with a pretty face and a tight pussy. Pulling out my phone, I scrolled through my contacts, finding Juliette's number. I had said I wasn't fucking with this bitch no more, but I'd give her this chance to redeem herself.

Me: Send someone tonight.

She responded almost immediately.

Juliette: Can't believe you reached out. Your usual type?

Me: Surprise me.

Juliette: What time?

I looked over at Kam. Having a kid fucked with my style.

Me: 9

Juliette: Usual spot?

I knew my ass was out here bad as I typed my response. Dream was the only girl I'd fucked at my house. Only a handful of people knew where I lived. But shit, I was trying to shake whatever hold she had on me and my space.

Me: Nah. I'll text the address. Delete my shit immediately. I get any unexpected visitors, I'm coming to see you.

Juliette: Understood.

It was exactly nine PM when the little Porsche pulled into my garage. Juliette's girls were always on time, a fact that I appreciated. I crossed the kitchen to open the door. The woman standing in front of me was flawlessly put together, from the top of her bone straight, black hair to the bottom of her crazy high stilettos. She was slim but curvy, her light skin smooth and unblemished. Her almond-shaped, amber eyes and full, pink lips were perfect. She smiled, revealing pretty, white teeth and dimples. She introduced herself as CoCo. Shorty was gorgeous but, ten minutes later, when she had my condom-wrapped dick lodged deep in her throat, I realized her looks weren't the only thing that made her perfect for this job. She deserved a gold medal for the way she was sucking me off.

So, it made no fucking sense that my mind was preoccupied with thoughts of a thick, brown-skinned beauty. I kept thinking about the light, sweet scent Dream wore and the feel of her soft body against mine and all the different ways she said my name. Pissed me off because I didn't do that shit, fixate on one woman. I had seen some powerful niggas fall off behind a bitch, and I wasn't going out like that. I was about to dive in this pussy and clear my mind.

But as pretty and talented as CoCo was, my dick wouldn't cooperate. Shit was sadly deflated and suddenly, I didn't want her hands or lips on me. Wordlessly, I pulled out of her mouth and walked out of the guest room. My weak ass hadn't even been able to take her to my room where Dream had just slept. I headed for the shower, needing to wash away CoCo's touch.

She was still there when I reappeared minutes later in a wife beater and joggers, looking at me in confusion.

"You ready now?" she asked softly.

"Nah, you can go," I told her abruptly.

She frowned. "But—"

"I already paid Juliette. You good. Let's go."

Shrugging, she stood from the bed, pulled her dress back on, grabbed her bag, and preceded me down the stairs. I opened the garage door as I walked her to her car. I was about to give her instructions on forgetting my address when I noticed the little Benz on my driveway.

Fuck no! I thought that all the way until I saw Dream's curvy silhouette, standing perfectly still in front of my house. CoCo tossed me a grin over her shoulder.

"That's why? She fine. You had a bitch about to doubt herself."

I barely heard her. All my attention was on the speechless chick who stood on my driveway. But she recovered quickly, pushing her long hair over her shoulder.

"Dream—"

"I—I—I just wanted to check on you and Kam, but it was inconsiderate of me not to call first. I see you're busy. I'll just text him," she said, her voice cold and stiff.

She turned to make her way back to her car. *Oh, well,* I thought. I knew what she was thinking, but I didn't owe her any explanations. She wasn't my bitch. I was in charge of this deal, and I'd call for her when I wanted her to come.

All that shit ran through my head, but as she got closer and closer to that car, I knew I had to stop her.

"Dream."

She held up a hand as she kept walking. "You good, Demon. I'm sorry for the intrusion. I'll be in touch."

My mouth tightened at her use of that stupid ass nickname and all that shit about not explaining flew out the window. I was on her in five seconds, in her face and about to grab her arms, when she held up both hands.

"Please don't touch me," she said.

She whirled around to open her car door.

"It's not what you think," I told her.

She shrugged. "It's not my place to think anything. Please move."

She tried to open the door again, but I held it closed.

"So, you drove over here and you just gon' leave?"

"I have the gas and the time. It's not a big deal."

She pulled on the door handle, then let out a frustrated breath when I didn't move.

"Damien, I need to go—"

"Nah. You need to talk to me."

"About what? What the fuck do we have to talk about?" she snapped, letting her cold mask slip as she turned to face me.

"You wanted to check on us—"

"I said I'll text Kam and I can see that you doing just fine," she said as CoCo backed down the driveway. "Maybe I should charge by the hour, too. You slut me out all night long, but she gets to leave at a reasonable time. Juliette is right. I do need some tips. My dumb ass letting you wear me out before the next nigga."

Ice trickled through my veins at her words, and I grabbed her face. "Ain't gon' be no—"

I cut my stupid ass off before I added, "next nigga." The fuck had that come from?

She pulled her chin out of my grip. "Can you just let me go... please?"

"No."

Moving quickly, I snatched her key fob.

"Damien—"

"Now, come check on us," I told her, walking back toward the garage.

"Give me my fucking key!" she shrieked.

I ignored her, listening as her footsteps clicked quickly behind me.

"I swear to God, I'll call the cops."

I shrugged, continuing at my leisurely pace.

"I hate you! Stupid ass!"

A second later, her fist made contact with my shoulder blade. This girl stayed choosing violence. I turned on her, ready to threaten her ass.

And then I saw the tears in her chocolate eyes. Confused, I frowned at her.

"Fuck you crying for?"

This time, her fist landed on my chest. "Will you just give me my keys, Damien?" she demanded.

"Stop asking me shit I already gave you the answer to."

She screamed in frustration before hitting me again. Then, suddenly, she was raining blows on my chest and abs, hitting me with all her strength as she cursed me and sobbed, her tears finally breaking free. They had me so confused, I didn't even stop her at first while she beat my ass and told me how much she hated me. But fuck, some of her licks were solid and that shit got old. Bending, I pressed my shoulder against her stomach and lifted her in a fireman's carry. She continued to beat my back and shriek obscenities at the top of her lungs as I walked into the garage and then into the kitchen. I wanted to dump her mean ass on the floor, but I set her on her feet and grabbed both of her wrists when she balled her hands again.

"Stop," I warned as I heard Kam's footsteps on the stairs.

Then his young ass was there, mugging me and trying to step between me and her.

"Why she crying? Did you hit her?" he asked, frowning.

I wanted to send the little nigga back upstairs and tell him to stay out of grown folks' business, but I knew exactly why he was acting this way.

He'd seen Melanie get her ass beat. He'd probably tried to stop it, maybe even got fucked up himself. And as he lay there bruised and hurt, he'd promised himself he wouldn't watch it happen to another woman. I knew because I'd been there. So, instead of going off on him, I took a few steps away from Dream, let him get closer so he could reassure himself that her crazy ass wasn't hurt.

"I didn't hit her," I told him.

She reached up and cupped his face. "He didn't. I'm fine, for real," she lied as tears continued to spill from her eyes.

Kam frowned.

"Why you crying, then?"

She tried to smile for him, but she couldn't.

"I'm just emotional sometimes," she finally said. "Your brother pissed me off, but I promise I'm good. You can go back to bed."

He looked at her, trying to read her damp face as she stood in front of him. Finally, he nodded.

"You just... just call my name if—"

"Go to bed, Kam," I ordered. He was doing a little too much, now.

He gave me one last nasty look before stomping back up the stairs.

"We upset him for nothing. Just let me go, Damien," she whispered.

"No."

An angry laugh, followed by a sob, escaped her lips.

"You can't possibly think you can fuck her, then me—"

"I didn't fuck that girl."

She laughed again as she waved a dismissive hand. "Nigga! Do I look that dumb?"

"Why you crying?" I asked again.

"Damien—"

"Tell me and I'll let you go."

She stood in the middle of my kitchen floor, wiping at her tears and weighing her options.

CHAPTER 54

Dream

I WAS SO fucking embarrassed I didn't know what to do. Was I really standing in this nigga's house, crying my heart out because he'd fucked somebody else? A gorgeous, slim, *professional* somebody else. Just like he liked. Where the hell was my pride? I was definitely not being the granddaughter of Lucien Dumont.

"Dream."

Damien's voice drifted to me through my thoughts. He was waiting for an answer. Nigga wanted to rub this shit in. But fuck it, if it would get me out of here, I didn't even care about my dignity.

"I keep calling you stupid, but it's me. I'm the stupid one. I can't believe… I… It's just…"

I wasn't making a damn bit of sense, and I knew it. And I still couldn't stop crying. My feelings were actually shattered. I didn't understand that shit.

"My crazy ass is actually bothered?" I wondered out loud, laughing at myself. "Cuz a nigga who fucking me because of a deal fucking another chick, too? Stupid. Cuz I'm out here fucking with my heart between my legs like I don't know better? Cuz you told me a little of your life story?" I scoffed as I covered my face. "I gotta be the dumbest bitch—"

"Shut the fuck up," he ordered, dragging my hands away from my face. "I didn't fuck that girl," he said again.

My head snapped up and I mugged him.

"What, she came over for fruit snacks and juice? Y'all watched a little TV? Played cards or some—"

The pressure of his lips against mine cut me off quickly. Heat flooded my body and, even with my pathetic heart hurting, all I wanted to do was melt into him. Apparently, I had a shred of pride somewhere, though. I yanked away from him.

"Don't kiss me! I don't know where your mouth been," I spat.

He trailed his lips along my jawline up to my ear.

"Yes, you do. It's been on your lips…"

He dragged his thumb across my bottom lip.

"On these titties…" he said, cupping my breasts and squeezing.

"On this pussy."

I bit back a moan as he brought both hands to the hem of my dress and started pushing up.

"My mouth only been on you. You need me to remind you?" he asked, dragging the dress above my panties.

"Damien, no," I snapped, pushing at his hands. "You not distracting me with sex and you not fucking me after that girl. You probably didn't even protect yourself. Just give me my—"

I squealed as he lifted me, my arms and legs instinctively going around his body.

"Put me down!"

"No," he said as he climbed the stairs with my heavy ass.

I hated when he picked me up.

I loved when he picked me up.

I wasn't surprised at all when he carried me to his bedroom. But again, he had me fucked up.

"Do not put me on that bed with all y'all juices and shit!"

Of course, he dropped me on the bed. I tried to scramble away, but his big ass got on top of me, holding me in place.

"I ain't fucked nobody in this bed but yo' dramatic ass and you the only girl I ever willingly fucked raw. So, shut up," he growled.

His use of the word "willingly" made my heart ache as I thought about what Angela did to him. He used the momentary distraction to kiss me again. I half-heartedly struggled. Stupid. I knew what I had seen, knew what probably had happened and I still wanted to believe what he was saying.

"Damien—"

"Dream. I have no reason to lie to you," he said, pinning me with his green gaze as he eased my dress up again.

"Then why was she here?"

The question brought more tears. Hell, I knew why she was here.

"Stop crying," he whispered, his fingers sliding under the seat of my panties.

I tried to close my legs, didn't want him to feel how, in the middle of feeling hurt and betrayed and as foolish as Ashanti's ass, I was still soaking wet for him. But then he brushed my clit and my hips jerked and parted even more.

"Why was she here?" I asked again, trying not to give in to the slow, sweet circles his thumb was drawing.

"Because I called for her," he admitted, sinking his teeth into my neck and sucking gently.

I closed my eyes and swallowed the moan caused by his sweet suction. *Focus, Dream,* I scolded myself.

"W-why did you call for her?"

He released his bite, then raised up to look at me.

"To fuck her."

A strangled sound erupted from me, half a laugh at his audacity, half a sob as his words stabbed me. I pushed against him with one hand, wiping my face with the other.

"Dream... *baby*. Stop crying. Please."

His words fucked me up, knocked me all off my shit. He never used endearments, never said please. But here he was, murmuring it like he was sincere, kissing away the tears that slid from the corners of my eyes.

"I hate you. Get off—"

But he was so damn fast. So fast, I didn't realize my panties had been pushed to the side. So fast that I didn't know he had released himself. So fast that the first delicious feel of him entering me broke me like it had each time. Made my back arch, my pussy gush, my thighs clamp against him.

So weak, Dream, I thought, even as I rolled my hips up to meet his, pressure already building in the bottom of my stomach and between my legs as he stroked me.

"I hate you," I lied again.

"I hate you, too," he whispered, his mouth hovering right above mine, his body sinking deeper and deeper into me. "I hate you cuz I wanna get bored with you, but I can't. I hate you cuz I wanna get tired of yo' pussy, but I can't. I hate you cuz I wanna feel annoyed when you say my name, but I can't. I hate you cuz my muhfuckin' dick wouldn't even work because she didn't smell right or feel right or sound right."

He pounded me harder, like he was really mad about that shit. I wanted to cuss his ass out, but I was too busy shaking, my eyes rolling back from the force of his thrusts.

"Yeah, so, I hate yo' ass, too. Fuck you, Dream," he whispered.

"Fuck you, Damien!" I whispered back. "Oh, my God, I'm gonna cum!!!" I wailed.

"You better," he hissed, right before his lips crashed into mine and the orgasm crashed over me.

A long time later, after we somehow actually undressed and I lost count of how many times he sent me spiraling, we lay there, my head on his shoulder, my hand on the chains around his neck. I realized this had to be the shit Yana called "toxic."

So, so bad.

So, so good.

"I really didn't fuck that girl," he said.

"Whatever," I mumbled.

But I believed him. Dumb ass.

"I wasn't tryna make yo' soft ass cry. I'm… I'm sorry."

I froze, shocked. I didn't even know what to do with that.

"You called me 'baby'," I whispered instead.

Like his apology, that had surprised me. It must have surprised him, too, because he was quiet for a minute. Finally, he did what he always did.

"Go to sleep, Dream," he said softly, holding me against him.

I wanted to protest, but hell, I *was* tired. I closed my eyes. Just before drowsiness claimed me, he whispered, "Good-night, baby."

Smiling, I went to sleep.

CHAPTER 55

Dayana

IT WAS our last full day here and I still hadn't gotten enough of the warm, white sand or the sparkling, clear water. I definitely planned to come back, maybe with my sister and a couple of our girls. This trip had been everything. Jenesis was my shadow, full of questions and thoughts about my status as "Princess Yana." Smoke and Ms. Stephanie constantly complimented me on how well I handled her, but it was no hardship. She was a smart, wiggly, giggling sweetheart and loving on her was easy.

Loving on all of them was easy, to be honest. Ms. Stephanie was funny, direct, and so much fun to talk to. I swear, between her cooking and the upscale restaurants we visited, I probably gained ten pounds on this trip.

And Smoke. Every day, he catered to me, waking me up to share the breathtaking sunrises with him, taking me on long walks and listening to me dream out loud, buying me little gifts everywhere we went, and constantly checking on me. And the nights. Oh, my God, I knew now why Daddy had kept Dream and me under lock and key. If I'd known my body could feel the unbelievable pleasure Smoke gave me—and of giving my partner that same pleasure—my ass

would've been wilding. So many positions. So many sensations. I could've spent every day, all day, in bed with Cartier
Salinas.

"Princess Yana, you ready?"

Jenesis bounced in front of me, pulling me out of my
thoughts. She was too cute in her snorkeling gear, and I
couldn't help bending over to kiss the top of her swim-cap
covered head.

"Yes, Princess Jeni, I am," I told her.

Minutes later, we were literally swimming with the fishes,
vibrantly colored schools of them I watched in awe. I grabbed
Cartier's hand and moved closer to him as I spotted two sea
turtles nearby. Letting out a soundless scream, I ignored his
shake of his head. Yep, I was a little scared.

Jenesis's little fins passed by me, her grandmother right
beside her. She pointed excitedly at a starfish. I could tell she
wanted to touch it, but during our safety training, they'd
emphasized that we shouldn't touch the sea creatures and her
father had repeated it to her several times. Hell, I was glad for
the lesson because I was beyond tempted to touch the beautiful, multi-colored reef. I knew life beneath the waters could be
dangerous, but it was also stunningly beautiful.

Two-and-a-half hours later, we were back at the house,
showering to get ready for the lunch that Smoke was having
delivered. Later in the afternoon, we were supposed to go
dolphin-watching at Jenesis's request, but after we ate and
she drowsily curled into my side, I wondered about that
particular plan.

"Princess Yana?" she asked.

I waited until she got her yawn out before answering.
"Yes, Princess Jeni?"

"Are you gon' stay with us when we get home, too?"

I froze, my eyes darting to where Ms. Stephanie sat,
reading a book on her phone. She didn't look up, but a small
smile curved her lips.

"No, Suga. Your daddy and I—"

I stopped as I tried to think of age-appropriate words. "We're just friends," I finished lamely.

Curious, bright brown eyes stared up at me suspiciously.

"None of Daddy's other friends sleep in his room."

I coughed, but she kept talking.

"Mommies and daddies do that. Are you gon' be my new mommy?"

This time, Ms. Stephanie looked up at me and she opened her mouth like she wanted to say something, but no words came. I cleared my throat, wishing Smoke would bring his ass in here, but that didn't happen.

"Cupcake," I said gently, using the nickname I'd given her. "Even though your mommy is in heaven, she's still your mommy and she loved you very much. No one will ever take her place."

She sighed and cuddled closer to me. "I know. But kids get step mommies. That's what Trina told me at school. She got a step mommy and a step daddy. She likes them. And I like you."

My heart melted as I pulled her onto my lap.

"I like you, too, Suga. Very much," I murmured.

"So, you can be my step mommy. I promise Daddy will be a good prince. He's even better than Naveen!" she coaxed, mentioning the prince from *The Princess and the Frog*.

Ms. Stephanie laughed as her son appeared in the doorway.

"I heard that, Jeni-face. Turn yo' daddy up, baby girl!" he said, coming to scoop her off my lap.

She giggled as Smoke covered her face in kisses. Smiling at them, I wondered how much he'd heard. The last thing I wanted was Jenesis to put either of us on the spot about that step mommy stuff. He sat down on the couch beside me, and Jenesis splayed her little body over both of us. A few minutes later, she was sleeping.

"Spoiled rotten," Ms. Stephanie said softly as Smoke lifted her to carry her to the room.

His mom followed, leaving me with my thoughts until he reappeared. He lay on the couch, his head in my lap, and I absentmindedly stroked my hand across his soft waves.

"You thinking too hard," he said finally. "She ain't never seen me with anybody and she likes you. I'll explain shit to her later."

"What you gon' tell her?"

I didn't mean to ask, but I wanted to hear how Smoke would describe our situation. He shrugged.

"Shiii, I'on know. Tell her we friends, and I'm not thinking about getting her a step mommy right now. Some shit like that."

I was glad his eyes were closed. He couldn't see the look that I'm sure passed across my face. So, we were "friends." That was good to know. I knew it was the same thing I said, but it hit differently coming from a man I was spreading my legs and opening my heart to.

Stop it, Dayana. The man only promised you a week, I reminded myself.

He was keeping his promise.

And I still wasn't happy.

CHAPTER 56
Smoke

SHE'D SNUGGLED UP with Jenesis on the boat ride to see the dolphins. She'd laughed with my mother over dinner as they both had a little too much wine. But she had barely said a word to me since our time on the couch. I knew I'd said the wrong shit even without looking at her. I felt her body tense against me, and I wanted to kick my own ass. I hadn't figured out what the fuck we had going on, but I knew it was more than friendship. I just wanted to put it in the simplest terms to my four-year-old, though, so she wouldn't be bugging the hell out of Dayana. I assumed she'd understand.

I assumed wrong.

So, I was surprised when I stepped out of the bathroom, freshly showered, and found her in my bed. I stopped for a moment, and she looked up at me. She squirmed around a little bit, a blush on her cheeks.

"I can leave, if you w—"

"Hell nah. I thought you were mad," I said.

I wasn't going to let her run away from how she had acted. And I wanted to know, if I were being honest, how she wanted me to describe us.

"Not mad… exactly," she dodged.

I looked at her as I crossed to the dresser and pulled out a pair of boxer briefs.

"Hmmm," I grunted, dropping the towel and sliding into the underwear.

She looked at me boldly, her tongue running over her plump lips. My dick responded instantly, growing hard as fuck. Dayana learned quickly, and her mouth was wicked.

"I mean, I understand we really don't have a label and I'm not pressing for one. And I don't expect you to explain 'friends with benefits' to a preschooler," she said softly.

I raised an eyebrow. "But?"

She sighed. "But I don't know. And I don't want to think about it. Just come to bed. My week isn't quite up."

She was avoiding something we needed to deal with, but when she pushed the sheet down and revealed the sheer, lavender silk shit she had on, I said fuck it.

A couple of hours later, I spooned her tightly, high off her perfect pussy and the blunt we had just shared.

"Cartier?" she asked drowsily.

"Huh?"

"What's gon' happen when we go back?"

Fuck! I'd been hoping she didn't ask that because I owed her a truthful answer.

"I don't know," I admitted. "We just go back to regular life, I guess."

She stiffened, like earlier. I hated that shit.

"I'm s—"

"It's okay. You gave me what you promised," she whispered. "Goodnight."

But it was a long time before either of us went to sleep.

———

(*Saturday, June 19*)

After the longest, quietest day-long flight of my life, we

were back on U.S. soil. Riding in the back of the short limo, all of us were silent, even Jenesis. My baby could feel the tension.

"You going home or to my place?" I asked my OG.

She looked between me and Dayana before answering.

"My place. I think the two of you need to—"

"Actually, I'm going to grab a hotel," Dayana interrupted.

I frowned at her. "The fu—"

"Cartier! Language," Mama snapped.

"I'm disowned, Smoke," Dayana said with a soft laugh. "My mama wants me to come over for brunch tomorrow to try to sort it all out, and I don't want to deal with my father before then."

"Then you stay at my place. You ain't gotta face this sh—stuff alone," I told her.

She shook her head. "Nah. We're going back to our regular lives, remember? So, I know you live on the far Northwest. Anything decent around there—"

"Dayana," my OG spoke up.

"It's good, Ms. Stephanie. For real."

Her smile was fake, and her stubbornness pissed me off. Fuck it. If she wanted to stay by herself in some hotel instead of in my home, that was on her dumb ass. A little while later, we dropped her off at one of the resort hotels. The driver got back in, but before he could pull off, my mother tapped on the partition. He lowered it and she ordered him to wait. Then, she looked at me expectantly.

I mugged her meddling ass. "What?"

"First, watch how you look at me and talk to me," she said.

"Yeah, you not too old for GiGi to mess up, huh, GiGi?" Jenesis piped up.

"Right, baby."

I shook my head. They stayed double-teaming a nigga. Sighing, I rubbed a hand over my face.

"OG, what you want me to do?"

"Cartier Alaric Salinas, do I really have to tell you every time you need to go after that girl?"

"Ain't nobody finna keep chasing Dayana, Mama."

"Go get her. Talk to her. Fix whatever," she said, settling into the peanut butter leather, a stern look on her face.

"Ma—"

"You want regrets? Cuz we can pull off right now, if that's what you want," she challenged.

I looked at her and she glared right back. Her bossy ass wasn't budging.

"Swear to God," I mumbled as I opened the damn door.

Seconds later, I was in the lobby. I spotted Dayana quickly —my eyes were always drawn to her. I walked up behind her just in time to hear the receptionist say, "I'm sorry, Ms. Castle. That one was declined, too," in a hushed voice.

"But… how is that possible?" Dayana asked.

It didn't take a rocket scientist to figure out what was happening. Darius Castle had really cut off his twenty-one-year-old daughter. Shit ran me hot as fuck. What that piece of shit didn't realize was that, as long as I had breath, Dayana would never need him for a muhfuckin' thing. I grabbed her arm, turning her to face me.

"Let's go," I said.

Her mouth fell open as a blush heated her skin. She was embarrassed. Shaking her head, she looked down.

"I can call my sister or brother—"

"Yana, bring yo' ass on. You going home with me," I told her.

I guess she read my tone right. Her argument dried up and she let me lead her back outside. I saw the tears in her eyes, and, for a minute, I thought about sending one of my niggas to Darius Castle's house. I knew she didn't want that, though. I stopped her beside the car.

"I know you wanna cry, Yana, and you can fall apart as

soon as we get home, shorty. But you probably better keep it together for your little homegirl in here," I said softly.

She sniffed, then nodded.

"Okay," she whispered.

Leaning down, I kissed her forehead. "I told you don't have to do this shit alone. I got you, Dayana."

She nodded again and I opened the door. Watching as she climbed in, I thought about how this was my second time sparing Darius Castle. I wanted to kill him for trying to force her into that marriage and now for humiliating her like this. One more strike, and I was gon' take that bitch ass nigga out.

CHAPTER 57
Dream

(*SUNDAY*, *June 20*)

I opened my eyes with a groan when my alarm went off. My family had a standing brunch date after my parents finished their nine AM church service. I needed to have my ass in someone's sanctuary, hell, but looking down at my naked body clasped against Damien's solid frame and feeling the throbbing soreness between my legs, I decided my fornicating ass wouldn't even play with the Lord like that.

"Shut that shit off. You not working today," he growled against my ear.

"Brunch with my family. It's my turn to cook and Yana is back. I need to be there because Daddy still has an attitude, but Mama said he's crazy if he thinks he's banning her baby," I explained, reaching for the annoying device and shutting it off.

My mind whirled as I thought over what I'd just told him. Since when did I offer explanations? Hell, since when did we talk this easily? This week had been different, our "deal" was looking less like business and more like... something I didn't want to think about. I stretched and yawned, about to get up.

"Always the fixer, huh?" Damien taunted.

Sighing, I pulled away from him. "Damien—"

I shrieked when he tumbled me back against the sheets and took my hand, bringing it to his rock-hard dick.

"Fix this, then," he challenged.

Instantly wet, I moaned as he pushed into me. Needless to say, I was running around like crazy forty-five minutes later. Mama was going to kill me! Damien and I showered together and dressed simultaneously. I wondered where he was going, especially when Kam knocked on the door and announced he was ready.

"We'll be downstairs in a minute," Damien responded.

Curiosity got the best of me. "Where y'all going? To see your moth—" I cut that off as he grilled me. "Melanie?"

"Fuck that bitch," he mumbled, fastening the Cuban link chains around his neck. "We going where you going."

I was just about to launch into my speech about how Kam probably missed his mother and was worried about her when I realized what he said. My eyes flew to his.

"What? Are you crazy? My daddy will—"

"I was invited. Ordered, actually," he said.

I stepped back from the dresser, my hands going to my hips. "By whom?" I asked, twisting my lips in disbelief. No one gave Damien Montana orders.

"Your grandfather. That was his condition for letting me and Eve into the wedding. I had to come to the next brunch so the nigga could basically interrogate me."

Closing my eyes, I blew out a deep breath. That sounded like Grandpapa. He had some kind of grudging respect for Damien, and he was particular about me, so it made sense. I just hoped he'd told my father. Then again, Daddy might be so focused on Dayana that he paid us no attention. I didn't wish that on my little sister, but shit! My eyes snapped open at the soft smack against my butt.

"Hurry up. We gon' be late," Damien smirked.

Oh, so this shit was funny to him? *Asshole.* I sent up a

quick prayer that he and Daddy didn't get over here, tearing shit down. I hadn't forgotten his promise to say something to my father about my bruised neck. Considering the fact that he killed the last man who touched me in anger, I guess I should be grateful he just planned to talk.

He insisted I ride with him to my house, but then his rude ass didn't say a word to me the whole way there. Instead, Kam and I talked about the camp I'd found him and his artistic interests. The easy conversation didn't stop the tension that was building in my chest as we got closer to my neighborhood. By the time Damien pulled into our circular driveway, I was on the verge of sweating. He looked at me and shook his head.

"Getcho nervous ass out my shit."

I flipped him off before opening the door. He grabbed my arm and I sighed.

"What, Damien?"

"Look at me," he demanded.

Reluctantly, I obeyed.

"The fuck you scared for? You act like I'ma go in here and shoot up y'all shit."

I side-eyed him. The nigga must really be crazy to be asking that.

"My father hates you, Damien. This shit could go very, very bad. He already pissed at Yana and now he gotta break bread in his house with you? Grandpapa is crazy!"

"You think your grandfather ain't told him what's up? Give that man more credit than that. Nigga is old school and yo' father is his family. He ain't about to let it be an ambush or no surprises on his watch. Now, chill with all the drama," he ordered.

I didn't say anything to him, but his words made me feel a little better. I climbed out and led them to the front door. Except for Mary, the housekeeper and sometimes cook, the house seemed empty. I was glad—I could use the time to get myself and brunch together before most of my family got here. I showed Kameron and Damien the theater room and gave them basic operating instructions. So, when Damien followed me out, I was surprised.

"You need the bathroom or something?" I asked.

"Nah. I'm going to the kitchen with you," he said nonchalantly.

"Mary will help—"

"Dream."

That was his "Don't argue with me" tone. I rolled my eyes but kept walking. Ten minutes later, I had him peeling potatoes while I cut up onion and peppers for a baked Denver omelet. I shot sneaky glances at him, unable to believe how sexy he could look in a pink and purple apron with "Kitchen Diva" scrawled across it. Life was unfair.

We worked in a nice silence, so caught up in our own thoughts that when a bright voice exclaimed, "Y'all are too cute, cooking together!" I almost jumped out of my skin.

I dropped my whisk and ran to my sister, and she giggled as we crashed together. Kissing each of her cheeks, I hugged her tightly.

"Damn, Ms. Celie, Nettie ain't been gone that long," Damien said dryly.

I whirled on him, sticking out my tongue.

"Fuck you, Damien."

"We can if yo' sister takes over brunch, cuz I definitely been wanting to bend your ass over that balcony railing."

My mouth fell open as he smirked, and Yana giggled. Speechless, I went back to my whisk…

…and wondered who would be able to see us if we did what he suggested.

Damn! This rude ass nigga had me all off my shit.

CHAPTER 58
Demon

I ALREADY KNEW Dayana was as dramatic as her sister after that *Color Purple*-ass greeting they did. But when she finally left Dream's embrace and hugged me from behind, I figured shorty might be over the top.

"Hey, Bestie!"' she crooned.

I raised an eyebrow as Dream repeated, "Bestie?"

"Yep. That's what I decided. He saved me from Jordan and took me to Smoke's house in my hour of distress and he stood up for me at that bullshit wedding. He like my ride or die. Definitely my new bestie," she announced breezily as she made her way toward the sink.

I stood there with a peeler in one hand and a potato in the other, confused as fuck.

"I don't do that," I finally spoke up.

They looked over at me.

"Do what?" Dayana asked.

"Have friends."

"Oh. Okay. Well, I do," she said, like she was dismissing what I said.

And for some reason, I didn't even argue with her extra ass. She washed her hands and I guess Dream thought the water was going to hide her voice as she asked, "What's up with Smoke?"

Dayana tensed for a minute before shrugging. "He promised me a week and he delivered. Now, let me get my apron and you tell me what you need me to do."

Dream looked at her for a moment, then nodded.

"I'm glad you came back home. Daddy be talking shit—"

"Girl, the only reason I'm here is because Mama said I better be. Dream, that nigga really cut me off. I was going to rent a hotel room when we got in last night, but my cards were declined. Credit card accounts all closed, bank accounts behind my debit cards emptied. Mary had to let me in a few minutes ago—my access code and thumbprint were not recognized at the front door," Dayana said.

Dream's eyes got big. "Bitch, you lyin'!"

"On God and Grandmama. I had to make myself laugh about how petty he is to stop crying."

Darius Castle was bitch made, for real. I started to announce it, but the shit wasn't my business. I peeled another potato. Shit, how many fucking potatoes could these people eat? Dream was definitely gon' have to bust it open for a nigga on that balcony for all this.

The sisters talked for a few minutes before the house-keeper walked in and cleared her throat.

"You good, Mary?" Dream asked.

"Yes. Dayana, there's a Mr. Cartier Salinas here to—"

Before she could finish, Smoke stood in the kitchen, grilling Dayana. Mary frowned her disapproval.

"Sir, you were supposed to—"

"Nah, shorty, I don't need to be introduced," he cut her off as he stalked over to Dayana, who was keeping her head down. "You gon' act like I ain't standing right here?"

Looking up, she rolled her eyes. "What are you doing here, Cartier?"

"The fuck I tell you? I'm not leaving you to face this bull-shit by yourself."

"First of all, I figured the faster I left, the faster you could go on with your future… or stay stuck in your past—which-ever one you plan." Her voice was bitter and for a minute, I wondered what that was about before remembering, once again, that none of this shit was my business. "Second, I'm not alone. I got my sister and my BFF—" she pointed at us as she spoke.

Smoke looked at me, confused by that BFF shit. I shrugged and picked up another fucking potato.

"—and the rest of my family except my daddy. I'm fine!" Dayana exclaimed. "You can go—"

"Shut the fuck up, Yana," he growled.

Her eyes narrowed, but she must've known that nigga was serious. She went back to laying out bacon on a sheet pan without saying a word. Smoke walked toward me, a smirk on his face.

"Damn, Kitchen Diva. They done domesticated you like this? Simp ass nigga," he teased.

"Fuck you," I said nonchalantly. "You out here on yo' Yung Bleu shit, stopping weddings and kidnapping brides, but talking shit to me?"

He laughed. "Touché, nigga."

"You want a peeler?"

Holding up both hands, he shook his head.

"Hell nah. This kitchen shit ain't for me. I can barely feed me and my daughter."

He leaned against the counter, focused on Dayana and Dream's conversation.

"Don't they call each other bitch and tell each other to shut up a lot to be sisters?" he whispered a couple of minutes later.

"I guess it don't count cuz they obviously ignore the 'shut up' part," I muttered.

"Bestie, you know we can hear you, right?" Dayana inquired, turning to glare at me.

Smoke looked at me. "How you get to be her—"

"Don't even ask me about that shit," I snapped.

"Bitch, everything been so crazy, we still ain't made plans for your birthday Saturday," Dayana said.

That caught my attention. *Fuck!* Dream's birthday was Saturday? How the fuck did I miss that? How was I gon' get her a decent gift in under a week?

Wait, what the fuck was I thinking? In twenty-nine years, I hadn't ever bought a woman I fucked a birthday gift. Why would I start now?

But even as I asked myself, I knew shit was different with her. I had already given her money and bought her jewelry. Now, I wanted to get her a gift and Dayana was going to have to compromise with whatever she was planning because I wanted some of Dream's birthday time, too.

"We can just go out. It doesn't have to be anything big," Dream said.

"Want me to get everybody together and we go back to Bliss? That shit was nice," Dayana commented.

Dream shot me a look before rolling her eyes. "As long as ain't nobody tripping."

I shrugged.

"As long as you ain't falling over," I said.

She glared at me, ready to pop off. I meant what I said. She could get a little tipsy for her birthday, but sloppy wasn't happening. Dayana clapped her hands, breaking the sudden tension.

"So, I'll see if I can pay extra and maybe get a VIP spot for Saturday, cuz I know they sold out."

"You don't have to pay, and get it for Friday instead," I instructed.

"Why I ain't gotta pay, and her birthday is Saturday," Dayana said.

"Because I own that shit with Dante, and she got Saturday plans."

My eyes were on Dream as I spoke. She looked surprised, but didn't argue. She was learning.

"So, bottles and everything on you?" Dayana asked slyly.

"Whatever."

She smiled brightly. "That's why you my best friend!"

I side eyed her before turning my attention to her sister.

"Dream, that's the last fucking potato I'm peeling," I told her, tossing that shit into the bowl of cold water.

She looked and nodded. "Okay. We got this thing that dices them—"

She paused as the sounds of her grandfather's motorized chair reached us. He rolled into the kitchen and stopped, looking me up and down.

"This girl got you looking fucking ridiculous," he said, shaking his head.

I glanced down at the apron. "So, she lied when she said pink was my color?" I joked, surprising myself.

"Yeah, Diva, she lied," Lucien said. "Y'all gentlemen join me on the back patio," he ordered before taking off.

———

Lucien was a smart ol' cat. Nigga didn't really question us, just kind of made observations and waited for our reactions or opinions. He didn't bring up his granddaughters directly, just sat back and sized us up. Finally, he nodded like he was satisfied.

"Just tryna make sure my girls in good hands," he said.

"I'on know about Smoke, but you know my... situation with Dream comes with time limits," I reminded him. "You ain't gotta worry—"

He stopped me with a small smile.

"I'm not worried. You putting niggas in the dirt and

crashing weddings and wearing pink and purple aprons. You the one oughta be worried about yo' level of denial."

I wanted to argue, but Smoke spoke up.

"Did he say 'niggas,' as in plural?" he asked me, smirking.

I ignored the shit.

"I think you have your own situation to be worried about, the way Yana was looking at you," Lucien said calmly.

Smoke's smile disappeared.

"A misunderstanding," he said tightly, like he didn't want it brought up.

"Hmmm. Make sure you clear it up," the old man advised.

The patio grew quiet for a moment until Dream stepped out the glass doors, her eyes wild, her hands twisting in her apron. I was on my feet immediately, scowl on my face as I walked toward her and grabbed both her arms.

"What's wrong with you?" I demanded.

She swallowed as she looked up at me, then shook her head.

"N-nothing. Y'all should wash up. My parents are here."

CHAPTER 59

Dream

THE SILENCE. That was the part that was getting on my nerves. The awkward silence that revealed the tension in the room like nothing else. I was glad Kam had let me fix his plate and deliver it to him in the theater room. That baby didn't need to be here for this.

We were in the formal dining room to allow for enough space. Daddy sat at the head of the table, his eyes narrowed, his mouth a tight line. On his left was Mama, and on his right was DeAngelo. Dayana and Smoke sat next to Mama. Crystal, Damien, and I sat beside D. Grandpapa was at the other end of the table, his shrewd eyes taking in everything.

If it weren't for the clink of silverware against the delicate China, I don't think there would've been any sound. We'd exchanged greetings, but when Dayana tried to speak to my father, that nigga had looked at her so coldly, I wanted to stab him. That had pretty much set the mood for this meal, and I was already wishing I was back at Damien's, watching some mindless shit with him and Kam.

I was going to have to get my own place. It was past time anyway, but Daddy always fussed when I mentioned it. I liked being close to family and stacking my money, but not if he was going to be on bullshit like this. My sister looked so sad, and the shit had Smoke looking pissed as fuck. My mother cleared her throat and all eyes snapped to her.

"Dream, first of all, the food is delicious, baby," she complimented me.

"Thanks, Mama. Everybody helped," I said.

My father smirked at that. "Everybody, huh? Y'all so cozy. You playing house with a nigga who supposed to be just business and your sister sitting up here like she welcome here," he said snidely.

Damien let out a low chuckle as Dayana threw down her napkin and slid her chair back, ready to leave. Smoke caught her arm, holding her in place as his eyes clashed with my father's. Only the fact that I could tell he was about to say something kept me quiet. I was tired of letting Daddy slide.

"What you want, Castle? Money? How much is your baby girl worth to you? Let me pay that shit so you can stop whining," Smoke spat.

"Ay, he might be outta line, but watch how you talk to my father in his house," DeAngelo spoke up.

Smoke's gaze shifted to his. "Or what, li'l nigga?"

"Or else the disrespect will have consequences," my brother promised.

Damien chuckled again and I froze. I knew he didn't care for D, so I knew he was about to say something reckless.

"You talk a lot of shit for a nigga who alive off the strength of his sister," he said calmly.

"Damien," I pleaded softly, touching his arm.

DeAngelo glared at him as Crystal whispered something.

"If you remember, I didn't agree with that bullshit deal. I don't think—"

"Yeah, you don't think. Like, what the fuck did you think was gon' happen when you ran off with the daughter of the most powerful man in the city?" Damien challenged.

DeAngelo fell silent, guilt all over his face. I felt bad for him.

"D—" I said, about to console him.

"I wish the fuck you would. Fuck that nigga," Damien snarled.

"I—"

"Dream."

Ugh! I hated when he said my name like that! Crossing my arms over my chest, I sat back. I didn't miss the smile that decorated my grandfather's face, though. He really liked this crazy ass nigga.

My father raised an eyebrow. "He got you trained already? Do you bark when he tells you to speak?" he taunted me.

Anger exploded in me, and I opened my mouth, ready to go the fuck off.

"I suggest you focus on what Smoke saying cuz you in the same boat as ya pussy ass son. I'm sparing yo' life because of her. But if you ever put yo' hands on her again, I'ma put mine on you," Damien said calmly.

Daddy sputtered as my mother and grandfather both demanded to know what Damien was talking about. Smoke held up a hand, silencing the room.

"Like I was saying, how much?" he spoke again.

Daddy looked him up and down. "We can talk after we eat. It's not just about the products. I'm building alliances, networks of mutual protection. But the first thing I'ma need is the money for the shipment Middleton is now refusing to pay for."

Smoke nodded. "Done."

"No!" Dayana's voice surprised me and apparently caught Smoke off guard, too.

He frowned down at her. "Yana, what—"

"I know what you're doing, Cartier, and I appreciate it. But one thing I realized on our trip is that I don't want my

father to sell me. And I don't want any man—not even you—
to buy me. I want to be free" she explained, grabbing his
hand. "You understand?"

He looked at her for a minute, like he was thinking over
what she said. Finally, he spoke.

"Yeah. Yeah, I do, Princess, as long as you understand.
You may be free, but you definitely gon' belong to
somebody."

My heart melted as she blushed, and he leaned over to
kiss her forehead.

"Corny ass nigga," Damien mumbled.

"You betta get like me," Smoke shot back.

Daddy clapped slowly. "So sweet. Unfortunately, that's
not how this shit works. I'm in a rebuilding phase, trying to
ensure my legacy so my ungrateful ass children and even
their children won't have shit to worry about. A long time
ago, my wife asked me to scale back. She saw what happened
to her parents and she worried about our small children. But
y'all grown now and it's time for me to expand again. That
takes money, alliances, deals. Each of you have a role to play
and all of you seem to be saying fuck what's best for this
family. Where the fuck is your honor and loyalty? Do you
know what I sacrificed for you? Do you—"

"Stop!"

Grandpapa's voice was quiet, but full of authority. Daddy
stopped.

"You can build your fucking empire, but it won't be on the
backs of my grandchildren. They don't owe you for taking
care of them, looking out for them. You're their fucking father
and you lost sight of that somewhere. These are not your
pawns, your property. These are your children. There should
be nothing more precious than that!" Grandpapa raged, his
tan face red with anger.

I moved to go to him, not wanting him so upset that he
hurt himself. Damien grabbed me and I turned on him

quickly. Nothing would make me back down when it came to my grandfather. Not even him.

"You need to learn to let men be men," he said softly, before I could go off on him.

"Tell her, Bestie. Let them fix their own shit," Dayana agreed before eating another bite of her omelet.

I mugged both of them, but I sat down. My father looked surprised, then turned his attention back to Grandpapa.

"Papa Lucien, with all due respect, I handle my children how I see fit—"

"And I handle my money how I see fit. Now, if you want to lose your most important business partner, keep fucking with these children," Lucien warned. "I might be a silent partner, but remember, there is no empire without me, Darius."

Daddy's mouth tightened as he glared at all of us. He pushed back from the table and stood up.

"Fine. But this is my house and this girl—" he pointed at Dayana, "destroyed something I'd been working on for a long time. She ain't even apologize. She's not welcome here and I'm not bankrolling her disobedient ass," he snarled.

"Stop!" Mama said suddenly. "If my child isn't welcome, then I'm not—"

"She ain't apologizing and she don't need shit from you," Smoke interrupted coldly, standing and pulling Yana with him. "You a bitch ass nigga."

DeAngelo rose and threw down his napkin. "I told you to watch yo' muhfuckin'—"

Damien moved so quickly that I didn't have time to process his standing and reaching across Crystal to drag DeAngelo onto the table. China and glass crashed to the floor and Crystal screamed as Damien's fist smashed into my brother's eye.

"Damien!"

I grabbed his arm and he snatched away.

"Didn't I tell yo' weak ass to shut the fuck up? You

couldn't even protect yo' fucking family from the consequences of yo' bitch ass actions and you wanna act stupid,
nigga?"

He punched the bridge of D's nose. My hands covered my
mouth as DeAngelo struggled against Damien's hold. My
father tried to move toward them, but the distinctive click of a
safety being flipped off stopped him. Our eyes flew to Smoke,
who was coolly aiming at Daddy as Damien continued to
mangle D's face.

"I suggest you think about that shit before you walk yo'
old ass around there."

I raised my hands, trying to stop this fucked up situation.

"Y'all... please d—"

"It's good that this little nigga is learning how real niggas
handle shit, but I'm gon' have to ask y'all to stop," Grandpapa said calmly, a smirk on his face.

"Papa, this not funny," Mama fussed.

"Girl, that nigga will be all right. He needed his ass
whooped, all the shit he been getting people into," Grandpapa waved her off. "He betta learn to back his shit up."

I watched as Smoke slowly lowered his gun and Damien
released DeAngelo's shirt. His petty ass pushed D off the
table and onto the floor.

"Get the fuck out my house. All of you!" Daddy snarled.

Smoke laughed as a small smile curved Damien's mouth.

"Nigga, shut yo' ass up," Smoke said as Damien picked
up two bananas and tossed him one.

"A nigga ain't leaving brunch hungry," he taunted, grabbing my hand.

Silently, we went to get Kam. My mind was whirling,
unable to believe what had just happened. I was worried
about my brother, but instead of going so hard for Daddy, he
should've done more to defend his twin. Damien looked back
at me just outside the theater room. Whatever he saw on my
face had him backing me against the wall and tilting my chin.

"You upset about that li'l nigga."

It wasn't a question, so I didn't answer. He leaned closer to my ear.

"Dream. I didn't kill him. For you," he said, his voice low.

"I-I know," I whispered.

"I don't know what else you want."

His lips grazed my skin as he spoke. I closed my eyes. I didn't know what I wanted either.

"Let's just go home," I said, overwhelmed by this crazy morning and unwilling to figure out why it was so easy to think of his place as home.

His mouth pressed against mine briefly before he walked in to get Kam.

CHAPTER 60

Dayana

(*MONDAY, June 21*)

When Cartier Salinas had something on his mind, there was no changing it. Ever since the brunch ended like it did yesterday, he was determined that I wouldn't go back to my parents' house or ask them for anything. We had already spent the day shopping for a new wardrobe, and now we were in my favorite grocery store picking up foods I liked. I told him it wasn't necessary. He said he didn't cook, and if I wanted something to eat quickly, he needed to stock up. Otherwise, Ms. Stephanie would be doing most of the cooking.

"Make sure you get whatever you want," he said for the hundredth time. I looked at the cart that was damn near overflowing. If I liked something, he insisted on getting five of whatever it was. I wondered how long he planned on my being there.

I wondered a lot of shit, like why he seemed to want me, told me I would belong to someone, but once again, kept me in a separate room and didn't touch me. If this was what he meant by us going back to our lives, I didn't like it!

"What you daydreaming about?"

He broke into my thoughts as I stared blindly at the juice display. I smiled slightly as I grabbed a bottle of cran-apple.

"Nothing."

He snagged four more of the juices before walking right up on me. I didn't resist as he kissed me in the middle of aisle eight, where anyone could see. I was breathless, my lips wet with his taste by the time he pulled back. See? This was the shit that had me confused. He kissed me until my panties were soaked, until I wanted to say, "Fuck these groceries," then... nothing.

"Don't lie to me. What's on your—"

He stopped as his phone rang. Pulling it out, he looked at the number and cursed.

"I gotta take this, Princess. I'ma go outside. You good?" he asked.

I nodded as I took his place behind the cart.

"Go. I'm almost done, anyway," I told him.

He had barely disappeared before I was half-running, ready to set my spur-of-the-moment plan in place. I was going to seduce the hell out of his ass. I picked up a nice loaf of French bread and three kinds of cheese. Sprinting to the produce section, I grabbed grapes, sliced apples, and straw-berries. Luckily, this H-E-B had a pretty nice wine selection. I studied the shelves slowly, trying to remember what Smoke had drunk in the Maldives.

"I knew something was telling me to stop by here tonight."

I froze for a moment at the sound of the familiar voice. Hesitantly, I turned to meet Jordan's eyes. I laughed as I noticed the chick from the swing with him. *This nigga...*

"Bunny, why don't you go pick up the ice cream you were talking about?" he suggested.

"Bunny" frowned, her deep red lips pushed into a pout.

"But—"

Jordan silenced her with a look.

"Do you want to earn more punishment, pet?" he asked.

Her eyes dropped as she whispered, "No, sir."

I watched as she obediently headed for the dairy section. She cut her eyes at me, and I smirked. Then, Jordan and I were alone on the aisle.

"You didn't have to send her away because of me. And 'pet?' Really?"

I shook my head. He walked closer, way too close. I wasn't going to let him see how uncomfortable I was, though.

"I'm disappointed in you, Dayana. So disappointed. You gon' have to pay for that," he said softly, reaching out to stroke my cheek.

"Are you crazy? And don't touch me," I snapped.

He laughed softly. "I'ma enjoy taming you more than I thought. I'ma break you and that attitude, Sweetness. You gon' make this up to me."

Okay, he had officially lost it. I needed to get away from this lunatic. *Walk away, Dayana,* I instructed myself. But I never did what I should.

"Make what up to you, with your cheating ass?" I spat.

He stepped closer. Too late, I realized I had nowhere to go. I gasped as he grabbed me by the throat.

"Leaving with Salinas. Giving him what was promised to me. I can't marry you until you make this shit up to me."

His face loomed over mine, twisted into a scowl. I should probably be more scared, but not my stupid ass.

"Yo' ass must be dreaming. I would never—"

I stopped as his hand tightened around my neck. That shit pissed me off. I clutched the loaf of bread in my hand and swatted him with it. It broke, of course, but before I could swing on him with my fists, he released me. Still mad, I charged at him, shrieking as a pair of strong arms held me back. I wanted to fight, to kick Jordan's ass, but slowly, I became aware of the calm voice calling my name.

"Ms. Castle, please!"

I looked up, recognizing Ammo through the haze of my anger. I hadn't even known he was here.

"Nah, Ammo! This nigga acting like he wanna choke me out? I'ma fuck him up! Move!" I demanded.

"Sweetness, it wasn't even like that," Jordan said hastily, his tone totally different all of a sudden.

It didn't take me long to find out why.

"Let her go, Ammo. Yana, dial your li'l ass down," Smoke instructed, appearing out of nowhere.

Like Ammo, he didn't raise his voice, but I was glad I wasn't on the receiving end of his deadly gaze.

"What part of her leaving the wedding with me didn't you understand?" he asked Jordan calmly.

Jordan swallowed, his eyes wide. The reappearance of Bunny made his bitch ass bold, though.

"She was promised to me. She don't get to just walk—"

Smoke moved then, so quickly that he was on Jordan before any of us knew it, an old-school, dark red switchblade pressed to my ex-fiancé's throat.

"Cartier," I whispered, not sure of what else to say.

He looked at me, a dark smile covering his lips.

"You want me to use Scarlet to cut this nigga's throat or gut his ass?" he asked.

I blinked several times, dumbstruck by the question. One look at him let me know he was serious.

"Here? Cartier! You can't do that here!" I hissed.

He looked at me, that evil, strangely sexy smile spreading.

"I can do whatever the fuck I want, Dayana. So, which is it?"

"Dayana…"

Jordan's voice was small and weak. Shit, it must be hard to face your untimely demise. Suddenly, I felt sorry for him. I sighed.

"Neither," I mumbled.

Smoke's eyes snapped to me as if he didn't trust his ears.

"What?"

I dropped the ruined bread. Twisting my hands together, I looked at him plaintively.

"Can't you just kick his sorry ass?"

It was his turn to blink several times.

"You fucking with me, right?"

I sighed.

"Don't... don't kill him. Please, Cartier."

He scoffed, his handsome face sporting a frown.

"You pleading for this nigga?" He chuckled softly. "Maybe you should've stayed at that church," he said, retracting the blade.

That shit ran me hot. Nigga better be glad I didn't have another loaf of bread. Before I could pop off, his attention was back on Jordan.

"Thank her soft ass for yo' worthless life. Get out my face, bitch," Smoke ordered.

Jordan scurried to obey, Bunny on his heels like the pet he called her. He turned at the last minute to grill Smoke.

"This ain't over, nigga," he spat.

Smoke chuckled, twirling the knife in his hand. "I know. That's why I let yo' ass go. I'll see you." He released the blade suddenly and Jordan paled. "Soon."

I watched as Jordan disappeared before looking over at Smoke again. He stared at me for a few seconds before speaking to Ammo.

"Take care of this," he said, gesturing toward the basket.

Ammo nodded and Smoke's eyes returned to me.

"Let's go."

I wanted to argue, but the coldness of his eyes and his voice changed my mind quickly. The ride to his house was quiet. I kept expecting him to lash out or something, but he didn't. Even after we arrived, the only sign I had of his temper was the fact that he told me good night and walked back out the door.

Fuck this, I thought, yanking it open.

"Just so you know, I won't be here when you get back," I announced bravely.

He looked at me, his caramel eyes heated to gold.

"Tonight is the night you wanna try me, Dayana?"

"What you gon' do? Spank me?" I said, throwing the threat he'd used on me a couple of times at him. "Nigga, you will *never*—"

"I'll spank your ass and make you like it. Take your ass to bed."

My pussy jumped, just like it did every time he mentioned that. Still, I wanted to talk my shit, but the quietness of his tone...

"Fuck you, Cartier," I mumbled finally, slinking my ass back into his house and into the guest bedroom where I'd been sleeping.

But I slammed the room door behind me, hell. Dayana Dionne Castle feared no man!

Well... not much.

CHAPTER 61

Demon

(*WEDNESDAY, June 23*)

I was closing the door of the room I called my sanctuary when my phone rang. I locked it before pulling the vibrating device from my pocket. Looking down, I saw Dream was FaceTiming me. She did that on her lunch break sometimes, called just to talk about random shit or nothing at all. I had never done that before and I didn't understand the purpose, but it made her happy. For some reason, I liked her happy. I answered and waited for her pretty face to appear.

"What you doing?" she asked, smiling hard as hell.

"Why you so nosy?" I shot back, fucking with her.

She rolled her eyes at me but kept talking.

"Kam at camp?"

She'd found his ass some kind of arts and sciences camp. Little nigga loved it. My weak ass didn't want to tell either of them no, so I had to have a talk with the camp directors about why a security detail was going to be allowed there.

"You wanna talk to me or that li'l nigga? Swear you got his number."

The lips I'd watched her line and fill with a matte purple this morning pushed into a little pout as she frowned.

"Well… I didn't really want anything. I'll just talk to you later," she said quietly.

Damn! I'd hurt her feelings. I had no idea why I was learning to read her emotions or why I gave a fuck, but I did.

"What you eating?" I asked suddenly.

"What?"

My question surprised her, and she looked at me like I was crazy.

"For lunch, Dream. What you eating?"

"Nothing," she sighed.

It was my turn to frown. "Why?"

"Oh, my God, we're so busy! I don't really have time for a full lunch break. I forgot to bring something, and I don't have time to go out."

"Order something."

She shook her head. "By the time it would get here, I would need to be working again. I didn't think this through too well."

I scowled at her. "You can't work if you don't eat."

"Oh, yes, I can. I'll just be grouchy and starving tonight."

She dropped her head in her hand dramatically before looking up at me and smiling again. I didn't return that shit, though. I didn't want her skipping meals. Yeah, my feelings about that came from my fucked-up childhood, but it was what it was. Before I could say anything else, I heard a knock on her end.

"Hold on," she told me.

I watched as she looked up and smiled.

"What's up?" she asked.

"Dream," I heard Parker say her name in a singsong voice.

"Whatever it is, I already know I should say no if you're saying my name like that," Dream responded, shaking her head.

"Stop thinking negative. I just came to let you know that

the grand opening of Malia's Smokehouse *y Taqueria* is today!" Parker sang out.

Dream's eyes widened.

"Malia, our classmate?"

"Uh-huh!"

"Malia, who can cook her ass off?"

"Yep."

Dream moaned. "Parker, why do you do this shit to us?"

"I just figured you'd wanna go support. It could be like a birthday lunch," Parker coaxed.

"My birthday's not till Saturday!"

"Pre-birthday, whatever. Work with me."

I heard another knock, followed by Paul Arceneau's voice. "I'll even drive," he offered.

A chill swept over me as I thought about killing his weak ass.

"Tell that nigga you good," I ordered.

"Damien!"

"Shit, you want me to tell him?"

"No!"

I chuckled. I'd handle that nigga myself. Dream closed her eyes like she was thinking hard. Finally, she sighed loudly.

"We can't," she said, sounding pitiful.

"Dream—" Parker began.

"Ay, I'll see you tonight," I broke in.

Dream looked at me and nodded. I disconnected, then immediately Googled Malia's Smokehouse *y Taqueria*. I was going to feed her stubborn ass, then make sure I was the only nigga on her mind while she was at that office.

———

Rayleigh Jones—that's what the nameplate on her desk said—looked up at me, her eyes wide as hell. Shorty looked half-scared and half-curious. I didn't want to freak her little ass out any more than she already was, so I held up the bags of food wordlessly.

"Y-y-you remember where her office is?"

Her voice was a nervous little whisper.

"Yeah," I responded.

I moved toward the hallway in the suite of offices, then stopped. Shorty couldn't be out here letting people in Dream's office, not when Keith was out here on the loose.

"Rayleigh?"

Her gaze snapped to my face.

"Don't let anyone else into her office without her knowing."

She nodded so hard that she looked like a life size bobble-head.

"O-okay, of-of-of course, Mr. … umm… Demon… sir," she stammered.

Parker's name was engraved on the plate by the first door. It was partially open, so I knocked lightly. She called out for me to come in. I entered silently, waiting for her to look up from her computer. When she did, she looked surprised, then gave me a big smile.

"What's up, Demon?"

"I heard y'all talking about this place. Get some of this food," I said abruptly.

I would never be a greetings-and-small-talk kind of nigga. It didn't matter how much Dream called me rude. Parker squealed as she stood up. Swear women be extra about food. Dream's ass sang and danced when she ate.

"You're so sweet, surprising her with lunch—"

"Nah, shorty. I'm not sweet," I corrected. "She gotta eat, though."

Parker clasped her hands together and looked up at me like I was Jesus or somebody.

"Awww! She needs that. She'll work all day without stop-ping for anything. I'm glad she has you."

She gave me a quick hug, her words and her actions knocking me all off my shit. Did Dream have me? And why did the chicks around her love to hug? I knew damn well nothing about me looked huggable, but they kept doing it. I just stood there as she took the bags and set them on her desk. She turned back around and looked at me like she was waiting for something. I shrugged.

"I just got a bunch of shit. I'on know what y'all eat."

Parker searched through the bags, reading labels out loud and talking so fast that I wondered how anyone kept up. Finally, she was still and smiling at me again.

"Thank you so much. I was starving, but we have so much to do and—" She stopped and waved her hands. "Anyway, I know you wanna see Dream. She's in Paul's office, I think. He—"

She kept talking, but I wasn't listening anymore. Grabbing the food, I headed down the hallway. I passed Dream's office, looking for Paul's. The soft sound of her laughter led me there. The icy feeling that had been building inside of me since Parker told me where Dream was grew. Like everything else about her, her smiles and laughter were mine. *For now,* I reminded myself. Keeping that shit straight was getting harder and harder. I stopped outside his slightly open door.

"Damn, your laugh is beautiful," his bitch ass complimented her.

"Well, thank you. But we really—"

"I see why that nigga so possessive."

So, he'd heard me and hadn't said shit, but wanted to hint at it to her? It took everything in me not to walk in and beat his ass lifeless. That nigga stayed violating, but this was her place of business. I was gon' catch him slipping.

"Paul, really—"

"Okay, okay. I wanted you to review this invoice from Chain Construction."

I turned around and walked back to her office. Her

personality was all over the room, from the yellow wingback chairs for guests to the mix of pictures and certificates on her baby blue accent wall. An open door allowed me to see into the little attached bathroom. Small sculptures adorned her tables and shelves, but the art piece that caught my attention was the K. Reid piece on her back wall. I hadn't noticed it the last time I was here. I took a minute to admire the way she had it displayed before setting the food on the small conference table. I bypassed the sunny ass chairs to sit in her girly-looking, velvet, blue chair and wait.

Twenty minutes later, she waltzed her thick ass into the room, the amethyst dress she wore swirling around her thighs. Her attention was on a tablet she held in her hands. I cleared my throat, then shook my head as her dramatic ass shrieked and almost dropped the tablet.

"I know you a screamer, but damn, shorty," I said dryly.

"Damien! What are you doing here?"

I ignored her question for now.

"Close the door and come here."

She frowned. "Damien—"

"Dream."

She stared at me for a minute before rolling her eyes and doing what I said. I stood up as she approached.

"I brought you lunch," I explained.

"Damien, I told you I don't have time."

"Make time," I said, backing her up toward the desk.

She brought both her hands up and rested them against my chest, trying to hold me back. I grabbed her ass before leaning down to run my lips against her throat. Shorty smelled so good that I wanted to taste her.

"W-what you doing?" she asked, her voice a whisper as her hands balled up my shirt.

I kissed the corner of her mouth before pulling back a little.

"Shit, what you think I'm doing?"

I nibbled on her bottom lip, then pressed my mouth against hers. She opened immediately for my kiss, her familiar taste of apple and mint going straight to my dick. She moaned softly before turning her head to suck in a deep breath.

"Damien, we have to stop. This is my office. I can't—"

She let out a cute little squeal as I picked her up and sat her on her desk.

"I can do what the fuck I want," I said, sliding my hands under the full skirt to rub the thighs she hated, and I loved. "That includes you."

"You so nasty!"

She kept talking her shit, but she opened her legs so I could get closer. And when I leaned down, she pressed those soft ass lips against mine. She gasped when my fingers stroked across the seat of her panties before diving beneath. I smirked at her.

"Making all that noise and this pussy soaking wet."

"Shut up," she moaned, her head falling back as I tapped her clit.

"Lay back," I instructed.

She looked at me, hesitating. I waited silently. Finally, she did what I said, her curvy body pressed against the mahogany of her desk. I grabbed one of the yellow chairs and set it in front of her legs before settling my body into it. I heard her draw in a sharp breath as I reached under her dress again. My hands eased up her thighs until I found her panties. I pulled on them and she lifted, letting me draw them slowly down her legs.

"Come here," I said softly.

She raised herself on her elbows and frowned at me.

"Now, you just told me to… Damien!"

She shrieked my name as I grabbed her thighs and pulled her closer to me. I shook my head.

"So smart to be so dense," I mumbled before pushing the dress up and placing a kiss on top of her pretty pussy.

She shivered and I used two of my fingers to part her lips. I licked her slowly from her juicy opening to just below her already swelling clit. Sighing, she gripped the desk and let her thick thighs fall open further. I bit the smooth, soft skin of her inner thigh before sucking it gently.

"What were you doing in that nigga's office?" I asked before giving her pussy another slow lick, still avoiding her clit.

"W-w-what?" she whimpered.

I sucked on one of her lips before responding. "You heard me."

"Damien... you know... mmm...w-we work...oh, my God... together... *Damien!*"

She struggled to put words together as I licked and sucked on her sweet pussy. She was extra agitated because her clit was getting no attention. I wasn't going to let her ass cum until we came to an understanding.

"You acting like you don't know that nigga tryna fuck?"

"He's... *ohhh*... n-n-not serious," she whimpered.

I stopped mid-lick as shorty tried to play with me. I bit her thigh again, harder. She squirmed against the desk.

"Damien!"

"You ain't that naïve, Dream."

"What that mean?"

I ignored her. My tongue traced the seam of her pussy and she moaned and twisted her thick body. Sinking my fingers into her thighs, I held her still as I licked her everywhere but where she wanted most. She lifted her hips, trying to get into my mouth where she needed it.

"Help that nigga save his life, cuz if he move recklessly one more time, I'm laying him down," I warned her.

"O-okay. Damien, *please*," she whined.

I smiled at her. "'Damien, please'," I teased. "You so

polite, Dream. That's why you always calling me rude? Maybe you need to be a little rude, too. I don't know what that 'please' means. What you want, shorty?"

She raised her head to look at me like she was shy or something.

"Y-you know."

I kissed the creases of her thighs.

"Nah, I don't know. Tell me."

"I can't," she whispered.

"I can't, either."

I sat back and stood up.

"Noooo!"

She used her legs to try to hold me in place. I lightly smacked the outside of her thighs.

"Nah, let go. You busy with work anyway."

She held on, her hips moving restlessly, her pussy glistening in front of me. Shit, it took everything in me not to dive back in. My dick was rock hard for her. She threw her arm over her eyes and whispered something.

"What? I can't hear that," I said.

She let out a deep breath.

"Please... lick my clit, Damien," she mumbled a little louder.

I smiled smugly before doing as she asked. She came as soon as my tongue stroked across her pearl, screaming softly when I sucked it into my mouth. I ate her pussy relentlessly, making her cum twice, ignoring her when she tried to push my head away.

"It's too sensitive," she moaned.

I had mercy on her and stood up, unbuckling my belt and grabbing the condom I had stuffed in my pocket with this in mind. I lowered my jeans and boxer briefs in one move before rolling the condom on. I didn't want to make her at-work clean up hard. I lifted her right leg, resting it in the crook of my left arm while guiding myself with my right hand between her dripping lips. I had to bite back a groan as I slid into the slippery, tight heat of her pussy. She moaned as I filled her, stretching to accommodate my girth. I moved slowly, giving her long, deep strokes.

"Damien... no," she said suddenly, shaking her head.

I stopped immediately, looking down at her. I didn't play about a chick saying no. Bad as I wanted to fuck her speechless, I wanted her to want it, too.

"I don't like it. Take it off."

I frowned at her, lost. I reached for the hem of my shirt.

"Noooo... The condom. It feels... funny," she said.

I leaned forward, bracing myself on my palms on each side of her.

"You wanna feel me raw, shorty?" I teased.

She threw her arm back over her eyes as she blushed, but her pussy clenched my dick. Dream could play proper, but she liked my dirty mouth.

"If I take it off, I'm not pulling out. You gon' be leaking my cum while you work."

Hell, I couldn't lie; that thought made my shit harder. She nodded and I pulled out, discarding the condom in her little trashcan before easing back inside her. I picked up the same rhythm, loving the feel of her tight walls gripping me. I fucked her slow, watching her pretty ass sex faces as she tried to hold in her moans.

"Oh, my God... I'm about to cum... *Damien*," she wailed my name as her pussy convulsed.

"Tell me it's mine," I demanded, thrusting harder as she exploded.

Caught up in her orgasm, Dream didn't hear the quick knock on her door before it opened. Paul walked in, smiling and about to say something. His expression changed fast as hell. I smirked as I continued to fuck her. I didn't care if that nigga watched; maybe he'd finally understand. I was focused on pleasing her and getting the nut I felt building.

"It's yours, Damien," Dream moaned, tightening her legs around me.

Her words pushed me over the edge. I groaned as I erupted inside her, her pussy milking my seed from me. I made a few more shallow strokes before I collapsed on top of her. She wrapped one arm around me as we struggled to breathe.

"I can't believe we did that," she murmured.

I rose a little bit to look into her eyes.

"However, whenever, wherever," I reminded her, as I slowly withdrew. "Get up so we can washup and you can eat."

"Damien—"

"Dream."

I didn't want to hear her bullshit. Sighing, she let me help her up and off the desk.

"You're too bossy," she mumbled.

I smacked her ass as she walked away. "You like it."

She sucked her teeth, then said, "Boy, shut up," in that way chicks say when they don't mean it.

I needed to check her on that shit. No one had told me to shut up in forever. Shit was unacceptable. I opened my mouth...

Then she giggled, like the shit was funny.

Like she was happy.

I decided to let her make it.

This girl, man. I was in trouble.

CHAPTER 62

Dream

(*FRIDAY, June 25*)

I was going to fuck Dayana up. I mean, anytime I agreed to let her buy my clothes, I knew her choices were going to be a little bit more risqué than mine. We were both thick, but Yana was a size and a little change smaller than I was, a fact that she seemed to forget. Like tonight. I stared at my reflection in the bodycon, one shoulder white dress. It clung to every inch of me, down to just above my knees. That alone would've been enough, but not for my hot ass sister. Oh, no. The dress had a split that basically bared my whole right thigh. Like, I was glad she bought skimpy underwear to match, or else I would've been panty-less.

I looked at myself again. Dayana knew how I felt about these thighs. This display was too much. Fuck it. She was going to have to give me something else or take me home to raid my closet. I was not about to—

There was a knock on the door right before my sister stuck her conniving ass face in.

"Bitch—" I began.

She waved me off, sashaying her ass into the guest room she'd been sleeping in at Smoke's house. She hadn't been home this week, understandably and, between work and my nights at Damien's, I hadn't been there much myself. What I didn't understand was why she was in a guest room. She'd told me enough that I knew she was feeling Smoke *and* his bedroom skills, but they had been acting strange this week since they'd been back. That wasn't the issue tonight, though. The issue was my looking like... this.

"Don't start your shit, Dream. You in here looking like you stepped straight from God's imagination, so I don't want to hear about your thighs. You ain't showing no more than I am," she argued, pointing at the strapless red dress that hugged her body and featured a deep split in the front.

"But you like showing it!" I protested.

"Breena laid the fuck out of your hair and makeup."

She changed the subject, letting me know she didn't give a fuck about what I had to say. That was Yana for your ass. I sighed loudly, before sliding my feet into the green Aquazzura stiletto sandals she'd chosen. My sister was thorough—a matching clutch and jeweled accessories rested on the dresser. She'd chosen flawless, emerald-accented pieces, and I wondered about her selections for tonight.

"Why green?" I asked.

She smiled. "His eyes."

I knew who she was talking about, of course.

"His eyes aren't this dark," I mumbled.

"They are when he looks at you."

I had no comeback for that. So, I waited as my sister snapped pictures of us for social media. Finally, her ass was happy.

An hour later, we met Parker, Crystal, and a few more friends at Bliss. While I was usually a little reserved, I enjoyed how over the top Yana had gone. Sparklers and dancers and a four-tier cake were just the tip of the iceberg. All my girls were dressed in red to make my white attire stand out even more. I could feel eyes on me as niggas didn't even try to hide their lustful looks.

"I guess you were right about this dress," I told my sister as we made our way to the main dance floor.

She rolled her eyes.

"Ain't I always?"

We vibed along with the DJ's selection, Parker's wannabe hood ass singing and rocking the loudest. I was happy just dancing with my girls, until Big Latto came on. It was a must that I pop my ass and I wanted to do it on some fine ass nigga. It was my muhfuckin' birthday, hell. But while many of the muhfuckas were eyeballing me, none of them stepped to me.

I spotted a nigga named Presley whom I had gone to high school with, standing near us as he chopped it up with one of his corner boys. Press was fine as fuck but way too deep in the game for me to ever take the few advances he made seriously. That didn't stop me from bopping over to him and grinding my ass against him. A few seconds later, his strong hands were on my waist. But they weren't pulling me closer like I expected. Instead, he was holding me still.

"Dream," his deep voice rumbled against my ear. "Shorty, you fine as hell and you smell good enough to eat. A month ago, I woulda been tryna take yo' pretty ass up outta here and taste that sweet pussy. But Demon not about to be tryna lay my ass down."

I frowned over my shoulder. "What?"

"Happy Birthday, Gorgeous. But you gon' have to go back over there, witcho pretty li'l crew."

Shocked, it took me a moment to process what he said. Rejection was some shit I was totally unused to, and I didn't like it. Plus, Damien wasn't my man, had no claim beyond thirty days on me, and niggas were acting like I was untouchable? Hell no.

"Sorry," I finally mumbled before moving to rejoin my sister and friends.

I grabbed Yana's arm to get her attention.

"What's wrong? That nigga talking crazy?" she asked, on go as usual.

"Girl, he wouldn't dance with me because of Damien," I said, getting pissed off the more I thought about it.

"What? Is that why—"

"Dream, just do us a favor and tell us Sunday what that birthday dick was like," Laina moaned, interrupting us.

"Ugh, Laina! That's my uncle," Crystal muttered.

I frowned at Laina. "The fuck, Laina? Where that—"

But already the telltale tingles were erupting over my body and butterflies took flight in my stomach. I spotted Damien seconds later and I could've killed Dayana, because I knew she was behind this shit, somehow. He literally matched my fly, the green blazer he wore accenting his muscular frame covered in a white button down and white pants. Green and white Prada sneakers kept his outfit some-what casual, but I would've put him up against any formally dressed nigga. His locs were braided up in a neat bun, allowing the ice sparkling at his ears to standout, even in the club's dim lighting. Damien looked so good that I almost forgot to breathe as the usual pulsating between my thighs started. He walked toward me, stopping about a foot away to stare me up and down. His eyes fell on the dress's split, and he frowned before shooting Yana a look. Her ass was suddenly all caught up in a conversation with Parker.

I stared up at him, ready for whatever he had to say. He bit his bottom lip as he studied me, and the unexpected sparkle of diamonds and metal caught me off guard. I swear I came as I realized this nigga was wearing platinum and diamond fronts. I was Texas born-and-bred, but my mama and her family were from Louisiana. The Louisiana girl in me could not resist locs and a grill. I entertained the thought of fucking him right here and now... as long as he didn't piss me off. But he never spoke. Instead, he walked past us, probably about to go to VIP. My heart rate was on the verge of slowing down when I felt a single, sharp slap against my ass.

I made a soft little sound, whirling on my heels.

"Damien—"

"Don't let that little ass dress get a nigga fucked up in here."

His gaze moved to Press before he smirked at me and strolled off.

Rolling my eyes, I turned back around. Press looked at me, one eyebrow raised, like he was saying, "I told you so." My childish ass stuck out my tongue and he laughed.

"So, y'all niggas coordinating outfits and shit now?" Parker teased.

I glared at Dayana, who shrugged.

"Crystal mentioned her mama styles him for special occasions, so I might have dropped a suggestion," she said breezily.

That explained a lot about the tailored clothes and designer brands I'd seen him in, because I could tell he didn't give a fuck about stuff like that. I just couldn't believe Sherrilyn had gone along with Yana's simple ass.

"I'm going to the restroom," I announced, exasperated.

Crystal, Laina, and Sasha went back to our section. Parker and Dayana volunteered to go with me, and we set off toward the hallway nearest us.

"Personally, I think Demon is a good look for you. Y'all obviously feeling each other and—"

I waved my hand, cutting Parker off. "Girl, no. This is just me having a quarter-life fling," I lied.

She didn't know the details of our deal and she didn't have to.

Dayana sucked her teeth. "You can't tell her ass nothing. This ain't no fling and—"

I covered my ears and ducked into the bathroom before either of them could say anything else. I handled my business quickly before rejoining my girls, who were still talking their shit. We were almost back in the main part of the club when I noticed four women walking in our direction, talking among themselves.

I recognized Juliette instantly and one of the women with her was the little trick Damien had tried to fuck. *Bitches*, I thought. I couldn't even front like I wasn't jealous.

"Excuse us," Dayana said politely.

Juliette looked up, smiling, until her eyes landed on me.

"Well, well, well. If it isn't the little lady who has cost me a lot of money," she taunted.

Lord, could this night get any more awkward?

CHAPTER 63

Demon

I STOOD at the front of Dante's VIP section, watching as Dream, Parker, and Dayana disappeared down one of the hallways off the main floor, Dream's detail following at a discreet distance. Dayana didn't know it, but if she ever put her sister in anything like that little shit they were calling a dress again, our so-called friendship was going to be over. It outlined her curvy body and her whole fucking leg was out. All I could think about was how warm and soft it felt when it was wrapped around my waist. I had no doubt ninety percent of the niggas in here were wishing they knew that feeling.

"I can tell Yana been in Dream's ear."

The voice came from the left, just outside the section. I shook my head as Smoke chuckled. Dante's security eyed him, but made no attempt to move.

"Let him in," I ordered.

They stood down immediately, and Smoke walked in. He dapped me up, then let his gaze follow mine.

"That little shit she got on ain't much better," he muttered as we waited for them to reappear.

"You oughta rein her little ass in," I said, only half-joking.

He made a frustrated sound. "You her bestie; you try. Shit, can't nobody tell that crazy girl shit."

Noticing his tone and the frown on his face, I raised an eyebrow.

"Trouble in paradise?"

"Trouble since we got back from paradise," he corrected.

I nodded once, then sipped from the glass I'd been nursing. Having an addict for a mother meant I was always conscious of how much of anything I put in my body, and I never let go of my control.

"The two of y'all over here looking like what you are for once," Dante said, smirking as he approached us.

"What? Killers?" I asked dryly, not in the mood for his shit.

"Nah. Soft ass yella niggas. Them Castle girls got y'all in ya bag. I'm surprised yo' crazy ass didn't try to break Press's hands."

The thought had crossed my mind and I guess it showed on my face. Dante laughed as he and Smoke shook it up. I didn't see shit funny. I couldn't believe she had been grinding on that nigga in that washcloth she had on. One wrong move and her pretty pussy would've been on display for all these niggas. That was definitely for my eyes only.

For twelve more days, I reminded myself, trying to get my head right.

"Damn, Juliette's ass knows how to pick them," Dante said, his eyes glued to the first floor.

I looked at Juliette and her girls and shrugged, my interest stolen by Dream's frustrating ass. Then I realized where they were headed.

"Shit," I cursed, pressing my drink into Dante's hand.

He tensed immediately. "What is it? You need us? You—"

"Nah. It's... I got it," I assured him before I headed toward the stairs.

I made it just in time to hear Dream pop off at Juliette.

"If you and your stable would move, it would be appreciated."

Juliette shook her head, laughing softly.

"Oh, no, love. We should catch up. Maybe you can tell me—"

"Maybe you could do what the fuck she said," I cut in.

All of them looked at me. Juliette's jaw dropped, but she recovered quickly.

"Look at you, Mr. Protector. You finally falling? Let me find out you out here eating pussy and fucking missionary," she taunted, bitterness in her hazel eyes.

"Raw and all that shit," I shot back, walking up on her. "You sound jealous, Juliette. That's bad for business, right?"

I leaned down to whisper in her ear. "You coming up missing would be even worse for business. I don't usually give second chances. And I never give a third," I warned.

Her mouth tightened as she stared at me, suddenly scared. The bitch composed herself quickly, though.

"Whatever, Demon. It's not that serious." She smirked. "See you around. And, oh… y'all look cute in your white and green."

She and her girls continued down the hallway. Dream looked up at me, her brown eyes shooting daggers, before easing past and following Parker and Dayana upstairs.

"What the fuck?" I mumbled.

———

I watched her for an hour as she danced with her friends and sipped from a glass of white liquor. She was smiling, but something seemed off. Maybe it was because her sister had disappeared downstairs minutes ago. Maybe it was because she knew my eyes were on her. I didn't know, and I didn't know why I gave a fuck, but I didn't want her birthday to start like this.

I nodded once at my brother, and he returned the gesture. I left his section for Dream's. She was sitting on a love seat by herself, and I settled beside her. She rolled her eyes but said nothing.

"I'm tryna understand what all the attitude is for."

She sighed. "Nothing."

"What I tell you about lying to me?" I asked, pulling on her high ponytail.

"Damien... not tonight. It's my birthday, hell."

She turned slightly, giving me her back.

"I know. And I got your gift, but since you wanna lie..."

I let my voice trail off. Eve had been right about one thing: Dream's bourgeois ass loved presents. She fussed and frowned when I gave her shit, but best believe, she didn't return any of it. Just like I expected, her body softened, and she looked over her shoulder.

"You gave me money earlier," she mumbled.

"That wasn't your gift, Dream."

Yeah, it had been stuffed in a new Chanel backpack, but she seemed to like those.

She sniffed, then turned toward me more. "What is it, then?"

"Tell me why you in here with yo' face looking ugly," I said, sprawling more comfortably against the couch.

She sucked her teeth. "Whatever."

I shrugged. "A'ight."

We sat there for a couple more minutes and I could feel her stubborn ass fighting her curiosity. I managed not to smirk when she gave in.

"I just don't understand why your little tricks talking sideways to me, but I can't even get a nigga to give me a birthday dance," she spat before pouting and crossing her arms over her chest.

"Fuck you talking about now?"

"So, you haven't noticed that not one nigga has approached me? And then you smacked my ass like you own it—and don't say you do for now, or I swear to God, I'ma fuck you up!"

I guess I was supposed to feel bad. And I should feel some type of way that this was more evidence of how well Dante manipulated me. But I was glad these niggas knew. Reaching in my blazer pocket, I pulled out a box and tossed it in her lap.

She mugged me before slowly picking it up. I heard her gasp as she opened it. The eighteen-karat pink gold Audemars was as beautiful as she was. It sported hundreds of tiny diamonds, including the baguette-cut hour markers.

"Damien... it's too much! I can't—" she started breathlessly.

"Girl, be quiet."

She looked like she was about to cuss me out, but I guess the ice had her mesmerized.

"Thank you," she said softly, caressing it with her index finger.

"Let's go downstairs," I said suddenly, standing up and holding out my hand.

For once, her bossy ass didn't argue. I put her watch back in my pocket and led her toward the staircase.

"Where we going?" she asked as we stepped off the last stair.

"I mean, you bitching about a dance..."

Her eyes widened in shock as I led her to the middle of the dance floor just as the old school Jodeci changed to Daniel Caesar and H.E.R.'s "Best Part." I pulled her plush body against mine, ignoring all the stunned eyes on me.

"You dance?"

"My father had me doing all types of shit, trying to take the rough edges off. He said I couldn't be hood in all our business. But I leave most of this shit to Dante," I explained abruptly.

We swayed for a minute, but she tilted her head back to say something else. I stopped her, running a thumb over her eyelid as Daniel Caesar crooned about brown eyes. That shit hit too close to home. One look in her brown eyes and I was ready to do whatever her ass wanted. I brushed my lips against hers.

"Damien?"

Her voice was breathless.

"Yeah?"

"Wh-what did Juliette mean? About... about you fucking missionary style?"

Damn, she didn't miss anything. And I wasn't about to lie, even if my answer revealed too fucking much.

"I guess they tell each other that I only fuck them from behind," I admitted.

Her nose wrinkled as she thought, and I wanted to kiss the tip. *Where the fuck did that come from?*

"Why?" she asked.

I kissed her again, trying to make her focus on something else. But her stubborn ass wasn't having it. As soon as I released her lips, she repeated her question. I sighed.

"So I don't have to look in their eyes or talk to 'em, Dream."

"But—"

I had to change this subject before this girl had me admitting shit that I didn't even want to acknowledge.

"Let's go," I said.

"It's my birthday. Why you wanna leave? We can talk about something else," she murmured, snuggling closer to me.

"I got your other gift," I coaxed.

She narrowed her eyes. "What?"

I grinned down at her. "This birthday dick. I know you feel it."

She scoffed. "Please! I can get that whenever."

"So, you don't want it?"

She rolled her eyes before smiling at me.

"Let me get my stuff."

CHAPTER 64

Dayana

"SO, what? Smoke just rescued you and set you free? You single now?" my ex-friend-with-no-benefits, Benzo, asked loud enough to be heard over Money Bagg Yo.

Smiling, I danced closer to him, letting my breasts graze against him. He looked at me skeptically, but that didn't stop him from tracing the split in my dress and rubbing my inner thigh.

"Why all the questions, Benz? Can we just dance, nigga?" I asked, sliding my arms around his neck and watching the colored lights play over his smooth, dark skin.

I was trying to enjoy my sister's birthday, even though she was upstairs in a mood, mad at Damien and every nigga in here. I chose Benzo because he was fun and harmless. We'd dated some my senior year in high school and my first year of college, but that had ended when Daddy made it clear that he was looking for a suitable husband for me.

"Shorty, you playing with fire right now and I ain't tryna get burned. You left your wedding to Jordan with Smoke. That kinda shit, with them two cats, starts wars, and I'on wanna be in the middle of all that!" he said.

Rolling my eyes, I pulled away from him.

"If you scared, just say that, Arbenz," I popped at him.

His face immediately changed, anger tightening his handsome features. "Ain't nobody scared, Dayana. I just don't like unnecessary confusion and you definitely coming off as confused, baby."

"Whatever," I mumbled, getting ready to walk away from him.

He grabbed my arm, stopping me because I didn't want to risk falling in my four-inch heels.

"Don't be like that, Beautiful. Come here," he said, lowering his voice.

Once upon a time, that would've had my heart fluttering. It did nothing for me now and I almost continued my walk off. But then, I remembered I was being petty. This wasn't about Benzo and my lack of response to him. This was about that nigga who had the nerve to move me into his house, basically ignore me all week, then watch me tonight like I was his or something. Fuck Cartier Salinas's hot and cold ass. He might not want to be with me, but plenty of men did and I was going to show him. I let Benzo pull me into his thick frame. My fingers tiptoed from his chest up to his jawline.

"I don't understand why you tripping. I told you what it was," I said coyly.

He gripped my ass and nuzzled my neck before bringing his lips close to my ear. "I'm just saying..."

His voice trailed off, and I felt him tense. I gazed up at him. His eyes were directed over my shoulder. Turning, I felt my stomach drop at the sight of Smoke standing there, hands in his pockets, watching us. I swallowed, then lifted my head.

"What's up?" I asked bravely.

One corner of his mouth lifted in a half-smile.

"Nah, go on with your performance, love. That was for me, right?"

His voice was nonchalant, but his caramel eyes were

unreadable. I realized this may have not been the best idea, but I was gon' ride this shit out.

"I don't know what you're talking about."

The lie tripped off my tongue as I turned to face Benzo again.

"Oh, okay. Then, if you done, my car is waiting," Smoke said.

I waved a hand over my shoulder.

"Don't let me hold you up. I'm talking with a friend."

Smoke chuckled, but it didn't sound amused at all, and I felt a current of fear slither down my spine.

"Benzo, right?" he said.

Benzo nodded.

"See, Benzo, this is the part where you move around before you can't," Smoke said calmly.

Benzo's eyes widened as he held up both hands.

"She said she was single—" his scary ass started.

"Bye," Smoke interrupted.

Benzo glared at me before he and his boys took off. I whirled around to face Smoke.

"Nigga, who do you think you are—"

My voice stopped at the look on his face. *I'm in trouble*, I thought, then shook my head. I was grown and unattached. Just because I was staying at his house—

"Oh, I'ma show you who I am, but do you really want it to be here?"

I knew the answer from his tone.

"I need my—"

"Ammo has your shit outside. Walk."

I rolled my eyes.

But I walked.

The ride to his house was silent, giving time for my righteous anger to grow. This nigga had me fucked up if he thought he was gon' ignore me most of the week, then lay some kind of claim on me. He better stay focused on his dead wife—no offense.

He had barely turned the car off before I was out and standing by the garage door, waiting to be let in. Smoke stopped in front of me, his eyes boring into mine.

"Dayana—"

"I don't wanna talk to you right now," I snapped.

He smirked and let me in. I stormed up to my room, slamming the fucking door just in case he missed the point. Yanking off my shoes, I threw them toward the closet, feeling satisfied as they clunked against the door.

"Stupid bastard," I mumbled, reaching for the zipper on the side of my dress.

I froze when my door banged open, and my eyes tangled with the angry caramel ones of Cartier Salinas.

For one minute, I was a little scared, but anger won, and I straightened to glare at him. I was glad his ass was here.

I had plenty to say. Even as he strode into the room and into my space, I stood my ground.

"What the fuck is wrong with you?" he demanded.

"With me! Nigga! What th—"

I gasped as his hand tangled in my hair and yanked my head backward. Oh, he thought he was going to handle me? Hell n—

"Watch yo' mouth, Dayana. The bullshit you been on this week—"

"You know what? I'ma just get out your house, cuz this shit ain't working," I announced. "Now, let go of my fucking hair!"

"Nah. And yo' ass ain't going nowhere. You gon' tell me why you been tripping," he demanded, his eyes narrowing.

"I ain't telling you sh—"

I shrieked as he moved suddenly, backing me into the wall.

"Cartier!"

"Dayana." His voice was low, calm, as he stared down at me. "I know you done had a rough couple of weeks, shorty. Longer than that since you had to put up with yo' bitch ass daddy. So, I been trying not to show you the other side of me. You know who I am, what I do, right?"

I rolled my eyes. "Yeah. And?"

"And I know you fucking smart enough to know that you don't get to where I am by playing nice and letting people talk to you any kind of way."

I nodded, about to bite my tongue in half.

"So, stop tryna son me, Dayana, cuz if you keep acting like a brat, I'ma treat you like one. Talk to me like you got some fuckin' sense. What's wrong with you? Is it cuz we saw that fuck boy the other day?"

I sighed.

"Cartier, look. I don't want to talk to you right now. I just want to go to bed, and tomorrow, I'll be out of your space," I said, unable to stop the attitude dripping from my words.

He looked at me and smirked.

"Oh, yeah?"

"Yeah." I could've left it right there. Probably should have. But not Dayana Dionne Castle. I always had to say what I had to say. "I mean, you talking about I'm tripping, but what was that shit at the club tonight? You walking up on me like you have some say in my life when you don't."

"I don't?"

"No. We had our week together, and you said we were going back to our regular lives. That means I'm single, boo. And I'm going to explore *all* my options."

"Options?"

I rolled my eyes. *Why was this nigga repeating everything I said?*

"Yes. Like Benzo and whoever else I might wanna fuck. It's not your business. Now, if you'll excuse me…"

I gave him a smug smile, happy to get the last word. I

wasn't interested in fucking Benzo or anyone else, but he didn't have to know that, and he needed to understand that he wasn't running—

I stopped as his hand tightened in my hair. My eyes flew to his and my stomach dropped at what I saw there. *Oh, fuck.* He was furious, his caramel eyes molten as he glared at me. His other hand curled into a fist beside my head.

"Cartier—"

He brought his mouth within an inch of mine.

"Fuck him if you want, Dayana. But be ready when I bring him to you and peel his skin off. You ever seen someone flayed, shorty? You'd be surprised what people look like under their pretty outside. And the screams—"

"You're crazy," I whispered. "You want to lock me down when you can't even commit. I want someone that wants me, Cartier."

My eyes filled and I let the tears slip down my face. His expression softened.

"Yana. *Princess*—"

"Just me, Cartier. I deserve that. I deserve someone who wants *just me.*"

He looked at me for a minute longer before releasing my hair. He stepped back and rubbed his face.

"*Fuck!*"

I jumped as he punched a hole in the wall above my head. With one final, regretful glance, he left me. I tilted my head back, refusing to let another tear fall. I'd be dumb as fuck to let the same nigga keep hurting me. Demon had plans for Dream this weekend, but early Monday morning, I'd be calling my sister, asking her for help to get my own place, just until I got a second job. I didn't know what I was going to do exactly, but this wasn't it. I couldn't win against a dead woman, and I shouldn't have to try.

CHAPTER 65
Dream

(*SATURDAY*, *June 26*)

The hand cupping my pussy stroked between the folds and eased upward to tease my clit. My eyes were closed as Damien's mouth found my neck, sucking gently on the skin there. His morning wood pressed against my ass. How could this nigga be ready to go again? We had driven up to the lake house after leaving the club, and he had kept his promise to give me birthday dick... over and over again. Moaning, I opened one eye, then closed it as bright sunlight streamed in.

"Wake yo' ass up. It's eleven o'clock," he rasped against my ear as his hand picked up its pace.

"Nooo," I whimpered, working my hips against his fingers.

"Bet."

He moved suddenly, and I immediately missed his warmth at my back and his skilled fingers. I turned over on my stomach and glared at him as he climbed out of bed.

"Damien..."

I was whining and I wasn't even ashamed. He smacked my ass through the covers.

"Stop all that pitiful shit. You 'bout to sleep yo' birthday away. It's a pretty ass day."

"But I'm tired."

He shrugged. "Do what you want, shorty. I'm finna go fishing."

"Why you start something you ain't gon' finish?" I grumbled.

He smirked down at me. "You know damn well you need to soak that li'l pussy before I get back in it."

"Ugh! Whateva," I muttered, hugging a pillow and closing my eyes.

"Ay! Before I go out here, do you need to go back to the city?" he asked suddenly.

I frowned. My brain was too fuzzy for this. "What?"

He looked awkward and uncertain for a minute, a look I wasn't used to seeing on him. I rolled over onto my side to stare up at him. I didn't know where that question had come from. He rubbed a hand over his braided locs.

"I mean, yo' family may have planned something for you or some shit. You need to go back?"

I sucked my teeth. "Now is a good time to ask," I responded sarcastically.

He gave me a look that said he wasn't with my bullshit. Sighing, I shook my head.

"You know my family is a mess right now. Yana already did what she wanted to do last night, and my mama is in her feelings about the whole situation. She gave me my gift already. So, I'm good."

He raised an eyebrow. "You sure?"

"Yes, Damien, I'm sure. I want to spend my birthday with y—here," I corrected quickly.

His eyes darkened as he gazed at me, their usual iciness warmed for a minute. I snuggled back down into the softness of the California King and let my eyes drift shut. I didn't go to sleep, though. Instead, I listened as he got ready for his fishing adventure. Finally, I heard him leave out of the room and then out the front door. I hopped up, headed for the suitcase that he'd brought for me—I smelled Dayana all over that. I pulled out underwear, a T-shirt, some leggings, and a cute pair of Chucks. He'd been right about one thing—I soaked in the ridiculously large garden tub after taking my ponytail out. Then, I jumped in the shower to quickly wash my hair with his loc shampoo, hoping I wasn't fucking my head up. With my body and my hair wrapped in towels, I made my way to the guest bathroom, hoping for any kind of conditioner. I found a leave-in one and a detangler. I side-eyed that shit skeptically, but at least he had put the bitch in his guest room. Plus, I needed the products to bring out my natural curls. I worked with my hair for a little while, then got dressed.

I was going to surprise Damien by joining him on his fishing escapade. I knew I'd need a fishing rod and some other stuff, so I searched around the house, wondering where he kept things like that. I hit lucky in the extra-large mudroom near the back door. Not only did I find a rod and reel, but I also saw a few of those waders I had seen people fishing in. I slipped into a purple one, refusing to think about who may have worn it before I did. The bitch was obsolete now!

I found him outside, a few feet into the lake. He wore black waders and gripped a rod as he stared out into the water. I guess I wasn't as quiet as I thought. He turned around as I walked towards him and glanced at me. One side of his mouth lifted in a small smile as he took in my appearance.

"The hell you doing, Dream?"

The nigga was clearly mocking me. I turned my nose up at him.

"Going fishing for my birthday," I snapped.

"Oh, yeah? Yo' bourgeois ass know how to fish?" he asked, eyeing me up and down as he lazily spun the reel.

"It can't be that hard. I watched a special about it once."

He nodded once, and the other side of his mouth curved. I took that as an okay and stepped into the water to get closer to him.

"Your rod and reel are straight, but you need bait first," he said, inclining his head toward a cup that sat on the bank.

Oh, yeah, bait! Had to attract the fish with something. I expected a tackle box, but maybe he put a few lures in the cup. I made my way toward it and bent down. I quickly stumbled back, my heart racing. My eyes flew to him.

"*Worms?*" I spat in disgust.

"Yep," he said nonchalantly. "The fish love 'em."

He pointed toward a bucket that I assumed held the fish he had caught.

"You keeping them?"

I couldn't hide the horror in my voice. He was supposed to catch them and throw them back. My tone didn't affect him at all. He just shrugged and kept fishing.

"Do you wanna eat tonight?"

"But I don't know how to eat fish with bones in it," I complained.

"Girl, get the worm."

I shook my head. I wasn't going to be able to do that.

"The documentary said they like bright, flashy, jiggly things. You ain't got none of those fake bait?"

"Nah, your highness. The only thing bright, flashy, and jiggly out here is you."

Jiggly? This muhfucka... I put my hand on my hip and looked at him arrogantly. Well... as arrogant as I could look in waders with my hair in wild curls all over my head.

"Well, you gon' have to do something. I don't do things that creep, crawl, or slither."

This nigga didn't even look at me. Just kept spinning that damn reel as he spoke.

"I did do something. I dug up them damn worms. You can creep, crawl, or slither yo' ass over there to that cup and get one."

I blew out a loud breath. "Damien!"

He grilled me, but I hid my smile as he walked back to the bank. Snatching the rod from me, he baited my line and handed it back to me. I squealed a little when it seemed the worm might swing back toward me. He shook his head like I was pathetic. With my head held high, I marched into the water. I figured I could just throw the fishing line a few feet away. But that shit was harder than it looked. I tried to watch Damien out of the corner of my eye to see how he did it. I thought I finally had it, so I tried again... and threw the whole rod into the water. Shrieking, I picked it up quickly before looking back at him. He wasn't smiling, but I swear his green eyes were laughing at me.

"Chill, mama. You over there screaming and splashing. Fish don't like all that noise. I don't either."

"Fuck you, Damien."

"You definitely better at that than fishing," he said as a chuckle escaped.

I sucked in an offended breath and moved to climb out of the water. Fuck this fishing shit anyway!

"Wait, witcho spoiled ass," he demanded.

I mugged him, but I waited. He waded over to lay his rod and reel on the pier before coming to stand behind me. For a few minutes, he showed me how to properly cast the rod. He was silent and then I felt him lightly touch my hair.

"I like it like this," he said, surprising me.

"Thanks. I had to use yo' girlfriend's products," I said slyly.

"Ain't never had one of them and I don't think Sherrilyn would like you saying she fuckin' two brothers."

I bit my lip to hold back my smile at his words.

"Jealous ass," he muttered.

I wanted to deny it, but I shrugged. "So are you."

He ignored me, walking through the water to retrieve his rod and reel. I squealed when I cast mine perfectly. He shook his head. We stood there for about ten minutes before I second-thought this bright idea. June? In Texas? I was fucking wilting!

"It's hot, Damien," I pouted.

"Dream. I look like I pay the light bill for outside? You think I got a switch that turns off the damn sun? I'on wanna hear all that shit. I came out here for peace and you fucking with that, shorty. 'Bout to drown yo' ass for real. Take yo' ass in the house," he fussed.

Oh, wait! He had me fucked up! I looked all upside his head.

"Not until I catch a fish!"

"Then be yo' ass quiet."

I cast my rod again before flipping him off. But five minutes later, I was ready to say fuck it. And then, something tugged on my line. My eyes flew to Damien.

"Something is pulling!" I exclaimed.

"Reel it in," he said.

He coached me through it until, finally, I pulled a flipping, flopping, silvery fish out of the water. I was proud for all of five seconds before I realized that slimy, angry thing was coming near me. Screaming, I dropped the rod and turned to run. In my hurry, I fell my ass right into the lake water. It took me forever to splash my way up in those waders, and Damien's smirking ass didn't even help. I was .38 hot by the time I was back on two feet. This nigga was laughing. I had seen him smile, heard him chuckle, but an all-out laugh like this? Ah, hell nah!

"I hate you!" I yelled, like I was six years old.

"You a lie. And while you scared of that one little fish you caught, you done fell in the water in them waders. They probably full of fish, snakes, frogs, and everything else that creeps, crawls, or slithers," he said casually.

I screamed again as I struggled out of the water, trying to take off the waders. Just to be safe, I pulled my t-shirt off and reached for my leggings. Then I caught a glimpse of Damien. He was looking at me with lust in his eyes.

"Hell nah. You not about to get this nasty ass lake water in my little lady. I ain't fucking with you, Damien Montana!"

I splashed my way up to the bank. I heard his annoying ass behind me.

"I'm not playing with you," I popped, taking off running.

"We'll see," he said, chasing me.

I was mad, but I couldn't help giggling. It turned out I was such a liar. We hadn't even been in the shower ten minutes before he was giving me powerful back strokes. And after we bathed and he gently washed my hair again, he fucked me on the bed, both of my wrists held in one of his hands above my head. His other hand held down my hip as he pushed into me so slow and deep. When I struggled against his grip, wanting to match his movements, he leaned down and whispered in my ear.

"Nah, shorty. Just be still and take this dick."

His words had me soaking him instantly. I stayed still and took the dick until we came together, my tightening walls pulling his seed into my greedy channel. When we finished, he made French toast and sausage that we ate in bed. Well-fucked and well-fed, my drowsy ass couldn't move.

"Go to sleep, baby," he said softly.

I went to sleep.

CHAPTER 66

Demon

A SOFT SNORE followed by a little sigh let me know Dream was really asleep. I moved slowly, easing my body away from hers. She mumbled my name and reached for me, but the Hypnos mattress did its job—she was sound asleep again in seconds.

I liked the fact that she reached for me too much. I liked a lot of things about her too much and my simp ass had given up trying to fight it. Shit was crazy. I could admit she had the best pussy I'd ever had. It was so hot, wet, and tight that a nigga could happily live between her thighs. I wanted to keep her in my bed, underneath me 24/7. If it were up to me, she'd never make it to work or anywhere else.

But it wasn't just the sex that had me off my square. I couldn't stand to see her sad, tired, or worried. I constantly wanted to give her stuff that would make her show all thirty-two of those pretty, white teeth. If another nigga laid a hand on her, I would kill, literally. The strangest part was that I constantly needed to touch her, and I liked when she touched me. I knew what all that shit meant. I don't know how the fuck it happened, but I cared about her. That was new territory for me, and I could admit that I didn't know what the fuck I was doing. I had eleven and a half days left with Dream. Either I was gon' get over this infatuation bullshit or I was gon' have to keep her. It was a done deal in my mind. I didn't need her input. I didn't know what that shit would look like, but we'd find out.

My phone buzzed on the nightstand, and I grabbed it. Seeing the number, I answered and said, "Hold on," while I walked into the hallway, then into the living room.

"What's up?"

A soft, feminine voice whispered, "Eagle Team One, this is Falcon Team One reporting. Falcon Team One has left the nest—"

"I'on think falcons build nests, love," I heard a male voice say.

"Could you not interrupt this important transmission?" the woman clapped back.

Sighing, I rubbed my temple as they argued a little bit. Finally, I spoke.

"Dayana?"

"Yes, Bestie?"

"Can yo' ass just speak some ol' regular, degular English?" I requested.

There was a long pause, then a sigh. "I mean, that's no fun, but it's whatever, nigga. We got everything and everybody and we on the way. Where my sissy?"

"Sleep."

"That's what I'm talking about! Keep putting it on her ass!" Dayana crowed.

"Yana, hang the damn phone up," Smoke said.

I hung up in the middle of her protests. I had something planned for Dream for her birthday dinner, but I'd had to get a few people to assist me. Dayana had been clutch in helping me get this whole weekend together, from shopping for clothes for Dream to schooling me on her favorite foods. She'd even given her opinion on the AP I chose for her sister.

She really was a cool little mama and a good look for Smoke if they could get it right.

I needed Dream to stay asleep for a little while longer while this shit came together. I knew fucking and feeding her would knock her ass out, but I didn't want her too tired to enjoy the evening. I headed for the guest room to take a quick shower, then grabbed her gift and all the shit that accompanied it before walking outside. I had just finished setting it up when I heard a vehicle pulling up. I turned to make sure there were no surprises, but relaxed when I recognized the darkly tinted Grand Wagoneer. Smoke eased into a stop, then jumped out and walked around to the front passenger door, but Dayana was out before he made it. He gave her a look that she ignored as she moved away from him. Neither of them looked happy.

One of the back doors opened and I watched as Eve climbed out, a big smile on her face. Shorty was about to talk shit, I knew. I'd take that, though, as long as she set shit up perfectly. She was a visual merchandiser, and her work was flawless.

I walked over to help them unload the stuff they'd brought. I nodded at Dayana and Eve, but they just grinned at me before continuing their own conversation. I walked to the back of the vehicle. Smoke had opened it and I half-smiled as I saw all the shit I needed to make this evening special for Dream.

"You setting the bar high, ain't you? Tryna show the rest of us niggas up," Smoke ragged me.

"Pretty sure that was Cartier I saw Dayana dripping last night. Shit, those panthers look good on her wrist and around her neck today, too," I shot back, smirking.

"Mind ya business, nigga," he said, chuckling.

But as the women walked toward the big ass gazebo where I wanted them to set up, he got serious real quick.

"The Keith nigga?" he asked.

I shook my head. "Swear somebody hiding him. He came out to put the price on my head, but nobody has seen him since then. He gotta be itching to make a move."

"I know y'all got the best in the business, but let me shake a few trees. See what falls loose," Smoke offered.

My first instinct was to say no. I was used to handling shit my way, usually on my own. But the fact that Dream could be in danger had me swallowing my pride.

"Yeah. Do that," I responded.

"And I got this shit. Go get yo' girl ready."

I shook my head. "She not my—"

He smirked at me. I knew my actions didn't match my words, and I didn't even want to attempt to explain. I just walked off.

———

Dream was still pouting as she slid into a bright yellow, strapless maxi dress. I hated to see the view of her thick body in the purple lingerie disappear. Her favorite color was yellow, and her skin did pop and glow against it, but there was something about her in purple. Shorty was beautiful.

"Fix your face," I told her.

"I'm tired," she grumbled. "I don't know why I had to get up."

"If you stop pouting, I might tell you about your birthday surprise."

Her expression immediately brightened. This girl loved surprises. A smile was already curving her lush mouth at the thought.

"A surprise? Damien, I know you didn't get me anything else. You really shouldn't have... but I wouldn't be upset."

I shook my head just as my phone vibrated. Pulling it out of my pocket, I rolled my eyes when I saw a FaceTime notification from Kam. I answered and was met with the sight of a long, skinny middle finger.

"Nigga, you ain't gon' be happy till I make you take a dirt nap," I said calmly.

Dream huffed and walked over to me, still holding one sandal and her chains. She smacked my chest lightly and sucked her teeth.

"Damien, stop talking to that baby like that," she fussed.

I looked at her incredulously. "Baby? This nigga a whole con artist out here. I don't know why—"

She shushed me, squeezing her thick body between my torso and my arm so she could see the phone screen. I swear, no one ever tried to handle me like this girl did. Kam rolled that damn finger up fast as hell and smiled into the camera.

"Hey, Dream. I just wanted to tell you happy birthday again."

She oohed and ahhed and thanked his bad ass as I glared at him.

"Are you being good for Dante and Sherrilyn?" she asked.

"Yes, ma'am. DJ and I are going to a birthday party tonight. Ms. Sherrilyn is going to take us to look for gifts," he said, sounding excited.

"Oh! Do you have money? Damien, send him some money. Kam, do you have Cash App? I guess you're not old enough—"

I mugged her little ass as she kept rambling, trying to spend my money.

"I do have a Cash App in Melanie's name. I could use a little more money," Kam spoke up, trying to sound pitiful.

The look I gave this little nigga... "I gave you two Gs before you left yesterday," I reminded his hustling ass.

"And he obviously needs more. Here, fasten my chains," she ordered, grabbing my phone and handing me the jewelry. "Kam, baby, what's your Cash Tag?"

Then, her manicured fingers were flying as she entered the

passcode that I didn't realize her sneaky ass knew and trans-
ferred Kam another two racks. I thought about choking her
bossy ass with them damned chains, but, in the end, I let her
live. She was still chopping it up with Kam as she bent over to
slide on her shoe, resting her soft ass against my pelvis. I
grabbed her hips, grinding my dick against her.

Perv! she mouthed, looking over her shoulder. I smiled at
her and did it again. She stood up suddenly and elbowed me
in the stomach as she wrapped up the call.

"I gotta go, Suga! Damien has another surprise for me."

"As he should!"

I frowned at his ass. "Don't be saying that gay ass shit!"

Another elbow to the stomach. "Don't be homophobic in
front of this child. Bye, Kam! Be good."

She handed me the phone and went back to her suitcase. I
looked at the screen. This spawn of Satan had sent me a text. I
opened it to read, *Bye, gay ass nigga.* But this girl wanted to
beat my ass for being homophobic. I banged on his bad ass. I
wanted to show Dream the message, but I wasn't a snitching
ass nigga. I was gon' fuck that kid up, though.

"I'm ready!" she announced, bangles and earrings clicking
and clacking as she walked toward me. She'd smoothed her
curls into a bun on top of her head, and the only hint of
makeup I saw was lip gloss. Made-up Dream was beautiful,
but this version of her was damn near perfect. I had to force
myself to lead her outside instead of right back to bed.
Dayana, Eve, and Smoke stood near the gazebo, waiting.
Dream squealed when she saw her sister. They hugged each
other, dramatic as usual, before Dream broke away to kiss
Smoke on the cheek. I smirked as she and Eve looked at each
other and exchanged a couple of cool hellos.

Dream gasped and I nodded my approval at the setup
inside the gazebo. Eve had gone all out. A round table stood in
the center, covered in a white tablecloth with a deep purple
overlay. She had set the table with beaded chargers and white

plates with scalloped purple borders. Polished silverware and delicate wine and water glasses gleamed against the backdrop. The purple and yellow flowers I'd requested were pretty in the rectangular vase. I didn't regret asking for them, even though Eve had popped off, "Oh, *now*, you a flower-buying nigga."

"Oh, my God! Damien, it's beautiful!" Dream exclaimed.

"Thank you," Eve said saucily.

Heavily insulated containers rested on the bench that encircled the interior of the gazebo. Eve had numbered them, so I'd know how to serve the meal. Wine chilled in buckets on stands around the space. They were numbered, too. There were two blankets on the bench, as well. I looked at Eve.

"What are those for?"

She cleared her throat, refusing to meet my eyes. "Just in case y'all get cold."

It was June. In Texas. We were not going to get cold. Little freak. I looked over at Dream and smiled at the blush covering her cheeks.

"Y'all sit down," Eve instructed, trying to change the subject.

Dream and I sank into the satin-covered chairs and waited. Dayana stepped up, rubbing her hands with sanitizer. Food had been her job.

"I'ma go ahead and serve your first course," she said.

She moved the plates in front of us to a little stand next to the table. The bottom shelf contained extra plates and cutlery. The top held two cloche-covered plates. Dayana set them in front of us, then yanked off the tops like she was doing some big reveal, before taking a deep bow. I looked down at the spinach and shrimp enchiladas covered in a cream sauce. It wasn't a typical starter, but tonight was all about Dream's favorite foods. She clapped her hands as her sister poured us some pinot grigio from the first bucket.

"Enjoy," Dayana said softly.

And just like that, my three accomplices disappeared. I could tell that Dream really liked the set up and the food. After saying grace, she smiled and moaned through the enchiladas, the lamb chops with Greek potatoes, and her mom's blackberry cobbler with homemade vanilla bean ice cream.

"Damien, thank you. This is seriously like the best birthday I've ever had," she said as she swallowed the last of her dessert.

That shit made a nigga feel good, but I wasn't one to show that. Instead, I smirked at her.

"Even with the shit that creeps, crawls, and slithers?"

She giggled as she stood up, grabbed the flute of the champagne we'd had with dessert, and rounded the table.

"Can I sit with you?" she asked softly.

I didn't say anything, just slid back and let her climb in my lap and snuggle against me. I liked the soft, warm weight of her in my arms. I held her for a few minutes as she took lazy sips of the Dom. Finally, she finished and yawned, settling closer.

"Ah, shit. Let me show you your surprise before yo' ass fall asleep."

She looked up at me, shocked. A small frown formed between her arched brows.

"Damien, I know I always say, 'you shouldn't have,' but I get excited, anyway. But really, this dinner was perfect. You didn't have to do anything else. Between the watch and the fishing and this dinner, nothing can top this weekend," she said sincerely, her espresso eyes shining.

I smiled down at her. "That's like a challenge to me, shorty."

I set her on her feet and stood up behind her. I pointed behind where we'd been sitting to an easel that held a covered canvas. I knew she liked black art and I was counting on this gift being the best one yet. She gasped and covered her mouth before looking back at me.

"A painting? You got me a painting? Oh, my God! Damien," she said in a hushed voice as I led her to the easel.

I moved behind her once we were in front of it. She continued to just stare at the hidden canvas like she was in shock.

"Uncover it," I prompted gently.

She reached for one corner of the fabric and slowly pulled it away. She gasped again as she took in the work in front of her. A woman sat on her porch steps, her arms crossed and resting on her knees, her face lifted toward the dappled sunlight as it filtered through the trees in her yard. Toys were scattered across the lawn and the front of a muscle car was partially visible, hinting at the busy family inside the house. But this was a moment she had stolen for herself. She looked happy and at peace.

"Damien," Dream breathed my name. "It's beautiful. I love it! You... oh, my God! It's a K. Reid? You got me a K. Reid?"

She spun around to hug me tightly. I shrugged like it was no big deal.

"I saw the one in your office. I figured you liked the artist."

I doubt that she even heard me with all the exclamations she was making over the painting. I was relieved that she liked it—there was no way she could fake this reaction.

"I haven't seen this one before and I thought I knew all K. Reid's work. How—"

"I know people who know people. This one ain't never been on the market, ain't never even been exhibited," I explained, hoping she didn't ask any more questions.

Her eyes got even bigger. Shorty had no intention of letting this shit go. She started talking about insurance and appraisals and safely displaying it. I let her go on as I moved to where Eve had placed the blankets. Grabbing one, I spread it out near the bench. I walked back towards her and scooped her up, bringing her to the blanket. She shook her head, then smiled as I worked the dress up and over her head.

Twenty minutes later, she was riding my dick reverse cowgirl, her hips keeping a slow, rolling pace. My back was propped against the bench as I sucked on her neck and cupped one of her full breasts. My other hand played between her thighs as she moaned my name. Shit was perfect. I was in my new favorite place—inside her—on a warm summer night, lulled by the gentle lapping of the lake, the insistent chirping of crickets, and the sultry rhythm of Dream's body.

"Thank you," she whispered suddenly.

I smirked against her nape. "For this dick? You wel—"

She smacked my thigh. "I'm serious! Thank you for this weekend and the gifts. You really thought about what I like, and you delivered. It means a lot. It means… everything."

Shit was getting too emotional for me. I could admit I had feelings for her, but that didn't mean I knew what to do with them. I swirled my thumb around her clit, trying to distract her. But she wasn't having it.

"I loved it all. Damien… I love you."

I froze, knocked off my shit by her words. I couldn't remember anyone aside from KiKi saying those words to me. Maybe Ms. Hazel. Definitely not my bitch of an egg donor. And I knew my father and Dante gave a fuck about me, but they weren't the type to say those words. Anyway, it was too soon. It was probably the dick or that damn painting. I tried to dismiss it, but I couldn't.

Dream had opened something inside me, found a longing I didn't even know I had. *She loves me.* I didn't even know that shit was possible. I lifted her off me, only to reposition us so that I was on top, pressing back inside her.

"Say it again," I demanded, surprising myself as my eyes locked on her soft, brown ones.

"I love you," she whispered.

She grabbed my face and kissed my brows, my nose, my cheeks, my chin, murmuring she loved me after each soft brush of her lips.

"You're mine, Dream. *Mine*."

I growled the words against her ear, accepting what I'd known since the moment I laid eyes on her in Dante's office.

Dream belonged to me.

And thirty days wasn't nearly long enough.

CHAPTER 67

Smoke

(*SUNDAY*, *June 27*)

I just kept fucking up. There was no other way to put it. I looked at Dayana as she talked softly to Jenesis over the breakfast she'd made for us. My OG was coming to get my baby a little later for church, and Dayana wanted to make sure she ate before the service. I mean, I would have fed my shorty, of course, but it probably would have been a bowl of cereal. Surprisingly, Dayana cooked enough for me, but she still wasn't really fucking with a nigga. She said as little to me as possible and I knew once my Jeni-face left, she was going to disappear into her room.

She was upset about what I had and hadn't said the other night. A nigga was just so confused. Yes, it was about my promise to Jenna. But it was also about my own feelings. I wanted Dayana bad as fuck, could see myself loving on shorty long-term, and even giving her a few babies. But putting my all into another woman was a risk I wasn't sure a nigga's heart could take. She was right; she deserved more. The thought of another nigga giving it to her made me sick, though.

We finished our waffles, eggs, and bacon, and I took care

of the kitchen while Dayana helped Jenesis finish getting ready. Once I was done, I walked into the living room and crossed to the TV stand to grab the remote. My baby reappeared with two of the cutest curly ponytails with ribbons that matched her little green dress. I grinned at her and opened my arms. Baby damn near tackled me.

"Daddy!"

"Hey, my Jeni-face. Princess Yana got you looking good, girl!" I complimented her.

She giggled and hugged me tightly. Over her head, I saw Dayana standing at the bottom of the stairs, smiling softly.

"Thank you," I told her.

She didn't say anything, just nodded once and walked back upstairs. I couldn't stand the way she was acting, but I couldn't blame her. Sighing, I carried Jenesis to the couch and sat her beside me to watch TV. We were halfway into an episode of the new *Fraggle Rock* when my mother let herself in.

"Hey, GiGi!" Jenesis exclaimed as I stood up to greet my OG.

I walked to her and dropped a kiss on her forehead before hugging her soft frame. Mama looked good in her light blue, a true beauty inside and out.

"You must got yo' eye on one of them deacons. I need to know that nigga's name so I can let him know what's up," I teased her.

She smacked me lightly on the shoulder. "Boy, hush."

She took my seat beside my baby, snuggling her close. I loved watching them together. It was crazy how good my mama had been to us since Jenna died. I sat down in the recliner and leaned forward.

"You a little early, aren't you? If you were planning to stop for breakfast, Jenesis already ate."

Mama sucked her teeth. "Uh, cereal doesn't count as Sunday breakfast," she fussed.

I mimicked the sound she had made. "For your information, old lady, Dayana cooked a real breakfast."

I ducked as she tossed one of the throw pillows at me.

"You better watch who you calling old!" she snapped, brushing a hand over one of Jenesis's ponytails. "Straight as that part is, Dayana must have combed her hair, too. Where is she?"

"Upstairs. She ain't beat for a nigga right now," I admitted, rubbing my hand over my wave cap.

The look she gave me said so much, but she didn't say a word about what I revealed.

"Actually, I came early because I wanted to ask you to go with us," she said.

I blew out a long breath. I denied my OG very few things, but I wasn't in a churchgoing mood this morning.

"Mama—" I began.

"Please, Cartier, I feel like you need this."

How could a nigga argue with something like that? Sighing, I stood to go get ready. I arranged for Ammo and Anthony to watch the house, just to be safe. We took two separate cars, in case I needed to leave, and I had a couple of my guys follow. I regretted it the minute we turned into the church's small lot. We finally found some spots and I escorted my family into the building.

Even though you couldn't tell from my father's and my line of work, Stephanie Salinas had raised me in the culture of black Baptist churches. From Sunday School to Youth Choir to Vacation Bible School, she had me there. Although I didn't come much anymore, the traditions would always be familiar and comforting and I settled into the service easily. I couldn't lie—I usually preferred the singing to the preaching, but this Sunday, the pastor preached from Jeremiah 29:11. My mother grabbed my hand after the sermon that had seemed to be directed at me.

"You hear that, baby? God has plans for you. Plans that

will give you hope and *a future*. Stop fighting your future, love," she whispered to me.

Choked up, I swallowed hard and nodded. We grabbed Jenesis from Children's Church after the benediction. My OG turned to look at me as we crossed the parking lot.

"Let's visit Jenna," she said.

Damn, she wasn't playing with a nigga today. As usual, we had Jenesis stand in front of Jenna's tomb and rattle about what she'd been doing. Her attention span wasn't long, so after a few minutes and a bright little, "Bye, Mommy!" Mama took her out of the mausoleum to give me a minute. A gust of wind ruffled my baby's ponytails as she walked out, and she giggled. I stood there, throat aching as I tried to get my words right.

"Hey, baby. You always told me to give it to you straight, so I will. I met a girl. She's beautiful, sweet, and funny and she doesn't take any shit, kinda like you, baby girl," I chuckled as I thought about Dayana's attitude.

"I think I halfway fell in love with her the first time I talked to her. Jenna, no matter how I try to cut her off and let her go, I can't. And honestly, baby girl, it's because I don't want to. I want her, Jenna. I want to love her, to protect her, to take care of her," I admitted, tracing her name.

"It's not about replacing you; it could never be about that. It's about learning to live and love again, and I realize, I want that with this shorty. I never meant to break my promise to you, but in my heart, I know it's not a promise you would have ever wanted me to make. I will never forget you and I will always love you. Aside from my OG, you were the first woman in my heart, but somehow, God made room for someone else. I wanna see what that's about."

I kissed my fingers and pressed them to her tomb.

"I love you, Jenna. I'll be back to see you soon. Rest easy."

I rested my head against the front of her grave. A light breeze stroked against the back of my neck. I smiled, the dampness in my eyes drying and the heaviness in my heart lifting.

"Thank you, baby girl," I whispered as I made my exit.

My mama eyed me like a hawk as I rejoined them.

"You okay?" she asked.

I nodded, wrapping an arm around her shoulders.

"I'm good, OG. You really gained more wisdom with that old age. Thank you."

She rolled her eyes and opened her mouth to speak, but stopped when Bruno stepped away from the blacked-out Tahoe. He walked over to us, his phone in his hand.

"Boss man, Ammo said he couldn't get you on your phone," he explained, handing me his.

"Yeah?" I said once the phone was against my ear.

"Mr. Salinas, Ms. Castle left."

My mood changed instantly, taking me from mellow to pissed the fuck off. I'd just made peace with going after her ass and she thought she was gon' leave? She was bringing her hard-headed ass right back, even if I had to drag her.

"Fuck you mean, she left? Fuck I leave you there for, Ammo?" I raged.

"With all due respect, sir, I tried to call while she was leaving," he said in his proper ass accent. "I didn't have instructions to restrain her."

His voice was as calm as it always was. While I usually appreciated the fact that he was unshakable, the shit was fucking with me right now.

"How she leave with no car? She called an Uber or some shit?"

Ammo paused. My anger ratcheted up about a hundred notches.

"What?" I bit out.

"Sir, a gentleman arrived to retrieve her."

I pulled the phone away from my ear and stared at it. I

had to be hearing shit. Wasn't *no* way my right hand just told me that my girl left my house with some other nigga.

"You following her?" I asked softly. I didn't need Jenesis seeing my rage.

"Of course, Mr. Salinas."

"Keep me posted."

I disconnected the call and handed Bruno his phone. Mama peered up at me.

"Everything okay?"

I thought about her question. Aside from giving another nigga my address, Dayana was going to say she did nothing wrong, because we weren't in a relationship. I knew she was tryna prove something to me, but I wanted to slit that nigga's throat in front of her. My OG and my baby were watching me, though. I couldn't follow my first instinct and go after Dayana because shit was liable to get fatal. Plus, I'd promised them lunch. I was going to have to trust Ammo to stay on her. I was calling my tech, Kat, as soon as I got home and telling her to put a rush on the bracelet I had her adding a tracking device to. Sighing, I nodded at my mother.

"Yeah. Everything's okay. Y'all want *Stephanie's*?" I asked, naming one of my restaurants that was close by.

Ammo called when we were about five minutes away from *Stephanie's*. I was glad again that Mama and Jenesis were in another car.

"Yeah," I answered.

"It appears that they are about to have lunch. Would you like me to approach or retrieve her?" he asked quietly.

I wanted to give him the go ahead so fucking badly, but I knew that shit wouldn't end well. Ammo would snatch her ass in broad daylight and stay completely unbothered. But Dayana would act a damn fool and probably never speak to me again.

"Nah. Just stay on her. Let me know what's next. I'll get up with you after I'm done with my OG and Jenesis."

I hung up and finished my drive. The hostess gave me a big smile when I walked into the restaurant right behind my family.

"Would you like to choose your seat, Mr. Salinas?" she asked.

"That's cool," I said, then held out my arm to let Mama and Jenesis know to precede me. Mama chose a booth by a window and slid in. Jenesis was about to do the same when her face lit up and she gasped.

"Hey, Princess Yana!" she exclaimed.

Before I could grab her, she'd taken off for a booth across the restaurant. My eyes followed her, only to see Dayana sitting across from some tired ass nigga in a blue polo. A smile curved her pretty lips as Jenesis approached and leaned into the booth to wrap her arms around Dayana's waist.

"Hey, Cupcake. How was church?" Dayana crooned, hugging my baby.

Jenesis launched into a rambling description of Children's Church as I slowly walked toward them. I stood by the booth, letting her chatter fill the air as I stared down at Dayana. Shorty met my eyes once and looked away. I smiled smugly.

She knew I was about to get in that ass.

CHAPTER 68
Dayana

WITH HIS TALL, slim, good looks and laid-back manner, Cartier Salinas seemed like the most easygoing man in the world. Rumor had it that by the time you knew how dangerous he really was, it was too late. I was feeling like that now as his caramel eyes stared down at me, almost molten gold with anger.

"Jeni, go ask GiGi to take you to the bathroom to wash your hands," he instructed Jenesis, his eyes never leaving my face.

"But Daddy, is Princess Yana gonna eat with us? I was just 'bout to 'vite her," she said, all soft voice and puppy dog eyes.

Oh, my God, she was too cute and too good at manipulating her daddy.

"Yeah," Smoke said, "Princess Yana is eating with us."

My mouth dropped open, and I looked up at him as Jenesis skipped off to where Ms. Stephanie sat. I don't think I could ever be ready for this nigga's audacity. I knew I could never when he slid into the booth beside me.

"Cartier, what—"

"Why you leave?" he demanded before I could finish my question.

I snaked my neck as I looked at him. "Because I'm grown and I had plans," I snapped.

His mouth tightened, but other than that, he didn't show his anger. He leaned back against the booth. His golden gaze settled on my date, Brady, who was looking confused as fuck. Brady had been another possibility my father considered for me. A clean-cut bank manager, he had the pedigree, education, and drive to become a billionaire financier. Since I was "exploring my options," I figured I might as well look out for my future.

"This your plans?" Smoke asked conversationally.

"Dayana, what's going—" Brady began.

"Nah, playboy. I'm talking to her right now. I'll let you know if you get a turn."

This insolent muhfucka! "Cartier, I know you see that I'm in the middle of something. I'll talk to you later."

He chuckled as his eyes drilled a hole in me. "You funny, shorty. You gon' talk to me now. Why I didn't know about these plans?"

"Didn't we just discuss this? My life and I are none of your business, Cartier," I reminded him angrily.

Brady tried again. "Dayana, we could resch—"

Fast as hell, Cartier palmed Scarlet and grilled my date. "Didn't I tell you to shut the fuck up?" he growled, flicking that wicked, blood-red thing open.

"Cartier!" I hissed.

"Nigga needs to learn to listen. And don't be over here calling my name when you saying stupid shit—"

I would never know why Brady decided that this was the right moment to defend his masculinity. He cleared his throat and I looked over at him. He was obviously pissed off, his eyes narrowed, his nose flaring.

"So, what? I'm supposed to be scared now? You don't—"

Smoke moved quickly, and I heard Brady's anguished scream tear through the air. Horrified, I looked to see what caused his agony. His hand was now pinned to the wooden table by Scarlet and all eyes were pinned on us. My mouth fell open at this wild muhfucka. A few people stood, including two scary-looking men. Cartier shook his head at those two and they slowly sat down. He rose, his hand still on the knife's diamond-encrusted handle.

"It's okay, y'all. I apologize for the disturbance. I'm Smoke Salinas, the owner. Please don't let this ruin your meal. Everyone's lunch is on me," he said.

Heart beating wildly, I shook my head as his tone and that charming smile actually worked to calm people down—that and the offer of a free meal. His staff kept circulating, greeting and seating and serving. These muhfuckas were really acting like nothing was going on. He sat back down and turned that smile on me.

"Now, tell me why I didn't know about these plans," he said, ignoring Brady's whimpering.

For a full thirty seconds, I couldn't speak. I just stared at his crazy ass. Finally, my brain and my body got it together, and I pushed against his shoulder.

"You fucking lunatic! Let him up!" I whispered, my voice beyond heated.

This maniac just kept smiling at me. The fucked-up part was that his actions and that slightly sinister smile had my body caught up in a sick reaction. My pussy was throbbing and dripping wet, and I prayed he couldn't see my hardened nipples. I wanted to climb in his lap and – I shook my head, trying to clear it. *Get it together, Dayana.*

Smoke turned the knife a little bit and Brady moaned before glaring at him.

"You don't know who the hell—" Brady started.

"And I don't give a fuck. You can stay stuck to this table like a fucking butterfly in science class, or you can listen to me carefully. I'ma give you a couple of options, cuz a nigga is thoughtful like that. My princess is pretty, isn't she?" he asked rhetorically, stroking my cheek with his free hand.

At this point, I was convinced that he had more than a few screws loose. I looked up helplessly as Ms. Stephanie reappeared with Jenesis. She took one look at our booth and shook her head.

"Always so dramatic, Cartier!" she fussed, using the same words she'd spoken when he saved me from that wedding.

She turned and led Jenesis to a booth far away from us.

"Sorry, OG. It's Dayana's fault," he said, his caramel eyes shifting to me.

I barely swallowed an outraged scream. "How is it my fault that you're a damn psychopath? Who does shit like this? *Why* are you doing shit like this?" I demanded.

Brady was saying something in the background, but I was too fucking mad at this point to hear him. He sucked in a breath, biting back a sob as Smoke twisted the knife again.

"What part of 'shut the fuck up' are you struggling with?" Smoke asked him before narrowing his eyes on me. "You left without saying shit to anyone—"

"Oh, excuse me! I thought I was a guest, not a prisoner. And I told Ammo 'bye,'" I shot back.

He ignored me and continued with his stupid explanations.

"You brought a nigga to my house. As if that's not enough of a violation, you brought him to my restaurant—"

"I didn't know you owned this! You act like—"

I stopped as a server approached us. She smiled nervously, her eyes flitting from the knife still embedded in Brady's hand to Smoke's face.

"Umm... Mr. Salinas, Ms. Salinas said I should come over here to get your order," she said hurriedly.

He actually sat there and thought for a minute, as if he didn't have a man trapped on this table with a deadly weapon.

"You can get me the large ribeye, medium, and a baked potato with everything. Add a side of broccoli with butter. Thank you," he said, smiling at her. "What you want, Princess?"

I looked at him incredulously. How the fuck could he even think about food? Hell, how could he even think that I was about to sit down and eat with him?

"Nothing," I gritted out.

He turned back to the server. "Get her the braised short ribs with mashed potatoes and some kind of green vegetable. You pick."

He winked at her and her ass giggled before gushing, "Okay, Mr. Salinas. I'll get that in for you." I shook my head. I had to be in an alternative world.

"I'll deal with you in a minute," he said to me before turning back to Brady. "Now, where was I? Oh, yeah. We were agreeing that Yana is fucking beautiful. I'm sure you had hopes of wining and dining her for a little bit, then fucking on her. I gotta admit, the pussy is sublime, so I don't blame you."

"I swear to God, I hate you," I interrupted furiously.

He rolled his eyes. "Chill, girl. I gave yo' ass a compliment. So, this is where those options come in. Yana, you should appreciate this, because you love options, right? But here are your options, my man. You can get that idea about fucking my girl out of yo' head and walk out of here with a hole in yo' hand, but alive. Or you can keep doing like you're doing, and I will be forced, unfortunately, to relieve you of yo' skin and yo' life. I promised her I'd do it, and I'm serious about my promises."

Cartier really sounded regretful… and serious as fuck. I wondered if Ms. Stephanie had ever had him evaluated. Brady's eyes widened as he shook his head.

"Just let me go, man. I can block her on everything right now. She's all yours," his weak ass said hurriedly.

Cartier smiled. "I'm glad we were able to come to this

understanding," he said before yanking the knife out of Brady's hand.

Brady grunted in pain but caught the napkin Cartier threw at him.

"Use that to keep pressure on it, but you probably should get that looked at. Oh, and remember—I don't want to have to skin you alive, but I will."

I stared at him wordlessly as Brady nodded and scurried away. Cartier looked down at me as he dipped a napkin in my water glass and wiped Brady's blood from his hand. A concerned frown creased his handsome face.

"You okay, Princess? You look upset."

For a long moment, my mouth gaped. Finally, I regained my ability to speak.

"What the fuck is wrong with you?"

He shrugged. "Nothing, now. Go sit with Mama and Jenesis while I go wash my hands for real."

I made a strangled little sound. "You think I'm eating with you after what you just did? Something is wrong with you."

He laughed softly. "Shiiiit. Ain't nothing wrong with me. Something wrong with you if you think you about to be with another nigga."

"I told you I was exploring my options," I sighed, dropping my forehead into my hand.

He pulled my hand away and tilted my chin, making me meet his golden gaze.

"You don't need no options. You said you wanted someone who wanted only you. You got that."

His words left me breathless for a minute. I swallowed before asking, "What do you mean?"

"I want you, Dayana."

I inhaled sharply. Then... "As... as what?"

He stared at me, his expression serious. "As my bottom bitch, shawty," he said, then fell out laughing.

I smacked his shoulder. "Cartier! I'm serious," I whined.

He grabbed my hand. "Stop beating on me, girl," he said, before leaning in and nuzzling my neck.

"Cartier—"

"As mine, Dayanna Dionne Castle. I want you, just you," he said before his mouth pressed against mine.

I slid an arm around his neck and pulled him closer as I opened for him. My heart swelled as happiness spilled through me. But I couldn't let him off that easily. I pulled back a minute later, wanting to make something clear.

"I'll consider you among my other options. But your behavior today was crazy and unacceptable," I scolded.

He chuckled. "You still talking about options. I can show you better than I can tell you, shorty. And my behavior today wasn't shit. Keep fucking around with these other niggas and you gon' see my other side. I been told you I was possessive, and I don't share."

"Can we discuss this later?" I asked, sighing.

"Oh, we definitely discussing it later."

He slid out of the booth and held out his hand. I took it and let him lead me to his family's table. This shit was crazy. He was crazy.

And I couldn't wait to get back to his house and tempt him into filling the aching emptiness between my thighs.

CHAPTER 69

Smoke

MY OG HAD TAKEN one look at my face over lunch and offered to take Jenesis to her house to change and then to a playground near our houses. I sent Bruno behind Dayana's little date—his name was Brady Nielsen, we learned—to make sure he understood how this shit was gon' go. Brady's father was some big deal lawyer and state politician, but I didn't give a fuck. He trespassed and I handled it accordingly.

So, now I was standing in my bedroom, staring at Dayana as she looked at me defiantly. Shorty was already skating on thin ice with this little shit she had worn for this nigga. It was almost as bad as that dress she'd had on Friday. Then that stupid shit about considering what I had said? She was gon' learn real quick that the time for considerations was over. We were about to sit our asses down and figure this out.

"What is your problem, Cartier? I swear, you on some good bullshit," she popped, hand on her hip as she rolled her eyes at me.

I moved closer to her. She backed up one step, then thought about it and stood her ground. I loved her attitude, even when she was pissing me off.

"My problem? I mean, I got several right now. I told you

about some of them at the restaurant. But I can continue. First, these little ass shorts you got on—"

"It's a romper!" she protested.

"I'on give a fuck what you call that shit. It's easy access for that bitch ass nigga."

She sucked her teeth and glared at me. "Easy access? Oh, yeah, that's me. Easy. I was a fucking virgin until a few weeks ago, but now I'm offering easy access?"

I shrugged. "You were easy for m—"

If a nigga really thought about it, I probably deserved the jab she threw at my mouth, cutting me off. The shit still shocked me. And her little ass was in a full fighting stance, like she wanted to square up. I would have probably laughed if she didn't look so serious and if my damn lips weren't actually hurting. Shorty had some hands on her. I threaded my hand through the back of her hair and pulled her head back.

"Ay, girl. Don't do that shit again," I warned.

"Fuck you, Cartier Salinas!"

She swung again, but I caught her wrist. I walked her backwards until she was up against the wall. She struggled, but I held on to her mad ass.

"I'm serious, Dayana. Chill yo' ass out."

"I am chill," she gritted through her teeth. "Get the fuck off me. You've been very clear about where your heart is, but when I respond like I should, it's an issue. So, yeah, I'm weighing my options. And if I don't choose you, whoever else I might wanna fuck is none of your business. I'm not sure why you having a problem getting that in yo' damn head. Just sit back and watch me go be easy with whoever the hell I choose."

Her options? Whoever else she might wanna fuck? Yeah, I went a long way with Dayana, but her mouth and her attitude had me seeing fucking red. Letting go of her hair, I brought my hands to the front of the strapless romper, grabbing it on each side of the split that put her cleavage on display.

"You been showing out all day, starting with putting this shit on," I told her before grabbing the material and tearing it straight down the front of her body.

Her mouth fell open right before she started cussing me.

"You stupid muhfucka, you gon' pay for this," she yelled, trying to swing on me again. The ruined clothes fell off as I swept her up in my arms, revealing the scraps of red lingerie she wore underneath. Shit pissed me off that she was out with that nigga with only that on beneath them tiny ass shorts, but it made my dick hard as fuck. I carried her ass to the bed and dumped her on it before sitting and pulling her face down across my lap. Her ass was revealed in that little ass underwear, and I smiled as I trapped her legs between mine.

"Cartier, what the fuck? I swear if you don't let me go, I'ma—"

She screamed as I landed the first smack on her ass.

"Nigga! Are you crazy? That hurt!"

"It's supposed to. What I tell you about your mouth?" I asked, popping her again.

"Fuck you, Cartier! You make me sick!"

Oh. She wanted to get serious. Okay, then.

"You remember your safe word?"

"M-mango. Cartier, you b—"

That was all she said before I brought my hand down again. Over and over, I spanked her as she yelled and squirmed. Her skin warmed beneath my hand and her fat ass jiggled as it took on a reddish color. I swear my dick was hard enough to cut glass.

Shorty was stubborn, but so was I. She called me everything but a child of God, but she refused to say "mango." She finally broke, twin tears sliding down her pretty face.

"I'm sorry, Cartier. Damn, you can stop!"

My hand connected with her ass a few more times before I acknowledged her words.

"Nah, shorty, tell me about ya options and these niggas you about to fuck," I said mercilessly, swatting her ass again. "Tell me about how you want them niggas, Benzo and Brady," I taunted.

"I don't want them!" she wailed.

She was still moving as I spanked her, but not the same struggling as before. Her motions were more rhythmic, her legs slightly open. A glance between her thighs revealed her pussy was glistening with her essence as it slipped from her. Shit, I wasn't the only one turned on by this spanking. I smacked her again before letting my fingers slide down and slip inside her. She was soaking wet, her walls greedily clamping against my fingers. A soft moan tumbled from her lips.

"What do you want then, Dayana?" I asked, working my fingers in and out.

"You," she whispered. "I just want you."

Freeing her legs, I removed her thong in one quick movement.

"On the bed, on your stomach," I ordered.

She obeyed as I stripped out of my clothes. I pulled her to the edge of the bed, then stepped between her legs. Pressing on her back, I pushed her into a perfect arch. I fisted my dick before guiding it to her soaking wet entrance and easing in. I didn't stop until my hips met the red skin of her ass and she whimpered.

"That ass hurts?" I asked.

"Yes," she moaned.

I smacked one of her punished cheeks.

"Good."

"Fuck you, Cartier!"

I pulled all the way out, then banged back into her. She

squealed and tried to move away, but I gripped her thick ass hips, holding her in place as I fucked her.

"Nah, what I tell you about that mouth? You stay wanting to talk crazy but wanna cry now."

"Smoke, oh, my God! It's too much! I can't—"

"Shut up," I snapped, moving my hand between her thighs and finding her pearl.

I pinched it, then pulled and my shorty came so hard that I thought the contractions of her tight pussy were going to break my dick off. She screamed my name as she gushed around me, and I fucked her harder.

"I don't want to hear about your fucking options, understand?" I bit out as I pounded into her.

"Y-y-yes," she stuttered, her hands twisting in the sheets as she tried to hold on.

"On God, Yana, this my pussy. You want a dead nigga on your conscience, let me find out you giving it to someone else."

She nodded as she pushed back against me, crying about how deep I was and begging for more at the same time. It was too soon for how I was feeling, but I meant every fucking word. Dayana was mine, and I needed to make sure she understood that. I had spanked her ass for her actions and words, and now I was punishing her pussy, my dick ruthlessly making her tight, almost resistant, walls spread over and over.

This time, when her walls started pulling on my dick, I was ready.

"You coming again, Princess?"

"Cartier... yessss," she sobbed, her pussy milking my dick.

I leaned over, burying my teeth in her neck as I did something I had never done—let go inside her with nothing between us. Fuck it. I was more than able to handle the consequences, and she felt way too good for me to pull out.

CHAPTER 70

Dayana

WHO THE FUCK AM I? I asked myself that as Cartier lay against my back, still inside me. I loved when he lay on my back. Shit just made me feel safe and warm. But I couldn't believe what had just happened.

This nigga spanked me. Hard. And I liked it. The blows from his hand were red hot, but somehow that heat had spread across my ass and changed into something tingling and warm and way more erotic than I would've expected. I was wet as hell by the fifth smack. He did just what he had promised; he spanked me and made me like it. Then, he mounted me and fucked me like an animal... and I came twice. I mean, yeah, he wasn't usually gentle, but he wasn't usually like *that* either. I thought he was going to push me through the damn mattress. Nigga had claimed my pussy as his and just to show he meant it, I guess, he came inside me. What the fuck?

"Cartier?" I called softly.

"Hmmm?"

"We gotta get a Plan B. I haven't been taking my birth control right with all the shit that's been going on."

He was quiet for a minute before finally pulling out of me.

"Roll over," he said.

I turned so we could face each other, and he settled between my legs as his gaze captured mine.

"You worried?" he asked.

I frowned, not sure what he was asking. Before I could ask him to explain, he kissed me softly. When he finally pulled back, his caramel eyes were gold with emotion.

"I would never abandon you with my seed, Dayana. Never," he vowed.

"I know that. I see you with Jenesis. But I'm only twenty-one and I'm not done with college, and I still haven't made up my mind what I want to do. And you…" I let my voice trail off.

He nipped my chin.

"I what?"

"I want you to be sure about what you said earlier. I have to know that I'm enough for you. I want my children's father to be fully with me," I said.

I probably sounded naïve as hell. And what was worse, I could easily, happily imagine having his babies, given how I had fallen for him. But I didn't know if he'd ever feel that way about me.

"Part of me will always love Jenna, Yana."

"I know."

And I could understand that, honestly. I wasn't tripping about his love for her. It was the fact that he loved her to the exclusion of everybody else… including me. He looked down at me before dropping another kiss on my lips.

"But a feisty little twenty-one-year-old taught me something recently," he continued.

I gave him a half smile. "Oh, yeah? What's that?"

"That a nigga definitely got room in his heart for someone else."

I sucked in my breath, almost scared to believe this could

be true. I had been turning his words over and over in my head since earlier.

"Cartier—"

"Tell me why you had the attitude all week," he said suddenly.

Wait, what? Just when we were about to get serious—

"Yana."

I sighed. "You put me in that other room and basically ignored me. I never know what to think with you."

"I didn't want you to feel like I expected you to sleep with me cuz you were staying here. But if you wanted to be up under a nigga, why you didn't just say that instead of walking around salty?" he teased.

"I'm not about to be that clingy virgin you described."

"What if I want you to be?"

His question caught me off guard. I couldn't answer for a second.

"Do you want that?" I asked hesitantly.

"Yeah. That's what I've been trying to tell yo' mean ass all day."

"Cartier, are you sure? I need you to be sure."

"I swear that shit on Stephanie Salinas. You mine, shorty. And you enough. Hell, with that mouth and that jab and this sweet ass pussy, you more than enough."

I smacked his shoulder before looping my arms around his neck. "You nasty *and* crazy."

He smiled. "You like it, though," he said smugly before capturing my mouth with his.

I moaned as he eased back inside me. My ass was sore pressed against the bed and my pussy was sore from his earlier ravaging, but I still wanted him. I tilted my hips to meet his first thrust.

"You really was gon' try to fight me?" he whispered against my ear.

"You better be glad I didn't have my bat," I popped off.

He chuckled softly. "We'll get the Plan B until you sure about shit. But start taking those pills right or get a shot or whatever," he said.

I looked up at him and nodded as he grabbed my hips.

"Cuz now that I nutted in this little pussy, I ain't never pulling out again."

CHAPTER 71

Dream

(*MONDAY*, *June 28*)

I needed a break. Numbers were swimming in front of my eyes, my mouth felt dry, and my stomach was growling loud enough that Parker probably heard it in her office. Lifting my hands from the keyboard, I rubbed my eyes and sighed. I wondered if anyone on my team wanted to grab food. I swore there were some wings somewhere calling my name.

I wanted a nap, too. I was tired from this weekend. Clubbing, sexing, and emotional encounters were exhausting. I couldn't believe I had told Damien I loved him. But more unbelievable was that I had meant it. Somehow, in the six weeks since I'd first lain eyes on him, I'd fallen hard. Of course, he didn't say the words back; I wondered if he could. I didn't know what this meant for our thirty-day expiration date, and when I tried to ask him, he just said, "I told you, you belong to me." Whatever that meant. I was too tired to figure it all out. The fixer couldn't fix her own shit.

The intercom sounded, and I didn't know whether I wanted to frown or laugh. Rayleigh was a mess and there was no telling what she might be calling to say.

"Yes, ma'am?" I answered.

"Boss Lady, you got a delivery," she announced in a singsong voice.

I rolled my eyes. "Rayleigh, sign for it and bring it to me. Why you acting brand new?"

"He said he has to deliver it directly to you. Mr. Arceneau said it was okay." Her voice dropped to a whisper. "And I'on know what you been on lately with all these fine men coming up here, but I wanna be like you when I grow up. I don't know where all the regular couriers are, but Mr. New Delivery Man is a sugar daddy. Go 'head—"

"Rayleigh!" I snapped, dropping my forehead into my palm. "Show him back."

"Yes, Ms. Castle. Right away," she said sweetly.

I shook my head. I swear she had a split personality. Drumming my fingers against my desk, I waited for whatever the hell was coming. Had to be something one of Daddy's clients didn't want anyone else to see. The thought made the little headache I was nursing explode. I was getting tired of this shit. Just like I didn't want a man who lived on the wrong side of the law, I didn't want to launder money and settle fights between gangsters my whole life. I came to work for Daddy out of a sense of obligation, but that was wearing off.

I stood up at the knock on the door. Rayleigh opened it and stepped back to let the courier in. I bit back a smirk when she winked from behind him before walking off.

Smiling, I focused on the man now taking up a lot of space in my office as he stared me up and down. Rayleigh hadn't lied. He was an older guy, in his forties, maybe, and sexy as hell. Tall and stocky with skin the color of bittersweet chocolate, his face was damn near perfect. Not as beautiful as Damien's, but—

Wait, I had to stop doing that comparison thing. Mr. New Delivery Man was cute in his own right, but I was skeptical about a middle-aged man who worked as a courier. Still, I smiled at him.

"You have something for me?"

I was just being polite; I could see the manila envelope in his hands. I held out mine, waiting. But he surprised me. Instead of handing me the envelope, he stared at me and smiled.

"Can I verify that you're Ms. Castle, please? Don't wanna get in trouble with my new job."

The request wasn't too crazy, given the sensitive stuff I worked on, but something about his eyes had my nerves up, my instincts telling me shit wasn't right. But he didn't seem really threatening. His body was relaxed, and his smile didn't waver. Plus, he'd passed through building security and the eyes my father kept on me and they were thorough. *Stop being paranoid,* I told myself. I grabbed my purse and pulled out my wallet. Handing him my license, I waited. He studied it for a few seconds before those dark eyes met mine again. His smile stayed in place, but his eyes were cold and black as night. Nigga was freaking me out.

"If I could get the—"

"Dream Dior," he drawled, giving me my license back. "That shit fits yo' pretty ass."

I coughed, uncomfortable as fuck. "Thank you, but I need to get back to work."

He pulled the envelope closer to him as he studied me. I held his gaze, refusing to back down.

"What I'm tryna figure out is why a beautiful, cultured lady such as yourself is laying down with a coward ass nigga like Demon," he asked casually.

"Wh-what?" I stuttered.

His response was as a cold little smirk. I swear I blinked for a full minute as my heart rate sped up and my throat closed.

"You heard me, Ms. Castle. How a chick like you end up fucking trash like Demon Montana? You Ivy League and he a gutter rat. Used to watch that nigga tear open trash bags looking for food," he said, chuckling.

Fuck. This must be the nigga from Damien's past. Okay, I had to get my shit together. My smile disappeared as I stared up at him. I didn't appreciate him bringing his shit to my office and the way he laughed at how desperate Damien must have been as a child pissed me off.

"You need to leave," I told him, my voice tight.

Crossing my arms over my chest, I leaned against my desk, waiting for him to do as I said.

"The only thing I can think of is, maybe you not as classy as you seem, Ms. Castle. What the old people say? Niggas be attracted to bitches like their mama, and his mama definitely a ho. A nasty one, too," he said, his smile spreading as he walked closer to me. "You a ho, Ms. Castle? I know the nigga got a little money. How much he pay you to—"

"Get the fuck—"

My words dissolved into a shriek as he moved, pinning me against the side of my desk. I'd been raised not to show fear, but it snaked through me, and I felt myself trembling as he pressed his body against mine.

"Maybe I should find out?" he whispered, using his free hand to trace my jawline before he grabbed my neck and squeezed. "I mean, I planned to just kill his bitch, like he did mine, but maybe I'll see what got that nigga changing up."

I froze as he nuzzled my throat, inhaling deeply.

"You smell good, shorty. I can't wait to find out if that pussy as sweet," he taunted.

"If you don't get the fuck off me, I'm gon' scream this bitch down," I hissed.

This nigga actually had the audacity to laugh at me. He took a few steps back before stroking my cheek again.

"Nah. No need to scream, Ms. Castle. Today ain't yo' day. I just wanted to deliver yo' package and let yo' bitch ass nigga know he can be touched at any time."

He tossed the envelope on the desk. With one last smile, he walked out.

For a long moment, I rested against my desk, trying to calm my racing heart. I held out my hands, watching how they shook. Finally, I turned slowly and grabbed the envelope. It took a few tries because my fingers felt clumsy, but I finally got it open. Reaching in, I pulled out three pictures and a folded sheet of paper. I barely had time to make it into the attached bathroom before dry heaves and my weak knees had me bent over the sink.

Three pictures.

Three dead bodies.

Three women burned until they looked like something from a horror movie.

One brief note: *Do you really know the nigga you fucking?*

CHAPTER 72

Demon

OTIS REDDING CROONED in my ear as I looked at the view in front of me. I nodded once. The shit was dope and allowed me to work my way through some of my thoughts. I stepped back to look again before I walked out of the room, careful to lock it behind me.

My phone rang suddenly, and I grabbed it from my pocket. *Dream.* I answered and just held the phone.

"Damien?"

Her voice was soft. Too soft. I knew something was wrong.

"What happened?"

She cleared her throat and hesitated for a minute.

"Dream."

"The guy you took me to the lake house to tell me about?"

My hands clenched into fists as the familiar icy feeling overcame me. I rested my back against the wall, waiting, trying to hold back the rage.

"Damien, I'm pretty sure I-I-I just met him," she stuttered, and I realized she was scared. Ignoring the chill that seized my body, I hung up, then dialed another number immediately.

"What's up?" the man on the other end greeted.

"Bring Dream to me at the guest house."

"Demon, what—"

"Now!" I raged.

———

"What you gon' do?" Dante asked me.

He sat on the couch in the small living room of his guest house. It was a crazy name. People didn't come here to stay. They came to die. I looked up at Dante.

"Fuck you think I'ma do? I was gon' kill him, anyway. Now, he gotta hurt first."

Dante nodded. "Because of the girl."

I rubbed a hand over my face, ignoring what he wanted me to admit. He laughed softly.

"I did good," he said.

My head jerked up and I grilled him. "What you say?"

He shrugged. "I said—"

He stopped as the doorbell rang. I shot him another evil look before crossing the room to open it. Dream stood there with two of Dante's guys, her eyes big and worried.

"Where's Kam?" she asked.

"At the main house with DJ. I didn't want to leave him at camp."

She nodded as I stepped back to let her and the detail in. I closed the door behind them before leading her a little bit away and pulling out a burner phone. I went to the photos and showed her the one I had of Keith.

"This who you saw?"

She squinted at the screen, then nodded. "He was bigger, and his hair is different, but that's him," she said, hugging herself.

"Tell me what went on. I need to know everything that nigga said."

Slowly, she told me what had happened. This sorry ass nigga posed as a courier and the shit really worked. My fists tightened as she described him calling her a whore and promising to rape her. I was going to cut the nigga's tongue out for talking like that to her. The part about how he pinned her up against the desk and touched her sealed his fate— Keith was going to die slowly. Very slowly.

"He gave me this," she said, pushing the envelope she'd been holding into my hand.

I opened it, looked at the contents, then replaced the shit. She bit her lower lip as she studied my face. Finally, she spoke again.

"Did you… did you do that, Damien?"

"Yeah."

I wasn't about to lie to her. Dream knew what I was. The fact that she was seeing it up close was bound to happen.

"Why?" she asked, her voice a whisper.

Instead of answering, I looked past her at the two men who were supposed to be keeping an eye on her.

"Y'all let this nigga get past y'all?" I asked calmly.

The one named Khaleef spoke up. "He went through the building's security. That's her dad's team. They let us know if someone is going to the suite of offices where Ms. Castle works. I guess he lied—"

I shook my head. I didn't have time for excuses.

"We showed you his last picture from the Department of Corrections. How the fuck did you miss him?"

Khaleef looked at his partner, Emil, like he needed help. Emil cleared his throat before speaking up.

"Like she said, he changed up some shit, Demon. And it ain't like we were face-to-face. I swear we didn't recognize him."

Raising an eyebrow, I stared at him.

"Oh, yeah?"

He nodded hastily. "Yeah."

"If you can't recognize or stop the nigga, what the fuck you being paid for?" I quizzed.

It was a rhetorical question. Before either one of them could respond, I had palmed my Glock. I lifted it quickly and fired twice, giving them both a grim third eye in the middle of their foreheads. Dante jumped up from the couch.

"Goddamn it, Demon Montana, why I always gotta remind you we have a room in this house called the 'kill room' for a reason? Now, these niggas bleeding into Sherri-lyn's rugs, and you got brain matter everywhere! Do you know how hard it is to get up all the brain matter? You—"

I tuned his ass out as a shocked Dream stared up at me, frozen in place. I walked to her, but she tried to move away from me. Grabbing her arm, I made her face me.

"Damien, oh, my God. Why—"

"They didn't do what they were supposed to. That's how this shit goes," I said with no remorse.

"Y-y-you could've just fired them. You killed them, Damien. You keep killing people and I *hate* that..." she covered her face with her hands.

I understood she wasn't used to seeing shit like this, but her reaction pissed me off. Dream knew the world we lived in. I shook her a little bit, making her look at me again.

"That nigga could've killed or raped you in that office while they sitting outside chopping it up. That shit is unac-ceptable," I told her.

"The nigga wouldn't have been there if you hadn't killed those women. Women, Damien?!" she shot back, her usual attitude showing itself.

"Ay, calm yo' ass down, Dream," I warned her.

"Getcho crazy ass outta here so I can take care of the cleanup shit," Dante said suddenly.

I knew he was giving me an out so I could get Dream away from this shit. Nodding once, I handed him the gun and turned back to her.

"Let's go," I said.

She hesitated for a moment, then locked eyes with me. I guess she saw that I wasn't entertaining her bullshit right now because she headed toward the door, careful to avoid the bodies I'd dropped.

"I need to go get my car," she mumbled once we had picked up Kam and pulled away from Dante's estate.

"Your car has to be swept. Nigga coulda put anything on it."

I checked the back seat to make sure the kid still had his Air Pods in. The way his head was bopping as he worked in one of his sketch pads let me know he did. I turned back to Dream.

"Ask me what you wanna know about the pictures," I demanded.

"You ignored what I asked, so whatever, Damien."

She crossed her arms over her chest and stared out the window. I should've left the shit at that. But I kept remembering how she looked when she said, *"Women, Damien?"* and I didn't like that.

"You know who those women were?"

"That man said one of them was his bitch. I guess you killed her to get at him."

I side-eyed her. "You guess wrong. The nigga who came to your office is named Keith McKellar. The first picture in the envelope is a picture of his sister. She was my main target."

She turned in her seat to look at me. "Why? And what about the other two?"

Rubbing a hand over my face, I took a minute to respond. "The first time I went back to my hood after my father came and got me was when I was nineteen to take care of that problem. The first woman is Angela, Dream. She was Keith's sister. She was into some twisted shit. There were times when she wanted to put on a performance for her friends or she wanted them to sample my…" I cleared my throat, unable to finish.

"Oh, my God, Damien," Dream whispered.

"She would give me Viagra and I would… anyway, the second chick, Mindy, she *was* Keith's bitch, but she also liked Angela's games. I didn't know she would be there that night, but I was glad she was. I went to Angela's with this crazy ass plan. I knew she'd let me in. People who do shit like that think they control your mind. Anyway, I got there, and Angela had just had one of her little parties. Had a little nigga there."

My jaw tightened at the memory. Dude looked around fourteen or fifteen, with eyes dead as hell. I knew then that Angela hadn't stopped, was never going to stop until a nigga like me stopped her.

"She sent him home when she saw me. Nobody was left but her and Mindy, I thought. I offered to fix them bitches a drink, and they let me. I knocked their asses out, turned the gas on, and poured gas around that bitch. Waited outside a while and lit that bitch up."

Dream gasped. "Do you know how dangerous that was for you? What if—"

I shrugged. "I was nineteen and pissed the fuck off. I was ready to die if I could get at her ass."

"And the third woman?"

"I didn't think about checking the house. She was asleep in another room. I'on know if she participated or not. I didn't find out till later she was there. Went back to my pops' house and Dante happened to be leaving. He took one look at me and knew I had done some shit. He took care of it, made sure they only reported the gas leak part of it. Keith started asking questions, but the fire department stuck to the story. He didn't believe it, but he went to jail before he could dig any more. He just got out."

"And he still wants revenge," she finished.

"Yeah."

She was quiet for a minute, chewing on her bottom lip like she was processing everything I said. Finally, she looked over at me again.

"What are you going to do, Damien?" she asked, her voice a whisper.

I glanced at her before returning my gaze to the road.

"That nigga put a price on my head, and he touched you. You already know what I'm gon' do, Dream. I'm gon' kill his bitch ass," I said calmly.

She was silent again for a few minutes. I didn't like her lack of response. One question bounced through my brain, fucking with my head. I shouldn't care, and I felt like a pussy ass nigga asking it, but I couldn't stop myself.

"All this shit change how you feel?"

I kept my eyes in front of me, trying to seem nonchalant. But her answer mattered more than it should. The fact that it took her a while to reply had a familiar coldness spreading through me. Fuck this. I had never needed anyone's love and I didn't need hers. I was just about to tell her that shit when she frowned and opened her mouth.

"No. Why would you ask me that? You think I'm that shallow? My feelings don't just change like that."

The way that she crossed her arms and pushed out that bottom lip let me know she had an attitude. But she'd said what I wanted to hear, so I let her ass make it. Besides, I now knew one way to get on her good side.

"You hungry?"

She sniffed, like she couldn't be bothered with my question. Then, in a small voice, she said, "I could eat."

CHAPTER 73

Dream

I HAD CONFESSED my love to a certified killer. I mean, I knew he was a killer, but before today, I had never actually seen him in action. Damien had stood calmly and blown off the heads of two men that I had just conversed with hours before. The fucked-up part was that I watched him and, while the shit bothered me, I didn't run away screaming from his ass. In fact, after what he asked me in the car, I just wanted to hold him close and reassure him of my feelings. I had to be going crazy. Since Dayana had gotten herself involved with a man in a similar line of business, I made a lunch date with her to talk this shit out.

Damien thought he was smart. Nigga was developing this habit where he fed me real good, then fucked me incoherent. He'd done it tonight, ordering from my favorite Italian place and making my plate while Kam and I argued over movies. Once Kam had disappeared for the night, Damien had lured me into the shower and started his seduction there. After two rounds, I had tapped out. I was lying here now, curled against him as his big hand rubbed my back and ass. His touch usually put me to sleep. I knew that's what he was counting on, but not tonight. My brain was a jumble of Keith McKellar and eye-witnessed murder.

One of Damien's phones vibrated on the nightstand. Sighing, he grabbed it. I shook my head at his attitude. He hated getting phone calls, which was probably why my evil ass called him every day.

"What?" he answered rudely. I lazily smacked his chest for his lack of manners. "Just send me the bill for getting the brain matter cleaned."

I was close enough to hear Dante's laugh.

"Nigga, I don't need yo' money. How's yo' girl?" he asked.

Damien was quiet for a minute, then, "You really gon' act like we have conversations like this?"

Frowning, I rose a little to glare at him. "Be nice," I whispered.

He frowned right back. "A'ight," he said, before talking to his brother. "She here overthinking shit in her big ass head. I must not have eaten the pussy as good as I thought."

My jaw dropped open as he smirked at me. Dante laughed again.

"If you need some tips from ya big brother, just say that," he taunted.

Damien disconnected the call.

"Oh, my God! I don't believe you said that!" I exclaimed, trying to sit up.

He held me down easily. "You told me to be nice. You leave me alone and let me be what you call rude, then I don't discuss my personal life with that nigga. You tell me to be nice, I gotta open up a little bit. Make up your mind," he said, smirking.

"Damien, don't fuck with me! There has to be some middle ground between being rude and discussing your sex life."

He grabbed my hair, still in the natural curls and coils he liked, and pulled my head back, making me look at him.

"Chill, mama. I discussed your big head, too."

I sucked my teeth. "I was here. And for your information, I'm not overthinking. It's a lot to think about," I countered.

He scowled down at me. "It's really not. It is what it is, Dream. Accept that shit and move on."

"Damien! You—" I stopped to look around the room as if the police were going to pop out at any minute. "You know killing people is not normal, right?" I whispered.

He smiled at me. "Why yo crazy ass whispering like somebody in here wearing a wire? People been killing people forever, shorty."

I sighed. "Not like this! Damien, look. The first night I met you, you were covered in blood. I assume you…"

He nodded nonchalantly.

"Then, Isaac and the two guys today. Damien, that's four people in under two months!" I countered, trying to make him see how crazy this was.

He yawned. "I mean, if you talking about the last two months, you gotta include Eve's baby daddy. He got a little too friendly with his hands. And that little nigga in the club that you gave your number to. He asked me about sharing you."

I blinked several times. That was all I could do as his words sank in.

"Go to sleep, Dream," he commanded as usual.

But for once, I couldn't. Six people in less than two months and he was totally unbothered. That couldn't be right.

I was still thinking about it Tuesday afternoon at lunch with my sister.

"I mean, I'm not the crazy one, am I? That shit is not normal, right?" I quizzed Dayana before biting into a fried shrimp.

She rolled her eyes, but took a sip of her water before responding.

"Sissy, you fucking a nigga named Demon who was splattered with blood when you met him. His father was Dixon Ware, the biggest crime boss in the state, who left his empire to his sons, including Demon. So, no, this is not your normal, but it is his," she said, her tone making it seem like I was unreasonable.

"But I love him," I admitted. "I love him, and I just want a regular—".

I stopped at her shocked look. She was paused with a spoon full of gumbo halfway to her mouth and staring at me as if I had suddenly grown horns. The spoon and the gumbo splattered back into the bowl.

"Bitch, wait, wait, wait! Did you say love? I know yo' practical, logical ass ain't fell in love, Dream Dior," she teased, smiling hard as hell.

I sighed. "I'm stupid, huh?"

Dayana's smile quickly turned into a frown.

"No. Hell no. You're not stupid. But you can't expect his normal to change, at least not overnight."

"He's so traumatized, Yana, and the shit he's doing is traumatizing. I swear, he needs therapy and to leave some of that shit alone," I argued.

My sister grabbed my hand and squeezed it.

"Give him time. He's always known violence. Maybe you can teach him something else."

I nodded, hoping she was right. For a few minutes, we ate in silence. Then my sister called my name as she smiled slyly at me.

"What, girl?" I asked, already rolling my eyes.

"When he's in that mode, you don't get a little... tingly?" she whispered.

I looked at her, confused. "Tingly?"

"Like... Sunday. I had a lunch date with Brady. Smoke popped up. Yada, yada, yada, he ended up stabbing Brady through the hand. I was pissed off. But I had a mini orgasm," she admitted shamelessly.

I shook my head, my top lip curling. "Bitch, you sick."

"Come on… you didn't get a little wet?"

"No, Dayana Dionne, seeing him blow two people's heads off did not make me cum," I said in a low voice, my eyes darting around us.

She sipped on her gumbo before trying again.

"Okay, maybe not when it's outright murder, but just the way he bosses up? Like handling Isaac. And how he stood up at my wedding. And the way he gave my twin that well-deserved ass whooping. Ooh, and how he just says your name… girl, I'm getting hot for you," she said, fanning herself.

"You have a problem, I swear. But…" I drawled.

"But what, heffa?"

"I may have gotten a little damp."

I winked at her, shimmied my shoulders, and we burst into laughter. My amusement lasted until my detail had seen me safely into my car and I had pulled back into traffic. Then my phone rang and Damien's number appeared on my dashboard. I answered quickly and sang out a little, "Good afternoon!"

"The fuck you at?" he asked grouchily.

I sucked my teeth before replying. "We gon' pretend that you don't know exactly where I am? But anyway, I'm on my way to get Kam."

He didn't say anything for a minute, so I knew where this was going.

"I'm not cool with this shit. It's not a good time and too much could go wrong. Y'all not going," he said suddenly.

I sighed loudly. "Damien, we already discussed this. You can't do that to him. He wants—"

"He twelve-years-old, Dream. I'on give a fuck what he wants. I gotta look out for him. Something happens to the little nigga, you gon' be the first one falling out and shit."

I banged my head against the headrest as I tried to figure

out how best to win this argument. Last night, Damien had explained a little bit to Kam about why he pulled him out of camp and why we had to be more careful right now. Kam had been silent then, but this morning, he had asked if Melanie was in danger, too. Of course, Damien's crazy ass had said, "I hope so." It pissed Kam off, but it also made him want to see his mother. Damien refused to go anywhere close to her. I volunteered to take Kam; as long as we had security, I didn't see the issue. Damien clearly did not feel the same way. We had argued until he reluctantly agreed. But apparently, his doubts had come back.

"Damien," I began slowly, knowing I had to tread carefully. "She's his mother. He misses her and he's worried about her. I know you can't understand why anyone would feel that way about her, but she's all he's had."

Obviously, my words had no impact. He bulldozed right over what I said.

"Well, he ain't had shit and he ain't risking his life for her. That nigga already came to your office. My brother and my... you together are sitting ducks for him. I'ma go tell the kid no. You can—"

"He will never forgive you if you do this," I said softly.

He went quiet again. I gripped the steering wheel tightly, waiting for his response. I hoped he could admit to himself that he cared enough about his little brother that my words mattered. Finally, he spoke.

"He got thirty minutes to visit. Anymore, and he won't see her until she's discharged or embalmed."

I mouthed, *Thank you,* as he hung up on me.

Kam and I went with a detail of four and the knowledge of one angry Demon Montana with us. It wasn't hard to see that Melanie Montana used to be a model. It also wasn't hard to see that her modeling and party days were behind her. Already, she looked sicker than she had in Damien's yard. Knowing how he felt about her, I tried to stay cold and quiet.

But it was clear that she loved Kam, and from the looks she shot me after he said, "You remember Demon's girlfriend," I couldn't help feeling a little bit sorry for her.

"You're beautiful," she said after one of those furtive looks.

Lost, all I could say was, "Thank you."

"I'm glad for Da— for him," she whispered as she cuddled Kam close.

I nodded quickly and stepped out of the room. Damien was gone when we got home, and Kam wasn't his usual talkative self. I made him dinner and sat with him for a while. In the middle of an episode of *Stranger Things*, with his eyes glued to the TV, he said, "She gon' die, Dream."

I respected him too much to lie. I just pulled him against me and turned the TV up a little.

"I ain't gon' have nobody," he whispered.

I squeezed him tightly. "You have me. You have your brother."

"He don't want me."

His voice broke and I gently dragged a thumb under his eyes, wiping his tears.

"He does want you, Suga. He *needs* you."

We both went to bed early, his brother missing. Knowing Damien was angry at me, I didn't even bother to call. And when he called me, I was half asleep and irritable.

"Get up. Come here. A couple of my guys waiting on you," he demanded.

"Damien! No…" I whined.

"Dream."

He spoke my name in his usual commanding tone, but even that wasn't enough. It was only when he added, "Dream, I need you," that I sprang from the bed.

"Here I come."

CHAPTER 74
Demon

(*TUESDAY*, *June 29—a few hours earlier*)

"Ay."

I looked over at Smoke as he spoke. He stood, leaning against the wall, rolling a switchblade over his knuckles.

"What?"

"How did you know what to get yo' girl for her birthday? Yana birthday coming up in August and I gotta outdo yo' ass."

I glanced at the blood-splattered, staggering man in front of me, then back to Smoke.

"You really wanna do this now?" I asked, gesturing toward the man named Kedrick.

Smoke shrugged as I dodged a weak, sloppy uppercut.

"I mean, you 'bout to knock that nigga out and put him out of his misery. What else you gotta do?"

I thought about it as I landed a right hook against Kedrick's jaw, sending him crashing to the cold, concrete floor of the warehouse.

"First of all, nigga," I said to Smoke as I stepped on Kedrick's chest, "you not gon' outdo me."

Kedrick whimpered and I looked down at his fucked-up face in disgust.

"Did you mean to leave his right eye open?" Smoke asked conversationally.

I turned my grill on him. "Can you let me do what I do?"

Kedrick coughed weakly before addressing me.

"Demon, I'm sorry, man. I was just tryna make a little extra. I wasn't tryna put yo' bitch—"

I smiled at the sound of his knee cracking as my boot made contact with his leg. Smoke let out a low whistle.

"Damn, them shits steel-toed?" he asked before looking down at Kedrick. "My bad, I coulda warned you. He get a little sensitive if you call her the B-word."

Kedrick was currently the target of my icy rage because he was the delivery man who had given Keith the truck and uniform that enabled him to get into Dream's office. Smoke had heard one of his crew talking about a nigga who did that shit because local dealers paid nicely to move product right under the police's nose. For a few stacks, Kedrick Martin would hook you up. Until Smoke snatched him up and called me. I'd beat his ass as I interrogated him about Keith. Nigga didn't know shit. He was useless, and that had me raging. I leaned down in his bitch ass face.

"I think I'm most fucked up cuz you put my shorty at risk for five Gs," I gritted out.

"Yo' shorty?" Smoke repeated before chuckling. "Nigga, let me find out you had sense enough to claim yo' girl."

I hadn't meant to say that. That shit was a total slip up. I mean, yeah, Dream was mine, but I didn't know about no titles like "my girl" or "my shorty." Of course, Smoke's aggravating ass had caught that shit. I shot him a nasty look and that nigga laughed harder.

"So, the last time you heard from Keith was when he returned your truck?" I asked Kedrick, ready to dead his ass and move the fuck on.

"I swear, man! He brought me back the truck and the guy who put the shit together sent the rest of my money," he sniveled.

"And you still saying you don't know who this mysterious other nigga is?"

He shook his head as best he could. "Said he heard about me in the streets."

"How did he send the money?" I pressed.

"W-wire. Sent it to Mr. Prentice's shop."

"Who was it from?"

"I... I don't know. The nigga you call Keith told me where and when to pick the payments up. Mr. Prentice always had the shit ready for me. Only reason I know it was wired is cuz he said it."

I looked over at two of my guys. They nodded immediately.

"Soon as Prentice gives you a name, I need it, and so does Li Jun."

My attention returned to Kedrick as they exited the building. Removing my foot from his chest, I reached for his shirt, pausing only because Smoke's dumb ass spoke again.

"Is this the part where you beat a nigga to death?" he asked, sounding excited.

I held out both my hands toward him. "I mean, if you don't object," I replied dryly, then blocked out Kedrick's crying.

Smoke walked toward me. "I've always wanted to see yo' ass in action, but you got better shit to do this evening. I asked for pointers."

Before I could say anything, he squatted, pulled Kedrick up by the shirt, and slit his throat. I debated being pissed off, then shrugged. That was one way to handle this shit. This wasn't the end game. When I caught Keith McKellar, no one else would have the pleasure of taking his life.

———

Smoke and I weren't out long after cleaning up. The only advice I could give him that mattered was to listen to his girl, pay attention to what she loved. I was currently on my way home, ready to see Dream and that bad ass kid at my house. Their detail had reported no problems, but I needed the reassurance.

I took a quick detour from the route to my house, stopping at a corner store. I pulled up on the side of a Valero, a few spaces down from a beat-up old Dodge Neon. I walked past it, but something out of the corner of my eye had me stopping and turning back. *Nah,* I thought, *my mind gotta be playing tricks on me.* Then, I saw it again—a little flash of pink and a small arm from the backseat. The front seat was empty, but as I walked up on the car, I tried to convince myself that there had to be somebody grown in the back, even though I couldn't see them. I got close enough to look in and my blood froze.

Two little girls, one of them a baby, were alone in the car. The baby was sleeping in her car seat, not strapped in, wearing a t-shirt and an obviously pissy diaper. The other one didn't look old enough to be in school. Her face and her pink shirt were dirty, and her hair was all over her little head. She was looking at me without saying a word. I reached for the door handle.

I'm gon' kill somebody, I thought as the door opened. Stupid muhfuckas couldn't even take the time to lock them in? But then again, the windows were halfway down. The little girl was still eyeballing me quietly.

"Ay. Where yo' mama?" I asked her.

She didn't say anything at first, just kept watching me. I recognized the look in her eyes—she was deciding whether to trust me. I knew because I'd had to make that decision myself a lot at her age. I stood there, waiting for her to make up her mind. Finally, she opened her mouth and whispered something I couldn't hear.

"Huh?"

"Her gone," she said, her voice a little louder.

What the fuck? Who the hell would leave their babies in a gas station parking lot? Hell, it wasn't even quite dark. The heat was still crazy, and they were sweating heavy. I looked around, hoping the silly bitch who birthed them might walk up. Maybe she was in the store. I didn't see any young women, but I saw an old drunk I knew walking toward me. He froze when he saw me, before turning and trying to walk back the other way.

"Melvin! Bring yo' ass here!" I ordered.

His shoulders slumped, but he headed toward me.

"Look, Demon, I ain't done shit, I ain't seen shit—"

"Shut the fuck up. Go in that store and see if you see these jits' mama in there."

He shook his head. "She ain't there."

I narrowed my eyes and stared at him. "How you know?"

"Saw a woman get out this car about fifteen minutes ago. She got in the truck with some nigga. I ain't know she left no kids back there, though."

He shook his head and tried to peek around me to see the girls.

"Demon, you gotta call the police. What you gon' do with some kids?"

Frowning, I vetoed his idea.

"I'on fuck with twelve like that."

Melvin looked at me like I was crazy.

"So, you babysitting now?"

Ignoring him, I turned back to the kids.

"Y'all hungry?" I asked.

The little girl hesitated again before finally nodding. I reached into my pocket and pulled out a wad of money. Pulling off a bill, I waved it in Melvin's direction.

"Go in there and find some shit kids can eat and drink."

His eyes lit up. "What about the change?"

"I'on give a fuck about that! Get what the fuck I said, then whatever."

His ass damn near ran in the store. I surveyed the parking lot again, hoping this bitch pulled up. Suddenly, I felt a light tap on my leg. I looked down to see the little girl touching me.

"What's up, little mama?" I asked.

"Wass you name?"

She looked up at me with those big ass eyes.

"De—Damien," I mumbled. "What's your name?"

"Mia."

"What's your sister's name?"

"Hailey."

She leaned back against the busted seat of the car and watched me. She had old eyes, eyes that had seen too much. It made me remember myself as a kid, shit I never wanted to do. I turned away from her and waited for Melvin. He came back a couple of minutes later with a bunch of shit for them and a six-pack, of course. The baby girl was finally moving around. She opened her eyes, took one look at me, and broke out crying. Mia tried to see about her, but the baby wasn't having it. I hurried up and opened one of the sandwiches Melvin had bought. Reaching across Mia, I picked the little girl up. The smells of sour milk and urine met my nose. Their parents needed their asses whooped. On God, I might dead their sperm donor tonight if he showed up.

"Ay! Ay, little mama! You gotta chill with all that," I said, bouncing her.

I held the sandwich up to her mouth and she got quiet almost immediately as she ate. She only had a few teeth, but she was producing enough slobber to soften the shit up.

"You need to change that diaper," Melvin said.

I shot him an evil look. He held up both hands and

stepped back. Carefully balancing Hailey, I reached for my phone. Dialing two of Dream's detail, I gave them quick instructions and sent my address.

Then I called her. I could tell she was already asleep, but I needed her for this.

"Get up. Come here. A couple of my people waiting on you," I said.

She told me no.

"Dream."

She made a whining sound. I had to admit something I never had before.

"Dream, I need you."

A pause and then, "Here I come," she said softly.

"Damie?"

Mia's soft voice fucking up my name drew my attention from what I had just done. I had a flashback, a quick memory of KiKi butchering my name the same way.

"Yeah?"

"Can you open my juice?"

Seeing me holding the baby, Melvin spoke up.

"I can do it, sugar," he offered.

For some reason, I couldn't let him. "She didn't ask you, nigga."

He shrugged as I adjusted the baby in my arms and reached for the juice. I opened it and handed it back to her.

"So, what you gon' do now?" asked Melvin.

"Wait for their mama, I guess, hell."

How did I get into this shit? I couldn't leave them, though. I knew the kind of things people did to abandoned kids. At first, I thought about giving their sorry ass mama one hour before I took the kids in the store and had the cashier call the police. I abandoned that idea quickly. The system was no place for babies. I knew where they could go for now, if their mama was a no-show.

Melvin helped me grab their food and move to my car. I

didn't want little kids eating in my shit, but it was just too fucking hot. I needed to get some air on them. We waited while they worked their way through the stuff Melvin bought. I didn't realize how much sugar they'd had until the baby started babbling and Mia started singing. I rubbed my head at the noise. If this woman didn't hurry up...

"Damie?"

I sighed heavily. "Yes, Mia?"

"I gotta pee."

Aww, fuck, nah! No way in hell was I taking shorty in a women's bathroom, and I knew the men's would be too fucking filthy.

"Yo, shorty, can you hold it?"

She shook her head as she stuck a hand between her legs, trying to hold it for real. I looked at her, in her juice-stained shirt and then to her little sister, who was even more of a mess after slobbing that sandwich down. Closing my eyes, I shook my head before holding my hand out to her. Seconds later, I walked into the store, daring a muhfucka to say something. I scanned the premises, my eyes landing on the woman behind the counter.

"Ay," I said, "I need you to take her to the bathroom."

Her eyes got big as fuck. Timidly, she shook her head.

"I'm sorry, sir, I can't leave my register like that. Somebody might try to steal—"

I twisted my lips as I looked at her. "Shorty, you think somebody gon' try to steal anything with me in here?"

"Damie..." Mia whined, dancing around.

I sighed and looked back at the cashier. "I'll pay you, but come get her now or you gon' be sorry."

I swear she suddenly sprouted wings, making it to my side and whisking Mia to the bathroom in seconds. A sudden little pull on my locs had me eyeballing Hailey, whose sticky hands held on to my hair. She gave me a slobbery grin. I sighed again. This couldn't be my life.

CHAPTER 75

Dream

AS JUAN PULLED into the convenience store's parking lot, my mind was racing, wondering what Damien needed. Juan parked, and Stella climbed out to open my door. I got out anxiously, searching the lot for Damien's face. I saw his car, but not him. Instead, standing next to it was an obviously very angry, obviously very high woman yelling at an older man. She was too thin, her body movements jerky as she scratched at her arms and went off.

"Hold on, Ms. Castle," Stella said calmly, putting one protective hand in front of me and reaching for her gun with the other.

I heard Juan's door opening and closing. Just as I was sure there was about to be a problem, Damien rounded the corner, cradling one baby girl and holding the hand of another. Surprise had my mouth dropping open and I guess it caught Stella off guard, too, because she didn't stop me as I made my way towards him.

"You see, you stupid bitch? Ain't no pedophile got your children. This nigga was trying to see about them!" the old man raged.

But she was too far gone. She looked at Damien and sneered.

"You fucking pervert. What, you thought you were gon' get my kids out the car and steal them?" she raged at him.

For a minute, Damien ignored her, even as she kept talking her shit. Instead, he turned to me and handed me the baby. She was a cutie, but the smells coming from her were almost overwhelming. I bounced her nervously as he squatted to talk to the older child.

"Mia, this is Dream. She's gon' help you, okay?"

My anxiety was immediately on a thousand. Dayana was the child expert. I had very little experience with babies, and I had no idea what to do. It didn't help that the little girl shook her head and leaned into him after giving me a skeptical look.

"Want you, Damie," she pouted, not even looking at her mother.

"Damien—"

He shook his head once, silencing me.

"Stella and Juan know where to take you. Tell Ms. Hazel I sent you and she'll take care of everything." He turned back to Mia. "I really need you to be a big girl and go with Dream. I promise I'm coming to see you."

"How the fuck you talking about somebody helping her? Get your fucking hands off my kids before I call the cops. Mia, you know yo' little ass supposed to stay in the car. I'ma beat yo'—"

Mia flinched and reached for Damien. But he moved so quickly that I was barely aware of it. One minute he was giving me soft-voiced instructions, the next he had the woman backed against his car, his hand around her throat, his glare stabbing into her. Her eyes were wide and scared as she grabbed his forearm.

"The only things keeping you alive are the facts that I try not to fuck bitches up and yo' babies right here. You left them in a wide-open car in this fucking heat, hungry and dirty.

Now, you wanna act worried? You lucky a real pervert didn't get them. I suggest you shut yo' trash ass up before I let Stella have some fun," he hissed at her.

Cracking her knuckles, Stella smiled at her boss's words. All these muhfuckas were blood thirsty.

"I-I-I'm sorry, mister, but I had to work—" the woman started backtracking.

He smirked at her. "Work, huh?"

"Damien, let her go. Please—" I started softly.

"Get in the car and do what I said, Dream."

His response was low, but his tone let me know he wasn't beat for my arguing. I was worried about him, though.

"There are cameras and witnesses. Let's just—"

"It'll be taken care of. You—"

He stopped as a white Cadillac CT4 pulled behind his car. Juan and Stella were instantly on alert as a stocky, middle-aged man stepped out, a greasy smile on his face. Letting go of the woman's neck, Damien flexed his fingers and then balled them up.

"Is there a problem here?" the man asked.

The woman flew to his side, linking her arm through his.

"Yes, daddy. This nigga all in my business cuz Mia and Hailey had to wait in the car while I handled my last customer."

That shit pissed me off. I was speaking before I realized it. "Wait, bitch. You mean to tell me you were off somewhere on your back while your babies were suffering in that car?" I asked, my voice incredulous.

For the first time in my life, I wished I had Dayana's fighting skills, or at least her bat, because this bitch needed her ass whooped. She grilled me and opened her mouth, but the man held up a hand.

"I'm not sure how that's your business, little lady," he said, eying me up and down as he licked his thin lips.

My skin crawled. I looked up at Damien. His eyes were

the glacial green I knew meant trouble. I touched his arm, but it did no good.

"Don't talk to her. Don't even look at her," he said, his voice cold, expressionless.

"But you can talk to and touch my property?" the man chuckled. "Nigga, please. Give us the girls so we can go. Amira and I have more business to handle tonight." He turned to her, like he was dismissing us. "You gon' have to drive yo' car cuz they too dirty to get in mine."

Juan looked at Damien. "Demon, you want me to—"

Damien shook his head just as the other man's head snapped up. The fear on his face was proof that he recognized Damien's street name. He stammered an apology, tried to gobble some explanation like a desperate turkey. but I knew there was no use.

"Just call Li Jun. No footage from the store or the surrounding area," he instructed.

Juan nodded, immediately grabbing for his phone. *Oh, shit*, I thought. This was going to get bad. I held Hailey tighter. Stella looked at me.

"Ms. Castle, we should probably go," she said.

"You should definitely go. This bitch not getting these babies back until she's sober. Stella, take them," he said.

I wanted to argue. I didn't wanna leave him. But suddenly, I realized the look in his eyes and that this situation triggered him, probably more deeply than I understood. A young mother, neglecting her two children to sell her body to please some man… and the man had disrespected him. Damien was further gone than I could ever imagine. I wanted to pull him to me and just hug him, but I felt the soft pressure of Stella's hand against my lower back. The man from the Cadillac was going to die tonight and there was nothing I could do to stop it.

Hailey fell asleep in my arms on the way to Ms. Hazel's house and, surprisingly, Mia curled into my side. I understood why Damien felt so protective. I would rather have died than let them go with that Amira chick. I wasn't expecting for Eve to answer the door. She took one look at me and said, "Mama, Demon sent you something!" I rolled my eyes.

Ms. Hazel was there almost immediately, fussing at Eve for calling him Demon and clucking and cooing after the babies. She was amazing. She had clothes in so many sizes and several boxes of diapers. I bathed the girls and washed their hair. Eve detangled and combed it so gently that they went to sleep.

"Gon' home, baby. He gon' need you soon. Tell him I got this till he's ready, and then he got something to tell Ms. Hazel," the older woman said, brown eyes twinkling.

I was fresh out of the shower when he made it in, and I was so glad that Kam was in bed. There was very little of him that wasn't splashed in blood; the fact that he'd come home without cleaning up said a lot. He was eerily silent and mostly still. I had watched him shoot two men in the head and not blink. But tonight was different. I swallowed my horror and walked closer to him. I didn't know what to do, how to handle someone who was so obviously in a place not here. But I loved him, and I knew he needed to feel that. So, I held out a hand. It took a minute, but he finally slid his into it. Wordlessly, I led him into the bathroom. While he stood mute in the middle of the marble floor, I started the shower. I left the water to warm while I attended to him. I lifted the bottom of his shirts, pulling him towards me and down so that I could tug them over his head. After removing his socks and shoes, I quickly got rid of his jeans and boxer briefs. My own sleep shirt was next, before I led him into the cavernous shower.

He was still so silent that it scared me, but I figured he needed his time. So, I washed him. Beginning with his beautiful face, I lathered and loved his amazing body. And his hands, his beautiful, graceful, long-fingered hands were bloody and swollen. I washed them gently before kissing every digit as I stared into his distant eyes. I took another quick shower before leading him out onto the thick rug and warmed floor. He was still silent as I dried him, still silent as I lotioned him, still silent as I pulled him into the bedroom.

The silence was too much for me, so I began to talk. Not about anything in particular, just random shit about my life. I dressed him in basketball shorts and a wife beater as I discussed my frustration with my job. I pulled one of his wife beaters over my head as I talked about Dayana's crazy ass. I led him to the bed as I reassured him what good hands Hailey and Mia were in. I talked about Kam as I climbed into bed and pressed my back against the headboard. I revealed how I wanted him to take me for dinner at a trendy, new steakhouse as I spread my thighs and invited him to sit between them, his back against my chest. And then I rubbed his temples, stroked his scalp, and ran my mouth as I tried to get him to unwind. Long minutes later, I slowly felt his body relax into mine. Still, I held him, my hand caressing every inch of him I could reach and my mouth whispering how much I loved him. My heart swelled for him as I felt the patchwork of faint scars and dents hidden by the ink of his tattoos. Finally, I murmured to him the words he always said to me.

"Go to sleep, Damien... *baby.*"

He went to sleep.

CHAPTER 76

Demon

(*WEDNESDAY*, *June 30*)

Waking up between Dream's thighs was everything. I couldn't resist rubbing them before moving so I could adjust our positions to something more comfortable for her. I stared at her as we lay side by side and she slept peacefully. Shorty was perfect; thick, brown, beautiful, brilliant and, for some reason, she rocked with a nigga, even knowing how fucked up I was.

I still wasn't sure I believed love existed. I had very little experience with it, receiving or giving. But whatever it was that Dream talked about, that made her soft and open to me, that made her treat me like I was the center of her world… I wanted more of that.

Part of me knew it was selfish. I couldn't give that shit back to her, but I wasn't so much of an asshole that I didn't try to give her something. I couldn't handle her heart, so I took care of her body, pleasing it, protecting it, providing for it. And I could give her things, whatever her high mainte- nance ass wanted, and some things she didn't know that she did. She could have the world if she kept caring for me the way she had a few hours ago. Starting now.

"Dream," I called her name softly.

She let out a little moan but didn't move.

"Wake up, shorty."

Another, longer moan and then she cracked open one eye.

"Whyyyy are you on your bullshit this morning? I swear you light skins be doing the most. First, staring at me while I'm asleep, creep ass. Now, you talking about wake up? Hell no, Damien. Take yo' yella ass to sleep," she snapped before closing that eye.

"Keep talking yo' shit, shorty. I'ma fuck you up," I warned her as she stretched and moved closer to me, shivering.

She and Kam whined so much that I turned the AC all the way up to sixty-two. She still claimed she was cold and stayed under me. A nigga couldn't complain. I lowered my mouth to her ear, nuzzling it before I spoke.

"What if I wanna feel you?" I asked.

Eyes still closed, she slapped around for my arm until she found it. She pulled it to her body, placing my hand on the curve of her hip.

"There. Now you feeling me. Go to sleep," she mumbled.

I couldn't help chuckling at her smart-mouthed ass. Shorty said I wasn't getting back between them thighs, and I could respect that. That wasn't why I wanted her up, anyway.

"Dream—"

"Damien!" she whined, burying her face in my chest.

I slid my hand underneath her ugly ass bonnet, threading my fingers through her hair so I could hold her close to me.

"You told Dayana—"

"Your bestie?" she teased.

I ignored her. "You said you needed something to wear to Dante and Sherrilyn's all white party on the Fourth of July. That's Sunday. It's already Wednesday. You need to grab that shit soon, huh?"

She sighed and I felt her pull back a little bit to look up at me.

"Damien, are we really up at dawn to talk about my fashion choices?" she popped.

"I need to know when and where you going for the detail so I can give you five or ten dollars on that shit."

She laughed, a sound that I liked way too much.

"Damien, I have my own money. Take your ass to sleep. You got a busy day," she murmured.

"I do?" I waited to see what she thought my day looked like.

"Mm-hmm. You gotta check on Kam. He's sad cuz Melanie looks... I-I don't know if her treatment is working."

I frowned. "Hopefully, it's n—"

She pushed my chest. "Damien, don't. I'm serious. You also gotta check on Mia and Hailey. Mia was looking for you last night."

I shrugged. "Little mama don't need to get attached."

She sucked her teeth. "Yeah, okay. And don't forget we have a date tonight!"

She sounded excited, but I still wasn't comfortable with the idea of a date, despite the fact that she had dragged me on several at this point.

"Plus, you probably have gangsta shit to do, too," she added.

I smiled at her bourgeois ass. "Is that what I do, shorty? Gangsta shit?"

"Hell yeah. But back to the other subject. You don't have to buy me things all the time, Damien. That's not all I want."

I tensed as this conversation took a turn that I wasn't comfortable with. I wasn't prepared, couldn't give her every-thing she wanted. Suddenly, she stroked my arm. I looked down to find her cocoa eyes staring up at me.

"Chill. Right now, all I want is for you to lie with me. I'm going in late," she said softly.

"Just lay with you, huh?" I asked as I pulled her closer.

She snuggled into me. "Hmm... and maybe rub my booty."

I chuckled lowly. "That jiggly thing?"

She smacked her lips. "You like it."

I couldn't argue. I did. I liked it like I liked everything about her.

This girl, I thought as I buried my face against that stupid bonnet and palmed the luscious curve of her ass. *This fucking girl.*

———

Dream didn't lie about my day. I left her warm and drowsy in my bed, still lying like she was going to work, even though it was around eleven. I found Kam downstairs in the game room that I never used, playing his new PS5. I just stared at him until he looked up and mugged me.

"Nigga, what's wrong with you?" he snapped.

"Go eat," I ordered before walking away.

That nigga was okay. I needed to find him a private art tutor or some shit, though. He wasn't gon' be on that video game all day, every day.

I let Stella in to keep a close eye on Dream and the kid. Juan and Melo were outside on duty with a couple of other hittas. With the detail settled, I was ready to go. I decided to drive my truck today. I was going to have to have the Jag detailed after having the girls in it. I had a call from Li Jun that I returned as I pulled away from my house.

"The wire for your friend came from a company called Distinctive Dynamic Designs Architecture. Haven't found much on them—a few jobs, but the company seems to be mostly a shell. Give me a couple of days to link it to something," he said abruptly.

"Let me know," I ordered before disconnecting.

I had barely made it through Ms. Hazel's front door before

Mia was attached to my leg, demanding, "Where you been, Damie?" Hailey grinned at me from her perch on Bryson's lap. They looked so much better today. Stella had had food, clothes, toys, and car seats delivered before she found a sixty-day rehab for Amira. A nice donation meant they were willing to accept her tomorrow. She was currently at one of Dante's safe houses, throwing a fit. My next stop was there to make sure she understood that if she didn't get and stay clean, Mia and Hailey would no longer be hers. I had no idea where I'd place them, but I'd never let them live the horrors KiKi and I did for as long as we did.

I explained all that to Ms. Hazel as Mia sat in my lap, occasionally calling my name so I'd pay attention to something on her tablet. The only thing the older woman objected to was the twenty thousand I slid her. I shook my head as she fussed about it being too much. Finally, she accepted it, then looked at me with a sly smile.

"The pretty thing who brought them..." she said coyly.

I was very interested in Mia's tablet for a minute before meeting the sweet brown eyes of the woman who had been more of a mother to me than my own. She was waiting hopefully, and I could never disrespect her.

"Dream," I said slowly.

"Yes," she chirped. "She your girlfriend?"

"She's my... mine."

It was lame as fuck, but I didn't know what else to say. I guess it was enough, though. She reached out and squeezed my knee as she squealed a little.

"Damien... baby! I'm so happy for you," she crooned softly.

Thankfully, she let that shit be. I tried to leave a few minutes later but Mia cried so hard that I had to take her and Breshay, Ms. Hazel's granddaughter, to the store and bend a few corners until her little bossy ass dozed off.

Dealing with Amira's ignorant, screaming ass next had a

nigga ready to buss on that bitch. I swear Mia and Hailey were all that stood between her and Hell. They were still young enough to need her, to care about her. She better take this chance and make the most of it.

I didn't feel my temperature thawing until Dream and I had been seated at The Rustic a few hours later, and she was chattering about the menu and asking my opinion. The effect this girl had on me scared me sometimes.

She asked to order for me since I didn't particularly care what we got. Her choices were good, even though she definitely picked shit she liked, too. Dream had started doing this weird shit where she could have her own food, but she still wanted to taste mine. I had heard other niggas talk about it but never experienced it. The only other girl who had ever eaten out of my plate was Kiana. I realized I'd let this girl have my last bite if she wanted it, though.

After dinner, we made our way to the mall that housed the damn paint and sip location she'd chosen for tonight. It was funny to me that this was the shit she wanted to do. She stopped suddenly at the Louis Vuitton storefront.

"I wonder if Mama ordered our new luggage," she murmured.

"You need to go in?"

She shook her head, curls bouncing. "Nah. We don't really have t—"

Her sentence trailed off and her body tensed. I was instantly on alert, ready to give the signal Dante and I used to call up our soldiers. Her eyes were on a couple of niggas who were walking toward us, one of them with a smirk on his face. Even in plainclothes, they had cop written all over them. I slid an arm around her waist as they approached.

"Ms. Castle," the smug ass black dude greeted.

"Detective Poole, Detective Jimenez," she said icily.

Poole's eyes flicked to me. "And I believe this is **the** Demon Montana? I thought you were an urban legend, my man. People whisper your name, but they never really seem to see you."

"I'm not your man and we don't wanna talk. Let's go, shorty," I ordered, grabbing Dream's hand and leading her away.

"This makes it so much more interesting, though. Ms. Castle, maybe we really should meet again," Poole taunted.

"As long as you arrange it through my attorney," she responded, her smile as fake as his.

I walked back over to him, getting in his space, throwing him off balance. He swallowed and took a step back as he looked up at me.

"I told you we didn't wanna talk. That means never. I find out you been pressing her, you gon' find out how real the legend is," I said calmly.

His mouth opened and closed several times before he spoke.

"You threatening a cop?" he finally asked.

I smiled at him. Scary ass niggas loved hiding behind a badge.

As if that would stop me.

"You better pay attention to those whispers. You'd probably know I never make threats, nigga."

Poole stood there, stuck, as fear flashed in his eyes. He took another step back, staring at me warily.

"Nick, we're going to be late," the other guy said suddenly, helping his partner save face.

Poole nodded and shot us one last look before rushing off. I turned back to Dream, looking at her expectantly. She clutched her little purse closer and looked down.

"Dream."

She sighed. "They came by about Isaac right after he... died."

I mugged her. "And you didn't think you should tell me that?"

Shrugging, she kept toying with her purse. "You weren't really approachable then, and they didn't know shit."

A second later, I was up in her beautiful face, scowling. She grabbed my arms, her chocolate eyes pleading with mine.

"Damien, it really wasn't a big deal. My lawyer will take care of—"

"Nah, fuck that. I'll take care of it. Don't fucking talk to them again. Understand?" I growled.

She got an attitude, of course, turning that little button nose up as she stepped back.

"Yes, I understand. I'm far from stupid and you don't have to curse me," she snapped.

I had been letting her make it, not checking her little ass when I should. But not today. Grabbing her hand, I dropped my lips to her ear, not giving a fuck that people were having to walk around us.

"I suggest you chill with that attitude shit you got going before I take you home and fuck it up out of you. So, unless you want that little pussy aching and the imprint of the head-board on yo' forehead, fix yo' pretty face," I whispered, before pulling back to grill her.

"Damien!" she gasped.

Shorty was acting all proper, but I could tell her breathing picked up and she was chewing that bottom lip. Panties were probably soaking wet. That thought had my dick instantly hard. This little "date" was about to be over early.

"You think I'm pretty?" she said suddenly, squeezing my hand.

I twisted my lips as I looked down at her. "You know you're pretty, Dream."

She looked at me shyly.

"But you never say stuff like that."

I pulled on one of her curls before tracing her chin with my thumb.

"You need me to gas you up like every other nigga in the city?" I teased.

She didn't like that. Her gaze dropped and she was quiet for a minute.

"It's just nice to hear it for once from you, Damien," she said softly.

Her words and tone made me feel some type of way. I stroked the back of her hand.

"You're not just pretty, Dream. You're beautiful. Inside and out, baby," I told her sincerely.

She tried to hide her smile as a blush rose on her cheeks.

"Really?" she pressed.

"Hell yeah. You beautiful and fine as fuck with them titties and ass. So fine that if you don't start walking to this damn place right now, ain't gon' be no paint and sip tonight. It's just gon' be suck and fuck."

Dream's jaw dropped, but she recovered quickly.

"Damien!" she hissed, scandalized.

Then, a sneaky smile curved her full lips.

"Why can't it be both?"

CHAPTER 77
Dream

AT FIRST, I thought paint and sip with Damien was going to be a complete bust. He talked shit from the moment we sat down and were served our wine.

"This sweet ass, cheap ass shit must be for lady's night," he muttered.

I rolled my eyes. "Now, who's being bourgeois? This is not cheap; it's just not a thousand dollars a bottle!"

Then our little canvases were passed out with the outline of a woman with a huge Afro, a little smile, and a glass of wine of her own. He frowned.

"Who drew this? Mia? These lines—"

"Chill, Picasso!" I whispered, smacking his arm as I looked at the scowling instructor. She walked closer to us.

"Is there a problem, sir?" she asked.

Damien looked at her, green eyes frozen. Her eyes widened and her hand went to her throat, literally clutching her pearls.

"No problem," I said hastily. "He just—"

"I ain't painting this shit. Give me a blank canvas," he demanded.

She nodded and scurried to do it. I shook my head at him. He held up both hands like, *What?*

"These the only brushes you got?" he asked when she exchanged his canvases.

"Y-yes, sir," she whispered.

"Hmph," he grunted, feeling the bristles as he stared at them.

The instructor almost ran away.

"Niggas take one painting class in high school and think they da Vinci," I popped.

"Oh, yeah?" he smirked. "That's what it is?"

I thought he was going to die when he saw the paints. He shook his head so quickly and so hard.

"I'm not using this dollar store shit. Ay, shorty!" he called for the instructor. "Just bring me some pencils."

Five minutes later, his ass was finally quiet as he stared at the canvas. Sighing, I started painting my own. After a while, I spoke.

"We're supposed to talk as we work. Get to know each other better," I said.

"I done had my face in yo' pussy and my dick in yo' stomach. How much better you want me to know you?"

I curled my top lip as I dipped my brush in the brown that I had mixed. "Nasty ass. That's not what I mean. Like… what's my favorite color?" I challenged.

"Yellow."

"Where I go to school?"

"B.S. from Yale. About to complete your MBA from Rice."

I paused and side-eyed him.

"Don't ask. You know I already know your favorite food," he said.

All right. Let me make this a little harder.

"My favorite musician?" I asked.

"Beyoncé or Summer Walker. You be walking around singing them when yo' ass call yourself mad at me."

I couldn't stop the giggle that escaped me. Nigga was telling the truth. I flipped him off.

"Definitely," he said.

I sucked my teeth. "Perv. My sorority?"

"I know that, too, Ms. Crimson and Cream. Now… what you know about me?"

"Hmm," I mused, tapping my chin. "Your favorite colors are blue and black. You don't really have a favorite food, but you cook sweet potatoes a lot. You rude as hell, but you like kids. You the only gangsta ass nigga I know who loves that shea butter and vanilla Dove—"

"First of all, you gon' stop calling me a gangsta. Second, how many gangstas you know to know their soap preferences? Third, gangstas got sensitive skin, too," he defended.

I laughed again, turning to look at him fully. Before I could say anything else, I caught sight of his canvas and stopped in amazement. I knew Kam could draw and apparently it ran in the family. I forgot all about my sad little painting as I watched a scene take shape beneath his pencils.

Long minutes later, I realized more people were watching him. Right before the session was over, he stopped. It was unfinished, but what was there was absolutely breathtaking. Rendered in pencil, in a mix of soft and bold strokes and a perfect blend of colors, was a view of the lake from the front of the lake house. The gazebo was there and the Black Willow and huge Cypress trees. And off to the side, looking at it all, was a woman. He had sketched her from the back, so all you could see was a shock of brown and blonde curls and a thick, curvy body. My eyes flew to him.

"Is that m—"

"Dream."

He gave me a silencing look. I knew the answer, though. I bit my lip to keep from smiling as the instructor oohed and ahhed over his drawing. He didn't like the attention, of course. We left so fast, I forgot my half-done painting.

We had to go to Dante's estate to pick up Kam. As always, I was awed by the sheer decadence of the place. The landscaping alone had me mesmerized.

Just as we pulled to the top of the circular driveway, Dante surprised us by calling. He said both of us should get out because he needed to run something by Damien. Damien cussed his ass out, but we did what he suggested. Surprisingly, Dante opened the door himself.

"The fuck you want, Dante?" Damien greeted.

Dante smiled. "You always show so much love, Demon. Shit just warms my heart," he said, touching his chest. "I'm trying to return the favor, keep you and everyone that matters to you safe from that bitch ass Keith. Come into the living room."

Damien grilled him, but we followed him into the expansive living room. Sherrilyn was there with two other women. One of them stood immediately, her eyes glued to Damien. She was fucking gorgeous. There was no other way to put it. Light, honey-colored skin and eyes, a mass of thick, natural red-brown curls, and a slim-thick body that looked flawless in her blue and white Dolce and Gabbana sundress. Jealousy spiked through me, but I kept my face composed.

"Damien," she whispered.

Suddenly, she ran across the room, not stopping until her body crashed into his. He caught her, steadied her, then dropped his arms. She linked her arms around him tightly and cried against his chest. Damien didn't move, didn't speak, didn't even seem to breathe. After a minute, he reached behind himself and gently pulled her arms apart. Wordlessly, he turned and walked out. Stunned and feeling awkward, I stood there for a minute, strangely sympathetic toward the crying woman. Unsure what to do, I finally followed him outside.

He stood motionless by one of the front pillars. I crossed my arms over my body as I watched him. The fact that this woman affected him so much played on my insecurities, reminded me that this wasn't a love match, just a business deal. I shook my head to clear it, then looked at him again.

"Is she your ex?" I asked, although the answer was obvious to me.

But he was back to the Damien I had first met, the Damien I hadn't seen in weeks. He didn't say anything in response to my question. I tried again.

"It really looks like you should talk to her. She was crying hard."

Still, no reply.

"I feel like my presence might be making this awkward. I'm gon' call an Uber and go—"

Finally, he looked at me, his beautiful face marred by the meanest mug.

"Make me fuck you up, Dream."

I glared at him. "You out here acting—"

I stopped as the door suddenly opened and that pretty *heffa* stepped out.

"I'm... I'm sorry, Damien. I understand you have a new life..." Her eyes flitted to me before returning to his hard expression. "And I don't mean to intrude. But your brother Dante explained to me what was going on and offered me the chance to- to see you. I met Kam. He looks like you and it made me miss you more. But if you don't want..." she swallowed hard, tears brimming in her honey eyes. "Anyway, I won't bother y—"

She didn't get the chance to finish before he grabbed her. He hugged her so tight, I worried she'd suffocate. She burst into tears again.

"I missed you, Damie," she sobbed.

"I missed you, too, KiKi," he whispered, kissing her hair and forehead.

Oh, my God! Kiana... My heart swelled and I had to fight back my own tears. A decade and a half, he'd been missing her and now she was here. I was so happy for him, but this was their moment. I took a step toward the door, but he grabbed my hand. I looked up in surprise.

"Stay," he said, his eyes unexpectedly wet.

I squeezed his hand.

I stayed.

———

We had finally made it home and I was glad. I'd thought I was going to have to watch Damien catch another body when he confronted Dante about Kiana.

"How long you been knowing where she was?" he asked.

His body was tense, his hands clenching and unclenching like he wanted to beat the hell out of his brother. Unbothered, Dante held up both hands.

"Just a few days. I wanted to reach out to her and get her here safely. You careful with a lot of shit, Demon, but for her, you would've steamrolled over everything and maybe led Keith to them. And I done told you before, nigga. You not about to beat my ass in my own house. Rest yo' fuckin' nerves," he said calmly.

Damien's eyes narrowed.

"You keep fuckin' with me, Dante. I—"

"I'm yo' big brother. I'm supposed to fuck with you. That and help keep you and what you care about safe. I'ma continue to do both, and I don't give a damn how bad you wanna box my ass."

Dante shrugged and sat on the love seat beside his wife. He was open about caring for his brother. Damien would probably never admit he cared back, but the fact that he wasn't drenched in Dante's blood was a sign that he did.

"How you find her? Li Jun?" Damien asked.

A shadow crossed Dante's face. His little smile disappeared, and he looked uncomfortable. Still, he met Damien's eyes.

"Apparently, Pop always knew where she was. My grandmother overheard Sherrilyn and I talking about finding her and told me.

Melanie gave Kiana to her sister Melody when you left. Pop found out a year or so later and went to her. Melody's husband had agreed they could keep Kiana as long as Melanie's lifestyle and Pop's was kept away from them. Pop wanted to take her, bring her to you, but she had settled in and was happy. He let her be, but kept an eye on her," Dante explained.

"So, because a pussy ass nigga—"

"Uh-uh, cousin. What you not gon' do is insult my daddy. He was doing what he thought was best and he's taken very good care of Kiana!" *the other woman spoke for the first time.*

Damien turned to sneer at her.

"The fuck is this b—"

"Damie!" *Kiana snapped as the woman stood and glared at him.* "This is our first cousin, Topaz."

She was an extra-curvy beauty who seemed fearless. I bit back a smile.

Damien insisted Kiana came home with us. He looked at Topaz and growled, "Bring yo' ass on, I guess."

And now he and a very excited Kam were helping them settle into guest rooms as I sat in one of the plush chairs in his bedroom. I felt so out of place, like I was in the way of Damien's family and their unexpected reunion. I needed to go, give them space.

I would just go crash with Mama and Grandpapa, who were staying at one of his houses right outside the city. Mama refused to stay with Daddy because of how he was treating Dayana. I didn't have anything there, so I grabbed my duffel bag and threw a few things in it. I picked up my key fob, backpack, and briefcase and got ready to go find him. Before I could make it to the door, he walked in. He didn't say anything as his eyes traveled over me and all my stuff. I fidgeted with the strap on my bag under his cool gaze.

"H-how are your sister and cousin?" I asked.

"Fine," he answered, his voice flat.

"I was thinking… I should go—"

"Oh, yeah?" His voice was low as he walked up on me. "That's what you were thinking?"

Swallowing, I nodded like a bobble-head. He grabbed my briefcase and dropped it.

"You know what I was thinking?"

"Uh-uh," I whispered as he slid the duffel bag off my arm and let it fall.

"Shiiii, a nigga was thinking, you been fucking with me all evening."

I clutched my backpack as he tugged on it. Of course, my strength was no match for his. He took it easily and it, too, landed on the polished wood.

"I really haven't..."

He took a step closer, and I stepped back. We repeated that little dance until the back of my legs hit the bed. I lifted my hands, but he gently slapped those down before picking me up and tossing me on the bed. I let out a soft scream as I bounced on the huge mattress.

"Now, Damien, let's be reasonable—" I began as he climbed over me.

"Fuck reasonable," he growled, flipping me over onto my stomach. "I told you what was gon' happen if you kept tryin' me."

Yes, he had, and my body was reacting, nipples hardening, pussy gushing at the memory of his erotic threat. *Okay, bitch, put up a little fight,* I told myself, biting back a smile.

"I mean, is this really the best way to handle our disagreements?" I asked as he pushed the skirt of my little forest green dress up my hips and over my ass.

No answer.

"Damien, I haven't been to work in a day and a half. I have to go tomorrow!"

"I'm not stopping you," he said.

The sound of his zipper sliding down almost made me cum.

"I can't go with a headboard imprint on my forehead," I whined, feeling my panties being pushed over.

"You better try bangs," he suggested.

I couldn't help it; I giggled. Until he pushed into me, bottoming out with one powerful thrust. I moaned as he began a savage rhythm.

Okay, bangs. I can do bangs.

CHAPTER 78

Demon

(*THURSDAY, July 1*)

Karma couldn't be real. I'd spent my fucked-up life brutally taking others', reaping the benefits of an illegal empire that ruthlessly crushed people. I always expected to reap what I sowed violently. Instead, fate or God or the universe—whatever the hell was real—had given me back the sister I valued more than my own life, a kid that was growing on me, and... Dream.

Seeing KiKi in Dante's living room had been surreal, a gift I didn't deserve but that I was so fucking grateful for. Dante had set her and Topaz up in their own suite, but I needed her under my roof, under my protection. I was even willing to put up with Topaz's bossy ass to have that. Last night had gone a long way toward fixing my fucked-up heart...

KiKi had loved on Kam for a while when we got home, and he put on his best show for her. Later, she laughed and said, "He bad, ain't he?"

"As fuck," I told her, sitting on her bed where she insisted I stay and talk to her until her eyes couldn't stay open.

"I looked for you for a long time," I told her softly as she lay

with her head in my lap, like she had when she was little. "*I guess Dixon and your uncle blocked me.*"

"*It's okay. I wanted to come to you when I turned eighteen. Uncle Jerome told me you were in prison with a life sentence. I still wanted to visit you, but he threw a fit. I was so naïve. I love him, have always trusted him. I never thought he'd lie to me, plus, Googling your name brought up nothing.*"

"*One of the benefits of money.*"

"*But I thought about you all the time. I missed you. I love you so much, Damie,*" *she said, tears in her voice.*

I swallowed hard. "*Same.*"

"You okay?" KiKi's voice broke me out of my thoughts.

"Yeah."

We had just come from lunch and were on our way to the hospital. I didn't understand it, but KiKi wanted to see Melanie. "Closure," she said. Her dying would be enough closure for me.

The drive to the hospital was mostly quiet. I could feel KiKi's nerves, and her mind had definitely been elsewhere. Topaz was talking softly to Kam. The kid was upset and ignoring me because I had tried to talk KiKi out of this shit. I wasn't trying to piss the little nigga off, but I didn't fuck with Melanie like that. I shook my head. This was some more of that Dream shit. I never gave a fuck about pissing someone off and suddenly, I was worried about this kid. We parked in the garage closest to the hospital and made our way in, still quiet. Stella was behind us, an extra gun and set of eyes, just in case. I followed them to Melanie's room, but I didn't go in. Kam looked at me expectantly, like he was hoping I'd change my mind.

"Don't play with me, little nigga," I said.

He rolled his eyes before walking in. KiKi was breathing hard as fuck, her eyes watery. Topaz grabbed and squeezed her hand. I walked up to her and pressed my lips against her forehead.

"You don't have to do this," I whispered.

"Yes, I do," she said.

She laid her head against my chest for a minute, sighed, and then walked slowly into the room. No way was I leaving them in there. I propped one of my feet against the wall and crossed my arms over my chest to wait.

My mind wandered to that shit Dream had done last night. Shorty didn't even realize how close she had come to getting some nigga iced. It fucked with my brain enough when she slid down my body and handled my dick like she was suddenly a blow job pro. I almost pulled all that damn hair out of her head when she introduced my mans to her tonsils. Then she climbed her thick ass back in the middle of my bed and bent over in the perfect arch. I was looking forward to banging that pussy out again as I worked my way in. But shorty did some kind of move, a fucking squeeze and snap or some shit and before I knew it, I was shooting off like a teenager. I may have won the first round, but she definitely KOed me in the second. I don't even think I made it two minutes. All I could do was roll over on my back, look at the ceiling, and ponder the mysteries of the universe as she cuddled up to me, laughing.

"My lessons paying off," she teased.

That shit snapped me back to reality real quick.

"What lessons?" I demanded.

She waved her hand dismissively. I narrowed my eyes. Reaching out, I grabbed her cheek, making her face me.

"I'm not playing with you, Dream. What lessons?"

I waited for her to tell me she had been practicing with some other nigga. I would kill his bitch ass in front of her, then fuck her in his blood until she remembered that this pussy and this mouth were mine exclusively. She slapped at my hand.

"Boy, gon'" she popped off.

I climbed on top of her, pulling both of her arms above her head

and holding her wrists with one of my hands. Settling between her
warm thighs, I glared down at her.

"Dream."

She sighed and rolled her eyes. "Parker, Damien. Damn! She
been giving me tips. Who else I been fucking? I'm always stuck up
under your ass!"

I smiled.

"You a lie. Sometimes, you on top."

"Demon."

Kam's voice brought me out of my reverie. I looked at him
as he stood in the doorway of Melanie's hospital room.
Raising an eyebrow, I waited for what he had to say.

"Mama wants to see you—"

If he weren't a kid, I would have laid that nigga out.

"Don't ever come at me with no bullshit like that."

"Demon—"

My phone rang, saving his little ass. I answered as soon as
I saw Smoke's number.

"Yeah?"

"If you not busy, you might want to get down here to
Methodist's emergency room."

I started to ask him what was going on, but fuck it. If he
was calling me, I obviously needed to be there.

"Already in the Medical Center. See you in a minute."

Even with Stella there, I made KiKi and Kam leave their
egg donor. The little nigga talked shit until I flashed my gun.
KiKi gasped and smacked my arm, but he was getting too
comfortable. I had to remind him how shit worked.

Smoke was waiting for me outside the waiting room. We
shook it up before I asked what was going on. He sighed.

"It's the Castles."

My eyes drilled into his. Dream had gone to work this
morning with a detail, but maybe some shit popped off.
"Where is Dream?"

Smoke rubbed a hand over his face. "She's not doing good, Demon."

He said some more words, but I didn't hear them. I was too consumed by the chill spreading through my body as I wondered what he meant by saying Dream wasn't good. I didn't wait for an explanation as I charged into the waiting room, ready to approach the admissions desk and find out where she was. Two steps away from the desk, I saw her. She stood huddled against Dayana. They were holding hands and their foreheads were pressed together as Crystal and DeAngelo whispered to each other. I walked up to Dream and silently turned her around. Tilting her chin up, I frowned as I saw the tears streaking down her face.

"What?" I asked tightly.

"Grandpapa," she sobbed.

"Sit down before you fall down," I told her.

I knew I sounded cold. Her tears fucked with me, though, and she really was shaking hard enough to fall. They all took seats next to each other, Dream and Dayana still holding hands.

"Demon, I called—"

My head swung toward Juan's voice. I hadn't even realized he was here. I spotted Melo at the back of the room, his eyes constantly moving. I held up a hand at Juan. I'd figure out the communication issue later. Right now, I needed to keep an eye on Dream.

Kam sat beside her, throwing one of his long, skinny arms around her shoulders. Smoke stood in front of Dayana, pulled her out of the chair, and sat down before easing her onto his lap.

I grabbed a chair near the window, next to KiKi and Topaz. I wondered what happened to Lucien, but what was important right now was that the old man rebounded. We sat in silence for about thirty minutes. Dream rocked back-and-forth in her chair until she sprang up and went to the admissions window. She had a quick, whispered conversation with the attendant before coming back to her seat and rocking even harder. Something inside me twisted as I saw she was still crying. A few minutes later, she blurted, "It's taking too long!"

"What did she say?" asked Dayana.

"She said we just have to wait. She wouldn't call back there because she said they'd let us know when they had news."

Tension gripped me. That bitch had life fucked up. Standing, I walked slowly to the admissions desk. The clerk was on her cell phone, but she set it down as she looked up at me.

"May I help you?" she asked dryly.

I grilled her ignorant ass as I picked up her phone. She sputtered and grabbed for it, but I ignored her. Some goofy ass nigga looked at me from the screen. He had the nerve to sneer at me. I laughed for real that time before setting the phone back down.

"The family of Lucien Dumont needs an update on his condition."

I tried to say the shit calmly. She rolled her eyes.

"I just told that lady that we don't call back there. They'll call us or come out when they have news for the family. Now, if you just have a seat—"

She stopped as my eyes pierced hers. Gulping, she looked at me and waited.

"I'm guessing that's yo' nigga on that phone. Now, either you or I are about to go on a fact-finding mission. You can *find* someone to come out here and talk to Lucien Dumont's family or I'ma find your little boyfriend and crack his skull."

I picked up her phone again before she could respond.

"Do you understand me?"

She nodded quickly and reached for the desk phone. I made my way back to my seat, feeling Dream's eyes on me.

"What yo' crazy ass do?" Smoke asked, shaking his head.

I just shrugged and sat down. I wasn't surprised when someone opened a door to the back and stepped out to call for Dream's family. They stood, and Dayana winced at how hard her sister squeezed her hand. Dream walked, but then she looked back at me. Wordlessly, I moved, following her toward the doorway. I stood behind her and she took a step back and leaned against me. I could feel how hard she was breathing. I bent down, placing my lips against her ear.

"Calm down."

She nodded, and I felt her attempt to slow her breathing.

"Are you my grandfather's doctor?" DeAngelo asked the man standing in the door.

This muhfucka had the nerve to look bored.

"Yes, I'm Dr. Harris Palmer. Mr. Dumont is fine. He needs to lay off the Cuban cigars and the butter-basted ribeyes he told me he likes, but other than that, his heart looks good. He's resting while waiting for a room. I want to keep him overnight for observation. Someone would have come to tell you. You have to understand that this is the emergency room, and we are busy," he said nastily.

Smoke and I looked at each other in disbelief. Smoke chuckled before addressing this clown. I was glad to let him do the talking. Shit, I was thinking about how I was gon' fuck this nigga up.

"So, you been knowing Lucien was okay and nobody told us? My girl out here about to worry herself to death and you got the nerve to be bitching at somebody? Seems to me you wanna end up in your own ER."

The doctor's mouth fell open and his eyes got wide. He started making some kind of stuttering noise, as his face grew red.

"I didn't mean to sound like I was scolding the family. We have nineteen people waiting for beds and even more—" he backtracked.

"Why the fuck you think we care? Apologize," Smoke

demanded.

I smirked as the doctor stammered out an apology. His eyes darted back to Smoke like he was asking was that good enough. Smoke nodded once.

Dream had turned sideways so that her shoulder and hip rested against me. She damn near sagged with relief.

"You wanna see him?" I asked.

She looked up at me, her brown eyes still teary, and nodded.

"We going with you," I told Palmer.

He started shaking his head instantly. "It's too busy. There's not enough room for—"

I sighed. Niggas was on bullshit today and I didn't want to hear Dream's mouth if I caught another body. I looked at Palmer and he squirmed.

"I'm just gon' be honest with you. I was gon' beat yo' ass for the way you talked to her, but I was gon' do my best to let you live through it. But if I'm not looking at Lucien in two minutes—"

"Just follow me," Palmer said hurriedly as he wiped sweat from his forehead.

I instructed Stella, Juan, and Melo to watch my family before Dream and I fell in step behind Palmer. We were halfway down the first hallway when she suddenly stopped in front of me and threw her arms around me.

Burying her face in my chest, she mumbled, "Thank you."

"Whatever. I was just tired of you sitting up there rocking like Rain Man," I smirked.

"Damien!" she whined, smacking my shoulder.

Lucien's old gangsta ass was cool, sitting up in the bed, flirting with his nurse. He took one look at Dream's puffy eyes and started frowning.

"Why you been doing all that damn crying, little girl? Bet y'all done called yo' mama and got her worked up on her little vacation. You think your grandpapa is that weak, *sha baby?*" he fussed.

She started sniffing again, big, chocolate eyes filling up.

"They picked you up in an ambulance and no one would tell us anything. So, yes, old man, I was worried. You scared me, Grandpapa," she said, wiping her cheeks with the back of her hand.

His expression softened immediately.

"Let this thing down," he ordered me, shaking the bed rail.

I stepped forward and lowered it quickly.

"Come here, Grandpapa's *bébé.*"

He beckoned to Dream, then patted the bed. She squeezed in beside him, curling into his side. He wrapped an arm around her shoulder and talked to her softly until her crying stopped. I was just about to tell her we should dip, give Dayana a chance to see him—fuck DeAngelo—when my phone buzzed.

Kid: ??? '

Me: What, Kam?

I had barely hit send on my message when a couple of pictures he forwarded came through. My blood froze. I called Juan. He answered immediately.

"Yeah?"

"I need you and Stella to come back here, ASAP."

I hung up and was already dialing Smoke. Dream rose slightly.

"Damien, what's wrong?"

Her grandfather squeezed her gently.

"Let the man handle his business, *bébé,*" he told her.

"What's up?" Smoke greeted me.

"You have people here?"

"Of course. Two in here, two outside. More, if needed. I got your people covered. What's going—"

"Thanks," I cut him off as my crew walked in.

"Dream goes nowhere without y'all. Don't make me make Gabriela and Nikki widows. Smoke's got the waiting room covered.

I didn't wait for a response as I strode out of the room. I knew, deep down, that I was already too late. That didn't stop me from heading upstairs.

The activity inside and outside Melanie's room was no surprise. Neither was the piercing, monotone sound of the heart monitor. Melanie was dead.

I'd known that the moment Kam sent me the pictures of her, looking scared as Keith smiled next to her, his arm resting on her shoulders.

CHAPTER 79
Demon

"SEND them back to the sixth floor," I told Smoke.

"You got that," he said simply, then disconnected.

The frenzy around Melanie's room was mostly gone. They'd worked for almost an hour, with no luck. The official cause of death would be whatever disease had attacked her body, but I knew better.

Keith McKellar had snaked his way into this hospital and killed my... killed Melanie. I needed to put some shit in motion, needed to get out and hunt him like the fucking animal he was. But right now, I needed to let my siblings say their goodbyes.

I looked up at the sound of footsteps. KiKi, Topaz, Kam, and Dream approached, led by Juan and Stella, with Melo and Ammo behind them.

Kam walked up on me, his face twisted.

"Is she... is she—"

He couldn't finish and I didn't know what else to do besides nod. He bent over, hands on his knees as a strangled sound escaped him. Topaz put a hand on his lower back, rubbing softly. He stood abruptly, mugging me again, and I suddenly understood why Dante described my eyes as ice cold.

"The pictures. That's the nigga you were telling me and Dream about?" he demanded.

"Yeah."

"Did he kill her?"

I shrugged. "Maybe."

Suddenly, he pushed me as hard as he could. Juan took a step, but I held up a hand.

"So, my mama is dead because of your bullshit?" he raged, pushing me again.

I blew out a deep breath and reminded myself he was a kid.

"Kameron, I suggest you keep them hands to yourself. I know you feeling a way, but you not gon' keep—"

"Nah, fuck you, Demon. What you gon' do? Kill me, too?" he shouted.

"Kam, suga—" Dream began.

"Fuck this nigga, Dream! He don't give a fuck about nobody, not even his own mama! My mama dead because of him—"

His words detonated something inside me.

"Yo' mama didn't give a fuck about me either. She probably dead because she was a junkie whose body finally gave—"

He swung on me, like I deserved. Still, I caught his fist and squeezed a warning.

"I hate you, you stupid muhfucka! I hate you!" he snarled.

"Good. That's smart," I said tonelessly.

I couldn't let this kid's words fuck with me. A month ago, I didn't even know him. A month from now, I'd be a bad memory to him. He'd definitely choose foster care over me. *Not that I give a fuck*, I thought.

Slowly, I let go of his fist.

He wrapped his arms around his middle and bent over

again, his breath heaving in and out. KiKi moved next to him and started whispering.

"Y'all better go in there and see her before they move her," I said.

Kam's head snapped up again. Tears slipped from his eyes.

"Why don't you care?" he asked, all of his rage from a minute ago drained away.

I would take his anger any day. I couldn't take his pain. I shifted, about to walk away, but he spoke again.

"Demon... why don't you care?"

I wanted to ignore him, but he looked like he was about to break. I didn't fuck with people and their emotions, but even I knew when someone was about to go down and not get up. Kam was bad and talked a lot of shit, but I didn't want that for him. I felt helpless, some shit I wasn't used to. I looked over at Dream, but her emotional ass was crying, too. My eyes went back to the kid. Little nigga looked like he needed a hug. I wasn't no affectionate nigga, but I could remember how it felt when Ms. Hazel hugged me when I was growing up. Against my better judgement, I slowly wrapped my arms around him as his narrow shoulders shook. KiKi walked up and wrapped her arms around both of us.

Kam was hurting and for some reason, the shit hurt me. Between him and Dream, all this new "feeling" shit was about to be too much. It knocked me off my square, made me feel weak. And now, my sister, my first soft spot, was back and I could see, even if I couldn't understand, that she was sad, too. I needed a break from all these emotions, needed to walk away before I exploded. My eyes found Dream's again. The look in their cocoa depths combined with the fact that she mouthed, *I love you*, calmed me. Everything about her calmed me. This had to be what niggas meant when they claimed someone was their peace. I had always thought that shit was weak.

I was wrong.

———

I let Topaz and KiKi deal with the doctors and hospital social worker and all the shit that went with releasing Melanie's body and planning to make arrangements. Li Jun had Kam's phone, even though I was sure Keith was using a burner. He was also tapping into the hospital's video surveillance.

We were back at my house and Dream was upstairs, getting the other women's dinner requests. I was sitting in the living room with Kam as he worked in his sketchbook. Kid was talented. I reminded myself again that I needed to get him a private tutor.

I heard footsteps on the stairs and Dream appeared.

"You know what you wanna eat?" she asked me as she sat on the love seat next to Kam.

I shrugged.

"Whatever you feel like you gon' wanna sample."

She sucked her teeth and turned to Kam.

"What about you, Suga?" she asked softly.

He hunched his shoulders.

"Not hungry," he mumbled.

"But you gon' eat something,"

He looked up long enough to frown at me, but I didn't give a damn. Since he was already aggravated with me, I might as well address the elephant in the room. I cleared my throat, the unfamiliar feeling of being uncertain gripping me.

"Ay, kid. Melanie was your guardian, so you got some choices to make about what you gon' do. I mean, KiKi and I are your older siblings, so one of us could probably get your bad ass, but you might not want us. Like, if you want one of them families with a mama and a daddy, you might wanna try the system. That's on you; that's yo' right. Dante and Sherrilyn would look out, too, if that two-parent thing is what you want. But you might want to stay with blood family. I'on know shit about kids, really, and KiKi a whole teacher out here. I know she wants you and she got to be good with kids, so a nigga understand if you wanna go with her. Really, that's probably the best thing. But yo' ass could always stay here," I said nonchalantly.

He didn't say anything for a minute, just kept drawing. Finally, he spoke.

"Do you want me to stay here?"

I shrugged. "Do you wanna stay here? It's on you."

More sketching. Then, "My stuff already here and I don't like to pack. I could stay, I guess."

He didn't even look up, acted like he didn't give a fuck one way or another. I didn't even realize I had been holding my breath until he spoke.

"That's cool," I said, playing that shit off, too.

Dream's eyes had been busy on her phone, ordering food, no doubt. I knew her nosy ass was listening because she was smiling. I pulled out my phone and sent her a G to cover what everyone wanted.

"Really, Damien?" she said a second later, rolling her eyes.

"What you working on, baby?" she asked Kam.

He handed the pad to her, and she gasped.

"Let me see," I demanded.

She turned it toward me. Shit made me speechless. Little nigga was drawing a picture of a younger Melanie. She was beautiful with her big smile, her green eyes sparkling as her long hair blew in the wind. I knew where he'd seen it. It was a picture she'd kept from her high school graduation night, and he had captured it almost perfectly. I nodded my approval. His bad ass was gon' be something special.

A little smile finally played around his mouth as he took the sketchbook back.

"Let me show you this other one," he said, flipping back, then handing it to Dream.

"Kam! Oh, my God! Damien look!"

She held it up, facing me. He'd drawn her, sitting on the couch, those crazy ass reading glasses on as she stared at her laptop. The detail was the shit— he got everything from the way she chewed her lip to how she always tucked one leg under her. Nigga was good. Better than good.

"It's beautiful," Dream cooed.

"It's a'ight," I fucked with him.

He raised an eyebrow.

"You think you can do better?"

I made an unexpected decision in that moment, one that I felt was justified after the day he had, and the love and trust Dream kept showing.

"I think I can. Come here."

I led them down the hallway and to one of my locked rooms. Opening the door, I flipped on the light and led them in. Complete silence reigned, and I smirked at the idea that I had left these two, who loved to talk their shit, speechless. This room, my "sanctuary," the place where I let everything go, was my studio.

"Damien," Dream whispered as she spotted the painting I'd begun of her.

She was sitting up in my bed, one hand holding a sheet against her lush body, the other holding back her hair that I had gripped and pulled until it was a wild mess. A drowsy smile curved her mouth and I hoped Kam wasn't old enough to recognize the look of a woman who'd been fucked good.

"Nigga, who shit you done stole?"

Kam was so shocked that he forgot to front for Dream. I chuckled at his bad ass.

"Oh, my God," Dream whispered as recognition dawned. "These are K. Reid paintings. Damien, you're K. Reid!" she squealed before jumping into my arms.

I had to catch her and manage to hold us upright. Her

short ass grabbed my face and pulled it down to hers. She pressed those soft lips against mine.

"This is so amazing. *You're* so amazing," she murmured.

"That nigga a'ight," Kam objected.

I turned my head enough to grill him as Dream laughed.

"I'ma fuck you up, Kam."

"Not even on your best d—"

Reaching around Dream, I grabbed a small drop cloth, balled it up, and threw it. It hit the door frame a second after his bad ass ran out.

CHAPTER 80
Dream

STEPPING OUT OF THE BATHROOM, I rolled my eyes. This man was seriously standing on the side of the bed, eating ice cream. Shaking my head, I walked closer to him.

"I still can't believe you like ice cream," I said.

He shrugged. "I'on know why you surprised."

He slid the spoon into my mouth and the flavor of chocolate exploded on my tongue.

"You know I like chocolate," he said, stroking a thumb across the smooth, brown skin of my cheek. "And you know I love everything cold… except that tight ass pussy."

I almost moaned as he withdrew the spoon and dropped a kiss on my lips. He dipped the spoon back into the bowl, pulling out more of the icy concoction. I squealed as he dripped some on my neck.

"Damien! I just took a shower and… *ohh*."

I sighed as he sucked the stickiness from my neck. And then, the ice cream was forgotten.

An hour later, I was draped across his chest, lazily tracing his tattoos as he rubbed my back. I grabbed his other hand, lacing my fingers through his as I lifted it. It was still hard to believe what he'd revealed earlier. That the fingers that stroked me to bliss created some of the most amazing works depicting Black life.

"You're K. Reid. That's crazy. You gotta take care of these hands. No killing five or six people every few weeks," I chided.

"Seven and a half," he corrected dryly.

I frowned. "A half?"

"I started. Someone else finished. And I got that reputation about my hands when I was younger. I'd beat the fuck outta anybody, bare handed. But I've expanded my range," he said smugly.

Shaking my head, I continued to quiz him.

"Where did the name come from?" I asked.

He sighed like I was getting on his nerves, but I didn't care.

"Nigga! Don't be blowing all hard at me. I—"

"You stay popping yo' lips, then be whining when I put this dick in yo' chest," he growled, reaching up to pull on my hair. "The K is for Kiana, nosy."

"And the Reid?"

He paused for a long moment, so long that I didn't expect an answer. I contented myself with listening to his heartbeat.

"Reid was Melanie's father. He came around a few times when I was a jit. Bought food. Bought other shit, but she sold it. Then, he didn't come no more."

He fell silent and I copied his energy for a little while, but I couldn't hold the question bubbling inside me. I rose a little to gaze at him.

"The hell you looking at?" he grumbled. "Go to sleep."

But I couldn't, not without addressing the elephant in the room.

"Damien?"

"Dream."

Smart ass. I rolled my eyes, but I pressed on.

"Are you okay?"

He looked at me, his green eyes freezing, his hand falling away from my body.

"Why wouldn't I be okay?" he asked coldly.

I should've taken the warning. I didn't want to trigger him, but this was important.

"Damien, I know you had mixed feelings about her, but your mother just died—"

He moved suddenly, pushing me off him as he climbed out of the bed.

"I keep telling yo' ass that bitch was nothing to me. I'on give a fuck about her dying. I'on know why Keith went after her ass if he was tryna get to me. Nigga really did the world a favor," he spat before stalking toward the closet.

I sat up, holding the sheet against me.

"Damien, I understand she was no longer a part of your life, but that doesn't mean that there aren't issues. And your sister and brother obviously feel a way. I really think all of y'all need to talk to somebody. It could help—"

He reappeared from the closet, yanking on some gray joggers and a black t-shirt. His eyes, cold as fuck, were focused on me.

"Shut the fuck up, Dream. God damn! You stay runnin' yo' mouth about shit that's not yo' business," he snapped at me. "I ain't talking to no fucking body. Shit don't work. Dixon had me up in therapy and nothing changed. Kameron and Kiana will deal with that shit. What you want me to do? You think yo' pussy so good that you gon' have me out here being one? Nah, shorty. I hugged that li'l nigga today and agreed to keep him. Fuck I know about raising a kid? I should be out right now, knocking niggas' heads together and finding Keith's bitch ass. But I'm here tryna make sure people okay and being stuck up under yo' Dr. Phil ass. You wanna make a nigga soft, always tryna make me be somebody else. Fuck that. Mind yo' business and I'll take care of mine!"

I swallowed and blinked back tears as he slid into socks

and some black and white Jordans and grabbed his key fob, phones, and wallet. Damien definitely had a way of reminding me exactly what I was to him. Right now, I wasn't anything but an annoyance, apparently. The shit was crushing —every time I thought I was getting close to his heart, he showed he didn't have one. At least not for me.

"You don't have to leave your own house. I can go."

I was proud of how steady my voice was. Tossing back the sheet, I got out of bed, throwing an arm across my breasts as I walked toward his dresser to find clothes. He was there before I could make it, pushing my arm aside.

"You hiding, like I ain't seen all that shit?" he taunted me.

Embarrassed heat warmed my body as I kept my eyes on the dresser drawers, reaching to open the one I had started using. If possible, his words made me feel worse. I bit my lip, determined to stay in control, despite the hurt. I covered my breasts again, rummaging through the drawer. He grabbed my arm.

"Don't do that. Don't fucking cover your body from me," he said.

His voice was calm, but his grip tightened as I tried to pull my arm away.

"Leave me alone, Damien," I said quietly, tired and dreading the drive I was about to have to make.

"Go to bed."

I shook my head. "I'm leaving."

He looked at me for a minute before a cruel smile curved his mouth.

"You in your feelings, shorty?"

Anger bubbled inside me. At this point, he was being an asshole for no reason, and I wasn't in the mood for the bullshit.

"Maybe. I don't expect you to understand that since you like to pretend you don't have anything as human as emotions. Wouldn't want people to think you're a *pussy* or influenced by one. Now, let me go and get out of my fucking way!" I snapped.

Reaching for the drawer, I wasn't prepared to be whirled around, then backed against the dresser.

"Watch how you talk to me, Dream. You got me fucked up. You ain't going nowhere. Get yo' ass back in that bed," he ordered, his voice tight.

"No! I—"

He pulled my hair, making my head tilt back and my eyes meet his. He lowered his head, bringing his lips a centimeter from mine.

"You what? You going to your family? Do that. Just know that I'm coming for you, and I don't care about any security. I'ma bury anyone who gets in my way. You worried about me killing so many people—make sure you don't get any of the blood on your hands," he whispered.

I opened my mouth and then closed it. His eyes, cold as he kept this damn house, revealed he meant every word. Angry, hurt, frustrated tears filled my eyes, and I gritted my teeth as he backed away.

"You ready to do all that? I thought you said my pussy wasn't that good," I mocked.

Silence. Then, "Go to bed, Dream," he ordered, walking out of the room.

I screamed as I threw the clothes that I had pulled out at his retreating back.

Then, I went to bed.

CHAPTER 81
Dayana

(*SUNDAY*, *July 4*)

A light knock on the door pulled my attention from the true crime marathon I was watching. Smoke had a little sitting area in his room, complete with a seventy-five-inch TV. I was being ridiculously lazy, draped all over the dark brown settee, eating gummies, and shaking my head at the women on *Snapped*.

"Come in!" I called, sitting up.

Jenesis popped her adorable little face in, then waved.

"Hey, Cupcake!"

I beckoned for her, and she skipped over to me, put her little sharp elbows in my thighs, and hugged my waist. I rubbed her back and we sat like that for a couple of minutes, until she started wiggling.

"What's up, ladybug?"

"I'm ready for lunch. Daddy working. I went in his office, and he said, 'Okay, Jeni-face. We can order something.'"

I grinned at her imitation of Smoke's voice.

"I'm 'posed to be thinkin' 'bout what I wanna eat."

She sighed and buried her face in my lap.

"Well, what's wrong? You don't know what you want?" I inquired.

She peeked up at me, all caramel eyes and pouting lips. I was about to get conned, and I didn't even care.

"'Member GiGi made that red soup and you made grilled cheese?" she asked in a small voice.

"Mm-hmm."

"GiGi put some soup in the 'frigerator…"

My smile widened. "You want me to make my famous grilled cheese?"

She nodded eagerly. "Yes, ma'am!" She looked around suddenly. "Daddy's be droopy."

This time, I laughed out loud. Twenty minutes later, she was sitting at the table, humming and swinging her feet with tomato soup smeared around her lips and her mouth full of grilled cheese. *Too cute*, I thought.

"You good, Suga?" I asked, turning back to the sink to wash the few dishes.

"Yeah, her spoiled butt good. She also 'bout to get a timeout after lunch," Smoke said.

I jumped at his voice, then frowned at his words. Turning, I knew I shouldn't interfere, but…

"Why?"

The word came out before I could help it. Jenesis looked so sad.

"Why you in trouble, Jeni-face?" he asked.

She chewed and swallowed slowly. She mumbled something while keeping her little head down. This girl was the best actress, looking all downtrodden, when in reality, her daddy had her spoiled rotten.

"What?" Smoke prompted.

"Cuz I wasn't 'posed to bother Princess Yana," she admitted. "But Daddy! She ain't bothered! Huh, Princess Yana?"

I opened my mouth to agree with her, and Smoke gave me a look. I rolled my eyes and went back to rinsing as he talked to her, then sent her to the upstairs den for a ten-minute time-out. As soon as she was out of earshot, I wrinkled my nose at him.

"She doesn't bother me, Smoke."

He walked up and dropped a kiss on my forehead.

"She will, if we let her. My little shorty wants all yo' time."

I linked my arms around his neck.

"You jealous?"

He smiled before leaning in to press his lips against mine.

"I'on mind sharing... as long as yo' nights all mine."

His kiss was passionate but quick.

"You don't have time to be cooking. Dante's party starts at three. You know it's gon' take you eight hours to get ready," he said as he pulled back.

"Lies!"

I swatted his shoulder. We had a busy Fourth of July planned. First was Dante and Sherrilyn's all-white day party. Next, we were grabbing Jenesis and hooking up with Dream, Demon, and Kam for a fireworks show. Then, we'd meet up with some people at one of Smoke's bars. I wanted to come back here after the party to shower and change, so it was going to be a whirlwind of a day.

"Let me see what little shit you plan to wear before Jenesis's time is up," he said suddenly.

"Don't start!" I popped. "You'll see it in a little while!"

"Smart-mouthed self. I'ma spank yo' ass," he threatened.

I tilted my head and smiled slyly.

"You promise?"

He pulled me into his body, burying his face in my neck. His response was interrupted when the doorbell rang.

"The fuck is this?" he mumbled, reaching for his phone.

I sucked my teeth.

"Like your guys would've let anyone close who wasn't approved," I said.

"You right. It's my OG."

He closed the security app and dialed someone.

"Ma? Let yourself in," he instructed.

"I thought she was programmed into the biometric system. Why she knock?" I asked when he hung up.

He shrugged. "In case I had you bent over the couch."

My jaw dropped. "Cartier!"

He chuckled. "It's the truth. Mama know yo' fast ass here and she respects boundaries."

"Ugh!" I mushed his head.

Ms. Stephanie was there to watch Jenesis. After a quick conversation, Smoke and I went to his room. I snuggled up to him to watch TV. After about an hour, we got ready. Just because he was rushing me, I put this pussy on him in the shower. His ass was dominant, but he wasn't gon' run every-thing with Dayana Dionne Castle.

Afterwards, I moisturized my body, applied sunscreen, and gave myself a light beat as he did his own thing.

"The hell is this, Yana?"

I looked over to see him holding up my outfit. It was a little skater dress with a short, flouncy skirt that would stop well above my knees. The top was sleeveless and fitted, with a plunging neckline and a low back. The sides featured little geometric cutouts. I was trying to be cool *and* cute. I sighed.

"My dress, Cartier," I said.

He looked down at it, twisting and turning it in his hands, before looking back at me, confused.

"Where the rest of it?"

"Cartier!"

We argued playfully as we got dressed. He steadily talked shit about my dress, and I steadily ignored his ass. I grabbed a few of the pieces he had copped for me, and he fastened the necklace and bracelet even as he threatened the lives of niggas who might get at me. Rolling my eyes, I was about to slip my earrings in when he grabbed my hand and gave me two flat boxes. I recognized the distinctive Cartier red, so I was already bouncing excitedly as I opened the first one.

My eyes widened at the large gold hoops inlaid with tiny diamonds.

"Oh, my God, Cartier! These are beautiful," I breathed, lifting one for a closer inspection.

He shrugged. Money really was nothing but a thing to this nigga.

"The other pair is for Dream. Figured y'all would like them big ass things, the way y'all walk around with them damn Forgiatos in yo' ears."

I stuck out my tongue. "Fuck you!"

"Shit, when?" he clapped back.

"You the one complaining about being late," I reminded him.

I was usually "fashionably late," but we actually made it shortly after the party started, since we had such a long day in front of us. My siblings were there with their partners. For the first time in my life, seeing DeAngelo was awkward. In my mind, my twin had chosen Daddy over me, when Daddy was clearly wrong. I quickly pressed my cheek against his and stepped back. Smoke just eyed my brother like DeAngelo was something on the bottom of his shoe. Crystal tried to make conversation, but the shit was uncomfortable. I was so glad when Dream and Demon appeared that I could have cried. I handed Dream her earrings, linked my arm through hers, and gave Crystal an apologetic smile, ready to get away. I looked over at Smoke.

"We about to check out outside," I told him.

He nodded and went back to talking with Demon.

The Wares didn't know how to do anything half-ass. The house was beautifully decorated with cold appetizers laid out on several surfaces and servers circulating with drinks. But outside was even more opulent. A whirl of red, white, and blue tents, servers with loaded trays, black-clad security, and guests in a sea of white were sprawled across the perfectly landscaped lawn with its groomed trees and riot of colorful flowers.

"A Cartier box! What you get me?" Dream finally asked.

"It's from Smoke. Open it."

She did and squealed like I did before changing her earrings out. I had grabbed two glasses of champagne and handed her one as I told her what Smoke had said about our love of large hoops. We were laughing when suddenly, another presence loomed over us. Our eyes swung to the tall figure and my heart dropped into my stomach.

"Daddy," Dream said coolly.

"That's the best you can greet your old man?" he said, smiling like he wasn't wrecking our family.

He pulled Dream into a hug. I looked down, trying to blink back tears. It was easy to say that I shouldn't care, that I had landed on my feet with one of the richest men in the state, but Darius Castle was still my father. His disappointment and rejection seemed so ruthless and complete.

Which was why I was I surprised when his strong arms wrapped around me.

"Believe it or not, Daya-baby, I miss you," he said softly.

Sniffing, I nodded. He probably just missed Mama and wanted us to put in a good word with her, but it was nice to feel like my father cared about me.

"Dream, you mind if I talk to your sister for a minute?" he asked.

Jaw clenched, Dream stared at him for a moment before looking at me. I nodded slightly.

"It's okay," I told her softly.

She blew out a long breath and rolled her eyes. Daddy's smile slipped.

"Nothing's changed, Dream Dior. I'm still your father and you gon' act like it," he warned.

Dream scoffed. "Yeah, okay. Yana, I'ma go find Kiana and Topaz out here. Text me when you're done."

She stalked off angrily, still mad at Daddy for me. I loved my big sister with everything in me. I turned to my father.

"What's up, Daddy?"

He smiled at me and wrapped one arm around my shoulders.

"I'm trying to see how we come back from this, baby girl," he said.

"I don't know. You cut me off. Pretty much threw me to the wolves—"

"No, baby. You walked willingly into the arms of one of the biggest, baddest wolves out here."

He kept his smile in place, but I could see the irritation in his eyes. Maybe there was no coming back from this, but that thought made me sad.

"Daddy, maybe we should—"

"Let's take a ride," he suggested suddenly. "I really want to talk to you and there's too much going on here."

His suggestion caught me off-guard. I didn't plan to spend my holiday debating with my father.

"Daddy, I—"

"Come on, Daya-baby. I don't like the way things are between us."

He looked so sincere, so concerned about our relationship. Sighing, I nodded. Giving him a few minutes wouldn't kill me.

"Okay. Let me just tell Cartier—"

"He's Cartier, huh?" he interrupted, a strange glimmer in his eye.

I pulled back, suddenly unsure. Reading my face, he recovered quickly.

"Baby, just come. You know Smoke ain't gonna want you to go," he coaxed.

That wasn't a lie, and I didn't feel like that argument. I

sighed again. His smile widened as he grabbed my elbow and led me around the side of the house. We exited through a guarded side gate and waited for a valet to bring his S 580. He opened the door for me, and I slid in. We rode in silence for about ten minutes. Finally, I felt him glance over at me.

"I know I went a little too far, Daya-baby. But you have to understand what you sacrificed. Daddy is in an expansion phase. The Middletons were ready to back my efforts financially. Significantly. On top of that, Talton was set to make a purchase to arm his own crew, enough to create his own fucking militia. When you walked out with Salinas, you left me holding the bag," he vented.

"I'm—"

I caught myself before I finished that thought. I refused to apologize.

"You really expected me to marry a man who was already cheating?" I asked instead.

"Dayana… baby… I know I kept you and Dream sheltered. Innocent. I taught you to… protect your virtue. But men are different. They have more… *urgent* needs."

My eyes widened at this explanation he was giving, straight out of the 1950s. I turned in my seat to look at him.

"Daddy, are you serious?"

His mouth tightened. "I know y'all got all that feminist shit in your heads, but I don't care what you learned in no fucking 'Women's Studies,' no nigga wants a woman who's been run through. Your innocence is priceless. It's different for men, and that's just how it is!" he ranted.

"So, my value is all about what's between my legs?"

"Don't be stupid, Dayana. I'm not saying that. I'm saying—"

Suddenly, I realized the direction we were heading.

"Where are we going?"

He sighed. "Daya-baby, I—"

"No!" I demanded. "Just take me back!"

We were a few minutes away from the Middleton estate. I couldn't believe this nigga's audacity!

"Listen. Jordan just wants closure. He deserves closure," he said.

"I don't care—"

"Dayana, I need you to do this for me. I need you to make peace with him because I need their support."

He lowered his voice, his tone desperate and pleading. I was torn in two. I didn't give a fuck what Jordan wanted, but I wasn't trying to destroy my father's plans. He picked up on my uncertainty.

"Please, Daya-baby," he pressed.

I crossed my arms over my chest and exhaled loudly.

"Fine. Ten minutes. I'll answer what he asks. That's it," I said, my voice firm.

He smiled and reached over to pat my knee.

"Good girl."

Jordan answered the door when we arrived minutes later. A small smile stretched his mouth.

"Sweetness," he said softly.

I shook my head. "Don't call me that."

His smile dropped.

"Dayana," my father chided.

"It's okay," Jordan mumbled. "I hope you're well, Mr. Castle. Let's go in the parlor."

I nodded and led the way.

"Is your father here?" Daddy asked.

"Grilling on the back patio, sir," Jordan replied.

"I'll go see him. Leave you youngins to work it out."

Daddy's voice was too eager for me and I didn't like the way he said that shit. Turning, I looked at him.

"Ten minutes," I reminded him.

He nodded. "I got it, baby."

Jordan and I walked on to the parlor. He gestured for me to sit on the love seat. Sighing, I did as he requested, ready to get this over. He sat across from me in a Louis XV chair, holding up a finger as he typed on his phone. I rolled my eyes.

"Jordan, I don't know what you want from me. You can ask me what you like, but please don't act like you're so surprised by my actions, like I didn't catch you cheating days before our wedding and didn't tell you I no longer wanted to marry you. I—"

I stopped as he laughed lowly.

"Look at you, all iced out. That's nice. Cartier jewelry for Cartier's property, huh?" he spat.

I stood, scowling at his ass. "See, what we're not doing is this."

Unlocking my phone, I began texting my father. I took four steps before a vicious pull on my hair had me shrieking.

"Nigga, have you lost yo' fuckin' mind?" I hissed, reaching behind me.

His hand tightened as he walked up to me, pressing his chest to my back.

"So damn feisty. You'll learn."

He snatched my phone with his free hand. Bringing my arm down, I elbowed his ass as hard as I could. The hand in my hair twisted so tightly that tears sprang to my eyes.

"Let me go, you lunatic!"

He lowered his mouth to my ear.

"Nah, I still got questions," he murmured.

"Fuck you and yo—"

"How many times have you let that nigga spread your legs so you could give him my pussy? Huh, Dayana? Do you suck his dick? Does he make you take it up the ass? Did you think I was gon' let that shit slide? Did you forget you were promised to me?" he raged.

I struggled against him, trying to work his fingers out of my hair. He dropped my phone, then wrapped his hand around my throat and squeezed. Before now, I'd been annoyed. That annoyance quickly became tinged with fear as I struggled to breathe.

"We gon' take a little trip, Sweetness. I'm gon' make sure you understand that you're mine. You gave yourself to Salinas, so you gon' make that up. Understand?"

He finally released my throat. Light-headed, I gasped greedily for air. He let go of my hair and it fell around my face as I bent over, sucking in oxygen. He yanked me up and spun me around.

"I said, do you understand?"

I shook my head. "I... I wouldn't cross the street with y—"

Jordan backhanded me, sending me tripping backwards until I fell hard onto the marble floor. An ache exploded in my head as I tasted blood. He straddled my body and kneeled. I screamed, but he clamped a hand over my mouth.

"Shh. Who you screaming for? Darius is gone. He wanted us to take time to work things out. I texted to let him know you agreed to stay for dinner."

Horrified, I shook my head as tears leaked from the corners of my eyes.

"I guess you don't understand, Sweetness. First, I'ma get rid of all this shit, cuz that nigga probably tracking you..."

I sobbed as he brutally yanked my necklace off, hurting me. My bracelet was treated similarly before he ripped my earrings out. He reached in his pocket then and pulled out the bridal set we had picked out.

"This is all the jewelry you need. But you gon' earn this back."

He chuckled as he stood, then pulled me up. Weakly, I fought him.

"You already made me hurt you. Don't make me hurt you worse," he warned, grabbing my wrists.

I twisted them, but he was too strong. Part of me was terrified. The other part was furious and needed to strike back, even though my head was spinning. I worked my jaws, gathering saliva before I spit in his smirking face. While he was reeling in shock, I spoke.

"You want answers? Fine. I can't count how many times he's spread my legs and made me cum on his d—"

I barely saw his hand move before pain crashed into my right temple.

The darkness came quickly.

CHAPTER 82
Smoke

DANTE WARE WAS A FUCKING CHARACTER. The streets claimed the nigga was a billionaire and he lived up to that reputation. But the more I got to know him, the more I suspected he was really laughing at all the shit that people assumed came along with being rich. The houses, the cars, the vacations, the parties—Dante had one setting for all of them: extravagant. Like the exclusive craft beer in my hand; as a bar owner, I was familiar with the brand and the price. Who the fuck served beer that cost thirty-two dollars a bottle at what was essentially a big cook out? Dante-fucking-Ware, that's who. Nigga had to be laughing at the ridiculousness of it all.

"You think that bottle gon' start talking or some shit?" Demon asked dryly.

I mugged his ass. Nigga had always had a smart mouth, but I'd rarely heard it, even though we'd been associates for a while. He talked a little more now, no doubt Dream's influence. I knew for myself how a Castle sister could start to change you in a short amount of time.

"Fuck you, crazy ass nigga," I said.

"Shiiii, talking about pot meet kettle..."

I took a sip of the overpriced—but surprisingly good—beer before speaking again.

"The family?" I asked.

He tensed for a minute. I guess the nigga wasn't exactly talkative yet. I could respect that. So, I was surprised when he responded.

"Kam is... it's got him fucked up a little. He been over here hanging with DJ. KiKi—" He stopped and sighed. "Mixed, I guess. I was glad she came today. She needed to get away from all the shit that's gotta be done to bury somebody."

I nodded, avoiding him not mentioning himself.

"McKellar?"

He shook his head.

"Came and left with Uber drivers. I grabbed them, but they didn't know shit. Picked him up and dropped him off at a big H-E-B on the Northwest side. He disappeared into the crowd. Store cameras don't show him coming out. No info on the phone he ordered the Ubers and texted Kam from. Nigga been having me on the defensive. That's changing," he vowed, his voice low.

"I'll keep my ears and eyes open," I said.

He nodded and took a swallow from his own beer. Frowning, he looked at the bottle.

"This nigga can't just get some Heinekens or some shit?"

I shrugged. "That's yo' brother. Shit is good, though."

A smile crossed his face. "You ol' juniper berry and chocolate loving, yella ass nigga."

"Nigga, I know yo' light bright ass—"

I stopped as Dream walked up on us. She smiled at me, and I gave her a nod. Her eyes swung to Damien before lowering.

"Are you hungry? There's food out back," she said, her voice flat.

"Nah, I'm good," he responded just as dryly, even though he didn't take his eyes off her.

"Okay."

She turned to walk off just as another woman was walking past. She bumped into Dream, making her stumble. Demon's hands shot out, but she caught her balance and stepped back, away from him.

"I'm fine," she told him and the apologizing woman.

I wondered what was up with the tension between them. Nigga had just given her a million-dollar birthday and Dayana had told me Dream was talking about the l-word. Speaking of Dayana...

"Where yo' sister?" I asked.

She rolled her eyes. "Daddy wanted to talk to her for a minute and she agreed to listen. They were outside."

I frowned at her. "You ain't see her after that? Cuz yo' Daddy over there, shorty."

I inclined my head toward the back of the room where Darius stood talking to a couple of other dudes. As if that nigga sensed us talking about him, he looked up. His mouth twisted into a smirk, and he saluted us with his champagne flute. I started walking before I even realized it. Dream caught my arm.

"I'll go," she said.

"Nah, ma. This nigga finna tell me something," I said, trying to hold on to the rage boiling its way through me.

Darius must've known I was about to embarrass his ass in front of his little buddies because he met me in the middle of the room.

"Where is she?" I gritted out.

"Hello to you, too, Salinas," he said, smirk still in place as he lifted his drink to his mouth.

I slapped that shit out of his hand. Surprised, he just stared at me. I took a step closer to him as people backed away from us and out of the room.

"What the hell is—" DeAngelo started.

"Shut the fuck up, D," Dream snapped.

"I asked you a question. You got three seconds to answer," I said, my voice deceptively calm.

He shifted his stance, trying to look unbothered as he slipped his hands into his pockets.

"I don't need three seconds. Dayana's with her fiancé, where she's supposed to be," he said, the smug smile returning to his face.

Dream gasped, and it was like I heard that shit from a distance. I had tunnel vision suddenly, every bit of my attention focused on Darius Castle's bitch-made ass as I balled his shirt in my hand and reached for Scarlet. Releasing the blade, I pressed it under his eye until I drew blood. A single drop of red slid down his face, then hung on the corner of his lips. He licked it before chuckling softly.

"You upset, Salinas? She was never yours—"

I shook the fuck out of him.

"She definitely mine and you gon' explain shit before I pop your fucking eyeballs."

I stared at him, part of me hoping he chose wrong so I could have the pleasure of sinking my knife straight through his pupils. That desire must have been in my own eyes because he started talking.

"She and I went for a ride and talked about fixing our relationship. Jordan came up—"

I snorted. "You mean yo' bitch ass brought him up."

He didn't bother denying it.

"She wanted to go see him. Apologize. See about making shit right if he'd have her back."

"You lying. She would never!" Dream spat.

She was right, and I wanted to kill this nigga for even suggesting it. I pushed the knife a little deeper, watched his skin split more as he swallowed.

"So, she suddenly wanted a nigga who just tried to choke her out in the middle of a fucking grocery store?" I asked him.

His mouth flapped open and shut before he let out a weak ass, "What?"

"Where did you take her?"

"It doesn't matter. She texted me. Said she and Jordan were going to take a few days and work on—"

Without thinking, without breathing, I flipped Scarlet, pressing the razor-sharp blade against his throat. Dream made a sound behind me. Again, I drew blood. Again, I waited.

"You wanna die in front of yo' kids? Keep fucking with me."

He stared at me for a few more seconds. Finally, his eyes dropped.

"Talton's," he mumbled.

———

Fury had me in my car by myself, racing toward the Middleton estate. Making calls at ninety miles per hour was probably stupid, but fuck it. I needed to set shit in motion and get people in place. One of my tech people confirmed that the tracker in her bracelet placed her at Middleton's. We didn't share locations on our phones, but I would definitely always know where she was from now on.

So, yeah, anger fueled me. But the other emotion I was feeling, the one that had my heart sitting in my stomach and chills tripping down my spine, that sickened me. Fear. I was scared for my shorty and for me—I didn't know if I could lose another love.

I shook my head, refusing to even consider it. I assumed Ammo and Anthony were somewhere behind me, but I didn't give a fuck if they weren't. It had taken all my discipline not to gut them niggas, but they hadn't thought anything was off about her walking off with her father. Logically, I couldn't really blame them. Emotionally was another story.

I called her repeatedly and got no answer. Darius Castle had forfeited his life if something happened to her, and that was on Stephanie Nicole Salinas.

A guard shack separated the entrance and exit gates and I stopped, letting down my window. Two men stared at me from behind what was probably bulletproof glass. Middleton was fucking extra, and I didn't have time for this shit today. A voice suddenly blared from an intercom system, demanding I state my name and what business I had there.

"Getcho weak ass on the phone and tell yo' boss or his simp ass son that Smoke Salinas is here, and my patience is just about gone."

I watched as one of them made a brief call, then came back over the intercom.

"The senior Mr. Middleton says Jordan and his guest are no longer here, so you have no business—"

I didn't wait for him to finish. I dialed the number I'd been supplied for Talton.

"Middleton," he answered after a couple of rings.

"Let me tell you what's about to happen. You about to tell these weak ass niggas at this gate to let me and..." I looked behind me and saw two cars, no doubt Ammo and Anthony and Dream and Demon, "the two cars behind me in."

"And why the fuck would I do that, Salinas?" Middleton snapped.

I chuckled. "One thing I am is thorough, Talton. You over here worried about Jordan like you don't have a little one and one on the way across town. You and Cara been real busy, I see. Now, I can make sure Mrs. Middleton knows all about that right before the niggas I sent to Cara's place in the Heights go in and snatch up your little family. You know how many couples would pay any price for a couple of babies, give them a whole new identity so they could raise them? You'll never see them jits again. Or you can let me in and I can check out this shit for myself."

My tone was conversational, but Middleton knew me, so he knew how fucking serious I was. I banged on that nigga as he sputtered over the line. A few seconds later, I saw one of the guards grab the phone. I smiled grimly as the gate slid open and I drove up to the sand-colored, Mediterranean-style house.

Middleton opened the door as I hopped out. He stepped back, allowing me into the house. He was flanked by two obviously armed men. If only he knew that shit wouldn't do him any good if I didn't like what he had to say. My team came up beside me and Dream was suddenly in front of us, phone in hand.

"Salinas, I told you—"

"My girl's tracking device is pinging from here, but you claim they gone. So, where's your son?" I cut in.

"Jordan left. He said he and his fiancée—"

My fist crashed into his jaw. One of his crew stepped forward, hand on his gun as Middleton fell back. My shootas reached for their own straps, but I held up a hand.

"Tell these pussies that you definitely don't want me shot," I ordered.

Middleton glared at me, but slowly shook his head. Dream moved suddenly and it took me a minute to realize that she was following the faint sound of a ringing phone. She looked over her shoulder.

"Smoke... it's her phone," she whispered, her anxiety obvious.

Demon was there in seconds, one hand on her back as we made our way toward the sound. My own nerves were on edge as I listened to the phone ring without being answered. Was she in here hurt... or worse?

Dream had to call it again, but finally we walked into

something like a small living room. Pointing to Dayana's phone on the floor, she made a pained little sound.

I curled my hands into fists as I saw her jewelry broken and thrown across the floor. Bending, I picked up her bracelet, rubbing it between my thumb and index finger. I turned back to Middleton, no longer in the mood to play with his bitch ass.

"Where did he go?" I asked, my voice a hiss.

"I don't know. I swear," he answered, his eyes everywhere but on mine.

I hated a muhfucking liar, especially when my girl's life was at stake. My hand closed around his throat. His guys moved, but I didn't give a fuck.

"Where is he?" I asked again.

"Oh, my God! Is that blood? Damien, that's her blood!" Dream cried.

I followed her gaze to the red stain smeared on the marble floor. My eyes flew back to Middleton's.

"I ain't telling you sh—"

I palmed Scarlet, the blade out and slashing across Talton Middleton's throat before he could finish his sentence. He grabbed his throat as blood sprayed, his eyes stunned, a gurgling sound escaping him. I watched emotionlessly as he fell to his knees, then onto his face. That's what this bitch got for raising a pussy ass son.

I looked up at his guards, who hadn't even drawn their guns. Money would do that. These niggas, Rigo and Smitty, had been happy to flip on Middleton. Their disloyalty disgusted me. They would be handled soon. I looked at Rigo. He did most of the talking for them.

"You were here? When he took her?" I asked coldly.

He held up both hands, like he was surrendering.

"We didn't even know she was in the house, Smoke."

I nodded.

"Take Ammo to the control room. Destroy all footage from

the gates up to here. Stop any recording. Ammo, call Kat and have her go behind you. Tell her I need her team to get me a list of every property the Middletons own," I said.

Ammo nodded as I turned to Anthony.

"Call clean up?" he asked.

"Yeah. And we got more people at the gate. Tell them to take it out if needed. We need them up here. We don't know who else is here."

"Got it."

I blew out a long, shaky breath, the fear that I had been feeling threatening to consume me. I looked over at Demon and Dream. He had moved closer to her, but she was looking at me.

"What... what now?" she whispered.

I rubbed a hand over my hair, confusion and dread tying me in knots.

"I'on know, shorty," I admitted. *"Fuck!* I'on know."

CHAPTER 83

Demon

I WATCHED Dream out of the corner of my eye as I talked to Ms. Hazel, letting her know

we wouldn't be picking up Mia and Hailey for the fireworks show. She was rocking again, and her right leg was bouncing hard as fuck. Her head was tilted forward as she hugged herself. Shorty was trying her best to hold it together, to keep in the tears that sparkled in her eyes. She'd given me an address to one of her grandfather's houses and asked that I drive her there. That was the last thing she had said. She was in her head, her teeth shredding her bottom lip.

"You didn't have to do that," she said suddenly. "You should go get them and Kam and DJ. Take them to the show. My family and I can—"

"Shut the fuck up," I growled.

I felt a muscle tic in my jaw as I clenched my teeth, mad as hell. Dream was tripping hard as fuck. Yeah, we had beef right now, but I wasn't leaving her.

"I'm just—" she stopped as my phone rang.

Her eyes snapped to the dash, looking for Smoke's number. But this was Dante. She went back to staring out the window. Sighing, I answered. Using as few words as possible, we arranged for KiKi, Kam, and Topaz to stay at his estate for the night. He discreetly asked If I needed help with the situation at the Middletons, but I declined. Even though he was obviously out of his fucking mind with worry, Smoke seemed to have it covered.

"How's your lady?" Dante asked.

I didn't know how to answer that, so I deflected.

"She's right here. She can hear you."

"Ms. Dream, I'm sure my brother has let you know our resources will be poured into finding your beloved... jewel and bringing it home," he vowed.

"Thank you," she whispered.

I disconnected the call as I turned onto the private road Dream had directed me to. A half mile and one gate later, I finally understood how big the legendary Lucien Dumont had been. The only word I knew to describe this house and its grounds was "palatial." Sitting on top of a hill, it had a low-lying roof, multiple columns, and I counted at least four wings. I saw a nod to the French Quarter in the French doors that opened up to stone terraces and balconies with wrought-iron railings.

We had to go through another gate that had an empty guard house. Pulling closer, I noticed the front yard was dominated by a French garden with a fountain at its center. I looked over at Dream.

"And you be amazed by Dante's shit?" I teased.

She shrugged. "I forget about this place. Only been here a few times. He was building it for Grandmama when she was..." Her voice trailed off. "Turn left right here," she said, changing the subject.

I followed her directions, coming to a stop a short distance later. I moved to turn off the truck.

"Wait."

I waited. Suddenly, the ground in front of us moved as a platform, enclosed on three sides, rose from beneath. Once it stopped, I pulled onto it and was quiet during our descent. Seconds later, I drove into the ten-car, subterranean garage, and picked a spot amongst the mostly vintage cars. I took one look at the 1950s-era Jaguar D-Type and for once, I was something like impressed. Those things could go for over fifteen million.

"Shorty, what the fuck kinda weight was Lucien moving?" I asked after climbing out and opening her door. Rolling her eyes, she led me to an elevator. We climbed on and she inserted a key and pushed a button. The elevator moved quickly, opening into a two-story foyer. We got off and Dream quickly walked across the natural stone floors and into a living room where her mother and grandfather waited. Lucien smiled affectionately as her mother walked up to us.

"Thought y'all had some big shindig to go—" he began.

"Dayana's gone. J-Jordan kidnapped her," Dream interrupted.

Silence. And then they were talking at the same time as Dream shook uncontrollably. I moved toward her, ready to hold her up, but she stepped away. Lucien's fingers flew across his phone as he interrogated his granddaughter.

"How the fuck did he get close enough to grab her?" he demanded.

"Daddy took her to him," she whispered.

The room was suddenly quiet again.

"I'm sorry... what?" Lucia asked softly.

Dream repeated herself. Two pairs of hazel eyes, father and daughter, met. The look that passed between them was enough to chill a lesser man. I was glad to see it.

"Where is Salinas?" Lucien inquired.

"He's... mobilizing. Papa, I need to sit d—"

She swayed on her feet, and this time, I didn't give a fuck about her objections. I swung her up in my arms before taking a seat on the cream-colored couch.

"Dream... baby... you gotta calm down. We gon' find her," I promised.

I was ready for her to fight me, to push her way out of my arms. Instead, she melted against me and the first of her tears fell.

"The blood... he hurt her, Damien," she sobbed.

"He gon' hurt worse."

Her mama sat next to us and grabbed her hands.

"He's right, my love. We're going to find your sister. And we're going to make sure everyone... *everyone* who had something to do with this, pays," Lucia vowed fiercely.

CHAPTER 84

Dayana

JESUS, *please turn off the bass in my head*, I prayed as the pulsing and pounding in my skull woke me up. I groaned and almost threw up at the taste in my mouth. If week-old sauerkraut had a flavor, it had to be what was between my lips. I moaned again and moved to sit up. Only, I couldn't. My eyes flew open and struggled to adjust to the pitch-black room. I'd been so focused on my head and mouth, I hadn't realized that I was restrained, some kind of restraint on each of my wrists and ankles. The last thing I remembered was suddenly at the front of my mind. I forgot all the other shit as rage boiled through me.

"Jordan!" I screamed, then collapsed in agony as my head almost exploded.

I slowly pulled myself back together and got ready to call this bitch ass nigga's name again. I had just opened my mouth when the door flew open. The light from behind the person revealed a feminine silhouette. She flipped a switch and bright light flooded the room. I squeezed my eyes shut and almost passed out again as pain pierced my skull. I took a few seconds to let the pain recede before I glared at Bunny.

"Where the fuck is Jordan, bitch?" I spat.

She turned up her thin nose. "He's busy, *bitch*," she snapped back.

With supreme effort, I rolled my eyes. "You little bleached blonde puppy, if you don't go get yo' owner—"

"You talk a lot of shit for a hoe tied to a bed," she taunted.

"And you talk a lot of shit for a bitch who follows behind a nigga who obsessed with another woman," I hissed. "Now, go get yo' handler and tell that pussy to bring me some water and pain medicine."

She stared at me angrily, but finally she turned to go do what I said. Trifling ass bitch slammed the door on her way out and I wanted to scream. As soon as she disappeared, the little bit of panic I was feeling threatened to overwhelm me. Where the fuck had this crazy ass nigga brought me? What if Smoke or Grandpapa couldn't find me? My heart rate picked up speed as I thought about the possibilities.

"Calm down, Dayana," I whispered.

I needed to try to figure out where I was, just in case I found a phone or was able to escape. I didn't recognize the overdone, fussy pink room that I was in, but that didn't mean anything. Jordan had brought me to a couple of their other properties, but it wasn't like I went through all the bedrooms. I thought I smelled water, but I needed a look out the windows. The heavy curtains with what I suspected were mechanized blinds behind them didn't look too promising from my position, handcuffed and chained to the bed. I'd been working my hands and feet the whole time, but this shit was secure. I was gon' kill this nigga.

I closed my eyes, focusing on my breathing and keeping it together, until I heard the door open again. My lids flew up and I felt my face twist into a mug. This bitch had the nerve to smile, Bunny right on his heels.

"Sweetness, welcome back to the land of the living," he greeted, walking closer to me.

"Where you won't be for long. Smoke is gon' kill yo' weak ass. Did you know he likes to flay people? He's—"

The slap didn't even surprise me. My spitting the blood from my re-opened lip in his face did shock him. Stupid ass motherfucker didn't learn before.

"Don't talk about that nigga to me," Jordan hissed, accepting the towel Bunny had run to the en suite bathroom to get him.

I smirked. "Why? You get scared? What if I say his name three times? Prolly about to piss ya self with that li'l dick I saw. I thank God for deliverance."

Bunny gasped. He raised his hand again and I braced myself. But he dropped it slowly and chuckled.

"No. That's what you want me to do, so you can act like Smoke is the hero. Fuck that, Sweetness. You loved me once. You will again."

I curled my top lip. "Now that I know what love is, I know I never loved you. I mean, you beat me, kidnapped me, and probably drugged me. No wonder the only way you were able to get a wife was for your daddy to offer to pay," I said, smiling evilly.

I watched with satisfaction as the color drained from his face. Nigga was so mad that his eye was twitching. I should be scared. I knew that. But he must've cracked my head too hard on that floor.

"Dayana, watch your fucking mouth, lovely. I won't keep saying that," he said softly.

"Good, cuz I won't be doing that. Unchain me so your Great Dane can give me that water and medicine."

Bunny sputtered, but I didn't care. She wanted to play co-kidnapper, that's how she'd get talked to. Jordan grilled me.

"Dayana, Bunny is here to serve us, but you will treat her with respect—"

I sucked my teeth. "Man, fuck you and that bitch."

He smiled. "You will soon."

"I'll drown myself in that sink in there first," I vowed.

He ignored that. "If I release you, will you behave?"

"Pretty sure I won't be doing that, either."

He laughed softly. "So stubborn, Sweetness. I think I'll let you keep a little of that fire. You're full of piss and vinegar as my grandfather would say."

"Nigga, I don't know about the vinegar, but the piss gon' be all over your feet if you don't let me go right now," I threatened.

He looked at me wordlessly for a moment. Annoyed, I rattled my chains. Finally, he walked over to me, pulling a key from his pocket. Seconds later, I was free. I moved to the edge of the bed, woozy as fuck as I rubbed my wrists. Jordan reached to touch my face... just as I brought up a wobbly knee as hard as I could. The sound of his pathetic whimper as I tried to send his balls into his stomach made me smile. I pushed him backwards. Bunny dropped to her knees, clucking and cooing as he fell on his back.

"Whew! That felt good!" I announced.

I bounced up and immediately regretted it as I almost fell, dizziness and nausea attacking me. I sat down heavily and grabbed my head again. Watching Jordan in the fetal position, cupping his balls, made me well enough to stand, snatch the water and ibuprofen from his ditzy broad, swallow some down, and head for the bathroom. I eyed the bedroom door, but I knew he'd jump his ass up or even trip me if I tried.

"Go with her," he wheezed to Bunny. "You know what to do if she gets crazy."

"Yes, sir," Bunny replied eagerly.

That stopped me in my tracks.

"Don't send that bitch in here to get fucked up," I warned.

He sat up slowly, gaze glued to me. "You touch her, Sweetness, and she's going to tase you until you're pissing the floor instead of in the toilet. Tread lightly, love. You're already in so much trouble."

Bunny smirked at me as she waved the taser he must have handed her. I sneered at Jordan.

"You need a bitch and weapons and you had to hit and drug me to take me? You really are a bitch ass nigga. What did I just knee you in? Couldn't be balls," I jeered.

He just smiled. "Hurry, love. I can't wait to begin your training."

Rolling my eyes, I stalked into the bathroom. Bunny watched me from the doorway, and I flipped her off.

"Fuck you looking at, Lassie?" I mouthed off.

"You're going to learn that he doesn't like his women to curse and be disrespectful," she responded.

"I'm not his woman."

"You'd better accept that you are. It'll make shit easier for your evil self," she advised angrily.

I wiped and flushed the toilet before standing.

"What is that? Stockholm Syndrome? Cuz you can't be dickmatized by what I saw!" I shot back as I washed my hands.

I made quick use of the gentle facial cleanser. Then, I grabbed the unopened toothbrush and toothpaste and took care of my nasty mouth while she carefully monitored me. Finally, I was ready to go back into the bedroom.

Jordan was waiting, watching me, the lust in his eyes obvious. It made me scared and more than a little sick. Would he try to take what I had no intentions of giving his weak ass? Lord, I hoped not. He turned sideways and adjusted himself, and I gagged.

"Don't act like you have to make room for that Vienna sausage," I snarked.

He chuckled. "That one was childish, Sweetness. And trust me, one day you'll beg for this cock like you probably begged for Salinas's. You're going to cleanse yourself and earn it first, though."

I tapped my chin with my index finger like I was thinking.

"Mmm... that begging part? That's not really accurate. The one time I tried to beg, he had his dick so far down my throat, I couldn't—"

The slap against my cheek wasn't even shocking. I actually laughed at his weak ass. He tried to cover up his annoyance immediately.

"You feel better?" he asked.

I shook my head. "Not until I get to watch Smoke leave you in that water I can smell. We're on the Gulf, huh?" I fished.

Ignoring me, he ran a hand over his smooth chin. "You gotta lot of faith in that nigga," he commented.

I shrugged. "It's a mix. I gotta lot of faith in him and none in you."

"I guess you hoping that faith is not misplaced."

"I guess you better hope that I'm not misplaced. If he doesn't find me soon, soon, he's gon' start shaking down yo' family. You ready to say bye to everyone you love?" I goaded.

That got a response. I watched as his eyes narrowed and his hands clenched into fists.

"You better hope—"

He stopped as a phone rang. Frowning, he pulled the device from his pocket. He sighed as he answered.

"Mother, I'm kind of busy right... What? What are you talking about? Daddy is not missing. He—"

Raising an eyebrow, I smirked at him. I could hear the older woman's panicked screams. Jordan's eyes flew to mine, the rage in them unmistakable. I shrugged and mouthed, *I told you so.*

Until that moment, I had doubted Jordan's desire to do me serious harm. But he hung up the phone and had me undressed and rechained to the bed, this time on my stomach, in minutes. My heart dropped. He opened a wooden cabinet mounted on the wall. I swallowed as I saw the things inside. Some, I had been curious about, even wanted to approach

Cartier about—the crops and floggers, smaller whips, and light paddles. All of those sparked my imagination and my desire when I thought about them in Cartier's hands. I got sick thinking of Jordan touching me with anything like that. And when he reached for a vicious looking whip that looked like it may have terrorized our ancestors, I almost peed again. But my mouth didn't betray that.

"I'm gon' teach you your first lesson. All this shit been funny to you, huh? And now my fucking father is gone—"

"Talton probably just had a meetup with this beautiful little lady named Scarlet," I said.

"Who the fuck is Scarlet, Dayana?"

I smiled at him. "Smoke's switchblade."

Even though I heard the crack of the whip, I wasn't prepared for the fire that shot across my back, excruciating in a way like nothing else I'd felt in my life. I screamed as I snapped against my restraints, but he didn't stop. Over and over, he unleashed the agony, the inferno caused by the whip, Jordan beat me until I could feel the blood running down my back, until my voice was hoarse from sobbing and screaming, until I went into some kind of numbed, shocked state, silent and shaking so hard that Bunny had to talk him off me. Finally, he bent to bring his sweaty face in line with my blurred vision, stroking my hair and my tear-stained face.

"You shouldn't have made me go so far, Sweetness," he whispered. "You better pray that my father is okay. It won't be good for you if you have to pay for Smoke's sins as well as yours."

He pressed a kiss to my forehead and the vomit I'd felt bubbling finally spewed forth.

"Clean her up," he ordered Bunny.

"Y-y-yes, sir," she mumbled.

I closed my eyes as tears leaked from them. I heard the door close and Bunny scramble across the room to the cabinet

Jordan had opened. Seconds later, I felt her looming over me as she hissed, "Bitch!"

A liquid sprinkled on my back. The unbearable fire blazed through my wounds again. Too weak to scream, I felt my body seize. Then, blessedly, blissfully, my consciousness was gone.

CHAPTER 85

Dream

(*MONDAY,* July 5)

I'd never seen Damien drive this car before. The Alfa Romeo Giulia Quadrifoglio, from its glossy red exterior paint to its luxe black leather interior, was gorgeous. If I were in my right mind, I'd have been begging him to let me drive it. Instead, I was nervous about the visit we were about to make to my father's home. Funny how it had stopped being my family's residence and now housed only the man I wasn't even sure I knew any more. I had wanted to come alone, but Damien refused to even entertain that. So, here we were, speeding along silently, awkwardly, because I needed answers. My eyebrows lifted as we pulled up. Then, I laughed angrily.

"He's comfortable enough to have company and leave the gates open?"

Damien shook his head.

"Hell nah. That nigga was probably hoping to leave and lay low for a little while. These are Smoke's people. He's not letting your pops get away until he gets Dayana back."

Dayana. My heart sighed. We had talked to Smoke a little while ago as he and Grandpapa exchanged notes and ideas for their teams. I had to give him credit—he was leaving no stone unturned in the search for my sister. He had reassured Mama and me he was going to find her. He'd even put a suddenly humble DeAngelo to work. D was sick over his twin. He'd literally gone from house to house of Middleton relatives and friends, enraged and trigger-happy, looking for leads. He'd been picked up after the third shooting, but I'd begged Damien to get Dante to make it go away. He hadn't given a fuck, but he'd done it for me.

Damien parked and we got out. I was a little surprised that my biometrics still worked on the front door. Damien and I walked into the quiet, darkened house. I'd grown up here and it had never felt this cold, this foreign, this empty. Part of me wanted to cry, but I was fresh out of tears.

Daddy wasn't hard to find, sprawled on the living room couch, leisurely sipping what looked like Hennessy from a Baccarat cognac glass. He gave us a twisted smile and held out the glass.

"Drink? Or are you here to put a bullet in your old man's head?" he asked.

Disgust roiled through me.

"I'm here to find out why you sold my sister out and what you know about where she might be," I said coldly.

He shrugged. "I didn't sell her out. She owed that man an apology for humiliating him—"

"He humiliated her first! She owed him nothing!" I hissed the words as I scowled at him. "Your baby girl is missing, thanks to you, and you in here relaxing? Are you even trying to find her?"

Damien moved closer to me, resting a hand on my lower back as I ranted at my father.

"I got feelers out. He's just mad and embarrassed. He gon' bring her back," he said before nonchalantly taking another long pull from his glass.

My mouth dropped at the audacity of his total lack of

concern. Before I knew it, I had launched myself across the room and slapped the piss out of him. He sprang up, but Damien was there, moving me behind him so quickly that I barely had time to realize what had happened.

"I wish the fuck you would," he gritted out.

"Who are you?" I asked my dad over Damien's shoulder. "You're not the father we knew."

He laughed. "Who are you?" he clapped back. "So brilliant at what you do. Washing the money, investing it, multiplying it, but you want to act like you're apart from my world."

"I do that for you," I whispered.

"You do it because you like it, Dream. You like the thrill, the risk. Instead of accepting that, you keep hollering about being legit. Being proper. But I gotta question. Do proper businesswomen lie on their backs on their office desks and let murderers fuck them blind?" he spat.

I gasped. Damien took a step forward. I grabbed his arm just as his fist tightened.

"Damien, no, let me...." My voice trailed off as I glared at my father. "You have cameras—"

"The fuck I need cameras for? Paul walked in on you and this nigga. He was so disappointed in you, Dream. *I'm* so fucking disappointed in you, Dream."

A year ago, hell, two months ago, those words would have crushed me. Now, with my sister missing and my family in shambles, I didn't have it in me to give a fuck.

"The feeling is mutual, Darius. This was a waste of time."

I tugged on Damien's arm, but he had his own words for Darius.

"As a courtesy to Smoke, I'ma let you keep breathing. But I know that you're behind Distinctive Dynamic Designs. You love them fuckin' "Ds." You helped McKellar—"

Oh, my God! I thought. *He'd set me up, too?* My rage exploded as he hurried to make excuses.

"Keith and I are old friends. He would've never hurt this girl. I just needed her to realize that you're not invincible, that you and the things you… prize can be reached."

"Of course, I can be reached when my own father is helping!" I screamed, trying to scramble around Damien.

He blocked my efforts as he stared down at my father.

"I'm going to enjoy finding out what you know about Keith McKellar. It won't be nearly as much fun for you."

Darius swallowed. "Get out," he whispered.

Damien chuckled. "Tick-tock, muhfucka."

Grabbing my hand, he backed us out of my childhood home. I looked up at the three-story stone house I had once loved. It was ruined for me now.

My own father had made sure of that.

CHAPTER 86
Smoke

(*TUESDAY*, *July 6*)

"Sir, pardon my forwardness, but I do think you'd be better prepared to continue the search for Ms. Castle if you would eat something and rest just two hours, perhaps?"

Ammo's proper voice stopped me mid-pace. He stood in the living room with me, had been with me since I found her broken jewelry and saw the traces of her blood. He'd been with me through so much more than that, and I usually respected every word out of his mouth. But right now—

"You want me to eat and sleep when she might be starving and sleep-deprived?" I snarled.

Logically, I knew it didn't make sense. I needed to be in my best shape to save her. But eating expensive food and lying up in my huge bed seemed like it would be a betrayal to her right now.

"I don't give a fuck what you think, Ammo."

"Of course, sir," he said calmly.

Always calmly. I sighed as an ounce of guilt snaked through me.

"Feel free to grab a nap and—"

"I'm fine, sir."

Nigga even cut me off politely and of course, he was standing by me. I made a mental note to include yet another big bonus in his monthly pay.

I scrubbed a hand over my face roughly. I hadn't been this restless since Jenna was sick. It was a little past three AM on Tuesday and I hadn't slept since early Sunday morning. Finding Dayana and bringing her back here with me and our families was all I could think about. We had no real leads yet, but Kat and the rest of my tech team were working around the clock. My crew and I were ready to go wherever they pointed. Once I had her back, I swear she was never leaving my sight again.

"Cartier, I need you to please try to eat, baby."

My OG's words broke me out of my thoughts. She set the tray of food she was carrying on a side table and came over to hug me. I let myself accept the comfort of her embrace, kissing her on top of her bonnet.

"What you doing up?" I fussed lightly.

"How can I sleep when my child's heart is so heavy?" she asked, stroking my cheek. "You gon' find her, baby."

"I know. I just need it to be now," I sighed.

She squeezed me tighter before stepping back.

"Come eat. It's just a sandwich and chips," she coaxed. "You, too," she told Ammo.

"Yes, ma'am. I thank you very much, Ms. Salinas," he said, giving her one of his rare smiles.

Stephanie Salinas would not be denied. She basically pushed me and Ammo into seats before digging in a small closet to pull out two TV trays. She had just started to put our food on the trays when my phone rang. I snatched it up.

"What?" I snapped.

"Boss, it's Ahmed. A couple of Humvees just pulled across the street. Looks like they're outfitted with armor kits, so we're opening the gates to approach."

Ammo and I were on our feet before he even finished. I

pushed the remote that would alert the other three guards in the house. One would get my mother and Jenesis into the safe room. The other two would join Ammo and me to back up the twelve guys outside.

"Go upstairs. Safe room," I told my mother.

She opened her mouth to protest.

"OG, not—"

I stopped as a sudden, bright light lit up the night and explosions ripped through the air. I could hear the agonized yells of my crew. *Flash bang*, I thought. Hell, I prayed. Flash bang grenades would stun them for five or ten seconds, leaving them momentarily blinded and deaf, but most likely not dead.

"Upstairs!" I roared at my mother as I reversed the gate operation on my phone.

"Closed?" Ammo asked as he opened the concealed gun closet and began to quickly select shit.

"Yeah," I said, catching my favorite sawed-off that he tossed to me. "The Humvees can take them out, but it'll take a minute. They can't get in, yet."

And then, we heard the helicopter. *Fuck!* I had assumed this was someone avenging Talton Middleton, an attack coordinated from afar by Jordan, who had probably heard of his father's death by now. But I should have known better. They didn't have the resources, Jordan didn't have the heart, and I had cut off the head of the family's snake. No doubt they were still shaken up.

Whoever this was, was next level. There was no way niggas across the street, still in their trucks, could have launched those grenades. And my gates and walls were high and smooth, almost impossible to climb from the outside. The helicopter that I'd only heard a minute ago was now over my property, meaning it was equipped with some kind of stealth modifications.

Ammo handed me a strapped, modified AR-15 that I

threw over my chest before I headed for the door. Unlocking it, I yanked it open, Ammo on my heels.

Too late.

Seven black-clothed, balaclava-wearing niggas were making their way up my front steps, discarded parachutes on my lawn. Behind them, my crew was just starting to recover, staggering as they attempted to aim their weapons. My eyes swung back to the tall, slim man in the middle of the lineup on my steps. I aimed the shotgun at the familiar figure, and he chuckled as he held up both hands.

"*Hola, mijo.* This is how you greet your father?" he asked.

"What the fuck are you doing here, Joaquín?" I growled.

Joaquín had this habit of popping up when the fuck he wanted and disrupting my life. I didn't have time for his shit now.

"Call off your *soldados* and we will talk."

"They probably can't hear me thanks to your fucking grenades. You do know stun grenades can still kill and you could have set my house on fire?"

I held up a hand, a silent order for my guys to stand down. Still, I was pissed the fuck off. This nigga could've seriously fucked up my operation when I needed it most.

"You think I would put my family in danger? That I would drop grenades, knowing *mi nieta* sleeps here?" he asked, sounding offended by just the thought that he would put Jenesis in harm's way. "No grenades, *mijo.* Plasma shields. Not lethal," he explained.

So, that was what the Humvees were for. I didn't even bother asking how the fuck he got his hands on that kind of technology. Joaquín was resourceful… and very, very rich.

"Joaquín, get off my fucking property before I put a hole through your chest," I advised calmly.

"But I come bearing gifts," he coaxed.

Before I responded, he had pulled a device from his pocket and pressed a button. A moment later, the door of one of the Humvees opened and another of his black-clad crew hopped down, then pulled another person out. I recognized the figure of a woman.

"The fuck is that?" I demanded.

"Trust me, *mijo*. Open your gates."

I grilled him before doing as he requested. The man walked through, gripping the woman's arm. When they were halfway up my driveway, I recognized Cassidy Middleton, Talton's wife. She hadn't been at home when I killed her husband and must have been warned some way, because she had disappeared. Trust my father to find her. A grim smile curved my mouth. I had questions for her.

"Thank you. Now, go before I call them alphabet boys on yo' ass," I told Joaquín.

The threat was fake, but I wanted him gone. I already knew that if he thought I needed him, though, he didn't give a fuck about no DEA, FBI, ATF, or none of those ABCs. All that mattered to him was DNA and I shared his. The nigga next to him suddenly pulled off his balaclava.

"Surely, there is no need for such hostility, brother. We come to help you retrieve your *mujer*," the young man said softly.

I didn't acknowledge Joaquín's other son. Four years after he'd been forced to leave my mother and me, he had a baby, Rafael, with a random hook up. It had crushed my OG when she found out. I hated that nigga for that. Rafael couldn't even be denied—nigga had my face, just lighter. We definitely looked like Joaquín.

"You brought this kid?" I spat.

Joaquín shrugged. "He is well-trained. How else will he continue to learn? And he was eager to help his older brother. You should…" his words trailed off and his eyes softened as he looked over my shoulder.

I knew damn well that nigga wasn't looking at Ammo,

Epps, or Sav like that, a thought confirmed a minute later when he whispered, *"Esposa."*

"I am *not* your wife, you fucking idiot! Skydiving from a helicopter? I guess a doorbell is too complicated for you," my mother snapped.

I turned to look at her, frowning. She was glaring at my father, her own silenced pistol pointed at him.

"Ma, safe room?" I quizzed angrily.

She rolled her eyes.

"I'm not about to hide in the wall while you fighting for our lives."

"First, Cartier will not allow me close enough to ring the doorbell and this way, I was able to use some of my favorite toys. Second, and most importantly, you will not put yourself in danger, *mi estrella*. You should be safe, where our *nieta* is," Joaquín told her quietly, his tone serious.

She swallowed, and I knew his use of the pet name he'd given her, *mi estrella*—my star—got to her.

"Shut up, Joaquín," she whispered, her hand shaking.

She rebounded quickly, though. "Didn't my son ask you to leave?"

"I will not leave *our* son until he no longer needs me," he countered. "Now, put your gun away and greet your husband appropriately."

Mama smiled. "Greet my husband appropriately?"

"Yes."

I shook my head, knowing his crazy ass had walked right into a trap. Close up, even a shot from a silenced gun is loud. Wincing, I grabbed my ears as Joaquín stumbled backwards and down a couple of steps from the force of Mama's shot. She knew her way around a gun, so I knew the shot wouldn't be fatal.

While most of his men turned toward him, one of the bastards pulled on my mama. I swung the shotgun in his direction as Joaquín roared, his own gun hand coming up. He fired and his shoota collapsed. He barked at the rest of them in rapid-fire Spanish, reminding them that Mama was off limits before returning his adoring gaze to her.

"You have wounded me. Are you satisfied now, *mi esposa*?" he asked, grabbing his upper arm.

"I am not your wife! And you're breathing, so, no, I am not satisfied!" she popped off.

"Then I will make sure you are before I must leave," he promised, his voice low.

I gagged. "Come on, nigga," I groaned as my OG marched into the house, cussing his ass out.

He laughed as he held his arm.

"*Dios*, I love that woman."

CHAPTER 87

Smoke

SHIRTLESS AND STRADDLING one of the dining chairs that had been moved into my office, my father sighed as my mother viciously stabbed a needle into his shoulder. She was closing the hole the in-and-out bullet had made in a part of his upper shoulder and arm not covered by the body armor he had worn.

"*Mi estrella*, you are enjoying this too much, no?" he asked.

"It's the only thing about your body I'll be enjoying, so let me have fun," she snapped.

I grilled them. Rafael looked amused, but I ain't wanna hear that shit at all!

"Y'all gotta be stopped, with y'all nasty asses," I groaned.

Mama paused, the needle held in mid-air.

"Who you talking to, Cartier Alaric? I owe you an ass whooping for the way you hollered at me earlier!" she threatened.

Joaquín's eyes flew to me. "You disrespected your *mamá*?" he growled.

I held up a hand. "Slow ya roll, nigga. She was trying to argue with me about the safe room."

He looked over his shoulder at her and made an irritated noise. Mama rolled her eyes and jabbed him with the needle. He hissed before turning back to me.

"Watch how you treat someone so precious," he said.

"Really, *Papá*? *¡Ella es difícil y obstinada! Tú lo sabes*," I argued. (*She's difficult and stubborn! You know that.*)

A pleased smile crossed his face. Too late, I realized I'd forgotten to call him Joaquín, instead referring to him by the title I'd used for him when I was a jit. But all he said was, "Your Spanish is still excellent, *mijo*."

Suddenly uncomfortable, I gestured to where Cassidy Middleton sat in a wingback chair, looking scared out of her fucking mind as Ammo and Rafael stood in front of her.

"Can I get on with this?" I asked sarcastically, withdrawing Scarlet.

I didn't wait for an answer as I crossed the room to take the chair in front of her. Her eyes widened as she visibly shook. I smiled at her, flipping my knife, blade retracted across my knuckles.

"Good morning, Mrs. Middleton. You good?" I asked.

She shook her head hard as fuck. Tears streaked down her cheeks. I tilted my head to the side and looked at her.

"What's got you so upset, lady?"!

"Y-you killed my husband?" she choked out the question, swiping at her nose.

I tapped my chest and did my best to look offended.

"Is that what you think of me, after my hospitality?" I mocked.

She swallowed, her head bent, her chest rising and falling rapidly.

"Are you going to kill me?" she mumbled.

I looked up at Ammo. "Am I gon' kill her?"

He'd gone through the phone Joaquín's crew had snatched from her.

"Her phone is new, a burner. Mrs. Middleton has made

calls to her sons, James and Jacob. Yesterday, at six PM, she received a call from a number that went unanswered. She called back to that number just after nine. They held a five-minute conversation. There is a missed call just after midnight. I assume she was in the elder Mr. Salinas's... care by then. Kat is currently working on the numbers," he said, handing me the phone.

I nodded once, then looked at Cassidy. "Living is up to you. Tell me about that phone call."

Her lips pulled into a tight line as she refused to answer. I laughed softly.

"You think Jacob and James are going to save you? They scheduled to land in under an hour. Had to cut their trip to Italy short. Something about their daddy and their brother missing. I got people ready to grab them. What happens to them after that is up to you. I'm treating you to the luxury of my office, but we can go to one of my... playrooms. Not the kind you thinking—get yo' mind out the gutter, ma. But there will be some sensory play." I released my blade and she whimpered. "I'll let you watch as I remove their eyes, ears, tongues, and hands. See how well they communicate with you then. You gon' sacrifice two of your sons for the one who fucked up?"

Blinking back tears, she looked at me.

"B-but you gon' kill him," she whispered.

"My shorty's blood was on your floor. Yeah, I'm gon' kill him. But if you don't start talking, I'm gon' kill him, your other sons, and you. Can you imagine what your daughter and granddaughters will have to do to survive?" I asked coldly.

She started sobbing for real then, shaking her head.

"You got five minutes to make a choice," I pressed.

My mother cleared her throat as she finished with Joaquín.

"I understand a mother's loyalty. But now is not the time," she told Cassidy, walking closer to me.

The other woman cried harder. I glanced up as something chimed in Ammo's direction. He pulled out his phone and looked.

"Sir, it would appear that James and Jacob Middleton have landed a bit early," he announced.

My eyes pinned Cassidy's. "Never mind about those five minutes. Time's u—"

"I don't know where he is! I don't," she exclaimed hurriedly.

My mother leaned forward.

"My son's being nice because you're a woman. I don't have to be. You saw me sew up that man's back?"

Cassidy nodded, eyes big as fuck. My OG smiled.

"If we find out you lying, I'm gon' sew your lips together and make sure we keep you until it's permanent," she promised.

I loved that lady with her gangsta ass. Holding Cassidy's phone up to her face, I unlocked it and went to her recent calls. I dialed the last number back and waited. Someone picked up after four rings. I switched to speaker phone.

"Mother, I told you I'd have someone retrieve you as soon as—" Jordan began, sounding irritated and sleepy.

"You talk to your mama like that? You young people have no respect," I scolded.

He was silent for a moment, then, "Where is my mother, Salinas?"

I rested my left ankle on my right knee and leaned back in my chair, eyes glued to Cassidy.

"She's right here, *dying* to be reunited with yo' bum ass father. Yo' turn. Where's Dayana?"

"Don't touch my fucking m—"

Something inside me snapped and I felt the raging heat of the anger I was trying to hold back roll over me.

"Where the fuck is my woman?" I roared at him.

"Upstairs in my bed," he taunted.

My vision blanked and I lost a few seconds. I heard my mother scream my name, felt hands suddenly holding me back. When the darkness cleared, Cassidy Middleton sat in front of me, sobbing and clutching the rapidly spreading bloodstain on her shirt. The tip of my knife was stained red. Shit, I had aimed for this bitch's heart.

"If you make me re-open my shoulder after your mother tortured me, I will fight you myself, *mijo*," Joaquín said, his voice low, trying to calm me.

He and Rafael had grabbed my arms. Ammo stood back, one hand on his gun. He wanted to respect my family, but he was ready to end their asses, too.

"Get your hands off me," I growled, tightening my grip on Scarlet.

"I know you are anxious to have your *mujer*. I know *el cabrón* on the telephone has angered you. But you should not kill her yet, *hermano*. She may be of use," Rafael spoke quietly.

I scowled at his ass, even as I silently admitted the kid was right. Cassidy Middleton was definitely a pawn I should use carefully. I yanked away from my father and brother. My OG handed me the phone I had dropped, and I could hear Jordan screaming. Good. He needed to be shaken up. His bitch ass had knocked me off my square—I never used Scarlet on women, but for Dayana, I'd carve this bitch like a Thanksgiving turkey.

"Salinas! What the fuck did you do? I swear to God if you—"

"I'm going to make you a onetime offer. You have twelve hours to return her, and I'll let you have your mother. After twelve hours…"

I felt a sinister smile curve my mouth. My office was quiet except for the sounds of Cassidy weeping and Jordan breathing heavily through the phone.

"Jordan, please," she cried. "Your father is missing

because you're obsessed with this girl. You can find another—"

"I don't want another girl. This one is mine. At least let me make Daddy's... loss mean something, Mother. Salinas won't... I can't... *Fuck*! I need to think. I need to—"

"Jordan!" Cassidy sobbed.

"Mother, please. I have—"

"Twelve hours. You have twelve hours or I'm going to cut her heart out and send it to your brothers in pieces," I vowed before disconnecting.

"Noooo! Wait!" Cassidy wailed.

My gaze swung to her and she clamped a hand over her mouth, trying to muffle her cries.

"That nigga don't give a fuck about you. If you wanna save your life, now is the time," I advised.

"But—"

"Girl! Don't be stupid," my mother hissed. "You wanna die for a nigga who wouldn't even negotiate for you? He's leaving yo' ass to die. Cuz trust me—that's what's gon' happen. You gon' die. You might live long enough to see your heart lifted out yo' chest. Is that what you want?"

Cassidy stared at Mama a minute before slowly shaking her head. I watched as the wheels turned in her head. She swallowed back a sob. Then, she started talking.

"He says... he says the girl is alive, but he fucked up. And I know he's near water. I heard the waves. The only house we have on the water is on St. Thomas. He didn't have time to get there. That's all I know. I swear that's all I know."

I shook my head. Jordan and Yana hadn't been on a plane, according to Kat's searches. She'd know if they'd boarded any flight, domestic or international. I looked at Ammo.

"Check again," I said. "Put eyes on their waterfront property."

He nodded once before walking just outside the room to make the call. He was back faster than I expected.

"She wants to talk to you, sir," he announced.

"Speaker," I said tightly.

"Hey, boss. Was about to call you," Kat greeted a moment later.

"Go ahead."

"Ammo told me about the water. I got a hit a little while ago— a car registered to Jordan was pulled over in Corpus Christi yesterday. It was driven by a Tandy Fairlie from San Antonio. She is a named insured, so there may be a relationship. Check your phone for the picture."

I grabbed my phone immediately, then sucked in a breath when I saw the pic Kat sent.

"It's the bitch from the grocery store," I told Ammo, standing. "Kat, I need you to find—"

"All due respect, boss man, let me finish," she interrupted gently. "I figured if she's with him and they snatched your lady, they're not at a hotel or rental, but I couldn't find a spot in Corpus in any of the family's names."

"I don't care. We can find that son of a bitch—"

"Uncommon Milieu," Cassidy whispered.

My head snapped toward her, then back to Ammo's phone when Kat said the same words.

"What?" I demanded.

"One of Middleton's companies, Uncommon Milieu, holds a house on North Padre Island, right off Corpus. I sent the address. I think that would explain the sound of water. It's the Gulf." Kat said.

For the first time since all this shit happened, I felt a sense of direction and something like hope. I was going to go get my baby. I handed Ammo the phone.

"Sir—"

I cut him off.

"Make the arrangements. We going to Corpus."

CHAPTER 88
Demon

DREAM TOSSED RESTLESSLY, so much on her mind that she was barely asleep. I was up, dressed except for my shoes, ready to make shit shake. And then, she frowned and made a soft heartbroken sound as she came awake. Somehow, I was sliding back into the bed, pulling her into my arms.

"Shh," I whispered, my lips pressed against her temple.

"My sister," she mumbled.

"Smoke sent word for you—he's gone to get her."

Her eyes blinked open, the chocolate brown bleary and unfocused. Shorty was exhausted.

"Wh-what?"

"Your brother is with him. Smoke will get her, baby. And I'll take you to her. But right now, I need you to sleep."

She pressed closer to me. If she was fully awake, she'd still have her little salty ass attitude. I knew because she'd barely been speaking to me before we went to bed and she'd made sure she was fully covered—big ass t-shirt, panties, and pajama pants. Dream was the only woman I'd spent the night with in fifteen years, so I didn't have a lot of experience, but I knew that outfit meant, "I might be lying next to you, but you better not touch me!" So, yeah, she was mad, but half asleep, she was warm and soft and melting into me.

"Promise you'll wake me up?" she pleaded.

I knew how much it had to cost her, my independent, in-charge shorty, to trust me for information on the sister she loved so much. I wouldn't disappoint her for shit.

"As soon as I know something," I promised.

She nodded, but I could still feel the tension in her usually soft body.

"What is it?"

"I should go to work, Damien. I don't want to go, but there's too much... I-I need to be on top of things. It's too much for Parker by herself and Paul..." She swallowed hard. I knew his bitch moves bothered her. She'd actually consid-ered the nigga a friend, but his jealousy got in the way. She spoke again, her voice softer. "I don't want to get in tr—"

"You not getting in trouble and you ain't going back to that job right now. We have accountants, money managers, all that shit. They used to... questionable accounts. Let Parker and a couple of your other people train them and they can help until you get back," I offered.

She squirmed against me, then finally met my eyes, her gaze doubtful.

"How do I know I can trust them? I can't—"

My arms tightened around her.

"Nobody in this fucking city would cross you."

She scoffed. "Damien, my family definitely has enemies."

I laid two fingers across her perfect lips, silencing her.

"And you definitely belong to me. You think these niggas don't know that fucking with you will end badly for them?"

She sighed. "Damien, you can't kill everybody!"

"Dream, there are things much worse than death. Trust me, shorty. Let me help you."

I don't know why I said it like that; it wasn't optional. She was going to accept my help, and she wasn't going back to that shit until she was taking it over.

"I belong to you?" she repeated, making it a question.

"I told you that. Is that a problem?" I asked, tensing as defensiveness kicked in.

She sighed, trailing her hand along my chest and up my neck until it rested on my chains. Baby obviously didn't know the power of her touch. I was about to say fuck my plans and her touch-me-not outfit.

"I didn't say it was a problem. But... tomorrow is our last day," she whispered, her eyes liquid as they met mine.

I wanted to lie like I'd lost count, like that fucking deal was the last thing on my mind. I had excuses—the Keith shit; dealing with Kam; the reappearance of my sister. I wanted to tell her that those fucking thirty days meant nothing to me, that she was mine until our caskets dropped, and that was the end of that shit. But part of me needed to know what *she* thought about those thirty days. And because I was a fucking coward, I slid away from her and stood up.

"You just not gon' say anything?" she pressed quietly.

"Go back to sleep, Dream," I deflected.

For the first time, she seemed to realize I was dressed. She frowned, white teeth worrying her bottom lip.

"Where you going?" she asked, sitting up.

"To take care of some shit."

"About Keith?"

I nodded before turning to grab my shoes.

"With... with my father?"

The words were soft, laced with worry. After all he'd done, she was still worried about him. I tried to understand, but this nigga kept hurting her and her sister, and she wanted to find something about him to believe in.

"Yes."

I heard her moving, felt her anxiety.

"I thought you were going to wait for Smoke."

I chuckled, turning back to face her.

"You think Smoke being there will make it better for him?"

She rubbed a hand across her face. "Damien, just don't —"

"Don't what, Dream? Kill that dirty muhfucka? Yo' ass needs to accept that some people need killing and yo' weak ass daddy is one," I growled.

She squeezed her eyes shut, breathing fast as she twisted the sheet in shaking hands. Finally, she looked at me again.

"I can't do this right now. I don't want to fight with you right now," she whispered.

"That's what you think I want? To fight with you? I go outside every fucking day and fight. Always have. I don't mind doing what I have to do out there, but I don't wanna come home and fight you, too. You for me. *Mine*. And I don't want to fight you," I admitted.

She was out of the bed and hugging me fast as hell.

"Damien," she breathed my name. "I love you."

I squeezed her tight, unable to give her those words. But I'd give her what I could.

"I'm not gon' kill him," I promised. *Tonight*, I added silently.

"Thank you."

"Probably gon' fuck him up a little."

She sighed. "He deserves it."

I held her a little longer, glad for the feel of her in my arms. No way I could let this shit go.

"So, no more fighting?" she murmured.

"Nah. And no more wearing this ugly shit to bed. That ugl'ass bonnet enough," I complained.

She giggled against my chest.

Thirty-five minutes later, I looked down at Darius Castle, snoring on his couch, an empty Hennessy bottle on the coffee table. This nigga looked like he'd given up on life. That was a smart move, because I doubted Smoke was going to leave any in him. If he did, I'd be happy to beat it out of him.

Reaching down, I grabbed his collar and pulled his ass up before backhanding him. He startled awake, fists swinging uselessly. When his eyes finally focused, he sneered at me.

"The fuck you want?"

"Keith McKellar."

I didn't have time to fuck around. He leaned forward toward the coffee table and I pulled back my fist. Throwing up both hands, he frowned.

"Damn, can I just get my cigar?" he spat.

I shook my head. "Nah, nigga. You ain't fucking up my lungs. Start talking."

"Why should I?"

I sighed. My promise to Dream was looking like it was going to be hard to keep.

"Cuz I'ma kill you if you don't. And yo' dumb ass keep putting yo' own flesh and blood in danger. The least you can do—"

"That nigga would never hurt my—"

I tried to knock the spit out of his mouth.

"Oh, yeah?" I asked as he cupped a hand around his bloody lips. "Nigga promised to see how sweet her pussy was before he killed her."

The memory of Dream telling me that had my fist crashing into his eye.

He sniveled for a minute before speaking.

"I'on know where the nigga is. He reached out to me. I helped with money and some shit, but that was it."

"You don't think that was enough?" I jeered.

"I ain't hiding him. He still got family here—"

"Them bitches been questioned. Thoroughly."

Hell, we'd had to send a couple on to Jesus to make a point.

"Nah. Nah, you ain't found the right ones," Darius insisted.

Nigga sounded sincere, so I decided to let him talk.

"How you figure?"

"Cuz somebody gotta be taking care of his daughter. That's the key to Keith. He loves that girl and, the way he talked, she's close by. I think her name was Bria... Briana... some shit like that. You find her, you find the way to him."

I nodded. Then, just because the thought of him playing with my baby's life pissed me off, I punched him in the temple, putting him back to sleep.

As soon as I was in my truck, I called Li Jun. Nigga had a whole team, but he was the best, so I refused to work with any of the rest of them.

"We may have missed some of his family," I said, pulling off.

"I'll look again immediately," he didn't argue.

"Including a daughter who might be named Bria or Briana, or some shit close to that. Possibly in the area. Check the schools and whatever shit you do," I instructed.

"On it," he said.

I called Dante next.

"You up causing problems already?" he greeted.

"How many people we got handling money?" I asked, ignoring his sarcastic ass.

"Layers of them. I'on trust nobody too much."

"Recommend a couple. I need to re-assign them temporarily."

He was quiet for a minute. I knew he wanted to ask what was up, but he was trying to fight the urge.

Finally, he said, "I'll let you know in a couple of hours."

"'Preciate it."

He called my name before I could disconnect.

"Yeah?"

"Did Smoke find—"

"He's on it now."

"And the arrangements for your... for Melanie?"

Shit turned my blood cold. Just when I was trying to get along better with this nigga...

"Why you asking me that shit?" Tried to get KiKi to light that bitch up and sprinkle her over the nearest landfill. She didn't agree, so I ain't asked about no arrangements.

"I wanna be there for y—"

I disconnected the call. These muhfuckas around me were losing their minds, trying to make me care about a bitch who let me be tortured and sold me away. Fuck Melanie Montana.

Turning up the music, I ignored the pang in my chest.

CHAPTER 89
Dayana

PAIN. It was the first thing I noticed every time my eyes blinked open. My back stung and throbbed. My head ached. My face felt tight from Jordan's repeated hits. And my eyes were so heavy, the result of Jordan and Bunny repeatedly drugging me. I had no idea where I was, just that the tang of saltwater lingered, even in the air-conditioned room. I didn't know how long it had been since the Fourth. I thought I had counted two mornings, but they could have been knocking me out for days.

My stomach growled and I knew Jordan would come to feed me in a minute. I hated it. He loved it, loved that I had to eat from his hand and depend on him for sustenance. He kept talking about breaking me, training me. I'd rather die first. Right after I slept some more…

"No, Dayana. Wake up!" I told myself.

I needed to stay awake, make a plan. But it was so hard when all I wanted to do was close my eyes and escape the pain. Maybe I could… just for a m—

My eyelids flew up as the door opened. Bunny stood there, glaring at me. From Jordan's rambling, I knew he had this crazy idea that he and I would be together, and that

Bunny would not only be our sexual sub, but some kind of servant. How the fuck he thought that would work when she was obviously so jealous that she hated me, was beyond me.

"How's your back?" she asked, smirking.

The last time I was awake, Jordan had tried to feed me breakfast for dinner, including grits, which I hated. He forced them into my mouth. By the third spoonful, I couldn't take it anymore. I spit them into his bitch ass face. He whipped me again, reopening the welts on my back and adding new ones to my ass and upper thighs. Afterwards, Bunny had sprinkled that damn ginger juice on me again, intensifying my pain. At this point, I wanted to kill her as much as I wanted to slaughter Jordan.

"Fuck you," I mumbled, struggling against my chains.

I was flat on my back, too dazed and disoriented to do much, but I had to keep fighting. I knew my family was fighting for me and, in my heart of hearts, I knew nothing would keep Cartier Salinas away. But I was starting to feel like Jordan might kill me before Cartier could find me.

Bunny walked closer to the bed and frowned at me.

"Why don't you treat Sir like he deserves so he'll let you take a shower? You look like shit," she said.

I looked up at her, ready to snap back on her ass. A clear look at her face had me pausing, though. Her eye looked as swollen as mine felt.

"You don't look too hot yourself. That nigga be hitting you?"

She shrugged like it was no big deal. "Because he loves me and it's his job to correct me when I mess up."

I stared at her blankly. I mean, I knew there were relationships where women were disciplined. Hell, Smoke had spanked my ass a couple of times when I was on my good bullshit. But this wasn't that. Jordan wasn't about loving correction. He was about control and power.

Suddenly, a new idea bloomed in my head. I half-smiled at Bunny, hiding the wince from the pain.

"I know you can't possibly like getting yo' block knocked off," I started.

"Mind your business," she spat.

"Bunny... you ain't gotta be with that nigga. You could get away—"

She leaned down, her face twisted into an angry mug.

"You mean, I could get you away! That's what you talking about. Bitch, you crazy. I'm not betraying him! I love him!"

My smile dropped. "You the crazy bitch, talking 'bout you love a nigga that got you looking like Martin after Tommy Hearne got ahold of him. I'm tryna save your life. Smoke is gon' kill Jordan and anyone helping him. I might be able to put in a good word for you if you just call him and let him know where the fuck we are," I suggested.

She was already shaking her head, looking at me like she was scared as fuck.

"You want me to lead him to Sir? To watch my love be killed?" she asked, sounding shocked.

Sighing, I pulled on my restraints again. If I could just get free, I'd kill this dumb hoe myself. I looked at her, deciding to try again.

"Bunny, let me break this down for you, honeybun. I'm fucking one of the biggest crime lords in Texas. I'm also my family's baby. I can guarantee you a few things. Smoke Salinas is looking for me with all his fucking resources. My grandfather Lucien Dumont, whose name still rings bells, is looking for me. My sister, who has a big, scary nigga who is crazy about her, is looking for me. Jordan doesn't even have his daddy to run to. In no situation does this look good for him. I'm gon' be found. He gon' be dead," I hissed as her eyes widened. "So which side you gon' be on?"

She was quiet for a long minute, then she spoke in a trembling voice.

"Maybe I'll think about it," she said, rumbling in the nightstand drawer where they kept the syringes and tiny vials

Angry tears welled in my eyes.

"Bunny, no. Are you tryna make me overdose? You gon' kill me. Jordan expects me up—"

"He's gon' be a little late this morning."

"Why?" I asked, stalling as she filled the syringe.

She stopped long enough to smile at me.

"He's thinking about moving us. I guess all yo' searchers ain't that good, huh?" she taunted, grabbing my arm and jabbing me with the needle.

And then we heard the distinct sound of glass breaking, followed by Jordan's scream. I smiled as Bunny froze.

"I guess they are."

CHAPTER 90
Smoke

(*A FEW MINUTES earlier*)

North Padre Island was so much more congested than the southern part of the island. That shit made a surprise attack almost impossible, but after my contacts confirmed three human-sized infrared signatures in this house, I didn't give a fuck about stealth. I should've waited until dark, but I couldn't take the risk of letting Jordan move Dayana. All I wanted was my baby back and I was about to get her.

Kat's team had gotten us through the front gate and disarmed the security system. The cameras would show looped footage instead of real-time activity. The locks were giving a little more problem, but they were currently trying to hack the app that controlled them. I wasn't waiting too much longer.

Ammo and Anthony were already moving quietly around the house. Jordan's bitch ass was apparently pacing the ground floor. I knew I had that nigga shook. The pussy was so fucking clueless that he didn't have a detail and he hadn't noticed the three SUVs carrying my crew parked along his street. Even though these houses had a little more privacy, someone in the neighborhood was going to notice our blacked-out vehicles eventually and probably call the cops. It's what these rich bastards did.

I sat in the driver's seat, just watching. My father and Rafael had insisted on riding with me, and I hadn't wanted to waste the time to argue. I'd already lost minutes arguing with my OG, who wanted to come. It took my father pulling her aside and telling her she wasn't going. When she'd protested, he'd said, "You will not like the consequences if you disobey me, *mi estrella*."

For once in her life, Stephanie Salinas actually kept quiet. Looking at Joaquín, I remembered suddenly where I got my dominant streak from. Then, I thought about *mi papá* spanking my mama and I had to shake that nasty shit off.

My other passenger was DeAngelo Castle. He'd pulled up a little bit before we left. Nigga was damn near desperate, but he was single-minded about rescuing his twin.

I glanced over the seat at Rafael. The kid was much calmer, way more composed than I had been at eighteen.

"You willing to risk yo' life for my shit?" I asked.

"*Sí*," he answered without hesitation.

"Why?"

I really was curious. I'd probably met him three times in eighteen years and I had never been friendly. I didn't dislike him; I just felt some kind of way. I remembered my mother being sad about Joaquín's cheating. Plus, I'd been my parents' only kid for eleven years by the time Rafael came along. I had still missed Joaquín living with us and being in my life daily. Knowing that he had another son in Mexico that he saw more regularly didn't set right with me.

Rafael cleared his throat before speaking.

"You have no brothers or sisters with your *mamá*, but I do. They are young, but I would do anything for them. Our *papá* speaks of you well and often. I know you do not know me and I understand you do not want to know me. But you are still *mi hermano*. I would do anything for you, too," he explained quietly.

I nodded. So, the little fucker was loyal. I could respect that.

"A'ight. All I can do is try to keep your head on yo' neck," I said.

He gave me a half-smile.

"Sir, any word on the locks? We feel that we have sufficiently monitored Mr. Middleton's movements. He is alone downstairs at present. I saw Ms. Fairlie ascend the stairs where Ms. Castle is most likely held. We have a clear shot at Mr. Middleton. Permission to proceed?" I heard Ammo's quiet, British-Nigerian accent through my earpiece.

"Hold," I instructed, hand on the door handle. "You not going in without me. And I want that bastard alive. I'm—"

I stopped as an Expedition pulled in front of the house and idled on the street. Seconds later, it pulled through the open gate and parked. Six men spilled out of the vehicle and made their way up the driveway. One of them surveyed the street and I felt his eyes land on my truck. I had waited too long—this muhfucka Jordan had finally organized back up. I banged my head on the headrest.

"Ammo—"

"I see, sir. Six, correct?"

"Yeah. We still outnumber them, but how the fuck we gon' get the jump on them?"

I watched as the guy who must've been the leader spoke. I knew we were made when he left two men outside.

"Ahmed, I need the guys in your truck to hold tight. My truck is emptying. Bruno, Quad, help cover and follow us in. Ammo, you and Anthony use the long-range tasers and take them niggas out in front. Someone might see, but I gotta get in ASAP," I said.

My team confirmed they understood. I watched as the guards in front collapsed, incapacitated by 50,000 volts. I quickly pulled the Tahoe behind the Expedition.

"They are still too close to the front door, sir. I'm going to take out a window, draw them away. Tell me when," Ammo said.

I looked at everyone in my truck.

"Ready?"

"Lead the way, *mijo*," Joaquín said, his voice low.

I nodded.

"Ammo, go!" I ordered as we sprang from the truck.

I heard the quiet *ping* of a silenced shot as we made our way across the street and through the gates. Joaquín and DeAngelo finished the niggas who had been tased. Ammo's call had been a good one. As I stepped through the door, three of those niggas were clustered around the window. I didn't know where Jordan found these niggas but they were clearly amateurs. I popped the one still near the entrance before he even got his mouth all the way open. Simultaneous shots–one from inside and one from outside–took out two of them. Jordan lay writhing on the floor, gripping his arm. My lips curled into a snarl. I was sure Ammo had only given his bitch ass a flesh wound. My right hand knew how much I wanted to handle this nigga.

Momentary distraction alost took me out. I heard a low chuckle and looked up to see the last of Jordan's detail aiming for me. His gloating was his downfall. I watched as a perfectly placed hole appeared between his eyes. I looked over my shoulder at the smoking barrel of Rafael's gun. Having a little brother may not be so bad after all, hell. I pointed at Jordan's ass.

"Grab that bitch, Bruno." I ordered, not even checking to make sure he understood.

It was beyond time to get my princess back. I climbed the stairs quickly, Rafael and DeAngelo on my heels. I found her in the second bedroom. What I saw made me glad I'd taken Jordan alive. He would pay for this. Dayana was chained to a bed, her hair wild, her face bruised and swollen, her lips cracked and ashy. Still, she smiled weakly.

"Bathroom," she whispered.

I nodded at Rafael, who immediately walked into the en suite. I heard a woman's screams and seconds later, my brother dragged out the bitch who'd been helping Jordan. She was babbling, crying, and trying to explain. She swallowed her sobs as I moved toward her. Yanking her from Rafael's grasp, I threw the bitch toward the bed.

"Unlock her," I hissed.

"O-okay," she agreed, fumbling in her pockets until she found a key.

Dayana moaned as she pulled her arms and legs closer to her body. I moved closer to her.

"Hey, Princess," I said softly.

I needed to get her out quickly, but I needed to know the extent of her injuries. I didn't want to make shit worse. If he'd broken her ribs, moving her could puncture a lung, for example.

"Hi," she murmured, her eyes dazed. "You have to excuse me. I forgot my tiara and I didn't have time to grab my makeup kit."

I smiled. Still my Yana. "You look beautiful."

She laughed, but it dissolved into coughs. I held her hand until it stopped. She turned her head toward her brother.

"Hey, D," she greeted lowly.

"Yana..." A tear streaked down his face. "I'm sorry. I swear—"

"It's okay. You just gotta do all my errands for the next decade."

He laughed through his tears.

"And you have a brother?" she asked me, looking at Rafael.

I nodded. "You can tell?"

"He has your face, your eyes. He might be cuter, though," she teased.

"Get fucked up, Princess. I need to move you, baby. You think anything is broken?"

She shook her head. "Weak ass nigga can't hit that hard," she said, talking shit as usual.

"I'ma pick you up," I said, unable to wait any longer to hold her, reassure myself that she was here with me. I slid my arms under her and lifted, frowning as the bottom sheet came with her. I laid her back down, this time on her stomach, so I could see the damage. My mouth tightened as I saw the blood staining the sheet. Her hair in the back was also bloody. What the fuck had he done? I looked at DeAngelo, then pointed to the sheet. Nodding, he grabbed one edge and I grabbed another.

"We gotta pull the sheet, Yana, okay?"

"O-okay," she agreed, fear in her voice.

I held up a hand and counted off to three. DeAngelo had the same thought as I did. We ripped it off, trying to get it over with. Her scream... Jesus, her scream would stay with me forever. Sobbing, she curled into herself.

"*Madre de Dios*," Rafael whispered as we looked at her back.

The crisscross of bloody welts and broken skin burned my eyes. Right then, I knew—he would suffer. He would suffer in a way he couldn't imagine, I vowed to myself, unfamiliar tears blurring my vision. Carefully, I picked her up again and DeAngelo came around to drape the top sheet over her front. She was shaking as I pressed kisses to her face.

"It's okay. I got you," I promised. "We have to go, love."

She nodded. "D?"

"Yeah, baby?" her brother responded.

She pointed at Tandy Fairlie, who was back in Rafael's tight grip.

"Kill that bitch."

"You got it."

Rafael released the woman. Screaming, she tried to run. I watched DeAngelo lift his gun and aim.

And then the screams stopped.

CHAPTER 91

Lucia Dumont-Castle

(*THURSDAY, July 8*)

I closed my eyes, thanking God as my baby girl's voice came through my speakers. She sounded almost normal, her usual sweet, feisty self. If I hadn't seen the injuries Jordan Middleton had inflicted on her, I might be able to convince myself that the last few days had been a long nightmare.

But they hadn't been. And I was incredibly glad and grateful to Smoke Salinas for reaching her when he did.

"Mama, everybody's here except..." she said.

I could imagine her little pout, spoiled ass. But that was my baby. I adored my kids—had given my life to them; would give my life *for* them. Which is why I had a stop to make right now.

"I'm coming, baby! Give me an hour," I coaxed.

"Maaaaa!"

I shook my head but smiled at that whine.

"Girl! You know how I am."

She sucked her teeth. "Yeah. You're beautiful no matter what, so stop all that dressing up or whatever you doing and come on!"

My eyes watered at her words as I pressed my head against the headrest.

"You're beautiful, too, beloved. So beautiful and I'm so glad you're here," I whispered, sniffing.

She was quiet for a minute before speaking again. "None of that. Dream done snorted enough for both of y'all. Crybabies!" she teased. "Mommy, you got fifty-nine minutes and thirty seconds or I'm throwing a fit!"

I laughed quietly. "See you then, crazy girl."

I disconnected the call and turned up the sound of Heather Hedley. I would always love this lady and right now, she was singing everything I felt. I wish I didn't love this nigga I had married and blessed with three children. I couldn't believe how he was treating those blessings. Darius Castle had to see me. Something told me I better make it soon. I knew Smoke probably wanted to kill his ass, but my husband always had a plan b.

The gates to the home we had made together were open and I pulled onto the circular driveway, on the opposite side of the blacked-out SUV parked there. I had spotted another on the street—it stood out because our neighbors weren't all that close. I got out of my car, then reached back in for my crossbody bag. As I stood back up, the door to the SUV opened and a man held up a hand as he spoke into his phone. I rolled my eyes.

"I'm Lucia Castle and I am not gon' be kept out of my own house," I snapped, striding toward the door.

"Ma'am! Just wait on—"

He stopped suddenly then nodded at me once. "All right. You good, Mrs. Castle."

I flipped him off and he laughed as I let myself in. The house that was once filled with the sounds of a busy, happy family was cold and quiet. For a few minutes, I silently searched for my husband, walking room to room, swallowing my tears as I walked into our empty bedroom. I didn't even bother going upstairs; I knew where he was.

I had no doubt that Smoke had found the couple of safe rooms—one down here and one upstairs—that we'd built. But this other space... the one that neither my kids nor my father knew about, wasn't so easy. And if he were there, it would tell me everything I needed to know. Slowly, I walked to the kitchen and made my way toward the pantry. I kneeled and pulled out the bins of sprouting potatoes and withered onions. Reaching to the back, I slid the panel over and ran my fingers along the wall until I found a slight depression. I pressed it and waited as the two gliding shelves parted, revealing a knob-less door with an access panel. I entered the code and pressed my thumb against it. Seconds later, the door slid open and I came face-to-barrel with a Smith & Wesson pistol. I met my husband's startled eyes. Smiling coolly, I stepped into the chamber, not bothering to close it behind me.

"Aww, baby. You weren't gon' invite me?" I asked, sarcasm dripping from my tone.

It was the only way I could hide my hurt.

This room was full of emergency supplies and packed bags. It was a small bunker, but more importantly, the back wall contained an entrance to a tunnel. I didn't know it at the time, but Darius had our house built at the highest point in this neighborhood, allowing him to construct the bunker underground—something rare in Texas—and the tunnel that led outside our back fence. I watched as he lowered the gun.

"Lucia... you left me, Little Light," he said quietly, looking lost and tired.

For one moment, my heart softened. He looked so much like the nineteen-year-old boy who had first enchanted me when I visited here one summer. He'd promised me the world, charmed my mama, and impressed my daddy. Darius and I had truly loved each other, but in the last few years, something had been lost. His focus changed and our relationship—and our daughters—paid the price. I walked farther into the room until a couple of feet separated us.

"I can't believe you're running like a coward, Darius. You owe Dayana an apology. You could have gotten our baby killed and for what?"

He shrugged, like what I said made no difference. "I plan to talk to Yana soon, but that nigga ain't gon' let me nowhere near her right now. He out for blood, Little Light. Mine. We need to let shit calm down. I'll be back and we can fix this, we can fix us."

He smiled then, that smile that could always get me to stand beside him and do what he wanted. It wasn't working this evening, though. I shook my head. I couldn't believe how out of touch he was.

"Fix this, Darius? I supported you when you talked about arranging Dayana's marriage. You were supposed to give her good choices, men who would love her and take care of her and her children. Yeah, I knew you'd get something out of it, but that was supposed to be secondary. You tried to push her into something she didn't want for *your* benefit. Our baby, Darius. Her feelings—"

He threw up a hand, stopping me. Frustration and anger were written all over his face.

"Her feelings, Lucia? You worried about her feelings and I'm trying to secure her future?"

I scoffed. "*Your* future."

"*Our* future," he argued, walking across the room.

I watched as he threw his bag on the little oak table in the corner. Unzipping it, he picked up a couple of stacks from the table and stuffed them in. I stood in silence for a moment before trying to reach him again.

"Darius, we had a vision of our future and it was fine. You started wanting some different shit and you forgot about—"

He whirled on me so fast, that I jumped.

"I forgot? *I forgot?* No, you forgot, Little Light. You forgot that we had dreams bigger than a little change and a nice house in the suburbs. You forgot that we wanted to run shit. You forgot—"

"I didn't forget, Darius!" I yelled, tears springing to my eyes. "Yeah, we talked big, but we grew up. We had a family. We watched my mother slaughtered because of those same dreams. My priorities changed; I thought yours did, too. Obviously, I was wrong. What do you want all of that for, Darius? Our lives were fine. Our children were happy. We had plenty of money. You just can't be happy until—"

"Until I have it all. Until I have everything that I ever said I'd have when I was cold and hungry and didn't have shit," he hissed.

I rubbed my hand across my eyes. "Darius... Baby..."

He was unapologetic and I didn't know what to say. He grabbed his bag again, walking back toward me. He jabbed the pistol in his back holster before reaching out and cupping my face.

"I love you, Lucia. You could walk through this tunnel with me. You could stand with me and we could come back and rule this shit. You worried about them kids, but they grown. They gon' do their own shit and where will that leave you?" he asked.

"You think you gon' walk back into this city without apologizing to our daughter? You think Smoke gon' let that shit ride?" I laughed, but there was no humor in my voice. "My staying here makes me the parent who didn't abandon them. That's where it leaves me."

His hand dropped and he took a couple of steps back to just stare at me before shaking his head.

"I got shit I gotta do, Little Light," he said.

I heard no regret, no apologies. *When did he get so heartless, so fucking greedy?* I wondered. Anger swelled in me, blurring my vision. It was like I didn't know this man at all. I'd shared a home, a family, a life with him for over twenty years, and I didn't know him. He was hurting us, ruining us, and he didn't give a fuck.

"You really just gone walk away from us? Like that? Like it's nothing? You willing to sacrifice our daughters, our everything, and for what?" I whispered.

He snapped. "Lucia, get yo' fuckin' head out yo' ass. Sacrifice? Those girls happily laying on their backs every night—"

"My baby can't even lay on her back right now because of shit you did!" I screamed, fury roiling through me. "You almost got her killed, and you not even sorry! You sat back and let Dream—"

"*Laying on their backs,*" he insisted, "thinking they on some love shit, when they really just getting slutted out liked the average street walker. Instead of being free pussy, the least they dumb asses could do is profit from it. Hell, no, I'm not sorry for having a bigger plan for them, bigger than spreading their legs like a couple of wh—"

The loud *BOOM* stopped Darius's tirade and caught me off-guard. I didn't realize what it was until he looked down, his hand clutching his chest where a dark stain crept across it. A look of betrayal, of hurt crossed his face.

"Little Light..." he muttered before collapsing.

It was then that I realized the little Ruger he always insisted I stash in my purse was in my hand. It slipped from my grasp as I brought my hands up to cover my mouth. *What the fuck did I do?* Speechless, I stared at him The stain on his shirt was so big, now, and his chest wasn't moving. Could he really be dead? Could I have killed the man that I loved and hated?

"CPR, Lucia. CPR," I told myself.

I lost myself in the rhythm of breaths and compressions, my hands and my face smeared with his blood. It wasn't working. Jesus, it wasn't working. Finally, with one last compression, I stopped. Resting my head on his chest, I just lay there, missing the rise and fall of his breaths and the cadence of his heartbeat. After what felt like a long moment, I found the strength to rise. Pressing one last kiss to his forehead, I lowered his eyelids. I stood up, biting back a sob as I looked at his lifeless body. *Why did you change up on me, baby? Why weren't we enough?* I sat down heavily on one of the chairs at the table, resting my face in my hands. I let the tears I'd been holding slide down my cheeks.

I had loved this man for most of my life, but what he had done... the way he had tried to traffic in our daughters and talk about them like they weren't his flesh and blood... The part of me that was his wife mourned. But the part of me that was Lucien Dumont's daughter accepted that he had brought death upon himself. I just never thought it would be by my hand.

Suddenly, a pair of large hands grabbed my arms, pulling me up. I fought instinctively, screaming and struggling, but he was too strong.

"Lucia. You gotta get out of here so we can get this cleaned up," a deep, calm voice rumbled at me.

I froze and looked up into the eyes of Demon Montana. I didn't know why he was here, what he was saying. I just stared at him.

"Darius—" I mumbled.

He shook his head. "It's too late. You need to come with me."

I stood there for another long moment, eyes closed, not knowing which way to go. I didn't want to leave him. I *had* to leave him.

"Lucia—"

I nodded, cutting him off. Straightening my shoulders, I lifted my head, then glanced back at my husband one more time. Words gathered in my throat, fighting to get out. But it was too late for reckonings or goodbyes. *Next lifetime*, I thought. I turned and for some reason, I rested my forehead against Demon for one minute. He patted my back awkwardly.

"Okay," I finally whispered to him. "Okay."

CHAPTER 92
Demon

(A COUPLE of hours earlier)

I opened my bedroom door only to come face-to-face with my sister whose hand was lifted like she was about to knock. I gave her a half smile and dropped a kiss on her forehead.

"What's up, little baby?"

She returned my smile, then looked down at the shit in my hands.

"You leaving? I can wait," she said.

Shaking my head, I slid my wallet and my work phone into my pockets.

"I always got time for you. Run it."

She linked her arm through mine and pulled on me.

"C'mon. I'll walk you down. Where's Dream?"

"With her sister. She'll be back later."

Kiana glanced up at me as we neared the stairs. I knew a question was coming. Sighing, I looked at her.

"What?" I asked.

"What's up with her? She lives here, but she doesn't live here. You told me no titles, but you crazy possessive. She seems cool as fuck, so why you dragging your feet, Damie?"

I rubbed a hand over my face before sighing. "KiKi—"

"If it's none of my business, you can say that, too," she popped, a grin lighting her pretty face as we walked down.

"Nah, it's not that. Shit just... complicated," I responded, lame as fuck.

My little sister eyeballed me. "So, now you a social media status? It's okay, brother. I been there."

I stopped and grilled her. I knew she was grown, but hell, nah! "With who?"

Her smile turned mysterious. "Anyway... I wanted to run a couple things by you."

"Don't be tryna—"

"All the arrangements for Melanie's service are done. Saturday at eleven, we lay her to rest."

Her expression was suddenly serious as she gazed at me. I shrugged, immediately feeling myself go cold.

"And? You need more money?"

She sucked her teeth. "Don't play with me like that, Damien Montana. You been generous and I ain't exactly hurting. I had a couple of things to ask," she said.

Instead of asking, though, she played with her ponytail and rocked from one foot to the other as we stood in the middle of my living room. I looked at her expectantly. Finally, she spoke.

"Damie... are you coming to the service?" she asked quietly.

I crossed my arms over my chest and dropped my head, thinking. I didn't want to hurt my sister's feelings, but I was tired of everybody around me suddenly having amnesia about my relationship with Melanie. After a long minute, I met her eyes again.

"I mean, you and the kid will be there, so I'll be around," I answered.

She nodded, then hesitated again.

"KiKi—"

"I think you should go see her... at the funeral home, so

you won't be... caught off-guard at the funeral," she uttered in a rush.

I was shaking my head before she finished. "I'm good. You need anything—"

"We have to decide what to do about Kam," she cut me off.

I tensed as I looked down at her. "What you mean?"

"After the funeral, Topaz and I are going back. Do you want him to go with me?"

I ignored that question for now. "You can't just go back. Not til I get this nigga—"

"Damie, we'll be protected. Uncle Jerome has connections. Plus, Topaz's boss—"

I scoffed, not wanting to hear any of the shit she was spitting. "Her boss? Why some random nigga gon' look out for her like that? I'on trust that shit. You gotta stay—"

"Paz's boss ain't no random nigga, brother. It's Saadiq Masters and—" she paused and looked up the stairs and toward the kitchen to make sure no one was coming, "Paz don't wanna hear it, but that nigga half in love with her. He having a fit right now, tryna get her to come back. Ain't shit gon' happen to her, to us, under his watch."

I knew Masters's name, and had to give him, grudgingly, a little credit. Nigga was on the up and up now—mostly—but he'd proven himself in the right circles. Still, after fifteen years, my sister's safety wasn't something I played about.

"So, he got her. I ain't trusting him with you. You ain't going—"

"Damie... my job starts back next month," she coaxed. "Talk to Uncle and Saadiq. Let 'em know what you wanna see. But I gotta go back."

"We'll see," I muttered.

She rolled her eyes, then tugged on my arm.

"And Kam? When I go back, what about K—"

"His bad ass wanna stay here."

The words came out too quickly. She looked at me, her eyes knowing.

"Is that what you want, Damie?"

She was asking too much right now, wanting a confession I didn't know how to give. I swallowed hard, eyes focused above her head. Suddenly, I felt her arms slide around me and squeeze.

"It's okay," she murmured. "Keep his bad ass."

We talked a little more before I let Stella and another hitta in and myself out. My first stop was an art supply store. Kam and I both could use some things. I finished up quickly and headed to my next destination. Smoke had brought my little bestie home, so I knew Darius's time was ticking. I wanted to talk to that nigga one more time before Smoke slumped him.

I parked across the street from his house and jogged up.

"The Mrs. just went in there," one of Smoke's crew informed me.

I nodded and let myself in. I wasn't ready for what unfolded over the next several minutes. The secret room; the argument; the gunshot. And now. Fucking with Dream kept putting me in these unfamiliar situations. I glanced over at her mama where she sat staring sightlessly out of my windshield. Both of us sported a little of Darius's blood although she'd washed a lot off in the bunker's tiny bathroom before I hustled her out. She looked like she was in shock and I didn't know what to do except take her to her children who were at Smoke's where Dayana was recovering. I called him before we got there, wanting to make sure we could get in and that he'd be in the room for Dayana.

We made it through the gates with no problem. I parked behind Dream's car and hopped out before walking around to help Lucia out. She took my hand and then leaned against me heavily. She shook her head.

"I killed—"

"You can't be saying that shit out here," I interrupted as we made our way past Smoke's crew and to the front door.

There was a moment I was sure Lucia would never forget, the last moment her children would all be together looking happy for a while. Dayana was sitting with her injured back toward the arm of the couch, her socked feet in Dream's lap. Crystal and DeAngelo sat on the loveseat while Smoke, Rafael, and Ammo stood a few feet away, watching. Always observant, Lucien Dumont sat in a corner to himself, watching them all. Smoke gave me a grim look and a single nod. I returned the gesture. Then, Dayana saw her mother and me. The smile slowly left her pretty face.

"Mama?" she whispered.

Dream's head snapped up. One look and she was moving Dayana's legs and standing. She walked across the room to us, her gaze on the blood still smeared on her mother's clothes.

"Daddy?"

Her voice trembled. Lucia looked at her and shook her head. An anguished sob tore from Dream's throat and I thought she was going to collapse as she pressed her fists against her mouth. She moved past her mother toward me. I reached for her...

And all hell broke loose. She slapped the fuck out of me as voices erupted in the background. Caught off-guard, I looked at her in disbelief. She rocked back on her heels, grilling me.

"You promised me!" she screamed. "How could you, Damien?"

What the fuck?

"Dream!" Lucia snapped, whirling around.

But Dream had already made up her mind. Face wet with tears, shorty went in. "He did wrong shit. Bad shit. He had to pay. But with his life, Damien? That wasn't your decision! You always show me I don't mean shit to you, but you outdid yourself tonight. You make me sick!" she ranted.

She raised her hand again. I caught it, squeezing her wrist. If that's how she wanted to play this shit, that was fine. I showed her she didn't mean shit? All the ways I had changed? All the shit I had given her? All the things I wanted to do for her? *Fuck that.* Something in me closed down, iced over as I felt my lips curl into an ugly smile. She cried harder, struggling against me.

"Keep your hands to yourself," I said coldly.

She yanked her wrist and I released my grip, watching her stumble back.

"Dream, baby, listen—" Lucia tried again.

"Nah, she good," I interrupted as I backed up to lean against one of Smoke's walls. Crossing my arms over my chest, I smirked at her. "Go off, shorty."

She glared at me, looking like she wanted to spit on me. So much for that love bullshit. She'd judged and condemned me faster than a fucking lynch mob. I knew better than trusting her, knew better than showing her the other side of me. She was just like everybody else.

"I'm good? *I'm good?* You don't know shit about me. You just killed my father—"

"Dream!" Dayana snapped. "Daddy wasn't even the same anymore. The only thing he cared about—"

Dream shook her head. "Yana, he—"

"*Chère,* if you would let the man talk," Lucien fussed at her, wheeling his way across the room.

He grabbed his daughter's hand and looked up at her. A soft moan escaped her as tears slid down her face.

"Daddy, I—"

"It's okay," he whispered, squeezing her hand, before looking back at Dream. "Listen, baby—"

Dream's mouth tightened. "I- I can't right now. I just need..." she waved her hands aimlessly. "He has to go. He can't be here right now. Not with what he did. I need to—"

"Shorty, this ain't yo' crib," I reminded her.

Yeah, I was being an asshole, but Dream had me fucked up. Part of me, the part that she made so fucking soft, wanted to care about the tears on her face and the hurt in her eyes. *Fuck her,* I told myself, *she don't mean shit.* Her eyes blazed at me.

"It's not my house, but there's nothing for you here," she hissed. "Our thirty days are up, remember? You obviously don't give a fuck about me and my feelings and that shit is mutual."

"Okay, now y'all just saying shit. Stop, please? Just—" Dayana began.

"That shit is mutual, huh? Crazy how that ain't what you say when I got yo' ass all spread out," I taunted.

It was a low blow, something beneath even a fucked up nigga like me, but she always pushed my fucking buttons. Watching her mouth drop open and her face redden, I knew this shit was going too far. She was right; I needed to leave. And then, she spoke again.

"You are ignorant and disrespectful and I hate you. I can't believe I thought—"

She stopped as my eyes pierced hers. Pressing her lips together, she shook her head. I chuckled even as something sharp and uncomfortable ripped through my chest.

"You thought what? That you were in love? It's okay, shorty. You a good girl. You had to make yourself feel like shit was more than it was, that you were more than a fuck loaned out to me. I hope it helped you enjoy that thirty days. Shit was fun, but—" I let my eyes travel up and down her plush body. "Maybe I'll get back to model types."

At this point, I was just fucking with her and it was working. Fresh tears pooled in her distressed brown eyes.

"The softer ride was cool, though."

She made a soft, hurt sound that would've broken a nigga's heart if I had one.

"That's enough, Montana," Lucien spat.

Dream squeezed his shoulder as she glared at me.

"It's okay, Grandpapa. He's right. It wasn't love. How could I love him? His own mother couldn't."

Her voice was soft, but the words were razors, cutting open places that had never really healed. Blinded by anger and something else I couldn't name, I moved toward her. I heard Smoke call my name, heard Dayana call Dream's. I picked her up quickly, walking her backward and pressing her ass against the mural that decorated one of the walls. Her eyes were big as she stared at me. I lowered my lips to her ear.

"I don't want your love, bitch, just your pussy. Fuck your thirty days. You a sweet little wet pussy for me to buss in, Dream. That's it. So, it's however, whenever, wherever until I get tired of using you," I snarled.

"Damien…" she whispered hoarsely as she shook in my grasp.

I dropped her and she slid to the floor, soft sobs racking her body. Smoke's hand was on my shoulder and I yanked away. He sighed, rubbing a hand over his face.

"Demon… come on. Y'all need—"

I shook my head.

"I'm good," I said, moving away from him, away from her.

Approaching the door, I turned around to give her one last look. "You probably wanna shut up and listen to your mama now," I advised.

I let myself out.

CHAPTER 93

Smoke

(*FRIDAY, July 9*)

The soothing rasp of my blade sliding across the paddle strop was one of the few things helping me keep my shit together right now. I had managed to last three days. Three days from the time I found my girl until I decided it was time to destroy the stupid muhfucka who'd hurt her. I waited because what I was going to do to him required a softening, a loosening of the skin. Joaquín, who'd given me my love of knives, told me to boil the nigga for a couple of minutes, but I didn't want him to die too fast. I decided to starve him, but every day I looked at the damage to my baby's back and remembered her scream, my patience faded. Last night, when she'd had another nightmare, that patience died.

Like Jordan Middleton would today.

I stroked Scarlet down the strop again, wanting to make sure she was as sharp as possible. Peeling someone top to bottom—or as far as I could get before he died—needed a razor-sharp blade.

"Cartier... I don't understand why I can't go," Dayana complained from the bed behind me.

I looked over my shoulder and struggled to keep from grinning at her pout. She was definitely feeling better and ready to raise hell.

"No," I said simply.

"But why not? Vengeance should be mine," she huffed, aggravated.

"Why? You the Lord or some shit?"

"No, but I'm the vic— the survivor."

Her voice faded and I turned to look at her. She had the heels of her hands pressed into her eyes as she took deep breaths, trying to calm herself. I set my shit down and went to her, scooping her off the bed and rocking her back and forth.

"Ay, Princess. It's all right. I got you," I whispered, squeezing her tight.

For a few minutes, I just held her silently, until I felt her start to soften, the rigid tension leaving her body.

"I swear on my life, no one will hurt you like that again. But this is how I know you not ready to see that nigga and what's gon' happen to him. Let me handle this for you, Princess. I'll get your vengeance. I promise."

She buried her face against my chest and sniffled a few times.

"Will you do me a favor?" she asked finally.

"Anything," I vowed.

"Cut off his dick and feed it it to him."

I looked down at her twisted up face in shock. Those words had me wanting to protect my shit from her little bloodthirsty ass.

"Maybe I should say 'anything but that.' Really don't wanna touch another nigga's junk, love," I said wryly.

She sniffed again before sighing.

"Okay. I guess I really don't want you to, either."

She giggled at my look of relief and I dropped a kiss on her forehead. Ten minutes later, I was ready and she was back to herself. She whistled as I walked across the room in my all black gear.

"You looking all sexy and murderish. Damn, hurry back," she purred, winking at me.

"Not until you're healed," I reminded her.

"What? We can't eat popcorn and watch Oxygen until I'm healed?"

She tried to look innocent, but failed. Laughing, I doubled back to the bed to kiss her.

"Be good, mama."

"I will," she promised.

At the door, I turned to look at her again.

"Yana? That cutting off the dick thing—you wouldn't really—"

Her eyes narrowed and she crossed her arms over her breasts.

"You just keep yours outta these bitches and Scarlet and I will never have to come at you like that," she said before smiling sweetly.

I got the fuck outta there.

———

"The USDA wouldn't like this shit," Ahmed mumbled as we strolled into one of the large rooms of the slaughterhouse.

I side-eyed his OCD ass. He liked quick, clean kills. Tonight's events would be neither quick nor clean. He shrugged.

"What? I'm just saying, boss."

Shaking my head, my gaze turned to the middle of the room where Jordan Middleton lay naked, restrained against a metal table. I smiled. He tried to say something but the gag muffled it. The terror in his eyes said enough. Pulling out Scarlet, I watched his eyes get bigger. I handed the knife to Ammo before pulling my black t-shirt over my head.

"I'm tryna think if I've ever had the pleasure of killing father and son with my knife. I don't think so, but there's a first time for everything," I drawled.

His face reddened and the veins in his forehead stood out as he screamed something.

I chuckled as I slid on the plastic suit and pulled water-proof covers over my shoes.

"You feeling talkative, nigga? Too bad I ain't got no interest in hearing that shit," I commented, walking closer to the table. I noticed that Rafael shadowed me; little nigga had been having my back since he got here. He wasn't playing about this brother shit. I appreciated that, even though I had a team that could easily handle my light weight.

Ammo handed me Scarlet. I extended the blade with a satisfied sigh. Smirking, I took a last look at Jordan Middleton with a whole face. The nigga started shaking his head wildly as my blade appeared. His fear energized me, made me laugh harder.

"What? You scared of a li'l ol' flaying? That's what you tried to do to Yana, though, right? Tear her flesh with that whip? Make her skin break and bleed?" I asked viciously as the first strip of his face gave in to my knife.

I flung it on the plastic-covered ground as he wailed behind the gag.

"You know my OG reads all kinds of shit."

My tone was conversational as I placed my hand on his forehead and turned it left and right, trying to decide where to peel next. "Read this book a few years ago about these immortal brothers. One of 'em got kidnapped."

I slid my knife behind the skin near his ear. Scarlet was so sharp, she almost did the work herself. I heard a hissing sound, then smelled the sharp, ammonia scent of urine. I shook my head.

"Aww! Now, you gotta lay in blood and piss," I fake sympathized. "Anyway, like I was saying. You know how hard it is to kill an immortal? But his kidnapper came up with something better."

I paused as I figured out the third piece of flesh I'd relieve Jordan's crying ass of.

"¿*Hermano?*" Rafael prompted. "The kidnapper?"

I removed slice number three before half-smiling at my brother.

"Yeah. For centuries—hundreds of fucking years—he peeled that nigga each night. Drove him fucking crazy."

I leaned closer to Jordan, wanting to make sure he could see me. "I'd do that to you if I could," I hissed then grinned as the fourth piece of his face succumbed to Scarlet.

This time the nigga almost seized, screaming and shaking so fucking hard that we had to remove the gag for a minute before his dumb ass choked. I shook my head.

"Damn, I'm sorry!" I lied. "You gotta forgive me if I'm a little rusty. I ain't done this in a minute and peeling a nigga's face is an art. I gotta go fast enough that the shock don't set in too soon but slow enough that you have plenty of time to regret ever touching what is mine."

My last words were a violent hiss as I went back to work. I'd made it to his neck when Ammo spoke.

"Sir, someone is outside the slaughterhouse. We are initiating a shutdown," he announced suddenly.

I stopped. The high-gauge, bulletproof steel doors would be shutting down now, the windows darkening, the sound-proofed rooms doing their job. Still...

"Who's on the fucking cameras, Ammo? His brothers?" I asked tightly.

"Only a car for now, sir. Too darkly tinted—" he paused. Several seconds ticked by.

"What?" I finally demanded.

I watched his body partially relax.

"Your father and it looks like... Ms. Castle. *Your* Ms. Castle," he said.

I felt the frown tear up my face as I strode across the plastic.

"Open this shit back up."

A minute later Joaquín was there, Dayana's arm threaded through his as she walked slowly. Anger boiled through me.

"What the fuck, Joaquín?" I raged at my father.

He shrugged casually. "Your *mujer* was feeling left out. What else could I do as a future father-in-law?"

Nigga was trying to sound helpless, but I knew better.

"You could have left her where I did," I spat, my gaze on Dayana's hard-headed, unapologetic ass. "What if Mama—"

"If your mama thought she was wronged, *mijo*, I could never have kept her away. But I could have made sure she faced the consequences of her choices later."

He gave me a knowing look. *Jesus.* This nigga really did discipline my stubborn mother. I tried to do a quick scrub of my brain.

"Cartier," Dayana began softly.

I narrowed my eyes. "As soon as you heal—"

"I'll take that. I know you have a method," she said, peeking around my shoulder. "You're meticulous. Careful. But me? I just need to get my lick back."

She held out her hand and for the first time, I noticed the barbed wire-wrapped bat that Joaquín held. Smiling, he gave it to her. She looked at me again.

"Can I get that?" she asked.

I glared at my father, gesturing toward her weapon. "You did this?"

"*La belleza* had the bat. She simply allowed me to reinforce it," he explained.

Wordlessly, I stepped back. She shook a little as she saw Jordan's full form. I wanted to grab her, but she made her way to the table.

"Jordan?" she whispered.

Nigga was beyond speaking, but somehow, he turned his almost skinless face toward her. My shorty smiled.

"I tried to warn you. Maybe next time, you'll listen. But... don't look like it'll be a next time. Smoke toying with you a little bit, huh? I'ma help you along."

Then, she swung, landing that shit on his chest. Ahmed groaned at the ripping sound her bat made as she yanked it from Jordan's flesh. She attacked his thighs next, skin and tissue flying as Jordan convulsed. On her next strike, I knew if that nigga hadn't been restrained, he would have folded in half and passed out. Dayana pulled the back bat, removing most of the skin from his genitals. Even Ammo winced.

"Rot in hell, you son of a bitch," she jeered.

Dayana dropped her weapon, suddenly shaky on her feet. My father slipped a supportive arm around her—I was too covered in blood and gore to touch her.

"You did good, *mija*," he told her softly. "We will leave it to my son now, ¿*no*?"

She nodded as he led her out. I looked back at Jordan, but he was a barely alive carcass. My work here was done. I'd leave him to die from the shock and blood loss.

Clean and composed, I slid into bed with my fiery little lady three hours later, pulling her closer to me. She murmured my name sleepily. I gave her a soft kiss then pulled back to look down at her.

"Yo' ass gon' be so red," I warned.

"You'll rub it better," she said, snuggling into me.

"Brat."

She laughed quietly. I held her until she was almost asleep.

"Dayana?"

She yawned before responding.

"Yes, Cartier?"

"I love you, Princess," I whispered against her ear.

"As you should," she popped.

But then a soft hand cupped my face tugging me down to her.

"I love you, too. It's the only option I'd choose," she said before pressing her lips against mine.

CHAPTER 94
Dream

(*WEDNESDAY*, *July 14*)

It was nine AM. I knew that because my alarm was blaring, tempting me to throw my phone across the room. Yeah, it was sad that I needed a nine AM alarm, but all I wanted was to sleep the day away, tucked here, in my beautiful hotel suite, with the sunlight blocked and the temperature way too low. *He* had rubbed off on me, I guess, but without his warm body to cuddle close to—

"Okay, enough of that!"

I sat up abruptly, willing to do anything to avoid thinking about him. I couldn't stay in bed, anyway. I didn't want to hear Yana's mouth. She had a lunch-and-shopping day planned for us. I knew I needed to get up—for our outing and for my life in general. I wasn't the first woman to have her heart broken and I knew that was exactly what was wrong with me. I'd given my love to a damaged man who'd rejected it. I could admit, I'd fumbled badly. I knew how much Damien trusted me. I knew he had opened up to me. And the minute shit looked shady, I accused him, never mind that he'd never lied to me.

So, he responded the way he knew how to. It hurt more than almost anything I'd ever experienced. I'd spent the first couple of days afterward sobbing my eyes out, my grief over him twisted up with my grief over my father. I'd been sick ever since. Even now, I couldn't see the light at the end of this particular tunnel, but I prayed that it was there. I just had to keep moving toward it.

That's what today was about. I didn't know if she was really up to it, but my sister was determined to cheer me up. Hell, I knew I wasn't up to it, but I had no choice with that girl. My saying that I had a doctor's appointment this morning did no good—she just invited herself along to that.

I guess we could get ready for Saturday's funeral—had to make shit look as normal as possible so we didn't arouse any suspicion. I blinked back more tears. So many funerals... Melanie's had been quiet and quick, heavily guarded with few words spoken. I had hugged Kiana and Kam. Damien had acted as if I were invisible and I returned the energy. I prayed to God he didn't show at Daddy's.

I took a long, leisurely shower, unwilling to get out until thoughts of Damien invaded my mind again. Images of him pushing my hand away and rinsing my neck before burying his nose and then his lips and teeth against it played through my head.

"You smell so fucking good," he'd growl against my skin as he lifted me against the shower wall and impaled me on his—

Yeah, I had to get out of here. I rinsed off quickly, oiled myself, and wrapped a towel around my suddenly restless body. I guess that was the bad thing about being introduced to sex—I missed it. That had to be it, because I refused to miss him.

Treading out of the bathroom, I stopped in the bedroom long enough to replace the towel with a sleep shirt before making my way into the kitchen for coffee. I didn't remember programming it, but I was glad I did. I opened the bedroom door to step out into the living and dining area of the suite.

To my credit, I didn't scream... much... when icy green eyes landed on me. For a moment, we just stared at each other. I hated him. He was fucking perfect in a gold-embossed Fendi tee, Amiri jeans, and metallic gold Jordans, his locs pulled back in plaits. The scent of Dove wafted from his skin and I knew he'd be solid and warm and delicious. I suddenly wanted to cry again, had to bite the inside of my jaw hard as hell to stop it.

"What the fuck are you doing here?" I hissed when I could finally speak again.

"The fuck are you still doing here?" he asked, his voice calm.

As if he hadn't almost broken me. As if he had no fucks to give about anything. I shook my head, laughing bitterly.

"I'm not doing this with you. Get out before I call security."

It was his turn to laugh. "What they gon' do, Dream? If they were as good as they should be, I wouldn't be in here."

"Then just have the decency to go."

"I will, as soon as you leave. Like I said, security here is a joke. We can't guarantee your safety because this place has too many variables, too many people, too many ways in and out. You leaving here, shorty."

His tone told me not to argue. I no longer had to listen.

"My grandfather—"

"Agrees with me and knows I'm here. Get dressed and get yo' stuff."

He turned, took down two mugs, and rinsed them, before starting to fix the coffee. My jaw dropped. *The audacity!*

"You must have cream in that refrigerator, cuz they ain't got enough for you," he mumbled.

"Even if I didn't, I could call room service. You are not needed," I spat.

"That's the kind of dumbass mistake that could get you killed. You don't know who might deliver shit to this room. You should've learned that from yo' office."

He opened the fridge and pulled out the caramel creamer as I stood there, mouth opening and closing. Pouring some into my mug, he glanced at me.

"Go pack."

Scowling at him, I rested a hand on my hip.

"I'm not going anywhere and you don't get to give me orders, *Demon*."

He moved before I knew it—nigga moved way too fast for a big man—fisting my hair and pulling my head back. Now, I screamed as fire danced across my scalp.

"You jackass! These braids are new!"

"You don't call me 'Demon.' You do what I say. That shit ain't changed. Understand?"

I stared at him defiantly, my lips sealed. His hand tightened. I folded. Weakest bitch ever.

"What the fuck ever," I mumbled.

He let go and stepped back, a grim smile curving his lips. Rolling my eyes, I spoke up again.

"I don't have time today. I got—"

"A doctor's appointment and an afternoon with Yana," he supplied.

Speechless, I stared at him. His smile widened.

"Did you really break into my calendar?" I demanded.

"How else I'ma keep you safe, Dream?"

"You worry about the safety of all your fucks?" I taunted.

At my words, the eyes that had started to thaw froze again. His smile disappeared.

"I'll have some people pack your shit. Go to your grandfather's estate when you get done," he instructed coldly.

I smirked, glad to have gotten under his skin.

"I hope yo' niggas enjoy going through my lingerie."

The muscles in his jaw worked, but he was silent. I was

bold but not completely reckless, so I shut up. Forty-five minutes later, I left him at the hotel—without my coffee—to pick up my sister.

I shook my head when we finally pulled up to Dr. Butler's office. I didn't have to wait long after signing in. I knew I'd probably be in and out—I'd had a Pap smear and multiple panels run before I started fucking Damien. She just wanted to check in to see how I was doing on the Pill. Weight, blood pressure, urine sample, short interview, and I was waiting for the doctor. She came in ten minutes later, her beautiful face adorned by a smile as she shook my hand and settled in her chair.

"So, this was supposed to be a six-week checkup, but you were last here May 24?" she asked.

I shrugged helplessly.

"Life just kinda… happened."

Her brown eyes were sympathetic as she opened her tablet. "As it does to all of us. You were due to start your period that week which meant you started the Pill…"

"May 30," I said.

"And you took it every day as scheduled?"

I nodded. "Yes."

"And did you notice any changes in your body or your period?"

Tilting my head to the side, I thought for a minute.

"Some nausea at first, but that's better. No period, but you told me that might happen. That's about it."

Nodding, she looked up from taking notes.

"And you were previously… well, do you remember when you became sexually active?" she asked.

Hell, how could I forget? "June 8."

More typing and nodding before she leaned back in her chair.

"Dream, your reactions sound perfectly normal—"

I smiled. "Good!"

"—but your missed period is not because of the Pill. According to your urine specimen, you're pregnant," she finished.

My smile froze in place. I couldn't even... *wait, what?*

"Dream?"

Suddenly, the illusion of being okay that I had projected the last couple of days began to fall apart. I shook my head rapidly as tears welled in my eyes.

"No. No, Dr. Butler, I can't be. You have to do it again. I can't. He and I aren't even... *No!*"

I guess in ten years of practice, I wasn't the first blubbering fool she had in her office. She talked to me soothingly, asked did we use a backup method, told me I had options— even if the state was working its hardest to limit them— offered me a blood test.

I finally got myself together enough for the blood draw, but I knew. We'd fucked like rabbits, every chance we got. Damien's seed had filled me almost daily, multiple times a day. What the fuck had I been thinking? I walked out of the exam room after Dr. Butler promised me that, at my request, no record of my results would be stored electronically. I could tell that freaked her out a little bit—she asked about my safety. Back in the waiting room, Yana took one look at my face and was ready to go off. I just shook my head, not wanting her detail or mine to hear anything. She made it all the way to the car, where she insisted on driving before the question came.

"What the fuck, Dream?"

I buried my face in my hands. "I fucked up, Dayana. I fucked up so bad."

"What? Girl, don't tell me that nigga gave you something. Dirty dick bastard! We can go kill him. Like, right now. We can go—"

She was banging the steering wheel with her open palm. I shook my head.

"I'm... I'm pregnant," I whispered.

She stopped, her head whirling toward me. "Huh?"

"Dayana, I'm pregnant."

My sister was quiet for a minute, but I could feel the tension leaving her.

"Oh. Dream... this isn't... we can handle this, sissy. You know how I am with kids and you gon' be a great mama—"

"No, I'm not," I said softly.

She frowned. "What you mean, you n—"

Silence settled in the car as my meaning sank in. Dayana's hands tightened on the steering wheel. I knew she didn't agree. But I just... I couldn't. Even with the idea of a baby tempting me, even with my heart already trying to overrule my brain, I couldn't. I'd die a little more every day, attached to him like that. Being close but never close enough. Dayana spoke up suddenly.

"Dream... you not thinking right now. You don't have to—"

"Saltgrass," I interrupted her.

She frowned. "What?"

Sniffing, I patted my face dry.

"You asked earlier what I wanted for lunch. Saltgrass. I want some Range Rattlers."

"Dream—"

A sharp knock at the window had us jumping, my hand already sliding into my bag.

"You ladies okay?" Juan asked.

I nodded, fake smile in place.

"Deciding on food."

"Okay. Please don't sit too long in one place like this," he warned.

"Pulling off now," I promised.

Nodding, he walked back to the truck. Dayana shifted gears but shot me another look.

"Dream—"

"You know what? Maybe fajitas," I said brightly. "Those would be good, too."

I wasn't discussing this pregnancy. Not at all.

CHAPTER 95

Demon

(*THURSDAY, July 22*)

Rubbing a hand across my face, I slumped back against the dining room chair, lost in my thoughts. My life hadn't been this chaotic since Dixon Ware rescued me from Melanie. Kam was on my mind heavy—little nigga was struggling to shake back, even with KiKi and me taking care of him. KiKi sounded like Dream at this point, talking about therapy, so I told her go ahead and sign him up. I ignored her question about me.

And Keith McKellar… all this shit with him was beyond old. Bitch ass nigga needed to show his face. I wanted to protect my family, and a part of me, a little part that I couldn't silence, wanted to avenge Melanie. He had overdosed her, given her enough heroin to kill a fucking whale. I had made deals with the lab and had the toxicology report changed before the medical examiner received it. She officially died from the fentanyl being administered to ease the pain her cancer caused. But we knew better.

Dante was about to blow. Nigga cared about me, yeah. But he also couldn't stand the idea of being outsmarted and outmaneuvered, and McKellar was definitely toying with us right now. Melanie's murder, the message through Dream—

Fuck! Dream. As pissed off as I was at her, her assumptions, and her fly-ass mouth, I missed my shorty. A little over a month with her and I was one of them longing, sad ass niggas I hated. She was supposed to be for my bedroom, but Dream had sneaked her way into every part of my life. I had to figure out how to get past this shit, maybe find a new escort service or kill a couple of niggas. Something.

I hadn't talked to her since last Wednesday and hadn't seen her since spying on her at the cemetery Saturday. She'd distanced herself from her family, even Lucien and Dayana, standing at the foot of her father's grave. I could tell she was holding herself tightly, her only movement twisting the clutch and the stems of the flowers she held in her hands. A veiled hat and sunglasses hid her face and only when her cousin linked his arm through hers and tugged did she move. Since then, she had been outside her grandfather's house only once —another visit to her doctor. I'd had Li Jun break into her records, but nothing was out of order. Shorty was grieving hard and that shit was fucking with a nigga.

"What wrong, Damie?"

Mia's sweet voice broke my reverie as she rested her little body against my leg.

"Yeah, what's wrong, Damien?" Eve teased, Hailey on her hip as she set an empty plate in front of me.

I almost flipped her ass off, but Ms. Hazel was right behind her with serving dishes. I stood up to help her, but she shook her head.

"Uh-uh! I got this. You think about that baby's question," she fussed.

Shit, I didn't want this breakfast to turn into an interrogation, but I couldn't just leave after she'd fixed all this food. Stalling, I turned back to Mia. She was looking up at me, real concern in her big, brown eyes. I didn't want this baby to ever worry about anything else. Giving her a little smile, I shook my head.

"Nothing, little mama. What you got going?"

She chattered a little bit as Eve and Ms. Hazel laid out the meal. Eve put Hailey in a highchair, then called her son and Breshay. Eve and MJ were staying with Ms. Hazel because I needed to keep an eye on all of them.

"Y'all take Mia, wash your hands, and go to the table in the kitchen. Mama Hazel already hooked y'all up," she instructed.

The kids cleared out quickly and I was left with two women who could outdo the damn FBI. Taking their seats at the round table with its lace tablecloth and woven placemats, they let me eat in peace for a few minutes. And then it started.

"I know that you lost your mo- that Melanie died, but I'on think that's why you looking like that," Ms. Hazel said between sips of her coffee milk.

Dream would probably love that shit, I thought before I could stop myself. I shook my head. My eyes snapped up as Eve sucked her teeth. Her irritating ass rolled her eyes at me.

"Mama, stop playing! Where Ms. Bourgeois, Demon?" she asked, smirking.

Ms. Hazel popped her fork right out of her hand. "Don't call him that!"

"Ma!"

I returned Eve's smirk until Ms. Hazel eagle-eyed me. "Where *is* Dream? Y'all shol' was acting funny at Melanie's homegoing service."

I shrugged. "She around. That situation is... over," I explained awkwardly.

Shit, when did I start doing awkward?

"Whatever," Eve mumbled.

Ms. Hazel side-eyed her again before addressing me.

"Only girl in twenty years you describe as 'yours,' and it's just over?" she asked skeptically.

Speechless, I shoveled in a bite of eggs.

"You welcome to say it's none of our business, baby. Especially Evangeline's," Ms. Hazel teased her eye-rolling granddaughter. "But I just want to see you with some happiness, Damien. That's all."

"And Ms. Bourgeois did make yo' mean tail happy. Need to fix whatever you did. Told you: spend some money, buy some flowers, don't be tryna kill the girl," Eve popped.

"Yo, you mad annoying, girl," I said lowly, then held up a finger as my work phone rang.

I didn't recognize the number. Grabbing my glass of apple juice, I excused myself to step out the back door.

"Yeah," I answered.

"A nigga gotta go through serious channels to get yo' number, huh? You a long way from that half-homeless, hungry ass bastard Melanie pimped out, I guess," Keith McKellar said before chuckling.

My hand squeezed the phone almost to the point of breaking, but I reined my temper in quickly. Staring at the neatly cut grass at my feet, I breathed in and out slowly before acknowledging him.

"Come find out," I invited.

"I'm having too much fun visiting yo' ladies. Too bad about Melanie, but at least I sent her out in her favorite style. Fucking junkie still owed me. I'd like to see Kiana close up after all these years. Pretty little yella muhfucka. And yo' other bitch... what's her name? Eve?" He whistled. "That's a tight little piece right there. Not as luscious as Dream, though, huh? She probably looking for a new nigga since you got rid of her daddy. I can't wait to hit all that ass from the back," he taunted.

The glass in my hand shattered from the force of my grip. Still, I kept my voice calm.

"I'm gon' kill you and I'm gon' like doing it," I vowed.

He laughed. "Nah. You gon' watch me make yo' bitches

suffer like you made my sister and my woman suffer. They gon' pray that I light they asses up when I'm done."

It was my turn to laugh.

"What I did to Angela will look like a game compared to what I'll do to your daughter if you touch anyone else around me."

He was suddenly silent, probably shocked that I knew about his kid. I revealed my hand too fast—he'd probably move her, but in his hurry, the nigga might slip up. I'd be waiting.

"If you ever—"

"You could always be a real nigga. Leave the women outta this. Face me yourself or we can see—"

"You keep my baby out yo' mouth, you fucking trash," he growled.

"You stay away from what's mine and I just might," I said before disconnecting.

The calm attitude I'd put on for him disappeared. Cursing, I threw the phone across the yard. On my own, I could deal with McKellar. But there were too many innocents around me now, women and children and a badass little brother whom I didn't want to lose. I had to find Keith McKellar. Soon.

I heard the back door open and a moment later, a soft hand squeezed my arm.

"Tell me," Ms. Hazel murmured. "You know I'll always listen to you. I might be able to help."

I shook my head. "You can't help with this one."

"You never know what an old lady knows. And maybe just talking about it will help you figure some things out," she coaxed.

Frustrated and damn near desperate, I was persuaded. I let her lead me to the patio furniture to take a seat. I explained the reason for the detail and why I had encouraged Eve to move back in with her for a minute. She mostly nodded but asked a few questions. When I was finished, she sat quietly. Then...

"Is his daughter with Angela's boy?" she asked.

I frowned. I vaguely remembered Angela having a son a little younger than I was. At some point, he had disappeared.

"You know he moved away when—"

"His daddy took him. Cut all ties to Angela cuz of her lifestyle. Changed his name and I think Pearline said he sent him off to some fancy school. Pearline was Angela and Keith's auntie, but she was a good woman, God rest her. But maybe that'll help ya, baby," she said, patting my arm and rising. "Find that boy. Maybe Keith did. And come eat. You can't do nothing on no empty stomach."

"Yes, ma'am."

"And maybe I can help you get ya girl back, too. She good for you, Damien Montana. You can't just let her slip away."

I sighed. "Yes, ma'am."

CHAPTER 96
Dream

(*TUESDAY*, July 27)

"Dream... I don't know about this. It just don't feel right," Dayana voiced her opinion, her eyes moving around the large parking lot as she clutched her phone.

I scoffed. "You know what don't feel right?"

"What?"

"Me being pregnant by that crazy ass nigga. Let's go."

She shook her head.

"But getting rid of your baby? Dream—"

I hopped out of her car as she hesitantly opened her door. Striding to the sidewalk, I waited until she joined me. We made our way up to the red brick building, a flurry of thoughts swirling in my head. Despite the brave face I gave my sister, I was torn. I had a lot I wanted to do before I had kids. Damien and I weren't even a couple, would never be on speaking terms again, and I always wanted to have kids with my husband.

But part of me wondered what if. What if I didn't end this pregnancy? What if I turned out to be a good mother? What if this baby turned out to be the biggest blessing of my life, like Dayana had been trying to convince me? Then, I thought about Damien, cold-eyed and hateful. I shook my head as I reached for the handle of the glass door. He was even less ready than I was to be a parent and I had no intention of doing this alone. His hands were full with Kam, anyway.

I walked into the building, ready to get to Dr. Butler's office. I had been back for my blood test results, an ultrasound, and counseling. Today, I'd get a dose of Mifepristone that would start early contractions. Technically, I was two weeks past the time limit for medication abortions. But my last name plus a little money meant Dr. Butler was willing to give me the pill, especially since I was within the seventy-day window of when it was most effective. Dayana and I headed for the bank of elevators. Once we were in one of them alone, she started again.

"Dream, are you sure? You don't have to do this. If it's because you and Demon are..." Her voice trailed off for a minute. "We'll help—"

I raised a hand, cutting her off.

"Yana, I'm not going to be tied to a man called Demon who hates me for the next eighteen years. And you know what he said. He's not interested in anything beyond fucking me."

"You making a mistake. You emotional and hurt and grieving. You can't decide something like this right now. You can't get rid of my niece or nephew. I'll take the baby, sissy. Just, please—"

I interrupted her passionate speech, tears welling in my eyes.

"I asked you to bring me because I needed the support. Do I think this is the best decision? Probably not! But my life had an order, Yana. I had steps I knew I was supposed to take. This was not supposed to happen! I-I don't know how to just leave my path. And for what? A man who's always gon' think of me as a piece of pussy? That man is fucking colder than ice. Yeah, he thawed out some and I fucked up and misunderstood. But allowing a child into a situation as fucked up as this? We supposed to be breaking generational curses, Yana. Can you please just offer the support that I need right now? Can you please just do that?" I begged, tired of the back and forth.

She looked at me for a long moment.

"I can be here for you and with you, but I can't offer support for something I can't agree with," she whispered.

The elevator doors slid open before I could respond. We made it to the suite of offices quickly and I took a deep breath and exhaled before walking in. My nerves were all over the place as I signed in and took a seat to fill out more paper-work. I was terrified, scared of making the wrong decision. I was definitely pro-choice, but that didn't mean I wanted to go through this myself. Leaning back in my chair, I squeezed my eyes shut. They flew open seconds later when a deep voice sounded in my ear.

"I thought you hated when I killed people."

I sat up, twisting my body to look at the chair next to me where Damien now sat.

"Wh-what are you doing here?" I stuttered. "How did you—"

My voice trailed off as I answered my own question. Only one person knew about my situation. I looked up at Dayana, who was suddenly glued to her phone. My eyes narrowed on her traitorous ass.

"I got a better question. Who you gon' make me kill today?" he asked calmly.

"What are you talking about? Just go back wherever you were, Damien. This is my body and—"

"My seed. You not getting rid of my baby, Dream."

I looked around, making sure no one else was close by, before turning back to him.

"You really wanna have a baby with someone who was

just a 'wet pussy for you to buss in?'" I asked sarcastically, repeating his words to me.

He looked at me for a moment before he spoke. "Dream, I—"

I waved him off.

"Anyway, you just came in here talking about killing some-one, but you ready to be a father? Get the fuck on!" I hissed.

His eyes cooled as he stared at me. "This blood is on your hands."

Frowning, I glared at him. "What—"

He leaned in closer, his face blank, but I could feel his anger.

"If you let Dr. Butler suck my baby out of you or give you a pill to destroy my unborn, I'm killing her for killing my child. That goes for any doctor you take your ass to."

The words were little more than a whisper, but I heard each one. I swallowed hard as I stared at him, realizing he meant exactly what he said.

"Damien, isn't this every nigga's dream? A girl who is willing to end a mistake without—"

He grabbed my chin and squeezed, shocking me.

"Don't ever call my baby a mistake. Ever. Whatever happens, it's your choice."

His fucking audacity made rage flare in me. This nigga had just reminded me that I was a short-term fuck, then dismissed me.

I opened my mouth just as the medical assistant called my name. Slowly, I stood. Making my way over to the desk, I felt Damien and Dayana's eyes on my back. I returned the clip-board as the woman started telling me the next steps. Squaring my shoulders, I looked her in the eye. I didn't want to let Damien Montana intimidate me. I wanted this final decision to be mine. It was my body that all the changes were going to happen to and I knew women took on most of the responsibility for babies. This was my life that was about to change drastically and he needed to understand that!

I made the mistake of glancing behind me. Damien sat quietly, busy on his phone, his decision already declared. My shoulders slumped. There was no way I could have Dr. Butler's death on my conscience. She was too kind. Too good at what she did. Too needed by other black women.

Then, there was the other consideration… the stifled part of me that wanted my little bit so bad, that wanted the child Damien and I had made more than anything. I refused to listen to that part, was terrified to listen to a clueless, dreaming girl. But…

Lowering my eyes, I shook my head quickly at the assistant.

"I changed my mind," I whispered before damn near running for the door.

CHAPTER 97
Demon

SHE WOULDN'T SPEAK to me. Dream lay in her bed, her back to me as I sat in the chair that I'd pulled from her desk. Dayana had let me in because her sister refused to even acknowledge my presence. Shorty kept coming through for a nigga today. Her text while they were on the way to that fucking clinic was much appreciated. Bestie, indeed.

I wanted to explain some shit to Dream, but I didn't know how. If I was honest, the way she felt about my little one growing inside her fucked with me. I didn't want my baby to ever experience what I did with my sorry-ass mother.

"I don't want you. I never wanted you. You ain't been shit but trouble." Melanie had spat those words at me over and over when I was a kid. Dream might not use those words, but my kid would sense it, know his or her mother resented their existence. I wasn't letting that shit happen. I rubbed a hand over my face before I started talking.

"Ay. If you don't wanna be a mother, you don't gotta be one."

I stopped after I said it. The shit bothered me. I didn't want my baby to be unwanted by its own mother. That was something that would stay on a nigga's mind forever. I was a fucking witness.

"I just need you to carry my seed and take care of it while it's inside you. Then, you won't ever have to see the baby again."

Each word felt like it was pulled out of me. I wanted her to stop me, to say she'd never give away our kid like that. But she was still silent, refusing to acknowledge anything I said. And what the fuck was I saying? I didn't know shit about being a father. The idea of me with a baby of my own was ridiculous. Hell, I wanted to hit Kam with a two-piece some days. But, from the moment I got Dayana's text, I knew I wanted my child. Shit would just be easier if Dream wanted it, too.

"I know you mad, but I can't let you destroy my seed. You can get that idea out yo' head. I'll fuck everything up behind mine, Dream. Do you understand?" I growled at her.

More silence. I felt the anger stirring, wanted to grab her ass up until she said something.

"What the fuck is it, Dream? Huh? My baby not good enough for you? You embarrassed to be pregnant by me, worried about disappointing all the fake ass people around you?"

I knew the moment I spoke that I was revealing too much, giving the impression that her opinion of me mattered. But what I said finally got a response from her. She sat up and glared at me.

"You don't know what the fuck you talking about, *Demon,*" she said.

She threw the bright yellow blanket off and moved to the edge of the bed, ready to fight. My hands clenched into fists as I fought the urge to yoke her up.

"That's not my name."

"That's who you are," she spat. "At least, that's who you acted like today with your threats. Leave me the fuck alone."

"Once you give me my baby, I will."

"You really wanna bring a baby into this? Cause I could have sworn you were the same one who told me, and I quote, 'If you not on birth control, get on it.' I got on the shit to avoid this and now we here. You talking about don't kill your seed but what about my garden? I have to grow and nurture a child with a man that doesn't give two shits about me? If that isn't enough... I don't even have a house, I'm trying to establish my career, we're not married, and you have this little annoying habit of killing people. Yeah, we'll be great parents," she snapped, her voice bitter.

I rubbed my forehead, reminding myself to keep it together before I responded to this girl.

"I'll buy you a fucking house. You can still establish your career. You wanna be married before the baby comes? We can do that shit."

She stopped me with a shocked laugh. "You must be crazy. I'm just somebody you fucked, remember? And now, you ready to marry me?"

Hell, my words surprised me, too. I had never thought about being permanently attached to one woman but shit with Dream had been different from the first time I saw her. If marriage would reassure her about our baby, I was willing to do that shit. I didn't address what she said about her getting on the pill because she was right. Those were my words. I couldn't lie and say I hadn't meant the shit because I did. I never thought we'd make a baby. I wanted to tell her that everything had changed, but my tongue was tangled or some shit and the words wouldn't come out. Only with her did I have this issue—this need to make sure my words were right. Only with her had I ever considered marriage and fatherhood. Bitches were for fucking and that was it. Yet, I just offered to attach the old ball and chain to my ankle. *Fuck is wrong with me?* I wondered.

"Dayana should have never called you—" she began.

"But she did. Bestie really got me, I guess. You know you were foul as fuck for even considering killing a nigga seed. You don't want it? Like I said, give the baby to me at birth and I will never ask you for a single thing. Got me out here begging like a fucking simp. But I said all that to say… I'm gon' protect mine," I cut her off.

She sighed. "Okay. You made your point. You can leave now."

I wanted to press the issue, make her listen to me, make her want my baby. But I could tell she wasn't having it right now. I stood up and walked toward the door. I turned to look at her one more time before leaving.

"Take care of my unborn, Dream."

"Or what?" she asked, eyes tangling with mine.

I looked at her for a good minute. I felt one corner of my mouth lift in something less than a smile.

"I suggest you don't find out, shorty."

CHAPTER 98
Dream

(*FRIDAY*, *July 30*)

Pretending to study the menu gave me a break, allowed me to catch my breath and refocus my attention as I tried to gather myself enough to survive this impromptu lunch date. My date, Eric Vaughn, had been nothing but polite and charming. We'd made a dinner date a few days ago, but I'd asked him to switch to lunch at the last minute. Less romantic; less pressure; fewer expectations. So, here we sat, in a glass-encased conservatory overlooking the Riverwalk. Everything was so beautiful, so perfectly laid out and orchestrated.

And I was still miserable.

"I really recommend the fish tacos if you can't decide. They're my favorite appetizer, but my mother thinks they're enough for a meal," he suggested helpfully.

I smiled at him and nodded before taking a sip of my water. Truth was, I probably wouldn't eat anything put in front of me. I had already been having slight nausea since Daddy died and the run-in with Damien earlier this week had destroyed any appetite I may have had. Mama and Grandpapa had tried to feed me all week, especially once I broke down and told them I was pregnant. They couldn't hide their joy. My family had lost their minds, apparently.

Our server appeared and I gestured for Eric to order for me as I prepared myself to be a good date. I'd decided that was the only way I was going to survive the next eighteen years—by finding a man who could take my mind off this baby's father. I knew word had circulated that Damien and I were done—Parker had hinted about it—but so far, Eric was the only one bold enough to text my previously busy phone. I'd gone from hot commodity to damaged goods in under two months, apparently.

I jumped as Eric reached across the table to interlace our fingers. I gave a nervous little laugh as he gently squeezed my hand.

"How are you doing for real, baby girl? Again, I'm sorry for your loss. Darius was a great man and I hope they get justice for your family," he said softly.

My eyes dropped for a moment, but I nodded.

"I don't want to talk about anything that makes you uncomfortable. That's not what today is about, especially since I know this must be extra hard for you and your sister."

Sympathy dripped from his voice and my hand froze on my water glass. Confused, I frowned.

"Why you say that?" I asked.

He looked at me, suddenly uncomfortable. Trying to cover it with a smile, he squeezed my hand again.

"Dream—"

"No, tell me," I insisted.

For a moment, I thought he would ignore me. He toyed with his silverware and smoothed invisible wrinkles from the pristine white tablecloth. But then he sighed and gave in.

"The streets talk, baby girl. Demon and Smoke look like the most likely candidates for killing your father. And seeing as how you and Demon called it quits right around that time..."

His voice trailed off, but I didn't need to hear anything else. The streets, indeed. Gossip was gossip, wherever it came from.

"People assume I was fucking a nigga who iced my father. Led him right to Daddy's doorstep, huh?" I said softly, lifting my water.

I laughed quietly. Suddenly thirsty, I almost drained the glass as he scrambled around for words to say. He was saved by the unexpected appearance of the maître d'. We looked up into the man's red face.

"Mr. Vaughn, you have an urgent matter requiring your immediate attention in the manager's office," he announced nervously.

Eric scowled. "Urgent? My phone hasn't rung. How can it—"

"Sir, I was simply told that your presence was needed as quickly as possible." The man stopped to look around and lowered his voice even more. "Something has occurred with a high priority shipment."

Eric tensed, dropping my hand as all his attention went to the maître d'.

"Where?" he asked tightly.

"If you'll follow me," the man said.

Eric stood and turned to walk off. Almost as an afterthought, he turned back, pulled his wallet from his pocket and dropped several bills on the table.

"In case I get caught up. I'm sorry, Dream," he said.

"Don't be," I murmured, but he was already damn near jogging behind the maître d'.

I meant the words—I no longer wanted his company. Maybe I could choke down a taco and leave before he reappeared. I looked around, trying to spot our server. I needed more water. I wanted something stronger. My nerves were everywhere. Closing my eyes, I inhaled deeply and pushed the cleansing breath out. I sucked in another, this time more sharply as goosebumps beaded my skin and butterflies went wild in my stomach. Slowly, I let my eyes flutter open. Damien Montana gazed at me from across the table.

There was no use asking him why he was here. He'd be any-fucking-where he wanted. I'd learned that by now.

"If you wanted lunch, I would've fed you, baby," he said smoothly.

"Why are you bothering my life?" I whispered, eyes darting around the conservatory.

I didn't want to make a scene here. I'd made far too many with this man. His eyes lit up at my question.

"Just checking on my unborn."

"Your unborn is just that—*unborn*. We don't need to see each other until I'm in labor."

He drummed his fingers on the tabletop. "You crazy as fuck. We'll see each other at your appointment with Dr. Butler in two weeks. I guess I'll let you keep going to her—bitch was way too ready to off my baby for me."

I couldn't even comment. I hadn't recovered from the fact that he knew my appointment schedule and that he planned to be part of this pregnancy. Despite my attitude toward him, part of me was happy about that.

"You should leave before my date comes back," I mumbled.

He chuckled. "Is that what this is? A date? We gon' have to talk about that."

"Nah. We don't have to talk about anything except this child."

Cold eyes pinned me to my chair. I stared right back, refusing to be intimidated. He smiled slightly.

"Vaughn's not coming back. He'll be busy with that shipment for a while. Missing cargo, nosy ass police, pissed off buyers." He shrugged nonchalantly.

Of course, he was behind this. I should've realized the

minute his ass popped up. Anger blazed through me at his attempt to interfere in my life.

"What did you order anyway?" he asked.

I balled up the napkin in my lap and tossed it on the table. "It doesn't matter. I'm leaving."

"How?"

I scowled at him as I stood. "In my car!"

He leaned back in the chair, smiling as he looked up at me. "You know, I saw them towing a little Mercedes Coupe as I pulled in. I thought it looked familiar."

My eyes narrowed on his smug face. "You didn't."

"Who knows? I'd be glad to give you a ride, though. In my car, I mean," he teased.

"I wouldn't ride with you if—"

My words disappeared as he rose to his full height, green eyes glacial. I wasn't scared, exactly, but I knew when to be quiet.

"Shorty, I been real nice considering what you tried to do today. My nice is running out. Now, if you ready…"

I didn't say another word to him until we were out of the parking garage and headed for the freeway in his sleek-bodied Jag.

"Where is my car, Damien?" I demanded.

"Put up," he said in a tone that let me know he was done with the subject.

My grandfather had a detail on me, too; if my car was taken, his old ass was probably in on it. I swear, they made me sick.

"And what you mean by what I tried to do today? We not together, Damien. Never have been, remember? I can date or do whatever," I snapped.

He looked over at me as he switched lanes. "Keep trying. Get all them niggas killed. Especially for that 'whatever' part."

Crossing my arms over my chest, I stared at him. "So, what, you gon' kill Eric now?"

"Fuck, yeah. Second time he touched what's mine. He already had his warning."

I stared at him, looking for a glimmer of a smile or any sign he was joking. I saw none.

"Damien! I'm not yours! You can't fucking—"

I couldn't even get the words together. This nigga and his nerve. And his murderous streak. Jesus, what if this child inherited that? I watched as he shrugged again.

"Been told you that you belong to me. And don't shed no tears over that nigga. The shipment I interrupted today was a shipping container full of women and girls he and his father had sold. I'm doing the world a favor."

I gasped. "You lying!"

"When you gon' realize I don't lie to you?"

I looked down, feeling guilty suddenly. He'd never lied, even when I didn't want to hear what he had to say.

"We need to set some boundaries around this pregnancy and this baby. You have claims on this child, not on me," I changed the subject.

"Say what the fuck you want, shorty. Ain't no dating. Ain't no boyfriends who gon' be around my seed. Ain't no marriage, unless you change yo' mind about my proposal," he rattled off like this was some random list and not my life.

I scoffed at his ass. "You think I'm going eighteen years like that? Nigga! You out yo' fucking mind! And that wasn't a proposal!"

"Dream."

He spoke, used to silencing me with that one word. But not today.

"No. *No!* I had a plan for my life. I followed all the right steps. Valedictorian, Ivy League, good job, great reputation," I vented. "And now, no one will touch me and I'm about to be a single mother and—"

His head whipped toward me so fast that I did a double take.

"You might be unmarried, but you not having this baby on your own," he growled, his green eyes flashing cold flames.

I slapped the dashboard in frustration.

"I don't just want a co-parent, Damien. I want a husband. Someone who loves me and wants me and touches me—"

"You wanna be touched, shorty? I can't help you with that love shit, but I'll touch you, I'll *fuck* you as much as you want."

His voice was low and husky, his eyes heated with sexual promise. It made me sad, the way he kept emphasizing how little I meant to him. I hugged myself as I stared out the window.

"What do you want to eat?" he asked a few minutes later.

"Nothing," I whispered.

He sighed deeply. "I'on care how mad at me you are. You gotta—"

"I can't. I get sick."

My explanation was short, clipped. He was quiet for a minute.

"Is it bad?" he finally asked.

I frowned. "What?"

"The morning sickness… is it bad?"

I shrugged, my eyes on the cars he was whizzing past.

"Dream—"

"Don't act like you care, Damien. Your baby won't starve."

We finished the ride in silence, without even the mindless sounds of hip-hop radio to break the tense quiet. He dropped me off at the front of Grandpapa's house.

"Your car is in the garage," he said tightly.

I nodded once before escaping into the house. I walked through the foyer slowly to where my grandfather sat in the living room. He looked up at me, a smug smile on his face. It faded when he looked at my face. I walked up to him and dropped to my knees, burying my face in his legs. I felt his hand stroke across my braids.

"What's wrong, my *bébé*?" he asked.

"Grandpapa, I love him," I wept.

"I know, *chère*. I know."

Unable to talk anymore, I cried silently and he let me.

"Dream," he said softly when my tears were nothing but annoying little hiccups. "Demon cares—"

"About this pregnancy."

"About you, too," he pressed.

I shook my head stubbornly. "He said—"

"Sha, you ever consider that you hurt that man feelings?"

I ran my fingernails along the polished stone floor. I didn't know how to respond to that, didn't want to fool myself into believing that our entanglement had ever been more than what it was.

"He says he doesn't have those."

Grandpapa scoffed. "You know better than that, girl."

I closed my eyes again and just lay against him as he stroked my hair.

"I don't like to get in your business," he started after a while.

I sucked my teeth at that lie. Lucien Dumont stayed in my business.

"Hush, sha. But I think, all the drama with your father and this situation with Demon and now the little one you are carrying, maybe you need a little break. Could you take some more time from work?"

Sniffling, I nodded.

"Okay. Let Grandpapa arrange some things. We gon' give your mind and your heart a rest. You gon' be good as new," he said.

I nodded again, loving the idea more and more. A get

away sounded perfect. Time to think about my next steps. Time to accept my coming motherhood.

Time for my heart to start to heal.

Two days later, pretending to go to my parents' house for more of my stuff, I slipped my detail. My mother led me into the secret room where she had taken my father's life. She hugged me tightly before directing me down a tunnel that took me past our backyard, up some stone stairs, through a small wooded area, to a narrow road. My cousin Rhythm waited for me in a nondescript little SUV.

I left the city with my backpack, a single suitcase, no electronics, and my grandfather's promise to keep my location secret.

I hoped he kept it.

CHAPTER 99

Demon

(*SATURDAY*, *August 21*)

Just out of the shower, the memory of the satisfying crunch of bone beneath my fists fresh on my mind, I climbed into my new G-Wagon and started toward Dante's house. I'd copped the SUV for Dream with plans to have it customized and make it her mommy car. But she was gone and I was sure my seed was, too. My hands tightened on the steering wheel as I thought about her grimy ass. Her family wasn't saying shit, but that was okay. I was going to find her, bring her back, and make her regret killing my child. She'd be lucky if I didn't put another baby in her and then chain her to my bed where I wanted to keep her. That was, if McKellar didn't get her first.

A few miles out from Dante's, I called Kam.

"What's up?" he answered.

"Get yo' shit together and be outside in ten minutes," I told him.

"Demon, I—"

I hung up on him. I ain't have time for whining and protests right now. Kam and DJ were close as hell and probably causing all types of problems, but I didn't want Kam to wear out his welcome. I frowned after I made it to the front of Dante's and Kam wasn't waiting against one of the pillars as usual. Putting the truck in park, I got out, jogged up the front steps, and rang the doorbell. Kam answered a minute later.

"Didn't I tell you be ready? Let's go," I said.

I was on my way back to the G-Wagon when I heard him say, "I ain't going."

I felt my blood starting to freeze and reminded myself he was a child. I couldn't fuck him up.

"Kameron, get yo' shit and bring yo' ass," I said, my voice low.

"Nah, I'm good."

I turned to look at him. Nigga stood there stiffly, arms crossed, green eyes defiant. Tonight wasn't the night for his shit.

"I ain't playing these games with you, Kam. You getting in this truck one way or the other," I threatened.

"I don't wanna go home yet."

Little stubborn muhfucka. My patience was hanging by one thin ass thread.

"I don't give a fuck what you want, you going and you going now. If I gotta tell you one more time—"

"Why? Why the hell I gotta go? You just gon' go in the studio and ignore me! And yo' work ain't even been good since Dream left! You shoulda let me go with KiKi," he raged, hands balling into fists.

Guilt punched me in the stomach at his words, but I shook that shit off.

"I mean, if that's what you wanna—"

"Demon!" Dante snapped, appearing behind Kam. "Let me talk to you."

I scoffed at him. "I don't wanna talk."

"That's fine; you can just listen, then," he said tightly, nostrils flaring. "Kam, gon' back with DJ."

So, my fucking brothers were teaming up against me. I laughed humorlessly. These niggas better be glad for grace.

"Let's go to my office."

He led the way, sliding behind his desk as I sat across from him.

"What?" I asked, patience gone.

He put his elbows on his desk and steepled his hands, just looking at me. I stared back. Finally, he spoke.

"Justin Robinson."

I sat back in the chair, smirking at him.

"I handled that. Why you fucking with me about shit that's done?"

He glared at me incredulously.

"You snatched that nigga in broad daylight from a fucking airport!"

I shrugged. "You realize how much harder it woulda been to get him if he got his ass on an international flight?"

"Four deaths. Three weeks. Loose fucking ends and sloppy behavior everywhere. Even we don't have enough money and influence to cover everything. Then you out here arguing with yo' brother like you ain't got sense?" he spat.

Fury roiled inside me. Nigga was overstepping boundaries by a whole lot.

"I did what I needed to do. And mind ya business. Kam ain't it," I warned.

"Kam is very much my fucking business now. You don't think so, ask Sherrilyn. She bout ready to gut you."

"Man, fuck y'all and—"

"It's his birthday, Demon. I know he bad and grown as fuck, but he still a kid and his grouchy ass big brother forgot his birthday."

That shut me the fuck up. My childhood had been nothing but disappointments like forgotten and ignored birthdays and here I was doing it to Kam. I rubbed my hand over my face.

"I knew I had no business with a kid. Fuck!" I said, slamming my fists against the arms of the chair.

"You good with him. You just need to find yo' girl and get yo' head on straight," Dante said.

My eyes snapped to his.

"I'on have a girl."

He shook his head. "We still doing this? That's part of the problem."

I frowned. "Did I ask you for advice?"

"Nah, but you need it. Li Jun and the team can't find her?"

"Not yet," I admitted.

"And Lucien?"

"Ain't talking."

It pissed me off to think about it. I wanted to box his old ass but Dream would never talk to me again and I respected the nigga too much, anyway.

"Why she leave like that?" my brother pushed.

I sighed at his nosy ass. "We were having disagreements." Hell, I might as well put it all out there. "She was pregnant and wasn't sure she wanted to be. I had to convince her she needed to stay that way."

Dante's eyes widened. For once, he seemed shocked. He sat back on that damn throne, speechless for a minute.

"A baby? Fuck, Demon, you made a...Did you do that shit on purpose?" he asked, eyes narrowed in judgment.

Elbows on my knees, I leaned forward with my face in my hands.

"Hell, no. I ain't want no baby. At first, I was just fucking her. Then, I was just—" I stopped, not sure what to say.

What the hell had I been doing?

"Loving her," Dante said quietly.

My head snapped up. "What?"

"You were just loving her."

I shook my head hard as fuck. "Nah. Nah, I ain't on that shit at all."

He sighed. "You make this so fucking hard. You been in denial since the first night you saw that girl. It's all right, little brother. Even the best of us fall."

I sprang from the chair. I had heard everything I needed to.

"It's okay if Kam stays a few more hours?"

Dante waved his hand dismissively. "Kam is fine. We'll probably take him out tonight. You invited if you get over yo' damn self."

"Nigga, fuck you," I mocked.

"Go get that girl. And stop lying to yourself," he said as I walked out.

Kam and DJ were still in the living room as I got ready to leave. I looked at the kid but he ignored me.

"Sup, Unc?" DJ greeted.

I bumped his fist then turned to Kam.

"Ay... that shit a little while ago, a nigga was wrong. I shouldn't have come at you like that. And, um, happy birthday. I got you tomorrow," I promised.

He ignored me for a few more seconds, then a sly grin lifted his lips.

"Tomorrow? You can CashApp me right now."

———

I didn't know where I was going when I left Dante's. I just needed to clear my head. How I ended up at this particular office building in this particular office was a mystery to me. Technically, the office closed at five. But it was 5:30 and the door was unlocked, so...

A pretty, dark-skinned woman emerged from the back hallway. Her attention was on the mail in her hand. Not wanting to scare her, I cleared my throat. She looked up and her eyes widened. I could see the fear in her eyes, but she kept herself together.

"How did you get in here?" she asked calmly.

"Shit, the door was open," I replied with a shrug.

Holding her ground, she studied me. I knew she was trying to figure out the best approach to take and I waited, curious to see what she would say.

"We... the deposit for today left with the admin who obviously left the door open," she said.

"I don't want your money, Dr. Monroe."

If she was surprised that I knew her name, it didn't show. She nodded before speaking again.

"So, what do you want, Mr...."

Her voice trailed off as she waited for me to fill in the blank.

"Montana. Damien Montana. My brother Kameron is one of your clients," I said.

A small frown creased her face. "Is something wrong with Kam?"

"Nah."

We stared at each other awkwardly. For some reason, I couldn't voice what I wanted. Instead, I studied the warm beige and blue space, thinking about the color choices. She smiled slightly.

"Well, Mr. Montana—"

"I thought maybe I could talk to you, too," I said in a rush. "I mean, not now. I know you leaving now, so I can—"

"No. Let's talk now," she interrupted softly. "Where would you like to start?" she asked me minutes later as we sat in her office.

I blew out a deep breath, my fingers drumming on the arm of the blue chair.

"I guess it starts with a girl," I said.

"A girl?" she pressed.

"Dream."

"She's your..."

Again, she waited on me. I shook my head.

"She's gone."

"She… passed away?"

Shit, even the thought of that made me sick, had my stomach twisting and flipping until I had nausea.

"She left town," I clarified.

"And you don't want to tell me Dream's relationship to you?"

I sighed, thinking of the right words. Finally, I had to fall back on the only ones that had ever seemed to fit.

"Dream is… mine. She's just mine."

Dr. Monroe looked at me thoughtfully.

"Then let's talk about what that means—to be yours. Did Dream understand what that meant?"

I leaned heavily against the back of my chair.

"Nah. I don't think she did."

"Maybe we should start with how she came to be yours," she said pensively.

CHAPTER 100
Dream

(**MONDAY**, *October 4*)

Two months. I honestly didn't think this "vacation" would last this long. I just wanted…no, needed to get away before I lost myself in everyone else. Sighing, I rolled over onto my side while thinking about my life. I'd been doing that a lot lately, trying to figure out my purpose and where I went from here.

For so long, I'd been the fixer of my family and now, look at us. Our mother killed our father. Dayana and I were a little distant because I felt she violated my trust, in a way. DeAngelo was quiet toward everyone, thinking about the problems he'd created or supported because of his blind dedication to Daddy. I didn't even know if we could be fixed. Guess I failed at that, too. Feeling myself rapidly going down that rabbit hole, I grabbed my journal. That was pretty much all I did out here: think, write, and repeat. Today's prompt almost made me close the damn book right back up. "If you could have anything you wanted, what would it be? Why? How would it enhance your life?" Fuck this journal writer. Like, why in the fuck was this even a question? Everyone knew exactly how they would answer that question… it took absolutely no thought. Or did it? Eyes closing, I started to envision what I wanted. What if my father were still alive?

Walking into the house, I gasped when Daddy walked in and asked about work and when I would be going on a date with Paul... My imagination abruptly stopped. Hell, no. As much as I missed my Daddy, I had to realize he had started to get a lot wrong. He caused so much pain and lost so much of himself because of his quest for power. I could admit now that it was no wonder that his time had expired.

A light knock at my door had me glancing up.

"Yeah?" I called.

"Just checking on you," Rhythm said.

"I'm good, cousin!"

"Okay! I'll be back in a little. Don't forget, we leaving soon!"

Smiling, I shook my head and read the day's prompt again. As much as I fought it, my mind started to wander, thinking about what I really wanted. Wondering that led me to my headache, my heartache, my frigid Damien. Thinking of him in terms of mine was crazy. It had been months. He had probably forgotten about me and was more than likely living his best life with Juliette's latest flavors. Fuck what that looked like and extra fucks for what it made me feel like. I needed to unload some of this shit, work harder to clear him from my mind and heart. For the journal entry, I was just going to pen a letter to him to cleanse myself of all my feelings.

Damien,

It's been a while and since I'm being honest, I can't believe I made it this far without seeing your face. I miss it. I even miss being frozen in the tundra you refer to as home. I guess I can finally speak words that you doubted and I tried to take back. I love you. This isn't a thought or an assumption. It is, without a doubt, the truth. The downside? You're closed off and don't want a thing from me besides my pussy and a seed that was not meant to be. From the beginning, that was made clear, but somehow, we managed to make a fairytale out of a grim reality. This letter would clearly piss you off if I had the nerve to send it. But I just can't do that. I am afraid to bare my soul to one who wants so badly to be soulless. You held me and told me I was yours. But what does being yours even mean? A lifetime of one-sided love and constant insecurity because you can't get over your past?

I want more from my life and come hell or high water, I am going to get where I want to be. Hurdles, mountains... unrequited love, I DON'T CARE WHAT IT IS! I WILL MAKE IT! (lol) Even while writing, I know that yelling will lead me nowhere. You shut down and I try to get in. It's exhausting. I had to leave because I needed time to grow stronger. I couldn't continue to see you and not want you; hell, not love you.

Of course, I bear plenty of the fault for our ugly end. Was I wrong for what I said to you at Smoke's house? Yep! One-hundred percent. I made an assumption and made an entire ass of myself. I knew that you would kill for me and I assumed you snapped. There was blood on you and my mother. What was I to think? That my mother did it? My proper, cookie-baking, pearl-wearing mama? It didn't even register. I couldn't understand the lengths one will go through to protect their child.

Damien, I am sorry for all the hurtful things that were done to you, things that make it impossible for you to believe that love is real and that you deserve it. You absolutely deserve all the love I have for you, but until you accept that, I can't empty myself by pouring into a void.

I'm going to answer the questions for today to you. If I could have anything in this life, it would be you. The whys of life usually leave me stuck but not now. I want you in my life but not in just any way. You have already offered to protect me, to provide for me, to please me, to marry me... everything except to love me, and I want that most of all. I don't regret meeting you, but I regret meeting you in those circumstances. Until you choose me, well, choose to love me, it will always be on my mind that fate and Dante *chose me for you. Would you have looked at me twice if you passed me on the street? It's the little shit that triggers me. I am stuck loving you, yet you can move on as if I never existed.*

You kill for me. You kill this pussy, lol. But you are always killing my heart. And still, my simp ass (I sound like you) would always CHOOSE you. (So glad you won't read this.)

Soooo… how would this enhance my life? Hmmmm. You add value to me even when you don't see it. Somedays, it feels like I'm losing my mind being away from you. But I have to stay away before you kill my spirit next…

"Dream, are you ready to go? You know the traffic will be crazy getting there and back, especially since you got this detail and shit, your highness."

Listening to Rhythm, I rolled my eyes as I eased from the bed. "Ay, I'm ready to go, but I need you to keep your head on your shoulders. I know you 'bout that life, but this nigga makes the Grim Reaper look like a slacker."

She knocked quickly before opening my door as I grabbed my bag.

"Baby, I am not worried about this nigga. When it's time for me to join the ancestors, then so be it, but I am not going easy. He gon' have to Bruce Leroy my ass to Elvis," she popped

"Ummm… why are you going to Elvis?" I asked.

"Shit didn't Tamela Mann say, 'Take me to the King?' You know Tamela gives good advice."

Laughing hard as hell, I hugged her ass because I needed that laugh.

"Bitch, you could have at least said Michael Jackson! I'm gone!"

CHAPTER 101
Demon

(*WEDNESDAY*, *December 15*)

I set the barbell back on its rest, sighing before picking up the insulated bottle of water I'd brought into my gym.

"Stop making all that damn noise. That's not good gym etiquette," Kam snapped in his cracking voice as he walked on the treadmill.

"Who invited you in here anyway, lil' nigga?" I asked, wiping my face with a towel before draping it around my neck.

"Nigga, I'on need no invitation. This my crib!"

He smacked his bird chest a couple of times as he spoke before grilling me.

"Shut yo' ass up before you be wrapped around the belt on that treadmill."

"You gon' make me call them people on you," he threatened.

I smirked. "Betta be good before Santa Claus don't bring you nothing."

"Shiiii, I hope he don't. I been having nightmares about seeing yo' big ass coming down the chimney."

This nigga... I couldn't help it. I laughed at his bad ass as I walked over to him. Catching him off guard, I pushed the button until the treadmill was on ten miles an hour. He cursed me as he started running hard as fuck. I was still laughing when my phone started to ring. I strolled over to pick it up, frowning as I saw the unknown number.

"Yeah," I answered.

"I found her," Li Jun said, speaking as abruptly as I had.

My heart jumped on some weak shit before I got it under control.

"Where?" I asked through gritted teeth.

"She's actually not far. Been searching for anyone or any residence under any combination of her immediate family's and grandparents' and great grandparents' names. Colette Le Blanc finally showed—"

"Where?" I growled again, cutting him off. "Where is she?"

He rattled off an address in another South Texas county.

"Thanks," I muttered.

"Demon?"

Li Jun's voice sounded hesitant. That instantly put me on alert.

"What?"

"I already have eyes on it. You should probably know there's a... man there with her. I haven't identified him yet," he said quietly.

I hung up, even as my body went cold. I was trying hard to remember all the shit Dr. Monroe said over and over, but other shit, bigger shit like the fact that she had gotten rid of my baby only to be with another nigga months later was crowding out all that fucking positivity. Dream was mine. I had searched for and found her so she'd know that and now, this shit? My hands balled into fists and my blood froze with the desire to hurt someone. Badly. I took several deep breaths before trusting myself to address Kam.

"Go get ready. You gotta go with Dante and Sherrilyn," I told him.

His face brightened. "Is it Dream? You found her?"

I nodded once. Nigga did some crazy little dance before giving me a serious look.

"You over there looking mean as hell. Don't fuck this up, Damien Montana."

"Mind yo' business, Kameron Montana," I growled at him.

He was too fucking restless to care. He jumped off the treadmill and scrambled over to me.

"You need to get our girl back. Let me give you some tips." He threw an arm around my shoulders. "Don't worry, awkward big brother. I got you."

———

It was almost dark by the time I stepped out of the car and onto one of the streets in the exclusive, gated community where Dream was staying. According to Li Jun, she'd left a while ago with a woman he'd identified as her cousin and her two-man detail. The only person in the house was the nigga I was more than ready to meet. I reached in my pocket as my phone vibrated.

Sure you don't want us to come in? Juan had typed.

Looking through the windshield of the truck that had parked behind me, I shook my head. Measured steps carried me across the street, up the long driveway, and to the front door. The alarm system had been disabled—way too easily, according to Li Jun—so I let myself in, entering a foyer. I wasn't worried about running into him unexpectedly. I wanted an excuse to kick his ass.

"About time y'all got back!" he yelled.

I followed his voice silently. Apparently, I was a lot better at moving quietly than he was, which is why when he stepped out in front of me, Sig Sauer pointed, I was ready. Grabbing his gun hand, I squeezed as I brought my other hand up and slammed it, open palm, into his nose. The gun fell as he went down, landing on his knees while clutching his probably-broken nose. I picked up the strap, the urge to pistol whip him lifeless so strong that I clenched my teeth until it felt like they might break.

"Get yo' ass up," I spat.

He shook his head, sitting on his ass. "Nah, fam. I'm good down here. I ain't into that Jackie Chan shit. Who the fuck are you?"

This was the nigga Dream picked? His goofy ass was worse than Isaac Stone and he looked young as fuck. I walked slightly past him, reached down, grabbed the collar of his shirt, and started dragging him toward the nearest room. Nigga made all kind of noises, but I didn't let go until we were in the living room. Standing in front of him, I aimed the gun.

"Stand yo' ass up before yo' head go missing."

He looked up and frowned, blood dripping from his nose, down his lips and chin.

"You gon' shoot me with my own gun? Bruh, that's some cold-hearted shit. And I still don't—"

I racked the slide of the gun. He threw up both hands before scrambling his ass off the floor.

"I'm up! Damn. A nigga injured and—"

"Where yo' phone?" I asked calmly.

Swallowing hard, he reached into his pocket and pulled out his phone.

"Call Dream. Tell her to come back now," I demanded.

His eyes changed once I said her name. His blood-soaked lips curved into a smirk.

"Ohhh... you must be..." he stopped.

She had talked about me? What the fuck had she told this nigga? I was struggling to hold onto my shit, as it was. If this pussy knew what was good for him, he'd change the subject real quick. Then, he spoke again.

"You ain't gotta worry about Dream. She's not yo' concern no m—"

Cold fury flooded me and I throat punched his bitch ass. He bent over, gagging and grabbing his neck with one hand and slapping his leg with the other. *This weak ass muhfucka.*

"Dream is always my concern," I informed him. "You done with the theatrics yet?"

He held up one finger and coughed again, then stood.

"I think I'm finished."

"Good."

I grabbed his throat and squeezed.

"You think this shit is a joke? You think I'm playing with yo' bitch ass?"

"I... I don't think that at all. This feels very serious," he wheezed.

"This is how this shit about to go. You gon' call her. When she gets here, you gon' leave. You gon' never talk to her again."

A minute passed as he blinked. "I'm waiting for the 'or.'"

I chuckled lowly as I used enough pressure to cut off his breath for real. "Nigga, what you think the 'or' is?"

I waited as he beat my hand and turned an interesting shade of purple. Finally, he held up a finger again. I eased up enough for him to gasp several breaths before talking.

"I'll call her. But the rest of that shit is dead."

My eyes narrowed. "Like you, if you try me."

He reached for the phone that had slid from his grasp and unlocked it to look through his contacts. Seconds later, the phone was ringing.

"Put that shit on speaker."

He sighed loudly but did as I said. That was safest. It was taking every bit of willpower I had not to beat his face into the back of his skull. Two rings in, the voice I hadn't heard since July was on the line.

"Hey, love. You good? We really are about to be on our way. Just on our way to pick up food," Dream said, the affection in her voice clear.

Something icy washed through me. She really cared about this pussy. A feeling that I'd never fully experienced consumed me. I'd felt a little bit of it when other niggas touched her or when she gave them her smiles or laughs. But this, the shit I was feeling now twisted and turned through me, a mix of rage and... and... something painful. The stupid ass nigga grinned smugly. Then, he spoke.

"Dream... run, baby!" he ordered.

My fist connected with his eye and I snatched the phone from him as he fell backward.

"West, what—" Dream's panicked voice floated from the phone.

"You come here *now* or I will finish him and light this bitch up," I promised.

"Damien... Damien, wait, please—"

I wasn't about to listen to her beg for this nigga and I had said way too much on an unsecured line. I disconnected the call.

I knew that she was coming for him.

I was mad that she was coming for him.

I looked at the nigga she called West, rolling on the floor and groaning. I kicked him in his side viciously, feeling a deep satisfaction as his body bucked off the floor.

"You called her 'baby.' She's not your fucking 'baby,' bitch," I snarled at him.

He smirked.

"She's not yours, either," he whispered.

I smashed the pistol into his head twice before I could stop myself. His ass was knocked out, his mouth still curved into a smile that mocked me. I took a few steps back and waited.

Not even ten minutes later, I heard the front door open and voices.

"Dream, you crazy as hell if you think I'm letting yo' ass go in by yourself!" some woman yelled.

"It's good, Rhythm," Dream said as footsteps came closer.

"Ms. Castle, I have to insist that you let us—" a man started

"Anand, please! Just wait outside, please? Y'all gon' only make this worse!"

And then she was walking into the living room, the other woman, Rhythm, rushing behind her. Rhythm screamed and dropped to her knees beside West's still body. Dream's eyes flew to mine.

"What did you do? Oh, God, Damien! What did you do?"

I heard her, but it was like I had cotton in my ears or some shit. I was too busy looking at her to focus on her words. In a red pea coat and a tan sweater dress with boots, she was beautiful. Her hair was straight and parted down the middle, falling to her breasts. Her lips were as luscious, her eyes as big and deep, her skin as perfect as ever. Only her button nose looked a little different. But my eyes were focused elsewhere, on her body. She followed my gaze, then wrapped her arms around her middle, as if she had to protect herself from me. That snapped me out of my daze and my eyes tangled with hers.

"Damien—" she began again.

"You're pregnant," I interrupted hoarsely.

I moved toward her. Suddenly, West and Rhythm, her detail, and Stella and Juan, who had burst in, were all forgotten. For months, I had been looking for her, wanting her to feel my anger, wanting some kind of retribution because she had the nerve to think that she could walk away and destroy my seed. But... she hadn't. Shit wasn't a question to me; I knew this baby was mine. Before I could accept how right that shit felt, another idea came to me, one that almost had me turning to kill West even now, with Rhythm crying and fussing over his weak ass.

Dream backed herself against the wall then put out one hand, trying to hold me back as she turned to look at Rhythm.

"Is he—"

I held out West's gun behind me and Stella immediately stepped forward to take it. I pushed Dream's hand away until only her stomach separated us.

"Nah, he ain't. You sho' got a lot of fucks to give for this nigga. I spared his life because…" I stopped. She didn't need to know everything I'd learned in therapy. "I let him live. But if you been fucking this nigga with my baby inside you—" I grabbed her hair, pulling her head back gently. "I'm glad I waited to kill him in front of you."

It was hard to focus on what I wanted to say, to stay as mad as I was when her sweet scent was suddenly surrounding me and her eyes were drowning me. I wanted… *needed* to touch her so badly I could taste it. And speaking of taste, my eyes shifted to her lush mouth. She was nibbling on her bottom lip like crazy. I wanted to pull it loose, soothe it with my tongue.

"Dream, what—" Rhythm shook me from my thoughts.

"Shut up," West ordered, sounding groggy as fuck.

I hadn't even realized that nigga had come around.

"Ms. Castle, would you like us to remove this… potential threat?" one of her detail asked.

Juan laughed. "And how you gon' do that?"

"Please… Anand, Jamal, it's okay," Dream reassured them.

"Who is this nigga?" I asked her.

"Dream, you don't owe him any explanations—" West interrupted.

I reached for my own gun. Dream grabbed my arm. I froze at her touch. Fuck, I had missed that.

"No," she whispered. "I'm not fucking him. Rhythm and West are my cousins."

West blew out a breath. "Thank God. I was gon' ride with you, Cousin, but I'm definitely more of a lover than a fighter. You ain't tell nobody the Hulk knocked yo' ass up," he fussed.

I mugged him. "Nigga, you ain't safe, yet," I warned. "How come Li Jun didn't know this nigga was yo' relative?"

I shot the question at Dream.

"Cuz I'm a love child and my daddy—Rhythm's daddy— didn't know about me until a couple years ago. My last name ain't Dumont and I don't live in Texas," West explained as Rhythm helped him off the floor.

Nigga ran his mouth entirely too much for me. I wasn't even talking to his ass.

"Surely you can understand the daddy part," Dream said, her voice low.

My eyes narrowed on her. *Shady ass.* I guess she was still mad at me. That was all right. She was about to get madder.

"Yeah, I can understand it, which is why that shit won't be repeating. Tell yo' cousins bye. You bringing my seed home," I told her, tightening my hand in her hair.

She sucked her teeth. "I never planned to keep this baby from you. I don't know why you acting all surprised when you knew I was pregnant. I'll be home next week for the holidays. I'm not going anywhere with you."

I smiled down at her, looking forward to the challenge. Her eyes were flashing, angry and defiant. My dick was instantly hard.

"That's yo' word, shorty?"

CHAPTER 102
Dream

I CROSSED my arms over my chest and glared at him. This nigga had me fucked up.

"We going to my room. Now," I said through my teeth.

"Lead the way," he responded, smirking.

"Move!"

I wanted him to move, not just because I wanted to go to the room, but because he was too close. His familiar scent of Dove and clean man was way too tempting. And even though I hated him, the way he towered over me, his locs pulled away from his perfect face, his muscular frame evident despite the hoodie and joggers, had my body on fire for him, my heart racing, my breathing shallow. I wanted to press my wobbly self against him and melt in his arms. But I just couldn't let go of all the words and time that had passed between us. He leaned in, bringing his mouth a breath away from mine. I inhaled sharply.

"Fuck, Dream. You pregnant."

His voice sounded strange, the words almost choked out.

"Why do you keep saying that? You knew I was pregnant," I snapped, suddenly irritated. "You stopped the abortion, remember? So, congratulations, Damien. You gon' be a father. Not that either one of us knows what the fuck we're doing," I muttered the last sentence, before turning to march out of the living room and down the hallway that led to my room. Reaching my door, I pushed it open before I stepped into the small sitting room that fronted my bedroom. Moving to the side, I let him enter. I barely had the door closed before he had me pressed against it.

"Damien—"

"We can learn, Dream. We can learn what to do—"

I scoffed before laughing bitterly. "We can learn? We are probably the most unfit... I mean, you do the shit you do and I planned to be a full-time career woman for another decade. I hadn't even made up my mind about kids! I had goals, dreams—"

His eyes were getting colder with each word I spoke so I stopped and just stared up at him.

"You still don't want my... this baby, huh?" he said, voice low.

What? I wanted this baby more than my next breath, loved it with my whole heart already, but I was terrified of fucking up. Even now, the feel of my child moving had me wanting to rub my belly and reassure it. I was too stubborn to tell him that, though, so I just dropped my gaze. He tilted my chin up.

"It don't fucking matter. You and the baby are mine, and I'm taking you home. You'll adjust."

My head was shaking already. "No. No. This baby is yours. I am not," I corrected, hoping he couldn't see the lie in my eyes.

One corner of his mouth lifted in a twisted smile.

"I told you, you belong to me. Shit hasn't changed."

I sucked my teeth. "Shit expired, remember?"

"We'll see."

Before I could object any more, he brushed a finger across my nose.

"Your nose different," he said, changing the subject like our argument was over.

I sighed. "Pregnancy. It's so ugly and big now."

He cupped my face and just looked at me for a minute, his thumb stroking my cheekbone.

"Still beautiful, shorty."

The compliment caught me off-guard. I didn't want to acknowledge how it made me warm, made me want to sink into him even more. I waved a hand, trying to dismiss the effect his words and his presence had on me.

"Lies you tell. And I'm not about to go nowhere. Rhythm and I been shopping and you interrupted what was supposed to be our dinner. I'm about to order food, shower, and go to bed. You need to go to your hotel and we'll talk about this child and whatever else tomorrow," I announced.

He chuckled lightly. "Yeah, okay, mama. Order me whatever you get."

"Ugh!"

I blew out a heavy breath as I threw my hands up. Damien Montana could manage to piss me the fuck off, but I knew once he made up his mind, there was no changing it. I ordered food for the both of us, getting him sweet potato fries instead of the truffle ones I chose. His cocky ass arranged to have clothes and toiletries delivered. Without saying a word to him, I walked into the bedroom, grabbed stuff for the shower, and stormed into the bathroom. I locked the door, knowing his infuriating ass would get in if he really wanted to.

As the warm water cascaded over me, I thought about how good he looked and smelled. Images of him played in my mind as my fingers eased between my thighs. It had been so long and this pregnancy made me so horny. The moan that escaped my lips as I stroked my already swollen clit made me stop. I would not give that nigga the pleasure of hearing that. I got my fast ass out of the shower, oiling myself and drying off before wrapping a bath sheet around my body. Padding back into the bedroom, I rolled my eyes at my annoying baby daddy before walking toward the dresser. Two seconds later, I squealed as he lifted me and walked toward the bed. *What the—*

He laid me down gently then looked at me, green eyes full of some emotion I couldn't name.

"I just wanna see," he said quietly.

I didn't stop him as he pulled the edges of the towel apart and rose over me. He stared down at my body, and his words from months before about model types played in my head. I squirmed uncomfortably. I couldn't hide my belly or my thighs, but I draped an arm across my breasts and a protective hand across my pussy. He moved them instantly, mugging me in the process.

"I told you, don't do that shit," he growled. "I've seen every inch of yo' body and it's mine, Dream."

I rolled my eyes. "We'll see," I mumbled his words back to him.

"Yeah. We will."

And then he was touching my stomach, soft, hesitant brushes as he took in the ways his baby was changing my body. Suddenly, my insistent little one pressed against my abdomen, as if it were pushing back against its father's touch. Damien inhaled sharply but didn't comment.

"This line is new," he murmured, tracing down the center of my belly.

"*Linea nigra*," I named it quietly.

He continued his slow exploration as I fought not to moan beneath him. I knew he was just curious, but his hands on my body, *oh, my God*! I had been thinking about his touch for so long and now he was—

My mind blanked, just fucking blanked for a minute when his hands landed on my breasts. I almost chewed my bottom lip in half.

"These are different, too," he said all clinically.

"Too... too big," I managed to push out, looking up at him.

His eyes finally changed, something hot and sexy in his gaze.

"Nah, shorty. They perfect," he whispered, letting his thumb graze my suddenly hard, aching nipples.

This time, I couldn't help the way my body arched and the moan that slipped between my lips. Damien, more beautiful than any human being had a right to be, gave me a dark smile before lowering his head...

...and freezing as someone knocked on the door.

"Dream? Food... and other shit," Rhythm called.

I could have cried as he lifted his solid frame and pulled me up. But gratitude washed through me as I wrapped the towel back around my body. What the fuck was I thinking? I might be attracted to this man and hornier than a toad convention, but I was not fucking him.

At all.

Ever.

Again.

I glared at him and his smile widened, smug and dark and gorgeous all at once.

Bastard.

"Here I come, Rhythm!"

CHAPTER 103
Demon

I FOLLOWED her into the sitting room and watched as she opened the door to let her cousin in. Rhythm's eyes swept up and down Dream, dressed only in that towel, before they shifted to me where I leaned against a desk. Her top lip curled as she eyeballed me and turned up her nose. I smirked at her, before grabbing the food and the shit I had ordered. Turning my attention to the desktop, I looked it over. Except for a few scattered business cards, it was neat and uncluttered. One of the cards caught my eye and an idea unfolded in my head.

"Are you all right, cousin?" Rhythm asked loudly as I opened my phone to type a message to Li Jun.

Dream sucked her teeth. "I'm fine. Girl, he ain't gon' do nothing," she popped off.

I stopped typing but decided to let her make it.

"Mmm. That ain't what West said," Rhythm shot back.

"She ain't West. Mind your business, shorty," I warned, my patience getting thin. "I don't hurt what's mine."

I added that for Dream, but Rhythm scoffed, reminding me of Dayana's bold ass.

"Oh, you don't?"

"Rhythm," Dream said softly, but her cousin stepped around her.

"She wasn't hurt when she first came here crying cuz her heart was broken? She wasn't hurt all those times I showed up to go to her doctor's appointments? She wasn't hurt every time—"

But I had heard enough. Dream's pain wasn't shit I wanted to hear about, especially if I played a role. Even after all the shit she'd said in Smoke's living room. I slid the phone in my pocket as I moved toward them. Dream's eyes widened. I wouldn't hurt that worrisome ass girl, but Dream walked between us like I would.

"Damien," she pleaded quietly, before focusing on her cousin. "Rhy, I got this. Thank you for the food and I'm sorry about West, but I promise—"

"You got this and yo' ass half-naked?" Rhythm shook her head. "Just be careful, cousin."

With one last glare at me, she stalked out. Dream was quiet as she opened and separated our food, handing me a Styrofoam container then a paper plate.

"Drinks in there," she said tightly, nodding toward the mini-fridge close to the desk.

I grabbed two waters before moving to sit across from her. She put everything else on the low table between the chairs before groaning. My eyes instantly moved to her.

"What?"

"They forgot my honey mustard!"

We had chicken strips, side salads, and fries. I looked at the containers on the table before shrugging.

"You got barbecue and ranch."

"I know," she said, but I heard the catch in her voice.

I frowned as I looked at her. Shorty really looked ready to cry.

"Dream—"

"I don't really want this without the honey mustard."

She set her plate down and stood up. I did the same, grabbing her arm gently. She glanced up at me and her glassy, tear-filled eyes had me confused.

"You really about to cry about—"

Fat tears slid down her cheeks as she sniffed.

"Leave me alone, Damien!" she whined.

"Yo, you serious, mama?" I asked in disbelief.

"You don't understand! I really wanted that because I was hungry and—"

She hiccupped and cried harder. It suddenly dawned on me that this must be the damn pregnancy hormones even I had heard about. Shit was ridiculous. So was the fact that I shook my head then walked out of the room. I found the kitchen easily, washed my hands, and threw open the refrigerator. Dijon and yellow mustard, mayo, a lemon from the counter, some seasonings from the cabinet, honey from the pantry. I didn't say shit as Dream and her cousins watched me work from across the island. Sticking a spoon in the finished product, I held it out to her. My dick almost ripped my pants when her tongue eased out to taste the honey mustard. Her pout shifted into a smile as she nodded.

"It's better than the restaurant's," she said, tasting it again.

A small drop clung to her lip. I clenched my fists to fight the urge to lick it off. Instead, I swiped my thumb across it before bringing it to my mouth to suck off. She pulled in a breath as her eyes heated. I wanted to fuck her right then. Hard. Bend her over the granite countertop and make her remember whom she belonged to.

"And on that note..." I heard Rhythm mumble.

"But she said the honey mustard was better than Belle's. I wanna—" West began.

"Bring yo' ass, West."

I was walking around the island before they even disappeared. This shit was crazy. One minute, I wanted to be mad at her; the next, I wanted to be inside her. I could see my confusion reflected in her pretty face. Bending closer, I let my lips trail along her jawline up to her mouth. She sighed, leaning into me, her fists balling in my shirt. I could kiss her right now and she wouldn't even fight me. As badly as I wanted to, I wanted to get her fed—and check out some other shit—first. I pulled back, resting my forehead against hers.

"C'mon, before your fries get cold. Then yo' ass will be crying about that," I said.

Frowning at me, she stomped off to her room. Shorty grabbed that honey mustard first, though. Forty minutes later, we had eaten and brushed our teeth. She climbed into bed as I showered, took care of my skin, then pulled on the pajama pants I had ordered.

"The couch in the sitting room pulls out. There's a blanket in the closet," she murmured when I stepped into the bedroom.

"Okay," I replied before slipping into her bed.

She made a frustrated sound before turning her back to me. I slid toward the middle and reached for her plush frame. She let out a little shriek and slapped at my hands as I wrapped my body around hers, her softness and sweet scent relaxing me in a way I hadn't felt in months. She still fit perfectly against me, a fact that her body recognized, although her mouth refused to admit it. Dream snuggled into me even as she talked shit about me touching her.

"Damien, you can't—"

"Shut up," I mumbled, easing my hand under the shirt she wore to stroke the silky skin of her stomach.

I was still struggling to wrap my mind around the fact that she was pregnant, that my baby was living and thriving in her womb. Hell, I had even forgotten to ask her what we were having, but I now understood why people said it didn't matter. Fuck a sex; I just wanted my little one to be well. Shit was making me soft... hell, softer toward her. It was some shit a nigga wasn't bending on, though. Tomorrow, she was coming home with me. She could be mad, she could refuse to speak, but she'd be doing all that at my spot, where I could take care of her and my seed. As if it agreed, my baby kicked the hell out of my hand. I cupped Dream's belly more possessively.

Sleep didn't come to me as easily as it did Dream. She was too tempting, from the flowery scent of her hair to the softness of her curves to the sweet scent of her skin. I wanted to be inside her too bad to do something as boring as sleep. I held her for a few hours until Li Jun texted that he had sent me a file. That nigga never slept, I swear. Switching to my email, I opened the file.

Thirty minutes later, I knew the most important facts. Dream was twenty-nine weeks pregnant and she and the baby were healthy as fuck. I had stopped myself from touching her like I wanted, scared of causing her pain or hurting my child. But between her file and Google, I realized that it was okay to touch her, taste her, fuck her, and that she might even want it.

She didn't wake as I shifted our bodies, lying her on her back and sliding down to ease up the nightshirt she'd been wearing once I was between her legs. I brushed kisses against her stomach before letting my lips travel lower. Her fresh scent drove me crazy. Hungry as fuck, I let my tongue explore the sweet entrance to her body. She moaned and her body arched. My tongue connected to her clit and she shot up.

"Damien..."

My name was a breathless moan on her lips. She gripped my locs, moving her hips and feeding me her juicy pussy.

"W-w-we can't," she whispered.

"Why?" I asked before sucking her clit into my mouth.

"You know why!"

I didn't bother to answer; I just kept making love to her pussy with my mouth. Shorty tasted so fucking good. She didn't hold out long. She gripped my hair tighter as I slurped and licked on her. I felt her shivering, felt her body tense.

"Damien... oh, God, yes," she moaned as she came in my mouth.

She was still the best-tasting thing I had all year. Her body quivered and shook as I inserted two fingers inside her. Shit, she was tighter than I remembered. I worked my fingers in and out of her.

"Please, Damien. I can't take any more. Oh, God," she whimpered.

I buried my face in her pussy and had her cumming again. Dream was soaking wet and I had to get inside. Climbing off the bed, I walked to the side. I pulled her to the edge and let my gaze pierce hers just as I leaned forward to kiss her. We kissed like lost lovers, like two people who didn't want to let each other go.

I stripped out of my pajama pants and stepped between her legs. I squeezed her thighs gently.

"Fuck, I missed these," I murmured.

"I thought you preferred the model type," she whispered, the hurt in her voice evident.

I hated that I'd ever said that to her. It was a stupid, petty comeback that I'd used in the heat of the moment and I was sorry. But all I said aloud was, "Your body is perfect, Dream."

I eased into her as gently as I could. Halfway in, I had to stop. So, this was that pregnant pussy niggas were always dreaming about? This super wet, super-hot, impossibly tight channel that was sucking my dick right up? I almost came immediately. A nigga couldn't move; I just savored this moment as she moaned for me.

CHAPTER 104

Dream

AT FIRST, I thought it was the same delicious dream I always had—Damien's head between my thighs, feasting on me like I was his favorite meal. Then I realized, his tongue between my lips and his locs beneath my hands felt too real.

I knew I should stop it, should push him away and close my thighs, but it had been five months and it felt too good. Hell, he felt too good and as he rocked into my eager and willing body, I moaned. Damien stretched and filled me to capacity. The shit was exquisite and I wanted to cry.

"You missed me?" he asked, his voice deep and rough.

"No," I lied stubbornly.

He laughed. "The way this pussy clenching and milking me, your body did. It knows who it belongs to."

I wanted to argue, but how could I, when he was telling the truth? I was about to cum again, my pussy contracting and releasing and he was barely moving.

"Damien, please... move," I whined, pushing my body against his.

"Not too deep. The baby—"

He was talking, but he picked up his pace, almost like he couldn't help it. His dick rasped against that sensitive place deep inside me and I went spinning out of control again. I screamed his name as I came all over his thick rod.

"Say you're mine," he whispered, stroking me relentlessly.

I shook my head, too overcome to speak.

"I told you that you belong to me, and you want to take that away? Why do you keep taking things, Dream?"

"I don't," I whimpered.

He leaned over me and I closed my eyes against his piercing ones.

"Nah, shorty. Open 'em while I talk to you."

Reluctantly, I obeyed. I almost closed them again when his teeth sank into my neck, his mouth warm as he bit and sucked me. Finally, he lifted his head.

"You took so much from me when you left. You took your body. You took this time with my baby. You took my calm, my peace."

I tried to listen as his hips moved slowly, deliberately between my thighs. His mouth trailed kisses and love bites down to my breast. I gasped at the sharp bite then the gentle pull of his mouth on my nipple.

"Damien…"

"You took yourself. You took your love," he continued, his eyes on mine again. "Well… you tried to take your love, but that's mine, huh, baby?"

This time, I did close my eyes again, not wanting him to see the truth there. I shook my head furiously. He chuckled against my ear before biting the lobe. His thrusts picked up and his hand snaked between us to tease my clit. Incredibly, I felt a fourth orgasm building.

"Little liar. Tell me you love me, Dream," he demanded.

I moaned a weak ass "no," my body too caught up in the rhythm of his.

"That's all right. You will."

His confidence should have pissed me off but I was

beyond sparring with him, my body tight and tingling and so ready.

"Fuck, Dream. You keep cumming and you so wet and tight. I'm about to cum in my pussy."

His voice was a gruff whisper that set me on fire and multiplied my shivers.

"Tell me who owns this body, Dream. Tell me who you belong to," he growled.

He pinched my clit and the little bit of pain rocketed me into a universe of pleasure. Damien fucked me as I came, until his own rhythm was jerky and offbeat. He pulled out before he released, palming his dick. I gasped as I felt the warmth of his seed hit my thighs and my pussy. Still disoriented from my own orgasm, it took me a minute to think.

Did this nigga cum on me? I looked at him in shock. He knelt between my legs, a small smirk playing around his mouth. Immediately, the shit clicked. I refused to say I was his, so he was fucking marking me? I had a sudden vision of what I must look like to his smug ass. His teeth print on my neck and chest. His baby swelling my belly. His seed spattered on my sex and thighs. And he was arrogant enough to know he had my heart in his hands. Here I was denying his claim and if anyone saw me as I was now, I'd sound ridiculous. In this moment, it was clear who possessed me.

This cocky muhfucka pissed me off.

"Get away from me," I hissed.

He did as I asked, but only long enough to get a warm, wet towel and wipe me up. Then he was pulling me against him and I didn't even fight as angry tears slipped down my face.

"Stop crying," he said eventually.

"I'm not leaving with you later," I whispered.

"Then I'll take you, Dream. I'm not leaving without you. I'm not leaving without my child. Keith is still out there. That shit been in my head since you decided to play hide-and-come-get-me. You and this baby are my responsibilities. I'ma keep you safe."

I sniffed. "And then what? We just play happy family?"

He sighed, hugging me tighter.

"It ain't gotta be for play. I'on understand why you crying. What you want? I'm in this long-term. I told you ain't gone be no boyfriends and stepdaddies; not after what niggas like that did to me and my sister and even Melanie's stupid ass. I'm gon' protect you and my seed. If you like being a mama, I'll give you more babies and I'ma be there. I'ma take care of you. You ain't gon' want for nothing. Not financially, not physically…"

He rubbed my hip suggestively as he said it.

"Just emotionally," I interrupted. "You want me to go at least eighteen years without the emotions. What if you fall in love with someone, Damien?"

"I'm committing to this, Dream. I ain't falling in love with no fucking body," he vowed.

Including me. That shit hurt my heart. I wanted to ugly cry but the lamp was on, so I bit my lip and tried to suck it up. Sighing, he turned me to face him.

"You and these hormones, shorty," he murmured, kissing the tracks of my tears. "You crying for nothing. I'm giving you more than I'll ever give another woman and you tripping about feelings. You know a nigga care about you, but what you want… I'on think I'm built like that."

I frowned at his words. For a minute, I just moved rest-lessly against the soft sheets, my mind a blur.

"So, you want me to love you, but you refuse to love me?" I finally asked.

For the longest, I got no response. Then, "Go to sleep, Dream. That drive gon' make you tired later."

———

(*Sunday, December 19*)

Mama was thick into last-minute planning for Christmas, about to drive Dayana and me out of our fucking minds. DeAngelo was no better—Crystal was due any day now and he was frantic, running in and out with no idea of why he came in the first place.

"So, Dream, you got the ham and mac and cheese?" Mama double-checked, looking at her iPad.

We had a million events catered over my life, but Christmas dinner was always homemade.

"Yes, ma'am," I replied.

"Whew, I'm so glad you back!" Yana said dramatically from her seat across the slice of tree trunk that Grandpapa had made into a glossy, lacquered table.

"Fat ass," I teased.

I had been shocked to come home and find my little sister with her own little baby bump. Their baby had been unplanned, too, but her nasty ass had confided that when Smoke finally felt she was well enough for sex, she'd damn near held him hostage for a week. This baby was the result. She said she wanted to tell me in person. Like me, they were waiting to know what they were having. Damien's ass knew the sex of our baby because he'd stolen my medical file and seen all the scans. The tension between Dayana and I lasted all of five minutes before we were on what Damien called our Celie-and-Nettie routine.

The tension between Damien and I was ongoing. I knew both of us thought the other was selfish. He thought I was selfish for wanting more. I thought he was selfish for expecting me to accept less. So, while we had fucked every day since I'd been back, we hadn't interacted much beyond that. Kiana was gone, but thank God I had Kam and the guards around for company.

Distracted, I yawned and rubbed my back as Mama reviewed her list. This baby was huge and I was paying the price in back spasms and aches. DeAngelo had suggested a massage therapist that Crystal used, but Damien had vetoed that instantly once he found out it was a man.

"Ain't no other nigga touching you like that. I got it."

And he had been rubbing and soothing the aches.

"Bestie!" Dayana called suddenly, breaking my reverie.

I frowned at her. Damien was in the next room playing chess with Grandpapa. Dixon Ware had really tried to smooth the rough edges off his youngest son.

"Why are you calling him?" I asked, my voice low.

She ignored me as he appeared in the doorway.

"Yes, Dayana?" he asked.

She looked at him, waiting patiently. He sighed.

"Yes, Bestie?"

She applauded as I rolled my eyes.

"Dream's tired. Take her home and don't try to get none, either," she said, grinning.

"Dayana!" Mama groaned as my jaw dropped.

"Well… at least make sure she's not on her back. Is that better, Mama?"

Mama sputtered for a minute. I just shook my head.

"You are a sick, terrible little person," I told her.

"So, you'll call me later?" she asked brightly.

Damien's eyes were on me, scanning me up and down. Wordlessly, he walked over, pulled out my chair, and extended his hand. I thought about trying to argue again, trying to insist that I could stay right here. I knew I'd lose, though. Damien wanted his baby under his roof, and that's where we would be.

The ride home was mostly quiet. Halfway there, he asked me about dinner.

"Mama cooked for me and Yana, thank you," I answered politely.

"You don't want nothing else?"

He was fascinated by my cravings. He watched as I

slapped the strangest shit together in his kitchen. I exaggerated my tastes just to give him a show, but today I really wanted the unusual.

"I want strawberry and mint chocolate chip ice cream on a waffle cone. With caramel syrup. And some salt and vinegar chips."

He side-eyed me. "For real, shorty?"

I dropped my head self-consciously, the waterworks about to start. I hated these fucking hormones.

"I know you think I'm fat and disgusting," I whined.

"What? Dream, a nigga always all over you. What the fuck are you talking about?"

"But you said... and then I'm pregnant... And I'm not some damn model—"

I was blabbering and making no sense. I had never had low self-esteem but I hated the thought that he found other bitches more attractive. He sighed heavily.

"That night... we were on some tit for tat shit. I regret the shit I said to you. Yeah, I fucked a lot of wannabe models, but I don't prefer none of them bitches to you, Dream. On God or whoever. And you being pregnant... fuck, baby, knowing I planted that seed while inside that sweet ass pussy makes my dick hard as fuck!"

My eyes widened. "Damien!"

He smirked at me.

"Stop fronting. That little thang jumping now. You like it when I talk dirty. Fix your face," he said, pulling into my favorite local ice cream shop. "You about to get snot in this ice cream."

I couldn't help the giggle that escaped me. Things with Damien could be so great...

If only he could love me.

CHAPTER 105
Demon

(*TUESDAY*, *January 25*)

The house was crazy quiet when I stepped in. I dropped my key fob in the little bowl and slid out of my shoes. Crossing the kitchen floor, I heard soft sounds from the TV as I approached the living room. I walked in to see Dream curled into a ball beneath a blanket. Her braids were in a bun and her glasses sat on her nose. She didn't look up from the screen as I moved closer. The last few weeks had been tense, full of tears, arguments, and the silent treatment. I wanted to get shit straight before I told her the suspicions Li Jun just revealed to me.

"Hey," I greeted, watching her.

"Hi, Damien," she replied, still avoiding my gaze.

"If you cold, why you didn't turn the heater on?"

She shrugged. "It's your house."

I started to argue with her, but I didn't come home with that energy. I let the comment slide.

"Will you come somewhere with me?" I asked instead.

That finally brought her eyes to me.

"What?"

"I need you to ride with me real quick."

Sitting up, she frowned at me. She patted her head and closed her eyes like she was thinking hard.

"Where?" she asked.

"Dream, will you just trust me?"

She opened her mouth but closed it just as quickly. Sighing, she started to push up from the couch. Shorty was all belly and I reached to help her. Surprisingly, she let me.

Dream did whatever freshening up she needed to do. Fifteen minutes later, we were in the truck, on our way. I made a mental note that I needed to get another car or drive the one I had copped for her. The Jag was too low and the truck was too high for her to get in comfortably. I could get a dad vehicle, but it wouldn't be a damn minivan.

The drive was quiet. She didn't ask any more questions and I didn't offer any answers. I pulled into the parking lot of the medical office building and shut the truck off. After opening her door and helping her down, I held on to her hand. She didn't fight me.

The waiting room was chilly and she shivered. I wanted to pull her closer to me on the small couch, but I didn't want to push my luck.

It didn't take long for me to be called back.

"Come on," I said, standing and holding out my hand again.

She stared up at me. "She didn't call me."

"Dream."

She rolled her eyes before grabbing my hand. The assistant led us to Dr. Monroe's office. The therapist greeted me and then gave Dream a curious look.

"This is Dream," I explained, awkward as fuck.

Understanding lit her brown eyes and she ushered us to a couch. Tablet open, she looked at us.

"Damien, can you tell me why Dream is with us today?" she inquired, her voice mellow.

"I'd like to know, too," Dream said, shooting me a look.

I blew out a long breath. This was going to be harder than I thought.

"She... wants to talk about feelings and shit," I mumbled.

"And you'd like me to act as mediator?"

Dream held up a hand. "With all due respect, Dr. Monroe, I don't think that will be necessary. Damien says he doesn't have messy things like feelings," she said, sarcasm coating her voice.

I focused on the sound of the small fountain in the corner, letting the trickling water ease my frustration. Shorty had to give this a try.

"And do you believe that, Dream? That he has no feelings?" Dr. Monroe asked.

Dream's lips pressed into a thin line before she spoke.

"No. He cares about some people, but not—"

She stopped suddenly, twisting her hands. Her head was down, eyes in her lap.

"But not?" the doctor prompted.

Dream shook her head. I sighed.

"But not her. She keeps saying that," I responded.

She looked at me upside my head. The little sound of disbelief that she made annoyed the fuck out of me.

"I'm just saying it? You don't give me any reason to say it?" she charged.

I grilled her. "I give you more reasons not to say it."

"Damien, tell us what reasons you give her to believe you do care," Dr. Monroe instructed.

"I—"

"He thinks because he gives me things, I'm supposed to understand what he's thinking or may be feeling," Dream interrupted. "I mean, he gives me really nice, really expensive things, but then he turns around and reminds me that I'm a possession, something he thinks he owns."

Dr. Monroe typed furiously. I wondered what the fuck she

was saving. But fuck that. Dream wasn't about to get away with her shit.

"I only give you things, Dream? You standing on that, shorty?" I asked.

She dropped her head, refusing to answer. She knew she was wrong as fuck, but I needed to get this point across to her.

"So, fuck the time we spent together right? Fuck my talking to you and telling you about my trash ass life. I let you into who the fuck I am and you say I only give you things? C'mon, baby. You don't even believe that. If I didn't give a damn about you, I would have moved around after the thirty days were up. I would have fucked you stupid and left yo' ass there. I damn sure wouldn't have given a fuck if you aborted my child. Hell, if I didn't give a fuck, I would have driven you to the clinic myself. I only give you things, but I gave you a baby. Nah. It wasn't planned, but I realized I wanted my baby inside you. I trust you to keep my child safe; I trusted you with me, too. I never had too many in my corner and I thought, for a minute, you were my biggest champion of all. But you stay assuming the worst about me."

I stopped suddenly and shook my head. Turning to face Dr. Monroe, I was about to end this hopeless ass session. Dream touched my arm before I could say anything.

"Damien..."

I looked down at her hand.

"Like this shit? I don't let people touch me like that. Just you. I give you more than I give anybody else and it's not enough."

The room went completely silent for a minute. Finally, Dr. Monroe cleared her throat and looked at Dream.

"Can you tell me how his words make you feel?" she asked.

Dream twisted in her seat, shifting to cross her ankles and

rest a hand on her belly. She looked up at the ceiling, chewing on her bottom lip as she thought.

"I... I don't want him to think his actions don't mean anything. They do. They mean a lot and they give me hope. But when he refuses to say exactly what he feels, it makes me doubt things. It's the one time I don't want to make assumptions. But I treasure everything he's shared with me. His past, his trust, his art... his baby..."

My head snapped up at her last admission. The baby. She treasured my baby. That had to mean something.

"Dream, let me ask you something," Dr. Monroe said, setting her tablet down. "I've been working with Damien for a little while now. I find it significant that he is so open with you. I want you to think about what that means. If you were just an object, would that be the case?"

Dream glanced at me, her hands twisting nervously. I was glad the good doctor was getting her ass straight. But then she turned those eyes on me.

"Damien, I want you to listen to her. She is telling you the things she needs—affection, assurance, love—but you don't seem open to hearing her. You are selling yourself short because you are more than capable of providing those things."

I rubbed my face as I took that in. She was right. I brought Dream here to tell her how I felt, but she was making that hard. "I–"

"You love your siblings, even Dante's meddling self," Dream interrupted, tears shining in her eyes. "You love Ms. Hazel and Eve. Part of you loved Melanie–"

I started to object to that shit, but she raised a hand.

"No. I don't want to hear it. It's the only way you could have been so mad at her for so long. You love everyone except me, Damien. It makes me feel like you have this power over me because you know how I feel about you. I don't want–"

I had to respond to that shit, and this time I wouldn't let her stop me.

"You wanna talk about power, shorty? You got it. All the power. Dante guessed that shit right from jump. For you, I'll give anything, do anything. You know why I brought you here?" I asked roughly.

She shook her head, her eyes glued to me.

"I read your journal. The letter to me. That shit you talked about? That's how I feel. If I could have anything in the world, it would be you. You gotta understand, letting people in means they can hurt you. Look how Melanie did me. Look how I lost Kiana. That shit is a risk. I hurt people; I don't let them hurt me. And you... Dream, you could hurt me. Because I... umm... I love you. I'm not good at that shit, yet. But as long as I got you and my little one, I'm fine. That shit ain't easy for a nigga to admit, so don't be out here doing me wrong. I don't wanna do you dirty, shorty."

It took everything in me to admit that, to open myself up to her, leave my heart out there like that. But I wasn't a stupid nigga. I could tell her how I felt, or I could lose her.

She scoffed. "You ain't gon' do shit." But her face softened. "I love you, too. Now, say it again."

I kissed her instead, my mouth crushing hers as I held her neck gently. I devoured her with my lips and tongue and teeth as I pulled from her mouth. She kissed me back with the same energy, like she was trying to mingle our essences, entwine our souls. At some point, I pulled back to stare at her perfect face. Her ass was insistent though.

"Damien, say it again!"

I pulled on her hair as I grilled her. "Nah, now. You doin' too much. A nigga ain't—"

"Please, Damien?" she pouted.

I sighed. "I love you, witcho worrisome, big-headed, bossy, bourgeois, pretty, good-pussy-having ass."

Dr. Monroe laughed out loud as Dream smacked my shoulder. "Damien!"

"Shit, stop me when I start lying," I mumbled before taking her mouth again.

She giggled against my lips and I realized that just might be my favorite sound in the world.

CHAPTER 106

Dream

(*MONDAY*, *January 31*)

Walking into the building, I was on cloud nine. I still couldn't believe that I was going to meet my baby in a month. What was more shocking was that Damien had managed to say words that I knew he never thought he'd say to any woman. And he'd said them to me! I was in love with a man who was in love with me. We were starting a family of our own. Getting on the elevator to my office, I realized that some things had to change. I was in the process of taking over my father's empire, but, with a baby on the way, I knew I didn't want to continue his illegal activities and put my child in danger. I knew that Daddy would be rolling over in his grave with the way that things were about to change around here, but I was creating a new legacy. *My* legacy.

It would have to be slow and steady, but I wanted to raise my child... my children... without having to worry about shoot-outs and their being in danger of being kidnapped by our enemies. Well, looking at who their father was, I knew that the shoot-outs were still liable to happen once in a while, but maybe I could simmer it down a bit with the moves I planned to make.

The elevator door opened and I felt flutters in my stomach. Having a new life to solidify our oneness was beautiful. It was all so exciting to me. Smiling and resting my hand on my stomach, I rolled my eyes at the sight of Rayleigh.

"Hey, Boss Lady! Man, I'm glad to see you. And you all glowing this morning. Well, more than usual. How you feeling?" she asked, her bright, perfect smile spreading across her face.

"Hungry," I joked, rubbing my swollen belly. We both laughed.

"I can order you something. What are you craving?" she asked.

Just the thought of food had me salivating, but I had some business to handle before I could indulge in all the things that came to mind when she asked that question. I'd just eaten before I left the house, so I shouldn't have been hungry again so soon, anyway. But then, I had to think about whose child I was carrying. My baby was off the charts.

"Let me handle a couple of things first, and then we'll talk about the spread that we're going to order for lunch," I promised, walking towards my office, Melo behind me.

When I got inside, I kicked off my shoes, and sent a text. I could've just had Rayleigh make the call for me, but this was something that I wanted to handle on my own. Rubbing my stomach, I smiled at the flutters of my little one moving inside of me and closed my eyes and daydreamed about who it was going to look more like. I knew spoiling wasn't even a question, but the thought of a perfect mixture of Damien and me being grown inside of me made me happy. The sound of my vibrating phone brought me out of my reverie. I smiled when I saw the message.

Damien: *WYA, baby?*

Office, I texted back.

Three knocks on the door had my head snapping up. "Come in," I said, knowing who it was already.

I could see Damien was typing a reply, but I sent a quick, *Call you n a little while. Love you!* Before turning it off.

"Hey, Dream," Paul greeted with a big smile on his face as he walked in. "You wanted to see me?"

"I did. Have a seat." I motioned towards the seats in front of my desk.

He sat down, eyeing me in the way that had prompted me to meet with him. It wasn't creepy, exactly, but I could tell that he really thought he had "feelings" for me.

"What's up?" he asked, and I could tell from his demeanor that he had no idea that I knew what he'd done. "Are you finally going to let me take you out?" he asked, and that was all I needed.

"No, Paul, I'm not. And that's why I wanted to meet with you. As you know, I'll be taking over the business soon, and there will be some changes. I need people that I can trust here and—"

"Well, you can definitely trust me. You know that, Dream. Your father did for years, and—"

"But can I really trust you, Paul? And funny you mentioned my father because that's what prompted this meeting."

"I don't understand," he said, his brow folding.

"I know that you took it upon yourself to tell my father what happened in this office between Damien and me. That wasn't your business to tell," I said pointedly, my face remaining stoic.

I didn't want him to think that there was anything emotional in this. This was truly business—at least it was for me.

"You didn't know who you were getting involved with, Dream. I was protecting you. I knew that you could do better than Demon. You deserved better. A woman like you didn't need to be involved in with—"

"And yet, you continue to try to think for me and speak

for me. That was my father's problem as well. I'm not a little girl, Paul, and I didn't need you running and telling my father about me. That action, and your words today, make me wonder if I truly can trust you. My father may have been able to, but I don't know."

"I apologize," he said, throwing me off.

I searched his eyes for something to tell me that he wasn't genuine in his apology, but I didn't see anything, so I continued to listen.

"You're an amazing person, Dream, and I thought I was doing what was best for you. I overstepped and want the chance to show you that you can trust me and I can serve you just as well as I did your father."

I leaned back in my chair because my stomach was pressed against my desk and my baby didn't like that very much. Paul looked at me and something flashed in his eyes. He corrected it quickly. Placing my hand on my stomach on instinct, I thought about what Paul was saying. Part of me was telling me that I couldn't trust him, but I didn't have a real reason to get rid of him. I didn't need a lawsuit while I was cleaning up the companies and making them legitimate. And I surely couldn't have him in his feelings and not where I could keep an eye on him. I knew that Damien would say just kill him, but that wasn't what I wanted to do, either.

"Listen," I said, making his eyes come up from where they had been glued to my stomach. "I don't have a reason to fire you, based on just that one act. And you have worked closely with me. To be fair, if you really understand that the only kind of interactions that will happen between you and me will be business related, then we can continue this relationship. You said I can trust you, right? Well, this is your opportunity to show and prove."

"Thank you, Dream!" he said, standing and extending his hand. I stood to take his hand, and when he took it back from our shake, he took a good look at me. "Congratulations are in order," he added.

"Yes," I smiled, glad my swollen belly was in full view. "Yes, they are."

"Well, since you're eating for two, and we're turning over a new leaf, let's break bread to seal the deal."

I thought about his offer for a second, knowing that he couldn't have gotten rid of his feelings for me just that fast. But I also knew that if I said I was going to trust him, I had to be a woman of my word and do so, until he proved himself untrustworthy. It didn't help that the second mention of food had me about to eat my desk, I needed to get something in me soon.

"Still trying to get me on a date?" I asked, trying to check his intentions in the moment.

"No. Trying to take you to the food court in the building. That's far from what I would do for a woman that I was trying to date. Don't play me like that, Dream," he said with a smirk and I had to laugh with him.

"Well, as long as I can bring a friend," I said, walking around the desk and towards the door.

"A friend?" Paul asked, confused. He opened the door and when we walked outside, Melo was waiting.

"Yes. A friend," I said, motioning towards Melo. "You hungry, Melo?" I asked.

He smiled at me while keeping his eyes on Paul.

"I could eat. Looks like Lil' Demon could, too," he said, watching my stomach jump on the side.

I rubbed it to settle the baby down, but he was right. I was starving.

"Oh, nah. I don't mind if you bring a friend," Paul said, with an edge to his voice.

I shook my head because I knew how men and egos went.

"Okay, then. Let's go."

I walked towards the elevator with Paul beside me and

Melo watching my back. Well, more like watching Paul.

"Rayleigh, I'm going to the food court. Want me to bring you back anything?" I asked as I passed her desk.

"Nah, Boss Lady, but thank you! See you when you get back. I'll call or text you if there's anything pressing that comes up while you're gone."

I loved her. She was silly but efficient and I knew she was going to help me take the company in the direction that I needed it to go. Getting to the elevator, it opened and Parker stood in front of me.

"Hey, Dream! I was with the crew downstairs, but I heard you were in the building. I was just coming to see you," she said, but she was looking at Paul while talking to me.

"Hey, girl. I'm headed to the food court."

"Already?" Parker laughed, and I joined her.

"Yeah. This one is already like its daddy, it wants what it wants when it wants it," I joked, making her chuckle again. "I won't be long. You want me to call you when I get back to the office?"

"Girl, yeah. I'm gon' talk to Rayleigh for a few. I need those laughs"

"She definitely got 'em," I said, scrunching my forehead a little because she was still staring at Paul.

Something about the way she looked at him had me curious. I was going to make sure that I found out what this was about as soon as I got back. But first... I was going to feed this baby so it would stop beating me up from the inside out.

Parker hugged me and then moved to the side so that we could step into the elevator that Melo had been holding open during our little chat. He stepped in last, with his back to the door, and his eyes on Paul. When the door dinged and opened, he moved to the side and let us out first.

"What do you have a taste for?" Paul asked, motioning around with his hands that I could have anything I wanted.

Hell, my ass wanted it all, but I chose a burger and fries, a slice of pepperoni pizza, chicken strips with honey mustard, and a smoothie. I didn't want to seem greedy.

"What are you having?" I asked Paul when I noticed that he'd bought all my food but there was nothing on the tray for him.

"I have to make a call, and then I'll grab something for myself. I didn't want to keep you waiting. Looks like your little one is a little demanding," he laughed.

"Well, thank you!" I said, before taking a bite of a chicken strip.

Damien's honey mustard was much better. I tried the slice of pizza. Paul walked off and Melo looked at me, shaking his head, before watching Paul like a hawk. When Paul made it back to the table with his food, I looked at Melo and realized that he hadn't gotten anything.

"Melo, you not eating?" I spoke my thoughts.

"I'm good, Dream," he said, and I shook my head.

"Nigga, go get you something to eat. Nothing's going to happen in that short amount of time," I fussed.

I gave him a look that told him not to challenge me, and he responded with a slight nod before walking towards the restaurants.

My bladder was full from that smoothie, so I stood to handle that. I swear it felt like my life was consumed with eating and peeing and sleeping. Walking towards the bathroom, I saw Melo turn around with his tray and give me a look that asked where I thought I was going.

"I have to pee, Melo. I think I can handle that by myself," I said. "Be right back. Go keep Paul company," I said over my shoulder, knowing that I was being petty. But I mean damn, can a girl at least pee by herself?.

I knew he was struggling with whether to sit down and eat or stand guard outside the women's bathroom, but his even thinking that I would allow that was ludicrous. I wiped down the seat and just when I was about to close the door to the stall, it was pushed open so forcefully that it shocked me for a second.

"Who the fuck are you?" I asked, looking at the woman who was standing in front of me in all black.

She didn't say a word, and my hand went to my stomach protectively. She sprayed something in my face. I raised my hand to slap the piss out of her, but I was suddenly weak. My vision blurred and then it was completely dark.

I woke up when I felt movement and wondered how I'd gotten in this... this... this... I realized it was a van as I came to fully.

"Hey there, beautiful," Paul said, looking in my face with a scary ass grin.

"Paul! What are you... Okay, now you're fired!" I mumbled, cursing myself for not following my instincts.

"We'll see if you still singing that same tune when yo' man is out of the picture. He lets you get away with talking and acting like the spoiled brat yo' daddy made you. I ain't tolerating that shit or that nigga's bastard. You gon' bear my seed and mine alone. But we'll get all that squared away shortly."

He reached out to stroke my cheek. I snatched my head back so hard that I hit it on the side of the van. He looked insulted and like he wanted to hit me, but then he smiled again.

I stared at him like he'd lost his mind and wanted to slap myself for putting my baby at risk. I knew I couldn't trust him and here I was, in a van, kidnapped. Suddenly, my heart dropped. What happened to Melo? I tried to sit up, and that's when I realized I was handcuffed. There was no way they were able to do this with–

"Melo..." I said his name, just above a whisper, and my eyes welled up with tears.

"Oh, he's leading the way for his boss to come after him real soon. Something he ate didn't agree with him," Paul said laughing.

The laughter from the front of the van made me turn towards it. The woman who had sprayed me in the bathroom was driving. She wasn't what had me panicking. It was who was in the passenger seat. Keith! How did we not know that he and Paul knew each other?

"Good job, nephew," Keith said, looking back over his shoulder at me.

The way his eyes gleamed when he stopped at my belly made me wish I wasn't cuffed. I wanted to bash his bitch ass head in because I felt like just that look alone would hurt my baby.

"Nephew?!" I hissed. "You sneaky son-of-a-bitch! You mean to tell me you infiltrated my father's organization and–"

"Shut up! Too late to try to figure it out now," Paul snapped. He'd never talked to me that way. No one had. "There wasn't any big plan against your dad. When he hired me, Demon was the last thing on my mind. It wasn't until you started dealing with that nigga that I... how do I want to say it... reached out to my uncle to eliminate a mutual problem."

"So, neither of you have the balls to face my man alone," I said with a laugh, knowing that was true, but also knowing that I really wasn't in any position to be coming at them like this.

But I didn't care. I knew that Damien would make them regret even coming up with this not-so-bright idea.

"That means y'all know Damien, and you know he's going to come looking for me and his child, and to avenge Melo," I snapped the threat. "He's not going to stop until he's killed both of you! All of you," I said, adding the stupid bitch who was chauffeuring them to their deaths and anybody else involved in this shit.

"That's what we're counting on," Paul laughed before spraying me in the face until I was out again.

CHAPTER 107

Demon

MELO CALLED me and told me that Dream was meeting with that nigga Paul. I knew his ass worked with her, but I knew, too, that he had a crush on her and that he couldn't be trusted. More importantly, I knew that Li Jun had finally discovered who Keith's relative was that cared for his daughter. I wanted to handle that nigga Paul away from Dream—her heart was too damn soft. But I had fucked up.

Now, Melo wasn't answering the phone, and I knew something was wrong. I was in my car and headed to Dream's office, calling her phone repeatedly, but it was going straight to voicemail. She was so stubborn, and I loved that about her, but this shit was about to stop. Yeah, her pops was dead, but she was still mine and now she was determined to lead his empire, which made her double the target. Add my seed to that shit and she was in danger every time she left the house. We were going to talk about her working after the baby got here for that reason. She could never be unprotected.

Seeing an ambulance and cop cars in the front of the building made my blood freeze. Who were they here for? There were a lot of people working in this building. One of them could've been who they were called for, but something was telling me that it had something to do with Dream.

I pulled into the parking lot on two wheels. I would've driven in the building itself, but I ain't know how I was going to get this big ass truck on the elevator. Hopping out and jogging through the doors, I ignored the valet, the receptionist, and everybody else that I passed who tried to stop me from getting to my destination.

"Demon!" Hearing a familiar voice made me pause and turn to face the direction it was coming from. "It's Melo," Stella said, walking up to me.

For once, my usually cool, calm, and collected guard was shaking with anger. Melo was her cousin and she'd brought him to work for Dante and me.

"Stella! What the fuck—"

"I think he was poisoned," she answered before I could finish my question. "He was working the inside and I was outside the building. He FaceTimed me while he was eating and then his mouth started foaming. When he fell on the floor, that nigga Paul was there. I'm gon' take his life when I cross paths with him again, Demon."

"I'll save him for you," I promised, feeling colder by the second.

By this time, we had made our way to the elevators. I needed to get to Dream and see her and that she was okay– ASAP. If Paul had killed Melo, that meant he was after my babies. The elevator was taking too long to get to me, so I ran for the stairs, taking them two at a time till I got to Dream's floor. When I opened the door to her suite, Rayleigh and Parker looked up at me, then at each other. Their faces confirmed what I knew but didn't want to admit to myself. She was gone.

"Where is she?" I gritted out, not realizing my voice was booming through the floor until a couple of heads peeked out to look at us. I didn't give a fuck. If one of their asses had answers, then they needed to speak the fuck up, too. I marched to Dream's office and the three of them followed me, Stella closing the door behind us.

"She…she…she…" Rayleigh started as soon as it clicked closed.

She looked like she was about to burst into tears.

"She went to lunch in the food court with Paul. I knew something was up with him. I should've gone with her. Damien, I'm sorr–"

My phone rang and I held up my hand to stop her because it was a private number. I put the phone on speaker and sat it down on Dream's desk. Rayleigh was inconsolable, and I knew that she blamed herself, just like Parker did.

"Damien… I have something that you want," Keith said with a laugh.

"If you hurt her…" I spat, not even needing to finish that statement.

"Threats won't make this any easier for her, Demon. Meet me at the location I just dropped to your phone in an hour. And come alone!"

I slammed my fist on the desk and then picked up the phone and turned to leave. I knew that he wanted me, and I would sacrifice myself a thousand times for that girl and my child.

"This office is closed for the day! Rayleigh, Parker, get these damn people outta here and stay by your phones."

I didn't wait to for an answer because they knew that Dream was in danger. I didn't want anybody calling the cops or telling somebody else what the fuck was happening.

"You not really going by yourself, are you?" Stella asked, following me back to the stairwell.

I handed her my phone that was already pulled up to the location that we were going to meet.

"What the hell is this?" she asked running down the stairs and keeping pace with me.

"He's making sure that I come by myself," I informed her, because we were meeting in an open field in the middle of nowhere. "And I can bet he has people set up to make sure that nobody follows me, too."

"Damn."

When we got to my truck, Stella opened the passenger door and hopped in. I looked at her like she'd lost her damn mind. She knew the terms and I loved that she was riding for me, but she was gon' get Dream killed playing these games.

"Don't look at me like that. I'm not letting you go alone. And you said I could kill Paul, so, I'm going," she advised me matter-of-factly.

The location was fifteen minutes away from Dream's office, so I knew this nigga was setting up his people and that's why he'd given me that much time. Stella and I rode silently for about a mile.

"You know it's three o'clock, right?" she finally spoke up.

I wanted to smack the phone out of her hand because she was talking about irrelevant shit instead of what we had going on. Then it hit me. Fuck! Kam! Today of all days, I had promised to get him from school at 3:30. I ain't wanna take him to this fucked up situation.

"See, this is why you shoulda took your ass on. You could pick him up so I could go get Dream."

"Yeah, I could have. But then, you would've missed out on your leverage. I've been texting with my girl Leandra. She works on Li Jun's team. He had more info for you."

I looked over to Stella's phone that was in her hand. She had a picture of a girl, about my brother's age, pulled up.

"That's Kalylah. She takes private art classes with Kam," I was tired of the riddles and wanted her to get to the point of this shit.

"Yeah. She's also Keith's daughter. Paul has shared custody of her so that nobody would be able to connect her to Keith. Nobody but us. They must've been trying to get close to Kam, too. Guess what school she goes to?" Stella said.

"Get that Leandra chick to call the school. They gotta call the school and get them to tell Kalylah she's supposed to ride home with Kam. And whoever her ride is supposed to be... make sure they don't get there."

Stella went to work. By the time I pulled up to the school, Kam was strolling down the walkway to the truck, talking to Kalylah. A smile came across my face. I didn't want to involve her in this shit, but her father and her cousin started it. I didn't plan to do anything to her, but they didn't have to know that.

"Kam!" Stella yelled out the window, catching their attention. "Y'all come on!"

Kam and the girl exchanged looks and then blushed. Kam opened the back door for her, letting her get in first. We pulled off and headed to the location I was given. I knew what I was about to do was going to make the kid act up and I would possibly have to knock his ass out. It was obvious he liked the girl, but that shit was going to be dead once we got to where we were going.

"My house is right... you missed it... that's okay, you can turn right... what's going on?" the girl asked, her voice starting to shake.

"Demon, what's going on, man?" Kam demanded but he knew as soon as we met eyes in the rearview mirror what it was.

"Man, fuck!" he cussed and threw his backpack onto the floor of the truck when the realization hit.

I was going let him have that because the situation was really fucked up.

"This about that nigga that killed Mama?" asked.

I nodded and he slumped against the seat.

"Did you call him Demon?" her voice was still trembling when she asked.

"Yeah," Kam's voice was flat and I could tell he was hurt. "Kalylah, meet the other side of my brother—Demon."

"Are you gon' kill me?" she asked me.

"Not the plan. But your dad and cousin have my girl and child hostage, so—"

I didn't even finish my statement because I didn't hurt kids. Ever. But for Dream and our baby...

"I get it. They always getting into some dumb mess. I can't wait until I can move out. If I live that long," she said, folding her arms across her chest.

I had to say that I loved that she didn't start crying and begging. That told me that she knew enough about her family to know that this was a possibility. Her words told me, though, that she might've been the only one in their whole bloodline with some damn sense. She must take after her mama.

"Man, Demon. Ain't no other way?" Kam asked, reaching out and taking Kalylah's hand like she needed him to comfort her.

His ass was making a love connection like we weren't headed into a hostage situation.

"Kam, this isn't the time," Stella spoke up.

"When is the time? When she gotta gun to her head? Like, this ain't the way to live. What if she was your daughter—"

"My daughter wouldn't be in this situation," I snapped, slamming on the brakes and pulling to the side of the road.

We were still about ten miles out and had some time. I turned to face my brother, ready to pull him out of this truck and leave him on the side of the road in the middle of nowhere. At this moment, I wished I had come by my-damn-self. I didn't need all this when I was walking into a life-or-death situation.

"You say that but look at what's happening. Your child is in this situation, Demon. And its mother, too," Kam snapped.

The fact that he was fighting for this girl, even if the shit was just puppy love, told me the kinda man he was going to be. I was proud and frustrated at the same time.

"What, you got suggestions?" I asked, taking a long, deep breath.

I knew if it was me and Kalylah was Dream, I would be acting the same way.

"She don't like them folks, Demon. Ask her what she thinks," Kam shot, making me talk to the girl, even though that would only make me less likely to do what I had to if it came to that.

"Do what you have to. I don't want your wife and child in danger. If you can keep from killing me, that would be awesome. If not, I won't haunt you when I'm dead," Kalylah said, making Stella chuckle.

"You heard her, Kam," I said, turning around and putting the truck in drive, trying to hide my smile.

I liked her more than I wanted to admit her family was going to decide her fate. I looked her over and hoped she wasn't in on this bullshit with her folks.

We rode to the destination in silence but I could hear Kam huffing from the back seat and knew he was heated with me. He would just have to be mad and accept that sometimes, life was fucked up and there wasn't shit we could do about it but get over that shit.

Two miles out, Juan sat in a darkly tinted Escalade, waiting.

Stella opened her door. "C'mon, Kam."

He looked at her like she was crazy. "Hell, no."

I rubbed a hand over my face. "Kam. Get yo' ass—"

"No. No. I'm not," he refused, shaking his head.

"Kameron—"

"Demon, I'm not leaving her!"

I turned to look at that little nigga. He was damn near vibrating with rage, a sheen of tears in his eyes. I sighed. Shaking her head, Stella got back in.

I turned into the field, and saw a car parked in the middle. A woman had Dream, and I wanted to shoot her ass in the head first. Paul and Keith, I wanted to torture for even playing with me like this. I was stopped by two niggas with AKs strapped to their chests. They picked them up and pointed them at me when I got to the top of the road leading to the field.

"Get down, Kam," I ordered and he seemed like he wanted to protest. Kalylah looked at him and gave him a smile that made him slide off the seat. These women, boy. We were really whole other beasts for the right ones. I cracked the window on my side when they walked over to it, trying to look intimidating.

"He told you to come alone—" one of them snapped seeing the silhouette of another body through my tinted windows. I rolled down the window just enough to give them both a smile.

"I know what he told me," I said.

"Hey Mr. Levi," Kalylah greeted the one who had been trying to scare me with that weak ass mug on his face.

His jaw dropped and he dropped his gun reaching for the walkie talkie on his hip. That was a mistake, I slid my silencer through the window and took his ass out.

"Sir, he has Kalylah," the other got out before I made his ass a memory, too.

That was all that I needed them to know to make sure they wouldn't hurt Dream. And the way that their bodies shifted told me that they'd got the message.

I pulled up until we were inches away from where they had Dream and threw the truck in park. Stella knew what to do, so there were no words necessary. Kam needed to stay his ass down. I just hoped he would and not try to play action hero to save Kalylah if shit got hot. I'd already lost one person who was important to me in Melo and now, my family was in danger. I couldn't fathom losing him, too, over some shit that didn't have to happen that way. But he was a Montana, so I was banking on him having more sense than he'd shown so far on this damn car ride.

"Kam, stay down," Kalylah said, making me look over at her for just a second. Seemed like we were thinking the same thing. "Trust your brother. I do."

Blowing out a breath, I hoped that her trust wasn't in vain, because if it came down to her or Dream...

"Get out," I ordered her, and she stepped out of the car and stood behind the door. I walked around to her and grabbed her arm.

"Grab my hair or something. Just don't mess it up. And where's your gun? This doesn't look like a hostage situation," she said.

I paused for a minute. She was as bad as Kam. I grabbed her by the back of her neck with one hand and put my gun into her back. I knew not to grab her hair. She was a black woman and I wasn't trying to get stabbed if she got out of this alive. I had to admit I was slipping, though, because seeing Dream with a gun to her pregnant belly had me not thinking worth a damn. Not to mention that little interaction with Kam's save-a-hoe ass. We closed the door and walked around in front of my truck.

"You're playing with fire, Demon," Paul said, upset about my hold on Kalylah.

"No, I just leveled the playing field," I said with a shrug. "So, what you say? Your family for my family."

That last part was a statement and not a question. Paul's eyes shot to Keith, whose face hadn't changed. Kalylah was his baby, but she wasn't an acceptable exchange. He wanted me too badly.

"Okay," Paul said, ready to hand Dream over for Kalylah.

"No!" Keith shouted, showing just how fucked up he was.

"No?" Paul and Kalylah seemed to say at the same time.

"It's Demon or no one. K, listen to Daddy. He's not gon'

hurt you. You're a kid. He won't do it," he tried to coax Kalylah without even looking at her.

That made me freeze because this nigga was rotten to the core. What business could we have that was worth the life of his child? My face twitched and I looked at Dream before sliding the gun into the waistband of Kalylah's pants. Pretending to put it away, I released the back of her neck and raised my hands in the air.

"Let her go, then," I ordered, and Keith's face raised into a smile like he'd just won the lottery.

"You can't be seriou–" Paul started, but Keith slapped him with his gun so hard he took a knee, holding his mouth.

"You'll find another bitch, Paul. She's used goods, anyway," Keith seethed at his nephew before nodding to the woman that had Dream.

"When Dream gets in the truck, you can end this," I said, hoping that Kalylah could shoot a damn gun.

"You have my word," Keith rubbed his hands together and said.

His word wasn't shit to me, but then the woman let Dream out of her handcuffs. She started to stop in front of me before going to the truck, but I shook my head at her, while looking in her eyes so that she could see just how much I loved the both of them. Walking up to me still, with her stubborn ass, she slapped the shit out of me, and then ran off, making it to the truck with no problem.

As soon as I heard the door close, I stepped from behind Kalylah, with my hands still raised.

"Looks like she's been waiting to do that for a while. Guess everybody hates you," Keith laughed. "Search him," he snapped towards the woman who'd had Dream.

She came to do just that. She was enjoying that shit way too much, spending extra time around my dick, when she knew wasn't no damn gun there. Sick, disrespectful ass.

"No guns," she said, backing up to her place beside Keith, her eyes on me, licking her lips.

Once she cleared me, Keith's coward ass walked up and hit me in the gut with the butt of the AK that he'd been holding to my unborn child. I buckled and dropped, like that shit hurt more than it did and he took that opportunity to hit me in the face with the gun.

Pewn! Pewn! Pewn!

Three shots and two bodies dropped to the ground. The girl that was feeling me up was face down with the back of her head blown open and Keith was on both knees his hands red with blood from two shots to the gut. Paul was frozen and I couldn't tell if he was struggling with being upset about their deaths or being glad they were dead and he was still.

"Kaylyah, you... shot... me..." Keith grunted, blood leaking from his mouth.

"You were going to let him kill me, Daddy. You're supposed to love me!!" she yelled, her hand shaking with the gun still trained on Keith.

I reached for it and gently took it out of her hand. "Go back to the truck."

"Will you take me home when you're done with...with... with..." she whispered almost inaudibly, unable to finish her statement.

"Yes," I promised, rubbing her back with the gun on Keith, in case he got any ideas.

My heart hurt for Kalylah because she was losing her father, but I knew that she never truly had him in the first place. Still, I knew that it hurt. A loss like this, for any reason was hard. She had tears leaking down her cheeks, but she obeyed me and went back to the truck. I didn't want her to have blood on her hands, especially not her father's blood, regardless of how fucked up the nigga was.

I heard footsteps coming my way and knew it was Stella. She walked right up to Paul and kneed him in the face, making him fall backwards. She was huffing and I knew that even getting this revenge for Melo wasn't going to make his loss hurt her any less.

"You killed him for pussy that was never gon' be yours," she said, her voice cracking, before she fired two shots into his head and one in his dick.

That shit made me jump a little because I knew it hurt, even though it was done after death. His ghost felt that shit because I felt it in my spirit from just watching it. "Boss... can you finish Keith's bitch ass so we can go home?" she requested, wiping the tears from her face with the gun still in her hand.

"I would take my time with you, but the kids have homework and shit. You know how it is."

Pewn!

I checked my body because I knew I hadn't fired yet. But the hole in the center of Keith's forehead told me that somebody had.

"That was for my mama, fuck nigga," Kam barked, walking up and spitting on Keith's leaking body.

I looked at my little brother and nodded. I was proud but wanted him to have a life that was nothing like the one that I'd led. He had a choice. He had promise. And with me in his life... he had a future. I thought about how many people I had in my life now that I loved and would never want to put in danger like this again.

I had a family now. A nigga could live with that.

CHAPTER 108
Dayana

(*THURSDAY*, *February 24*)

I dropped the grapes, peeled and cut in half, next to the strawberries on my Cupcake's plate. She smiled up at me and I dropped a kiss on top of her head as I listened to Ms. Stephanie's instructions for this chicken dish Cartier loved.

"You got it?" she asked finally.

"I think so, I'll probably have to call you again when I actually make it," I said, laughing.

"You know you can!"

I sat down at the table, my expanding belly making my body tired as hell.

"When you coming back? We miss you! Tell Mr. Joaquín we need our time," I said.

She had gone with her husband to his estate in Mexico and the nigga didn't want to bring her back. He wasn't hiding any more. Years of retirements, resignations, and bribes had weakened the case against him. The loss of crucial evidence and two key witnesses recanting meant that it had been dropped altogether. Joaquín Salinas was a free man, but he loved his home country and wanted to spend most of his time there. He wanted his wife with him.

She sucked her teeth. "Joaquín play too much, hostage-holding ass. I'm coming back next week. I miss my baby. Y'all, too. And he's bought so much stuff for her, he oughta be ready to deliver it. I'm not leaving again until after the baby comes," she vowed.

"Mm-hmm," I said doubtfully.

Stephanie Salinas was a strong, outspoken woman. No one walked over her, but I had learned that when Joaquín Salinas decreed something, it usually happened. I looked up as Cartier walked in. He kissed a giggling Jenesis, then pressed his lips to my forehead and stomach.

"Tell that weak ass nigga yo' man is here and you gotta get off," he popped.

I rolled my eyes. "I'm sure yo' Mama heard that," I said.

He pressed the side of his fist against his mouth.

"Oh, damn! Sorry, OG."

"Tell him watch his mouth before I whoop his ass. I'll let you go, though. Joaquín in there burning up that damn kitchen, anyway. Tryna fix me lunch. Let me go tell Rafael to pick something up for me and him. His daddy can eat that charcoal he in there making. Bye, my love! Love y'all. Kiss everyone for me."

"We love you, too. And I will," I promised, laughing as I disconnected.

I glanced over at Cartier, who was watching Jenesis. She ate her fruit and he swept her and her plate up, carrying both to the sink. He helped her wash her hands and then washed the plate.

"You ready?" he asked her.

"Where y'all going?" I asked.

He hesitated which set off alarm bells for me. Cartier was always straightforward with me. I trusted him, but I wanted to know what had him dodging my question. I stood up.

"Let me change shoes. I'm going, too."

He sighed. "Yana…"

I waited, silently daring his ass to tell me no. I wasn't as hormonal as Dream's ass, but he and I could tear this bitch down today!

"Get your shoes," he said.

Ten minutes later, he had buckled Jenesis and me into his Mercedes and we were pulling off.

"Where we going?" I asked after a few minutes.

He glanced at and smirked.

"You wanted to ride, so just chill, Princess," he said.

Huffing, I crossed my arms over my breasts and pouted. That pout quickly turned into wide eyes and a look of disbelief when he took a left turn into a serene, tree-lined locale.

I looked over the seat at Jenesis to make sure she was preoccupied.

"Cartier!" I whispered fiercely.

He shrugged. "You wanted to come."

He parked a few moments later and turned off the car. My head swiveled toward him.

"What you doing? Leave it on!"

"Nah. Get out and say hi. It's about time."

He didn't give me time to argue, taking Jenesis out and grabbing her hand as I sputtered. Then, he opened my door.

"Are you for real?" I demanded.

"Dayana, get out."

I gave him one last crazy look. He was unmoved. Grumbling,

I climbed out with his help. We walked up the shaded path into a beautifully kept mausoleum. I stood back quietly as Jenesis chatted with her mama. I wanted to give Cartier a moment of privacy as he kissed his fingers and pressed them to her tomb, but he grabbed my hand.

"You can stay. She'd like you," he said softly.

I didn't know about that, but I nodded.

"Oh, Daddy! A squirrel!" Jenesis yelled suddenly, running out the doorway.

"Jeni!"

Cartier took off after her, leaving me standing there awkwardly. I started toward the door, then stopped.

"Hi, Jenna," I whispered. "I just want you to know you have the most beautiful little girl in the world. Getting to know her has been a joy. I truly love her. I... I love her father, too. You are so special to him and will always have a sacred place in his heart. I want you to know that I would never try to take your place—I never could. But I am going to love and take care of them to the best of my ability. You can take your rest knowing that I promise that. I should—"

I stopped as an unexpected breeze, cool but gentle, brushed my cheek. My nervousness suddenly disappeared and I smiled as I made my way to the door. Cartier and Jenesis were approaching and he was fussing her out.

"Cartier," I scolded softly as I stepped out.

It crossed my mind how still the late winter air was out here. I frowned a little.

"What?" Cartier asked.

"Nothing. The mausoleum had a breeze but—"

"Yeah," he cut me off, a small smile on his lips. "It must have a draft or something."

I narrowed my eyes. "Or something," I muttered as he dug his vibrating phone out.

He read the screen then looked up at me.

"Let's go, Princess," he said.

"You not gon' talk to her?" I asked, ready to fuss.

I didn't want him changing his routine for me.

"Well, I could..." he began. "But..."

"But what?" I asked impatiently.

"Dream's having the baby. Thought you might want to go the hospital."

A grin broke out on his face as I screamed right there in the middle of the cemetery. I was about to be an auntie for the second time and I couldn't wait.

"Hurry up, Cartier," I said, grabbing Jeni's hand and taking off. "TeTe's baby is waiting!"

A joyous laugh escaped me as a sudden wind ruffled my hair. Scratch that!

Our whole lives were waiting.

And I was ready.

CHAPTER 109
Declan Montana

(TEN YEARS later)

"Baby! Come check my room!" my nine-year-old brother Dex yelled.

He was calling our mama, Dream. I mean, we mostly called her "Mama," but our pops called her "Baby" so much, sometimes we forgot and called her that, too.

"Dexter, I'm not coming up there right now. Just know, if that room ain't right, I'ma have a case for the blunt force trauma I'ma cause!" she yelled back from the bottom of the stairs where she was bouncing my baby brother Denim on her hip. I smiled at her as I walked down on my way to the living room. She grabbed me and kissed both my cheeks, before rubbing her hand over my locs. Mama was cool, but she couldn't accept that I was turning into a man! I let her kiss me and stuff, but she had to be extra.

"Baby!" I groaned, but I gave her a quick snuggle.

She was warm and smelled like cookies and strawberries. I almost forgot how grown-up I was as she gave me a one-arm hug.

"I can't help it. You so handsome. And y'all better call me 'Mama,'" she fussed, but her voice was soft.

She shrieked as Pops sneaked up behind her and pulled her against him before kissing her neck. I rolled my eyes. My dad was the toughest man I knew and I had mad respect for that. This nigga played no games with anybody else but was a simp for my mama, always touching and kissing her.

"Leave my seeds alone, Baby," he told her.

"Umm, speaking of yo spawn, where is Dylan? It's your turn to keep an eye on him. I swear if he causes an explosion today, Damien—"

She made a mad face.

"Chill, Baby. He knows if a science kit comes out today, my foot going in that ass," Pops tried to calm her.

I shook my head as I kept walking. Dylan was my five-year-old-brother, a mad scientist for real. Nigga was always in the kitchen or the lab Pops built for him. He wasn't allowed to use heavy chemicals, but he was *still* always blowing and blasting shit up. I didn't understand it, but I knew he better do right today.

Today was the party celebrating my uncle Kam's graduation from my mom's old college. That was my nigga. He was an artist like my pops and me, but he was into a bunch of other stuff, too, and I liked hanging with him.

The doorbell rang suddenly and I walked over to see who it was, something Pops had just let me start doing. I grinned when I saw my TeTe Yana, my uncle Smoke, and their kids on the screen. I opened the door and before I could blink, my TeTe had pulled me into her arms.

"Hey, TeTe's F—"

"TeTe!" I stopped her just in time.

She was about to call me TeTe's Fat Man like she'd been doing since I was a baby. I had to remind her to keep that between us. She winked at me as she walked in. I hugged my cousins Jenesis and Amaya, who was my age, then gave my little cousin Cartier and my uncle a pound as they all walked in. TeTe Yana was pregnant now and she swore this was it.

"Be looking for your Aunt KiKi and her people," my Pops called out as Maya pulled me to the side. "Your uncles should be close, too."

"Yes, sir," I answered. "Hold on, girl," I told Maya.

She was my cousin and best friend so I knew she probably wanted to talk to me about something. I'd get up with her in a minute. I needed some water and a snack first, cuz ain't no telling how long it would be before we had lunch or whatever. Baby said my legs must be hollow as much as I ate.

Maya and I walked into the kitchen where Papa Lucien was sitting, talking on the phone. We knew to be quiet, but Maya ran over to hug him before helping me make a couple of PB and Js. A little while later, most of my family was there. I opened the door for my Auntie Eve, Mama Hazel, MJ, Mia, and Hailey.

"Where's Jenesis?" MJ asked as soon as the adults walked off.

"My daddy gon' fuck you up," Maya warned.

He grinned and walked off with Mia to look for Jeni anyway. Suddenly, I heard a *BOOM* and saw a cloud of smoke before Dylan's skinny ass appeared, goggles crooked and lab coat stained as he coughed. Baby glared at Pops.

"Don't worry!" Dylan finally said, catching his breath. "But I apologize. The chocolate slime fountain won't be ready for Uncle Kam's party."

Pops lifted him by the back of his coat and shook him.

"Nigga! What I tell you about upsetting yo' mama today? She pregnant and—"

My mama's gasp was loud, cutting Pops off.

"You *still* hadn't told her, Bestie?" Aunt Yana asked, shaking her head. "Sister, you know I can't be pregnant without you."

Just like Amaya and me, Dylan and Cartier were the same age, too. Pops swore he always knew Baby was pregnant before she did, except with me. I guess he was right. She looked mad as hell.

"Ooh," Maya whispered next to me. "TeTe Dream gon' kill your daddy."

Mama let out a little scream and stomped toward the stairs.

"I hate you, Damien Montana! I can't believe you did this to me again!"

"Now, Dream—" my MawMaw Lucia began, but Pops waved her off.

He followed behind my mama. "I just wanna know why you always act like you don't want my babies!"

She turned on him so fast, she kind of scared me.

"I love my children. But every one of those boys weighed over nine pounds, Damien, thanks to yo big ass! They killed my back. And look at their heads!" she wailed.

"They do have some big heads," TeTe Yana agreed.

I frowned at her. She shrugged.

"Sorry, F—"

My eyes widened in warning. She cleared her throat and said, "Nephew."

Pops grabbed my mama as people started congratulating them. "This is our daughter, Baby. I feel it. She gon' be smaller. And them boys' heads didn't mess up nothing. Trust."

I didn't know what that meant, but from the way the adults laughed and Baby smacked his chest, I figured I wasn't supposed to know.

"You buying me a new body," Mama grumbled as Pops hugged her.

"Nah, I want the one you got," he told her.

I fought back a gag. Five of us kids? Bad as my little brothers were? And a girl? I scratched my own head, thinking.

But then the door burst open and my uncle Kam stepped

in, smiling big as hell. I smiled back, already moving towards him as he yelled out, "Family!"

I stopped, though, as a pretty lady in a long-sleeved black dress with a long skirt walked in. She looked scared, her eyes moving around the room before she looked at the floor. My uncles' and my pops' smiles disappeared as they walked toward Kam. The lady moved closer behind him.

"Fuck is she doing here, Kam?" Pops growled.

Uncle Kam grinned. "Her? Oh, you remember Kalylah. She's my fiancée."

Want to be a part of the
Grand Penz Family?

To submit your manuscript to Grand Penz Publications, please send the first three chapters and synopsis to grandpenzpublications@gmail.com

Made in the USA
Middletown, DE
05 October 2023